Green☩⚲

THE FINAL PROJECT

A Novel
By Stephen Goldhahn

To Frances
I hope you enjoy the read.
(But watch out for the greenhead flies!)
Best Wishes!
Steph Goldhal
6/3/17

Rigel Publishing
http://www.rigelpub.com

Paperback ISBN-10: 0-9965551-0-2
Paperback ISBN-13: 978-0-9965551-0-4

e-book ISBN-10: 0-9965551-1-0
e-book ISBN-13: 978-0-9965551-1-1

Manufactured and printed in the United States of America.

All maps, diagrams and illustrations were drawn by the author.

Lyrics to "Green Eyes" © 2012 reprinted with permission from Kevin Goldhahn and The Gantry

Cover design by Deborah Bradseth of Tugboat Design.
http://www.tugboatdesign.net

To my wife, Janet, and our two sons, Kevin and Michael

Map: New Jersey circa 1774

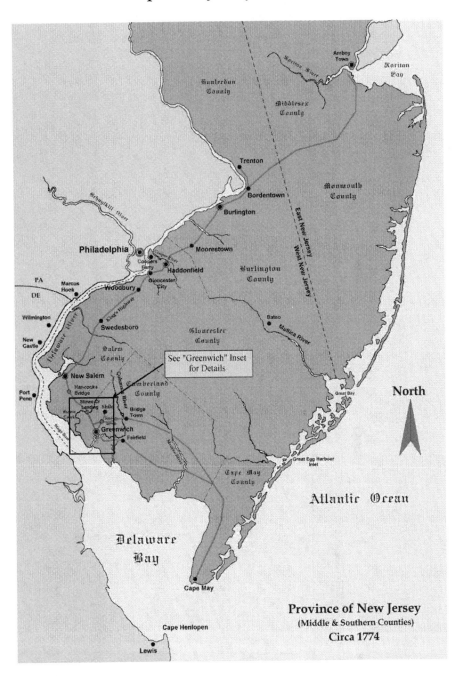

Province of New Jersey
(Middle & Southern Counties)
Circa 1774

Greenwich Map Inset

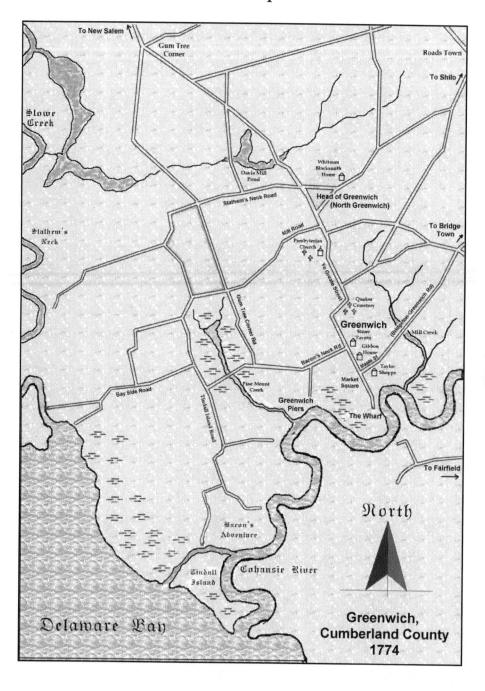

Greenwich,
Cumberland County
1774

Contents

To The Reader

Greenwich is a work of fiction, a story told against the backdrop of real places and historical events of eighteenth-century colonial New Jersey on the eve of the American Revolution. While the main characters of the story are imagined, certain persons of history are referenced and make cameo appearances from time to time. I have tried to make these interactions as seamless and faithful to the character of the persons represented as possible, but in no way imply that such encounters actually occurred. Where appropriate, footnotes are inserted to clarify the historical context of these interactions. Beyond this, any resemblance of fictional characters to persons living or dead is purely coincidence.

Historically, the colonial story line revolves around major political events of 1774: what might be dubbed "the year of tax revolt." Triggered by the 1773 Tea Tax—the latest of many tax burdens imposed on the colonies—unrest soon led to action, culminating with the famous Boston Tea Party of 1773. This event spawned a series of what, in today's parlance, might be called "copycat crimes" against the Crown, hitting Parliament where it really hurt—in the pocketbook. The burning of the merchant ship *Peggy Stewart* with its seventeen chests of tea in Annapolis Harbor in October, 1774, was arguably the high mark of expression of discontent. However, it didn't end there. Two months later, on the evening of December 22, 1774, a cargo of tea, recently off-loaded from the brigantine *Greyhound*, was burned by a band of patriots in the open market square of Greenwich, Cumberland County, West Jersey Province, in a final act of defiance against Parliament and the Crown. That this event happened is an indisputable fact of history…at least, that's how modern historians now record it.

While all reasonable attempts were made to avoid anachronisms, some liberties were taken with certain historical dates and events to better support the fictional narrative. For example, the current Indian King Tavern building, which plays a key role in the novel's 1774 colonial story line, did not, in fact, acquire its name until 1777, when both ownership and name were transferred from another nearby tavern operated by a Sarah Norris. It is hoped that such occasional lapses in historical accuracy will not offend the purists among us. *Greenwich* is, after all, first and foremost a work of fiction.

Prologue

Like hordes of angry fireflies bent on a common mission, streams of glowing embers ride the hot currents of air high into the cold, night sky, challenging the moon's dominion over its star-spangled realm, rising ever higher against the broad canopy of stars, mingling at last with the ancient gods-strewn constellations in a final moment's burst of glory. Their fiery tracks, traced back to earth, reveal the source of their being: flames rising from a great fire, spawning and spewing forth fresh embers in crackling pangs of birth, the newly born gushing upward in great swarms, playing catch-up to their brothers and sisters gone before, dispersed on cushions of a calmer air high above. Orion the Hunter looks down from his celestial perch with passive, star-eyed wonder.

Now, against a backdrop of orange flame and smoke, vague new forms in erratic motion appear and disappear, coalescing at last into a vivid collage of images and sounds: human silhouettes in wild, dancing rhythm; men, some naked to their waists, joined in common celebration around a raging bonfire; human voices, chants, and shouts of victory; and then an odor, pleasant, sweet, and familiar, but difficult to place.

Focusing on the heart of the flames, the vision of a woman's face slowly takes form. It is the face of an older woman, worn and haggard, wrinkled, discernible now as the crackle of flames is replaced by the sinister cackle of an old crone. A frightening specter! Lingering awhile, she fades back into the flames, her laughter supplanted by the muted cries of a much younger woman, affronting the senses in a crescendo of torment—they are the cries of anguish and pain. (I try to run, but my hands and feet are tightly bound, somehow.) The sweet scent is replaced with the stench of burning flesh, the cries fade, the dancers dance on, as cooling embers dissolve deep into the cold, long night of a distant winter solstice sky...

PART ONE

"The body is often curable, the soul is ever so"

Marble inscription above the main entrance to
Our Lady of Lourdes Hospital, Camden, NJ

Chapter 1

1999
Thursday, 16 September
Camden, New Jersey

Noon. John Samuel Weston lay on his back, motionless, eyes closed as self-awareness slowly replaced the fog of troubled sleep. Images and echoes of a bad dream faded to join the crushed remnants of discarded memories buried deep inside his mind. Nearby, a low, mechanical hum muffled the more reassuring sounds of human activity farther off.

Open your eyes, John! commanded a voice from within.

Reluctantly, John obeyed, forcing his lids apart, slowly, painfully dragging the sandy remnants of sleep across his eyeballs. Mind and eyes now connected, he found himself staring blankly at the bare, white tile ceiling above, and for a fleeting moment he was lying in his own bed, back in his home in Haddonfield, New Jersey. His eyes scanned slowly, left to right and back again, surveying the full extent of this small room: bare white walls melting seamlessly into ceiling, filling the room with the brilliance of the noonday sun. This was not his home, and this was not Haddonfield.

Reacting to a lingering ache in his wrists, John lifted his hands to his face, rotating them for a thorough inspection. He tried massaging away the burning soreness of the red, banded indentations left by the leather restraining straps, which he now recalled as only part of a bad dream. Feeling a similar ache in his ankles, he lifted the sheets and looked down: no problem there. He was now free to move about.

To his left, a soft summer breeze tossed the window curtains lazily aside from the only window in the room: a tall, double-hung sash with a heavy metal grill cage mounted to the outside, similar to what you might find in an inner city high school. He identified the source of the mechanical hum as coming from the AC unit located just below the window.

John flinched as the door to his room suddenly burst open. Entering was a thirty something, medium-sized man sporting a tweed jacket with patched elbows and a mismatched tie, clipboard in hand. Dr. Aldus Caldwell's stocky build seemed more suited to rugby than psychiatry; thick, straight shocks of blond hair covered his ears, and his mouth was buried under a bushy Roosevelt-style mustache in need of a good trim.

Dragging a metal classroom chair away from the wall in one quick, continuous motion, Dr. Caldwell flipped it around and sat down, straddling it like a barstool, his arms folded across the back of the chair, clipboard dangling from his left hand. Like the screech of a subway train, the mostly empty room reverberated with the sound of metal against hard tile floor.

John was fully awake now.

"Good morning, John. Welcome back to the land of the living," barked Caldwell, with the bedside manner of a high school football coach. "How are we feeling today?"

Today? What day is today?

Dr. Caldwell gave him a moment to get his thoughts together. "Do you know where you are, John?"

John glanced at the name tag on Dr. Caldwell's jacket. "Our Lady of Lourdes Hospital?" he offered.

Looking down at his own name tag, a dead giveaway, Dr. Caldwell smiled knowingly. "Very good, John."

John knew Lourdes, of course, a familiar South Jersey landmark rising ten stories above the streets of east Camden, a multitiered, orange, brick structure, like a large wedding cake, with "Our Lady of Lourdes," the very bride of God, set high atop its crowning pedestal in gleaming white marble. With head bowed, hands clasped in prayer, she stood as a beacon of hope to all who passed through her doors. And John knew he could use a little prayer right about now.

John massaged his left wrist with his right hand and directed his eyes toward the caged window. "And more specifically," he continued slowly, testing his hypothesis, "I would say we are in the psych ward of your hospital."

"Astute observation, John. I'm glad to see that your presence of mind appears to have returned. But," corrected Caldwell, "we prefer to call this our Crisis Intervention Unit, or CIU for short." Caldwell sensed John's concern. "Don't worry, John, this is a not a locked-down unit. But, we must employ a certain level of security for everyone's safety and well-being."

"Guess you still don't want *supermen* flying out the windows to test their wings, eh?"

Caldwell smiled and pursued his original line of questioning. "John, do you know how you got here?"

John was stumped now. Then all at once his mind was filled with an unwelcome stream of disturbing images....*Swampy water. A great bonfire. Screams. Shouts of celebration. Large green flies. Then swarms of flies in ever-increasing numbers*...Fragments of a dream trying to emerge and reassemble into a more coherent memory of events, people, and places. Then suddenly, as quickly as they came, they were gone!

Was it real? Or just more pieces of a bad dream?

"John, are you OK?"

John snapped out of his stupor. "Sorry, doc. Guess I'm just...tired."

Sitting up on the side of the bed, John planted his bare feet on the cold tile floor, took a deep breath, and wiped back a wisp of mainly brown hair from his eyes. At forty-one he was beginning to show streaks of gray. "You tell me, doc. What the hell's going on?"

John's attention was drawn to the clipboard. Cocking his head, he began reading aloud from the doctors' notes:

"...patient admitted Monday, 12 September, '99, in an extremely agitated state exhibiting signs of psychosis and delusional behavior. Suffering from physical exhaustion and dehydration. External examination revealed a 2 cm abscess on left side of neck just below ear, with localized inflammation. Flush around eyes and face. Moderate edematous swelling in neck, face, and throat consistent with allergic reaction..."

Dr. Caldwell flipped the clipboard over as if to say, "okay, I'll take it from here." Shifting position to get a little more comfortable, he took a softer tone as he sought to explain events as he understood them. "John, you appear to have suffered from an acute psychotic episode of some kind—what may be known on the street as a *nervous breakdown*. When you were brought in three days ago you were, well, in pretty bad shape. Physically and mentally exhausted, dehydrated, and delusional to the point of hallucinating, with periods of uncontrolled outbursts, ranting, and raving"—Caldwell looked down and read directly from his clipboard—"insisting you needed to 'go back and save her.' I believe they were your words." Caldwell looked up. "We initially thought drug overdose or adverse reaction of some kind. But your blood tested clean for the usual recreational drugs."

Caldwell folded his arms and made direct eye contact with John. "So tell me, John. Are you presently taking any prescription drugs, medicinal herbs, anything like that?"

John was quick to respond. "No, doc. I do my best to avoid drugs. Just the usual stuff. You know, vitamins, dietary supplements, Tylenol for a headache." He smiled. "A good run around the track usually gives me all the lift I need."

"Hmm. Okay," Caldwell pondered, consulting his notes again. "I'm not surprised, John. Your cardio checkout showed you to be one healthy specimen."

"So, what then?" John replied.

"Well John, sometimes a traumatic event following a prolonged period of stress can trigger an episode like this in susceptible individuals. Have you been under any stress lately? Maybe at your job, or with a relationship? Any headaches or backaches?"

John hesitated, with a faraway look in his eyes. "No, not really," he said finally. "Not in recent years, anyway. Just the usual day-to-day stuff we all deal with while trying to make an honest living."

"So, you've never been treated for emotional problems of any kind. Depression? Anxiety? Or perhaps someone in your family—"

"No, doc. Nothing like that," John interrupted, shaking his head. "Doc, I really think you're barking up the wrong tree with this line of questioning."

Caldwell scribbled some notes on his clipboard before continuing. "John, do you have any known allergies? Foods, drugs, plants? Childhood asthma?"

John considered this. "Well, now that you mention it, me and poison ivy never got along. Very sensitive, well into my teen years. Even the smoke of burning leaves would cause me to break out. Also had to use an inhaler on a number of occasions for what the doctors called 'reactive airways.' But I outgrew those allergies as I got older."

"Hmm. Well now, that may be part of the problem," Caldwell observed, guardedly encouraged. "A severe allergic reaction perhaps."

"Allergic reaction? From what?"

"Well, we think it may have had something to do with that abscess on your neck."

John reached up and touched the bandage on his neck. He honestly hadn't noticed it before.

"When you were brought into the ER," Caldwell continued, "that carbuncle was quite inflamed and your swollen neck was threatening to close your air passages. The ER took the usual precautions and treated you with steroids for the swelling, then ran the usual blood work and lab cultures. You were cleared for killer staph, but put on broad-spectrum antibiotics just in case. Dr. Ritchie thought it may have been an insect bite somehow gone bad."

"Dr. Ritchie?"

"Yes, Dr. Alex Ritchie. He was the on-call physician in the ER the night you came in. A damn good internist, with a special interest in infectious and parasitic diseases."

"I see," John nodded.

"But quite frankly, John, I've never seen an allergic reaction manifesting the kind of psychosis you exhibited. We're not really sure if there is a connection with the bite, if that's what it is. It may just be a coincidence."

Dr. Caldwell stood up and slowly pushed the chair away. "John, if you don't mind, we'd like to keep you here for a few more days for observation and testing. We want to be sure there's no"—pausing for a moment—"relapse of any kind. We'll need to determine, if possible, what actually precipitated this episode. Then we can determine the proper course for follow-up treatment. Capiche?"

John sighed. "Well, you're the doc, doc."

Caldwell smiled. "Anyway, I think you'll find the accommodations around here quite, well…quite accommodating!" Caldwell pronounced with a wave of his arms, in the manner of a Maître d'.

Dr. Caldwell sat back down in the chair, folded his legs, and began tapping his pencil slowly against his clipboard. Taking a more subdued tone he proceeded slowly, choosing his words carefully.

"John, have you ever been placed under—hypnosis?"

John's eyes widened. "You mean, as in *mind control?* Magicians' parlor tricks?"

"No, John," Caldwell objected condescendingly. "I mean as in a safe and proven method of psychoanalytical inquiry. When administered by a trained professional, that is. I've found it to be a very useful tool in cases like yours, and often quite effective in helping to identify the deeper, rooted causes of a person's neurosis. If, in fact, that is what we are dealing with in your case."

John chuckled. "Like—you think maybe I want to knock off my father to marry my mother?"

"Well, I don't think it will come down to that," Caldwell replied stifling a laugh, "but you'd be surprised what secrets we find lurking in the subconscious."

Shifting to find a more comfortable position, Caldwell placed the clipboard under his left arm and reached into the left inside pocket of his jacket. Removing a small black notebook he thumbed through its pages until settling on a page with a turned down corner. Without looking up he asked, "John, what can you tell me about—a *witch burning?*"

John reached up and touched the bandage on his neck. *Witch burning? What kind of question is—?*

Suddenly, another torrent of disturbing images, just like before! Only this time they were accompanied by strange buzzing sounds…*Swampy water. A great bonfire. Screams. Shouts of celebration. Large green flies. Then swarms of flies in ever-increasing numbers. An old woman, laughing…*

And then in a flash—it was gone!

John took a deep breath, wiping away the beads of sweat from his brow. "I'm…not…sure I know what you're talking about, doc."

Dr. Caldwell just stared at him, drumming his fingers across the open pages of his notebook in slow rhythm.

John focused on the motion and sound of the fingers, moving ever more slowly in hypnotic rhythm:

    …thud-thud-thumb…thud-thud-thumb…

"Doc, may I"—*thud-thud-thumb*— "please have a"—*thud- thud-thumb*— "drink of water?"

The drumming stopped. Then, like a host who suddenly remembered his manners: "Yes, of course, John. I can arrange that."

Caldwell stood up, regaining his professional composure as he returned the notebook to his inside jacket pocket.

"John, if it's okay with you, I'd like to schedule a therapy session in the morning. For the time being, I'm going to maintain your Seroquel at 200 mg, two times a day. It appears to have gotten your psychosis under control, and your body seems to tolerate it well enough." Caldwell cocked his head to get a closer look at John's neck. "How's the neck feeling?"

John reached up and gently massaged the surrounding area. "It's feeling pretty good. Like I said, I hadn't even noticed it until you mentioned it."

"Good. But I'll let Dr. Ritchie make that call. He'll probably want to continue the antibiotics. Capiche?"

"Capiche," John echoed.

"Good. And I'll also let Dr. Ritchie know you're feeling well enough to see him. Probably drop by during his afternoon rounds. I'm sure he'll want to run more tests to rule out anything organic. Okay by you?"

"I'll have to check my appointment calendar to see if I can fit him in," John deadpanned.

Dr. Caldwell smiled. "Glad to see you're feeling better, John. So, I will see you in the morning then?"

John nodded.

Caldwell smiled, turned, and left the room.

After just sitting there for a moment, John took a deep breath, stood up by the side of the bed, and looked around. A small plastic bin on the night stand contained the usual complementary toiletries: toothbrush, toothpaste, comb, a pair of floppy slippers, and a terry cloth robe folded and over-wrapped in a poly bag. John tried on the slippers, then ripped open the bag, and removed and donned the robe.

"One size fits all," he mumbled.

The robe barely reached his calves. But that was okay. He was feeling a bit chilly, so anything helped. *They keep the rooms so damn cold in these places.* He walked over to the window and peered out.

John's room was located in the west wing of an upper floor of the hospital. From his window, he had a good view of downtown Camden, with Philadelphia's modern center city skyline visible in the distance, just across the river (the Delaware River) separating the two cities. Spanning the river were two great suspension bridges bearing the names of two famous native sons hailing from opposite sides: the Ben Franklin and the Walt Whitman.

Focusing just outside his window, John followed the antics of a gray squirrel as it leaped from its treetop nest onto and across the rooftop shingles of the neighboring church, exchanged some nervous chatter with another squirrel it met along the way, then darted off in a new direction with the other in close pursuit. Leaping into space from roof to limb and back to roof again, from one gray stone building to another, they danced their way across the church and convent grounds and onto the six-foot gray stone wall that surrounded the compound, scampering along the top of the wall until they disappeared in a dense patch of vegetation that bordered the gardens. *Seems like a nice, safe place to hide away*, John thought.

John remembered now having been treated at Our Lady of Lourdes Hospital on one previous occasion, about fifteen years ago. He was suffering a chronic infection of the prostate. His urologist said it had to be "massaged," a polite way of saying "lanced from inside." "A good job for Roto-Rooter!" John had remarked. Ouch! He recalled being sedated with a twilight anesthesia that worked really great. Even asked the nurse for a "six-pack to go" as he was coming out of it. But once it wore off, well, it was like pissing nails! Just the thought of—

"Hello, John."

A soft, familiar, female voice broke his meandering thoughts. John turned to see a woman standing just inside the doorway—medium build; sturdy, but not too stout; a pretty, round face framed in a blonde, page boy cut—appearing smartly attractive in business casual attire: pants and a jacket. "I—brought you a pitcher of water," she said hesitantly. "Dr. Caldwell said you might be needing it."

"Katie? Katie Fenwick." John looked puzzled. "What are you doing here, Katie?"

"Well, for one, I *do* work here, John."

Yes, of course! Katie, the wife of his good friend and partner, Bob Fenwick, was a certified occupational therapist and activity director of Lourdes' Crisis Intervention Unit. He knew that, right? He just forgot what he knew, for the moment. He would instantly recognize Katie in her role of soccer mom or gracious host, but seeing her out of familiar context caught him off guard.

"Sorry, Kate. I'm still having trouble piecing things together."

Katie poured a glass of water and handed it to John. He took a long drink and returned the empty glass to the bedside table.

"John, you really gave us a scare. Are you—feeling alright?" she inquired. She spoke in the caring tone of a good friend, or surrogate mom.

"I think so, Kate. But I'm still trying to figure out how I got here."

Seeing the pained look on Katie's face he drew closer and added, "Kate, I haven't forgotten *everything*. Tell me, how is Bob doing?"

Katie's head drooped, the corners of her mouth quivered slightly as she wiped the moisture from the corners of her eyes; then, looking up, she took John's hands in hers and squeezed them tight.

"The kids are doing better, John. They spoke with their father the other day. He was actually able to carry on a conversation with them, and"— Katie stopped mid-sentence and broke down. John braced her to keep her from falling and continued to hold her in a gentle hug. Sobbing, Katie tried to speak.

"Bob is going to Lakeland, John. They're afraid he might try to harm himself. And he should get better treatment there."

"Lakeland? You mean the psychiatric hospital?" John asked.

Katie simply nodded yes.

John knew the name. The county operated a number of public health and human service facilities at its Lakeland complex, located in Blackwood, NJ, about eight miles south of Camden. But when one heard the name *Lakeland*, it was the psychiatric hospital that most often came to mind.

Regaining her composure, Katie released herself from John's hold.

"There's a Dr. Alexander there who wants to try a new kind of treatment for this form of"—she found it hard to say the word— "schizophrenia."

John's memory was returning now. He recalled the last time he'd seen Bob. It was less than two weeks ago, Labor Day weekend. John had been invited over for a cookout at their Moorestown home. He remembered bringing some legal papers over for Bob and Katie to sign. On the surface, Bob appeared normal and was able to engage in intelligent one-on-one conversation. But in his delusional state of mind, he had become increasingly obsessed with a messianic mission of some kind, and when the subject turned to events of *that day*, something was triggered in Bob's head; his countenance had turned sullen and strained, the color fading from his face, as he'd stared distantly into space.

John tried to reassure her. "I'm sure he'll be getting the best of care possible, Katie." But he found it difficult to hide his own concern.

Changing the subject, John asked her about Dr. Caldwell. "The doctor seems a little rough around the edges," he said. "Like a bull in a china shop. Is he for real?"

Katie laughed. "He's got a unique style, I'll give you that. But, he's really quite good at connecting with the patients in here, John. You must know how difficult that can be"

"Takes one to know one. Capiche?" John rebounded.

Katie laughed knowingly, recognizing Caldwell's trademark expression.

"Funny, he doesn't look Italian," John said.

"No, but his wife is. Grew up in South Philly."

"Oh, I see. Well, that explains it." John paused. "And who is this Dr. Ritchie?"

"I don't know too much about him," Katie replied. "Just that he's an Internist and a pretty good infectious disease doc. I think he specializes in parasitic diseases, or something. Why do you ask?"

"Dr. Caldwell said he wanted to drop by and talk to me."

"Well, come to think of it. I believe he was on duty Monday night, the night you were brought in. Probably just wants to evaluate your progress." She glanced at her wristwatch. "Oh m'gosh! John, I'm gonna hafta go. Gotta set things up in the activity room for this afternoon's events."

Katie, in her role as CIU Activity Director, was responsible for keeping the patients occupied and entertained as part of their treatment program. The activity room was her domain. Located in the east wing on the same floor, it was equipped with a TV, a computer station, ping-pong table, and an assortment of tables and chairs for arts and crafts.

"Why don't you drop by after lunch, John. I've got a live classical guitarist coming in at two o'clock. Should be nice. Good therapy, too."

"Well, that sure as hell beats a *dead* classical guitarist," he chortled.

"Great! See you there." Katie turned and left the room.

John took a seat in the same clanking metal chair used by Dr. Caldwell. He closed his eyes and allowed his thoughts to drift back to his Haddonfield home. That's where he longed to be, back in his restored Victorian home in the middle of a town rich in family and local colonial history. A little nap, a little day dreaming, just before lunch couldn't hurt.

Chapter 2

1774
Friday, 16 September
Haddonfield, Province of West New Jersey

The Union Jack flew high and proud over the courthouse of the thriving colonial market village of Haddonfield, West New Jersey. Partly frayed, colors fading, the flag drew new vitality from a cool, stiff breeze starting up out of the northeast on this clear and pleasant September evening, and few could foresee the coming gales of political change that would tear asunder the very fabric of British rule in North America.

By 1774 the village of Haddonfield, founded seventy-three years earlier by Elizabeth Haddon, a Quaker, had grown into an important hub of transportation and commerce for the province of West New Jersey.[1] Located where King's Highway crosses the Cooper River, its proximity to the major shipping port of Philadelphia fostered growth and prosperity for its area's growers, trappers, craftsmen, and merchants. Just a five-mile barge trip down the Cooper took you into the Delaware River and from there to just about anywhere else in the colonies—or world—you might want to go.

The pre-autumn sky was ablaze in shifting shades of crimson as the sun slipped softly behind a layered cloud bank on the western horizon, while high overhead, cottony wisps of fair-weather clouds in ever-changing hues—from white to orange to red—caught the last rays of the setting sun. A distant flock of Canadian geese in shifting tiered vee formations raced the daylight in search of warmer climes, their faint honking lagging far behind as they faded slowly into the southern sky.

---

[1] Sailing alone from Southwark, England in 1701, twenty-one-year-old Elizabeth Haddon (1680-1762) arrived in the colony of West Jersey to claim and manage the 500 acres of land purchased by her father, John Haddon. Taking separate passage, her longtime friend, John Estaugh, a young Quaker minister, arrived in the New World in the same year. While legend has it that it was Elizabeth who proposed marriage to John, it is more likely that their intentions were mutually understood prior to departing England. They were married in 1702. With the establishment of their New Haddonfield Plantation in 1713, and a new Quaker Meeting House in 1721, the role of this growing settlement as a center of commerce for the region was assured.

A short, stocky, middle-aged man with sandy beard and weathered look, sporting a blue homespun coat, buckled shoes and a corncob pipe, paused for a moment, setting his duffle bag down on the red brick sidewalk. With wrinkled brow he looked up and studied the sky.

"A good day's sailing on the morrow. Mark me words," he commented to his traveling companion, a younger man of medium height.

"Yes, sir!" the younger man agreed. He likewise paused to regain his grip on his own duffle bag, which he had flung over his shoulder.

Walking with a slight limp, the older man approached the door of a handsome, three-story brick building, his friend following close behind. A sign hanging to the left of the door announced the establishment as: The Indian King Tavern and Inn, Est. 1750.

Wiping his boots on the wrought iron boot wipe to the right of the main entrance, the young man opened the door, inviting the older man with the limp to enter first.

The door entered upon a foyer and central hallway which ran straight back, connecting the various dining rooms, the bar, and food preparation areas of the twenty-four-room establishment. Located off the hallway to the left, was the largest of the public dining rooms, its walls lined with large wooden booths and benches, not unlike a modern diner in concept. To the right, a door opened into the tavern's bar, a central gathering place for the sharing of news and tales of the road, for both locals and travelers alike. At the far end of the hall and to the right, was a smaller dining room, reserved for the better-paying clientele, which also connected directly to the main barroom through a second set of double doors capable of being closed off to provide a more private dining or meeting experience.

As the two men entered the dimly lit tavern bar, they were swathed in the din of animated conversation and the odor of stale, spilled beer. The bar itself occupied a corner to the immediate left upon entering the room. Completely enclosed in a locked, barred cage (hence the derived appellation 'bar' for such establishments), access to the bar's interior was jealously guarded by the barkeep, who maintained a set of keys hanging from his belt. This evening's business was especially brisk, with all tables and chairs occupied. Our two new arrivals stood near the bar, scanning the room for an open seat or familiar face, their eyes slowly adjusting to the dim light.

The barkeep gave a nod of recognition to the man with the limp. "The usual, Captain?"

The man with the limp held up two fingers. "Aye, make it two pints o'ale, Jake. One for meself and one for me first mate here. The trip up river from Cohansie parched me throat quite sorely, it did."

The barkeep poured two drafts and passed them through the cage to the two thirsty men.

"Thanks, mate."

The captain took the two pints and gave one to his friend, then turned back to the barkeep. "Tell me, mate. Have ya seen the master 'ere abouts?"

The barkeep tilted his head in the direction of the rear dining room. "He's been expecting you. You should find him in the back room."

"Much obliged, mate," the captain replied with a tip of his cap.

Holding their duffle in one hand, a tankard of ale in the other, the two men drudged and nudged their way through the crowded room to the double doors at the rear. The older man knocked first before entering.

The dining room was better lit and appointed than the other rooms: curtains hanging from the window, Irish linen covering its tables, and silver and Wedgewood china replacing the pewter and earthen dinnerware found in the more common areas of the establishment.

Seated at a table on the far side of the room two men, nursing their glasses of brandy, engaged one another in quiet conversation. Two long-stemmed, white clay smoking pipes rested, smoldering in their trivet stands, their charge of tobacco mostly spent. The older gentleman paused to take a sip when he noticed the two men who had just entered the room, his countenance changing immediately from worried anticipation to relaxed recognition.

"Captain Jack McElroy! You are indeed a sight for sore eyes." The older gentleman stood up and offered the men two chairs. "Please, come join us!" He received the captain's handshake with enthusiasm, placing his free hand on the captain's shoulder in a near embrace.

"So, how was your trip from Cohansie? Did you come overland or by river?"

The older gentleman was approaching his middle years, handsome, medium build, standing five-feet-eleven inches tall, considered tall for his time, obviously a man of means and influence, eschewing the more fashionable powdered wigs of his day and preferring the tied-back ponytail hairstyle favored by artisans and laborers.

"Ah! Master Bartholomew," the captain replied, "ye must know me old bones can't abide the shock o'the road. We took the new stage boat service from Cohansie up river to Philadelphia, a bargain at four shillings six pence. Made it just under two days, with one night's stay in Marcus Hook. For another six pence, and two extra hands at the oars, the good Cap'n dropped us off at Coopers Ferry."

Cooper's Ferry, the site of present day Camden, was one of several ferry systems operating along the Delaware in 1774, providing vital transportation and commerce links between West New Jersey and Philadelphia.

"So, how is the missis and the young'uns?" the captain inquired.

"Sarah and the children are fine, thank you for asking. They are presently in Philadelphia, visiting with her mother and father. Did I tell you that Sarah is with child? She is expecting in the early spring."

"My! That is cause for celebration!" the captain beamed. "We must surely drink a toast to that bit o'good news!"

Bartholomew Weston was almost forty years old when he married Sarah, the young daughter of a well-to-do Philadelphia barrister. Their oldest child, James, was now eight years old; followed by Matthew, six; and Emily, a toddler of two.

Bartholomew smiled and acknowledged the captain's toast with a raise of his glass. "Thank you, Captain. Now, if you would please allow me to introduce my business associate, Jonathan Bigelow. Jonathan, this is Captain Jack McElroy, the man whose sea prowess I was boasting to you about."

His young associate, who was already standing, offered his hand in turn. "I am delighted to meet you at long last, Captain." The young man spoke with the quivering voice of a schoolboy. "Let me assure you, the master's boasts were most genuine and not at all lacking in candor."

"Arrgh, pure embellishment, fer sure," the captain replied. "Must 'ave been the brandy speakin'."

The four men laughed.

"It is indeed a pleasure to see ya again, Master Bart," the captain said. "I hope ye don't mind, but I took the liberty of bringin' along me new first mate."—turning to introduce his young traveling companion—"This is Paul. Paul McKenzie."

Bartholomew looked Paul straight in the eyes and studied him. Without blinking, Paul offered his hand and spoke boldly and deliberately. "It is truly an honor to make your acquaintance, sir. Your reputation precedes you, and I look forward to placing myself in your service."

Like the captain, Paul hailed from a long line of seafaring Irishmen. Unlike the captain, his impeccable King's English did not so readily betray his Irish lineage. A thick crop of auburn hair, as unruly as a horse's mane, crowning a long head with a pinkish-olive complexion attested to his Celtic origins.

Bartholomew took his hand and spoke slowly. "I am glad to see the captain has retained his gift as a judge of fine character." Turning to the captain he then took a more solemn tone. "Jack, I am truly sorry over the untimely demise of your former first mate."

Captain Jack looked down and slowly shook his head. "Aye, sir. He was a fine lad. And he left behind a handsome wife and young child."

"I am well aware of that. I do hope you conveyed my offer of a pension on her behalf. Until such time as she is able to re-establish herself and remarry."

"Aye. And she is most grateful for yer generosity, sir."

Master Bart smiled and motioned for them all to be seated. "Please, gentlemen, make yourselves comfortable. I see you have already drawn yourself a libation. Pray tell, when was your last meal?"

When it came to food, the captain was not bashful.

"Ahh, ye must be hearin' me stomach moanin'. I could down a whole side o'mutton were it set before me, now!"

Bart laughed. "I'm afraid the larder is void of mutton this evening. You may just have to make do with a fresh, steaming pot of venison stew."

The captain's eyes widened. "That'd be just fine!"

Bart nodded to Jonathan, who responded with a call to the waiter. Drawing a deep breath he spoke to his team gathered about the table. "Do you know why I summoned you from Greenwich, Jack?"

The captain paused a moment. "Aye. Well, I figured it had somethin' t'do with the large shipment ya spoke of in yer note. Also said it had something t'do with the current embargo situation."

"You are correct," Bart replied. "It has become my good fortune to find myself under contract to deliver a large consignment of goods to England. It constitutes a variety of goods, tobacco, furs, lumber, and cotton originating from diverse parts of the colonies—Virginia, Maryland, and Pennsylvania. Each lot is not sufficient by itself to fill a ship, but taken together they make a goodly load, enough to fill out the hold. It all must be carefully coordinated for scheduled pickup."

The captain took a hefty swig from his tankard of ale. "Sounds like ya need a good crew and captain t' make the trip."

"And a good, sound ship," Jonathan chimed in.

The captain turned and gave a worried look to Paul, his first mate. "Mr. McKenzie, can ye please enlighten us as to the condition of the *Richelieu*."

The *Richelieu* was the captain's ship, a sturdy brigantine which had made the ocean crossing countless times. Currently, the ship was moored at anchor fifty miles south of Haddonfield in the tidal port town of Greenwich, located on the west bank of the Cohansey River five miles upstream from where the river empties in the Delaware Bay. The area was also referred to as *Cohansie* or *Cohansey* by the locals, a derivative of the original *Cohanzick*, the name given by its founder, John Fenwick, when he established the sister towns of New Salem and Cohanzick in 1675. Now, a century later, New Salem and Greenwich were two of three port of entry towns in West New Jersey, the third being Burlington, located about ten miles north of Philadelphia, all lying on the Delaware River.

The towns of Burlington and New Salem were further connected by a north-south road, the King's Highway. Commissioned in 1681, the road would become a major thoroughfare connecting the new towns and villages soon to spring up along the way: Moorestown, Haddonfield, Woodbury, and

Raccoon—a small town located on the Raccoon Creek, later renamed Swedesboro after the original Europeans who settled in the area during the 1740s. In 1707 a second "king's highway" was commissioned—the Salem-Morris River road—connecting Salem to the new port town of Greenwich and the Morris River beyond. So, by the late eighteenth century, whether by road or waterway, the towns of West New Jersey were fast becoming connected for travel and commerce, and Bartholomew and company found themselves comfortably riding the crest of this colonial wave of economic growth.

Both the captain and Paul knew the *Richelieu* was leaking badly and in need of repairs; they were hoping to dry-dock the vessel in the Greenwich shipyards for the winter to effect these repairs.

"Sir, I fear we will have to look elsewhere for a sound ship," Paul said in response to the captain's question. "The *Richelieu* is in no shape to make such a demanding voyage. It is in need of much repair, which we were hoping to bring to fruition at a dry dock in Greenwich. The yard is well attended by the most able ship builders. But they would be hard pressed to complete such a task in the time to match your plan."

"Hmm, I suspected as much," Bart said as he took a sip of brandy. He turned to Jonathan. "Jonathan, my dear fellow, what recourse do we have? The Mr. McKenzie tells us that we have no ship at our disposal."

Jonathan suddenly perked up. Like a young thoroughbred too eager at the starting gate, he stumbled over his opening words. "Well, sir. I…that is to say, we have…well, given some thought to an alternative plan. One that I think will actually put us in better stead with the clock"—giving Bart a wink—"and with the customs officials."

Jonathan paused a moment, testing the waters, so to speak. The captain cocked his head to one side to better hear, as if perhaps he had missed the point. His voice turned low and gravelly.

"Aye, lad. So, what's yer plan?" he growled.

Jonathan swallowed hard before continuing. "Yes. Well, sir, we have contacted our agents in Virginia and Maryland, instructing them to send their shipments up the coast at once, to converge on Greenwich where the *Richelieu* is docked."

Bart interrupted. "We have contracted with local shipping firms, familiar with the intercostal shipping lanes used for trading between the colonies. They would be using the smaller schooner packet boats designed for speed and lighter loads, ideal for our purposes." He turned to Jonathan. "I apologize. Please continue."

Jonathan regained his composure and continued. "Yes, sir. The smaller schooners are definitely well-suited for the job. Now, all the while they are at sea, the captain and Mr. McKenzie would be bringing some measure of repair upon their good ship—enough to make it worthy for a single crossing. When the trade goods arrive in Greenwich, they—that would be you, sir—would effect a transfer and set sail. Upon arriving in England and delivering your cargo, you could dry-dock there to finish the repairs. Or, sell the ship for profit."

Bart turned to address Paul and the captain. "Two months ago I instructed my young brother, John, to travel to the Chesapeake region to coordinate these arrangements. He contacted Anthony Stewart in Annapolis, a longtime friend and respected shipping merchant in that area. Together they worked out the details, signed on the ships' captains, and made the final transactions with the suppliers in Annapolis and Alexandria."

Bart pulled a letter from his inside vest pocket and held it up. "Yesterday, I received this letter from John, confirming that the ships departed at first high tide on the morning of the ninth of September. Barring bad weather, they should make Greenwich within a fortnight."

The captain rubbed his bearded chin and turned to his first mate. "Tell me, Paul, d'ya think it can be done?"

Paul took a few seconds to respond. "It may be possible," he said at last. "A fortnight, you say?"

Jonathan nodded.

"Well, it will be close," Paul responded after a moment's pause. "But I think the necessary minimum repairs could be made; however, there is no time to lose. We must return to Greenwich with the first morning light."

"Argh! And I was hopin' to rest me weary bones and see something of Philadelphia," the captain moaned.

"Well, sir. Why don't you stay behind? There's no reason we both have to go back. I can return tomorrow and initiate the repairs."

The captain's eyes sparkled. "Ahh, now that's a fine lad! And I know it's not just the *Richelieu* ye be hankerin' t'get back to, eh?" He turned and whispered across the table in feigned secrecy. "I think there's a young lass who waits upon his return."

Everyone laughed—except Paul. His complexion turned a color that matched that of the room's interior, which was now awash in the red glow of the setting sun.

The captain continued. "On the way up river, the ferry captain said there's quite a stir and some goings in the city. Says business in the city has been brisk of late."

Bart nodded his head slowly. "Yes. Well, I'm not surprised. As you may or may not be aware, Philadelphia is playing host to a general congress of the colonies. As we now speak, delegates from up and down the colonies are meeting across the river to consider our future relationship with Great Britain and the crown. Hopefully, we have not progressed to the point of irreconcilable differences, and some restoration of imperial authority may yet be managed."

There was a moment of silence. Bart began drumming his fingers on the table. "So, my friend, with so many out-of-town guests," he continued, "you may have trouble finding suitable lodging in the city."

Bart took the bottle and poured himself another brandy.

The captain rocked far back in his chair and let out an audible sigh. Leaning forward with hands folded together on the table, he proceeded to speak softly but decisively. "Now, Master Bart, I mean no disrespect for mother England or the crown. But, it seems to me that little can be done at this point to re-establish respect for a King or Parliament that has demonstrated such meager regard fer the rights of its colonial subjects. As a man of business, ye canno' deny the impact the Townsend duties have had on trade. And the recent actions on the part of Parliament...the—" Pausing to find the right words, he turned to his first mate for help.

"The *Coercive Acts*, sir?" Paul offered.

"Yes, me lad. The bloody Coercive Acts, by God! Such arrogance! What could Parliament be thinkin'? They've only managed to prompt open rebellion with their iron-fisted handling of that tea dumping affair last year in Boston Harbor. I tell ya, many who weren't so inclined t'sympathize with those Bostonian hotheads at the time are now sidin' wid'em!"

The captain sat back in his chair, took a drink of brew, and wiped his mouth with his sleeve. Jonathan nervously studied Master Bart's expression for a reaction to this outburst. He knew, if the others did not, that Bart's young brother, John, was one of those "Bostonian hot heads" to which the captain was referring. John had long since taken up the cause of rebellion against the crown, and would have suffered the crown's justice had not his older brother intervened on various occasions, relying upon his influence and good standing with local royal officials. A silver crown gracing an outstretched open palm would most often suffice to soothe the wrong.

Bart's countenance remained congenial. His left cheek just below his eye twitched once, then twice.

"I take no issue with your position, captain," Bart replied at last. "The prospect of self-rule is fast becoming a popular notion. But I do object to certain incendiaries raising the ire of the general populace for no other purpose than the advance their own causes, for which little long-term common good can be gained."

Paul shifted nervously in his chair, glanced at the captain, and then turned to Master Bart. "Sir, while I consider myself a loyal subject of the crown, you must surely agree that there are certain causes worth fighting for...certain liberties worth preserving."

Bart was quick to reply. "Certainly! Fair trade would be top on my list of causes. The duties and taxes imposed by Parliament are at best ill conceived, and quite arguably oppressive in the manner of their enactment— lacking the proper colonial representation in Parliament. But even without the duties, it is becoming next to impossible for a well-meaning man of business to successfully navigate the shallow shoals of commerce these days, what with the morass of regulations, bonds, certificates of clearance, and the arbitrary enforcement of the laws by customs officials. There is rampant confusion and corruption at every turn."

"Although, you must admit, sir, that you have done quite well at navigating those 'shoals of commerce,' as you put it," Jonathan interjected with a self-congratulatory smirk.

Bart smiled. Of course he knew this to be true. He knew that he was well connected, having worked hard to become so. Just a year before, after Parliament had granted the East India Tea Company exclusive rights to sell tea in America, the company was permitted to grant monopolies to certain favored colonial merchants for purchasing and importing their tea. Bart was on this list of favored merchants.

"Yes, Jonathan, but only with the help of loyal, hard-working associates such as yourselves, I must add," Bart acknowledged with a look around the table.

They all nodded approvingly.

Bart leaned back and shook his head. "God knows, the duties are a burden. However, I must say, the embargoes imposed by colonial associations in reaction to these duties have placed a stranglehold on trade that goes far beyond the effects of taxation."

"Aye," the captain said. "I got t'agree with ya on that account." He looked down and took the lapel of his coat in hand. "D'ye think I prefer this Daughters of Liberty homespun coat to the likes of what ye be wearin'? I think not!"

They all laughed. The captain's indigo-dyed, homespun coat with pewter buttons was no match for Bart's smartly tailored, imported English jacket, with its solid brass buttons and gold cord trim. In New England towns, the "Daughters of Liberty" held spinning bees to encourage the use of homespun clothes in lieu of imported fashions from England, in support of the trade embargoes that had become widespread as a means of protest and resistance.

"But, sir, do you think free and fair trade is possible as long as we are subjects of the crown?" Paul challenged.

Bart was playing with the clay pipe on the table, trying to empty it of its ashes. He spoke to Paul as he continued to clean the pipe.

"I believe, when all is said and done, my good lad, that compromise is still possible. And we need not necessarily sever connections with the crown to implement self-rule."

A clump of ash dislodged from the bowl and fell to the floor.

"Aye," the captain said. "We need only convince Parliament that we can govern ourselves. Make our own laws. And heaven knows, it's becoming harder and harder to tell just who is in charge these days. What with every town and county forming their own association and provincial congress, where is it all going t'lead?"

"Hopefully," Jonathan interjected, "the general congress now convening in Philadelphia can resolve these issues. It may be our last chance at compromise." He spoke with a measure of exasperation in his voice, nearly swallowing his words at the end.

Everyone nodded in agreement.

Bart smiled and raised his glass. "So, let me offer a toast, then, to the general congress of the colonies. The First Continental Congress. May they succeed at reaching a suitable compromise, and may business thrive, both here and abroad!"

"Hear, hear!" the four men cheered in unison.

With a single clank, the four glasses and mugs met above the table. A splash of brandy and suds spilled onto the white linen tablecloth as the four men drank their toast.

The waiter approached the table with two steaming bowls of venison stew and a fresh loaf of bread wrapped in a towel.

"Ahh, just in the nick o'time!" the captain exclaimed.

The waiter set the meals down in front of the two hungry men. The captain leaned over the bowl of stew and inhaled deeply. "Mmm! Such a fine scent that truly sets me juices flowin'!"

"Would there be anything else, sir?" the waiter asked.

"Aye, be a good lad and bring us another round o' brew, if ya don't mind."

Bart then addressed the waiter on behalf of his two out-of-town guests. "Thomas, our two guests will be staying the night. Could you please arrange for their lodging? You can put their charges to my account."

"Yes, sir. But..." Thomas hesitated, turning to the captain. "I'm afraid that we are quite filled to capacity this evening. Unless you wouldn't mind sharing a small room?"

The captain looked at Bart. His raised brow said, *you'd better take it.*

The captain turned to Thomas. "Tell me lad, 'ave y'ever been to sea?"

The young waiter looked puzzled. "No, sir. In truth I have not."

"Aye, then ye canno' know that the quarters below deck to be tighter than a bosun's knot! I should think one shared room between us will do just fine!"

The four men laughed. The waiter smiled nervously and backed away.

"Yes, sir. I'll see to it straight away." He quickly turned and left the room.

The captain broke off a piece of bread as he spoke to Bart. "So, tell me sir, what of the return trip? In yer note ye mentioned something of the embargo situation."

Bart took the clay pipe and began charging it with fresh tobacco from his own pouch, which contained a custom blend of Virginia's finest tobaccos, as he spoke. "This summer I negotiated the purchase of a large consignment of black tea with the East India Tea Company for the purpose of importing into these colonies."

Bart paused. Holding the pipe firmly between his teeth, he ignited a piece of matchwood with the table candle's flame and drew it close to the bowl. Whiffs of white smoke swelled from the bowl and the corners of his mouth as his cheeks pulsed in accustomed rhythm, puffing like a smithy's bellows, until the whole company was enveloped in an aromatic cloud of smoke. Satisfied that the pipe was lit, he removed and held out the pipe with the one hand as he withdrew the match with the other, shaking its flame to extinction with a snap of the wrist, all performed in one synchronous motion; then, tilting his head upward and pursing his lips, he exhaled forcibly in one long breath, sending a plume of smoke to impinge on the rafters overhead.

Picking up where he had left off, Bart continued. "Captain J. Allen, commanding the brig *Greyhound*, is scheduled to set sail from England sometime in early November. His instructions are to ship the cargo of tea to Philadelphia, where I will pay the necessary duties and sign for its release." Bart took a long puff on his pipe. "Now, I have been told by customs officials across the river that the climate in that fair city of brotherly love has deteriorated to the point where English tea may no longer be welcome there. In fact, the contagion of discontent is so severe that it is feared there could be a repeat of the Boston Harbor incident of last December. Need I say that such would be a cataclysmic conclusion, indeed, to our sound enterprise?"

At this point the sound of cheering was heard coming from the bar. Someone shouted, "No taxation without representation!" More cheering. Another voice, louder than the first, exclaimed, "Massachusetts! A toast to your resolve!" More rousing cheers.

Bart motioned to the waiter, who had just returned from the bar and was hastening toward the kitchen. "Thomas, can you please tell me what all the commotion is about?"

Thomas turned in his tracks. "Yes, sir. A correspondent from the *Gazette* just arrived from Philadelphia. He announced that the Congress has just endorsed the Resolves of Suffolk County. Massachusetts, I believe he said. But, in all truthfulness, I'm not sure what that means."

"Thank you, Thomas."

Bart and company remained silent as Thomas continued his retreat to the kitchen. The captain spoke first. "So, ye were sayin', sir?"

Bart, distracted for the moment, snapped back to the present. "I'm sorry, Jack. Yes—as I was saying—a cataclysmic conclusion, indeed."

Unlike Thomas, Bartholomew knew exactly what was meant by this congressional endorsement. It meant that those wishing to break the bonds with Great Britain had won the first round in these deliberations; that reconciliation may not, in fact, be possible after all; and that long-term, life in the colonies may, indeed, be heading toward very difficult times.

Bart picked up on his original train of thought. "What I need for you to do, Jack, when you arrive in England, is to contact Captain Allen as expeditiously as possible. He must not deliver the tea to Philadelphia. I am thinking, in fact, that New Salem or Greenwich may prove a much safer haven for our tea." He looked at the captain and his first mate. "Tell me, how would you measure the mood of the people in Cumberland County?"

Paul and the captain exchanged glances. Paul spoke first. "Sir, I believe that Greenwich has not yet been touched by the fervor of resistance." The captain nodded in agreement as Paul continued. "The people are, for the most part, loyalist in their politics. And, I believe the town should prove to be a safe haven for holding the tea."

Bart took a moment to consider this. "In that case, let me propose the following. Paul, upon your return to Greenwich, I would like you to arrange for the safekeeping of the tea. Find a safe house in Greenwich for its storage until a final sale and disposition can be arranged. This should be done in secret. We cannot trust the usual public warehouse storage. That would be too risky."

Paul nodded. "Yes, sir. I think this will be possible. I have someone in mind who should be willing to do our bidding. Someone inclined toward neutral, if not loyalist, political views. Someone," he added, "in possession of a large cellar suitable for our purposes."

Bart smiled. "Good. And just one more thing, Paul."

Bart always saved the less agreeable aspects of the job for last. "Once in England, Paul, I would like you to accompany Captain Allen and the *Greyhound* back to America. He may not be as familiar with the shoals and channels in the bay as you are." Turning to the captain he added, "Jack, I would leave it up to you whether to return on the *Greyhound*, or to remain in England to effect repairs on the *Richelieu*."

Bart could see the captain was not enamored with the idea of giving up his first mate, even for just one ocean crossing. The captain rubbed his bearded chin and responded hesitantly. "Aye. Sounds like a—workable plan. It's all in the manner of execution, I suppose. As ye well know, there's many a slip twixt cup and lip."

They all realized that timing was crucial. Any delays brought about by bad weather, illness, or just the "bad luck o' the Irish," as the captain put it, would set the plan back and possibly jeopardize the tea shipment.

Paul posed the obvious question. "What if we should fail to intercept Captain Allen in time, before his departure?"

"In that case"—Bart hesitated—"well then, we must resort to an alternative plan. Plan B, as it were."

The company remained thoughtfully silent. It was Jonathan who spoke first. "Sir, if I may be so bold."

The others turned and studied the young lad.

"I could travel to Lewes, Delaware, at the appointed time in December, meet with the harbor master there, and try to intercept the *Greyhound* as she enters the bay."

The young man noted a look of incredulity on the captain's face. The captain knew the harbor town of Lewes was located near the wide mouth of the Delaware Bay, on its south side just west of Cape Henlopen, whose sandy reaches separated the bay from the ocean.

"I actually know the area quite well," the lad continued. "I spent my summers there as a child and young man—or, should I say, younger man," he corrected himself. Then, continuing with his original train of thought, "We would communicate our intent for a change of course from Philadelphia to Greenwich. It could be a simple lighted lamp signal in code. If Captain Allen responds in kind, we will know that Paul is on board and all is well. If he responds otherwise, then I would attempt an intercept on the open water in the harbor master's sloop."

The men looked at one another.

"That could work," Paul finally nodded in agreement. "Inbound ships oft times stop to check with the harbor master for changing conditions in the bay. The shifting sand bars can be treacherous, especially after a storm."

"Well! Plan B it is, then!" Bart concluded in a congratulatory tone. "Let's have another round to toast our scheme."

Just then, the sound of singing, accompanied by fiddle music, was heard coming from the adjoining barroom. An especially fine tenor voice, accompanied by at least two musicians on fiddles, was met with applause and cheers from a friendly, celebratory crowd.

Captain Jack's eyes brightened at the sound of the music. They were now playing a lively rendition of one of his favorite tunes, "The Rakes of Mallow":

> ...Beauing, belling, dancing, singing,
> Breaking windows, damning, sinking.
> Ever raking, never thinking,
> Live the Rakes of Mallow...

The blood began flowing anew, bringing a ruddy glow to the captain's cheeks, his toes tapping out the rhythm of the tune as it picked up speed with each refrain in the style of an Irish reel, with brisk hand clapping in unison from the tavern's company accenting each downbeat.

"Er, Master Bart, methinks I hear a reel playin' in the far room," the captain said. "D'ya think ye could spare me for a short time. I would sorely like t' get closer to that music, if ye don't mind."

"Please, by all means, Captain. Go! Enjoy yourself!" Bart smiled. "But, please mind the time. The tide goes out at eight in the morning. If you're considering a barge transport to the city down the Cooper, give yourself ample time to reach the landing." Then, as an afterthought, "Oh, yes, when you get to the city you may want to try the new City Tavern on Second Street. It's boasted to be 'the most genteel tavern in America,'" he said with a smile. "That is, if we mark the words of our illustrious delegate from Massachusetts, John Adams."

Then, looking around the table, Bart slapped both hands palms down on the table and added in closing: "I believe our official business is concluded for this evening, gentlemen. I now leave you to your own devices."

"Aye, and a good evening to you, sir," the captain replied eagerly. "Now, if ye would kindly excuse us."

The captain pushed back his chair and began to rise, but paused midstride in a crouched position, with both hands remaining on the table. "Oh, I almost forgot something I was meanin' t'mention."

"What is it, Jack?" Bart replied.

Bart was relaxed now. Sitting back in his chair, one leg crossed over the other, he held a snifter of brandy in one hand and a smoking pipe in the other.

"I was just meanin' t'mention," the captain continued, "that I came across one of yer relations, sir, earlier this week, as I was taking refreshment at the Stone Tavern in Greenwich. Said his name was John. John Weston. Not the younger John, your brother, mind ya. Rather, this one claimed to be—a distant cousin."

Bart cocked his head to one side and raised an eyebrow. "Are you quite sure of that?"

"Oh, yes sir! Quite positive. The gentleman—and I do mean to say he acted the gentleman part—he even knew yer missus by her first name, he did. Sarah. I thought that enough to vouch for' em. And, if I could be so bold, even in his manner and likeness, he did bear a strong family resemblance."

Bart pondered this for a moment as he stared off into space. Finally, he just shook his head. "I have no knowledge of such a…distant cousin with that same name," he concluded. He took another sip of brandy. "But then again, my family tree has many far-reaching limbs. Perhaps, from my great-uncle Andrew's lineage. We rather lost track of him when my grandfather emigrated from New England." He turned to the captain. "I should like to meet this man. This *other* John Weston, as you say."

"Yes, indeed, sir. He did say he was headin' up this way. Had an uncanny knowledge of Haddonfield, I might add. Like he lived here himself."

"Well, I shall have to keep one eye peeled for this mysterious gentleman, shan't I?"

"Yes, sir. And so shall I."

The captain turned to Paul. "Well, young man, shall we have at it? Music and shenanigans beckon in the next room!"

With that said, Captain Jack and Paul McKenzie adjourned to the tavern bar, where they passed the remainder of the evening in song, drink, and revelry.

The clock on the dining room wall struck ten. The music had ceased and the tavern crowd was beginning to thin. Tomorrow would come early for most; and more than a few would face the morning light with a shared measure of dread and discomfort, a fair price to pay, the intemperate would argue, for an uncommonly fine evening of camaraderie, entertainment, and celebration.

Jonathan spent some time with the revelers, but had returned to join his mentor at the table as Thomas was making his last call rounds among the late evening customers. Jonathan was feeling more relaxed, now, as he addressed Bart. "Sir, you quite surprised me when you introduced me early this evening as your business associate. It rather threw me off at the start."

"Why should you be surprised?" Bart replied. "As an apprentice to our firm, I should be permitted to introduce you as whomever I please, as the occasion requires. And besides," he added with a smile, "you certainly merit the appellation. You have proven yourself to be an industrious and trustworthy addition to our enterprise, my fine fellow. And, I might add, resourceful. Your Plan B took even the captain by surprise! Jack is not one who is so easily impressed. Personally, I consider myself fortunate to carry you as an apprentice."

Jonathan took a deep breath as he absorbed the compliment. "Thank you, sir. I...will continue to strive—"

"Now, now," Bart interrupted the struggling lad with a wave of his hand. "Enough said."

"Yes, sir." Jonathan settled back in his chair, feeling good, knowing somehow that he had reached a new plateau in his young professional career.

Bartholomew shifted his weight and continued. "And now, if we may return to the business at hand."

Leaning on the armrest of his chair, he moved himself closer to Jonathan who was seated to his right. He motioned Jonathan to draw closer, and began speaking in a tone that hovered just above a whisper. "About my younger...baby brother: *John.*" Bart drew a deep breath and sighed. "How should I put it? John has more than a fair share of his mother's blood flowing in his veins. He worries me in a way."

"How do you mean, sir?"

"Well, as you may or may not know, my family originally settled in New England. It is only since my father, Samuel, migrated to these parts have we called West Jersey our home."

Bart hesitated as he considered the approach he would take. "I was the youngest of three children. But, I never knew my mother. She died bringing me into this world. Needless to say, her loss put a terrible burden on my father. Although my two older sisters helped to raise me, my father, as I only learned later, became sullen and withdrawn. He eventually sought remedy by moving his family southward, to this fair village of Haddonfield, which had only recently come to be settled."

Bart took another sip of brandy.

"But, Father did not completely escape his connections with New England. Twenty years later he remarried. His new, young wife, Amanda, no more than half his age, came from a nouveau riche Boston family of barristers, bankers, and politicians. I am told that, as meek and gentle was his first wife, my mother, God rest her soul,"—lifting his glass of brandy in the manner of a toast—"was his new wife bold and vivacious! Less than a year later, young John was born," he said, setting his emptied glass down with a thud. "His sister, Emily, followed five years after. As my father's health began to fail, I took over more and more of the family business. Considering the span of years between myself and John, I became something of a surrogate father for him. Emily...well, she remained the special pride and joy of her mother. They began spending more and more of their time with her side of the family, in New England."

Jonathan sat still, not knowing how to respond. He felt somewhat uneasy, never having been brought so closely into someone's confidence before, someone so senior to himself, someone he deeply respected and admired. He understood, now, why Bart hadn't married sooner in life.

"I never knew that John was your...*half* brother," he said finally.

"Yes. Well, as John grew, he developed strong bonds with the cousins on his mother's side, in the Boston and Salem areas." Bart leaned forward over the table and added: "Of course, I mean the old Salem in Massachusetts, not our New Salem here in Jersey." He planted both elbows firmly on the table, hands joined, forming a single, tight fist.

"The point is"—speaking softly but firmly, punctuating each phrase with a tapping motion of his fist—"I came to realize that John had more of his mother's blood in him than his father's. A free spirit, like his mother. As such, he is attracted to other...free-spirited individuals. In these times, you don't have to go far to find such people," he laughed. "Wouldn't you agree?"

Jonathan squirmed in his chair. He was seeing a pensive, almost melancholy, side of Master Bart he had never witnessed before.

"Yes, sir. Most definitely. Especially in New England."

"Hear, hear!" Bart backed off and poured himself another glass of brandy.

"You know. Maybe there is something about the New England weather. Not surprising they call the worst kind of storm in these parts a nor'easter, eh?" Bart chuckled.

Jonathan smiled.

Bart coughed to clear his throat; then raised his snifter of brandy to study the currents of vapor condensing on the inside of the glass as he spoke very slowly, very deliberately. "John...doesn't know anything about the tea consignment. And I would like it to remain that way."

"Sir?"

Bart's speech was becoming a little garbled and Jonathan wasn't certain he had heard him correctly.

"What I mean is, I don't want John having to compromise his principles. I know how strongly he feels about the Tea Tax and the whole taxation and rights issue in general. I don't want to force him into having to choose between profit and principle. And God knows, we need the profit! You have seen the books yourself."

Jonathan knew the business was barely doing well, and could scarcely afford a serious setback.

"My concern is not so much with John, as with his associates," Bart added. "If they were to catch wind of this tea shipment, I'm afraid things could get out of hand."

Jonathan understood, now, Bart's ulterior motive for sending John to Annapolis and Alexandria to arrange for the southern shipments. In John's absence, Bart had a free hand to make the more sensitive tea deal arrangements. Considering John's intimate association with the Sons of Liberty and the whole Boston tea dumping affair, he knew this to be a fair precaution.

"Yes, sir. I understand."

Bart nodded. "You see, as far as John knows, the only ship returning from England will be the *Richelieu*, bound for Philadelphia."

"Then, we shall keep it that way, sir," Jonathan assured him.

Bart smiled and closed his eyes.

Jonathan caught a glimpse of the clock on the wall. "Sir, if it would not be too inconvenient, I should like to turn in for the evening. The evening hours have flown by and—"

"Now, now, my good lad," Master Bartholomew interrupted, "The 'healthy, wealthy, and wise' among us have long since retired, as our friend, Mr. Franklin from Philadelphia, would admonish us to do as well. Please feel free to go at any time."

Jonathan smiled, stood up, and bowed. "Very well, then, I must bid you good evening, sir. Would you be requiring my services in the morning?"

Bart's thoughts were elsewhere. Staring straight ahead, he seemed oblivious for the moment to Jonathan's presence. Jonathan began to speak again, but was interrupted.

"No, no. That won't be necessary," Bart replied, snapping out of his reverie. "It is week's end. Enjoy the day, and the Sabbath the day after. I shall see you bright and early Monday morning, at the office."

"Yes, sir."

Jonathan turned to leave, but had a second thought. "Sir, will you be in need of...any assistance getting home tonight."

Bart sat there for a moment. His three-story brick townhome at 14 Tanner Street was less than a ten-minute walk away, which he had negotiated in the past with a far greater number of brandies under his belt.

Bart smiled and patted Jonathan on the hand. "No, my good fellow. Thank you, but I shall be fine."

Chapter 3

1999
Thursday, 16 September

2:00 p.m. John was relaxing in an overstuffed lounge chair in the activity room of Our Lady of Lourdes' Crisis Intervention Unit when the music started. The guest guitarist played well and kept the attention of most of those in the room for the half hour or so that he performed, starting off with a classical medley of the familiar and the obscure, mixing it up with some Spanish flamenco, and ending on a modern note with a great rendition of Mason Williams' "Classical Gas." That seemed to perk up the room, turning the heads of all but the most self-absorbed patients, some of whom were obviously preoccupied with music or conversations of their own making. The most attentive were the visiting family members of patients, who were often invited and even encouraged to participate in the group therapy and activity sessions.

As the guitarist completed his final selection, he signaled Katie with a nod and a smile. Katie returned the gesture and quickly came forward clapping her hands briskly.

"All right! Let's give Mr. Osaka a big hand for that splendid performance!"

Scattered, half-hearted clapping rippled through the room. A young, angry-looking man boasting a green Mohawk haircut and assorted body piercings, mumbled something about "not sounding anything like Zeppelin," obviously disappointed with the performance and choice of songs. An older woman continued clapping long after the room fell silent. Her companion, possibly her husband, gently muted her hands and whispered, "Okay Jean. The show is over, Jean."

Katie turned to Mr. Osaka and shook his hand. "Thank you so much, Mr. Osaka, for sharing your time and talent with us. I know the patients and families really enjoyed it."

Mr. Osaka smiled and bowed politely, then quietly prepared to leave, placing his guitar in its case.

John turned to look out the window, as an orderly began opening the blinds to let in more light from the afternoon sun, which was beginning to cast long shadows over the east wing of the hospital. The view from the window presented a generally flat, but pleasingly green panorama of South Jersey's suburban sprawl, extending to distant towns and farms far on the horizon. Viewed from above at this angle, the arbored landscape resembled a vast field of broccoli, with the occasional church steeple or high-rise poking up like weeds.

The hospital was set back a hundred feet or so off Haddon Avenue where it intersected with Vesper Avenue, a small side street. Traffic was light as John followed its progress eastward down Haddon Avenue toward the neighboring towns of Collingswood and Westmont of Haddon Township. He squinted hard to make out a familiar landmark in his hometown of Haddonfield, just beyond Westmont, less than four miles away.

The faint sound of an emergency siren caught John's attention, growing louder as John strained to find its source. Separating the window blinds further to provide a broader view, he sighted a police cruiser turning onto Haddon Avenue heading in the direction of the hospital. Not appearing to be in any particular hurry, its lights not flashing, the cruiser was obviously not the source of the siren, but John nonetheless followed its progress as it turned right onto Vesper Avenue, drew near to the hospital, and pulled into the driveway which serviced the emergency room, and came to a stop just below his window. Two uniformed police officers emerged, one pointed, the other followed, and both were soon lost from view. The sound of the siren peaked and faded with a rising and falling pitch, signaling its passing into the distant, tangled heart of the city.

As he looked across Vesper Avenue, John's eyes followed a tall cyclone fence topped with barbed wire running toward Haddon Avenue to the right. Beyond the fence lay a green expanse of manicured lawns, gently rolling hills, and wooded gardens, through which John could just make out the Cooper River, about a mile away. A labyrinth of narrow, paved paths wound their way through the grounds, broken up by a system of interconnecting ponds, interspersed with white marble monuments of all shapes and sizes. John knew this place. It was Harleigh Cemetery.

He remembered first visiting here as a boy on a class school trip, and knew it to be the final resting place of some of South Jersey's more famous sons and daughters, including Walt Whitman, the "Good Gray Poet." There were later memories as well, some pleasant, but others too painful to recall. He quickly brushed them aside and continued his study of the wooded grounds. From this perspective he gained a new appreciation for its beauty: an island of serenity in an ocean of urban sprawl.

From the corner of his eye, John sensed a commotion on the other side of the activity room. He turned to see two uniformed police officers standing at the entrance of the room, speaking with Katie who was looking over and pointing in John's direction. John recognized them as the two officers who, minutes before, had arrived in the patrol car just below the window, and could sense from their gaze that he was the object of their visit. As they approached, John turned to greet them.

"Good afternoon, officers."

He offered an extended hand in greeting.

The officers ignored the offer. The taller of the two got right to the point. "Sir, are you John Weston, of Haddonfield, New Jersey?" he asked brusquely.

"Yes, officer. What can I do for you?" John responded, slowly bringing his hand back down to his side.

John couldn't figure out why two police officers would want to speak to him. Then the unthinkable crossed his mind. *OhmyGod! Did I do something terrible when I was out of it? Did I hurt someone?*

The smaller, younger officer spoke to the taller one in a Latino accent. "I told you, Bret. This was the guy we picked up the other night. I tell you, he was out of his fu-...."

"Ahem." Katie quickly interjected.

The taller, older officer looked disapprovingly at his partner and then turned to John. "Sir, are you the owner of a tan, 1999 Toyota Camry?"

"Why, yes, officer. As a matter of fact, I do drive a Camry," John responded, somewhat bewildered.

"Have you reported the vehicle lost or stolen in the past week or so?" the officer continued.

"No...I don't believe so," John replied slowly. He was puzzled by the line of questioning. At the same time, he was relieved that the questions were not being directed at him personally. His mind raced as he tried to remember the last time he'd seen or used his car.

"So, are you saying that you're still in possession of your vehicle?"

Katie jumped in. "Excuse me officers, perhaps I can help. As you may surmise, Mr. Weston here has been through some traumatic events lately, from which he is still in the process of recovering. If at all possible, could you please get to the point of your visit?"

"Yes, of course, ma'am." The older officer's tone softened a bit as he turned back to John. "Mr. Weston, it appears that your vehicle was recovered yesterday morning"—reading from his notebook—"'abandoned about fifty miles south of here near Bridgeton, along a back water road about four miles from the Delaware Bay.'" He looked up and continued. "We were notified by Cumberland County Police, who tracked the VIN number with the Division of Motor Vehicles. Your name came up as the registered owner. When we couldn't find you at home, and you failed to answer your phone, we followed the normal protocol and checked the area hospitals."

"And bingo!" announced his young partner.

The older officer produced a Polaroid print of the recovered Camry from an envelope and presented it to John. John nodded.

"Looks like there was no damage done to the vehicle," the officer continued. "Just a small dent on the left front fender, which could have been there before the incident. Very unusual." He was looking directly at John, now, trying to gauge his response. "Usually all we find is a stripped down frame sitting up on cinder blocks. You're very lucky."

This elicited a *gruntle* from the younger officer: half grunt, half chuckle.

John just stood there, silent, trying to piece things together.

Katie took the initiative. "So, what do we do now, officers?"

"Well, I'd like Mr. Weston here to make a written statement and sign these papers," the older officer replied. "Basically acknowledging that he read the police report, and that he is the registered owner of the vehicle."

"Okay if I help him with this?" Katie asked, reaching for the papers. Sensing some reluctance on their part, she added, "It will help expedite the process."

The older officer handed Katie the papers. "Fine. We'll just wait outside. Please let us know when they're ready." Then, almost as an afterthought he added, "Oh yeah. Here's the phone number of the garage where you can pick up your vehicle. The sooner the better. They charge by the day. There will also be a towing charge. Thought you'd like to know."

The older officer pulled a business card and invoice from the envelope and handed it to John, tipped his cap to Katie, "Ma'am," then turned and left the room with his young partner close behind.

A half hour later, John remained in the activity room while Katie escorted the police officers from the ward with their completed paperwork. He looked down at the invoice from the towing service and garage company. Twenty...dollars a day. *Hmm, if the car hadn't turned up for another couple days, it would've saved me how much?* John mused. No, he was glad they'd found it. Trouble was, he was totally clueless as to how it got there. Had it been stolen? Maybe he left the keys in the car before this episode, and someone ran off with it: young teenage kids on a joy ride.

Within minutes Katie returned with a folded copy of the police report under her arm and sat down at one of the activity tables. She had a concerned, puzzled look on her face.

"John, do you remember last Sunday? You had called and left me a message the day before, on Saturday, that you were planning to go to Fortescue to look for clues about what happened to Bob?"

John nodded. Yes, he now recalled it. Fortescue was a popular fishing town on the banks of the Delaware Bay, about sixty miles from Camden. *Was that just last Sunday? It seemed like weeks...no, months ago.*

"Yes, Katie. I remember," he said finally.

"And you drove your car there. Right?"

"Well...yes. Of course." John agreed with some hesitation.

Katie held the police report up to John's face, poking at it with her free hand to get his attention.

"John, did you not read the police report before you signed it?"

"Well, er, not every word," he admitted.

"John, that's not like you."

"Well, just in case you haven't noticed. I haven't been myself of late," John replied with a touch of sarcasm.

Katie ignored the slight and began leafing through the pages of the report.

"According to the police report, there was an eyewitness who saw you. A young boy on a bicycle. Here it is," she said, handing the report to John. "You may want to read it again—for comprehension this time."

> It was about nine o'clock, Sunday morning (September 12). I was going fishing, riding my bike down Bayside Road to the bay. I saw this older guy, standing on the road next to his car. He seemed lost. It was a brown Camry, or something. He asked me for directions to Cohansey Marina. When I left, I saw him get back in his car. Later, about three o'clock, I was coming back to town along Bacons Neck Road. That's when I saw the same car parked on the side of the road, near the corner of Gum Tree Corner Road, just above of the marsh. The driver's door was wide open. I waited for a little while, but no one else was around. There was a rag on the front seat soaked in red. I thought it was blood and got scared. When I got back home I called 911.

Katie paused, waiting for a reaction, but got none.

"So, it was late Monday, the next day, when they picked you up roaming the streets of Camden," she continued, exasperated by John's lack of recall. "You were incoherent, John! They found your car over fifty miles away. So how did you get back in your state? The officer who found you"—pointing at the door to indicate the young officer who had just left—"said you were ranting, insisting on 'getting back to save her.' Those were the exact words in his report—*your* words apparently."

John just stared blankly into space. Then suddenly...

...Swampy water. A great bonfire. Screams. Shouts of celebration. Large green flies. Swarms of flies in ever-increasing numbers. An old woman, laughing. The screams of a young woman...

"John. Are you alright?"

John shook his head to clear his mind. "I'm sorry, Katie. But, I'm thinking maybe what I thought was a dream was, well, maybe it wasn't a dream after all. I don't know. I do remember driving down to the bay, and stopping to ask directions. There were marshes all around, on both sides of the road. And the flies. You know, the big green-headed ones. Relentless. But I don't recall the ride back. In fact, I can't recall much after that. Just parts of a...bad dream."

Katie turned sullen, took a deep breath, and sighed.

"Are you all right, Katie?" John asked, returning the favor.

"It's probably nothing," she said. "But, Bob said the same thing when he came back from the fishing trip that day. Complaining of the flies. Only—"

"Only what?" John pressed her.

"Well, when he started acting strangely, I never thought to make the connection. But in his delusional state, he would sometimes talk about 'going back to save someone,'" Katie explained.

John stood up and moved to the window. Staring out and focusing on the lengthening tombstone shadows of Harleigh Cemetery, he spoke in a trance-like monotone, as if he was addressing the dead rather than the living. "The week following Bob's fishing trip—that was the Fourth of July week— he told me about something strange that had happened to him down there. He said, about an hour after returning to port, on the way home actually, he began to hallucinate. He thought he might be dehydrated, so he ripped open a bottle of Gatorade. He said that helped, enough that he was able to get back on the road and make it home."

John snapped out of it and turned around to face Katie, his backside leaning up against the window sill. "But, I could tell he was troubled by something," he continued. "Maybe something he experienced while he was hallucinating. He wouldn't elaborate. As his condition deteriorated over the next month or so, I started thinking that maybe someone down there would be able to shed some light on what happened. That's why I went down there on Sunday, Katie."

John sat down at the table across from Katie. "From Bob's day planner I got the name of the captain of the fishing boat he had rented, and intended to contact him. But I don't remember ever making it to Fortescue."

They both just sat there for a while, looking at each other. Finally, Katie took a deep breath and exhaled slowly. "John, why don't you keep the police report and read through it again. Maybe something else will come back to you."

Over Katie's shoulder, John had been following the approach of a tall, handsome, middle-aged gentleman in a freshly pressed lab coat, a stethoscope hanging from its waist pocket, the quintessential physician! As he came closer, John made out the name tag on his coat: Alex Ritchie, MD.

"Excuse me for the interruption, Katie"—the doctor spoke in a booming baritone voice, forcing Katie to jump in her seat—"but, I was told

Mr. Weston was feeling better, now. I'd like to ask him a few questions, if I may."

The doctor turned to John and extended his hand in greeting. "Hello, John. Happy to see you're feeling better. I'm Dr. Ritchie. But, please, you can call me Alex."

John stood up, reached out, and shook his hand. Dr. Ritchie exuded charm. He had that powerful, resonating TV announcer voice, the kind that instills confidence from the start, and his tall, handsome stature and slightly graying hair only reinforced the classic TV doctor image.

Katie stood up and excused herself. "John, I'll be leaving you now. But, you're in the best of hands." She turned to Dr. Ritchie, smiled, and said good-bye.

"Mind if I sit down, John?" Dr. Ritchie asked.

John nodded and offered him a seat at the table.

The doctor took a chair on the other side, and studied his clipboard briefly before looking over at John.

"John, I'm not going to bore you with a lot of numbers and statistics. Let me tell you what we've found so far." He placed the clipboard on the table. "First, I believe the abscess on your neck resulted from an insect bite that became infected. I've seen bites develop into nasty infections within just a few hours' time. Do you recall being bitten sometime recently? Say, over the weekend?"

John was quick to answer this time. "Yes, I do remember, now. It was a *fly* of some kind. One of those big greenhead varieties you find at the shore. I'm pretty sure it happened Sunday morning when I was touring the wetlands along the Delaware Bay."

"Ah! *Tabanus nigrovittatus*!" Dr. Ritchie sounded almost pleased, like his medical hunches had paid off. "The salt marsh greenhead fly," he explained. "I'm not surprised. They can leave a very nasty, bloody, and dirty bite. They're related to the horse or deer fly, which can also carry some pretty nasty diseases. When you came into the ER Monday evening, your neck and face were swollen and inflamed. Consistent with an allergic reaction, but could also be the onset of a serious infectious disease, *tularemia*. You weren't in any shape to give us information, so I was forced to cover all the bases. I treated you with steroids for the inflammation, and streptomycin for possible tularemia."

"Tularemia? What's that?"

"It's a rather serious disease caused by a bacteria, *Francisella tularensis*. The organism can enter the body from the bite of a tick or deer fly. Once inside the body, it finds a home as a parasite within a host cell, usually the white blood cells. Doesn't take much. Only a dozen or so cells to cause serious illness. Symptoms develop quickly. Headache, fatigue, dizziness, muscle pain. Face becomes flush, eyes inflamed. Inflammation can spread to the lymph nodes, which become enlarged, accompanied by a fever."

The doctor seems to know his subject very well, John thought.

"Now, in your case," Dr. Ritchie continued, "while you had a low grade fever, the lymph nodes never became involved. But that's not totally unusual with tularemia. The disease can manifest itself in a variety of ways, depending on where the bacteria reside in the body. So, I felt that streptomycin was indicated, as a preventive measure. Your lab work came back clean for *tularensis*. However, with your confirmed fly bite history, I recommend keeping you on the streptomycin for the full course."

"So, what about the abscess?" John asked.

"When we cultured the exudate, we got the usual flora. Nothing exotic. So, we put you on amoxicillin, an effective broad-spectrum antibiotic, to clean it up." Dr. Ritchie pointed to John's neck. "Mind if I take a look?"

"Be my guest."

Ritchie moved closer to John and removed the bandage. "Hmm, looking good! Let's continue with the amoxicillin for another five days. I'll get the nurse to change that dressing. I think a couple Band-Aids will do just fine."

John was already thinking about the doctor's next question. Dr. Ritchie must have read his mind. "Now, let's talk about the other problem," Ritchie said.

"The hallucinations?" John offered.

"Yes. The hallucinations." Dr. Ritchie leaned back in his chair. "As Dr. Caldwell probably explained, psychotic episodes can be tricky matters. It could be purely psychological, or what we call a functional, problem. Or there could be an organic basis for the illness."

"You mean, like a brain tumor?"

"Precisely!" Ritchie rebounded. "I took the liberty of contacting your family doctor. As far as he's concerned, you're as sound, mentally, as the Rock of Gibraltar. So,"—reaching for his clipboard—"this leads me to believe there's an underlying physiological problem at work here."

Dr. Ritchie turned a few pages on his clipboard. "When you were brought in to the hospital Monday evening you were delirious, hallucinating. Quite literally fit to be tied. Initially, I attributed this and the accompanying fever to your dehydrated condition. However, even after you were rehydrated with intravenous fluids and the fever broke, your mental state continued to deteriorate. We had to keep you restrained and sedated for your own protection."

"But, Dr. Caldwell told me what it was. He called it an acute psychotic episode, or nervous breakdown," John said.

"Well, John, you've got to understand"—resuming his teaching voice, as if he was addressing a freshman class of medical students—"the term psychosis refers to the set of symptoms, not the underlying cause. It's like saying, you have a headache. Yes, but what's causing it? Is it stress induced, or the result of a brain tumor? Dr. Caldwell treats the former, while I focus on identifying an underlying organic condition to explain your set of symptoms. Working together we can eventually nail it down."

"Eventually?" John repeated as a question. "And hopefully, before the patient succumbs from his…*symptoms.*"

John emphasized the word "symptoms," drawing quotation marks in the air with his hands.

"Yes, of course," Dr. Ritchie smiled.

"So, you're saying that we don't really know at this point what caused, or is causing, my mental condition."

"That is…essentially correct, John," Dr. Ritchie admitted reluctantly. "On Monday night we ran a brain CAT scan, which revealed nothing."

"So, you didn't find anything up there?" John chuckled. "That's what my associates sometimes say."

Dr. Ritchie corrected himself. "I should say we found nothing abnormal. No tumors, no aneurisms. But now that you're up and about and back to your somewhat ornery self, I'd like to schedule a few additional tests and an MRI. They can often pick up things that a CAT scan will miss."

"Sounds good," John agreed.

"John, the question that concerns me is why a perfectly healthy individual with no prior history of mental illness would suddenly suffer a near complete mental collapse. From what you tell me about how you spent the weekend, I'm thinking you may have picked up something down there along the bay. I mean, aside from the bite. Like, maybe something in the water." Dr. Ritchie paused. "Tell me, John. How is your sense of taste and smell? Notice any recent changes over the past week or so?"

John thought this strange. "Is this a trick question, doc?" he asked.

"No. Not really. Actually, it's something I'm loath to ask, considering the consequences. But, we have to cover all the bases."

John shook his head. "Well, in that case, doc, I've got to say no. Haven't noticed any change. In fact, I think I taste and smell as well as I ever have. Despite the fact that I haven't showered in three days."

"The orneriness coming out again, eh John?" Dr. Ritchie forced a chuckle. "I don't think I have a cure for that in my little black bag."

"So, what's your point, doc?" John pursued.

"Well, there are a few nasty parasitic diseases that attack the central nervous system. One of the worst is something called *Primary Amoebic Meningoencephalitis*, or PAM, for short. Fortunately not very common, but quite devastating when it does strike. It's caused by a free living amoeba, *Naegleria fowleri*, typically found living in the muck and slime on the bottom of freshwater lakes and ponds. But, if stirred up and inhaled up the nose, it can penetrate the mucosa, attacking and destroying the olfactory nerves. That's why I asked you about your sense of smell. Sensory changes are the first sign of infection."

"Well, I don't think that's my problem. My sniffer's in good shape," John assured him.

"And you haven't been swimming in any warm, stagnant ponds lately?"

"No. Not in this lifetime, anyway."

"Good. So I think we can write off PAM."

Dr. Ritchie made another entry in his notebook, as though he was keeping score, humming a little tune as he did so.

"So, aren't you going to tell me what happens next?" John pursued.

"About what ? Oh, you mean—," Dr. Ritchie said pointing to his head.

"Yes, the PAM thing?"

"Well, I don't think you really want to know," Ritchie replied.

"Try me. You said yourself I don't have the disease," John insisted.

"Well, okay then. You see, these amoebae are free living and free moving. Now, don't ask me how they know where to go or what to do. But somehow, these nasty little buggers make their way along nerve fibers, climbing up through the floor of the cranium and into the brain…"

John suddenly had a mental image of a Warner Brothers' Bugs Bunny cartoon with a sign post reading "This way to rabbit brain." John couldn't keep from chuckling.

"You find something amusing in that, John?" Ritchie asked.

"Oh no, nothing. Just a passing thought. Sorry, doc. Please continue."

"Well, once there, they begin feasting on brain tissue, growing in numbers. The hapless victim will start to experience headaches, fever, and maybe a stiff neck, similar to other forms of meningitis. But, in its final stages, as the brain is devoured from within, the victim will begin to exhibit signs of severe brain damage. Behavior changes, hallucinations, things like that."

"Whew! Sounds like some wild science fiction: the attack of the brain-eating amoeba!"

"Right. Not a pleasant thought."

"So, what's the usual prognosis?" John asked.

"Not good. Death almost always results within two weeks of infection. There's about a 97 percent mortality rate. Now, certain antibiotics can provide effective treatment. But the main problem is early detection and diagnosis. Because it's a relatively rare occurrence, typically the first doctor-patient contact is with the pathologist…at postmortem."

"Yes. Well, let me just say, thank you for that, doc. But, if I have a choice, I think I'll opt for Dr. Caldwell's 'nervous breakdown' scenario."

Chapter 4

1774
Friday, 16 September
Greenwich, Cumberland County, West New Jersey

Greenwich on the Cohansey was a picture suitable for framing: a thriving colonial village of farmers and merchants tucked away in the cozy backwaters of West New Jersey Province. In 1774, just ten years shy of its first centennial celebration, Greenwich was a growing, prosperous community—the largest in Cumberland County—populated with third- and fourth-generation Americans getting down to the business of building the new American dream. Located on a navigable inland waterway just five miles from the Delaware Bay, the town prospered as one of only three ports of entry for the province of West New Jersey. The area's fertile soil also made it a prime and central farming community for the region.

Greenwich was also a town with many names. Having established the village of New Salem, New Jersey, in 1675, John Fenwick's plans for a sister Quaker settlement, to be located sixteen miles away on the west bank of the Cohansey River, were never fully realized in his lifetime. When he died in 1683, it was left to his executors to carry out the plans for his new town, which was to be named "Cohanzick," a name thought to have been taken from the local Lenni Lenape Indian name for the river which flowed through the region to the Delaware Bay. Over time, Cohanzick became *Cohansie*, variously spelled as *Kohansey*, *Chohansey*, or *Cohanzee*, which, by the time of the American Revolution, had evolved into its modern-day form, *Cohansey*. One year after his death, in 1684, the town was finally laid out in strict accordance with the plans provided by John Fenwick in his will.

Initially settled by Quakers from New Salem, Greenwich was destined to be a town of Friends in more than name, its early settlers setting the tone for religious tolerance as Presbyterians, Baptists, and Episcopalians shared equally in the growing prosperity of this young farming and bayside shipping community. The town's idyllic setting and its citizens' reputation for tolerance and industry soon attracted people from other parts of New Jersey and its neighboring colonies. In the early 1700s the town received a great influx of immigrants from New England and Long Island who thought the interests of history would be better served if the town's name was changed to Greenwich.

But that didn't end the naming controversy, for there was still no universal agreement on how the name should be pronounced. Ask three different persons and you might get three different responses: "Green-witch," "Gren-itch," or "Gren-witch."

Like many planned communities of its day, the town featured a wide central avenue, one hundred feet across at its widest point. New Salem had its Broad Street; Williamsburg its Duke of Gloucester Street; and Philadelphia its High Street, or today's Market Street. For Greenwich it was Ye Greate Street, a two-and-a-half-mile stretch of road that connected the town's Head of Greenwich section in the north to the town's main center and Market Square in the south, terminating at the wharf at the river's edge. Initially, land was sold off along both sides of the street in sixteen-acre lots, which were later parceled off as the town population grew. On the other side of the river further upstream, a smaller, sister community, Fairfield, was established by migrating New Englander Presbyterians in the early part of the eighteenth century. Before long, a regular ferry service was operating between the two towns.

It was Friday afternoon, September 16, 1774, a typical late summer day, with clear skies and a steady breeze picking up out of the west. Three hollow, clear, glass globes the size of grapefruit, their surfaces decorated in swirling patterns of frosted glass, hung inside the kitchen window of a small cottage, gathering and scattering the incoming light of the early afternoon sun in shadowed reflections throughout the room. *Witch Balls*, the locals called them, for besides offering some measure of adornment to an otherwise austere environment, they were said to repel evil spirits—not a bad feature for an old people in a new, unknown world. Along with a desire to escape religious persecution, those who settled the new North American colonies also brought their European folk traditions and superstitions with them, taking many more generations before such beliefs were supplanted, or perhaps only suppressed, by more modern scientific thinking.

A young, black woman wearing loose-fitting sandals, a simple cotton dress, and an apron, her head covered in a brightly colored turban, entered the kitchen from the storage cellar with a basket of vegetables. She had a bounce to her walk, exhibiting an attractive vitality that belied her low position in life. Humming a little tune, she resumed her work at the hearth as she busied herself with the preparation of the family's evening meal. The distant ringing of a hammer striking cold steel could be heard through an open window.

Another woman, white and younger still, entered the kitchen from the front room, carrying a tall, folded pile of linen and fine, tailored clothes. More finely appareled, yet modest in dress, she wore a brightly printed calico gown with a spotted apron; a sky-blue shawl was draped over her shoulders. Her eyes were emerald-green, hair a light brown, almost blonde, combed back into a casual chignon bun and topped with a small gauze and lace cap. At eighteen years of age, the blossom of youth only accentuated the natural poise and beauty she'd carried with her from birth. Setting the bundle of clothes on the kitchen table, she addressed the young black woman.

"Isabel, I'm taking these mended items to market. I completed them a whole day early and should get a half shilling bonus for my added efforts. Please tell Papa I'll be home for dinner, but not before then."

"Yes, Miss Rebecca. But, you can tell 'em yourself," Isabel smiled, motioning with a wooden stirring spoon toward the outside kitchen door. She spoke in a choppy English dialect peculiar to certain regions of the Caribbean.

There, in the doorway, stood a large, imposing figure of a man: not simply tall, but broad at the shoulders and solidly built. His two arms, like cast bronze stanchions—clearly the strongest members of this brawny frame—hung naked, tan, and heavy by his side. Their molded buff musculature, from flexed biceps to clenched fist, gave evidence of a man well-accustomed to wielding an axe, hammer, or other heavy tool of physical labor. His cotton shirt lay open at the collar, exposing concentric bands of grime and sweat that filled the creases of his neck. His shirtsleeves, stained in sweat, were rolled up above his elbows. Clean shaven, he possessed a full head of chestnut-brown hair that was tucked beneath a simple leather skullcap and gathered and tied at the rear in a ponytail, which trailed a short distance behind. Draped about his neck was a tall, heavy, black leather apron which covered his front torso and extended to below his knees. He appeared to be a man in his prime middle years—say, early forties.

Immediately upon entering the kitchen, he paused to remove his cap and apron, methodically hanging each on separate assigned wall pegs just inside the door, taking a towel in exchange to wipe the sweat from his dirty hands and face as he sought the wash basin at the far corner of the room. The worn nails of his black leather boots struck hard against the flagstone kitchen floor, throwing an occasional spark.

"Did I hear you say you were going to market, Rebecca?" the large man's voice boomed in the stony confines of the small kitchen. Cupping his hands, he reached in and scooped up a handful of water from the basin and doused his face and neck with the cool refreshment.

"Yes, Papa. I finished my mending for Mrs. Mason two days early, in time for the weekend market. She promised me a bonus if I returned them before Saturday."

"Then, by all means, make haste, my child!"

Mr. Whitman wiped his face with the towel, then turned with a smile, leaned over, and gave his daughter a kiss on the cheek.

Thomas Whitman was a blacksmith by trade. His shop adjoined a simple stone and frame cottage home located on the north end of Greenwich. Twenty years earlier, Thomas had migrated to Cumberland County in the province of West New Jersey from East Hampton, Long Island, with his young wife, Elizabeth, and their firstborn child, Thomas Jr. Mr. Whitman was a young man of twenty at the time; Elizabeth was eighteen. They initially settled on the east bank of the Cohansey River in the town of Fairfield, joining the descendants of other Presbyterian families who had similarly relocated from Connecticut and Long Island in preceding generations. Having no close family in these parts, except for a distant cousin on Thomas's side, they relied mostly on ties with their church as they settled into their new way of life in the province of West New Jersey.

Within six months of relocating to Fairfield, young Thomas Jr. contracted measles, an especially virulent and pernicious childhood disease for which neither preventative nor effective cure existed in 1754, aside from the body's own natural defenses. As was often the case, eighteenth-century "cures" and medical practices only exacerbated the condition and hastened one's demise. The child died just before his first birthday.

In Fairfield, Thomas initially found work as a journeyman blacksmith. Two years after their arrival, learning that the neighboring town of Greenwich was in need of a blacksmith—old Mr. Barley had just passed away—Thomas took hold of the opportunity and moved across the Cohansey River with his young wife, now pregnant with their second child. He purchased Mr. Barley's estate lock, stock, and barrel—in this case, house, barn, and forge—located on the north end of town, an area known as the Head of Greenwich, or simply Northern Greenwich, less than two furlongs off Ye Greate Street on the road to Shilo.

It was here, in Northern Greenwich, where young Rebecca was born on August 8, 1756, a healthy, bright-eyed baby girl.

Desiring to expand their family, Elizabeth became pregnant for a third time. When her pregnancy ended with a midterm miscarriage, Elizabeth was advised by their family physician, Doc Woods, not to become pregnant again, as it could put both her and the baby at risk. However, throwing caution to the wind—after all, little Rebecca "needed a baby brother or sister"— Elizabeth became pregnant for a fourth time. She went full term, but as misfortune would have it, the doctor was correct: her labor was long and hard, and the birth was a breech birth. Doc Woods was able to save the baby, but there was nothing he could do to save Elizabeth once the infection took hold. She died within days of the child's birth. It was touch-and-go for several weeks, but the baby—a boy this time—did survive. Thomas named him Elijah, after the boy's grandfather and the Old Testament prophet. That was in the summer of '64.

Needless to say, Thomas was devastated by the loss. Almost equally difficult was having to explain to little seven-year-old Rebecca why her mother had gone away, since he didn't understand it himself.

"Rebecca, your mother told me, before she went away, that she wants you to take good care of your little brother. Do you understand?"

"Yes, Papa," Rebecca replied innocently.

Over time, Rebecca managed to cope with the loss. But after a year of struggling to raise two young children alone, build a business, and maintain a household all at the same time, Thomas realized he was going to need help—more help than little Rebecca and his local church congregation were able to provide. So, it was with some reluctance that he ventured to Amboy Town, a northern port city in East Jersey which prospered in the trade of Negro slave labor, where, in the autumn of '65, he purchased a young slave girl, just seventeen years old and recently arrived from the British Caribbean possession of Barbados. Her name was Isabel.

Isabel was a much younger woman than he had initially planned to purchase. While largely a matter of the purse—having sold a small parcel of his land to generate the needed cash, she was all he could afford—Thomas nonetheless took some measure of pity on this poor girl from the islands, so far from the only home she knew, with no mother, no father, and no family of her own. Born a first-generation child of slave parents on a sugar plantation in Barbados, she was taken from her family by the plantation owner and sold to slave traders bound for the English colonies in North America, to be placed on the auction block in Amboy Town. With the English cracking down on molasses smuggling, and the worsening embargo situation in the colonies, business was down, so the plantation owner had been forced to liquidate some of his assets to maintain a margin of profit, choosing to sell off some parcels of land which had not been so productive in recent years, as well as several of his slaves. Isabel was one of those liquidated assets.

Isabel took an immediate and genuine liking to little Rebecca, whose ingenuous and loving nature proved irresistible. Over time they became very close, almost as sisters. Thomas recognized this bond and the harmony that Isabel had brought to his household, so when Rebecca turned sixteen, he promised Isabel that upon Rebecca's attainment of her twenty-first birthday, or upon her marriage, whichever occurred first, he would manumit her, which is to say, release her from her bondage: Isabel would be a free woman.

But personal tragedy would again strike the Whitman household. Just past his sixth birthday, little Elijah was playing down by Pine Mount Creek not far behind their home. Running barefoot through the remains of an abandoned stable, he was injured when his foot came down hard on a rusty nail protruding up from an old board half buried in the ground. He ran home crying, and Isabel did the best she could to dress the wound, using an old home island remedy: cleaning the wound with turpentine and dressing it with clean linen wrapped in bacon fat. Incredibly, the wound healed without infection. However, ten days later the boy began to experience facial spasms and difficulty swallowing and opening his mouth.

"Lockjaw," Doc Woods had said with grim resignation. "I can give him something for the fever, but his recovery is…well…in the hands of God."

Over the next two weeks the boy's condition worsened. The stiffness in the neck soon spread to his pectoral and calf muscles, and the rigor progressed to the point where the boy's body was racked by whole body muscle spasms, coming in waves that lasted minutes at a time, throwing his tiny body into severely distorted, backward arched positions. Thomas agonized at seeing the boy suffer so, the child's whimpers and tears evidencing a clear mind that was only too aware of the paroxysms ravaging his body. Thomas prayed for the child's release. The next day his prayers were answered: little Elijah gave up the ghost and was at peace once more. The boy's tiny body was buried alongside his mother's in the family plot in the Presbyterian church cemetery.

Now, four years later, Thomas had emerged from this loss with an altered, cynical, view of the world, which translated into an obsessive devotion—doting, some would say—to his young, beautiful daughter, the only remaining love of his life. None dared begrudge him this fair obsession.

Standing there in the kitchen on this Friday afternoon, Mr. Whitman placed his large, rough, calloused hands on Rebecca's shoulders, studying her at arm's length. Rising to every bit of four-feet-eleven-inches tall with shoes on, she possessed her mother's petite frame, but carried it with greater strength and self-assurance.

"You are indeed the very image of your dear mother the day I first met her," her father said with moisture welling up in his eyes. "Such a beautiful young woman you have grown to be. If only she could see you now."

"I surely believe, Master Whitman, sir," Isabel interjected, "that Mrs. Whitman is looking down and smiling this very minute. Jus' as sure as those warm rays of sunshine are comin' through yonder window. Yes sir, I'm certain of it."

Mr. Whitman turned to Isabel with a broad smile. "And you, my good Isabel, have brought your own fair measure of sunshine to this household. You know my promise is good regarding your emancipation," he assured her.

"Yes sir. I'm much obliged by your kind offer. Why else you think I'm so eager to see Miss Rebecca married off? If only she can make up her mind, she got so many fine young men knockin' down the door to win her over."

Rebecca cast a stern look toward Isabel. "Izzy! That just isn't true. I've got two bona fide suitors, is all!"

Isabel put her hand to her mouth to stifle a laugh. Rebecca blushed, looking down, biting her lip to hold back a giggle.

Mr. Whitman shook his head. "Rebecca, I thought Mr. McKenzie was your only interest. Such a fine, upstanding young man with excellent future prospects. I understand he has received his first mate papers."

A new thought came to his mind. Taking a more firm, but still gentle hold of Rebecca's shoulders, he cocked his head to one side and challenged her directly. "Tell me, young lady. Is young Mr. Weston still sending you letters? I thought you had long gotten over your infatuation with him."

"Ohhh, Papa," Rebecca whined. "You know John and I have been friends ever since…well, since before mother passed away. Since the time of the Greenwich Fairs. And that's been"—thinking for a moment—"almost ten years ago since the last fair."

Her father released his grip and backed away.

"Besides," she continued, "I didn't think you were so…fond of the Irish."

His eyes widened, taken slightly aback by her comment.

"Well, if you ask me, a loyal Irishman is many times preferred over an English vagabond inclined to seditious points of view."

Rebecca moaned and began refolding the pieces of clothing that had fallen loose upon the table.

"What worries me," her father continued, "is that he would drag you into one of his ill-conceived Sons of Liberty schemes. How he has managed to escape the King's justice to this point in time is beyond my understanding."

"Well, Papa, I think Paul McKenzie is a very fine gentleman. But"—she paused, holding up a man's shirt for inspection, then refolding it—"there is something special about the way John and I feel." Turning to face her father, she added, "We really understand each another, Papa, and share…special feelings."

"Ah! I don't understand the younger generation these days," he complained.

Rebecca approached him and picked up his hand, speaking softly. "Papa, we are not any different than you were in your younger days."

He melted. Reaching out to rearrange a curl that had fallen out of place over her eyes, he finally gave in.

"Oh, just like your mother, bless her soul," he sighed reflectively. "She certainly carried the power of gentle persuasion in her tender look."

His thoughts snapped back to the present. "So, you will be in need of a carriage to go to town?"

"Yes, Papa. I have several bundles of clothes that are too unwieldy for horseback."

"Yes, of course." He thought for a moment. "You can take the Reverend's buggy. He won't be needing it until tomorrow afternoon, and has offered its use to us. As he himself said, it's the least he could do, since I made the necessary repairs free of charge."

Rebecca's face brightened. "Oh, Papa! You mean that handsome rig sitting to the side of the barn?"

"Yes," he confirmed, "the canopied carriage with the rosin glass windows and the tassels hanging all about. You'll make a fine ensemble. With your pretty face and handsome figure at the reins, you're bound to attract the attention of all passersby."

Rebecca squealed with delight as she flung her arms around her father and gave him a big hug. Backing away she added, "Thank you, Papa. I promise not to flaunt myself as to offend the sensibilities of our Quaker townsfolk."

"Well spoken, young lady. Fine, then. Give me some time to hitch up the rig. I'll give you the nice spotted mare. She knows her way around town even in the dark, should your chores delay your return."

Less than fifteen minutes later, Rebecca was in the front seat of the rig with a hold of the reins, the three bundles of mended clothes piled on the back seat.

"I'll be home by dinner, Papa," she called out.

He waved her off. Then, with a snap of the reins and a "giddyup," the carriage lurched forward and out onto the gravel road in the direction of Ye Greate Street. The carriage wheels made a familiar crunching sound against the crushed clam shell surface of their side yard where all the other rigs were parked. One belonged to the Whitmans. The others were in various stages of repair, belonging to customer townsfolk who relied on the local blacksmith for the servicing and repair of their carriages and farm implements.

The sun shone brightly in a nearly cloudless sky, as a cool breeze started up from the northeast, foretelling a shift in the weather. It would soon be autumn, the peak of the harvest season, and Rebecca liked this time of year best. With the heat of summer past and the cold blast of winter's chill still many weeks away, this was a time to relax and enjoy the changes of the seasons: the colors, the smell of fresh cut hay in the fields, and, perhaps most welcome, the demise of pesky crawling and flying insect hordes that proved so bothersome in this part of the world.

The nearby marshes and inland waterways offered fertile breeding grounds for a vast variety of annoying and disease-carrying insect pests: blood-seeking greenhead flies during the day and hordes of mosquitoes on warm summer nights were the norm, something her English ancestors across the sea, living in their open-window, thatched-roof cottages, could never have foreseen. In the new world, they learned from the local natives, the Lenni Lenape Indians—called the Delaware Indians by the English settlers—how to concoct lotions that proved at least partially effective in deterring the will of the mosquito.

But the greenhead fly, that was another matter! A persistent and pernicious adversary, the greenhead drew a nasty bite and was not so easily deterred from its attack with lotions or the mere shaking of the limb. It needed a more determined persuasion: a direct smack or swat with a paddle or willow branch. Now, with the coming chill of autumn, the flies would soon retreat into the marshes from whence they came, bringing welcomed relief to the people living along the bay and inland waterways.

Rebecca's spotted mare came to a stop at the intersection with Ye Greate Street, the wide, tree-lined main street which ran the length of the town. Past Stathem's corner store on the right, the street ran north past a line of framed cottages and shops, neatly aligned and maintained with their nicely trimmed yards and gardens. Crossing Pine Mount Run and the narrow, shady glen that transected this part of town, the road climbed a small rise—Mount Gibbon—as it joined King's Highway and continued toward the town of New Salem some thirteen miles away, running in twists and turns through smaller towns and settlements along the way, towns with colorful sounding names, like Gum Tree Corner and Stow Creek Landing. Rebecca had made this trip many times and knew its every rise, dip, and turn. As a seamstress for a local tailor and haberdasher in Greenwich, she would often accompany Mrs. Judith Mason, the tailor's wife, to buy and sell fabric and supplies with the local Salem merchants and shops. From Salem she had longed to turn up Broad Street, the town's main street, and continue northward along the main King's Highway toward the more distant towns of Raccoon (Swedesboro), Woodbury, and beyond. Papa had promised to take her to visit Haddonfield and Philadelphia before her twentieth birthday, and she harbored secret dreams of someday finding gainful employment in Philadelphia as a seamstress for a high fashion designer of women's apparel. "*Haute Couture,* that's what the French call it," she told Izzy. "Philadelphia? So, why not Paris?" Izzy would chide her in return. To a small-town slave girl from the country, one big city was as remote as another.

But Rebecca was not going to Salem today. With a deep sigh, she ordered the mare to make the wide left turn onto Ye Greate Street and proceeded south toward the town's center and her final destination, the Market Place, some two miles away. Approaching an ivy-covered, red brick church and cemetery to her right, Rebecca closed her eyes and said a silent prayer for her mother who was buried there. Dotted throughout with ancient elms and buttonwoods, the church grounds provided a quiet, shady repose— for both the living and the dead. Rebecca was seven years old at the time of her mother's death, and she cherished the small traces of memory she was able to retain of her: the bedtime stories, the times spent "helping" her mother with her embroideries, as she knew her mother was the inspiration and source of her sewing interests and seamstress skills.

This was the church to which Rebecca and her father belonged—the Greenwich Presbyterian Church—and it was this church's minister whom she had to thank for the use of his carriage. The Greenwich congregation espoused a more liberal view of fundamentalism than did their Presbyterian brothers and sisters across the river in Fairfield. Rebecca knew that her father, while he felt comfortable with the church's position on religious matters, was not as inclined to agree with the congregation's patriotic leanings and liberal political viewpoints. Such was the rift between them when it came to her relationship with John "Jay-Bird" Weston, as she'd playfully nicknamed him.

The avenue opened wide and straight before Rebecca as she continued south on Ye Greate Street through the Head of Greenwich. Large deciduous trees—elm, oak, maple, and buttonwood—lined the road, their sprawling branches meeting in the middle, forming an arched, shady canopy of forest green. Up and down the street, men and women set about their daily chores at a comfortable pace, some on foot, others on horseback or the occasional wagon or carriage. Single dwelling homes and shops, constructed of wood frame, stone, or brick in accordance with the particular means and bent of the owner, were set back and spaced a comfortable distance from the road, leaving ample room for picket fenced yards and well-cared for trellised, brick garden paths. A few original log dwellings remained, constructed by first-generation settlers almost a century before. They now served as barns and storage sheds or living quarters for slaves and indentured servants. Beyond the homes, split rail fences extended far into the checkerboard fields, which were dotted with farm workers and horse-drawn wagons bringing in the harvest of late summer corn, wheat, and barley.

Continuing down Ye Greate Street, the buildings gave way to meadows and fields as the spotted mare, sensing the open country, picked up her pace. Rebecca delighted in the cool breeze rustling through her hair, threatening to loosen her cap, as two field swallows swooped in from the left and gave her a start; but the mare continued her pace, steadfast and sure.

Rebecca pulled up on the reins as the road jogged sharply to the right, but the mare negotiated the turn with accustomed ease. A low stone wall running along the left side of the road enclosed another cemetery. This was the burial ground of the Society of Friends, or Quakers, although, on first passing this might be difficult to discern, for there were no tombstones to mark the grave sites, as was the custom of the early Quakers.[2]

Just past the cemetery, the road took another abrupt turn to the left, resuming its original southward direction. Here the road widened into a grand treelined boulevard, one hundred feet across, as it made its final, straight one-

---

[2] The early Quakers took a strong stand against ornamentation of any kind, in death as in life, and considered it especially improper to mark or decorate the remains of the deceased. "Ashes to ashes, dust to dust" was a scriptural adage they took especially to heart.

mile run toward the Market Place and the Cohansey River beyond. Homes and shops in this part of town evidenced a somewhat finer degree of affluence and activity than her "Head of Greenwich" neighborhood. A sign posted on the gray fieldstone tavern approaching on the left proudly announced the establishment as the oldest tavern in the county.[3] The building faced opposite the T-intersection with Bacons Neck Road, which branched to the right and ran through the west end of town toward the Delaware Bay and *Bacons Adventure*, one of the original grand estates of Greenwich established in 1682 by Samuel Bacon.[4]

Rebecca's passing caught the attention of a group of young men emerging from the Stone Tavern, one waving and shouting something to Rebecca. She recognized him as a local ne'er do well from the far side of the river, a tall, skinny young man with long, straight, unkempt hair. *Like a scarecrow*, she thought. As he spoke, all she could make out were the words "...Johnny Jay." Rebecca drew up on the reins and brought the carriage to an abrupt halt.

"Hello, Roger," she called out. "I couldn't make out what you said. Was it something about John?"

Roger Walker shuffled lazily toward the carriage, dragging his feet and kicking up little puffs of dust.

"A good day to you, Miss Whitman," he said with a squinty smile. He tipped his wide-rimmed farmer's hat in a half-hearted greeting, but mainly to shield his eyes from the sun. "I was just inquiring whether you had seen your Johnny boy lately. Did you know he was in town?"

Roger took the horse's bridle in one hand and began to pet the mare on the snout with the other in long, gentle strokes. He didn't bother looking up when he spoke, like he was talking straight to the mare.

"Yes ma'am. I heard tell that Johnny Jay was in town just a few days past."

Tilting his head and squinching his eyes, Roger looked up at Rebecca silhouetted against the afternoon sun.

---

[3] Having served in its earliest years as a courthouse for traveling sessions of the Salem County courts, the Stone Tavern continued in this capacity for the newly established Cumberland County, partitioned in 1748 from the parent Salem County. Eleven months later, Greenwich lost its bid for permanent county seat when nearby Bridge-town was chosen over Greenwich in a general election, to the surprise and disappointment of many of the locals.

[4] The titles of many of the early estates in Fenwick's colony assumed colorful names such as this, following the tradition of the English gentry from the old country. The Bacon family lineage would boast many accomplished individuals over the years, including actor Kevin Bacon, and noted architect and urban planner, Edmund Bacon, in modern times.

"It was said that he appeared a bit ragged. Like"—with a touch of mystery in his voice—"he was running from something. Or perhaps, in pursuit of some *clandestine* mission."

He took relish in saying that word, clandestine, as if it needed no explanation. Backing away from the mare, Roger just stood there, arms folded, like a lawyer making his final statement to the jury.

"They said he took the Cumberland stage to Haddonfield on its weekly run, this past Monday. I am surprised he didn't make his presence known to you, Miss Whitman."

Roger seemed to take delight in presenting bad or discomfiting news.

Rebecca was puzzled. "But how can that be? I received a letter from him just this past week. He was writing from Annapolis, Maryland. He reported that he was handling his brother's business, arranging for some shipments from the southern colonies."

"Well, I don't know anything about that," Roger admitted. "Like I said, I didn't see him with my own eyes. Just reporting what I heard."

Rebecca became annoyed, thinking she might be the brunt of a joke. "Well, I thank you, Roger, for that tantalizing piece of news." Glancing at his two drinking companions waiting for him by the tavern door, she smirked and added, "Perhaps the senses of your witnesses were dulled by one too many drafts of hard cider."

"I do beg your pardon, Miss Whitman." Roger bowed and waved his arm down and across his chest in the exaggerated manner of a gentleman addressing a lady on a ballroom dance floor. "But I remain true to my story. It came from a reliable source. Besides," he smiled, "*rum* is the drink more to our liking. They mix a heavenly *flip* here at the Stone Tavern."

Rebecca bristled and shook her head disapprovingly.

Changing the subject, the young man's attention returned to the spotted mare. "Tell me, Miss Whitman. Do you think your father would be willing to part with this fine animal? I could make it well worth his while."

"And what would you use for payment?" she challenged.

"What! Do you not think my handsome demeanor and ingratiating manners would serve as a suitable down payment?"

Rebecca laughed. "I think not," she replied. "But if you were able to secure a cash loan with such collateral as you propose, then Papa might be willing to talk."

"Ah, Miss Whitman, I pity the man who takes you for his wife. He must daily endure your sharp rebukes without recourse. I would have you know that I am on the brink of a grand venture that could prove very profitable for both myself and my colleagues."

Rebecca smiled. "I surely wish you well with your adventures, Roger. But, I must away and be about my business. And I would recommend you do the same. Your father's fields must be in need of harvesting. Now, what opportunity is that for cash return on vested effort!"

"Miss Whitman, are you suggesting that I resort to an honest day's labor for my support?" he quipped.

"It works for most folk. Of the upstanding sort, that is," she retorted. "Perhaps you should try it!"

With that she shook the reins and ordered the mare to move ahead. Roger pulled away and waved her by. Then, slowly backing up, he returned to his friends.

Rebecca continued down Ye Greate Street to the steady clip-clop of the spotted mare, tassels hanging from the rim of the buggy's canopy, swaying in the gentle breeze as pleasant thoughts of her childhood came back to her. A stately two and a half story brick home approaching on the left side of the street held a special place in her memory. This was the manor house of a sixteen-acre estate, built in 1730 by Nicholas Gibbon and his brother, Leonard. In the early days of Greenwich, the Gibbon brothers were responsible for much of the physical growth of the town and its burgeoning shipping business, with their ships carrying a majority of the region's imports and exports.

But to the young Rebecca, the Gibbon mansion sparked imaginings of princesses and Cinderella endings, whenever her mother would read bedtime stories to her.

"You mean, like the Gibbon House?" she would ask whenever the story called for a grand manor. She remembered as a young child visiting the Gibbon mansion on several occasions with her mother, where they would join in with other women-folk of the town in the manor's spacious kitchen with its immense fireplace and hearth. More than a kitchen, the room was a cottage factory where the women would spend the day in common industrious pursuit of the necessities and amenities of colonial life: spinning, weaving, and dying of cloth; sewing; and candle and soap making. To her young eyes and ears, the house was truly a mansion, and she would fantasize that one day she might live in a home as fine as this.

Young Rebecca had an eye for patterns, whether in nature, in her own weaving and embroideries, or in the man-made and finely crafted articles that surrounded her in her daily life. Viewed from the outside, the patterns in the mansion's front face brickwork especially fascinated her as a child, alternating red and blue brick of varying sizes, which created an interesting checkerboard pattern.

"Flemish bond brick," her papa would explain.

Mr. Whitman apprenticed two years as a bricklayer, before taking up the blacksmithing trade in his early twenties.

"You see," he would continue, "bonding is the method of laying brick. If you lay the brick lengthwise along the course, you see its long stretcher side. If you lay it crosswise, you see the shorter header end. By using alternate stretcher and header brick in the same course, you get what is called a Flemish bond."

"But how do they make the blue color in the brick? Do they dye it like cloth?" Rebecca would ask.

"Aha!" her papa replied, with a glad-you-asked smile. "That's the secret art of the brick maker. To get the brick to turn blue, you need to burn or toast it closer to the flame. It takes a special kind of wood fuel, as well."

Rebecca would simply nod, pretending to understand.

As Rebecca approached Maple Street and the Market Square, she knew she was nearing the end of her afternoon trek. Maple Street branched off to the left, across from the Market Square, and was the last of three roads leaving town to the east, all heading toward other smaller neighboring towns, with names like Roadhouse, Shilo, and Deerfield. Crossing and merging with one another, these roads eventually took the traveler to Bridge-town (modern-day Bridgeton), located six miles upriver from Greenwich where the river narrowed. As its name suggests, Bridge-town—sometimes called "Cohansie Bridge" or simply "the Bridge"—offered the only bridge crossing over the Cohansey River. But, for the citizens of Greenwich and Fairfield, a ferry service had long been established allowing them to make the wider river crossing between their two towns. Common family and business ties strongly united the two communities, so crossings were frequent and necessary.

With its wide open green and rows of neatly arranged vendor stalls, the Market Square and its neighborhood shops formed the hub of merchant and artisan activity in Greenwich. Its pleasant park-like setting also made the square a favorite gathering place for social and community events. Rebecca smiled as a group of young boys ran shouting across the green, chased by a flock of fluttering kites that competed for new heights in the clear, blue sky. With makeshift tails fluttering wildly in the breeze, the kites dipped and soared, teasing a pack of yelping neighborhood strays that followed in close pursuit, snapping and leaping to bring down their paper prey. It was a great day to fly a kite!

On the other side of the square, two young girls sought to gain the confidence of a gaggle of geese that were taking pause from their migratory flight southward, while the girls' mother sat on a nearby park bench engrossed in her knitting. Holding out their hands, the girls tried to entice the big birds with small morsels of stale bread. Just when it seemed as though they might succeed, an older boy came dashing from out of nowhere, shouting and charging the geese with arms waving wildly overhead. The geese quickly dispersed in all directions with a great honking and flapping of wings. The older girl stomped her feet in protest, the younger one started to cry, and the boy just gave a hearty, triumphant laugh, running off as quickly as he had appeared. An old man, preparing a stall for Saturday's farmers' market, waved his arms and shouted something at the boy as he whisked by, while the young girl sought solace in the arms of her mother, who hugged her, taking a handkerchief from her purse to gently wipe away her tears.

For Rebecca, the scene brought back pleasant memories of the Greenwich Fairs of her youth. Held twice a year in April and October, the fairs were originally established in 1695 by the royal governor to promote commerce and trade in the colony, and would go on for several days, attracting people from as far away as Philadelphia and beyond. However, in 1765 the fairs were discontinued for some reason or another. Rebecca never knew why exactly. Her father said it was because certain influential local retailers became wary of lost revenue to itinerant peddlers, and therefore forced their shutdown. He always suspected Richard Wood, who owned and operated a large and lucrative retail emporium on the corner of Bacons Neck Road and Ye Greate Street, just across from the Stone Tavern. Rebecca only knew that she missed the fairs and wished they would return.

The spotted mare paused at the corner of Maple and Ye Greate Street, waiting for the command from Rebecca to go either straight ahead or turn left toward Bridge-town. Continuing straight on Ye Greate Street—for the mare was accustomed to either route—would have taken her past the rectory and Saint Stephen's Episcopal Church on the left, followed several houses later by the newly built (1771) Orthodox Friends Meeting House, a massive brick structure located on a slight rise overlooking a bend in the Cohansey River, within direct sight of the ferry dock and wharf. There, several windowless structures served as temporary storage buildings, or warehouses, for off-loaded cargo or goods waiting to be shipped.

The house of John Sheppard stood close by, located on the second oldest property along Ye Greate Street. The property had been sold by Fenwick's executors eighty-eight years earlier to the house's builder and original owner, Mark Reeve. The Sheppard family founded and operated the ferry service that made regular crossings of the Cohansey River between the towns of Greenwich and Fairfield. If they were traveling to Fairfield today, Rebecca would have led the mare and carriage onto a waiting flat-bottomed scow, paid the ferryman, and enjoyed a short but leisurely cruise up river to the landing at Fairfield. The fare for such crossing was negotiable: a pint of rum oftentimes sufficed for a man and beast. Although the boat was equipped with a sail, more often than not it required the assistance of one or more oarsmen to navigate the currents and guarantee a proper arrival at the landing on the far side. The assistance of an able-bodied male passenger was always welcomed, and would sometimes win him and his party free passage.

But Rebecca and the spotted mare were not taking the ferry today. With a left tug of the reins and a "giddyup!" the carriage lurched forward and turned left onto Maple Street. Proceeding a short distance down the road, Rebecca brought the carriage to a stop in front of a modest two-story frame building on the right. A sign post announced the business establishment as: *Mason's Tailor Shoppe and Haberdashery.*

Stepping down from the carriage, Rebecca adjusted her cap, straightened her dress, then scooped up a bucket of water from a nearby trough and offered the grateful mare a much-needed drink, followed with a handful of oats scooped from a burlap bag hanging from the side of the rig. The mare giving a thankful nod of its shaggy head.

"Good old girl," she said, as the horse whickered between mouthfuls.

After a pat on the haunches and a few gentle strokes down the bridge of the nose, Rebecca tied the horse's reins to the hitching post and retrieved one of the bundles of clothes from the back seat of the carriage. It was only then that she noticed an older woman seated by herself in a farmer's wagon parked just ahead, a woman seated with her back to Rebecca, a white lace shawl draped about her shoulders. Rebecca thought it strange that the woman was rocking to and fro, front to back, and she thought she could hear the woman humming, or laughing to herself—she wasn't quite sure, as she couldn't see the woman's face.

Rebecca turned and approached the front porch of the shop with the bundle of clothes under her arm, just as an older man was leaving—a thin man with a ruddy, farmer's complexion and worn, baggy knee britches. She thought he looked familiar, but he didn't seem to notice her as he moved quickly, brushing against her as he passed by, almost knocking her down in the process.

"Pardon me, ma'am," he mumbled gruffly, realizing his mistake as he hastened down the walk, tipping his three-corner hat in a perfunctory gesture of apology without ever looking back.

Recovering her balance, Rebecca turned in time to see him climb up onto the wagon, taking a seat next to the older woman. Her rocking motion ceased for a moment as they exchanged some words, but once again resumed as the man commanded his two-horse team with a snap of the whip. The wheels creaked and groaned as the wagon made a tight one hundred-eighty degree turn on Maple Street and slowly lumbered back into town. Rebecca had never seen such a fine pair of steeds: two stallions, black as pitch; each with a distinctive white diamond blaze on its face. The wagon continued on, disappearing from view as it made a right-hand turn onto Ye Greate Street heading north.

Rebecca stepped up onto the porch and opened the front door of the tailor shop. The tinkle of bells announced her entry.

"Good afternoon, Mrs. Mason," she called out. "And a good day to you, too, sir!"

Mr. Mason nodded without looking up from his work. Seated on a three-legged stool, his white linen shirtsleeves rolled up to his elbows, he hovered intently over a wire-framed torso mannequin as he put the finishing touches on his newest creation.

Rebecca paused just inside the room and took a deep breath. The combined scent of fabric and perfumed candles filled her head. She felt right at home in Mason's Tailor Shoppe. Ever since she was thirteen, she had spent much of her waking hours working here under Mrs. Judith Mason's tutelage, learning the trade and skills of a seamstress. She very much liked the Masons, and had come to regard Mrs. Mason as the mother she had lost at so young an age.

Rebecca went directly to the counter on the far side of the shop where she placed her bundle of clothes.

"Hello, Rebecca," Mrs. Mason responded from her high perch atop the stepladder, where she was busy arranging bolts of cloth on the wall shelves behind the counter. Without looking down or turning around, she added, "Just set the clothes on the countertop, dear."

Mr. Mason looked up and smiled, peering over his spectacles set low on the bridge of his nose. "I think Rebecca knows her way around the shop by now, Judith."

Robert Mason was an accomplished tailor who took great pride in his work. In his manner and attire he was marked by a certain economy of expression. There was no waste in his work, and every motion and word served a direct purpose.

"My dear Judith, please recompense Rebecca for her added efforts. I do believe we owe her a bonus for her timely return."

Mrs. Mason stepped down from the ladder and turned to greet young Rebecca with a broad smile. A short, stout lady with a pudgy, rosy complexion, she moved quickly about the shop, rather like a mother duck gathering up her ducklings, bouncing endlessly from one task to another. Rebecca wished to have a fraction of her energy when she turned Mrs. Mason's age.

"Yes, of course, dear. I have your money right here."

Mrs. Mason opened the cash drawer and removed several coins, handing them to Rebecca.

"Thank you, ma'am."

Still troubled by the man she passed on the porch, Rebecca inquired after the gentleman. "Mrs. Mason, who was that man just leaving the shop? The older gentleman with the three-cornered hat. He looked familiar. But honestly, he would like to have knocked me over as I was coming in!"

"Oh, that would be Albert Greene, dear. He was bringing in some clothes for alterations and mending. You must know him. He has a wife and three daughters, and lives on a farm out toward Stowe Creek, northwest of here. Not far from the bay, actually."

"Oh, yes, I remember, now." Rebecca said. "Their youngest daughter is my age. Cynthia is her name. I remember playing with her as a child."

Rebecca thought about the older woman seated in the wagon outside, rocking to and fro, laughing to herself. Looking back toward the door, it suddenly dawned on her who she was.

"So! That was Cynthia's mother, Mrs. Greene, in the wagon. Oh my! I do recall her now. When I was growing up she always had a wild look about her—and such a piercing voice! I remember feeling so sorry for Cynthia and her sisters; her mom used to beat them so. And she scared me, too, with her big, bulging eyes." Rebecca laughed. "We used to call her the 'bug lady'—for those big, buggy eyes. She'd like to stare a hole clear through me!" Pausing briefly she added, "But...Mr. Greene. I always remembered him as a gentle and kind man. He looks so much older now, and so worn. It really hasn't been that long ago."

Mrs. Mason drew closer to Rebecca. "Well, if you'd been put through what she's put him through over the years, you'd know why. Especially, ever since..."

She hesitated, thinking maybe she had said too much.

"Ever since what?" Rebecca pressed her.

Mr. Mason spoke up from across the room. "Ever since Mrs. Greene took ill," he said without dropping a stitch.

Rebecca turned to Mr. Mason.

"Took ill? From what?" she asked.

"Melancholy. Nerves. Least, that's what Doc Woods called it," he replied.

"Well, if you ask me," Mrs. Mason added, "I think it to be something a bit more than what Doc Woods used to say, God rest his poor soul. After all, her behavior is not exactly...normal."

"What do you mean?" Rebecca's interest was piqued.

"Well, I really shouldn't be talking out of school, but"—Mr. Mason began humming a tune, as if he really didn't want to be hearing this—"I heard Mrs. Robins telling Abigail Stern the other day that she saw Mrs. Greene dancing in the fields under a full moon, wearing not a stitch of clothes, conversing with the trees, of all things. She continued in this manner until Mr. Greene finally showed up and wrapped her up in burlap. Had to pick her up bodily and place her in the wagon."

Rebecca gasped at the thought. "How did she ever come to such a state?" she asked.

"Well, dear. Of course, I don't know for sure. But, it is well-known that the bite of the *wolf peach* can produce severe upsets. Even death!" Mrs. Mason dramatized. "They're known to grow wild in these parts, you know."

"Yes, I've seen them," Rebecca acknowledged. "Low-growing green vines with pretty yellow flowers and soft, bright red fruit. Papa always said they were poisonous. Like deadly nightshade berries."

"Yes, like deadly nightshade," Mrs. Mason repeated for emphasis.

"Well," she continued, "when Abigail Stern was a young girl growing up in Fairfield, she reported seeing Agatha Greene actually eating a wolf peach. Right off the vine! Happened right in plain view at the Greenwich Fair."

"Really? And what happened?"

"Well, the story goes that nothing happened. Least not right away," Mrs. Mason explained matter-of-factly. "Then, all of a sudden, the poor woman simply went mad with rage, chasing people with a broom all about the Market Square. From that point on, well, that was about the time folks began to notice…her odd behavior," she added mysteriously.

"So, you're saying, that's why she's the way she is? From eating a wolf peach?"

"Well, I can't say for sure. But, it is an attractive explanation. I'd sooner accept that explanation than report what other folks sometimes say."

Mrs. Mason began sorting out the clothes from the bundle Rebecca had left on the counter.

"What is it that other people say?" Rebecca pressed her.

Mrs. Mason didn't say a word—just gave a worried look at her husband, like she was waiting for him to say something.

Mr. Mason finally spoke.

"What Mrs. Mason is trying to say, is that Agatha Greene is touched, my dear Rebecca. Even that she is…a *witch*!" On the word "witch" he raised one eyebrow and waved and shook both hands in the air like a madman. "Which is why, some would say, she didn't die from the bite of the deadly fruit."

There was a moment of silence.

Mr. Mason went back to his work. As an afterthought, without looking up he added, "But, fortunately for Agatha Greene,"—with just a touch of sarcasm—"we now live in an age of enlightenment. A hundred years ago we would have burned her at the stake and be done with it. Now, we just shun and gossip the poor woman to death and…Ouch!"—pulling quickly away from his work and shaking his hand—"I pricked my finger!" He put his finger to his mouth and sucked out the blood and soreness. "I hate it when that happens!"

Mrs. Mason just shook her head. "Tut-tut. It serves you right, for carrying on that way. 'Burn at the stake.' My word!" she laughed nervously.

"Maybe we should stop all this talk about witches," Rebecca replied. "It gives me the shivers."

She suddenly remembered the other two packages from the carriage.

"Oh, I almost forgot. I have two other bundles of clothes waiting in the carriage. I'll go get them."

"Tut-tut, my dear. You need help." Mrs. Mason turned to her husband. "Robert, why don't you give Rebecca a hand with her bundles."

"Oh, that won't be necessary," Rebecca objected. "I can handle them myself, really."

Mr. Mason backed away from his work and straightened up to his full six-foot frame. A tall, lanky man with sinewy features, his curly, thinning white hair lay in disarray atop his head, like windblown wisps of cirrus clouds floating high in a fair-weather sky. His legs seemed longer than they ought to be, out of normal proportion to his torso, like a man hiding a pair of circus stilts beneath his trousers. Rebecca once heard him confide to a friend, when asked how he had chosen his profession: "...I was obliged, dear sir, out of self-preservation to become a tailor, lest I be forced to wear a barrel or go naked through life, as no haberdasher on God's green earth I have ever found who could give this frame a proper fit." Rebecca could not keep from chuckling at the image evoked by these words, as he stood there before her now.

"No, I insist, dear," Mr. Mason responded as he removed his spectacles—taking care to fold them carefully—and placed them in his top shirt pocket. "I would actually welcome a break from my work right about now."

Mr. Mason braced himself at the small of his back with both hands and, arching his upper torso backward, gave his body a good stretch. Rebecca could hear his joints crack.

"Why, thank you, Mr. Mason. I'll show you the way to my carriage."

Rebecca was interrupted by the tinkling of bells. Reflexively, Mr. Mason's attention was drawn to the door—another paying customer.

Two ladies entered the shop: one very young, in her early teens, followed by a second older woman. Both were generously endowed in form and figure: the younger one, pleasingly plump, the older, a bit rotund and top-heavy, rather like bags of barley grain stacked to overflowing on an undersized pushcart. Mr. Mason greeted them both with a broad smile.

"Good day, Mrs. Robins. And your lovely daughter. My, how you've grown into such a fine young lady!"

Mr. Mason was generous with his compliments. It was good manners—and good business. The young Miss Robins tittered and blushed. Her mother forced a smile and nodded.

"And a good day to you, Mr. Mason. If you please, I've come for my mended garments. I trust they are ready?" she challenged briskly.

Before he could answer, the woman turned to his wife, Mrs. Mason.

"And Judith. I'd also like you measure my little Samantha for an ensemble and corset. I think you would agree, it is high time for her to dress like a lady."

"Why, yes, of course," Judith assured her. "One can plainly see that she is ready."

"Indeed," added Mr. Mason, assuming a thoughtful pose. "The young flower must blossom and bloom, if ever the hope for bee or groom."

"Why, Mr. Mason," Mrs. Robins reacted with affected coyness, "I didn't know you had the flare of the bard in you."

Mrs. Mason just rolled her eyes and shook her head dismissively, out of sight of the two Robins ladies.

"Ah, my dear Mrs. Robins"—Mr. Mason drew out the *ahh* and continued with magniloquent dramatic flair—"a tailor's eye and needle as much befit the form of art as prepare the form for fitting!"

Mrs. Mason paused in her tracks, wondering if he was quoting Shakespeare. She then turned to address young Samantha directly. "Miss Samantha. You shall leave this day with the full assurance of meeting the height of today's fashion."

Samantha cupped her hands over her mouth and gasped with joy. "Wonderful! Oh, Mother, I do so want to be fashionable."

Mrs. Robins smirked. "A proper fit is all I ask," she responded brusquely.

"Yes, of course. A proper fit. That is all anyone really needs," Mr. Mason conceded. Leaning over to address Samantha directly, his hands braced at the knees and with a quick glance toward his wife he added, "Samantha, why don't you and Mrs. Mason go into the back room to be fitted. I must attend to other business and assist young Miss Rebecca with her packages." He then straightened up and, after bidding the ladies adieu with a gracious nod—"Ladies!"—he took his leave, signaling Rebecca to follow him out the front door.

Mrs. Mason came from behind the counter to tend to Mrs. Robins and her daughter.

"I have your mended items hanging on a rack in the back room, Esther. Please don't let me forget to get them before you leave. Now, can we—"

"Shhh." Esther Robins interrupted. Raising two fingers to her lips she turned her head, checking to see that Rebecca and Mr. Mason had left the shop. Turning back to Judith, she spoke quickly but softly, her words barely making it past her tightened lips.

"Have you heard?" she started excitedly. "There's been another fire! Abigail Stern's barn caught fire, just last night!"

"Oh, my word!" Judith gasped. "Was anybody hurt?"

"No, not to my knowledge. I understand that Ralph"—Abigail's husband—"and his two sons managed to save most of the animals and livestock, getting them out of the barn before the flames grew too intense."

Judith considered this. "My, that's been three fires in almost as many months, hasn't it? And all the fires happened at night. Rather unusual for pure happenstance, wouldn't you say?"

"Precisely!" Esther Robins agreed enthusiastically. "I was thinking the same thing. You know, folks are saying it was"—cupping her hands around her mouth so Samantha couldn't hear—"*arson*! Deliberately set!"

Judith just shook her head in disbelief. "But, who would do such a thing?" she asked.

Ester Robins was ready for this. "Well, some are saying it's the work of roving gangs of thugs. A sign of these troubled times. Others, that it must be runaway slaves. But"—saving the best for last—"I think I know who is responsible."

Judith cocked her head, waiting for an explanation. Esther held off for a moment to intensify the impact of what she was about to say. Leaning forward, she whispered into Judith's ear. "I think it's the work of...Dan Fire Cloud...or one of his kind."

Judith's jaw dropped. Then she broke into laughter. "Dan! Dan Fire Cloud! That old Indian chief? You can't be serious, Esther?"

Judith couldn't keep from laughing.

Esther's face turned red with embarrassment. She looked around sheepishly to be sure no one else had entered the shop and overheard.

"Well, you must at least consider the possibility," she said in her own defense.

"But, why Dan Fire Cloud? Just because his name is *Fire* Cloud?" Judith broke into another fit of laughter.

"Well, I certainly don't think it's any laughing matter, Judith," Esther responded desperately. "And I'm not saying Dan actually set the fires. Like I said, could be one of his sons, or another of his kind."

Judith caught her breath. "I'm sorry, Esther. I certainly don't wish to demean the importance of what has happened, but the thought of Chief Dan doing something like that? Why, old Dan just keeps to himself most of the time, living in that old log shack, making baskets to sell at market. Can't imagine him doing such a thing."

"That's just the point," Esther retorted. "No one really knows what he could be up to. And, I heard tell that Chief Dan is trained"—lowering her voice again so Samantha couldn't hear—"in the magic arts, and can produce fire out of thin air."

Judith just shook her head. "Still, not exactly compelling evidence for the kind of thing we're talking about, I would say. That's a pretty serious accusation, Esther."

Esther stiffened and backed away. "Well, say what you will," she pouted, "I think he needs watching. I didn't want to say anything while young Rebecca was here. You know…her papa being good friends with the Chief, and all."

"Well, tell me, Esther, have you thought about confronting him with your suspicions?"

"*Humph!* Of course not!" Esther said, looking away and shuddering with frustration. "He would only deny it, anyway. He's got to be caught in the act."

"Well, okay, then," Judith replied, shrugging her shoulders. "So, are you volunteering for first watch?"

Judith grabbed a cloth tape measure from the counter and draped it about her neck. Turning to the young Samantha she quickly changed the subject, just as Rebecca and Mr. Mason were re-entering the shop.

"Well, Samantha, dear! What do you say we go into the back room and get fitted for that new ensemble?"

"Oh, yes. Let's do!" the young girl replied excitedly.

*****

The embers were still smoldering among the remains of Stern's barn that Friday afternoon following the night of the big fire. The barn itself was a total loss, but Ralph and his sons had managed to save most of the livestock. Ralph Stern was going through the rubble with a handcart, salvaging what he could of the iron and steel farm implements, as he thought back on the events of the past twelve hours.

It was Ralph's wife, Abigail, who'd first noticed the flames. Awakened at around two in the morning to a strange crackling noise, she opened her eyes to a bedroom lit up with the eerie, flickering light of flames reflected off the dresser mirror. Confused at first, she shook Ralph, trying to wake him up before jumping out of bed toward their second-floor bedroom window. The sight of the blazing barn took her breath away. Gasping, she let out a piercing scream that finally got Ralph's attention, and the attention of their two sons in the adjoining room. Once Ralph realized what was happening, he acted quickly, putting on his trousers and boots under his nightgown, hollering to Abigail as he fled out the bedroom door.

"Go get the boys! Tell them to meet me outside. You and the girls stay in the house."

Rushing through the kitchen toward the back door, Ralph grabbed his coat from its hanging peg, ripping the peg from the wall and propelling it across the room to ricochet off the stone hearth. As he grappled with the coat, Ralph was finally able to get it on over his nightgown. Then, he quickly grabbed a towel from the kitchen table and ran out the back door toward the burning barn. Passing a water trough along the way, he dipped the towel, completely soaking it, then draped the dripping cloth over his head like a drenched monk. He paused momentarily to size up the situation: the muted sounds of horses and cows in distress filtered through the roar of the flames, and it appeared that only the hayloft toward the back of the barn was burning at this point. But the flames were spreading fast and he knew he had to act quickly to save what he could of the livestock. Rushing toward the main door of the barn, he lifted its heavy timber latch, tossed it aside, and pulled open the doors, becoming instantly engulfed in gushing billows of thick, black smoke. Momentarily overcome by heat and smoke, he pulled back, but quickly recovered. With the wet towel wrapped across his face, he entered the barn, groping for the familiar, the railings and stalls, knowing his way even in the dark. When he came to the first stall on the right, he opened the gate and patted the two heifers, speaking to them in soothing tones as he took hold of their tethers and led them to safety.

"Good girl, Bessie. Stay calm, and I'll getcha outa here."

As he exited the barn he was met by his oldest son, Paul, sixteen year old.

"You okay, Pa?" he hollered out. "Let me go in there and get the other two."

"Let me go, too!" shouted his younger brother, who was just now running up the path from the house.

"No, Sam!" his dad responded firmly. Sam was only nine years old, two weeks shy of his tenth birthday. "You stay here and take the animals, while your brother and I bring them out to you. Keep away from the fire!" he ordered.

Glancing up, he looked over at a stand of young maple trees on the right side of the house. "Over there! Take the animals over to those trees and tie them up."

Ralph looked up to see Abigail approaching from the house with a shawl draped about her shoulders.

"Where are the girls?" he shouted.

"They're both fine," his wife answered. "Ruth"—their seven-year-old daughter—"is watching the baby. She's sound asleep."

"Good!" Then, turning to young Sam, "Momma will help you with the animals, son. Listen to your momma. Understand?"

Sam nodded his head, "Yes, Pa," and took the ropes of the two cows, leading them away to safety.

Ralph turned to Paul and offered him his head covering. "Here, son. You take this. It'll keep you from choking."

"What'll you do?" his son asked desperately.

"I'll be all right. Here, take it!" he commanded.

After fixing the towel about his head, Paul and his father went back into the burning barn. In the course of the next ten minutes—what seemed like an eternity—they managed to save all the horses and cows, and all but the largest of the pigs. After it was over, Paul lamented, "Oh, well. Guess it's gonna be roast pig for the rest of the week."

His father grinned. He just thanked God that no one was hurt.

The rising sun found Ralph exhausted and sound asleep in a rocking chair on the back porch, still in his nightgown, wrapped in a blanket. Abigail approached from behind and nudged him.

"I made a fresh pot of coffee," she said. "When you're ready I can fry up some eggs and pancakes for you and the boys."

She handed him a cup of hot mocha coffee.

Ralph opened his eyes and looked up. He took the steaming cup and wrapped both hands tightly around it, taking comfort from its warmth.

"Looks like the shed and chicken coop were spared," he said. "Chickens must be shaken up a bit."

The shed and coop were located across the yard, some distance from the barn. Fortunately, the fire did not spread beyond the confines of the barn.

"Yes, well, there were a lot more eggs than usual this morning. Almost more than I knew what to do with," Abigail commented.

"Like I said, shaken up a bit," Ralph chuckled as he took a sip of coffee.

Abigail handed him a towel. "Here," she said, "wipe your face and hands. You look like a chimney sweep."

Ralph grinned, took the towel, and wiped the soot from his face.

"How are the boys?" he asked.

Abigail sat down beside him on the porch. "They went back to bed after all the excitement. But I thought I heard them up, just now."

Ralph looked around, as if he was expecting to see someone else.

"What happened to Ben?" he asked.

Ben Simmons, their good neighbor from across the road, had also been awakened through the night by the fire. He'd responded by coming to the aid of his friend and neighbor, just as Ralph and Paul were bringing the last of the livestock from the barn. Ben found Ralph down on his knees, overcome by the smoke and heat, and came to his aid with a canteen of fresh water, dousing his head and neck with the cool liquid before handing him the canteen. Ralph drank long and hard till he almost choked.

"Ben said he'd be back after he milks the cows and is through with his morning chores," Abigail answered. "He said he has room enough in his barn for our cows, if they don't mind sharing the stalls with his Guernseys."

Ralph smiled. *Good old Ben!* Then a thought came to him.

"Hmm. Good thing Old Thunder wasn't in the barn last night," he said aloud. "No telling how he'd have reacted to all the commotion. Might've lost him."

Old Thunder was the Sterns's prized bull. Ralph had hired him out to the Stedhams for siring services just two days before, so his barn stall was vacant.

Providence, he thought, or just a bit of good luck.

Ralph took another sip of coffee and looked up to see his neighbor, Sid, approaching from across the field, silhouetted against the morning sun. He wasn't actually able to make out his face, but recognized Sid's gate.

"Mornin' Sid. Can I interest you in a cup of coffee?" Ralph hollered out as he raised his cup.

Sid put a hand up to his ear and shook his head. Sid was hard of hearing. Ralph took another sip and waited as Sid entered the yard, closing the gate behind him.

"That was quite a fire, Ralph. Could see it for miles around. Anybody hurt?"

"No, Sid. Thank God. I am very pleased to report that everyone is well. Just shaken up a bit."

Sid stepped up on the porch, turned, and gazed at the charred remains of the barn.

"How do you think it started, Ralph?"

Ralph squinted as the sun rose above the tree line.

"Well, I know it wasn't lightening. Not a cloud in the sky last night," he said standing up slowly and leaning against the porch post, his mind much clearer now.

"The fire…I know it started in the barn loft," he recalled.

Both men considered this for a moment.

"Maybe a lantern?" Sid suggested at last.

Ralph shook his head.

"No. Don't think so. I never keep a lantern in the loft," he puzzled.

Sid sought to change the subject.

"Well, listen, Ralph. Anything me and Annie can do t'help, just holler. When you get ready to rebuild the barn, we'll be here, you can bet."

Holler? Ralph chuckled.

"Sure, Sid. We much appreciate it."

As the morning wore on and the cleanup effort continued, there was no shortage of help. News spread quickly and over the next few days, neighbors came from miles around to lend a hand. Of course, some folks were just curious, and wanted to actually see what they'd been hearing about, but most were there to help. A tent was erected in the side yard to provide temporary shelter for the livestock, and the shed and chicken coop were modified to make room for the pigs, as Paul and his friends set about building a new pen from partially charred wood salvaged from the barn. The women-folk from their Presbyterian congregation would bring an endless train of food baskets to keep the Sterns provisioned until they were back on their feet; and the Baptists in Shilo, four miles up the road, would later chip in with the promise of lumber for a new barn.

Friday afternoon, Ralph resumed his cleanup chores, pushing a handcart though the rubble to retrieve salvageable articles, farm implements, and the like. A fully serviceable anvil lay on its side half buried in the smoldering ashes, still a little too warm to handle. By now the neighbors had all gone home with promises to return to help rebuild, but everyone was puzzled over the cause of the blaze. Some said it seemed similar to other recent fires in the area which also happened at night, their causes never fully explained, and they were beginning to entertain the real, and unsettling possibility that the fires may have been deliberately set.

Ralph was just about to turn back to the house when he spotted something in the bushes along the tree line which appeared to be a piece of woman's apparel snagged in a low-hanging branch. Drawing close and reaching down, he was able to disentangle it undamaged and held it up for closer inspection: a woman's monogrammed shawl, dirty but in good shape, couldn't have been there for very long. Placing the shawl in his satchel, he headed back to the house where Abigail greeted him with a pewter mug of cider, the hard kind.

"Compliments of Mrs. Stedham," she said.

"Ahh, God bless her!"

Ralph took the mug of refreshing liquid and gulped it down. Then, holding out the empty mug: "Refill?"

Abigail took the mug and began pouring more cider from a large earthen jug, as Ralph took the shawl from his satchel and laid it on the kitchen table.

"I think you lost your shawl, m' love. Must've happened sometime last night. I just now found it over by the west tree line."

Abigail studied the shawl for a moment.

"That's not my shawl, Ralph," she stated firmly.

He looked puzzled. "Of course it is. It's got your monogrammed initials on it."

Abigail smirked. "Look again, my dear. This monogram says 'A G.'"

Ralph inspected the shawl more closely:

"Oh. Well, that G looked like an S when I saw it the first time."

He lay the shawl back down on the table.

"So, who do we know with the initials A G," he asked.

Abigail shook her head.

"Hmm, could be"—shrugging her shoulders—"I really don't know."

Chapter 5

1999
Thursday, 16 September
Our Lady of Lourdes Hospital

4:00 p.m. Following his conversation with Dr. Ritchie, John remained in the activity room of Our Lady of Lourdes Hospital perusing an old copy of Psychology Today magazine when he decided to take Katie's suggestion and reexamine the police report she had left behind. Laying the magazine aside he picked up the report and opened it to the part describing where his car was found:

> LOCATION: Car found abandoned on Bacon Neck's Road, just east of intersection with Gum Tree Corner Road, Greenwich Township, Cumberland County, NJ.

John got up, went to the nurses station, and asked the nurse on duty if someone might have a map of New Jersey he could borrow. José, the young orderly assigned to the unit, overheard. He was eager to help and produced a road map from his locker.

"Keep it," he said, "I can get all I want from Triple-A."

Returning to the activity room, John sat down, unfolded the map, and laid it out flat on one of the long tables. Locating the city of Camden on the Delaware River, he began tracing the eastern shoreline of the river southward into the Delaware Bay toward Cape May, the southernmost tip of the state, until he found what he was looking for: the small coastal bay town of Fortescue, with its marina nestled between Beadons Point to the north and Egg Island Point to the south. About fifteen miles inland to the north, located on the Cohansey River, was the city of Bridgeton, the county seat of Cumberland County. *So, where was Greenwich Township?* Tracing the river's twisted southwesterly course to the bay, he located a small open dot on the map with the name *Greenwich*, about five miles upriver from the bay on the west bank of the Cohansey River. Other small dots appeared close by, with interesting names like Othello, Springtown, and Gum Tree Corner.

John leaned back in his chair and pondered the question: so what was I doing wandering around the back waters of the Cohansey fifteen miles from Fortescue, way off the beaten path?

"Must've really been lost," he mumbled.

He tried to locate Bacons Neck Road, but the map didn't detail the many small country roads in the area. Then he had another idea. He got up and went back to the nurses station.

"Excuse me, ma'am," he asked the nurse at the desk again. She looked up. "Sorry, but I was wondering if I could bother you again for my street clothes. The ones I was wearing when I was admitted last Monday."

She hesitated at first.

"I just need to check for something I left in my pants pocket," John explained.

"Well, I don't know," she answered nervously.

He tried another approach. "It's something that could help with the police investigation."

"Oh, I see." She looked relieved, got up right away, and disappeared. In a few minutes she returned with his clothes, wrapped and tied in a brown paper bag.

"Thank you, ma'am," John smiled, taking the package.

He found an empty lounge sofa just inside the activity room and made himself comfortable. Sitting cross-legged in his terrycloth robe and floppy slippers, with the brown paper-wrapped bundle nestled in his lap, he looked like a kid on Christmas morning getting ready to open the big one from Santa. The only things missing were the red ribbons and bows.

Unwrapping the packaged bundle he took inventory: one soiled pair of khaki cargo pants, one dark blue polo shirt, one dirty pair of socks, and one pair of Adidas running shoes. Yup, all there! Unfolding the cargo pants he reached into the right hip pocket and retrieved a small blue notebook, and thumbed its pages until he found what he was looking for: his original handwritten entry, "Fortescue State Marina," was crossed out and the words "Cohan-Sea Marina" was written beneath it in a different color ink, followed by some brief driving directions written in his own chicken scratch shorthand, which he now had trouble deciphering it, but it read something like this:

> Bridgeton Grenwch Rd south fm Bridgetn.
> Left on Baconek Rd past stone ruins
> South on Bac road to Del Bay

On the opposite page were the names of the boat and its captain, with another note:

> The Greyhound Capt – George Davies

Moved boat to new Marina (Cohan-Sea?). Will be there til
noon

John could only vaguely recall making these entries, but he did remember
placing a phone call to Captain Davies Sunday morning on his cell phone and
being told that he was no longer docked at Fortescue, but rather at Cohansey
Marina, located some fifteen miles up the coast at the mouth of the Cohansey
River. He wished now that he had asked for better directions, for he never
did make it to the marina. *Come to think of it, where's my cell phone, anyway?*

"Excuse me, ma'am!" John called out to his favorite nurse.

She looked up with a sigh.

"Besides my wallet," he continued, "were there any other personal
articles recovered when I was admitted on Monday night? Like maybe…a cell
phone?"

"Hmm." The nurse shook her head. "Something like that would have
been locked up for safekeeping, along with your wallet. But I can have José
check with security."

"Thank you, ma'am. I'd sure appreciate it."

John got up, taking his clothes and notebook with him, and returned to
the map on the table, picked up a crayon and began tracing his route as well
as he could recall, circling the towns of Fortescue, Bridgeton, and Greenwich.
Suddenly, soft breathing over his right shoulder and a warm breath on the
nape of his neck told him he was being closely watched. John turned around
quickly and was startled to see the young man with the green Mohawk and
body piercing standing close behind—the young man with a disdain for
classical guitar music.

"Whoa! You startled me," John exclaimed.

"S-sorry," the young man apologized, remaining there, nervously
rocking back and forth on the balls of his feet in a jerky rhythm. With his tall,
gaunt frame; haircut; and body decorations, he brought to mind a circus
clown teetering precariously on a high wire, with the audience holding its
breath, anticipating the fall.

"Are you going on a t-trip?" he finally asked.

"No. Just trying to figure out where I've been," John replied.

The young man looked down at the map. "I k-know that place."

"Really?" John looked up in surprise. "And where would that be?"

"C-c-ohansey. Greenwich," the young man stuttered. He pronounced
it as *green witch*.

"How do you know that area?"

"I g-grew up around there. Right there!" he said, reaching forward and
planting his finger on the map. "Sh-sh-shilo."

"Shilo? That so? Then maybe you can tell me where Cohansey Marina
is located. Can you point to it?" John asked.

The young man took the crayon and drew a small boat at the mouth of the Cohansey, with an arrow pointing to a bend in the river about three miles upstream, on the north bank of the river.

"Great! So, do you still have family down there, Mr.—?" John paused to elicit a name from the young man, but he ignored the cue and just continued.

"I think so. My mom's family goes back to colonial days. She said her gr-gr-great-great grand mom, or something, was a B-Bacon. One of the original families in the area. Least, th-that's what I was told growing up."

What with his speech impediment, John had trouble figuring just how many great generations that was, exactly, but he couldn't avoid the obvious question: "Any relation to Kevin Bacon?" he asked straight-faced.

The young man grinned and responded with practiced poise, like he'd been asked this question many times before.

"I th-think we're six degrees removed."

John chuckled. *Can't be too crazy*, he thought. *Must be more in tune than his demeanor would suggest.*

"So, what's your name? Certainly not Kevin." John asked. He was starting to take a liking to this young man, in spite of his apparent problems, or maybe because of them.

"Name's Doug."

"Doug." John repeated, testing the sound of it. "Good name. Got a last name to go with that, Doug?"

Doug hesitated before replying. "J-Justin."

"Doug Justin. Nice to meet you, Doug Justin. My name is John. John Weston." John reached out and offered his hand.

Doug held back at first. When he finally took John's hand, his own hand was limp, and John had to do the shaking.

"Well, I b-better be getting back to my room," Doug said. "Gotta t-take my m-meds." After starting to go, he stopped and added: "N-Nice to meet you John. Hope you f-find what you're looking for." He then turned and left the room.

John thought about Doug for a long while after that. He wondered where his parents were; where did he live when he wasn't in the hospital? Then it dawned on him why he liked the boy: Doug was about the same age as his nephew, Sam; just about the same height and frame, too. Of course, Sam didn't sport a green Mohawk, but take that away and you might mistake them for brothers. He thought about their differences, too. Had Doug inherited his problem, or had he acquired it? The old nature versus nurture thing. Yet, there was something about their two personalities that was similar, something lying at the core of their very being.

Finally, John returned to his map and notebook and the task at hand. He was returning the notebook to his pants pocket when he felt an unaccustomed bulge in the left hip pocket. Reaching in, he pulled out a rolled up wad of paper. He carefully unfolded it and spread it out on the table, pressing it flat with his palms to take out the wrinkles. The paper was heavy, unbleached parchment, of poor quality, a ticket of some kind, with the following words printed across the top: *Cumberland Stage-Wagon Service*. Below this it read:

> Good For One-Way Passage
> From: Greenwich – Cumberland County
> To: Cooper's Ferry
> Charge: 8 Shillings – Credit to Weston Account

Below the words Credit to Weston Account there was a signature, but John couldn't make out the name. Odd, he thought. He certainly didn't remember...then suddenly, in a blinding flash of white light...

...the smell of leather and sweaty horses. A coachman dressed in knee breeches and a white linen shirt speaks in an unfamiliar English accent. "I can take you as far as Salem this evening. There, we will find lodging for the night at Mr. Dickenson's Inn, and with a fresh team of horses, continue the trip north in the morning." Then a swarm of large horseflies set in flight with a single swoosh of the large animal's tail...

The vision was lucid, the smell real and persistent, but as quickly as it came, it was gone, and he was back in the present again.

"Shit! What the hell was that?" John stammered.

Wiping the beads of sweat from his forehead with his shirtsleeve, trying to regain his composure, he looked around the activity room: no one appeared to notice. After studying the ticket one last time, he refolded it and returned it to the lower left snapped pocket of his cargo pants, this time for safekeeping, his heart still racing as he tried to make sense of it. He carefully folded the map and placed it in the same pocket.

John turned to look out the window. The late afternoon sun was casting long shadows over the tombstones in Harleigh Cemetery as John began to focus his thoughts, reconstructing near and distant memories of people, places, and events. He started with the time immediately preceding Bob's illness, two months ago.

July the second to be exact.

PART TWO

How sweet the silent backward tracings!
The wanderings as in dreams – the meditation of old times resumed – their
loves, joys, persons, voyages.

Walt Whitman, "Memories," *Leaves of Grass*

Chapter 6

1999
Friday, 2 July
Haddonfield, NJ

6:00 a.m. The morning sun was just breaking through the trees of Cooper River's Pennypack Park as John Samuel Weston completed the last leg of a three-mile circuit leading up from the water's edge. More creek than a river at this point, its waters meandered gently through the outskirts of Haddonfield before widening into a more navigable stream on its six-mile course to the Delaware River. The park's tree-lined riverbanks and wooded meadows offered a network of primitive trails that was a favorite of local joggers and nature lovers alike. Having traversed these trails countless times, beginning years ago with his high school's cross-country running team, John could almost run them blindfolded.

Pausing briefly to turn down the volume on his Sony Discman and to adjust the sweaty headband slipping down over his eyes, John left the protection of the tree line where the trail divided and took the left fork across an open green meadow, now within view of his parked car. Stopping just short of the gravel lot, he checked his stopwatch: seventeen minutes, forty seconds. Not bad after all these years. At forty-one, he was quite proud of his just under six-minute mile. He took a final swig from his water bottle and climbed back into his car for the short mile ride into town and the start of another workday.

Like clockwork, four times a week John ran Pennypack's cross-country trails—addicted to it, you might say. It helped clear the mind and revive the soul, like a good tonic; it was a great stress reliever that had become as much a part of his daily regimen as a good night's sleep and vitamin C. From the first time he entered "the zone" running cross-country at Sterling High School, he had become a disciple of nature's own time-released cure for stress, the so-called "runner's high." In college, John's mantra to counter the popular drug culture of his day was: "Why walk a mile for a Camel, when you can run two more to get high?"

Driving into the village of Haddonfield's historic downtown district on such a gorgeous summer morning was tonic enough for the soul, jog or no jog. Entering town from the north along tree-lined King's Highway, John lowered his car window and took a deep breath of the clean, crisp morning air. Ah, the scent of history invigorated him! Continuing into the heart of town, passing one restored brick and stone building after another, he came at last to his favorite: The Indian King Tavern. Established in 1750, the Indian King was the largest of five taverns built during colonial times. Over the years it managed to survive the ravages of time and social change, operating as a dairy parlor during the temperance movements of the late nineteenth century, before being designated as an historic landmark, refurbished and opened to the public as a museum in the early 1900s. John knew its history well, having toured it many times.

The village of Haddonfield remained respectfully dedicated to its historical past. Building renovations were strictly governed by local zoning regulations and building codes designed to maintain that small colonial village feel. While some might complain, John felt comfortable with this. He chose Haddonfield to live and work as a way of keeping in touch with his family's roots and colonial past, to which he had always felt a strong connection.

The King's Highway became Haddonfield's downtown main street, lined with shops of all kinds, sidewalk cafes, and quaint boutiques spilling into small side streets and alleyways, bringing to mind a place from an earlier time. With the morning sun barely peeking above the low nearby rooftops, shopkeepers were busy setting up their sidewalk displays, and restaurant owners their tables and chairs for the early breakfast crowds. One block past Haddon Avenue, the town's major east-west intersecting thoroughfare, John made a right turn onto a quiet side street shaded by sycamores and maples. This was Tanner Street. Lined with an assortment of framed and red brick, three-story shops, townhouses, and professional buildings, the street ran for only a few blocks before ending in a Y intersection with Haddon Avenue. About halfway down Tanner Street, John made a right turn into the small, paved parking lot of Haddon Life-Tech Consulting Engineers and took the first reserved parking spot against the building—the one with his name stenciled in yellow paint on the asphalt.

Walking briskly up the brick path from the lot, John sidestepped the wrought iron boot wipe and took the three porch steps in a single bound. It was a few minutes past seven when he entered the front door.

"Good morning, John," Mary greeted him from her perch behind the receptionist desk.

Mary Hogan, retired Army WAC, was John's very capable administrative assistant, receptionist, and Jacqueline of all trades, performing "other duties as assigned" in keeping with her military pedigree. Although you'd never guess it by looking at her, Mary had bragging rights as a grandmother, with a second grandchild on the way. A smart dresser, now in her early fifties, she maintained a girlish figure that still turned an admiring second look.

John was still wearing his running clothes and sweaty headband, a towel draped around his neck and shoulders. Mary anticipated his next question.

"I don't believe there is anyone using the shower, John."

"Great. So, how's the new Afghan coming, Mary?"

Mary smiled. Reaching down into her yarn bag, she held up her handiwork.

"Ta-da!" she proudly announced. "I'm about half done. Should have it finished in about a month, in plenty of time for the baby shower—unless things pick up around here."

The comment was not wasted on John. Of all people, he certainly knew that business had been a bit slow of late, so he didn't mind her working on her Afghan during the day, as time permitted. Nancy was the second oldest of Mary's three daughters, and she was about to enter the second trimester of her first pregnancy.

"So, when's the baby due?"

"Officially, December twenty-second," Mary answered quickly.

"Oh, a winter solstice child," John noted.

"Yes, but don't count on it. The women in my family have always gone early. So, I want to be ready, just in case."

As John passed through the reception room into the office area, Mary hollered after him, "Oh, John, I almost forgot. Bob wants to meet you for breakfast at eight o'clock."

"Where?"

"The usual place."

"Tanner's Cafe?"

"That's right," she replied. "And he said to bring the notes from your meeting last Monday with Dr. Sam Li of GenAvance."

"Sure. Thanks, Mary."

"Oh, one more thing. Your brother called to say he was going to be in town the last week in August. He's bringing your favorite nephew to visit some colleges in the area. Wants to know if you could give him the grand tour."

John knew what that meant. They'd hop on the PATCO High-Speed Line to see the historic sites in downtown Philly: Independence Hall, Betsy Ross House, the whole circuit; then they'd cap it off with a tour of the Indian King Tavern right here in Haddonfield. He'd done it a thousand times with his out-of-town guests. His favorite was always the Indian King.

"Okay, Mary. Please put it on my calendar. I'm bound to forget."

John continued into the main office space, which was organized into cubicles with low, shoulder-high partitions, allowing one to survey the entire room from any location. An aisleway on the left ran past a row of private offices with outside-facing windows— "Executive row"—before taking a straight shot to the rear of the building where the print room, kitchen, and other service areas were located, including a small fitness room equipped with a treadmill, bike, Nautilus, and, of course, a shower facility. John encouraged use of the fitness room by his employees, feeling that, in the long run, it helped promote productivity.

"G'morning, John," a man seated behind two large CAD station computer screens greeted him, not even looking up as John passed.

Andy Benson, a man in his mid-thirties, medium height, slightly balding, was John's IT guy and CAD coordinator, who usually got to work before anyone else, and was often the last to leave. The print room was also his domain.

"Good morning, Andy. Got the new AutoCAD software loaded yet?" John asked.

"I'll have it by noon, John," Andy replied, again without looking up.

"Great, Ange. Right on the ball, as usual."

John Weston and his partner, Bob Fenwick, were principle partners of Haddon Life-Tech, LLC, a small engineering consulting company servicing the pharmaceutical and biotech industry. Bob was a year younger than John, having just celebrated his fortieth birthday. The two first met when working together at GenAvance Biologics in Thousand Oaks, California, in '89. John was a manager in GenAvance's Global Engineering Division, and Bob was a project manager working for a large east coast Architectural and Engineering (A&E) firm contracted for a two-year expansion project at GenAvance's Thousand Oaks site. Bob reported to John, who had owner responsibility for the project. The expanded facility was intended to produce a new cancer therapeutic drug which was undergoing the initial stages of clinical trials for FDA approval. Marketing projections were off the charts. To get a jump on the competition, GenAvance took the calculated risk of building the facility before the product was actually approved, which—given the lengthy federal approval process—could take another two or three years. The project was a great success, ahead of schedule and under budget. Unfortunately, the product failed in stage-three clinical trials and had to be shelved. With the facility 90 percent complete, GenAvance was left with a $120 million "white elephant"—a classic case of "operation was a success, but the patient died." Not long afterward, John was caught in a downsizing at GenAvance and was let go, after accepting a very favorable severance package.

In addition to developing a deep professional respect for one another, John and Bob had become close friends over the course of the project. Many a "team building" after-hours meeting at the local sports bars had helped to grease the wheels of that project, and cemented a firm friendship between them. When Bob heard of John's layoff, he contacted him and proposed partnering on an engineering consulting firm. They would focus on front-end studies, small design-build jobs, and process equipment modules—or *skids*, as they were known in the industry—for the fast growing biologics industry. Several locations were considered, but they eventually settled on Haddonfield, given its proximity to a major corridor of biopharmaceutical activity and manufacturing between Philadelphia and New York, and their own personal ties to the area.

*****

John took a seat at one of the small sidewalk tables outside Tanner's Cafe, located on the corner of Tanner Street and King's Highway, just two short blocks from the office. Going through the notes he brought along for his breakfast meeting with Bob, he could begin to feel the warmth of the new day sun as its golden rays peaked through the open bell tower of the church across the street. The usual morning crowd was out and about, sidewalk joggers, morning dog walkers, a young mom in sweatpants pushing a three-wheeled jogging stroller, its on-board yuppie guppy seemingly used to the routine and sleeping through it all.

Directly across the street was the popular twenty-foot tall town clock tower landmark, an impressive four-faced timepiece that resembled a bronze-green Chinese lantern set atop a single, matching bronze pedestal. John checked the time: 8:05 a.m.

"Care for anything else besides water and coffee, Mr. Weston?" the waitress inquired. Pronouncing water as "wooder," John would sometimes chide her for her Philly accent, but he let her slide this time without comment.

"No. Not just yet, Helen. I'll wait till Bob gets here. He should be coming by any minute."

Helen smiled. "Okay. Just give a holler when you're ready."

John looked around: still no sign of Bob.

Catercorner to the restaurant stood the First Baptist Church, a handsome gray stone edifice with a classic, square, castle bell tower. John figured there had to be more churches in Haddonfield than Starbucks and McDonalds combined, and most of them were located along a six-block stretch of King's Highway running through the center of town: Methodist, Presbyterian, Baptist, Episcopalian. Not surprising, considering the Quaker origins of the town. The early Quaker settlements of Pennsylvania and New Jersey were notoriously accepting of people of all denominations into their communities. As for himself, while raised a Methodist in the small nearby borough of Stratford, he was no longer affiliated with any particular denomination. On any given Sunday he might find himself at any one of the churches in town, and often entertained the possibility that he might just be a Quaker at heart.

"Good morning, John," came a panting voice from behind. "Sorry I'm running a little late, but the traffic on Route 38 was miserable. Accident I think. Should've listened to the traffic report before leaving the house."

Bob pulled up a chair and joined John at the table. Just a bit on the portly side, Bob played baseball in high school, but hadn't done much regular physical activity since then, just the occasional company softball team through the years. At forty years old, his waistline was beginning to show signs of neglect.

"No problem, Bob. I thought you might be having engine trouble. I was getting ready to call Triple-A," John taunted.

Bob commuted the six miles from his Moorestown home in his '88 Ford Taurus, which he'd maintained in mint condition since acquiring it secondhand a few years back. Machines were his passion. After receiving his mechanical engineering degree from Drexel University in '82, he was hired by a major South Jersey-based food manufacturing company. He'd worked in their corporate engineering department designing and troubleshooting high-speed filling- and sealing machines for soups in metal cans. In the late '80s the company was reorganized and began outsourcing most of their engineering development programs—"leveraging equipment vendor design expertise." Bob came to feel it was time to leave and was soon picked up by a large Philadelphia-based A&E firm specializing in the newly emerging biologics pharmaceutical industry. Since teaming up with John, Bob had handled most of the equipment module business, working with several specialty metal fabricator and model shops in the area.

Helen approached the table again. "So, what'll it be this morning, gentlemen?"

"The usual for me, Helen," John answered first. "Hot oatmeal, whole wheat toast, and a fruit cup."

"Hmm. Think I'll try the blueberry pancakes, with a side of bacon. Oh, and a cup of coffee. Thanks, Helen." Bob smiled and handed her back the menu.

"Great! Be back in a jiff with the coffee. Refill, Mr. Weston?"

"Sure. Thanks."

John leaned back in his chair. "So, does Katie have any Fourth of July weekend plans for you, Bob?"

Bob had married his high school sweetheart, Katie, soon after college. Their two children, Bob Jr. (fourteen) and Amanda (eleven), were normal adolescents with the typical peer pressure concerns and predilection for electronic gadgets, games, and cell phones.

"Well, I was planning to take the kids down to the bay tomorrow for some fishing. They've never been out on the water before. So, I arranged a rental out of Fortescue."

"Katie gonna join you?"

"Nah. I'm afraid she's not much of a fisherwoman. Gets sea sick. Hey, how 'bout you John? Wanna join us? The captain says the stripers are still running. Should be a good catch."

A distant memory flashed through John's mind: a young, beautiful woman on water skies, blonde hair blowing in the wind, holding the rope with one hand, waving with the other. John shook off the memory.

"No. I don't think so. Me and boats just…don't get along."

"Okay. Suit yourself. But how 'bout joining us for a cookout and some fireworks later on Sunday? Moorestown usually puts on a nice show. And I cook a lean, mean brat. King of the charcoal grill!"

"I just might take you up on that," John said.

Bob took a sip of his coffee.

"So, John. Did you bring your notes from your meeting the other day with Dr. Li?"

John slapped his hand on the black notebook lying on the table.

"Got it right here. What's up?"

"Guess who the keynote speaker is for the next New Jersey ISPE Chapter meeting?"

The International Society of Pharmaceutical Engineers (ISPE) was a major worldwide professional organization for the biologics and pharmaceutical industry, its members representing the broadest range of interests and disciplines in the industry, including process equipment suppliers and consultants. Local chapter meetings were typically held at either a sponsor site or a regional conference center.

"Let me guess. Dr. Sam Li?" John offered.

"Exactomundo!" Bob replied. He took another sip of coffee. "So, tell me, John. What did you and Sam talk about the other day?"

John shifted in his seat to escape the glare of the morning sun.

"He said they were looking to build a new pilot plant for clinical manufacturing. GenAvance is developing a new insect cell culture process that employs a continuous perfusion recovery process for excreted protein product. Unusual for insect cell cultures, which are typically grown in batch mode."

Bob's interest was piqued.

"So, d'ya think we may finally get to try out our design for continuous cell culture harvesting?"

"Could be. After all, it *is* a pilot plant. The time to innovate is during process development. Unfortunately, having worked at a mega pharmaceutical I know firsthand how difficult it is to get the scientists and the engineers to communicate, and once the process has been validated and filed with the FDA, it's often too late make changes."

Bob nodded. "So, what's the timing on this one?"

"Well, there's a good chance they may not go out on the street to bid the front-end study," John said. "I put a bug in Sam's ear that we could do the whole thing on a "design-build" basis, cutting cost and time to market. Also sounds like a good opportunity for process modules. Right up your alley, Bob!"

"Sounds great!" Bob replied. "So, do you think Rick has caught wind of this? He's bound to go after it tooth and nail. I hear things are a little slow over at PSE&C. He'll probably buy the job."

The "Rick" to whom Bob was referring was Rick Nuisom— pronounced "new-some"—the sole owner and CEO of Process Systems Engineers and Consultants (PSE&C). Rick was a major competitor of Haddon Life-Tech. His reputation was legendary, managing to show up at every pre-bid meeting like a lost relative at a reading of the will. He was known to lowball his bids to "buy" the job, and then hit the client with change notices as the job progressed to recover his losses.

John took a sip of coffee.

"God only knows. I just hope he's not aware of GenAvance's plans. Dr. Li said they haven't even gone in for funding, yet."

"So, maybe we should go to the ISPE meeting and try to close the deal with Sam over a nice meal," Bob suggested. He lifted his coffee cup to toast the idea.

"Sounds like a plan." John responded, clinking cups.

"So, where's the meeting?" John asked.

Bob took a brochure from his briefcase and studied it briefly.

"Rutgers University is sponsoring this month's event," he said. "Looks like...let's see...the Hilton East Conference Center in New Brunswick, just off exit nine of the Jersey Turnpike."

"When?"

"Three weeks from Tuesday," Bob said, checking his planner. "That would make it the twenty-seventh. Dinner at six, followed by the keynote speaker's address at seven."

Helen arrived with their tray of food. "Here we are, gentlemen. Blueberry pancakes, hot off the griddle."

"Ahh. Thanks, Helen. You're an angel."

"Enjoy!" And she was off again.

Chapter 7

1999
Sunday, 4 July
Moorestown, NJ

When John pulled up to Bob and Katie's suburban Moorestown home Sunday afternoon, everything seemed in order. Bob's Taurus was in the driveway parked alongside their '98 Dodge Caravan, the family car, decorated with a checkered bumper sticker advertising the minivan as "Mom's Taxi," an oblique reference to Katie's soccer mom duties. A portable basketball pole and net stood to the side of the driveway, with a pair of his and hers mountain bikes leaning against it. Inside one of three garage bays was an antique '67 Mustang up on a lift, being nursed back to health through Bob's tender loving care. A collection of hubcaps, license plates, and other machine head memorabilia lined the back wall of the garage.

Since returning to his childhood hometown of Moorestown, New Jersey—"the most livable small town in America" he would boast—Bob maintained his interest in all things mechanical by outfitting half the basement with a machine shop where he was able to perform complete engine rebuilds and dabble with his many inventions, some of which he had been able to patent. Their garage served as the neighborhood auto repair shop, complete with hydraulic and joist lifts. Machines were his passion.

"Hello, John. So glad you could join us."

Katie greeted John with a hug as he entered the front door.

"Too bad you weren't able to join Bob fishing yesterday. He came home with quite a catch."

The muffled, high whine of a table saw could be heard from the floor below.

"Bob's in his basement workshop," Katie explained, throwing a troubled glance toward the basement door. "I'll...tell him you're here, John. Please, just make yourself at home."

Katie turned to her daughter. "Amanda, be a good girl and show Mr. Weston to the backyard and find him something cold to drink."

"Sure, mom," Amanda replied without even looking back. "This way, Mr. Weston."

John noted a high-pitched nervousness to Katie's voice. Passing the basement stair door on their way to the kitchen, Katie opened the door and hollered down to get Bob's attention.

"Honey! The guests are all here. Are you going to join…"

The sound of the table saw revved up drowning out her words, and Katie's head dropped in annoyance. Flicking the basement light switch a few times brought a pause to the sawing, and she tried again.

"Honey, when are you going to join us for the cookout?"

"Be up in a minute, babe," came the distant reply. The saw resumed its high decibel chore.

Katie simply sighed and shook her head, then turned and marched toward the kitchen as Amanda led John out the back door onto their newly finished wooden deck overlooking the backyard. This was your typically well-manicured suburban lot, complete with terraced patio decking, barbeque pit, and in-ground pool. For the moment, Bob Jr. and his teenage friends were engaged in a spirited game of water volleyball, having all but taken over the pool, even the shallow end typically reserved for non-swimmers. The boys took every opportunity to impress, splashing the girls in great displays of pubescent exuberance, which was met with a chorus of squeals and shouts of feigned offense, resulting in playful jousts to right the pretended wrong, and the chanced close physical encounters welcomed by both offender and offended alike.

"So, did you remember to bring your swim trunks?" whispered a sultry voice from behind.

John turned. There was Sally Fielding, good neighbor and friend of Katie's, standing three feet away, holding a mixed drink in one hand, a bottle of beer in the other. A mother of four, Sally had managed to retain a girlish figure and looked rather stunning in her two piece bathing suit. The slight gravelly texture to her voice only accentuated her sensual appeal.

"Oh, hi, Sally. No, I don't think I'll be testing the water today. Although it does look very inviting."

"In that case, here, take this. It should take the edge off the heat. Your favorite brew, as I recall."

John read the label. "Sam Adams. Yup, you got that right, Sal. My favorite, next to my own homegrown brew, that is."

"Oh, so you brew your own beer?"

"Sure! What self-respecting chemical engineer hasn't tried it at least once in his or her lifetime? Got the perfect basement for it: cool and dark."

John took the open bottle from Sally and took a long, hefty swig. "Ah! Nice'n cold! Thanks, Sal!" he said at last coming up for air. "So, tell me," he asked, looking past Sally, "where's your less better half?"

"Oh, you mean Paul? He's tending the fire, over there. Filling in for Bob, it seems."

John followed Sally's gaze to the far side of the pool, to a shaded patio area with its own built-in brick barbeque, where he saw Paul wiping his hand on his apron and tending to the grill. Looking up, he saluted John with a wave of his spatula. John raised his bottle in the manner of a toast, giving a nod of recognition.

"So, tell me John," Sally asked, stretching her neck and looking around and over John's shoulder, "did you...come alone?"

"Afraid so, Sal. I'm going stag today."

Sally smiled. "You know, John, it amazes me how you've managed to avoid the state of matrimony all these years. Of course,"—quickly checking herself—"I just assumed you've never married."

"No, that's okay. You're right, Sal. I suppose...I was never much of the marrying kind." John's voice dropped off as he tried to hold back a painful memory. "Anyway, I promised myself to stay single, and raise my kids the same way," he added, forcing a smile. He meant it as a joke, but it didn't come across that way.

Sensing his discomfort, Sally quickly changed the subject. "Well, John, you are a native son of this great state of New Jersey, are you not?"

"That's right. Grew up in Stratford, a small town, not too far from here," he said, waving his free arm in a generally southerly direction. "Did you know that Walt Whitman had a summer home there? Well, not right in Stratford. It was actually neighboring Laurel Springs. But it was all just one big place back in those days, I guess. And it wasn't actually *his* home, but the home of a friend."

"And he didn't actually write poetry, but borrowed a few lines of verse. Is that what you're telling me?" Sally laughed.

"Touché! Actually, I know more than I let on. Did you know he used take walks in the woods in the nude?"

"Hmm, now I do find that interesting. Is that footnoted in his collections of verse?"

"No, I don't think so. But it must have been an inspiration to him. That's where he wrote *Leaves of Grass*, and much of his prose on nature."

"So, can I assume you're a Walt Whitman fan?"

"Yeah, I guess you could say that. Me and Becky, we used to..." John stopped and took a deep breath, then another sip of his beer. "I used to read Whitman whenever my studies became too overwhelming. Kind of helped put things in perspective."

"So, you never did tell me where you went to school, John."

"Well, after graduating from Sterling High School in '76, I enrolled at Rutgers University on a partial scholarship. In high school I ran cross-country. When I got to Rutgers, I rowed on the crew team in my sophomore and junior years. But I continued with my running. In fact, I'm still running to this day."

"Like, to this *very* day?" Sally queried.

"Yup. Ran three miles this morning. Up at six and once around Pennypack Park."

"My! Such energy!" she said in a beguiling tone. "So, what did you study at Rutgers?"

"Chemical Engineering."

"So, you do…chemicals? How does a chemical engineer end up working in the biotech consulting field?"

"Well, a chemical engineer doesn't so much deal directly with the chemical or product, like a chemist in the lab, but designs the process required to manufacture the chemical product on a large scale. The product could be just about anything. In biotech, it's usually a large, complex biological compound, like a protein, which may prove useful in treating or preventing disease," John explained.

"You mean, like a *drug?*"

"Right. But a very complex drug, which only living systems can produce. The job of the process engineer is to take the product from the lab, where things are done in buckets and beakers, to a manufacturing scale with large, sterile vats and clean rooms. All this while the FDA and other regulatory agencies are breathing down your back."

John was drifting into "professor mode," now, as if he were addressing a senior engineering design class. "Actually, the whole biotech industry has only emerged in recent years, owing to breakthrough discoveries in the fields of molecular genetics. It all started with Watson and Crick in the '50s, when they identified DNA as the basic stuff genes are made of…"

John could see he was beginning to lose his audience.

"I'm sorry, Sal. Guess I got carried away."

Sally lifted her sunglasses away from her eyes to nest high atop her head of jet black hair, revealing a pair of clear, emerald-green eyes that sparkled in the afternoon sunlight, feline in their intensity. *Why does she hide those beautiful eyes behind sunglasses?* John puzzled.

Sally continued her interview. "So, what happened after college?"

"*More* college. I continued at Rutgers, working full-time toward a master's degree in Bio-Chemical Engineering. My thesis sponsor was investigating the use of genetically altered insect cells grown *in vitro* for making therapeutic proteins." John paused to clarify. "You know, one of those large, complex biological compounds I was talking about. I spent the summer of '81 working in the unit operations lab, collecting data from a unique fermenter design the professor was developing."

"*Fermenter.* Let me guess. One of those large vats for making whatever it is you're making," Sally chanced. She was showing a genuine interest now in John's resume. Or maybe it was just the passion and gentle lilt of his voice that held her attention.

"Excellent! You got it, Sal. I'll make a bio-process engineer out of you yet." John tapped her glass with his bottle of lager, then held it up against the sunlight, studying its tiny stream of bubbles. "It's a little like brewing beer," he continued. "Only instead of growing a batch of yeast cells that make alcohol, you grow a batch of cells that have been genetically engineered in the lab to produce your protein."

"It all sounds pretty complicated," Sally acknowledged.

"Yes, it can be. But the whole idea is to simplify the process as much as possible, making it economical and safe, not just feasible." John paused for the clincher. "*That's* where the process engineer can make a difference."

"I see. So, where did you go after finishing up at Rutgers?"

"I spent the fall of '81 putting the final touches on my thesis before graduating with my master's degree in December. Anticipating my degree, I was hired by GenAvance Biologics in November at their Princeton research and development facility."

John spoke slowly now, choosing his words carefully.

"Er, later...I moved to their west coast campus just north of Los Angeles. That was after GenAvance was purchased by Aqua-Lyne Pharmaceuticals, a mega global pharmaceutical company looking to get into the biotech business. That's where I was working when Bob Fenwick and I first met."

Just then Katie hollered out from the back door. "Hey, Sal! Could you lend me a hand here in the kitchen?"

"Sure, Kat," Sally hollered back, "be there in a sec." Turning back to John she excused herself. "Sorry, John, but duty calls."

On the far side of the pool, a puff of smoke and flame suddenly erupted from the grill, forcing Paul to recoil with a shout.

"Looks like Paul might need a hand, too," Sally added. "Why don't you go apply your engineering skills to that problem grill over there and help get this show on the road. And maybe you can get him to put on his hat. He's gonna burn in this hot sun."

"Sure. I'll see what I can do."

John started off toward the grill on the far side of the pool as Sally shouted after him, "Hey, ya gotta let me sample some of your home brew sometime!"

John shouted back over his shoulder. "Sure thing. I got a fresh batch brewin' as we speak!"

Sally smiled and turned toward the kitchen door. Katie met her as she entered the house.

"So, I see John was bending your ear," Katie remarked.

"No, not really," Sally said. "He's a nice guy. Okay, a little bit self-absorbed, perhaps, but very interesting, nonetheless." Glancing back out the window, she added, "You know, I'm really surprised that some young kitten has never managed to get her claws into him."

"Or, even some not so young feline, eh, Sal?" Katie offered with a smirk.

Sally blushed. "Now, don't get catty on me, Katie! You're not suggesting that I—" deliberately pausing and not finishing the sentence.

Katie laughed. "C'mon, I'm just joking. Here, help me with the salad."

Sally picked up a fresh cucumber and knife and started slicing and dicing.

"Seriously, though," Sally continued. "What do you know about John's..."

"...love life?" Katie finished the sentence for here.

"Okay. That'll do," Sally answered.

"Well, not much, really. The only thing we know is that he was engaged to be married once, but it didn't work out somehow. John doesn't talk much about his past, the time before he and Bob first met."

"Was her name...Becky?" Sally asked.

Katie stopped in her tracks. "Yes, now that you mention it. I think that was her name. But, how would you know? Did he say something to you just now?"

"Not much really. Just a casual mention...in passing."

Katie nodded. "I see. Well, now you know as much as we know." She picked up the knife from the cutting board and handed it Sally. "Now, whadaya say we get back to work and finish this salad?"

John approached Paul just as he was bringing the fire under control. Paul, a tall, lanky man who had lost most of his hair as a young man to hereditary pattern baldness, was wearing a kind of safari outfit today, khaki shorts and a vest.

"So, is there a hat that goes with that outfit?" John asked.

"Hi, John. Actually, yes. I should be wearing my brimmed Aussie hat. I'm surprised Sally hasn't gotten on me for not wearing it. Ever since her sister was diagnosed with skin cancer, she usually doesn't let me forget." He looked up. "But, we're in the shade, here. Should be okay, right?"

John didn't pursue it further. Figured he did his part.

"So, how's business, Paul?"

"Ha! Do you mean as chief cook, or as county medical examiner?

"Take your pick."

Paul Fielding, M.D. was a boarded pathologist, with accreditation in forensics and skin pathology. As medical examiner for the county, Dr. Fielding was responsible for investigating all cases involving homicides and deaths resulting from injury or unknown causes. This included ordering and conducting post-mortems and laboratory tests, and testifying in court when necessary.

"Well, as holiday chef, things could be better. But, as for my daytime job, business is fairly brisk of late. Sorry to say, I might add."

"So, tell me. How come you're wearing Bob's apron? Has he abdicated his charcoal throne?"

Paul motioned toward the garage. "Well, the way I figure it. My friend, Bob, takes care of my four-wheel drive. The least I can do is tend the grill in his absence."

John looked back toward the house. "So, where is Bob?"

"To tell the truth, I haven't seen him since we arrived an hour ago. Katie said he's been holed up in his shop ever since he returned from his fishing trip yesterday. Katie's not too happy about it. You may have noticed."

"Well, she did seem a little bit on edge when I arrived."

A commotion at the house suddenly caught everyone's attention. Bob had emerged from the backdoor onto the deck wearing his dirty coveralls, waving his arms in the air, with Katie fast on his heels, obviously upset. She followed him across the deck, ignoring the stares of her startled guests. Almost crying, she shouted out, "I can't believe you, Bob. You ignore your guests. Then show up dressed like a…like a *grease* monkey. What's gotten into you? Look!" She pointed across the pool toward the grill. "The brats and burgers. They should've been done by now!"

John and Paul froze. In unison they looked at each other, then down at the grill, then back at the house again. The rendered fat from the brats began to sizzle, flowing in a steady stream onto the glowing bed of charcoal embers.

Bob had turned around, now, and was talking and walking backward across the deck in the direction of the garage. "I'm sorry, Katie. I…I can't explain right now. But, I just gotta finish what they started."

"Started? Started *what*? And who's *they*?" she demanded in exasperation.

Bob continued toward the garage and disappeared inside, as Katie just threw up her hands and turned back toward the kitchen, with Sally following close behind.

The neglected brats lost their sizzle and began a slow charring burn on the open grill.

*****

Pop! Pop! Pop! Bang!

"Ooooo."

The crowd expressed their approval as the sky erupted in starburst clusters of red, white, and blue, illuminating the ground below in staccato patches of light, revealing a field temporarily transformed from high school gridiron to town amusement park as families and friends, randomly assembled in assorted folding chairs and blankets, celebrated the sights and sounds of another Independence Day fireworks display.

Pop! Pop! Pop! Bang!

"Ahhhhhh." The smell of sulfur wafted over the packed bleachers, as coiled shards of cardboard and spent rocket embers drifted down upon the downwind crowd.

Flash! Pop! Flash-Flash! P- Pop! Pop!

A rapid series of brilliant white bomb bursts directly overhead was quickly followed by waves of concussive shocks to the chest. And then…*Ka-boom!* A gigantic starburst blast jolted the crowd into a round of cheers and applause.

John turned to his right to gauge the reaction the kids, Amanda and Bob Jr. "Nice display, huh?"

"Great! I think it's a lot better than last year." Amanda was first to respond.

"Yeah. I really like the bomb bursts. Ka-pow! You can feel it right there." Bob Jr. made a fist and pounded his chest to illustrate his point.

They had all arrived at the high school ball field about an hour before dark, in plenty of time to get the best seats in the bleachers. It was also enough time to pick up a couple of franks before the show as, unfortunately, not many of the bratwursts survived the grill at the Fenwicks' cookout and people were still hungry. Dr. Fielding officially pronounced the cause of death: "Major third-degree burns with irreversible fluid loss."

John turned to Katie, immediately to his left, and was about to say something when he noticed Bob, who was seated on the other side of Katie, bending forward with his head in his hands. Katie turned and whispered something to Bob, who slowly removed his hands from his face and sat up. A flash of light from an overhead starburst revealed a ghostly pale complexion, and his lips appeared to be moving, like he was mumbling to himself.

Bob looks sick, John thought. *Maybe it was the brats.*

Suddenly, the space in front of them erupted in a grand pre-finale ground display of flares and sparklers, turning night into day for a solid three minutes. Shadow figures silhouetted against the bright backdrop of illuminated smoke moved to and fro, tending to their pre-assigned tasks in choreographed precision, as a fire truck and emergency vehicle with crew stood by, prepared to respond to the slightest mishap.

Suddenly and without warning, Bob stood up, shouted out, "We must to go back and save her!" Then, bolting from his seat he bounded up and over the row to his front. Pushing people aside he quickly forced his way to the center aisle, paused momentarily as if to get his bearings, then turned and ran down the aisle, stumbling near the bottom, falling head over heels to the cinder track below.

Everyone was stunned, caught off guard by Bob's sudden, bizarre behavior. John was the first to finally react, rushing and stumbling forward in pursuit of Bob. Paul, who had been sitting with Sally in the row just behind John, turned to Sally, "Excuse me, dear," and then took off, taking the same path across the bleachers, which by now had been cleared of people.

John was the first to reach Bob. He found him partially recovered, sitting on the ground with his head in his hands. Bob looked up.

"What happened, John? How did I get here?" he asked, confused. He began to brush the dirt and imbedded cinders from his hands.

"That's what I'd like to know. Bob, are you all right?"

By that time Paul had joined them. "Here. Let me take a look at that, Bob," he said.

"What?" Bob pointed to his right arm. "Oh, you mean, that?"

"Yes. Looks like a nasty bruise. But can't really tell in this light." Paul looked up. "You'd think they could turn the lights on," he complained.

At that moment a young paramedic arrived, kneeled down and asked Bob a series of questions, confirming that he was conscious and coherent, then listened to his heart and examined him for broken bones and bleeding.

"You seem to be all right, sir. Do you want to be taken to the hospital?"

"No, I don't think that will be necessary," Bob replied weakly.

Katie was there now, cradling Bob's head in her arms. She was crying.

"Bob, whatever possessed you to do such a thing? Are you feeling okay?"

"I don't know. Something about those...fireworks set me off."

He glanced over his shoulder and stretched his neck, trying to see the field through the crowd that had gathered around him.

The grand finale was over now and the crowd started to break up and go home. Bob remained seated on the bleacher step with a blanket wrapped around him; Katie huddled close by his side. The field lights were turned on, allowing the crowd to find their way out.

"Honey, Paul said something about your arm. Please let him take a look at it in the light," Katie pleaded with her husband.

Bob opened the blanket and held out his right arm. Paul reached out and turned it over to inspect it. There was ample lighting, now. There, on the backside of his upper arm was a large, red, raised welt.

"Wow. You've got quite a nasty infection there, Bob. Looks like an insect bite of some kind. How long have you had this thing?"

Bob thought a moment. "Not long. Just since yesterday, actually. During my fishing trip. You know those big greenhead flies down by the bay?"

"Delaware Bay?"

"Yeah. The son-of-a-bitch bit me just as I was pulling in a twenty-pound striper. I couldn't swat it, you know, without losing my grip on the reel."

"Well, I'd seriously suggest you get yourself to a doctor and have that thing lanced, my friend. I'd put you on antibiotics, too."

Paul placed his hand on Bob's forehead. "You might even have a fever, be dehydrated. That might explain your...odd behavior. Have you had enough fluids today, Bob? I mean *aqua*, water or juice, the pure kind, not fermented. It's been a pretty hot day."

John took the cue by offering Bob a drink of his Gatorade. Bob obliged, taking a good, long drink.

"Thanks, John. I needed that."

"Sure. What are friends for?" John replied.

Chapter 8

1763
Greenwich, Cumberland County
Province of West New Jersey

It was a lovely crisp autumn day in October. The year was 1763. Little seven-year-old Rebecca Whitman was enjoying the sights, sounds, and smells of the Greenwich Fair, a popular county-wide attraction held twice a year, centered about the town's Market Square. Walking past the livestock display, her mother, Elizabeth Whitman, cautioned her away from a large bull tethered to a stake.

"Please, dear. Not so close."

Nervously steering little Rebecca away from the large beast, she spied a less threatening display of husbandry.

"Rebecca, do you see those chickens in the pen over there?"

Rebecca nodded.

"Yes, Mama."

"Well, they look mighty hungry to me. Why don't you go over and give them something to eat."

Elizabeth reached into her purse and produced two small coins.

"Here, honey, take this money and give it to that nice man. He will give you a small bag of feed for the chickens."

"Okay, Mama."

Rebecca took the two pennies and ran over to the man tending the chickens, as her mother moved away to find shade under a nearby willow tree. She was suddenly feeling very tired and in need of a place to sit down.

Just then the pleasing, harmonious sounds of a guitar and flute could be heard from a nearby stand of performers. The tune was a familiar one; a Scottish working song extolling the virtues of the weaver:

> ...The weavin' is a trade that niver can fail
> As lang as we need clothes for t'keep anither hale.
> Sae let us all be merry wi' abeaker of guid ale
> And we'll drink tae the health of the weavers!

Mrs. Whitman closed her eyes and began humming the tune. When they came to the chorus she knew the words and sang quietly along:

> …If it wasn'a for the weavers, what would ye do?
> Ye wouldn'a hae the clothes that's made of woo.
> Ye wouldn'a hae a coat o' the black or the blue,
> If it wasn'a for the work o' the weavers.

Little Rebecca was too preoccupied to notice the music. She took a small handful of corn and scattered it among the chickens. The birds reacted in predictable fashion, squawking and competing for every kernel thrown their way, attracting chickens from other parts of the pen. The commotion also drew the attention of some geese resting under a nearby elm tree. Tiring of the chickens, Rebecca moved in the direction of the geese. Taking a stale slice of bread from her apron, she began breaking off small pieces and tossing them toward the big birds. Before long she was surrounded by honking geese in search of an easy meal. Spying several goslings hidden among the weeds just beyond the elm, she grinned and advanced abruptly toward the young birds. Suddenly, from out of nowhere a very large gander charged to her front, placing itself between her and the young goslings. With a great hiss, the large bird spread its wings and lowered its head and, holding this threatening pose, began a slow advance toward little Rebecca.

"Shoo! Shoo!" Rebecca tried to fend off the bird with a wave of her arms. But this only emboldened the irate gander, which hastened its advance toward Rebecca. Rebecca began to cry.

Suddenly, before Rebecca knew what was happening, a young boy ran between her and the gander. Brandishing a willow branch and barking like a dog he caused the geese to scatter, with the gander the last to leave. The birds retreated beyond the elm tree and order was soon restored. The boy turned around to face the little girl, who was no longer crying but just standing there with her mouth agape.

"They won't hurt you, now, missy. Anyway, they're mostly all bluster and no bite."

The boy was taller and a little older than Rebecca, but carried himself with a kind of self-assurance that belied his young years. Tossing the willow branch aside, he removed his cap and bowed at the waist in the manner of a gentleman.

"Master John J. Weston, at your service, missy."

After straightening himself up he continued. "And may I ask to whom I have the pleasure of addressing?"

Rebecca was beside herself, rendered speechless for the moment.

"Er, my name is Rebecca. Rebecca Whitman."

Remembering her manners, she quickly curtsied.

"John J. Weston. So, what does the "J" stand for?" she asked.

"I just told you. John Jay Weston. That's 'J-A-Y.'" He spelled the name for her.

"Oh, like in Jay-Bird," she giggled.

"That's right, just like in Jay-Bird," he confirmed, matching her smile for smile.

"I'll tell you what, Missy Rebecca, I have two pennies in my pocket to spend as I choose. How would you like one of those nice candy apples they're selling over there?"

He pointed to a line of food stalls on the far side of the green. Downwind of the stalls, the air was filled with the tantalizing scent of the bakers' ovens, smokers, grills, and open-pit rotisseries, all manner of delectable fare being prepared as fast as the hungry crowds could consume them: pan bread, sausages, skewered beef and vegetables, rotisserie chicken, wild turkey, and fresh roasted corn-on-the-cob. There were also sweet, juicy melons of every sort freshly harvested from nearby fields.

"Okay. But I'll have to ask Mama first," Rebecca replied excitedly.

John followed Rebecca as she ran back to her mother seated on the park bench.

"Who is your gentleman friend, young lady?" her mother asked with a pleasing smile.

"His name is John Jay Weston, Mama. And he has offered to buy me a candied apple. Is that all right, Mama?"

"Well, I suppose so," her mother replied.

Mrs. Whitman leaned forward to inspect the young lad further. He appeared neat and well groomed.

"How old are you, young man?" she asked. Looking around she added, "And where are your parents? Are they close by?"

"I am nine years old, ma'am. But I'll be ten next month. I'm visiting the fair with my brother, Bartholomew. He's the tall gentleman over there talking to the ship's captain."

Mrs. Whitman squinted and held her hand up to shield her eyes from the sun.

"Yes, I see." She paused. "He...he looks so much...*older*."

Old enough, in fact, to be the young lad's father. She never recalled seeing either of them before.

"You're not from around here, are you, John?" she pursued, continuing to gaze over his shoulder.

"No, ma'am. We live northward, in the town of Haddonfield. My father...well, he doesn't travel much. But my big brother makes trips quite often. He brought me down to see the fair, and tend to the family business.

Mrs. Whitman looked down at the boy. "And what business would that be, if you don't mind my asking?"

"No, not at all, ma'am. He's in the merchant shipping business. Just like my pa."

"I see," she replied, turning to Rebecca.

"Well, my dear Rebecca. You and John go off and enjoy your candied apples. And be sure to thank John for the treat."

"Yes, Mama. And also for saving me from the big goose."

"It was a gander," John corrected her.

Mrs. Whitman laughed. "Yes, my dear. And certainly such heroism must be rewarded." She pulled out two more pennies from her purse and gave them to Rebecca. "And for your part, young lady, you may treat John and yourself to a nice cool glass of cider," she added, gesturing toward a nearby stall advertising "Sweet Cider from Fresh Pressed Apples."

Rebecca clapped her hands and jumped with joy. "Oh, thank you, Mama! I shan't forget my manners."

She turned and took the hand of her newfound friend. "Come, John! Let's go for the apples and cider."

John continued to speak as they moved on, removing his cap with his free hand and trying to bow even as Rebecca tugged on his other arm. "Yes. Well, it was a pleasure to meet you, ma'am. I promise to take good care of little Rebecca."

John and Rebecca ran off toward the food stalls.

"Just take care to keep within my sight," Mrs. Whitman called out after them.

John and Rebecca continued playing together the remainder of the afternoon. The next day at the fair, Rebecca kept a watchful eye out for her new friend. But, John found her first, sneaking up and surprising her from behind.

"Boo!" he shouted.

Rebecca jumped. "Oh, you frightened me!" she protested.

Today, John's older brother, Bartholomew, received permission from Mrs. Whitman to take the children for a walk away from town center in the direction of the lower landing piers and boatyards less than a mile away. Fairly half the distance to the piers the trail passed through a broad marsh, replete with turtles, toads, and other low crawling and swimming life forms certain to excite a child's curiosity. There they became lost in the excitement of new discoveries, exploring the wonders of nature, all under the watchful and diligent eye of big brother Bart. Flying insects there were, as well—the greenhead fly had not yet given up its hold on the summer season.

"Ouch!" young John shouted, swatting the back of his bare neck with a slap of a hand. "That one got me real good!"

"Oh, the greenheads really like you, Johnny Jay!" Rebecca laughed.

Once on the other side of the marsh, the trio continued toward the piers and boatyards located on a bend in the river where its generally southerly flow cut back sharply to the west—which is to say to the right of their line of travel. The children's eyes lit up as they were now confronted with a new kind of adventure: the heart of Cohansey's maritime activity. The boatyards were bustling with activity, reverberating with the sounds of hammer and saw; carpenters and laborers were busy at the craft of building and repairing ships; the voices of men giving and receiving orders mixed with the jovial laughter of those who took joy in their life's work and in the company of fellow workers.

Closer to the river, now, the piers came into view.

"Whoa! Look at that ship. I bet it's carrying gold doubloons from the Spanish Main!" John shouted as he started down a pier toward a large brigantine moored at its far end.

"Actually, I believe a cargo of tea from East India. But, almost worth its weight in gold, nonetheless," brother Bart replied. "And please watch your step, Master John. I don't want to have to be fishing you out of the water today."

"I think the ships are gorgeous!" Rebecca commented. "But, how are they ever able to mend all those sails? It must take lots and lots of cloth to make!"

"Indeed. Maritime canvas, a very strong and special kind of cloth," Bart explained. "It takes an experienced crew and a good captain and first mate to properly manage the sails," he added.

"That's what I want to do when I grow up," young John bubbled with enthusiasm, "to sail the oceans and seven seas!"

Something in the distance caught Rebecca's attention.

"What is that moving through the marsh on the other side of the river?" she asked.

Placing himself behind her to follow her line of vision, John replied, "What? I don't see anything."

"There, just on the horizon. Like a cloud or balloon or something. Don't you see it?" she pointed.

Across the river, the green expanse of grassy marshland continued unbroken to the shores of the Delaware Bay, with an occasional stand of low scrubby trees breaking up the monotony of an otherwise flat landscape. As the crow flies this was a distance of less than three miles; but by river, with its wide serpentine path winding its way through the low-lying marshland, the distance was closer to six miles. Bart knew the river and the lay of the land. While neither allowed a direct line of sight to the bay, he knew that the distant body of water was hidden just below the near horizon. The children stood quietly as Bart removed a small black tube with brass trim from his inside coat pocket. Young John's eyes lit up.

"Whoa! A ship's spyglass!" he exclaimed.

Bart extended the telescope to its full working length and raised the eyepiece to his right eye. He began to manipulate the tube as he brought the distant object into sharper focus.

"My, my, young lady, but you have exceedingly keen eyes!" Bart remarked. "I should like to have you for my lookout, were I a ship's captain."

Bart lowered the glass to Rebecca's eye level.

"Here, child. Take a look through this end. What you see are the topsails of the mainmast of a large merchant ship, fully rigged. It's actually much further off than it appears. You see. It's moving right to left. What direction would that be?"

Young John spoke first. "That would be southward, sir."

"Very good, John. Yes, that ship is out bound. Probably departed from Philadelphia early this morning with the outgoing tide. Heading for England, no doubt.

"May I have a look, brother Bart?" John asked impatiently.

"Yes, of course. Rebecca, let's give the glass to John so he can give us his opinion on the distant object."

Bart handed the glass to John, who handled it with some measure of familiarity.

"But, it looks like it's moving through the marshes," Rebecca insisted.

"Just an illusion," young John replied as he peered through the glass at the object. "Through the spyglass things appear altogether up close and flat," he added matter-of-factly, like someone well versed in such things.

In the course of their young years, John and Rebecca's friendship continued to grow, despite the miles that separated them. It was Rebecca who first began writing letters to John, under her mother's tutelage. Short little notes at first, it started out as much an exercise in penmanship and composition as anything else, but soon it developed into something more. John reciprocated, of course, and as they grew and matured, so did their communications.

John continued to visit Greenwich with his big brother, Bart, even after the fairs were discontinued in 1765. The family mercantile business would often take Bartholomew to Cumberland County, as Greenwich was a major shipping port in the New Jersey colony. Cohansey and the Jersey coast also became a favorite getaway spot to vacation and relax. Whenever circumstances permitted, John would tag along with his older brother on these jaunts, which always included a visit to see young Rebecca.

Chapter 9

1999
Tuesday, 6 July
Haddonfield, NJ

John spent the Tuesday morning following the Fourth of July holiday weekend going over the second quarter's profit and earnings with Gene Morris, the company accountant. They met in the conference room just off the lobby. Gene was concerned with the company's cash flow and gave John a long list of outstanding invoices, some ninety days overdue. John thought it might be time to take Bob's suggestion and hire that accounts receivable clerk he always talked about from Camp Hill Foods, a real "bull dog" at going after delinquent accounts. So where was Bob, anyway? John looked at the clock on the wall: 11:05 a.m. Bob hadn't called, and was not answering his phone. *Not like him*, John thought. *Maybe something's wrong.* He thought about Sunday night, the way Bob had flipped out during the fireworks display.

Just then the outside line lit up on Mary's phone. It was Bob. She patched the call through to the conference room. Bob was subdued and hesitant, but John was finally able to coax out of him what had happened following the incident at the fireworks display Sunday night. Turns out Bob spent Sunday night and the better part of Monday in the ER at West Jersey Hospital having that infected bite tended to. Besides the infection, he had become severely dehydrated. He was put on intravenous fluids and antibiotics overnight and had to have his arm lanced and opened up to drain the infection and give it some air. "Afraid of flesh eating strep," he said. But it proved to be *just* an especially virulent strain of staph. They were able to send him home late Monday afternoon with a two-week supply of antibiotics and a promise to follow up with his family doctor. He said he was feeling better today and would try to make it in sometime after lunch. John told him not to rush it, things could wait, but Bob insisted. Through it all, John couldn't wipe the image from his mind of Bob darting from the spectator stands at the Moorestown fireworks display like he was either hell-bent on a mission or scared out of his wits—or both.

It was almost noon when John and Gene finally wrapped up their meeting. On the way back to his office John stopped by the front desk, tapping it with a pencil to get Mary's attention.

"Mary, I'm going to take lunch in my office for the next hour and don't want to be disturbed. Would you please take my calls for me? And if I'm not out by two o'clock, please come get me."

"Sure, John. What if Sam Li calls?"

John thought a moment. "Well, in that case just come get me. I don't want to miss his call."

"Will do. Oh, and John, I left a newspaper article on your desk for you to read. Thought you might find it interesting."

"Thanks, Mary."

John retreated into his office and closed the solid oak door behind him. With the hum of the window air conditioner effectively blotting out all interfering outside noise, his private office became a special place of peace and solitude. But for Mary, bringing him back from these midday retreats was not easy. "Like raising Lazarus from the dead," she would say.

Sitting at his desk in his black leather, upholstered swivel chair, John clasped his hands behind his head and stretched back, relieving the stress in his back with an audible crack. After briefly fussing with the mail and other loose papers on his desk, he grabbed Mary's newspaper article, a letter to the editor circled in red pencil with a handwritten note: "Thought you'd find this interesting – Mary."

The letter was entitled, "History: Preserved or Entombed." Mary knew of John's interest in local history. The writer was complaining that local historical sites were not accessible enough to the public, citing the Indian King Tavern in particular. Because of limited hours of operation and staff shortages, visitors needed to schedule tours well in advance, and sometimes had trouble getting in at all. "…What's the sense of preserving an historical site if it's not going to remain accessible to the public? It then becomes a *mausoleum* and serves no public interest," the writer lamented.

John frowned at the writer's insensitivity. *History must be preserved! At all costs!* he silently reaffirmed to himself. Why? Well, just because! This is what he'd always believed.

Tossing the article aside, John sat back and surveyed the room. On the wall to his right, above the credenza and its clutter of day planners, file trays, and pencil holders, hung his diplomas from Rutgers University and various plaques and awards from high school and college.

To his left hung a beautiful, large wooden plaque carved with his family tree and coat of arms in bas-relief. Now a family heirloom, the plaque was a custom carving created by his Aunt Dee, whom John remembered as being a rather gifted artist. Neatly arranged around the plaque hung a gallery of framed family photos. The largest was a family photo of a much younger John; his younger brother, Matt; older sister, Laura; and his dad and stepmom, Richard and Eleanor Weston. The photo was the last family portrait taken before his dad passed away six years ago, less than a year after he and Eleanor had sold their home in Stratford and moved into a nearby retirement community. His stepmom's health started to decline after that, but she was still able to get around, even drive on her own. John would see her as often as he could, being the closest living relative and all. He fixed up the first floor guest room in his house so she could visit on weekends. Of course, he knew sooner or later she'd "graduate" to an assisted living home—or have to move in with him.

John didn't remember much about his real or biological mom. She left when he was only three years old. His dad always said she had a "wild streak in her," and couldn't be tied down. The last he'd heard she was living somewhere up in New England, taking up with a guru at a mountain commune or something. John and Laura continued getting birthday cards from her for a few years after that, until he turned about ten years old, but there was never any return address on the envelopes. From that point on they lost complete track of her.

His dad remarried a couple of years after the split up. Eleanor was a nurse, working at West Jersey Hospital at the time. They met when John was rushed there at the age of four with a ruptured appendix. She stayed with John through the crisis even after her shift was up. She and his dad struck up a relationship almost immediately and were married within six months. Eight months later brother Matt came along.

The most recent picture was that of his brother posing with his wife and three kids. Their oldest was Sam, now going into his senior year of high school. The picture had been taken last Christmas and sent to John as a gift. Matt enjoyed a successful career as an architect, living just outside Boulder, Colorado. He and John kept in touch, but seldom saw each other anymore. They tried to make a point of getting together around the holidays, but missed last year when Matt decided to take his growing family to Disney World on a winter holiday. John felt bad because Sam was his favorite nephew.

Funny, but most people would never take them as brothers—even half brothers was a stretch. Matt was on the short side, stocky build, with strawberry-blond hair, and was an above-average varsity wrestler in high school and college. John, on the other hand, had the frame and body of a long distance runner, tall—lanky growing up—with brown hair. They had different personalities and interests, too: John tended to be more introverted and cerebral, but over the years had learned to adapt and become more assertive; Matt, on the other hand, was an open book—artistic and musically inclined. Their father would sometimes joke that they were "from opposite ends of the genetic spectrum, with a little half-breed blood thrown in."

John pulled a key ring from his back pants pocket and, selecting one of the lesser worn keys from the ring, unlocked the right-hand file drawer of his double pedestal desk, reached in, and pulled out an imitation leather-bound scrapbook and placed it on the desk in front of him. The binding was old and worn, and the book's cover had developed small fissures across its embossed raised lettering.

John navigated his swivel chair toward the credenza, opened the credenza door, and produced a bottle of cognac and two brandy glasses. Coasting back to his desk, he opened the bottle and poured equal measures of cognac into the two glasses. He tore off a few pages of his desk calendar until he came to today's date: *Tue, 6 July*. Across the page in large block letters were the handwritten words: "Our Anniversary."

John opened the scrapbook to the first page. A much younger John Weston stared back at him from an assortment of high school graduation photos: John in cap and gown, John with family and friends, John running cross-country at Pennypack Park. *Turn the page*. There was John on his senior class trip to Disney World. Many happy photos filled the page. *Turn the page again*. John is posing with his crew team at Rutgers University, and there he is clowning around with—what was his name?—oh yes, Dan! "Dan da man," his friends called him. *Turn the page*. John lingered on this page for a minute or two. John is posing with a young lady: beautiful, tall, and slender; blonde hair; and green eyes. The caption reads: "John and Becky."

John thought about how he and Becky first met in college. She was a marketing major, same year as John. He remembered admiring her from a distance since their freshman year, but they never shared classes, so never actually met—until his junior year when he was voted "sorority sweetheart" of Becky's sorority. That's when Becky suddenly took an interest in the school's regattas, as she and her sorority friends would come out to see John at all his races on the Raritan River. After the events, John and his buddy, Dan, would join the girls to celebrate—win or lose—at the local brew pub. On one occasion, he found himself alone with Becky, with the others long gone, and spent the next few hours till closing time swapping stories and anecdotes of family and friends, and finally, sharing their own personal hopes and dreams. The night ended with each knowing that their stories together were just beginning.

John turned to a page marked with a small frayed tab. On the right page was an 8" x 10" portrait of a beautiful young woman in cap and gown. "Becky Bowden – Rutgers Graduating Class of 1980," the caption read. Across the bottom of the picture was a handwritten note: "John, now let's get on with our lives together! Your one and only love, Becky."

John studied the picture for a minute or so. He took one of the brandy glasses, touched it to the other, raised it to his lips, and took a sip.

The next page contained several photos of a beautiful young blonde in various fashion poses. They were each signed: "To John, with love, Becky." During a summer '79 internship with a New York advertising agency, Becky's interest in the modeling industry was tweaked, and upon graduating in May

'80 she took an entry level marketing position with the company's sister company, Modeline Fashions. With her brains, good looks, and keen business savvy, she quickly found herself in the fast lane of a promising career.

John took another sip of cognac and turned the page.

Several newspaper articles, now yellow with age, were cut and taped to the page, one from a small north Jersey town newspaper, dated May 20, 1980, proudly announcing the graduation of "...local hometown girl, Miss Becky Bowden, with a BA degree in marketing, from Rutgers University." Another, dated June 5, 1980, was cut from a Modeline Fashions, Inc. company newsletter, under the "New Hires" section. It read in part: "...and Becky Bowden, recent graduate from Rutgers University, has accepted a position in our expanding marketing department. Welcome aboard, Becky!"

John turned the page. More newspaper clippings. One announced: "Mr. John S. Weston, of Stratford, NJ engaged to Miss Becky Bowden, of Morristown, NJ. No date set at this time." The article was dated July 20, 1981. Two separate photos adorned the right-hand page, one of John and the other of Becky.

John raised his glass and gently clicked the other glass.

"Here's to you, Becky."

He took another sip of the brandy.

Turn the page. More photographs of John and Becky, now in their new apartment. John was sporting a new mustache and beard. Soon after John took a position with GenAvance in November of '81, he and Becky abandoned their separate efficiency apartments and moved in together, sharing a two-bedroom apartment in New Brunswick. They planned to marry in August of the following year.

The next few pages contained various candid shots of John and Becky. In one they were walking the sandy beaches of South Jersey's family summer resort town of Ocean City. In another, they were horseback riding along the wooded trails of north Jersey's Morris and Sussex Counties.

John smiled and wiped his eyes. He remembered now how he and Becky would engage in friendly jousts over which was better: North Jersey or South Jersey.

"North Jersey has the Jersey Devils hockey team. And there's the Meadowlands, host to the New York Giants," Becky would boast.

"Ahh, but South Jersey has Atlantic City and the Pine Barrens, the legendary home the *real* Jersey Devil," John countered.

"The devil with beaches and sand flies!" she'd reply. "You know I like horses. What better place to ride than in Sussex County?"

John couldn't argue with north Jersey's rolling hills and endless ribbons of white-fenced horse farms nestled at the foot of the Catskill Mountains. "The Northwest New Jersey Skylands," the tourist centers referred to this section of the state. Then, with a newfound spark of insight, John would try for the last word. "But, how do you think Jersey came to be known as the Garden State? South Jersey farms, that's how! They don't call Hammonton the blueberry capital of the world for nothing, you know."

And so on and so on it would go. The one thing they had in common: the Jersey Turnpike! They joked that their marriage would serve to seal the union of north and south kingdoms forever, like aristocracies of old.

John raised his brandy glass and sipped its remaining contents, then turned the page. There was a photo of John and Becky posing in front of a fishing boat, dated July 5th, 1982. That was the last photo in the scrapbook. The next page and all remaining pages were blank—waiting for life's story to resume.

After setting down the glass, John gently closed the scrapbook and returned it to the desk drawer.

*****

It was a few minutes past two in the afternoon when Bob Fenwick quietly walked into the conference room. John was seated at the conference table focusing on his new laptop, so he didn't notice Bob entering the room.

"Hello, John. New laptop, I see."

John looked up, startled. "Oh, Hi Bob. Didn't hear you come in."—glancing back at his laptop— "Yeah, the new Windows system promises a glitch-free transition into the new millennium."

They both laughed.

"Right. I don't think the world is ready for a glitch-less Windows system, no matter what millennium it is," Bob countered.

"Anyway, I think Andy has a good handle on the year two thousand," John offered. "We don't have any serious legacy issues with our finance and accounting systems anyway. I don't really expect any serious problems."

John sat up and studied Bob for a moment, really seeing him for the first time. *Boy, you look like shit, my friend!* Tired and disheveled, hair messed up, the back of his shirt hanging out, Bob looked like he'd just been in a fight. As Bob turned, John noticed a large bandage on his right forearm. You'd think it was broken the way it was wrapped, from his hand to just above his elbow, just his fingers protruding.

"Whoa! Looks like the ER did quite a number on you, my friend!"

Bob raised his bandaged arm and rubbed it gently with his left hand.

"Yeah. Never thought a little fly bite could create such a problem." He forced a laugh. "Happy Fourth of July! Eh?"

John smiled. "So, you feeling better, pardner? You did give us something of a scare the other night at the fireworks."

"Sure, I'm fine, John, really."

John wasn't convinced. Bob was obviously struggling with something as he sat down at the conference table across from John.

"Yeah, well, the doctors think my dehydrated condition may have contributed to my...odd behavior that night."

He still seemed troubled, like he was hiding something.

"Well, I'm sure if you follow the doctor's orders, everything will be all right," John offered hopefully.

Bob got up slowly and turned to leave the room. Then, stopping and turning around, he added: "You know, John. I just gotta say, that fishing trip was a little...*strange*."

"Whadaya mean, Bob?"

Bob leaned forward against the table, supporting himself with outstretched arms.

"Well, I remember, after being bitten by that fly, I started to feel, well...a little light-headed. I thought it might have been too much sun. But, driving home, I started...I know it sounds funny saying it, now, but...I started *hallucinating*."

John was taken aback. Finally, he asked, "What kind of hallucinations, Bob?"

Bob started fidgeting. "Well, sort of like an out-of-body experience of some kind. I imagined I was participating in some kind of...*witch burning*." He quickly lowered his head. "Jeez, I can't believe I said that." Slowly, he lifted his head and stared right through John. "I just...drifted in and out of this state for several minutes," he said with glazed eyes. "When I could, I grabbed a bottle of Gatorade and drank it down. That seemed to help. At least I was able to drive home."

"What did the kids think of all this?" John asked.

Bob just stood there, as if in a trance, before finally snapping out of it. "Oh, yeah...the kids. Well, they just figured Daddy wasn't feeling well. That's what I told them. That I had must've picked up a virus or something."

There was a moment of silence.

John spoke first. "That doesn't sound good, Bob. I mean, the hallucinations and all. Did you mention this to the doctor?"

Bob put his head down. "No. I didn't. I...maybe I was in some kind of denial—or just too scared to think of the consequences."

"What kind of consequences?" John pressed.

"You know. Like I'm going crazy, or something."

John hesitated, afraid to ask the next logical question.

"Bob, have you had any...any hallucinations since then."

Bob didn't answer right away. He just stood there, staring back into space.

"Bob? Are you all right?" John repeated.

Bob snapped out of it, again; shaking his head he responded. "W-What was that you said, John?"

"Oh…nothing, Bob."

John looked down, shuffling some papers on the table, as he tried to figure out what was going on with his good friend and partner.

"Bob, I was thinking you may want to take some time to shake this thing off, whatever it is. I can handle things around here for a few days. Whadaya say?"

Bob's head drooped as he weakly replied, "I don't know, John. Maybe you're right." Then it dawned on him. "But, what about the ISPE meeting? Dr. Sam Li?"

John tried to lighten things up. "Hey! That's a whole three weeks from now. We're just talking a few days, right?"

"Yeah, maybe you're right," Bob agreed reluctantly.

"Okay, then!" John said as he flipped down the lid on his laptop. "A little R and R can go a long way!"

Chapter 10

1999
Tuesday, 27 July
New Brunswick, NJ

The ballroom lights of the Hilton East Conference Center, just off exit nine of the New Jersey Turnpike, were dimmed as the man at the podium introduced the next speaker.

"And now, it gives me, and the ISPE organization, great pleasure to introduce our keynote speaker for this evening, the distinguished Dr. Sam Li of GenAvance Biologics. Dr. Li and his group at GenAvance have pioneered some groundbreaking work in the area of recombinant insect cell culture for the commercial production of therapeutic proteins. Working in close partnership with Rutgers University's entomology department at Cook College, Dr. Li's research team has developed a new continuous cell culture strategy for growing and harvesting target proteins produced from the"— pausing to adjust his bifocals—"Baculovirus Expression Vector System, or BEVS."

The moderator removed his spectacles, turned and looked down at the small-framed man seated to his right. "Did I get that right, doctor?"

Dr. Li looked up with a grin and nodded, yes. A murmur of light laughter filled the room. The moderator continued.

"Well, just so I don't risk getting something wrong, without further ado, I'm going to turn the podium over to Dr. Li. I would only ask that you hold your questions until the conclusion of Dr. Li's presentation." Turning to Dr. Li, "Doctor, the floor is yours."

Doctor Li stood up and stepped to the podium, smiled, and nodded approvingly to the man who had just introduced him, then turned to the audience and politely bowed in response to their accepting applause—not quite the formal bend at the waist, as was the custom in the land of his ancestors, but a more casual bow, evidence of assimilation into the western culture of his lately adopted home.

Dr. Li came to the United States from Vietnam as a young man in 1973, having lost most of his family to the "war of liberation," as his countrymen from the north referred to the conflict. Four years later, Sam graduated with honors from Berkley University, and was immediately accepted into a graduate program at Rutgers University in field of entomology and microbiology. Soon after receiving his PhD in '82, he was hired by GenAvance to head up their new biologics development program in the area of insect cell culture.

Dr. Li stepped up to the podium with notes in hand, reached into his inside jacket pocket for his reading glasses and put them on, then adjusted the microphone to his height, tapping and blowing into it once or twice to test its pickup.

"Am I able to be heard in the back?" he asked.

John Weston and Bob Fenwick, seated at a table at the rear of the large ballroom, gave him a thumbs-up. Dr. Li cast a long stare toward the rear of the room and smiled in recognition.

"I am glad to see so many familiar faces in attendance tonight. I can only assume there must be a beauty pageant happening in the next ballroom to attract so many on a rainy Tuesday night."

Congenial laughter rippled through the room.

With a customary nod to the gentleman who had just introduced him, Dr. Li continued. "First, let me say 'thank you, Peter'"—turning to the audience—"and thank you all for allowing me to intrude on your evening's festivities by indulging in one of my favorite topics: insect cell culture and Baculovirus Expression Vector Systems."

There were smiles and nods of approval from the audience. Dr. Li picked up the remote control from the podium and turned to his left.

"Lights, please."

The room lights dimmed as a white screen was slowly lowered behind the podium. Dr. Li turned to face the screen to begin his PowerPoint presentation. The first title slide read: "Continuous BEVS Insect Cell Culture for Commercial Production of Therapeutic Proteins"

"I don't know how many microbiologists we have here in the audience tonight," Dr. Li continued, "but, just for the record, let me repeat the word is 'bac – u – lo – virus.' As in the movie, *Back – to – the – Future*." He drew out the pronunciation, syllable by syllable, for emphasis and comparison. "Of course," he continued, "not to stretch the metaphor, I'm certainly not ascribing to the virus the power of time travel."

More smiles and open laughter this time from the audience. Sam had to chuckle himself, proud of the success of his little one-liner. One young lady seated at a table close to the podium jotted down a few notes.

Sam continued, occasionally glancing down at his prepared notes.

"Now, the use of certain insect cell lines for the production recombinant proteins has gained popularity in recent years due to the relative ease of growing these cells *in vitro*, that is, in a test tube or bioreactor, and the ability of these cells to generate large amounts of desirable target protein. But, how do you convince these cells to begin making the protein of your choosing? A therapeutic protein which may prove to be the next cure for cancer, or to combat mental illness?"

Dr. Li let the question sink in before bringing up the next slide. It presented a schematic diagram depicting the normal sequence of events for infecting insect cells with the *Baculovirus*.

"The genes which code for these proteins are not normally present in the insect cells. What we must do is enlist the help of a special naturally occurring group of insect viruses, called baculoviruses, which predominantly infect insect larvae of the order *Lepidoptera*, the moths and butterflies. In nature, once infected, the insect cell is forced to make more virus particles, which exit the cell and go on to infect other nearby cells. This continues until the cells eventually burst and die, what we call 'cell lysis.' However, just before this happens, a special gene, called a late viral promoter gene, instructs the cell to produce a special protein, called *polyhedron*, for encapsulating multiple virus particles together. So, this polyhedron coat allows them to survive in the environment when the cell bursts open. It functions as a kind of escape pod. They're released into the environment so they can go on to infect other insect larvae."

The next slide contained a cartoon depiction of the BEVS approach for inserting the gene of interest, or GOI, into the insect cell. The virus particles were represented as numerous miniature wooden horses.

"What we do is take advantage of this natural infectious system by allowing the gene which codes for our target protein to hitch a ride on the virus into the cell's nucleus. Like millions of little Trojan horses."

When Dr. Li gave the command, the cartoon horses suddenly became animated, invading the fortress cell and taking command of its nucleus.

Dr. Li paused, allowing the animated slide to run its course, eliciting smiles and a few scattered chuckles from the audience.

"So, you like my little Trojan horses? Yes, I do so admire the innovations of the ancient Greeks."

The room rippled with light laughter.

"Okay. Back to the present. First, you know, the baculovirus must be genetically altered. To do this, the virus gene which codes for the polyhedrin protein—*polh*—is replaced with the gene of interest, or GOI, which codes for the desired target protein. The polyhedrin gene is not essential for virus replication. But, the replacement gene now comes under the control of the late viral promoter gene, so that late in the infection cycle, the GOI is 'turned on' and starts instructing the cell to produce our desired target protein. The important thing is, the insect cell is not destroyed by the virus before it is able to produce *tons* of the desired recombinant target protein. I exaggerate of course."

More soft murmurings and light laughter.

"So, a typical process involves first growing up the insect cells in a large bioreactor to increase their numbers. At the proper point in the growth process, the culture is infected with the genetically altered baculovirus. As the virus imparts genetic control over the cell, the cell begins to produce more virus particles, infecting the entire culture. Finally, toward the end of the infection cycle, the GOI is turned on by the late viral promoter gene to produce the desired recombinant protein."

Dr. Li paused to take a sip of water from a glass resting on the podium.

"During the very late stages of BV infection," he continued, "very large amounts of protein can be produced within the cell. Up to 50 percent of the total insect cell protein, in fact."

The next slide depicted a typical scheme for the recovery of product protein.

"Now, some proteins remain inside the cell, while other proteins are excreted into the liquid medium. The recovery process depends on which type of protein you have. If the protein is *intracellular*, or *inside* the cell, the cells must be harvested and washed to remove the medium, and then the protein is extracted by breaking open the cells. This is done either mechanically, with something like a milk homogenizer, or chemically with a detergent-like buffer solution." Dr. Li turned to the audience and smiled. "Like they say, you have to break a few eggs to make an omelet."

More congenial laughter and nods of recognition, as many in the audience were familiar with this well-established scheme of protein recovery.

"Anyway, the timing of the harvest is very critical. Harvest too soon, and you don't get much protein. Wait too long, and the virus begins to destroy the cells, spilling their precious recombinant proteins into the culture media, which is typically discarded in the first steps of cell harvesting and washing. Up to 30 percent of the desired protein may be lost this way."

Dr. Li brought up the next slide, and adjusted his position at the podium, as though he was about to make a great pronouncement. The slide was titled: "A New Symbiotic Variant of Baculovirus."

"What our research team has developed is a variant form of the baculovirus, which I depict here as 'vBV.' Now, this variant form of the virus does not destroy the insect cell, but actually enjoys a kind of symbiotic co-existence with the infected cell. What we have managed to do is alter the viral genome such that, once a critical level of virus particles has been achieved within the cell, the genetic switch instructing the cell to produce virus particles is turned off."

Dr. Li paused and turned to the audience to elaborate on this last point. "We know there is some kind of biochemical feedback system at work here, but we are still not certain of the exact mechanism. What's more, the insect cell is able to continue to divide, partitioning the virus particles within between the two new daughter cells. Employing the same feedback mechanism, the switch is then turned back on until the number of virus particles in each daughter cell is restored to pre-meiotic levels, and so on. The daughter cells continue to produce the target recombinant protein at the same levels experienced previously by the parent cells."

The screen faded into the next slide, which presented two schemes for continuous insect cell culture and protein harvest.

"Now, the significance of this development is simply awesome, in terms of increased capacity and expanding the choice of proteins expressed."

On the word "awesome" Dr. Li's voice cracked with excitement, obviously impressed by the significance of this discovery.

"Now, for the first time, insect cell cultures can be grown continuously, with portions harvested on a daily basis for protein recovery. Premature cell lysis has been virtually eliminated, resulting in an immediate 20- to 30 percent increase in yield." Dr. Li turned away from the screen and spoke directly to the audience. "We have been successful in growing viable continuous insect cell cultures for up to thirty days, almost matching what can normally be achieved with mammalian cell cultures. Furthermore, a whole new class of excreted proteins can now be considered for insect cell culture, which is to say, proteins that are released into the surrounding medium, rather than being held within the cell. This greatly simplifies the recovery and purification process."

Dr. Li brought up his final slide: "Prospects for Future Development."

"Many challenges remain, of course. On the microbiological side we are trying to overcome certain stability issues with regard to the spontaneous retrograde of the BV genome. That is to say, the variant baculovirus has been observed to regress to its native form in the course of a single product run, resulting in a total collapse of the cell culture. We think this may have something to do with an interaction with the cell's mitochondrial DNA."

Dr. Li removed his glasses and looked up from his paper, speaking off-topic for the moment.

"As we know, mitochondria kind of have a life of their own. They exist as special, almost autonomous, structures within the cell, and contain their own unique DNA makeup, independent of the cell's nuclear DNA. Mutations are common. As a result, mitochondrial DNA can vary from cell to cell and tissue to tissue even within the same organism. It's always changing!" he exclaimed excitedly, with an added measure of frustration in his voice, raising both hands like he was conducting a symphony orchestra. "But…we are striving to better understand these changes, and their possible interactions with the baculovirus genome."

Dr. Li returned the remote control to the podium.

"That concludes my presentation. I thank you so very much, ladies and gentlemen, for your kind attention. I will now entertain any questions you may have."

Following a brief period of polite applause, the young lady at the front table raised her hand, stood up, and asked, "Dr. Li, can you tell us which insect cell line has been used in your experiments?"

Dr. Li thought for a moment. "As you may know, certain cell lines derived from the pupal ovarian tissue of the fall army worm, *Spodoptera frugiperda*, are commonly used in conjunction with the BEV system. Unfortunately, our variant baculovirus does not work well with these established cell lines. However, working in collaboration with Dr. Evert's group at Rutgers University, we have developed a special new cell line from another insect species that works very well with our variant strain of baculovirus."

"And what would that species of cell line be?" pursued the young lady.

Dr. Li forced a smile. "I'm sorry, ma'am, but for the time being that information is…confidential."

The young lady thanked him and returned to her seat.

"Any other questions?" Sam surveyed the audience. "Yes, the gentleman in the rear of the room."

A short, stocky man with a wrinkled jacket and loosely fitting tie slowly rose to his feet, tucking in his shirt as he stood up.

"Dr. Li," he began, leaning on the table in front of him, "your description of the symbiotic relationship between the insect cell and baculovirus particles sounds strangely reminiscent of the mechanism which, as many of my colleagues believe, may have contributed to the evolution of mitochondria in nucleated or eukaryotic, cells. If what you say is true, might we not be on the verge of a new evolutionary order of cell structure, and might this not possibly have unpredictable consequences on established ecosystems?"

Dr. Li took a deep breath. "My, that is quite a mouthful!"

Some light laughter broke the tension in the room.

"I believe you are referring to the 'endosymbiotic hypothesis' which suggests that mitochondria are actually the remnants of an ancient bacterium that once upon a time entered a primitive nucleated cell."

The gentleman in the back of the room gave a confirming nod.

Dr. Li continued to elaborate on the topic, playing to the audience. "Yes, well, as I understand the theory, once inside the cell, the bacteria neither destroyed the cell, nor was it digested by the host cell. Rather, the two entered into a mutually beneficial, or symbiotic relationship. On the one hand"—Dr. Li held out his left hand—"the engulfed bacterium provided energy to the engulfing cell, while on the other"—extending his right hand—"the cell provided the basic nutrients to the bacterium. Over time, and after many millions of generations, the bacterial partner became today's mitochondrion, which is characteristic of all modern eukaryotic cells. This includes the very cells that make up our bodies." Dr. Li looked directly at the man. "I take it *this* is what you are referring to?"

The gentleman nodded in agreement.

Dr. Li paused to take a sip of water before continuing.

"Yes, well of course, it is only a theory. But in our case, as far as a threat to the environment is concerned, let me say that every precaution has been taken to ensure that all experiments are contained. We conform to the strictest standards of biological containment as set for by the National Institute of Health. Until our BEV system is better characterized, all experiments with live viruses are performed under the highest biological safety level conditions prescribed by the NIH guidelines. Furthermore, the insects and cell lines themselves are maintained in a quarantined environment. So, we are confident that there is zero risk of environmental release or adverse effect on the ecosystem."

Dr. Li leaned forward on the podium. "Does that adequately address your concerns, sir?"

The gentleman hesitated. "Yes, thank you, Dr. Li." He then took his seat.

The room was filled with the low murmurings and bobbing heads of private conversations provoked by this recent exchange. Dr. Li sought to regain control.

"Well, then, if there are no further questions, let me again say, thank you for your kind attention. And please have a good evening."

The room broke into a polite applause, as many in the audience rose to their feet. Dr. Li smiled and bowed, then turned the podium back over to the evening's moderator.

With the formal portion of the program concluded, Dr. Li made the rounds through the ballroom, like a proud father at his daughter's wedding, moving from table to table, enjoying the notoriety afforded the evening's keynote speaker. An entourage of well-wishers and favor-seekers followed him, picking up and dropping off members as he meandered purposefully toward the back of the room.

Was that Rick Nuisom refilling Sam's glass of punch? Sure was. *What a leach!* John thought. *Sucking information out of Sam. He's bound to know about their plans for a new pilot plant.*

As Sam approached the table where John and Bob were seated, Rick excused himself and slithered slowly away.

"Rick Nuisance...I mean, Nuisom," Bob commented under his breath. "He's everywhere. Like *horseshit*, my dad used to say."

John stared at Bob with a surprised look.

"What?! It's just an old turn-of-the-century expression," Bob countered unapologetically.

"Sshh," John motioned with a finger to his lips, as Sam finally reached their table.

"John Weston, my old good friend! So happy to see you again!"

John stood up and offered Sam his hand. Sam took a firm hold with both hands and shook vigorously.

"I was hoping I might run into you tonight, John," Sam said. "It's too bad, having to travel clear across the country to see old friends and associates. I think the next meeting should be in Chicago. Then we could meet halfway. East coast, west coast."

"Well, let's put that in the suggestion box," John offered. He then turned to Bob, who was now standing behind him. "Bob, you remember Dr. Li?"

"Of course." Bob reached out and shook Sam's hand. "Good to see you again, sir."

John turned back to Sam. "Sam, can you join us for an after dinner drink? Maybe catch up on old times."

Bob moved aside, offering him his own seat at the table, and then took an empty seat next to Sam.

"I'd be happy to, John. I think my official duties this evening are over."

His remaining entourage finally took the hint and quietly melted away, as Sam took a seat at the table between John and Bob.

John and Sam had first met at GenAvance's R&D facility near Princeton, soon after John was hired by GenAvance. Later, when John transferred to the company's corporate headquarters campus in Thousand Oaks, California, John wound up working directly for Sam's development group as a process engineer and team leader. John and Sam quickly developed a warm friendship, which was facilitated by their mutual love of history. When the downsizing occurred, Sam did everything he could do to avoid the pain of having to lay John off, but corporate policy dictated the outcome. When John started up his consulting business, Sam gave him his first contract. It was a small upgrade renovation project for an existing pilot scale clinical manufacturing facility. That helped to kick-start the business, putting Haddon Life-Tech in the black in less than two years of operations.

"Sam, I must say, I certainly enjoyed your slide presentation," John said. "But, I was particularly disappointed to learn that BVs do *not* promote time travel."

Sam laughed out loud. "Yes, a little silly. But I think it got the audience's attention, don't you think?"

"You're a real showman, Sam."

"Yes. Well, sometimes that's just what it takes to get funding these days," Sam confessed.

"Yes. But I do believe your presentation was well received. Tell me, Sam, who was the guy asking the environmental questions? He seems to have done his homework."

Sam sat back and sighed. "Ah, yes. You mean Alex Preston of the NIH, our card-carrying Green Party member. Seriously, though, Dr. Preston's comments and concerns are certainly germane. But we have also done our homework and can assure you that every precaution has been taken with regard to biological containment. I'm not even convinced that an accidental release into the environment would be harmful. The insect-virus vector system that we have developed is so mutually dependent that it is doubtful whether either could survive without the other. The fly...err, I mean, insect...would likely die if released on its own. And the virus variant is not capable of infecting other insects."

"Well, that is good to know," John replied. "And Dr. Evert. That wouldn't be Dr. *Julie* Evert, would it?"

"Why, yes. Do you know her?"

"Not personally. But if she's the same Julie Evert, I was voted 'Sorority Sweetheart' of her sorority when I was an undergrad at Rutgers. She was a year or two behind me. Didn't really know her, just knew *of* her."

Sam laughed. "My, you are quite the popular fellow, John."

"Nah, that was really a long time ago," John said, brushing off the compliment.

"Yes, and time enough for Julie to have developed quite a reputation in the field of 'insect transgenics.' Perhaps I can reintroduce you to her once this pilot plant project gets underway," Sam offered.

"That would be great, Sam."

John was glad that Sam was the first to bring up the subject of the pilot plant project. He took the opportunity to pursue the subject.

"So, tell me Sam, what is the status of the project? Do you have the funding to pursue it?"

"Yes, well, I have managed to get some bridging funds approved, enough to engage a consultant to execute a feasibility or conceptual study establishing the scope of the work. I really like your 'design-build' approach, John. But to be honest, I'm having a little trouble selling corporate management on the idea. Still, there were a few people who were quite receptive."

Sam leaned forward, making a small tent with his hands, thumbs and index fingers joined. He spoke softly. "John, would you be interested in taking on the conceptual study, pending final funding approval for the engineering design?"

At this point, Bob, who had remained silent up until now, suddenly blurted out, "Does the Pope *shit* in the woods!"

John's jaw dropped, rendered momentarily speechless by Bob's outburst. An amusing mixed metaphor in a less formal setting, but definitely not appropriate for this occasion.

Sam broke the awkward silence. "Well, yes, I can understand your enthusiasm, Bob. We are all quite eager to get this show on the road."

"Sam, you mentioned previously that the site for the facility was still being studied. Has GenAvance made a decision on this?" John inquired further, keeping a nervous eye on Bob. That's when John became aware of Bob's lips occasionally moving as he stared away from the conversation at the table. He seemed preoccupied with something.

Sam perked up. "Why yes, John. You'll be interested to learn that the Princeton area, just south of New Brunswick, has been chosen for the site. Another reason why your firm would be the ideal choice for this project: *Location*. Since the facility will be focused on the new continuous process, we thought it would be better if it were close to our partners at Rutgers University."

"That sounds great, Sam."

John chose his words carefully for his next question, as he saw Rick Nuisom trolling for leads over by the dessert table on the far side of the room.

"So, has the decision been made...not to go out on the street for this one?"

Sam leaned back. "Well, not entirely. At least, not yet. But, even if we go out to bid for the engineering phase, you would be in a preferred position having done the conceptual design study."

"True. I was just thinking that it might be to everyone's advantage"— *and keep Rick Nuisom out of it*—"if we took the design-build approach from the very beginning."

"Well, we will see. What I'd like to propose is for you, and Bob here"—turning to acknowledge Bob's continued presence—"to come out to Thousand Oaks to meet the project team, and to kick off the conceptual study. I was thinking"—looking up as if the calendar were printed on the ceiling—"about the third week in August."

John quickly consulted his pocket day planner.

"It's a deal, Sam! Bob and I can fly out Monday morning, the sixteenth, and spend as much time as necessary to get the ball rolling."

"Excellent! I will prepare an agenda, and, of course, have a purchase order issued to Haddon Life-Tech, as soon as I return to the office next week," Sam concluded.

"What about 'confidentiality'?" John asked.

"Ah, yes, of course. I'm glad you reminded me. I will forward a copy of our standard confidentiality agreement for your review and signature. It contains the standard legalize on such matters. I don't think you should have any trouble signing it. But if you do have any questions, please don't hesitate to call. I wouldn't want the lawyers getting in the way of progress, eh?"

"Of course not, Sam. I'll bring the signed papers with me on the sixteenth."

John closed his planner and returned it to his pocket. "So, tell me, Sam. How long are you going to be in town? Wondering if we could treat you to a nice dinner. Say, Bookbinders in Philly; or, there are plenty of fine restaurants on the Jersey side of the river?"

"Thank you, John. But, but I'm pretty well booked till the end of this week. But I will take you up on your offer when you come out to the west coast next month."

"It's a deal!" John agreed. "I was just hoping you might've had time to explore some of Jersey's local history while you were in town."

"Oh, I would so like to, John. Perhaps the next time I'm back this way. I'll have to set some time aside. Then you can take me on one of your famous tours."

"I'd be only too happy to oblige, Sam. You know, my family goes back to colonial times."

"Yes, I remember. And did you not have a great-great-uncle in the revolutionary war? And his name was…Ah, yes! How stupid of me. His name was John Weston. Just like your own."

With talk of business over, now, Sam was starting to relax. It was beginning to feel like good old times again.

"Ah, you remembered!" John replied. "I am amazed! I think I only told you that once before."

"Well, maybe more than *once*." Sam laughed. "John, I've often thought that you must have a Buddhist monk hiding out somewhere in your family tree, what with your keen interest in ancestors and family history."

John smiled. "You might be right, Sam. You might be right."

*****

Bob remained quiet on the ride home from the ISPE meeting. The Jersey Turnpike was slick from the rain, which had been falling steadily most of the day, and truck traffic was especially heavy.

"You want me to drive?" John asked.

Bob didn't respond right away. It took another prodding from John.

"You okay, Bob? Maybe I should drive."

Bob finally answered. "No, I'm okay, John. I only had one drink all evening. Just a little tired."

John continued to study Bob. He was moving his lips again. This made John nervous. He tried to engage Bob in some light conversation.

"Tell me, Bob, exactly what was that basement project you were working on the other day. Seemed awfully important. Important enough to hand the grill over to an inexperienced grill master." John chuckled, picturing Paul Fielding in his khaki shorts battling the burning brats.

Suddenly, Bob blurted out, "God! Not you, too, John! I get enough of that from Kate! Can't you just leave well enough alone?"

The Ford Taurus suddenly swerved to the right. Bob turned the wheel just in time to avoid hitting the guard rail. John stiffened in his seat, bracing himself against the dashboard with both arms, heart pounding in his chest. "Jesus!" he screamed. With tires squealing, the car swung wildly to the left across traffic as Bob overcompensated to regain control of the vehicle. A pickup truck blared its horn and swerved just in time to avoid a collision, passing them on the right. Finally regaining control of the Taurus, Bob brought the vehicle back to the center of the lane and managed to settle down behind the wheel.

"Whoa! Bob. What got into you?" John scolded. "I was only trying to make conversation."

Bob slowed the vehicle and pulled over to the shoulder of the highway, bringing the car to a complete stop. Taking his arms off the steering wheel and looking straight ahead, he spoke in a low, weak voice.

"I think maybe you should drive, John."

Without waiting for a response, Bob unlocked his driver-side car door and opened it halfway, preparing to exit.

Suddenly a huge tandem diesel rig, which was bearing down on them with its air horn blasting and high beams flashing, passed them like a runaway freight train, coming within inches of the half-opened driver-side door. *Swoosh!* John could almost feel his ears pop as the air was sucked out of the car, setting it rocking and leaving them in a swirling mist of oil and water road spray.

"Damn it, Bob, not so fast!" John yelled. "Wait for the goddamn traffic to pass!"

Bob meekly obliged, closing the door.

John quickly jumped out of the car and crossed over to the driver side. "Move over, Bob!" John shouted above the rain and road noise.

John and Bob didn't say another word to each other the rest of the ride home. Forty minutes later they pulled into Bob's driveway, parked alongside John's tan Camry, and sat there for a few minutes reflecting on what had just happened. By now the rain had tapered off to a light drizzle. John looked over and thought he saw Bob's eyes tearing up. Bob spoke first. Staring down into his own lap, he said with a whimper, "I...I think I need help, John."

Bob clenched his fists to keep from trembling. Then, sitting up and looking straight ahead, avoiding eye contact with his friend, he said, "I don't think I can make it. The...*voices*. They..."

He stopped mid-sentence and turned to John.

"I think you're gonna have to make that trip to GenAvance yourself, John. Or get someone else to go in my place. I gotta try and get some help to fight this thing."

"Sure, Bob. Do whatever you have to do."

John paused a moment before asking: "Does Katie know what's going on?"

Bob sighed and shook his head. "How can she know what's going on, when I don't even know what's going on."

His tone turned real and serious.

"She's been dropping hints all this past week. About going to see a shrink. Okay, so those weren't her exact words. But, you get the idea."

John took a deep breath. "Yeah. I get the idea. Maybe she's right, Bob."

Suddenly Bob's mood shifted, becoming lighter, almost silly. With a burst of laughter he asked, "Hey! If you really want to know what I'm working on, I can take you down in the basement and show you, right now!"

John wasn't sure how to react. Was this the same Bob talking?

"Maybe another time, Bob. It's getting late, and with the bad weather and all. I probably should be getting home."

Like a hurt puppy, Bob took a deep breath and sighed. "Oh yeah, right."

He then mumbled something under his breath, sounding something like, "Anyway, I don't think you're *ready* to…" which trailed off into incoherence.

John tried to elicit a response, but got none. Bob just continued staring blankly into space. John unlatched the car door, then turned back to his friend.

"Try to get some rest, Bob. A good night's sleep can make all the difference, sometimes. Go ahead and sleep in tomorrow…just call me later. Okay?"

"Sure," Bob whimpered.

*****

The headlights of John's tan Camry illuminated the old carriage house as he pulled into the driveway of his Haddonfield home. A young rabbit caught off guard stood frozen in the beams for a moment, then scampered off into the lush greenery of John's backyard. The night was warm. After cutting the lights and killing the engine, John just sat there for a few minutes, savoring the soft patter of the light summer rain on the car roof. For the time being, all cares of the day were gone.

Finally, John got out of the car. Grabbing his briefcase and covering his head with a newspaper, he quickly made for the house, taking the red brick path which wound its way through the right side yard, leading to the wraparound porch of his restored, three-story Victorian home. Patches of soft-colored landscape lighting marked the way, betraying the night's hidden drizzle with illuminated streaks of silver-gray. Traversing the length of the side porch John turned past the corner and continued to the front door. Like an actor on stage, his progress was tracked by a succession of bright spotlights and beacons, triggered by the house security system's motion detectors. John checked the mailbox, removed a handful of letters and bundled mail, then opened the front door and entered.

Shaking off the rain, John entered the shallow vestibule and pulled the door closed behind with his briefcase hand as he focused on trying to read the mail with the other. From the vestibule he entered a large foyer, or entrance hall, which communicated to the other main sections of the house. The hall was sparsely appointed with a large grandfather clock standing against the right wall, a cherry Queen Anne side table with mirror and sconces on the far wall, and a lone coat tree occupying the left inside corner. A grand, oak staircase dominated the room's interior. The stairs began their slow climb to the left, went straight back to an intermediate landing, then continued to the right before terminating at a second-floor landing which overlooked the entrance hall. A second set of stairs continued unseen to the third floor above. The banisters and baluster posts were original, handcrafted mahogany with a restored red varnish finish, reflecting the craftsmanship of an earlier age. Each flight of stairs was accented with a wide, dark maroon runner which complimented the red mahogany finish of the woodwork.

A large, ornately patterned gold and maroon Persian area rug covered most of the floor. The underlying hardwood, which ran throughout house, was restored with wide oak planking, closely matching the original ancient hardwood flooring. The lower portions of the foyer walls were wainscoted in raised oak paneling, with the remaining walls covered in a textured floral print, accented with beautifully sculpted white molding—not the modern plastic imitation, but original handcrafted wood. A large Schonbek crystal chandelier hung just off room center, anchored high above in the cathedral, sky-blue coffered ceiling. Like a Foucault pendulum, it could be seen to sway at times, ever so gently, seemingly of its own accord.

John proceeded though a pair of sliding doors to his left leading into his study, just as the large grandfather clock in the hallway struck the hour, counting off eleven chimes. Turning on the room lights, he quickly rid himself of his baggage, dropping his briefcase to the floor with a thud and tossing the bundle of mail onto his desk: a large antique roll-up kind, a proud find which he acquired a few years ago at an estate sale and had since refinished. Pouring himself a glass of ginger brandy from the liquor cabinet, he dimmed the lights, kicked off his shoes, and flopped back in his favorite reclining chair. He liked flavored brandy best. It helped sooth his throat—and his nerves. He especially needed it this evening, having neglected his running regimen for the past few days.

His study occupied a portion of the first floor that included the house's corner cupola. The cupola structure, a signature architectural design feature of many Victorian homes, was largely what sold John on the house in the first place. This cupola was especially large, with four symmetrically arranged outside faces, each fitted with a tall double-hung window. Unlike many cupola structures which included only the upper floors over a wraparound front porch roof, John's cupola included the first floor and faced directly into the right front yard, away from the house, giving the study added space and contributing to its unique character. With its southern exposure and four tall windows arranged in a wide arc, east to west, this was one of the brightest rooms in the house. Only the second-floor observatory, the room directly over the study, was brighter. From there the cupola offered a splendid view of the skies on clear, starry nights. John had a hidden spiral staircase installed connecting the two rooms. In recent years he had taken up stargazing as a hobby. A six-inch Meade reflector telescope with equatorial clock mount was his new pride and joy, occupying a choice location by the upstairs observatory window. He had joined the local Stargazers' Club of South Jersey, which offered a nice change of pace and the opportunity to socialize, as the heavens allowed.

The room had a calming effect on John. His "inner sanctum," as he referred to it. In contrast to the austere modern furnishings of his workplace office, his home study conveyed a pragmatic turn-of-the-century opulence that would have made Thomas Edison feel right at home, from the rolltop desk and large earth globe cradled in its maple floor stand, to the glass front barrister-style bookshelves lining the walls. The imitation leather reclining chair in which he now found himself was his only concession to modern fixtures. "Genuine Naugahyde," the salesman had assured him with a wink, "straight from the Nauga herds of Naugatuck, Connecticut!"

So, John settled back in his Naugahyde recliner trying to piece together the events of the day. He thought about Dr. Li and his cell culture research, the strange behavior of his good friend and partner, Bob Fenwick, and their harrowing trip home on the Jersey Turnpike.

John stared at the windows, dimly illuminated by the scattered backlight of a distant street lamp, and followed the downward tracings of tiny rivulets of rain against the tall glass panes. Starting high on the pane, they took separate paths, slow and erratic at first, uncertain which way to go, competing for small droplets of rain along the way, picking up speed until, upon reaching a critical mass, they disappeared in a mad dash to the bottom sash.

Suddenly, a new light broke through the windows as the clouds parted momentarily, revealing a full moon seeking to reclaim its dominion over the night sky. John raised his snifter of brandy and studied the rising vapors of distillate condensing on the inside surface of the glass, catching the soft reflected light of the moon. The room was now filled with dancing shadows cast by the swaying boughs of nearby trees and the kinetic projections of raindrops against the window panes. It brought to mind another night such as this, many years ago.

He took a deep breath and recalled the words of Dr. Sam Li: "And did you not have a great-great-uncle in the revolutionary war?"

"Yes," John answered aloud, "and his name was John J. Weston."

John's mind cleared as he recalled the night he introduced Becky, his college sweetheart, to the ancestor whose name he was to carry into the new millennium. That was exactly twenty years ago this Thanksgiving. Walking over to a nearby bookcase, John's eyes scanned the shelves until they came to rest on an old, well-thumbed edition of Walt Whitman's *Leaves of Grass*. Pulling the book from the shelf, he placed it on the desk and opened it to a bookmarked page, the poem's title highlighted in fading yellow: "The Voice of the Rain."

Chapter 11

1979
November
South Jersey

Harleigh Cemetery, Camden, NJ. John began reading from a book of Whitman poetry, as a light rain tapped a soothing rhythm on the roof of his blue '74 Plymouth Gold Duster:

> And who art thou? Said I to the soft falling shower,
> Which, strange to tell, gave me an answer, as here
>   translated:
> I am the poem of Earth, said the voice of the rain,
> Eternal I rise impalpable out of the land and the
>   bottomless sea,
> Upward to heaven, whence, vaguely form'd, altogether
>   changed, and yet the same,
> I descend to lave the drouths, atomies, dust-layers of the
>   globe,
> And all that in them, without me were seeds only, latent,
>   unborn;
> And forever, by day and night, I give back life to my own
>   origin and make pure and beautify it;
> (For song, issuing from its birth-place, after fulfillment,
>   wandering,
> Reck'd or unreck'd, duly with love returns.)[5]

John put the book down, his left arm leaning on the steering wheel, and turned to Becky, waiting for her reaction. Becky sat barefoot next to him, her long legs folded up to her chest, leaning with her back against the passenger door.

"So, what do you think?" John inquired at last.

---

[5] Walt Whitman, "The Voice of the Rain," *Leaves of Grass*, 150th Anniversary Edition (New York: Signet Classics, 2005), 434-435.

"I like it. And, well…it certainly does fits the occasion," Becky replied tentatively, acknowledging the weather and the poem's author with a simple glance out the window—the Walt Whitman family tomb was located less than twenty feet away from the parked car.

John had invited Becky home for Thanksgiving break, partly to get away, but also as a perfect opportunity for her to meet the family. They had been dating since July, having first met in the spring of their junior year, and their relationship was now taking a more serious turn.

It was now Wednesday, the day before Thanksgiving. Soon after arriving home, and having made the customary introductions to his mom, dad, and younger brother, Matt, they were off again in his Plymouth Duster touring the favorite haunts of his youth, the schools he attended, his favorite hangouts, the malls and local coffeehouse, the trails he had conquered while running on his high school's cross-country team, and finally—saving the best for last—his favorite local historical sites.

This naturally put them on the trail of his favorite poet and local celebrity, Walt Whitman. He was never quite sure why he favored Whitman. Was it because of his local roots and celebrity status, or was it for the works themselves? He only knew that, whenever things got rough in his life, he could take solace in the verses or natural prose penned by the "Good Gray Poet," often while walking the same paths through nature which had inspired the bard a century before. Their explorations inevitably took them to Harleigh Cemetery, the site of Whitman's grave and family mausoleum, the poet's final resting place.

Entering the main gate to the cemetery, the road immediately split in three directions. The leftmost fork went past the main office building and parking area, from whence the road narrowed, curving downward to the right and passing through a shaded glen on the extreme western edge of the cemetery. There, in a sheltered grotto set into the hillside off the left, stood an unobtrusive gray granite structure: the family tomb and mausoleum of Walt Whitman. The uninitiated could easily pass it by without notice.

"So, how did he come to be buried here?" Becky asked.

"Well, when he died in 1882, the Harleigh Cemetery, which was fairly new at the time, donated a site for his burial. But he paid for the mausoleum himself, which he shares with his brother and mother."

Becky studied the site. "It's kind of isolated. Even spooky," she confessed.

"Well, he did live a somewhat isolated existence, especially in his later years. He received his inspiration from nature. So, this is probably as fitting a final resting place as any."

Becky's attention was drawn to a small black granite monument located just off the road. "What does it say on that stone monument?"

John strained his neck to see. "Dunno," he said. "Lemme go see."

He jumped out of the car and ran over to read the words inscribed on the stone.

"It's kinda hard to read. Can't make out the words," John shouted back. "Wait a minute."

He shifted position, catching the light at a new angle to highlight the words engraved in the highly polished black granite surface.

"It says, 'I bequeath myself to the dirt to grow from the grass I love. If you want me again look for me under your boot soles.'"

John jumped back into the car, shaking off the rain.

"He was not without a sense of humor," John chuckled. "Even in death!"

A chilly breeze, ripe with the scent of damp earth and decaying autumn leaves, swept through the open door of the car.

Becky laughed. "You're crazy. And you're gonna catch pneumonia running around in the rain like that. Gotta getcha warm."

With that she drew herself close to John and gave him a kiss. John felt the warmth of her body, and put both arms around her. She reciprocated. They kissed long and hard.

Becky whispered in John's ear. "Isn't there a blanket in the back seat?"

"Right! I can get it."

She held his face closely in both hands, and whispered softly. "I was thinking maybe that we could go to the blanket."

John understood. He looked around. "It's still daylight. Don't want to create a spectacle."

"Well, I think the rain is chasing everyone away. We have the place to ourselves," she giggled. On second thought, she corrected herself. "Well, alone among the *once* living, anyway."

Looking down the road, on the far side of a distant pond, John saw a pickup truck heading in their direction. Pausing at a crossroads, the truck made a quick left turn and took another path up the hill and out of sight.

"Groundskeepers," he said. "Let's find a more secluded place."

He put the car in gear and continued down the path, leaving Whitman behind for the moment. Becky huddled close to his side, stroking the inside of his thighs.

"Don't make me have an accident, dear," he whispered. "At least, not until we're both ready."

They continued down toward the river on the far side of the cemetery.

"The Cooper River," John announced. "Should be able to find some tree cover here."

The pristine view surprised even John. He had never been this far into the cemetery, nor had he ever seen the Cooper River from this perspective. The bend in the river offered a wide-angle view of the river and its wildlife, as all evidence of encroaching civilization melted into a distant cityscape. They took shelter along a secluded tree line, near the river's edge.

There, wrapped in a blanket and lying on the fold-down back seat of the Gold Duster, they made love, as the voice of the whispering rain, "duly with love," returned to caress the earth.

*****

Eleanor Weston basted the holiday turkey one last time with its own sizzling juices, before removing the steaming bird from the oven. The delicious aroma of this most welcomed traditional autumn feast permeated the Weston household as Mrs. Weston lifted the big bird from its roasting pan and set it on a carving board. It was Thanksgiving Day, 1979, and dinner was ready!

"Honey! Can you please carve the turkey," Eleanor hollered out to her husband, Richard, who was absorbed in a college football game on TV in another part of the house. "I *do* believe it's done!"

"Be there in a sec, hon!" Richard hollered back.

All manner of seasonal gastronomical treats assembled for what seemed to be the great and final assault on world hunger: stuffing, mashed potatoes, candied yams, cranberry sauce, string beans, and brussels sprouts. Hardly a square inch of empty space remained on the table and countertops, as the cupboards were emptied of all available bowls and utensils to support the preparation of this grand feast. As master planner and executioner-in-chief, Mrs. Weston directed all aspects of its preparation, enlisting the help of her household subordinates with a shout and a wave of the spatula.

"Matt, will you please help set the table," she ordered. "Use the good china from the dining room china cabinet. And don't forget to set a place for your Aunt Dee and Uncle Dan. They should be here any minute."

Matt, John's younger brother, responded slowly, but surely. Tearing himself away from his *Star Wars* video required a little help from the good side of "The Force." Matt was in his junior year at Sterling High School. He possessed a creative and artistic streak that would eventually lead him to a successful career as an architect. But for now, his main interests were science fiction and Marvel comics. He had a natural talent for illustrating.

"Becky, you don't have to do that. You've done enough already. After all, you're the guest," Eleanor said.

Becky had been helping John's mom in the kitchen for most of the day, while John and his dad tracked the college football games on TV.

"Oh, I don't mind, Mrs. Weston," Becky replied. "I really enjoy cooking, but I don't get much opportunity. I share an apartment, and the kitchen's pretty small. I'm afraid college has turned me into a fast food junkie."

"No way!" Eleanor exclaimed. "You certainly don't look like a fast food junkie."

Becky's figure was hard to ignore. With her slim, classic beauty and poise, she appeared a perfect match for a career in the advertising and modeling business.

"Well, I do work out. Something new, called Aerobics.

"Aerobics? Maybe I should try it," Eleanor considered.

She then turned to the unattended turkey sitting on the countertop and shouted over Becky's shoulder.

"Richard, dear, the turkey's not going to carve itself! I think it's cooled off long enough!"

With that Richard Weston leaped into the room. "Sorry, Ellie. I couldn't leave the game with only two minutes to go. What a nail biter!"

Spying the big bird and the great holiday spread staged for its final transfer to the dining room table he added, "Ah, what a site! Great job, as usual, honey!"

He gave his wife a peck on the cheek, then shouted, "All right! So where's the carving knife?"

The holiday meal was enjoyed by all. There was plenty to go around, with ample surplus to provide leftover meals for the long weekend ahead: turkey sandwiches, turkey croquettes, and finally, turkey noodle soup prepared from the boiled down carcass of the big bird. Truly the most economical meal purchase of all time!

"Okay, so who's ready for dessert?" Mrs. Weston asked rhetorically. This was her way of announcing the next and final phase of the meal—and a cue for Mr. Weston to start brewing a pot of coffee.

"Dee, the apple and pumpkin pies look simply scrumptious," Eleanor said. "You are definitely *the* baker *par excellence* in the family."

Dee was John's favorite aunt, his dad's oldest sister, but not just because she made great pies. Dee and Uncle Dan could never have children of their own. Never bitter over it, they redirected their love and attention to their nephews and nieces.

Dee smiled and nodded, graciously absorbing the compliment. "Thank you, Ellie. It's too bad Laura couldn't be here. She so enjoyed my apple pies growing up."

John and Matt's older sister, Laura, had recently moved to Paris, France, with her new husband and publisher, Jean Dupree. Laura graduated from Dickenson College three years earlier with a degree in journalism, and was now working as a syndicated columnist for Jean's magazine publishing company.

"Yes, Dee," Ellie replied. "But look on the bright side. Maybe next year she'll invite us to come to Paris to spend the holidays."

Young Matt corrected his mother. "Don't think they celebrate our Thanksgiving in France, Mom."

"Well, you know what I mean. With Laura living abroad, it could give us an incentive to travel. Yes?"

This last remark was meant for Mr. Weston. A gentle hint to get their vacation plans in order.

Getting everyone back on the holiday track, Dee addressed the table. "I brought some Cool Whip topping along, if anyone cares for some. It's in the refrigerator."

Ellie yelled out to her husband in the kitchen. "Richard! Would you please bring the Cool Whip with you when you come in?"

"Got my hands full with this coffee pot, dear" he shouted back. "Matt, why don't you help out and get the Cool Whip for your Aunt Dee."

Matt didn't hesitate. "Sure! Hey, Cool Whip's the shit!"

Mrs. Weston threw down her napkin and glared at her younger son. "Matthew, where on earth did you pick that up that kind of talk!"

"Sorry, Mom."

Mrs. Weston continued. "My word! You may talk to your friends that way, but not to family. And certainly not at the dinner table."

"Okay, okay! I get it," Matt hollered back from the kitchen.

Matt returned with the Cool Whip. Not far behind was Mr. Weston.

"The coffee should be ready in another five minutes," Mr. Weston announced. "When the timer goes off."

Settled back down in his seat at the head of the table, he reached for a piece of apple pie as he spoke. "So, Becky, did John give you the grand tour of South Jersey, yesterday?"

Becky put down her fork and turned to speak. "Why, yes, Mr. Weston. He showed me his high school. Then we drove into Haddonfield and Pennypack Park. Had a nice sidewalk lunch before heading over to Harleigh Cemetery and Whitman's tomb. But, then it started to rain and…"—John kicked her leg under the table—"…well, we had to cut it short."

She started to blush, but quickly redirected the conversation. "So, Mr. Weston, John tells me you're a history teacher. That's great! Where do you teach?"

"Sterling High School. Mostly early American history. But I also teach a few elective courses of my own making. Try to get the kids to think for themselves."

"Dad's holding back," young John interjected. "He's really quite the popular fellow among the students. Voted teacher of the year three of the past five years!"

"Well, I just try to do my best," Mr. Weston humbly acknowledged.

"That's great, sir," Becky exclaimed. "Wish my history teacher had been so interesting." She turned to John and smirked. "Then I might be able to keep up with your son, here. You must know he's a real history buff."

"Well, I'm glad something rubbed off," Mr. Weston said triumphantly.

"Not 'off,' dad—in! It's *in* our blood. Must be the Weston genes," John laughed. "They've endured the ages."

He raised his coffee cup in a mock toast.

Becky thought a moment. "So, how far back do the Weston genes go?"

"All the way back!" Mr. Weston laughed. "Actually, we've been able to trace the family name as far back as colonial times. Thanks to John's Aunt Dee, here. She's really the family historian." He turned to Aunt Dee. "Dee, tell John and Becky what you know."

Aunt Dee spoke deliberately, with authority. "Well, the best I've been able to determine, the Weston name, at least our family line, goes back to early Danver, Massachusetts."

"Danver? Isn't that what they used to call 'Salem'?" John asked.

"Very good, John. You get an 'A' in geography," his dad smiled, giving his son a congratulatory nod.

"Is that 'Salem,' as in 'witch trials'?" chimed in Becky.

Dee smiled. "Yes, the same. But, our family line actually starts a few years after those events. The Salem Witch Trials occurred in 1692. The best we can tell, Samuel Weston, already an established merchant, came over from England as a young man sometime in 1696. The church records record his wedding to an Elizabeth Goodall in June of 1702. Sam also had a younger brother or cousin, don't know for sure, who came over around the same time and settled in Boston. His name was Andrew, but we don't know much about his family line."

"So, what does that make Sam?"

"Let's see." Dee paused, counting off with her fingers. "That would make you…a ninth generation American-born Weston."

"Making Sam your seven times great-grandfather," Mr. Weston added.

"But I always thought our family was based in South Jersey. You know, the Haddonfield area," John questioned.

Dee answered. "Well, Sam and Elizabeth had six children: three sons, and three daughters. Samuel Jr. was the oldest, born in 1704."

As she spoke, Dee took a clean napkin and began sketching a family tree to illustrate her point. "Sam Jr. took over the family business at the age of twenty, when his father died in 1728. Young Sam married Regina Walsh and together they had two daughters and a son. His name was Bartholomew. Regina, poor soul, died bringing little Bartholomew into the world. That was in 1730. It was after Regina's death that Sam relocated his family business from Danver, Massachusetts, to Haddonfield, New Jersey."

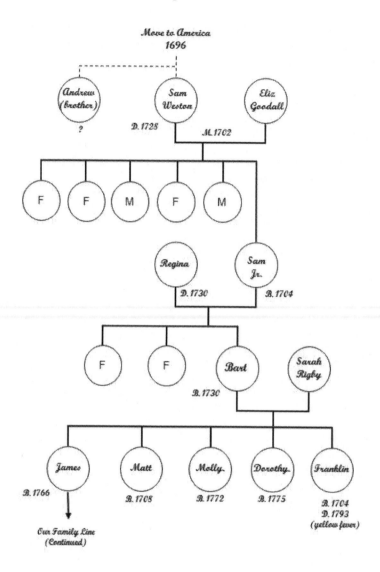

"When Bartholomew grew up," Dee continued, "he remained in Haddonfield and eventually took over the business. He married Sarah Rigby of Philadelphia, and together they had five children. That's how our family line, which is traced through Bartholomew and his oldest son, James, became rooted in West Jersey. Their youngest child, Franklin, died in the great yellow fever outbreak of 1793 in Philadelphia. He was only fourteen at the time, poor child."

Running out of space on one napkin, Dee picked up a second and completed the nine-generation male family line from Sam Jr., first American born in 1704, to John, born 1958.

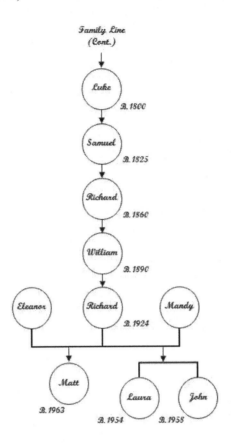

"Whoa! That's real interesting, Aunt Dee," John exclaimed. "Hey Dad, how come you never told us about all this before?"

"Well, you see, John, your Aunt Dee took a serious interest in genealogy after your grandfather died three years ago. So, most of this information is fairly new. Since you've been hitting the books at college, your Auntie 'gumshoe' here has been pounding the sidewalk getting the lowdown on our family tree. Isn't that right, Dee?"

Dee nodded. "Well, yes, in a manner of speaking. And it's all written down in this family bible"—patting the cover of a thick scrap book she was holding—"that I've been building up over the years."

"What I find interesting, Dee," Becky chimed in, "is how you were able to uncover this information after all these years. I mean, it's not like you can just go to your local library and look up 'Weston Family Tree' in the card catalogues."

"Well, in a manner of speaking that's what you *have* to do," Dee explained. "But instead of the library, you need to search church and municipal records. You know, birth and baptism records, death certificates, deed registers, tax records. And of course there are the occasional memorabilia—diaries and letters—left behind."

"So, were you able to find any old diaries, Aunt Dee?" John asked.

"Well, not so much a diary as a journal. Bartholomew was quite meticulous in keeping records of his business transactions and expenses. But he also used his journal to record personal happenings and events, his impressions and the like."

"Tell them about the love letters, Dee," Mr. Weston prodded.

"Yes, of course. That would be of special interest to you two." Dee addressed John and Becky with a sparkle in her eye. "We can't be positive who the author was, as he never signed his name in full. Most of the letters are simply signed with the letters 'J.J.' or 'J. Jay'. But you can tell from the handwriting that they're all authored by the same person. And, he always signed off the same way: 'Your true love till the end of time.'"

"Hmm," John mused. "Wasn't there a John Jay during the Revolution? One of the founding fathers, or something?"

Mr. Weston rocked back in his chair, arms crossed. "That's right, John. You would be referring, of course, to John Jay, co-writer of the *Federalist Papers* with Alexander Hamilton and James Madison. He later became the first Chief Justice of the US Supreme Court of the new fledgling republic."

"Right! Just what I was going to say," John smirked. "So, Dad, do you think these letters could have been written by the same John Jay?"

Mr. Weston paused. "Actually, I had entertained that possibility when Dee first uncovered the letters. But, after checking the handwriting against archived copies of authentic John Jay documents, I had to give up on that idea. There is absolutely no match."

"There is another possibility," Dee interjected.

"You mean the 'younger brother' hypothesis?" Mr. Weston replied.

"Yes," Dee nodded. She turned to John and Becky.

"You see, there are references in Bartholomew's journal to a 'younger brother,' and separate unrelated references to a 'young John.' We think the two may be one and the same. If true, that could mean Bart had a younger half brother. We think Sam may have remarried, although we don't know have any positive record of this, or to whom he married."

John rubbed his chin. "So, you think this 'J.J.' may have been Bart's younger half brother, John?"

Dee nodded. "Yes, quite possible. As far as the second 'J' or 'Jay' in the signature, it may have been his middle name, or just a nick name of some kind. Actually," Dee smiled, "some of the more interesting letters were signed '*Jay-Bird*.'"

John and Becky looked at each other, repeating the name in unison: "Jay-Bird?"

Dee chuckled. "Probably just a nickname or maybe a pet name his sweetheart gave him."

"Or, maybe they were having a secret affair, and didn't want to be discovered in case the letters were intercepted," Mr. Weston suggested with a sly rise of an eyebrow. "After all, if we're having trouble identifying the author, then perhaps that was his intent."

"Can we see these letters, Aunt Dee?" John finally asked.

"Well, the original letters are in a safe deposit box. But your dad should have copies." Dee turned to her brother. "Richard, can you get your copy to show the kids?"

"Sure. Give me a minute."

Mr. Weston jumped up from his seat and disappeared into his study.

"So, how did you come by these letters, Aunt Dee?" John asked.

"Well, dear, when your grandfather died…let's see, it's been over three years, now…we, of course, had to go through his things. We knew about the journal. In fact, I remember seeing it as a child, along with other artifacts and heirlooms that have been passed down through the years. But, in going through the attic of dad's old Haddonfield home, we came across a chest that *no* one…I mean, *none* of the children ever knew about. In the chest was a locked box, like a jewelry box. Its lid was decorated with elaborate hand-painted floral designs. Probably belonged to his wife or mother. We can't be sure. No one could find the key to unlock the box, so we reluctantly forced it open. That's where we found the letters."

Mr. Weston returned from his study with a large cardboard file box, the kind used to store important documents. As he placed the box on the dining room table, John timidly reached for the box and removed the lid.

"Go ahead, John, they're copies. Don't worry about damaging them," his dad assured him.

John removed the top letter and began to read:

2 September

My Dearest Missy

I pray this missive finds you well. I can scare bear the pain of our separation. You are the object of my dreaming, day and night. I had all intentions of bringing you good news of my early arrival, but events have forced a delay until November of this year. Brother is striving to succeed with his new enterprises, although my own

endeavors have proved to be far less promising. He has not
been so supportive as I had expected. Howbeit, I hold
onto the sanguine hope that time may yet be our ally.
Please strive to endure until a better fortune shines on the
course of our affairs. Remain steadfast in health and
purpose, as I endeavor always to do.

Your true love till the end of time,

Jay-Bird

John looked up. "It all sounds rather...mysterious. Dad, I think I like your
theory. Secret love affair and all that."

John's dad just smiled and gave a little nod.

"Interesting," John added as he examined the remaining letters, "All of
the letters are one-sided, from the guy to the gal. Are there any letters from
Missy to Jay-Bird?"

"No, unfortunately, there is no record of them, at least not in the
Weston family archives. They would be nice to have. Maybe help explain the
ambiguities."

"Right," John agreed. "And none of the letters are dated. I mean, no
year is given. Just the day and month. Is there any way to determine when the
letters were written?"

Mr. Weston anticipated his question. "Well, unfortunately, there's little
contextual evidence for dating the letters. He talks about his 'brother,' but
doesn't name him. An 'enterprise' is mentioned, but not identified. The letters
were more personal in nature, and made no reference to time or place.

"However," Mr. Weston continued, raising an index finger for
emphasis, "based on an analysis of the ink and the paper, we think the letters
were written sometime in the last half of the eighteenth century. Furthermore,
the remnants of the wax seals on two of the letters suggest they came from
the colonial era. They bore a royal seal, something that would only have been
used before the Revolution. So, we think that places the letters sometime
between 1760 and 1776."

Up until now, John's uncle Dan had been silent. He was a quiet man
and normally spoke only when spoken to, or after having had time to size up
a situation.

"It's really too bad you can't conjure the dead to conduct an
interview," he offered.

John turned to his uncle. "You can't be serious."

Dan addressed his brother-in-law. "Richard, didn't you tell me you
once tried to conjure up your ancestors with a Ouija board?"

Mr. Weston hesitated, and then replied sheepishly. "Well, yes, but that
was more of a fraternity prank. Anyway, I tried it and it didn't work."

John's young brother, Matt, suddenly chimed in. "Dad, I think it takes two people to work a Ouija board."

Everyone laughed. Mr. Weston turned to John and Becky and winked. "Oh! So *that's* why it didn't work!"

More laughter.

"Right. And I think it needs to be a guy and a girl. Two frat brothers simply won't cut it." Dan pushed the point home.

More laughter.

Mrs. Weston turned to Becky. "All this talk of Westons! Becky, you must be bored to tears!"

"Not at all, Mrs. Weston. I find it all very interesting. Anyway, a girl has to know what she may be getting herself into."

"Touché!" Dan interjected. "And, a *man* as well, I might add. Had I known what I myself was getting into, I'd have…"

"Oh, pshaw!" Dee didn't let him finish. "You entered this family with open eyes, my dear!" She gave him a pretend slap on his lap.

"And, an open heart, I might add," he apologized.

"Okay, you're forgiven," Mrs. Weston said. She then turned to Becky. "So, Becky, before we were so rudely interrupted, where is your family from?"

"Well, my family lives in Morristown, New Jersey. That's where my dad's family comes from. But my mom's side of the family is from the Boston area. I'm told they go back to colonial times, too, like the Westons."

"Oh, that's interesting!" Aunt Dee beamed. "Do you have any brothers or sisters?"

"I have one older sister, Pam. She's twelve years older than me, so we never interacted very much growing up. But, we have become good friends in recent years."

"Morristown? Not Moorestown?" tested Dan. "That's North Jersey, right?"

Dee spoke up. "Oh, don't start with that North-South Jersey thing, Dan."

There was some nervous laughter. While John and Becky would often joke about regional differences between North Jersey and South Jersey, Dan took it a little more seriously. He was part of a local movement to put a non-binding referendum on the ballot for next year's election calling for several South Jersey counties to secede from the state, actually creating two separate states: North Jersey and South Jersey.

John tried to thaw the momentary freeze: "Hey, why don't we break out the cards? How 'bout some hearts? Or sheeps-head?"

The table was cleared and a new pot of coffee brewed for the card game that followed.

*****

It was getting late, almost midnight. Aunt Dee and Uncle Dan had long since gone home, leaving John's mom and dad relaxing in the living room watching Saturday Night Live. Matt was up in his room listening to Led Zeppelin and doing some still life illustrations of his *Star Wars* memorabilia.

John and Becky, meanwhile, were sitting on the back porch listening to the softly falling rain, watching the distant sheet lightning illuminate the western sky. Counting the seconds between flash and sound, they were debating whether the storm was getting closer, or farther away. It was unusual weather for November. More like a summer storm, John thought.

It was Becky's idea to get out the Ouija board.

"Ouija board!" John scoffed. "You don't really believe that inanimate game board is going to conjure up the dead, do you?"

"You're not afraid, are you?" she challenged.

"Afraid?" John smirked. "No. I'm not afraid. Just hate to waste a perfectly fine evening hovering over a silly board. Why don't we just play Monopoly instead?"

"Aw, com'on. Let's just try it." Becky begged as she brushed herself against John's thigh.

"Well, since you put it that way."

John took Becky's hand and led her into the basement family room, a cozy knotty pine retreat which had served John and his brother well growing up. It was well-equipped as a game and TV room, and his parents let it be known that their friends were always welcome there. It made perfect sense, too, as they at least knew where the kids were. His dad would say: "As long as you don't set fire to the place, and keep out the drugs, we won't bother you." The outside basement door made it even more like a clubhouse. They could come and go as they pleased without bothering Mom and Dad—or being bothered by same.

John opened the bottom door of the bookcase and began reading off the names of games. "Let's see. Candy Land. Clue. Scrabble. Monopoly."—turning to Becky—"You sure you don't wanna play Monopoly?"

She sighed and shook her head. "Noooo. Not tonight. Anyway, it's too late. We'd never finish."

John finally located the Ouija board buried at the bottom of a stack of books and other game boxes. He had trouble pulling it loose without toppling the whole stack.

"Still don't know why they call it a 'game,'" he puzzled. "Games have winners and losers. How do you win or lose at Ouija boarding?"

"You don't win or lose," Becky laughed. "You just…well, you just experience the game."

John looked at the box. It was worn and splitting at the edges. He wiped off the dust and read the lid: "Ouija: The Mystifying Oracle Game. Contents: one game board; one plastic *planchette* ." He looked up. "Guess that's French for 'message indicator.'"

A flash of light lit up the room; four seconds later, came the slow rumble of thunder.

"Okay, so open the box already!" Becky said impatiently.

John took the board and the plastic planchette from the box. There was nothing fancy or complicated about it. It was laid out in typical Ouija board fashion: the twenty-six letters of the alphabet arranged in two arc-shaped rows across the middle of the board; ten digits 1 through 0 in a single horizontal row across the bottom; the words "NO" and "YES" set apart near the top of the board; and a large "GOODBYE" located at the bottom edge of the board.

The planchette was a flat heart-shaped piece of plastic about the size of one's palm, with a round clear window located toward the pointed end. Three stubby feet with felt pads allowed it to slide easily across the lacquer surface game board.

"So, what do we do, now?" John asked.

"First, we have to set the right atmosphere," Becky replied. "Do you have any candles?"

Before John could answer, Becky spied three scented country candles in their holders resting on the fireplace mantle. They had never been lit.

"Do you think your mom would mind if we lit them?"

"No, I don't think so. As long as we don't burn the place down," John smirked.

John lit the two candles as Becky dimmed the lights. The flickering glow of candlelight transformed the room into a magical chamber of shadows, with sporadic flashes of lightning creating a strobe light effect, which only enhanced the mystical mood.

Becky found two card table chairs and unfolded them, arranging them face-to-face in the middle of the room.

"So, you sit there, and I sit here, facing each other," she explained. "First, our knees have to be touching. Then, we lay the board on our laps."

John did what he was told. "Which way should the board face?"

"It doesn't matter," Becky answered.

"Okay, now what?"

Becky looked puzzled. "You really never have done this before, have you? I thought you were just joking."

"Sorry, luv. I led a sheltered life."

"But not *too* sheltered," she rebutted, thinking back over events of the past few days.

"Okay," she continued, returning to the task at hand. "Now, we place this indicator on the center of the board, like so." She placed the planchette so that it was centered and pointing to the right. "Now, place both hands over the board and lightly touch the indicator with the tips of your fingers, like this."

Becky demonstrated, her hands suspended over the indicator like she was getting ready to type a letter. John imitated her action. The top edge of the plastic indicator tickled the tips of his fingers. As his knees met Becky's knees under the board, he felt a sudden, electrifying tingle up his spine, raising goose bumps on his bare arms and the back of his neck.

"Now, close your eyes," she ordered.

With his eyes closed, John focused his thoughts on the board. Slowly, the indicator began to move in a lazy circle.

"You're moving it, aren't you?" John said, without opening his eyes.

"No, not at all. I'm just following it with my fingers. I thought you were moving it," Becky insisted.

The planchette continued to circle in an ever-increasing spiral until suddenly…it slipped off the board and fell to the floor.

"Now what?" John wondered. "C'mon. You're the expert."

Becky thought. "Well, I think maybe we need to both focus on something," she groped. "And it's got to be the same thing. It's as if…we have it turned on, but we're just not tuned in."

"You mean, like we gotta find the right channel?" John suggested with a silly grin.

"Yeah, something like that."

Becky looked toward to the ceiling for inspiration. "The letter!" she replied at last.

"What?"

"The letter. The one you read at the dinner table. You know, the one signed 'Jay-Bird,'" Becky reminded him.

"Right! Good idea. Maybe we can find out who actually wrote the letter. Give me a minute. I'll go get it."

John left the room and returned quickly with the letter. He unfolded it and placed it on the coffee table next to them, and then resumed his Ouija board position.

"Okay, let's try it again," he said, closing his eyes.

Rebecca closed her eyes and began to speak…softly and deliberately.

"To whomever may be listening. We are trying to contact the writer of this letter. It is addressed to someone named 'Missy,' and is simply signed 'Jay-Bird.' Is there anybody out there?"

Nothing.

"Any-*body*?" John smirked.

"Shh! Quiet!" Becky snapped.

The planchette nudged forward, gradually picking up speed and circling counterclockwise once, twice, before coming to a complete stop. Waiting a few seconds, Becky spoke first.

"Okay. Let's see where it stopped."

They opened their eyes and look down. The planchette was resting with its window over the word "YES."

"Okay! Seems to be working!" John said expectantly, his pulse quickening a bit at the prospect of actually making contact. "Tell us please, are we speaking to the author of this letter?"

Again, with eyes closed, they followed the planchette with the light touch of their fingertips as it seemed to move on its own accord until finally stopping over the word "YES."

"Look," John whispered. "We've got to raise the bar and ask it something a bit more challenging."

"Why are you whispering?" Becky asked, whispering herself.

John shrugged his shoulders.

"I don't know. Don't want to offend it. Whatever it is."

They turned their attention back to the board.

"Can you tell us your name? What is your name?" Becky asked.

It only took a minute or so for the planchette to spell out the letters of a name: "J-O-H-N-J-A-Y."

John and Becky looked at each other suspiciously, then closed their eyes and continued.

"Okay, are you 'John Jay,' signer of the Declaration of Independence?" John asked.

"NO" came the quick reply.

"Well, I guess that eliminates one possibility," John said.

"Can you give us your full name, John?" Becky asked.

The board responded without hesitation: "J-O-H-N-J-A-Y-W-E- S-T-O-N."

"Okay! That's good" John said. "Looks like we're definitely tuned into the right channel, now."

Becky resumed the questioning. "John, are you related to anyone in this room?"

The board did not respond right away. The planchette just continued to circle without stopping.

"Maybe it…or he…is confused," John suggested.

Becky rephrased the question. "Do you know if you are related to either one of us? Please, say 'yes' if you think…"

Before she could finish, the planchette spelled out the words: "N-O-T S-U-R-E."

"Hmm, not a very all-knowing entity, is it?" John said.

"Well, why should it know?" Becky countered. "Would you know if someone suddenly came back from the future and asked you if he was related to you?"

John considered this. "You got a point there. If this really is a voice from the past, how would he know anything about the present?"

Before Becky could answer he added, "So, let's put ourselves in his time and start asking the questions he can answer."

"Sure," Becky said. "You go first."

John paused to formulate the next question. "John, can you tell us who your father was? Can you spell your father's name?"

The board was quick to respond: "S-A-M-U-E-L-W-E-S-T-O-N."

It paused briefly before finishing with the word: "J-U-N-I-O-R."

"Sam Weston Junior," Becky repeated. She looked across the board. "John, wasn't that the name of your great-great-grandfather, or something, from the eighteenth century? The one your Aunt Dee was talking about at dinner?"

"That's right!" John replied. "So maybe this John is the half brother Dee was referring to."

His hope was suddenly deflated as a new thought crossed his mind. "So big deal," he sighed. "Let's ask it something we couldn't possibly know the answer to beforehand. After all, we may just be moving this thing around ourselves, subconsciously supplying the answers. Let's start asking it some tough questions. Things we couldn't possibly know the answers to."

"Okay," Becky agreed. "Let me try."

Closing her eyes, she asked: "John, if you can hear me, please tell us your mother's name?"

The board took a little longer to respond this time.

"Maybe it doesn't know," Becky thought out loud.

"Aha! Maybe it's not moving because neither one of us knows the answer!" John challenged.

"Shh!" Becky barked.

Slowly, the planchette began to move, spelling out a full name: "A-M-A-N-D-A-J-A-Y."

"Amanda Jay?" John confirmed. "Was that your mother's maiden name? 'Jay'?"

"YES," came the board's immediate response.

"So, if Amanda Jay was your mother, and Sam Weston Jr your father, tell us, John, who was Bartholomew Weston?"

"B-R-O-T-H-E-R."

Before they could ask another question, the board added: "H-A-L-F."

"So, Bartholomew Weston was your *half* brother?" John concluded.

"YES," it replied.

Great! Even Aunt Dee didn't know this stuff! It suddenly made sense! The signatures on the letters, even the pen name, "Jay-Bird." He was using his mother's maiden name as his middle name, and "Jay-Bird" was just a derived code name, or nickname, John figured.

Becky chimed in to change the line of questioning. "John, can you tell us please, who is this *'Missy'* person you were writing to?"

The planchette moved quickly, but somewhat erratically, now. At last it spelled out the words: "R-E-B-E-C-C-A W-H-I-T-M-A-N."

"Rebecca Whitman," Becky repeated.

John asked the board whether Rebecca was any relation to Walt Whitman, the famous American poet. The board simply didn't know.

"So, who was Rebecca Whitman, then?" John asked.

The answer came quickly: "M-Y-T-R-U-E-L-O-V-E."

John and Becky looked at each other.

"Wow," Becky sighed. "So, they were his love letters!"

She looked across at John.

"So, that would make this John your great-great-half-uncle, or something, right?"

"Yeah, something like that."

The interrogations were going easier now, as though they had established a kind of rapport with this…whoever, or whatever, it was. They learned that Rebecca Whitman lived in a place called "Cohanzie." Neither John nor Becky had ever heard of it. They each accused the other of moving the planchette, of "pulling the strings," as it were. They also learned that the letter was written in 1774, which fit in with the time period John's dad had calculated, and that John Jay would later be a soldier for the patriot cause, achieving the rank of Colonel in the 8th Massachusetts Regiment. He would die of "the fever" in the year 1779.

"Where were you when you became ill, John?" Becky asked.

"V-A-L-L-E-Y F-O-R-G-E," came the reply.

"And who was your commanding officer at Valley Forge?"

The board began spelling "W-A-…"

To speed things up a bit, John jumped the gun and asked, "Was that Washington? George Washington?"

"NO," came the quick reply.

"No? Well, who then?" John asked impatiently. This time he let the board finish the word it had started: "W-A-Y-N-E."

"General Wayne?" Becky wondered. "Was there such a person?"

"Yes, I think he was one of Washington's generals," John said. "They called him *"Mad* Anthony Wayne."

John addressed the board. "Was that your commanding officer, John? Was it Mad Anthony Wayne?"

"YES," the board answered.

Becky looked suspiciously at John. "So, how did you know about Mad Anthony Wayne, John?" She suspected John of controlling the planchette this time.

"Hey! I thought it was going to spell *Washington*," John protested. "I'm telling you, I'm not moving that thing."

"At least...not *consciously*," she said.

"All right, so let's ask about his girlfriend, Rebecca."

John closed his eyes and wiggled in his seat to get more comfortable.

"John, can you tell us what happened to Rebecca, your...girlfriend?—the love of your life?"

The planchette began to move erratically, circling many times before finally coming to rest on the first letter: "F."

Speeding up, it quickly spelled out the remaining letters: "I-R-E."

John and Becky exchanged troubled looks.

"Fire!" they said in unison.

The candle flames began to flicker as a cool draft passed through the room. John and Becky took their hands away from the board momentarily and looked around. The candlelight was casting gigantic versions of themselves grotesquely silhouetted against the dark, knotty pine paneling, bouncing, quivering erratically with each flicker of the flames. A shiver ran up John's spine. He took a deep breath.

"So," he said exhaling slowly, "the spirits appear to be...restless tonight."

Becky hugged herself. "Don't you think it's getting cold in here?"

John squirmed in his seat.

"A little. Must be getting cold outside. Weather's really turning nasty," he said.

"Well, I think we should finish up with this session," Becky suggested. "But first, we should ask if it wants anything from us."

"Whadaya mean?"

Becky sighed. "Well, we've been asking all the questions. Maybe we should give it a chance to ask us something."

"Fair enough," John agreed.

John and Becky assumed their former positions over the Ouija board. John took his time with the next question.

"John, is there anything you'd like to tell us? Anything you want ask?"

The board remained still.

"Maybe we scared it off," Becky suggested.

"Shh!" John said. "Let's give it some time."

After about a minute, the planchette began to move again. The first letter it came to rest upon was "C," then "U-R-S," and finally "E."

Puzzled, Becky repeated the word: "Curse?"

Just as she spoke, the clock on the mantel piece struck midnight. John and Becky jumped in their seats, and then sat quietly as the clock counted down twelve chimes. On the last *bong*, like a strobe-lit disco bar, staccato flashes of lightning filled the room, followed by the low rolling sounds of thunder. John thought he felt the floor rumble just a bit. He spoke first.

"What about this *curse*?"

The planchette spelled out the words: "G-O B-A-C-K S-A-V-E H-E-R."

"'Go back save her.' What does that mean?" Becky asked.

John looked up and studied the puzzled look on Becky's face. "Now, you know I didn't do that."

"Well, somebody is moving that thing, and it isn't me," Becky insisted.

John was about to speak when the silence was suddenly shattered by the loud crash of something falling down the stairs. John and Becky jumped completely out of their chairs, which sent the Ouija board flying.

"Oh, my God, Matt! You scared the 'bie-jeebies out of me!" Becky exclaimed, holding a hand to her breast to catch her breath.

"Gee-whiz, Matt! Was that really necessary?" John scolded.

Matt was at the bottom of the stairs by now, basking in the joy of the moment for having taken his older brother so totally off guard.

"I just came down to get my sketch pad," he chuckled nonchalantly. "I left it...over there on the shelf, behind the bar."

Crossing the room, Matt took note of the burning candles and the game board lying on the floor. "Hey, what're you guys up to, anyway?" he asked.

"Just trying to contact the dead," John deadpanned as he leaned over to pick up the board and plastic planchette.

"Whoa! Awesome! Hey, don't let me stop you," Matt said as he continued across the room

"Too late. You already have," John mumbled.

Matt picked up his sketch pad, turned around, and suddenly took an interest in the Ouija board. "So, how does it work?" he asked.

Becky suddenly got an idea. "Hey! Why don't we let Matt test this thing for us?"

John gave her a puzzled look.

"I mean," she continued, "you keep insisting that I'm the one peeking and pushing this thing around. But I know it's been you all along! So, let's see who's right. Let's put on blindfolds and let Matt read the message while we keep our eyes closed. He can be the referee."

John liked that.

"Good idea! *And* Matt can *rotate* the board so we can't possibly know which way the letters are oriented."

John looked at Matt. "Okay, Matt, make yourself useful and go get two towels from the kitchen."

John and Becky took their seats and resumed their Ouija board positions, as Matt quickly retrieved two towels from the kitchen.

"Let me tie them," Matt said, "just to be sure they're tight, and no one is peeking."

Once the two were blindfolded and seated, Matt took the board and replaced it on their laps so they couldn't know how it was oriented.

"Okay. Ready, set, go!" Matt said at last.

John and Becky tried to get back into the spirit of evening, as it were.

"Okay, Becky. Go ahead and ask a question," John said. "I just hope Big Foot, here, hasn't scared away the spirits."

Becky smiled and thought for a moment. The planchette began to move in a lazy circle.

"Whoa! Totally awesome!" Matt exclaimed.

"We haven't asked it anything, yet," John smirked.

"Huh? Oh, yeah."

Matt became quiet now, focusing on the board and the moving pointer. "Hey, wait a minute!" he said. Matt then he took one of the candles from the mantel piece and held it closely over the board. "Need to put a little more light on the subject."

Illuminated from below, his face, masked by the soft eerie glow and long contrasting shadows of candlelight, was transformed for the moment into a gothic Picasso still life.

"Are you ready, now?" John asked impatiently.

"Shoot!" Matt fired back.

But it was Becky who asked the question.

"Please, tell us your name! Would you please spell your name for us."

The planchette circled, picked up speed, and suddenly changed direction before coming to an abrupt stop.

They waited.

"Okay," Becky said, "I think it has definitely stopped moving."

John agreed. "Okay, Matt. Tell us where the thing is pointing."

Matt studied the board. "I don't know," he said. "It's not really pointing to anything."

"Hmm. Just as I thought," Becky said. "See, it must've been you, John, just as I suspected."

"Wait," Matt interrupted. "Am I supposed to be looking at where it's pointing? Or what's showing through the little round window?"

"What's showing through the window," John answered impatiently.

"Oh, well, in that case it's the letter 'J.'"

"No way!" Becky exclaimed.

"Yeah! Directly over the letter 'J.' See for yourself."

With that Becky ripped off her blindfold and stared at the pointer. Sure enough, the letter "J."

John did the same. They both looked at each other, stunned.

Keer-rack!

A great bolt of lightning shook and lit up the room all at once, rattling the basement window panes. Matt jumped back, almost dropping his candle as the remaining candles flickered wildly on the mantelpiece, threatening to extinguish themselves.

"That's it!" Becky shouted.

She sprang up out of her seat and turned on the lights.

"I'm not doing this anymore," she said nervously. "It's just...*way* too spooky for me!"

John picked up the board and planchette and began putting it back in its box.

"Well, I *told* you it wasn't me," he said. "And besides, whose idea was this in the first place?"

*****

Back to the present. The large grandfather clock in the foyer of John's Haddonfield home ticked off the final seconds of Tuesday, 27 July, 1999 as John closed the cover of Walt Whitman's *Leaves of Grass* and took another sip of ginger brandy from his snifter. Settling back comfortably in his recliner, he studied the remnants of the summer storm through the foggy windowpanes. The rain had stopped falling, and the moon was slowly reclaiming its hold over a clearing night sky.

It had been quite a while since John thought about that night with the Ouija board. For several weeks afterwards he had tried to uncover more concrete evidence of his great-uncle John Jay's existence, checking the DAR records at Valley Forge, local church records, even the national archives. But getting caught up in the day-to-day business of living, he soon lost the scent of the trail. Not as tenacious as his Auntie Dee "Gumshoe." Anyway, he never made it to New England, where he always felt he could have hit real pay dirt. Never even found out where Cohanzie was! Why hadn't he pursued that line of questioning the night of the Ouija board? Oh, well. That was years ago, past history, and tomorrow's another day.

Just then the clock stuck twelve midnight. Startled, John nearly dropped his glass of brandy.

"Looks like tomorrow is today!"

He toasted the new day and emptied his glass, then headed slowly up to bed.

Chapter 12

1774
Greenwich, Cumberland County, NJ
Agatha Greene's Story

It was the summer of 1774, and Agatha Greene, the middle-aged wife of Albert T. Greene of Cumberland Country, was acting in strange and mysterious ways. Of that there was no doubt. "Shameful depravity!" some were heard to say. "Consorting with the devil!" others whispered behind closed doors.

Then there were the eyewitness accounts of her dancing naked in the fields under the light of the full moon. After all, did her family not hail from the Salem, Massachusetts area, a town made famous for its witch trials less than a century before? It was even rumored her grandmother was named as a defendant in the trials, but none could say for sure.

"Of course, none could say," others rebutted, "she put a spell of silence on those who would dare to speak!"

And so on it would go.

But none could refute the strangeness of her behavior. Even the local Indians avoided her. Was it out of fear? Or a form of respect for one so touched—or *empowered*—as to be capable of conversing with the trees and woodland spirits.

But Agatha had not always been this way. In her youth she was known to be bold and vivacious. "A woman of fine lineage with bountiful potential," her father would boast. Not beautiful in the classic sense, but attractive in other ways. A weak chin, protruding nose, and generally mousy features were readily compensated by Agatha's jubilant nature and lusty love of life. Besides, youth and vitality can often hide, even pardon, nature's flaws.

Descended from a prosperous nouveau riche family of new world merchants, Agatha traced her lineage straight to the Mayflower and Plymouth Rock. But even a well-dealt hand, a rich dowry, sound pedigree, and a pleasing nature can be trumped by unforeseen circumstances. Call it fate, or just a hidden fault line running deep that shakes your world as life takes sad and unexpected turns for the worse.

Agatha was the eldest of four daughters born to Solomon and Claudia Jay of Boston Massachusetts. Their union produced no sons that lived past the age of two. It was not surprising, then, that over time Agatha became the son Solomon never had. A tomboy one might say today. Not surprising either that as a young woman, Agatha accompanied her father on two trans-Atlantic voyages—business trips—to England and France. She quickly gained a hearty appetite for the sea and all things nautical. This appetite soon extended to the men who sailed those ships as well.

It was on her second voyage that Agatha met Leftenant Jacob Allen, a dashing young firebrand of an officer serving in the His Royal Majesty's Navy. She and the leftenant suffered a whirlwind romance that quickly ran its course—as far as the leftenant was concerned. For Agatha it was an affair of the heart. For the leftenant, other body parts better served to define their relationship.

At first, Agatha's father encouraged their relationship. After all, the young man appeared to live up to his royally commissioned status as "officer and a gentleman." But in time it became clear that he was more the royal scoundrel than gentleman. By then it was too late. Soon after reaching home port, Agatha was found to be with child. The leftenant's whereabouts became more and more difficult to trace and in time, he failed to respond at all to any letter of inquiry.

Agatha became despondent. It was a difficult pregnancy, but in the end she gave birth to a healthy baby girl. Destiny was her name.

That's when her problems really began.

Post-partum depression we call it today. On one occasion she tried to drown the baby in her own bath water. Only the quick action of her attending nurse managed to save the child. From that point on she and the baby were never left alone together.

In the months that followed, Agatha would be seen staring out her bedroom window for hours at a time. Just staring, and then rocking gently, to and fro.

"She just rocks all the time," the nurse reported to Mr. Jay one day. "Has no need for a *rocking* chair. Just rocks in place by herself, head bobbing like a mother hen. I thought I heard her mumbling to herself, like she was talking to someone else in the room. But there was no one there."

"Yes, I know," Mr. Jay replied despairingly. "I don't know what can be done for her."

But Mr. Jay didn't have to do anything. After several months, Agatha just seemed to snap out of it on her own. One afternoon he passed by the nursery and was surprised to see Agatha holding little Destiny, singing her to sleep:

"…Come little baby don't you cry,
Mamma gonna sing you a lullaby;
And if that lullaby don't make you sing,
Momma gonna buy you a golden ring…"

So, for all outward appearances, Agatha was well again, and began talking about the future. The future came knocking at the door one mid-summer day in 1744. Agatha answered.

"Good day, ma'am. I'm sorry, but my horse threw a shoe. I wonder if I could impose on your good favor for the use of your stable. I promise I shan't trouble you for long."

Three hours later Mr. Albert Greene was seated in the Jay's kitchen enjoying his third pint of freshly brewed hard cider, compliments of Agatha Jay.

It didn't stop there. Over the next several months, Albert came to call on Miss Jay on a regular basis. Mr. Jay took a genuine liking to the young man, as much for the positive effect his visits had on his daughter as anything his character or social status had to offer. Agatha recovered to the point where her bouts of melancholy came but infrequently now, and never while Albert was around.

Twelve months later to the day, Miss Agatha Jay became Mrs. Agatha Greene; and little Destiny, just shy of her second birthday, had a new father. Albert, though a farmer at heart, was persuaded to join her father's merchant business as a junior partner. Solomon Jay was delighted! He now had a "son" to whom he could pass the family business. But of course, being of sound mind and body, he wouldn't need to worry about that for quite a few years, yet. Or so he thought.

It was a cold midwinter afternoon in 1746. Agatha's father sat by the fireplace in his study, cradling a snifter of brandy in his lap with one hand and holding an iron poker with the other as, in the adjoining bedroom, little Destiny was taking her afternoon nap and sleeping soundly. Agatha had gone downtown to the market with all the women-folk, leaving the baby under Grandpa's care for the day.

Solomon Jay reached out with the poker to stoke the fire, spewing sparks from the crackling logs onto the stone hearth. Solomon's brow furrowed: there was something wrong with the draft. Kneeling by the hearth he reached up inside the flue with the poker, testing it for obstructions. Ah, yes, that was the problem: the flue was partly closed! Pushing it full open, the flames surged, singing the hairs on Solomon's arm before he was able to pull away. But the fire seemed to be burning okay, now; so, returning to the comfort of his chair, he wrapped himself in a wool blanket, took a sip of brandy, and allowed the warmth of the brandy and fire to permeate his body. In a matter of minutes he was dozing. The empty snifter slipped from his hands, disappearing softly between the folds of his blanket.

It was almost dark when Agatha and her mother and sisters returned from market. As they turned the last corner and came within view of her father's townhouse, they could see something was wrong. A crowd of local townsfolk were gathered in front of the smoldering brick façade, as a line of men, young and old, were desperately filling and transferring buckets of water, one after another, from neighboring side yard water pumps through the front door of the townhouse. It wasn't much of a fire, actually, mostly smoke from a fire generated from the build-up of creosote in a chimney long overdue for the services of a chimney sweep; no, not much of a fire, but more than enough smoke to smother a tired man and young child in their sleep.

Agatha leaped from her carriage and pushed her way through the crowd, screaming for her father and baby, "Destiny!" A young man stood at the door, barring her from entering the house.

"Ma'am, I don't think you want to go in there."

"Please! My father and baby are in there!" she hollered frantically. "I must go to them!"

The young man lowered his head and pointed to the side yard. "Ma'am," was all he said.

Agatha turned and looked.

There in the side garden were two wrapped bundles, one about five feet long, the other less than half that size. Agatha's heart sank. Wide-eyed and screaming she ran and flung herself over the two wrapped bodies of her father and baby girl.

That's where she was when Albert found her an hour later, the tragic news reaching him just as he was closing up shop down by the harbor. And that's where she remained, weeping and sobbing, inconsolable, all through that dreadful night, rocking to and fro over the lifeless remains of her father and daughter. Albert remained with her, holding her close, wrapped in blankets to keep warm.

Hindsight is twenty-twenty, they say, unless you're looking at the past through the prism of mental collapse and confusion. For Agatha, life soon became a fun house of mirrored distortions, with reality shifting in and out of focus. Like the phases of the moon, her state of mind waxed and waned through alternating periods of highs and lows, lucidity and fantasy, and some would say even lunacy.

One recurring fantasy was the reliving of her high seas romance with Leftenant Jacob Allen, her first love and the father of her ill-fated child. With every handsome seafarer that came into port, she was at risk of falling into a "reverie"—that's what Albert came to call them—lasting days at a time. During such times Albert became, in her eyes, her dear, departed father. Wrapping herself in a shawl, she would go to the widow's walk of their three-story townhome overlooking the harbor where she would spend hours peering out to sea.

"Father, I must keep a lookout for my dear Jacob. I think I see his ship on the horizon. Don't you see it, just there, coming into the harbor?"

Albert would respond with an affirming nod.

"Yes, my dear. Shall we go downstairs to meet him, now?"

That was often enough to coax her down from the balcony. Once inside and distracted, her thoughts would turn to other things.

Albert was at his wits end, trying to run the family business and deal with Agatha's depressed and delusional states of mind at the same time. When asked what to do, Agatha's tending physician said that a complete change of scenery might be the only thing that could bring her around.

"She needs to distance herself from any device or situation capable of rekindling the painful memories of this event," the good doctor advised.

"Are you suggesting that we move away from Boston, from family business?" Albert asked.

"It is only a suggestion," the doctor replied. "I'm afraid there is nothing in my leather bag of curatives that can remedy her condition."

For months Albert wrestled with his emotions before finally deciding what they must do—what *he* must do. After all, he was a farmer at heart, so perhaps a return to the land, to the open spaces, would provide her the remedy that trained physicians and modern science could not offer.

The decision made, Albert acted quickly. He arranged to sell his interest in the family business to Agatha's uncle, Stephen, her father's younger brother who, at the age of forty, had amassed a fair portion of wealth as a respected banker and landowner. "Unky Steve" was Agatha's favorite uncle, and his youngest daughter, Amanda, her favorite cousin, though several years younger than herself. As young ladies growing up in Boston's emerging nouveau riche society, Agatha and Amanda Jay became the closest of friends. Amanda was named maid of honor at Agatha's wedding, and now was hard pressed to accept the reality of her older cousin's deteriorating mental condition.

Then too, Amanda was busy with her own courtship and soon to be wedding plans. Her fiancé, a Mr. Samuel Weston Jr., was a successful and wealthy merchant in his own right. A widower of twenty years, Sam had relocated his family and business from Boston to the up and coming village of Haddonfield in the Province of West Jersey, soon after the loss of his first wife, Regina, who died giving birth to their third child and only son, Bartholomew. Maintaining strong, albeit distant, business and social ties with the powerful and wealthy of Boston, Sam Jr. was to eventually reconnect in a more close up and personal way. In the old world one may have called it a union of the aristocracy, to ensure continued peace, prosperity, and maintenance of the royal lineage. In the new world it was more a marriage of convenience, a consolidation of power and wealth between two strong family business lines. Romancing the throne was now romancing the stone.

Albert sought the assistance of Agatha's Uncle Stephen in his search for an affordable tract of land suitable for farming and establishing a new homestead. It needed to be far enough away to quell the bad memories, but not so remote as to be primitive or inaccessible. Working through the Presbyterian West Jersey Society and following the trail of recent New England migrations to the fertile farming regions of the West Province of New Jersey, Stephen was able to arrange for the purchase of 200 acres of prime farmland located in the newly formed Cumberland County of the colonial province of West New Jersey. The new county was parceled from its parent Salem County in the year 1748, and for a short while the county seat resided in Greenwich, the prosperous sea port community located on the Cohansey River.

Eight months later, in the spring of 1749, Albert and Agatha Greene packed up their possession and booked passage on a packet ship sailing out of Boston Harbor, bound for Greenwich of West New Jersey, some three hundred miles to the south. Steering a course around Cape Cod with a strong northeast wind at their backs, the ship made Narragansett Bay and the port of Newport, Rhode Island midday on day three. There they held up for two nights, replenishing provisions, and exchanging mail and passengers before disembarking on day five for the final leg of their southward journey. Sailing past the eastern tip of Long Island the ship's progress was slowed as the winds shifted, blowing steady and less favorably now from the west. Taking a starboard tack, the ship's crew tracked a course south by southwest along the coast of New Jersey toward the mouth of the Delaware Bay.

The fresh salt air and the freedom of the open sea had a great calming effect on Agatha. Albert could see the change in her almost immediately. Standing hours on end at the ship's rail she recounted in vivid detail the exploits of her own voyages with her father years before. These were real accounts, not at all counterfeit or fanciful. The rise and fall of the ship's wooden hull through the ocean swells, the creak of its timbers, the flap and snap of loose canvas taking a new, stiff hold of a changing wind, brought every memory back to her in soothing clarity. Albert had to wonder if perhaps they should simply remain at sea indefinitely, turn fisherman or explorer. Perhaps this was the remedy missing from the doctor's bag of potions. But of course, his own aversion to sea travel produced a ready response, as he too spent long hours by the ship's rail—retrieving the remnants of unsettled and partially digested meals, offering them up to the sea as fresh warm chum to the hungry fish below. A true farmer at heart, his temperament and constitution were much better suited to the firm, non-shifting platform of God's good earth.

It was late on day seven when they reached the mouth of the Delaware Bay. Rounding New Jersey's southernmost land protection, Cape May, the captain dropped anchor less than a quarter mile offshore and contacted the harbor master for the latest report of conditions in the bay. There they remained for the night, waiting for the morning's first light to proceed into the bay.

A wide, expansive body of water on the surface, the Delaware Bay was deceptively shallow in most places, limiting navigation by larger oceangoing vessels to a few well-charted channels. Between Cape May to the north and Cape Henlopen—or Cape James—to the south, the mouth of the bay spanned a distance of some fifteen miles. However, a collection of sandy shoals, called the Overfalls, occupied a major portion of the bay's entrance, restricting a ship's passage into the bay via one of two navigable shipping lanes: the New England, or Cape May, Channel, which passed through the narrows between the Overfalls and Cape May to the north, and the wider Main Channel between the Overfalls and Cape Henlopen to the south. The former was so named as it was the preferred route for ships sailing from New England and points north. Ships sailing from Europe and points south most often took the Main Channel, taking their bearings on Cape Henlopen. Once inside the bay, these channels diverged and converged into a series of parallel, charted shipping lanes for navigating the numerous shoals and shallows throughout the bay.

By the new light of day eight, the ship's crew pulled anchor, hoisted sail and set out into the bay through the Cape May channel. Once past the cape the land fell quickly away and out of sight as they entered the widening body of water. Before long, the channel split into two: the Cape May Channel continued straight into the open water of the bay while the New England Channel took a more northerly route, heading toward the distant Jersey shoreline. Taking this northern route, the ship didn't reach landfall again until the late morning, the salty air of the open sea gradually giving way to the brackish scent of the bay's lower tidewater as the Jersey shoreline gradually reappeared along their starboard side. They continued on through the afternoon, sailing close hauled against a prevailing westerly wind, while keeping a safe distance from the shoreline from which they took their bearings.

It was early evening when they reached the mouth of the Cohansey River. Not much to mark the place, just a wide, lazy cove where marshy shorelines give way, concealing the first of many bends in the river's slow, meandering inland course. A colorful assortment of egrets, blue herons, and other shore birds, wading through the shallows of saw grass and cattails, dotted the shorelines, while flocks of squawking seagulls hovered overhead in a seeming display of welcome. While not apparent at first, the left shoreline was actually broken up into a collection of small islands separated by a network of marshlands and tidal creeks emptying into the Cohansey. The largest of these had a name: Tindall Island. It was here the ship dropped anchor for the night to await the next morning's incoming tide that would assist them with the final leg of their journey: six miles up the winding Cohansey to the port of Greenwich.

This is where the piloting skills of the captain and crew were truly put to the test. Navigating the river's serpentine path against an apparent ever-changing wind and narrowing channel, required the skillful management of the sails and tiller. Sailing with the tide, the crew slowly tacked their way upriver, sails luffing into the wind with each major bend in the river. As the channel continued to narrow, the crew reefed the ship's mainsails and employed a back and fill technique to maintain the ship in mid-channel, allowing the incoming tide to carry it slowly, but safely to port. As a precaution, certain of the crew took to the oars to keep the ship on a steady course and to avoid running aground.

After about two hours' time, the church steeples and boatyard of Greenwich at last came into view, and just around the final bend—the Greenwich wharf! Albert breathed a sigh of relief as the ship tied up to the dock. "Ah! Sweet terra firma!" The color returned to his cheeks as he quickly made preparations to disembark.

Albert and Agatha Greene were well received in the new land which they now called home. The local Quaker and mixed denominational townsfolk provided an earnest Christian welcome with many lending hands. In no time at all, it seemed, a cabin of logs was constructed as their first home; the fields were cleared, tilled and planted; and they were rewarded with a first year's bountiful harvest.

Agatha did well that first year in Greenwich, so much so that she and Albert decided to start a new family. Little Samantha came along in the early summer of 1750. Three younger sisters followed in quick succession, spaced about eighteen months apart—just about as close as Mother Nature would allow.

But over time Agatha's personality began to change. Her mood swings deepened and she became increasingly irascible and despondent. It seemed that each new pregnancy left her more melancholy and detached than the one before. Turning into something of a recluse, she rarely ventured into town anymore. Even on Sundays, when Albert took the girls to church, Agatha would remain at home.

"I'm afraid Agatha's not feeling...herself, today. A touch of consumption," he would offer apologetically to those who were kind—or curious—enough to inquire.

On the occasion she did accompany Albert and the girls to the town market, she often remained in the wagon, avoiding direct eye contact and interaction with the other townsfolk, her private conversations with persons or things not of this world going largely unnoticed.

But young girls are quite good at picking up on such things, and little twelve-year-old Abigail Bowen—later to be Mrs. Abigail Stern of Shiloh—was particularly astute at sensing the subtleties of inappropriate social behavior in others. Popular with her friends, she was not above prodding them into playful pranks when the opportunity arose.

Such was the case in the autumn of 1756, on the occasion of Cumberland County's bi-annual Greenwich Fair. The day was sunny and inviting, with just a touch of autumn chill in the air as the sun sank low in the afternoon sky. Agatha Greene had been shopping among the fresh fruit and vegetable stalls and was now resting on a half-log bench in the shade of a large elm tree with little six-month-old Cynthia sleeping comfortably in her carriage by her side. Albert had taken Cynthia's three older sisters to see the animal-judging contest, on the far side of the green, so Agatha was alone now with the baby. A small basket of freshly harvested apples rested on the ground by her side.

Abigail was playing jump rope with two of her friends not far off when she first spied Mrs. Greene. Her eyes widened as she anxiously nudged her two friends.

"See that woman over there?" she said, pointing to Agatha.

"Uh-huh," her friends said in unison.

As they watched they could see Agatha rocking forward and backward, not a gentle motion, but exaggerated and tense. Her lips moved as she rocked.

"Who is she talking to?" one of the girls asked.

"Maybe she's talking to the baby," the second girl offered.

Abigail handed her the jump rope. "No, I don't think so," she said, then paused before adding, "I think she's talking to the *devil* himself!"

The other girls gasped.

"How do you know that?" the first girl asked.

Abigail thought for a moment. She was studying a bunch of bright red fruit hanging from a low-growing green vine nearby. She then looked back to Agatha.

"You see that basket of apples next to her?" she said finally.

The girls nodded.

"Well, I'll bet they aren't real apples. I'll bet you anything that they're wolf peaches. Like the ones growing over there." She pointed to the low-growing vine with its hanging red fruit. "And only the devil, or a witch, can take a bite of a wolf peach and survive!"

The word "witch" really got the other girls' attention.

"How do you know that?" the second girl asked.

"It's just common knowledge, is all!" Abigail replied peevishly.

The first girl was wasn't convinced. "Oh really? Well, prove it!" she challenged.

Abigail puffed up and rose straight to the occasion. That's just what she hoped her friend would say. Actually, she didn't believe the whole wolf peach and witch thing herself. She had once taken a bite of the fruit on a dare and suffered no ill effects. But her two younger friends didn't ever have to know that.

"Okay, but you've got to do what I say. I'll prove she's a witch. Agreed?"

Her friends hesitated. "Well...all right," the first girl said. "As long as Betsy goes along with me."

Betsy, the youngest of the three girls, nodded.

With that, Abigail got her friends to pick several of the largest, red wolf peaches they could find growing on the nearby vine and put them in a small fruit basket, like the one the apples were in. She then told them to go over to the lady on the bench—the one rocking to and fro—and ask to see her baby. With Agatha so preoccupied with the two girls making a fuss over little Cynthia, Abigail exchanged the basket of wolf peaches for the basket of apples. When she gave the signal, the other two girls abruptly thanked Agatha for letting them see the baby, and then said "good-bye."

What happened next, no one exactly knows for sure. Some people say they were sure they saw Agatha calmly taking a big bite from one of those juicy wolf peaches. They were sure it wasn't an apple, because the juice and seeds just exploded from the fruit as she chomped down, spilling down over her receding chin and dribbling down her neck. To their surprise, she went back for another bite, and still another. Before too long a small crowd of curious townsfolk had gathered around, watching as Agatha consumed not one, but all of the fruit contained in the basket. They knew the nature of the fruit, but apparently Agatha did not. Finally, someone was sent to find her husband. When Albert arrived he was petrified at what he saw.

"Why in God's name did not someone try to stop her!" he cried out, ripping the basket from her hands.

At this point Agatha seemed to come to her senses and realized something was amiss. Bewilderment turned to disbelief, and then back to bewilderment again as the voices in her head grew louder.

That's when the rage set in.

Was it the voices, or the sudden realization that she was the brunt of a childish prank? Whatever the spark, in an instant her countenance shifted from blank unawareness to fear and maniacal rage! With a wild shriek she set out after the girls, but by this time they were nowhere to be found. That didn't stop Agatha. She picked up a broom stick from a nearby vendor stall and began waving it in the air, chasing and striking anyone who came within easy reach. Albert had his hands full as the he tried wresting the broomstick from her, positioning himself between Agatha and the carriage to protect baby Cynthia, as Agatha continued ranting and raving. In due time, Albert was able to subdue and calm her, politely waving off offers of help as low murmurs of "should see a doctor" and "must be possessed" rippled through the crowd.

Off in the distance, three young girls peeked from behind a large sycamore tree. There they had taken refuge, watching in wide-eyed disbelief as Agatha Greene became a public spectacle right there in the middle of the Market Square on the occasion of the bi-annual Greenwich Fair of Cumberland County.

None would soon forget that day, the day Agatha Greene went mad from eating not one, but a whole basket of wolf peaches! And where she had gotten them, no one would ever know.

Ironic that the very fruit thought to be poisonous by American colonists would later take its place as a sterling icon of the "Garden State's" agricultural economy: the prized Jersey Tomato! It's close resemblance and biological similarity to other members of the nightshade family—including deadly nightshade and wolf bane—was its undoing.[6] The popular notion was that this acidulous fruit was not fit for human consumption, and if ingested in sufficient quantity, could cause death. A plethora of lesser symptoms ran the full range of extreme imaginings, from appendicitis and stomach cancer to hallucinations and mental fatigue—and yes, even madness! Stomach upsets are easy to fathom, given the acid nature of the fruit, but no one was daring enough to challenge the limits of popular belief.

Was the wolf peach, or Love Apple, the cause of Agatha's madness? While public opinion definitely leaned that way, Albert and Doc Woods both knew better.

"It appears to be no more than a mild stomach upset," the doctor said on examining her after the incident.

Like a bright comet in a clear night sky, alarming and portentous, the event sparked a sudden public awareness of Agatha's condition and offered a convenient explanation for her strange behavior, which most townsfolk were ready to accept without question. To paraphrase the Zen query: If a person talks to oneself and there is no one else around to hear, then is one really crazy? Maybe yes, maybe no, but all it takes is one public outburst to make it so.

So, when *did* Agatha start hearing her voices? No one can say for sure. Perhaps they accompanied her on those long seafaring voyages with her father. If that be so, then she certainly kept it well hidden, perhaps even from

---

[6] Even its scientific name, *Lycopersicon esculentum*, which translates to "wolf peach," reflected a common distrust held by laymen and physicians alike for the tomato. In Europe the fruit would later be touted as an aphrodisiac, and given the name *pomme d'amour* –"love apple"—by the French. But it would be almost fifty years (1820) before Colonel Robert Gibbon Johnson, the grandson of maritime magnate Nicholas Gibbon of Greenwich, would stand on the steps of the Salem Courthouse in 1820 and daringly defy death by eating not one, but a near bushel of Love Apples, attesting to the true innocuous and nourishing nature of this luscious fruit of the vine: the humble tomato.

Albert, until the tragic loss of her father and daughter triggered her first breakdown and threatened to consume their relationship. But Albert did manage to keep the lid on things, to keep her condition a "private matter," until the notorious wolf peach-eating affair made it forever public knowledge. Now, everything she was to do or say—or not say—would be measured against her "feeble condition." When found frolicking naked in the fields and talking to no one in particular, rumors spread she was "talking to the trees," or as the local Leni Lenape would put it, "conversing with the woodland spirits." When housebound and reclusive, as she often was when her depression was at its worse, it was a case of "the nerves," or worse yet, "plotting with the devil" and a real cause for concern. And those periods of violent outbursts when the voices simply got too much for her? Well, that was just the "devil himself" acting up.

"You mustn't make eye contact with her," someone said, "lest you be stricken in the same manner." And woe to the person who remains the focus of her smiling gaze, the sure sign of a witch's curse!

Eventually, the tumultuous wolf peach-eating affair faded into no more than a good story, to be retold whenever the need or occasion arose, to account for some mysterious happening or, more likely, to deflect public attention from the real cause of something. Albert summed it up for Doc Woods: "Doc, I think people just need something, or someone, to blame for their own failings."

But even Albert couldn't keep the lid on one of Agatha's more troubling obsessions which developed over the ensuing years: her increasingly morbid fascination with fire—*pyromania!* That's what the doctors called it. He wasn't sure when it all started, but suspected it went back to the traumatic events surrounding the death of her father and baby daughter. But not even Albert made the connection at first between her occasional disappearances and the rash of fires that broke out from time to time throughout the county. Brush fires, barn fires that no one could explain, until the night the Sterns' barn caught fire. When Agatha returned home that night, her clothes reeking with smoke, Albert was forced to confront the agonizing realization that she was likely to blame.

Chapter 13

1999
Wednesday, 28 July

Bob Fenwick never showed up for work the day following the ISPE conference. Katie finally phoned John later in the morning to say that Bob had checked himself into Cooper University Hospital's psychiatric ward for "treatment and some well needed rest." Cooper was a major teaching and treatment center located in the city of Camden, New Jersey.

When John hung up the phone, he realized he was going to have to make some adjustments, as it could be some time before Bob would be back on the job. Near term, that would mean finding someone else to replace Bob on the GenAvance conceptual study in time to join him for the kick-off meeting in Thousand Oaks next month on August 16. He made a mental list of potential candidates, going through them one by one until he finally settled on Jim Connelly, a very reliable process engineer who possessed many of Bob's finer qualities, and was probably even better suited for a front-end conceptual study of this kind. Of course, he would also have to bring in Jacob Carlson, process architect, for doing the facility layout studies. Jacob had his own architectural consulting business and was often contracted by Haddon Life-Tech for his specialized services and experience in designing pharmaceutical and biotech facilities and laboratories.

But for this first kick-off meeting, it would be just John and Jim making the trip. John contacted Jim Connelly and filled him in on all the particulars. He then went to see Mary and had her make all the necessary travel arrangements. He and Jim would fly to LAX airport in Los Angeles, pick up a car, and drive the sixty miles up the coast to Thousand Oaks off Ventura Highway. Mary booked them two rooms at the Siesta Courtyard, about four miles from the GenAvance site.

"And don't forget to give me a window seat. I like the view," John added.

"Got it!" Mary said. "It's in your travel profile."

John was about to turn away when he looked down at her Afghan. "Hey, that Afghan is really coming along! Looking good!"

"Gee, thanks. Yeah, I hope I get it finished in time. I'm experimenting with a new stitch and pattern that I've never tried before. Hope I haven't bitten off more than I can chew."

"I'm sure it'll turn out great!" John reassured her.

He was turning to go back to his office when Mary added, "Oh, by the way, John. Here's an ad I cut out of this morning's paper. Thought you might be interested."

She produced a small piece of newspaper clipped from the classified section. John took the clipping and read it aloud: "Volunteers wanted to be trained as docents for Indian King Tavern Museum. Volunteers needed, all ages, from various professional backgrounds: gardeners, teachers, librarians, and more."

John looked down at Mary.

"So, what's a *docent?*"

Mary laughed. "Yeah, I had to look it up myself." She looked down at her notepad. "Docent: a college or university lecturer, or a knowledgeable tour guide, especially for a museum."

"Well, there you go," John acknowledged. "So why didn't they just say 'tour guide'?"

" Fewer letters?" Mary offered.

"Wise guy!" John snapped in jest, grabbing the clipping from Mary's hand. "Thanks just the same. I just might take them up on it. Something else to do in my spare time!"

*****

Monday morning, August 16. The flight to LA was late taking off, but the pilot was able to make up most of the lost time in flight. After going over his notes for the meeting, John was able to relax and enjoy the in-flight movie: The Blair Witch Project. About twenty minutes into the movie, an elderly, silver haired woman seated in the center seat next to him turned and asked, "When is this documentary going to end and the movie begin?"

John just smiled, responding politely and quietly: "Ma'am, I think this *is* the movie."

"Ohhh," the woman replied slowly. "I don't know, they really don't make movies the way they used to," she lamented. "I can't make any sense of this."

Shaking her head she just removed her headphones, opened a magazine and began to read.

John motioned to the stewardess, who was coming up the aisle pushing a refreshments cart ahead of her.

"Yes, sir. What can I get you?" she asked with a paste-on smile.

"What I'd really like is a glass of V-8 juice, if you have any," John replied.

"Oh, I'm sorry, sir. All we have is tomato juice."

"Well, okay. That'll have to do, I suppose."

John took the glass of tomato juice and nodded. "Thank you, ma'am."

The movie was just ending as they crossed the Nevada-California border, approaching the southern edge of California's Sierra Nevada mountain range. Flying across country was as much a transcendental as it was a transcontinental experience for John. It didn't have to be; he could have contented himself with a good book, in-flight movie or idle chatter, but he found the view from thirty-five thousand feet a totally absorbing, majestic experience, which is why he always insisted on a window seat. Beyond the beautiful transient cloud formations, it was the kaleidoscopic-changing patterns in the earth's surface that fascinated him most. At this altitude, all familiar features and details become lost in a higher order of geologic landforms.

Starting out in the east, the lush green piedmont rose to meet the ancient Appalachian mountain range, a vast broccoli carpeted geo-landscape, overlaid with the brown and silver threads of merging river systems. Interspersed throughout were patches of blue in varying shades, shapes, and sizes: the lakes, bays, and waterways of the eastern watersheds. Paler shades of brown and turquoise colored the shallows, with rippled patterns in lighter grays marking the silt and sand deposits along the water's edge.

Continuing westward, the undulating green hills transitioned slowly into the regular patchwork quilt of checkerboard farms and fields of the great midwest and central plains, primordial prairie grasslands cultivated and converted over generations of hard work into the vast fields of corn and grain of today's modern mechanized farms, the breadbasket of the modern world. Cities and towns were fewer and farther between, now, with interconnecting roadways laid out in regular square-grid patterns, so regular that one could gauge the plane's speed by counting the seconds between the road grids, spaced exactly one mile apart.

Then suddenly, in the distance, like a great wall rising abruptly from the high central plains, the leeward side of the first Rocky mountain range came into view, partially veiled in cloud cover spilling over the mountain crest from its windward side. Within minutes they were passing over the mountains, and when viewed directly from above, the rough terrain brought to mind the torn, crumpled remnants of gift wrapping strewn across the living room floor in the aftermath of a child's Christmas morning: craggy ridge lines converging, diverging in fractal geometries of alternating peaks and shadowed ravines, reaching majestic heights of jagged, snow-capped peaks; mile after mile of virgin wilderness; pine-forested slopes; cavernous canyons; and raging rivers.

John marveled how our pioneer ancestors ever managed to traverse this formidable barrier with ox and horse-drawn wagon. John smiled. *But then again, I suppose they would be equally amazed to see us passing so effortlessly overhead, at such a speed.* John figured this was as close as we ever get to seeing things from God's perspective—in this lifetime anyway.

Continuing on, the mountains yielded reluctantly to the desert canyon lands of the great Southwest: Utah, Arizona, New Mexico; a broken, alien landscape extending as far as the eye could see in blended tones of browns, rusts, and ochres; great gorges slashing deep into the earth's crust of soft shale and still softer sandstone, revealing the secrets of the ages in neatly layered patterns of rock, the fossilized and petrified remains of ancient worlds and epochs, worn away over eons by the power of wind and water, presenting a geological storyboard of earth's past.

Now, crossing over the southern Sierra range into California's central valley, the rugged wilderness was replaced by the tamer landscape of California's "gold" interior, amber fields sparsely mottled with tufts of green, ribbons of wet and dry river beds snaking their way down from the mountains, man-made irrigation canals slicing through the valley floor like a knife. As the plane made its final descent across the San Bernardino valley, the terrain became increasingly dominated by twentieth-century man, now an almost unbroken array of concrete and glass city blocks, multilane highways, and broad, palm tree-lined boulevards. The plane was now in its final approach to Los Angeles' LAX airport, the groan of the deployed landing gear signaling an imminent touchdown; this was followed by the jolt and screech of tires against the runway, the roar of the engines' reverse thrusters, and finally the gentle, bounce of the large plane taxiing to the arrival gate. *Ah, sweet terra firma!* John uttered a silent prayer of thanks for a safe and sound arrival.

After picking up their bags, John and Jim loaded themselves onto the crowded shuttle bus heading for the rental car lot. The summer tourist season was in full swing.

"Looks like Disneyland is having a special," Jim remarked wryly.

John just took a deep breath and smiled. For the few years he spent living in California, he never found the time to visit America's great theme park. He had always preferred nature's attractions, and there were plenty of those to see in this part of the country.

"So, you've got directions to the site?" Jim asked.

John poked the side of his head with his index finger. "Got it all up here." Reaching into the side pocket of his briefcase, he produced a folded road map of California. "But, just in case. I brought along Mr. Rand McNally to help us out." He handed the map to Jim. "Here you go, buddy. How 'bout I drive, you navigate."

John took his Nokia 8110 cell phone from his pants pocket to check his messages.

"Whoa! The *Matrix* phone. Nice!" Jim exclaimed.

"Huh? What's that?"

"The Nokia 8110! The cell phone featured in the movie, *The Matrix*. You didn't know that?" Jim snickered.

"My, you're just loaded with trivia information, aren't you."

"C'mon, John. Gotta keep up with the times. New technology and all."

John just groaned and continued working with the cell phone. After checking his messages, he programmed Bob Fenwick's cell phone number with a quick dial * 9 code. He did the same for Katie's number, with a * 8. He wanted to stay in touch in a moment's notice to check on Bob's condition.

The sixty mile trip via the "fast lane" up Interstate 405 took a lot longer than planned. Even though it was close to noon and long past rush hour when they hit the road, the interstate was still jammed with traffic, due mainly to some major ongoing road construction. As they approached the exit to Ventura Freeway north (US-101), the traffic finally began to thin out and move faster. Meanwhile, Jim wrestled with the large map as he tried to pinpoint their location and get a feel for the area.

"So, isn't your wife's family from California?" John asked.

"Right. But she's from up north. Sacramento area. It's really like another state up there."

Jim continued to struggle with the map. "Just like this blasted map," he said. "The north half of the state is on one side, and the south half on the other." He turned to John. "So, just like Jersey, California has this north-south thing going on," he joked.

John smiled. "Yeah, guess you just can't get away from it."

GenAvance's Thousand Oaks site resembled a large, sprawling university campus, the buildings and manicured landscaping, interconnecting brick paths, fountains and man-made waterfalls blending unobtrusively with the nearby foothills and local Spanish architecture, with its characteristic orange, clay tile roofs. There were no visible fences or gates to keep people out, but a sophisticated card reader security system provided controlled access to the more sensitive areas and building complexes. As the corporate headquarters for both GenAvance and its parent organization, Aqua-Lyne Pharmaceuticals, the site employed over 5,000 individuals. It was also the company's center for research and product development.

John Weston and Jim Connelly sat in the visitors' lobby of the main headquarters building waiting for their host escort. Jim was leafing through the latest issue of *BioProcessing International* magazine when the door opened and a young, attractive woman in a long, white lab coat appeared.

"Mr. Weston?" she asked expectantly.

John turned and stood up. "Yes, ma'am. That would be me...or us, actually. We're both here to see Dr. Sam Li."

"Yes, of course. I work for Dr. Li." She held out her hand and smiled from ear to ear. "Samantha Joyce," she said. Her manner was sweet and bubbly.

John reached out and shook her hand, then turned to introduce Jim.

"This is Jim Connelly. I think I mentioned in my e-mail that Bob Fenwick would not be joining us this trip. Jim will be working with me on the conceptual study."

"Yes, we were aware of that." Samantha took Jim's hand and shook it vigorously. "*So* happy to meet you, Jim."

Jim smiled and nodded politely.

"Well, if you're all signed in," she continued, "I can take you back to the conference room."

Samantha turned toward the receptionist. "Doris?"

Doris looked up and gave a perfunctory smile. "They're good to go, Sam. Visitor badge and all."

"Great! Okay, gentlemen, if you would please follow me."

Samantha briskly led the way, escorting them through the door and down a long, wide, marble hallway. The hallway ended in another lobby area, a large open sky-lit atrium with a fountain waterfall and island garden at its center. An assortment of lounge chairs and sofas filled out the remaining space. A wall placard read: "Conference Pod-A." Samantha directed them through a door into one of the larger conference rooms adjoining the pod.

In the room, they were greeted with the smiling faces of twenty or so GenAvance employees seated around a long, oval, mahogany conference table, some in white lab coats, but most were in casual business attire, polo shirts, and jerseys. Another ten or so individuals occupied seats around the room's perimeter. Samantha directed her guests to two empty chairs near the head of the table. Dressed in jackets and ties, John and Jim were the obvious out-of-town guests.

Dr. Li had not yet arrived. John noticed the large wall clock: 1:50 p.m. That's good; they were early for the scheduled two o'clock meeting.

John turned to Samantha, seated to his left. "So, Samantha, do you work directly for Dr. Li?"

"Yes! Sam's my boss! Actually, I think he only hired me for my name. Easy to remember." She laughed. "Sorry, just kidding. Anyway, you can call me 'Sam,' or 'Sammy.' I'm only called 'Samantha' by the IRS, or my parents...when I've done something wrong. No, just kidding again. Around here I usually get 'Sammy,' to tell me apart from the boss."

Without pausing she turned to face John, tucking both legs up under her on the chair. "I'm in charge of all downstream protein purification operations in the pilot plant. Whatever the cell culture or fermentation guys send me, I handle it."

"So, you do all the liquid chromatography and membrane separation steps?" John asked.

"That's right, except for the initial clarification and *Protein-A* capture chromatography steps. Those are special front-end recovery operations performed by the Cell Culture and Fermentation group, headed up by my good buddy, Ted Salmonson, right over there."

A young man in his late twenties, seated directly across from John, acknowledged his name's mention with a nod and half-hearted salute.

It was a few minutes past two o'clock when John heard the familiar sound of Sam Li's voice just outside the room in the atrium.

"Yes, so, can you please make twenty copies…no, make that thirty. Thank you, Nancy. You can bring them to me in the conference room."

Dr. Li walked into the conference room and went straight to the head of the table. He didn't seem to notice his guests at first. Sitting down at the table, he finally got the meeting underway.

"So, I do apologize for running late," he said hurriedly. Quickly regaining his composure he looked up and smiled. "First," he said, "let me welcome our esteemed guests, Mr. John Weston and his colleague, Jim Connelly, of Haddon Life-Tech, Haddonfield, New Jersey. I've asked them to join our project design team for the conceptual design portion of our new pilot plant project."

John smiled and slowly scanned the room, making direct eye contact with everyone seated at the table. He was also looking for another familiar face, someone he may have worked with fifteen years earlier. Most were just young kids in their twenties, maybe thirty, tops. But there was someone he thought he recognized, seated at the far end of the table. A woman, late thirties, maybe forty years old, small frame, petite, with a blonde pixie haircut.

"As some of you may or may not know," Dr. Li continued, "John used to work here at GenAvance. About fifteen years ago, wasn't it, John?" John smiled with an affirming nod. "At that time when many of you were still in high school, I might add."

Dr. Li's last comment was met with a mixture of grimaces and groans.

"But, I know there is at least one person at this table who knows John from a previous life." Sam directed his next remark at the pixie blonde haired woman seated at the far end of the table. "Does 'Sweetheart of Sigma Phi Delta, Rutgers University '78,' ring a bell with anyone at the table?"

The woman appeared to be expecting this. She smiled and leaned forward. "Well, hello, John. It's so nice to see you again. Julie Evert, Rutgers Class of '81."

John returned the smile. "Dr. Evert, the pleasure is all mine. I thought I recognized you, but didn't want to speak out of turn. I've been reading up on the work your research group is doing at Cook College. Very impressive. I'd like to learn more."

"Thank you, John. And I certainly think that opportunity will present itself. That is, once the project"—glancing at Sam—"is *officially* kicked off."

Sam was slow to react.

"Ahem. Yes, of course. There is the question of confidentiality."

He turned to John. "I trust you and Jim brought signed copies of our confidentiality agreement?"

John reached into his briefcase and pulled out a folder marked: CONFIDENTIAL. Opening the folder, he removed some official looking papers and passed them on to Sam.

"I think you'll find what you need here, Sam. All signed and notarized."

"Excellent!"

Sam took the papers and studied them briefly before setting them aside. Leaning forward and folding his hands, he took a more serious tone.

"Well, then, I think we can now get to down to the business at hand, the reason we are all here." Pausing for a moment, he smiled and added, "And let's hope it turns into a real…sweetheart of a project for everyone concerned."

More sour groans from around the table. John just had to chuckle. *Boy, he just won't leave that one alone, will he?*

At that moment Dr. Li's administrative assistant, Nancy, entered the room and handed him a pile of papers, all neatly collated and stapled.

"Ah, thank you, Nancy. Just in time! Please see that everyone gets a copy. That would be great!"

Once everyone was settled again, Dr. Li proceeded with the meeting. First, there were the introductions. Going around the table, it appeared that all invitees were present, except for one.

"Nancy, would you please try to contact Jennifer. I'm afraid we may have to start without her," Dr. Li said softly.

Nancy was about to leave when a strikingly attractive woman entered the room. Tall and slender with dark hair and a soft, flawless olive complexion, she moved gracefully to the only remaining empty seat on the far side of the table, almost directly opposite John and Jim.

"I apologize for being late, Dr. Li. I'm afraid my one o'clock meeting ran a little bit over."

She spoke softly, in pleasing, mellifluous tones. There was a hint of an accent to her voice, French perhaps, but her features suggested a mixed European-Asian descent.

"That's quite all right," Sam assured her, "we were just getting started."

Dr. Li completed the introductions. "Jennifer, this is John Weston and Jim Connelly of Haddon Life-Tech. Gentlemen, may I introduce Jennifer

Brady, Manager of Quality Assurance. Jennifer oversees all new products and processes, and will be working with the design team for the life of the project.

Brady? Must be her married name, John thought. He knew her as Jennifer Dupree. John repeated the name to himself as he stared into her gorgeous, cinnamon-brown eyes. Jenny, as he knew her, was just as beautiful as the last time he'd seen her, fourteen years ago. Her presence released a flood of memories from a tumultuous period in John's past. When he met her fourteen years ago, she was a new hire in the microbiology lab, fresh out of school with a biology degree from U of C San Diego. John had recently relocated from Princeton to Thousand Oaks, working as a process engineer and team leader in Dr. Li's Process Development Group. They were both dealing with recent losses in their personal lives, and each found in the other the strength that seemed lacking in themselves. Now, he wondered whether she remembered him at all, or was she deliberately avoiding making eye contact. Perhaps—

"...isn't that right, Mr. Weston?" Dr. Li asked.

Everyone's eyes were on John. He had missed the question.

"Yes, that is correct," Jim jumped in, breaking the awkward silence. "The conceptual study should fully define the scope of work for the design phase. At that point, we would propose taking a design-build approach to the subsequent engineering and construction phases."

John's mind was clear and back on track now. "Yes, and if agreeable to GenAvance," he interjected, "Haddon Life-Tech could be a single-source provider, picking up the contract for the new pilot plant."

Dr. Li smiled as a tall, slightly gray haired gentleman at the other end of the table spoke up. "Yes, I understand the benefits of design build," he said. "But, there are risks as well. Before a design scope can be defined for the engineering firm, we—and I mean GenAvance—must establish the User Requirements Specification for the new facility. I don't believe I've seen anything issued on this, Sam?"

Bruce Hanson, VP of Global Engineering for Aqua-Lyne Pharmaceuticals, GenAvance's parent company, spoke with confidence from years of experience on similar projects. He knew how difficult it often was for a company the size of GenAvance to nail down a design objective of this magnitude, especially when dealing with the moving targets of research and product development.

Dr. Li leaned forward and folded his hands. "Samantha and Ted are responsible for developing the User Requirement Specifications for the new facility. They plan to have a draft document finalized this week, ready to issue early next week for review and comment."

Dr. Li glanced at Sam and Ted for confirmation.

"That's correct, Dr. Li," Samantha responded on cue. "We were planning to meet with Mr. Weston"—glancing down at her day planner—

"tomorrow afternoon to discuss certain topics and ideas Mr. Weston had forwarded to us for consideration, for possible inclusion in the URS."

"Very good." Dr. Li seemed satisfied.

Judging from his expression, Bruce remained skeptical.

"I would recommend that AL Global Engineering be included in these discussions, so that certain aspects of facility design and infrastructure can be captured in the finished document."

"Yes, of course." Dr. Li responded, finding it difficult to conceal his annoyance. "Perhaps this can be handled as part of the review and comment process."

Bruce nodded. "As you wish. So long as it receives the proper attention," he concluded.

"Yes. Well, if we can return to the agenda for this week," Dr. Li continued. "You should find it in your handouts."

The meeting continued for the remainder of the afternoon, as they made final last-minute adjustments to the week's agenda. Jennifer had to excuse herself early to attend another scheduled meeting. On the way out she brushed against John's chair, touching his left shoulder ever so slightly with the palm of her hand. John felt a tingle. He turned his head and looked up, but she was already out the door.

Tuesday morning's meeting began with a discussion of the BEV cell culture process, expanding on the points made by Dr. Li in his ISPE slide show presentation. Next, Dr. Evert presented the most recent findings of her Rutgers research team, providing specific details on how new insect cell lines are developed in the laboratory.

The morning session was followed by a tour of the laboratory, a one-hour break for lunch, and a second tour of the existing cell culture and fermentation pilot plant. That's when John took the opportunity to bring up the ideas for continuous cell harvesting that he and Bob had been developing at Haddon Life-Tech. He produced some sketches to illustrate the process. There was general interest all around, especially after John offered to share the IP, or intellectual property, rights with GenAvance should the process pan out.

It was almost three in the afternoon when the tour wrapped up. At that point, John and Jim split up, with Jim heading off to meet with one of Bruce Hanson's people in Global Engineering to familiarize himself with GenAvance's engineering specifications. John, meanwhile, was scheduled to meet with Teddy Salmonson and Samantha Joyce to better understand the process and special needs for the new pilot plant. But that meeting wasn't scheduled until 3:30.

Since he had a half hour to kill, he found a quiet corner of the now nearly empty cafeteria, picked a clean table by the vending machines, and sat down to enjoy a hot cup of coffee. He began reviewing his notes of the past two days.

"Mind if an old friend joins you for a cup of joe?" came a familiar, soothing voice from behind.

He turned and looked up. There was Jennifer Dupree Brady, wearing a short white lab coat, hair tied up, just as tall, sylphlike and beautiful as ever.

"Jenny! You startled me!"

"Sorry," she said.

"Actually," John continued, "I wasn't quite sure you remembered me. You didn't have much to say at the kick-off meeting yesterday."

"Well, that wasn't quite the place to renew old acquaintances, now, was it?"

"I suppose not," he said with a smile.

Jennifer took a seat next to John and crossed her legs.

The legs of a model, John thought. He noticed she wasn't wearing a wedding ring.

"So, what'll it be. Regular or decaf? I'm buying," John offered.

"Decaf. Too late in the day for caffeine. I'd be up all night."

Well, that might not be such a bad thing, John thought as he took a Styrofoam cup from its stack and placed it in the automatic coffee maker.

"So, do you still take one sugar and two creams?" he asked.

Jennifer acted surprised. "Why, yes. You remembered. I'm impressed."

John took the freshly brewed cup and handed it to Jennifer. Sitting down, he took his cup and offered a toast. "To old friends?" he said.

"To old friends," she reciprocated.

She took a sip. Then, holding the cup close to her lips with both hands, she asked hesitantly, "So, John. It's been a long time. Tell me." She tilted her head to one side. "How have you managed the ghosts in your life?"

John would have been taken aback had he not been entertaining the same question.

"I was about to ask you the same thing," he said. He glanced at her name tag. "I take it you are…married, then?"

Jennifer held out her left hand, fanning her fingers. "Was married," she said. "You see. The gold band is gone." She set the cup down and smiled. "But, I do have a wonderful and beautiful daughter. So, I consider it all worthwhile." She reached into her pocket purse and produced a small picture album. "See, here's her latest picture. Her name is Renee."

John studied the picture. "She's a very pretty girl. Gets that from her momma."

Jenny smiled and returned the pictures to her purse. "She starts the third grade next month. Loves horses, and Nancy Drew stories."

"Then, I'd say she's a pretty well-rounded and well-adjusted young lady," John said softly.

Jennifer made a face. "You mean, unlike her mom, huh?"

"Now, I didn't say that," John protested.

"Well, we *both* have had to make adjustments in our lives," Jennifer conceded. "Following the loss of my parents, and"—she hesitated— "the loss of your fiancée."

Jennifer was the youngest of four children born to Jacques and Kim Dupree. Jacques Dupree was a young member of the French diplomatic corps stationed in Hanoi, French Indo-China, in the early fifties when he and Kim first met and fell in love. She was a local national, of Chinese descent, working as a clerk in the French embassy at the time. Looking at the two of them you wouldn't think them a match: Jacques, tall and imposing; and little Kim-Lan, not much more than half his size. Her name meant "golden orchid" in Vietnamese. He would affectionately refer to her as *ma petite fleur d'or*—"my little golden flower."

Sensing the threat of the rising nationalistic sentiment and the imminent fall of colonial rule in southeast Asia, Jacques and Kim were married in a hurried ceremony in February of 1954. In May of that same year, less than three months later, the final curtain came down on French colonial rule with the fall of the besieged city of Dien Bien Phu. Jacques Dupree was recalled to Paris and reassigned. Kim, his new bride, was permitted to accompany him. For the next ten years they lived in on the outskirts of Paris, where they started a family. Jennifer was born in September, 1961.

In the years that followed, Jacques was assigned to various posts taking him and his family to the Middle East, Canada, and finally, to the United States. Now in her late teens, Jennifer was preparing for college. She wanted to stay in the US and felt especially drawn to the west coast. Maybe because of its proximity to the Far East and her mother's side of the family, she entered the University of California, San Diego campus, in the fall of '79. After spending the summer of her third year interning at Aqua-Lyne Pharmaceutical, she was offered a job in the microbiology lab of the newly acquired GenAvance Therapeutics upon graduation in June of '83. Her parents flew in for the ceremonies, using the trip as a jumping off point for a flight to southeast Asia, where they planned to spend the summer vacationing and visiting Kim's relatives, whom she hadn't seen in almost thirty years. Jennifer was able to delay the start of her new job to join her parents on the first leg of their journey. Four weeks later she flew back alone to start work at Aqua-Lyne, but she kept her parents' itinerary in her desk drawer so she could follow their progress.

It was late August. Jennifer was watching a *Dallas* rerun on TV when the show was interrupted with a News Bulletin.

"This news just in." The voice on the TV announced stoically. "An Air France airliner, flight 783, has crashed over the Indian Ocean. The flight originated in Bangkok, Thailand, and was traveling nonstop to Paris, France.

No word yet on survivors. We will notify you of further developments as they become available."

The news didn't register at first with Jennifer, just another unfortunate turn of events for some nameless persons in a faraway place. Then suddenly, a cold chill ran through her body. Her parents! What day was this? She grabbed their itinerary from her desk drawer. Why, that's today, she said to herself. Then she confirmed the flight number. Oh my God! 783!

Things were very quiet at work the next day, as she and her new coworkers awaited some hopeful news on survivors. Finally, there came the news she was dreading: "No survivors. All lost!" the headlines read.

It was 3:15 p.m. John and Jennifer now had the cafeteria completely to themselves. Jennifer held her cup of coffee, sat back, and looked at John, staring right through him, as if in a trance.

"My solution was to run away to the mountains," she said. "If you recall, John, I accepted a transfer to Boulder, Colorado, about ten months after you were transferred to Thousand Oaks from the east coast."

John nodded. "Right, and I believe the day I started at Thousand Oaks was the day you received news of your parents."

Jennifer continued her blank stare. "Yes. Well, soon after arriving in Boulder I met and fell in love with…"Mr. Right." Only, once I finally got things sorted out over my parents, I realized that Mr. Right wasn't who he pretended to be. Or at least, not who I thought he was. He was in pharmaceutical sales, and unfortunately, he fit the typical traveling salesman stereotype: a girl in every port. I just turned out to be his convenient 'home port mama.' One day he left on a sales trip"—blinking her eyes to snap out of her trance—"and never came back home."

Jennifer took a sip of coffee. Moving closer to the table she assumed a more inquisitive pose, her chin resting atop her folded hands, elbows firmly planted on the table.

"So, John. I don't see any wedding band on your finger. Tell me, then, what was *your* solution?" she asked poignantly.

John closed his eyes, deep in thought, considering his response. Finally, opening his eyes, he asked, "You know the definition of a bachelor?"

She shook her head and replied in French, "*J'sais pas.*

"It's a guy who never makes the same mistake *once*," he said.

Jennifer backed off and smiled. "Cute, John. But that doesn't answer my question."

John was forced to turn serious. "Well, the truth is, Jen. The pain…well, it may have gone away, but the scars still remain. And…sometimes, you know, scars are what keep a person from doing certain things. Can affect one's flexibility—and performance."

Jennifer took a deep breath and leaned forward, taking hold of John's finger tips with both hands. "Well, John. Maybe I can help you with your...performance issues."

The gentle touch of Jennifer's hands and her soft words sent a surge of relief through John's body. Something he hadn't felt in a long time. He looked into her eyes. Why hadn't he seen it before?

Some commotion at the door to the cafeteria interrupted his concentration. He looked over to see Nancy, Dr. Li's assistant, motioning to him.

"Yes, Nancy. What is it?" he asked.

Jennifer released her hold as he stood up.

"Mr. Weston, I've been looking for you. Mary, from your office, has been trying to get in touch with you since noon. She said she tried your cell phone."

John pulled out his cell phone. It was turned off.

"Dammit!" he exclaimed. "No wonder she couldn't reach me. Thank you, Nancy. I'll phone the office right away," he said, turning on his phone.

He checked the time: 3:25 p.m. Only five more minutes until his scheduled meeting with Ted and Samantha. He turned to Jennifer. "Jen, why don't you join us for the three-thirty meeting. Might be beneficial to have someone from Quality Assurance present."

"Okay. Not a bad idea. Gotta keep tabs on what these young folk are up to," she joked.

"Great! Why don't you go on ahead and I'll meet you there, after I return this call. Can we continue our little meeting at a later time? Say, dinner tomorrow night? Or Thursday?"

Jennifer considered the options. "Tomorrow night isn't good. Renee's Brownie Scouts meeting, and I'm the Den Mother. Thursday night could work, though. But, I'll have to get a babysitter."

"Babysitter? Why? Renee can join us for dinner. I'd very much like to meet her."

Jennifer smiled. "Okay. Thursday evening it is, then. How about seven o'clock. Don't want to keep Renee up past her bedtime. Even though it is summer, I don't like her getting into bad habits."

"Sounds good. Be sure to give me directions to your place."

After Jennifer left the cafeteria, John pulled out his Nokia and dialed his home office number. His call was directed to Mary's voice mail.

"Dammit!"

Of course! It was already 6:30 at home, three hours and time zones ahead. He suspected the call was about his partner, Bob, so he decided to check the missed calls on his cell phone. Sure enough, there were two missed calls from Katie, but no voice mail messages. He punched * 8 for Katie's number. It rang once, twice...six times, before going to Katie's voice mail.

John left a quick message, asking how Bob was doing and to return his call, then returned the phone to his pocket.

*****

6:00 a.m., Friday, the twentieth. The coastal mountain range to the southwest remained shrouded in a low-hanging mist as daylight was breaking. John and Jim checked out of the motel, grabbed a cup of coffee for the road, and headed out toward LAX for their mid-morning return flight home.

"Okay, you drive and I'll navigate," John said as he jumped into the front passenger seat. "You're gonna need a stellar navigator to get over this coastal mountain range to the ocean."

"My, you're bright and chipper this morning," Jim said. "Judging by that shit-eatin' grin you must've had a pretty good time last night. So tell me, how was your rendezvous with the pretty Ms. Jenny?"

"We had a very pleasant evening, thank you very much. Just catching up on— some good old times."

"And making some good *new* times, too, I would imagine," Jim pressed.

"Well, you'll just have to read about it in my trip report," John quipped.

They decided to take the scenic route on their return to LAX, which would take them over the coastal Santa Monica mountain range to Malibu, and then up the coast toward the cities of Santa Monica and Los Angeles. Hopefully, the morning sun would burn off enough of the mountain mist for them to enjoy the scenery. John checked the map.

"Okay," John said. "Here's what you do. Take the N9 exit off the Ventura Freeway, US-101, and head south on Kanan Road. Cross Mulholland Highway and then just continue and follow the road over the mountains toward the ocean. Can't miss it. It's a large body of water with lots of fish. Okay, my job's done."

John reclined his seat and leaned back, laying the map over his closed eyes.

"Great!" Jim retorted. "Now all I gotta do is put this thing on auto-cruise-pilot control and I can take a nap, too."

"I wouldn't count on it. These mountain roads are really tricky. But Kanan Road is nowhere near as bad as Westlake, with its treacherous switchbacks. Lucky for you I'm not taking you that way."

As they climbed into the Santa Monica Mountains, the clouds began to lose their hold over the terrain. John had always been impressed by these mountains, how they concaved upward, like giant inverted teacups, very different from the hills back east. The homes and ranches scattered across the terrain, perched precariously on mountain tops, slopes, or cliffs, enjoyed splendid views, but suffered from a remoteness and inaccessibility that bothered John. There was simply no running off to a nearby corner store for a bottle of milk or forgotten newspaper.

"Well, I thought the week went rather well," Jim commented. "What do you think?"

John looked up from his day planner. "What's that? Oh, yeah. I thought the meetings went very well. I never expected them to commit to a design-build approach at this point in the project, but at least we got them thinking about it. So, according to the schedule"—consulting his day planner—"we need to be back out here the week of September twentieth to review the progress of the study. We should have the process flow diagrams completed by then, and, assuming they've nailed down their User Requirements Specification, we can get Jake Carlson to start the architectural programming of spaces."

"Sounds good," Jim agreed.

Jim swerved to avoid hitting a jack rabbit crossing the road.

"So, John. Did you ever get back to Katie?" Jim asked.

"Sort of. We played phone tag and exchanged voice mail messages. Cell phone reception in these parts isn't the greatest. The best I can make out, Bob seems to be doing better and says he wants to come back to the office to work. But I sensed a nervousness in Katie's voice, like she wasn't telling me everything."

John looked out the window and noticed a dark haze rising from the distant hills to the north.

"Hmm. Looks like a brush fire way off in the distance. See that smoke?"

"Are you sure it's smoke? May just be the morning haze," Jim suggested.

"*Shay pah*," John said reflexively.

"What was that?" Jim smirked.

"I'm sorry. Pardon my colloquial French. I mean '*Je ne sais pas.*'" John articulated each syllable this time.

Jim still looked puzzled. So, John kicked it up a notch. "That's French for 'I don't know,'" John explained. "When you say it fast it just comes out *Shay pah*, a contracted form of the expression. It's like saying" – John shrugged his shoulders to give it some body English – "'dunno' in English. Get it?"

"Gotcha! So why are we speaking French in the heart of a former Spanish colony?" Jim countered.

"Well…just preoccupied, I guess," John replied.

Jim smiled. "Jennifer?"

John just nodded.

"Hey! No need to apologize," Jim said.

The Pacific Ocean came into view just as they began their descent from the Santa Monica Mountains toward Malibu.

"See! What did I tell you?" John smiled. "Can't miss it. Once we're down from these hills, just hang a left on the Pacific Coast Highway and head right up along the coast to LA."

"Aye, aye, Captain," Jim replied with a pirate's growl.

As they continued their long gradual descent from the mountains, John looked toward the north again. Definitely smoke this time. He turned to Jim.

"I better give Mary a call to see if the office has burned down since we've been gone."

John punched the quick dial number for the office. It was just past nine o'clock back home. The phone only rang once before connecting.

"Mary Hogan, Haddon Life-Tech. How may I direct your call?"

"Good morning, Mary. This is John, just checking in"

"Oh, good morning, John. Is everything okay out in sunny LA?"

"Great, Mary. The meetings went well and we're still on schedule to touch down in Philly around six. How are the home fires burning?"

Mary hesitated. "Everything is…fine, John."

John sensed uneasiness in Mary's voice. "You haven't convinced me, Mary." John paused. "Have you heard from Bob?"

"Well, yes. Bob was actually in the office for a few hours yesterday afternoon. He…well…was behaving rather strangely."

John gave Jim a worried look and shook his head, then turned back to his phone. "So, Mary, were you expecting Bob back in the office today?"

"Yes," she replied. "He said he'd be coming in a little later today. He keeps talking about 'an important project' he's working on. Do you know what that could be?"

John thought a moment. *The invention. That must be it! The continuous cell culture harvesting system.* John knew that Bob had drawn up plans for the device, and even ordered the major components. Their plan was to assemble a working prototype in Bob's basement and use the yeast culture from John's basement brewing system to run tests. Yeast cells were almost as good as insect cells for testing purposes. If it didn't work for yeast, then it probably wouldn't work for insect cells.

"Chances are he's just working on that invention of his," John said. "Probably got a brainstorm. You know Bob. Can't let go of an idea till he gets it down on paper." He paused a bit before adding, "Does Katie know his whereabouts?"

"Yes, she's been keeping close tabs on him. But, I think it's beginning to wear her down."

"Tell me, Mary. Has he shown any signs of…violent or aggressive behavior in any way?

"No. But he's making everyone here very nervous with his inappropriate and random outbursts. Running back and forth to the plotter from his office. He's driving Andy crazy in the print room with his demands. It's as if...he's hearing voices, or something. Like someone telling him what to do."

John took a worried deep breath and sighed. "Well, just tell everyone to remain calm. Don't want anyone getting hurt. I'll touch base with Katie as soon as I get back. Okay?"

"Sure. Okay."

"See you on Monday, Mary. Have a nice weekend."

"Thanks, John. And you guys have a good flight. Things will be all right here," she assured him.

John hung up his cell phone and sat there quietly for a moment before turning to Jim.

"Okay, I guess you probably overheard. Let's be sure we don't miss that flight."

"You got it!"

Jim gunned the engine as they sped up the Pacific Coast Highway toward L.A.

*****

It was after eight when John and Jim arrived back in New Jersey that Friday night. It was a good flight: smooth, and on time for a change. Jim went straight home, but John decided to drop by the office first to check his e-mail and landline voice messages.

The office was quiet—like a mausoleum. The janitorial cleaning crew had already come and gone an hour before. John checked his voice mail. The first three messages were sales calls from equipment vendors. John made some notes and erased each one in turn.

The next message was from his brother, Matt: "Hi, John. Your brother Matt here. Listen, John, I'm sorry to say I'm gonna hafta postpone our planned trip back east. Turns out Sam, your godchild and favorite nephew, has decided to vacation with his girlfriend, Beverly, and her family before heading back to school in the fall. Sorry, but you know how it is. He's just got Bev on the brain! Anyway, give me a call when you get in. And give Mom a hug and a kiss for me. Later."

John smiled. "Bev on the brain, eh?" It then occurred to him that he hadn't seen his mom in quite a while. He'd make a point to see her this weekend.

The last message was from Kate, left this afternoon. Her voice was flat, not the bubbly Kate he was used to: "Hi, John. I spoke with Mary, so I know you're traveling. But, I just wanted to let you know, we're having a cookout on Labor Day. Not a big thing. Nothing like the Fourth of July. Just Sally and Paul Fielding...and yourself. And anyone you'd care to bring. I think it may do Bob some good...(long pause)...I guess you know, Bob has been going to the office this week. He insists, saying he's working on something...really important. Anyway, give me a call when you get in. Bye, now. Hope to see you on Monday."

John took a deep breath and sat back in his chair. "She sounded worried. What the hell's going on with Bob?"

He sat there for a while before getting up to make his usual final rounds through the office. The print room was tidy and clean, but there were a half dozen large, empty spools lying upright in the corner. It was unusual to go through so much paper in just a few days. Then he thought about what Mary had said over the phone, about Bob driving Andy crazy in the print room.

Returning to the front of the building, John paused outside Bob's office. A handwritten sign taped to its closed door warned people to "Keep Out!" John tried the doorknob and was surprised to find it locked. Hmm, what was Bob trying to protect—or hide? He went to Mary's desk drawer and retrieved a ring of master keys. Returning to Bob's office door he tried several keys before he found the right one. The door opened.

The room was a mess. Obviously, the cleaning crew had missed this one, heeding the warning posted on the door. Three wastebaskets were stuffed to overflowing with wads of paper, torn drawings, and crushed Styrofoam cups; stacks of paper, broken pencils, and paper clips lay in disarray across the desk and credenza, with piles of Styrofoam fragments from the whittled down rims of half-empty coffee cups littering the entire area. Definitely not the tidy guy John knew.

But it wasn't the inordinate mess that really caught John's attention. It was what decorated the walls and ceiling. The three inside walls were papered with full-size 36" x 48" CAD drawing plots, covering every available square inch of wall space. They appeared to be mechanical assembly drawings of some kind, but one thing John knew for sure: "This is definitely not the continuous cell culture harvesting device!"

Like a collection of unfinished DaVinci sketches, their assorted machine parts seemed to be related in some way, but lacked completeness. As John studied the drawings further, he realized that the isometric perspectives they intended to convey violated the rules of three-dimensional reality, like an MC Escher print; if you followed one line into the drawing, it eventually met up with a line in the foreground. It seemed right on paper, but couldn't possibly exist in real three-dimensional space; it was very clever, but mildly disturbing as well.

But the strangest things were the glass globes: hollow, clear glass spheres of varying sizes, some about the size of grapefruit, mostly just lying loose about the room and on the credenza; and hanging from the ceiling in front of the window were about a dozen glass spheres arranged in a kind of mobile structure fashioned from clothes hanger wire and fishing line, resembling something like a sixth grader's school art project.

"What the hell has Bob been up to?"

John stood behind Bob's desk and sorted through the stacked piles of paper and note pads. That's when he discovered the notebook, a black-covered, wire-bound, lined journal with the simple, but rather presumptuous title: *The Final Project*.

John began leafing through its pages. It contained a combination of annotated drawings and sketches, interspersed with written notes and passages of verse. Many of the sketches were smaller versions of the full-sized drawings spread across the walls, presented in different perspective views, mysteriously identified as: "Three-dimensional projection in xyz plane" or "Exploded view of core." They all embodied the same Escher-like quality of conflicting perspective. Other sketches depicted various mobile structures similar to the one hanging from the ceiling, only much more intricate in detail.

The written notes were difficult to decipher, sometimes reading left to right, then right to left or top to bottom, and even sideways. The size and style of font varied and sometimes approached calligraphic beauty in their intricacy and detail, like a map drawn by a monk from the Middle Ages. One page spoke of a curse of some kind, with such isolated, cryptic phrases as: "Go back"; "Save her"; or "The chosen one will come!" He finally came to a more coherent passage of verse written in fine calligraphy style, framed within a beautifully hand-drawn border, intricately detailed with repeated paisley patterns and French curve designs. It read:

> As Grey Hound calmly resting off bayshore,
> By cloak of night and misty moor,
> Did unburden itself of tea and crew
> To set in course this witch's brew.
>
> The cold night sky filled with the plume of her pyre,
> That so mixed with the sweet smoke of the patriots' fire,
> Would have caused no suspicion, being one and the same,
> In the course of midnight mischief and mayhem.
>
> And so heated was the bonfire's blaze
> That by morning light no ash remained
> That could point a finger of cause or blame
> To person, or spirit, or good family name.

And several pages later:

> And ne'er the curse shall it be lift
> Till the time of the winter solstice rift
> And The One whom time henceforth reclaims
> Returns to barter with his good name.

The next several pages were missing, torn from the journal, while the final dozen or so pages remained blank.

"Curse? What kind of curse?" John puzzled. "Whew! Weird stuff. Can't believe it came from Bob. He must have copied it from some other source. Mystical writings of some kind."

John closed the journal and returned it to its original, undisturbed position under the stack of papers. Standing there, he just reached up and nudged one of the glass globes hanging overhead, setting it in motion. This action in turn set the other globes and mobile in motion. He continued watching as the globes slowly bobbed and turned, revolving like a miniature planetary system, reflecting the last light of the setting sun filtering in through the window blinds, casting an eerie blood-red pall over the room.

"I gotta have a talk with Bob...and Katie—and soon!"

Suddenly, he thought he heard a sound from the main office, like a chair or table being moved. He looked up, alert for any other movement or sound.

"Who's there?" he shouted.

But there was nothing, just the steady hum of the ventilation system.

"Guess it was just the AC kicking in."

Exiting Bob's office, John's eyes panned the main office space for any sign of movement: everything seemed to be in order. Finally, he turned and closed Bob's door, locking it behind him. The hanging mobile continued moving, its suspended glass globes slowly bobbing and turning against the red back light of the setting sun.

Chapter 14

1999
6 September

Monday, Labor Day. Lounging on his back porch veranda, John took another sip of coffee from his favorite mug as he opened the Sunday's day-old newspaper. The world hadn't changed much in that short time. It promised to be another hot, humid day.

John had spent the better part of the weekend reworking the draft interim report for the GenAvance conceptual design study, due one week from today. GenAvance was late finalizing their User Requirements Specification, and when John finally received the final version on Friday, it bore little resemblance to the initial draft, requiring a major re-write of their project scope. If Jacob Carlson, his process architect, was to begin his space programming efforts this week, as called for in the schedule, it meant John putting in a little overtime this weekend.

But that wasn't all that was on John's mind. Lying on the table was a manila envelope with the names "Bob and Katie" handwritten on the outside. It contained application papers for long-term disability, and other legal forms giving Katie power of attorney over Bob's business affairs, which John planned to take with him to the Fenwick's cookout. Katie was expecting it. He and Katie had worked out the details over lunch the previous Wednesday with the help of the company lawyer. She was nearing her wits end over Bob's condition and coming to the slow realization that he was going to need long-term, possibly institutionalized, treatment—if he could be persuaded to commit himself.

John put the paper down and finished his coffee, then went back into the house to get ready for the cookout. Before heading out he grabbed a six-pack of his newest creation from the basement: a dark creamy stout with just a touch of honey. After four weeks of fermentation, it peaked out at 9.2 percent volume alcohol. Sweet!

*****

John pulled into the driveway of the Fenwick's Moorestown home and parked alongside their family car, the Dodge Caravan. The "Mom's Taxi" sticker on its rear bumper had faded from bright checkered yellow and black to a bleached white and gray. Bob's Taurus was nowhere in sight. Clumps of dry grass clippings littered a freshly mowed lawn, but the sidewalk and curb were in need of a good trimming.

John found the front door open, but rang the bell anyway. He stood there waiting on the front porch a few seconds before finally seeing the handwritten note: "We're in the back yard. Just go around the side."

John obliged.

"Hello!" he announced himself as he opened the backyard gate. "Kate. Bob. Anyone home?"

Apparently, he was the first to arrive. John looked out across the yard. The pool was green with algae, the flower beds overgrown with weeds, many of its blooms withered and dying. All in all, the yard was a mess.

Katie emerged worn and pale from the back door, carrying a tray of hors d'oeuvres, but on seeing John, her face brightened up a bit.

"Hi, John," she said weakly. "I'm so glad you were able to come. You don't know how much it means to me...and to Bob."

She set the tray down on the glass patio umbrella table, wiped her forehead with the back of her hand, and exchanged a quick hug with John, kissing him lightly on the cheek.

"Please help yourself to the hors d'oeuvres," she said, drawing herself away to resume her chores.

John took a decorated cracker and gulped it in one bite as he looked around. "Where are the others?" he asked.

"You're the first to arrive, John. Actually, it's just going to be us and the Fieldings. Sally called to say they were running a little late. She's putting the finishing touches on the desserts she's bringing. And Paul volunteered to work the grill today."

John raised his eyebrows. "Don't worry, John," Katie reassured him. "Paul promised to do better this time. Said he's been working on his 'grill skills.'"

John chuckled. "Well, just in case, I brought along something to help wash down the brats." He held up the six-pack. "A gift from the gods of the grain harvest!"

Katie smiled. "Nice! Here, let me put it in the fridge for you."

She took the six-pack as John looked over her shoulder toward the house.

"So...where's Bob?" he asked.

Katie took a slow, deep breath. "Well, he *was* in the basement working on his...project. But, I don't hear anything, now," she said, looking back at the house. "He must've gone to his room, or up to his study."

"And, where are the kids? I don't see them anywhere around."

Katie sat down at the patio table and planted her hands on her lap. "Well, Amanda is staying with her cousin at the shore this weekend. You know, they have a place in Ocean City. Bobbie Jr. is spending the day at a friend's house." She looked at the green pool. "*Their* family pool is still swimmable," she said with a nervous laugh. "But, I still expect him to join us later for dinner. As you can see"—purveying the yard with a sweeping glance—"our yard is, well, a bit of a mess, to say the least. Nowadays, it's all I can do to keep a paycheck coming in. As it is, I've had to cut back my hours at Lourdes to keep up with this place—and keep track of Bob."

Katie lowered her head and John noticed the corners of her mouth quivering.

"So, tell me, Kate. Have you actually seen what Bob's been up to in the basement? His so-called 'project'?"

Katie regained her composure and looked up. "No, not really. He keeps his shop door closed and locked. Won't let anyone in. I don't dare challenge him."

"Why? Has he ever threatened you in any way?"

"No, nothing like that. It's just that, well, it's the only thing he seems to have control over anymore, even though it's become something of an obsession. I dare not challenge it, because it's the one thing that seems to be holding him together."

"What do the doctors say?" John pursued.

Kate shook her head. "Pretty much the same thing. They're still holding out hope that, with the right combination of medications, they can get his delusions and hallucinations under control. You know…the voices," she strained to add.

"I see," said John.

Katie quickly changed the subject, trying to lighten things up.

"So, John, how did your visit go with the—who was it—the guy from the museum? Something about being a tour guide?"

"Oh, right, you mean the Indian King Tavern thing. Yes, I went Thursday afternoon and spoke with the museum curator. We really hit it off. Turns out I already know almost as much about the history of the place as he does. He was especially interested in my family history, which traces back to early Haddonfield."

"So, are you going to do it? Work as a volunteer tour guide?"

"Docent. The correct term is *docent*. Gotta get the terms right," he said with a chuckle. "Yes, I think I might. It should be interesting; might even learn something. And I'd feel like I'd be giving something back to the community."

Katie stood up. "Well, I better get back to work. Excuse me John. Gotta get the baked beans out of the oven."

"Oh, I'm sorry, Kate. Is there anything I can do? Just name it."

"Well, you could get the beer and soda up from the basement. That'd be a big help."

"No problem. Just show me the way."

Kate led John through the back door into the kitchen and directed him to the basement stairs. "You'll find them in the large fridge in the utility room, just off the family room to the right."

"Right! Be back in a jiffy."

The basement stairs took John into their large family and game room, beautifully decorated and appointed with pool table, wet bar, and stone fireplace. An outside door on the left side of the room opened directly to the yard. John located the refrigerator in the utility room, removed two cases of beverages, and was about to take them upstairs when he noticed the closed door at the far end of the room, on the other side of the furnace. It wasn't so much the closed door that caught John's attention, as it was the dim, flickering light coming from under the door. He figured this must be Bob's workshop.

Curiosity got the better of him. Setting the beverages down on the laundry table he slowly approached the closed door and knocked gently.

"Hello! Anybody there?" he asked softly.

No reply.

He remembered Katie saying that Bob kept the shop door locked. He tried the doorknob anyway. The door opened with a creak. John paused, feeling like a thief breaking and entering. Ridiculous! Bob wouldn't mind. He had even invited him in that rainy night of the ISPE conference.

He opened the door wider and entered the room. Letting go of the doorknob, he stood there as the door closed on its own accord behind him. Except for a flickering light, like a candle, coming from the far end of the room, he found himself in nearly complete darkness. He reached for the wall switch and flipped it on. It didn't work.

John remained standing there for a minute or so, slowly getting his bearings as his eyes became accustomed to the dim light, before stepping carefully into the room toward the flickering light. He had a sense of objects moving about him, hanging from the ceiling, reflecting and scattering the candle light from across the room. With his eyes now accustomed to the dark, he found himself in the middle of an elaborate scaffolding structure of some kind, constructed of narrow wooden beams and furring strips supported not from the floor, but suspended from the overhead ceiling joists. The structure extended throughout the room, leaving little space to navigate without tripping or knocking one's head, although the major portion remained close to the walls, terminating just in front of a small workbench at the other side of the room. There seemed to be no rhyme or reason to its form. It brought to mind the interior latticework of the Statue of Liberty that supported Lady

Liberty's outer skin, but in this case it was impossible to see what form the structure could possibly represent. Many of the wooden members, supported at one end only, simply ended in mid-air, like a bridge under construction.

"Maybe that's it. Maybe it simply isn't finished."

Then he thought of the drawings hanging on the walls in Bob's office: the MC Escher prints. Yes, it looked something like that, only in real 3D space.

Scattered throughout the labyrinth structure were large, hanging mobile units of glass spheres similar to the ones he had seen in Bob's office. But unlike the office units, these mobiles were stationary, fixed in space, connected to the ceiling joists and cross beams with rigid steel or clear plastic rods. There had to be over a hundred glass globes of various sizes, ranging from the smaller golf ball-sized spheres—like Christmas ornaments—to the largest, about the size of cantaloupes. Like the devil's own disco bar, they filled the room's interior, suspended at various heights, some almost touching the floor, others crowded against the ceiling and along the walls and periphery of the room.

"Crazy!" John said under his breath.

The room was much longer than it was wide. A workbench ran the full length of the left wall, while the opposing wall was covered with assorted cabinets and open shelving systems. Ducking under the hanging spheres and lattice structure, John made his way toward the flickering light and workbench at the far end of the room. What he found was not a candle, but what appeared to be an old whale oil lamp, the kind you'd see in a maritime museum, only it smelled like kerosene or Coleman fuel, the modern-day equivalent of whale oil.

On the workbench lay a pile of notepaper and drawings, similar to the ones that were hanging on Bob's office walls. He then recognized the loose pages from his notebook, the missing pages torn from his journal. One page read:

> When blood lines are at last restored
> And the anguished cries of the innocents implore
> The chosen one will at last awake
> To see the path that he must take.

John studied the words, reading the lines of verse several times to himself, and then repeating them in a whisper, hoping the sound of the words might somehow reveal their hidden meaning. The other loose page contained more verse.

> So standing at the crux of time
> Where merge the course of family lines

Discern in madness what once was true
When seen from a single eye's point of view.

"More mumbo jumbo," John said aloud.

"Ah, less jumbo and a bit more mumbo, John," an unseen voice calmly answered from out of the darkness behind him.

John gasped as his heart skipped a beat. Sounded like Bob. He quickly turned around to see a human form slowly emerging from the shadows, half-revealed, face concealed, standing just to the right of the door—the only way in or out of the room.

"Tell me, John. What do you think of my...masterpiece?"

It was Bob's voice, all right. Only, it was subtly different. Subdued and mysterious would sum it up best.

"Bob! You really startled me," was all John could think to say.

Bob moved forward into the flickering light. His features were visible now; his arms behind him, apparently holding something.

"But, it is I who should be startled, John. Isn't that right? After all, this is *my* house, and...*my* workshop."

John watched as Bob brought his arms slowly around. In his right hand he held a crowbar. With his left palm faceup, he proceeded to slap it slowly, deliberately with the curved end of the crow bar, held firmly in his right fist.

John stood there for a moment, anxiously considering his options. Should he holler for Katie? Make a break for the door? Or just try to talk Bob down from whatever it was he was intending to do?

"I'm sorry, Bob. But, I...I thought I'd take you up on your original offer, to see the project you were working on. Don't you remember? The night of the ISPE conference?"

"Yes, John, I do remember. But I really think it was the voices that brought you here, to this place in history."

John tried to play along.

"Y-yes, Bob. Of course, the voices. You know I've always respected the voices from the past, the voices of history."

John stepped slowly and carefully to the left, as Bob began moving slowly along the right side of the room.

"You know that's not what I'm talking about, John. I'm talking about the cries of the anguished, the cries of the innocent from the past—from *your* past, John."

John began to feel nauseous. Images flashed in his head, images he had tried to suppress ever since that horrible day in July, 1982. But he'd never told Bob about that, so how would he know?

"Yes, John," Bob continued, "not just from your past alone, but from your family's past, John. An anguish that has survived many generations—an anguish that persists to this day. It is a *curse*, John, a curse that must be lifted. Before too long, John, as I fear time is running out."

There was a sense of urgency in Bob's voice, but an unusual calmness and certainty as well. Bob had reached the far side of the room now, almost trading places with John as they each continued maneuvering about the center of the room, like two slow motion boxers in a ring each trying to size up the other. Much to John's relief, Bob set the crowbar down on the workbench, gently, and then turned to face John, leaning with his backside against the table.

John posed the obvious question. "So, tell me, Bob. If you don't mind my asking,"—scanning the room as he continued—"what is this…this *thing* that you have constructed here?"

"What is it?" Bob replied, half surprised by the question. Then, holding up his hand—like Moses parting the Red Sea—he added slowly, "Why, this is my *time machine*, John."

John simply nodded. "I see."

Bob grimaced mildly and raised a finger to his head, tapping his temple firmly several times and then pointing to John in a repeated jabbing motion.

"Ah, but you *don't* see, John. To see the real truth you must sometimes change your point of view."

There was a strange logic to Bob's madness, John thought. Perhaps he's not so bad off, after all. Or perhaps he's just sucking me into his little mad world.

"So, tell me, Bob," John continued, "How does it work? This…time machine of yours."

Suddenly there came another voice, a man's voice, bellowing down the basement stairs. "Okay, time's up, John. So where's the brew?" It was the voice of Dr. Paul Fielding. "Guess I'm gonna have to come down there and get it myself," he said with forced determination.

There followed the sound of heavy footsteps on the basement stairs as John turned and opened the door into the utility room, shielding his eyes from the glare of the incandescent lights.

"Sorry for taking so long, Paul," John replied with no small measure of relief. "I was just…having a little talk with Bob, here."

Paul appeared at the doorway to the family room. "Well, tell Bob he's got guests. No time to be languishing in the basement workshop."

As Bob emerged from the darkness of his workshop close behind John, his deteriorated physical condition became readily apparent. He looked like he hadn't shaved or slept in a week. He was totally disheveled, with calloused hands and dirty, unclipped finger nails; his hair and clothes were a total mess.

Paul paused to study Bob for a moment before turning to John. "Uh, okay, you grab the sodas, I'll get the beer. Bob…can you get the outside door for us?"

Bob went ahead and opened the outside basement door. "Go on," he said in a most pathetic whimper, "I'll catch up with you later."

His head was turned down and away; he avoided direct eye contact.

John and Paul exchanged stunned looks as they walked on past Bob and out the door.

The cookout proceeded with Paul Fielding presiding over the grill. Paul was true to his word: the bratwursts were much better this time around.

"All it takes is a good bed of coals," he said as he turned the brats over for the last time. "I prefer real charcoal to the gas-fired grills. You get that real smoked flavor. Not the fake stuff, but the re-e-e-al carcinogens, the way food was meant to be eaten."

"That's great, doc!" John said. "So tell me, can you give me a discount on my postmortem, when I keel over from your tasty, cancerous brats?"

"No problem, John. For you it's on the house," Paul acknowledged with a wave of the spatula.

Everyone was gathered around the patio umbrella table, with the grill just a few feet away. The stone grill on the far side of the pool was just too remote for this more intimate gathering, so Katie had picked up a Weber grill from the local K-Mart earlier in the week and set it up on the patio.

John broke out his home-brewed stout, which was a big hit with Paul. Sally reserved judgment. "I'm not really a beer drinker," she said, "but, this really doesn't taste bad…for beer."

Bob did eventually join them for dinner, but remained subdued and didn't have much to say. On occasion, John would notice Bob's lips moving as he slowly disassembled his empty Styrofoam cup into smaller and small pieces, like the faithful silently reciting the Rosary.

"So, tell me, John. How is the biotech business these days," Sally asked.

"Oh, things are starting to pick up, Sal. We're working with a client on the west coast on a new process. They want to build a pilot plant facility right here in Jersey, up near Princeton. It's a real good opportunity for us." He looked across the table at his partner, Bob. "Isn't that right, Bob?"

Bob nodded. "That's right, John," he replied slowly and mysteriously. "But, you know"— leaning forward on the table and whispering so as not to be overheard—"I don't think I would trust that Dr. Sam Li fellow, if I were you."

He then leaned back in his chair and began to rock back and forth, humming to himself.

Sally pretended not to hear, and quickly changed the subject.

Bob Jr. soon returned home with a friend and finished off the last of the brats before the coals completely died down. Then, turning to his mom he asked, "Hey, mom. Can Frank and I roast some marshmallows on the grill?"

Without thinking Katie said, "Sure. Just be careful with the grill. It's still hot."

"But there's no flame," he protested.

"No, but the coals are still hot enough for roasting," Katie replied.

The marshmallows weren't roasting quickly enough to the boys' liking. Bobbie tried dousing the coals with charcoal starter fluid. When that didn't produce the effect they desired, his friend, Frank, got another idea. Sneaking into the shed he poured some gasoline from the 5-gallon can into a small cup. Before anyone realized what they were up to, he emptied the cup onto the grill, and *Vroom!* With a great ball of flame the grill erupted like Mount Vesuvius, spewing hot embers in every direction.

"Oh, my God!" Sally exclaimed. Everyone jumped from their seats in unison, spilling drinks and tipping over chairs. Fortunately, the boys were lucky to escape with only singed arms and eyebrows.

As quickly as it happened, it was over. Except for Bob Sr. He continued to gasp in wide-eyed horror at the burning grill, repeating over and over again, "We've got to save her! Don't you see? We've got to go back and save her!" He continued pacing back and forth like an enraged, caged lion. John and Paul came to his aid, eventually calming him and getting him to sit down on the terraced steps leading down to the pool.

Katie, meanwhile, took immediate disciplinary action with her son, once she ascertained that he and his friend were all right. She sent his friend home and Bobbie Jr. to his room. She then turned to John and Paul who were tending to her husband. Bob was still shaking and mumbling something about a "curse."

"Please keep him calm while I go inside and get his medication."

"Don't worry, Kate. We have him under control," Paul replied.

A minute later Katie returned and administered a sedative to her husband. She was finally able to get him back into the house, where he collapsed on the sofa in the basement family room and fell sound asleep.

Back outside the mood was somber. For a few minutes no one said a word. Finally, Paul spoke.

"So, Katie, asking both as a friend, and a professional, how long has Bob been this way? If you don't mind my asking."

Katie took a deep breath and gave a long sigh. "Seems like forever, Paul." She paused to get her thoughts together. "But, no, actually. It's been ever since that fishing trip on the Fourth of July weekend. You remember? The fireworks display?"

"Oh, yes! I do recall. Something about an insect bite on his arm becoming infected. But I thought that was all taken care of?"

"Right, the bite healed just fine. But, whatever it left inside of him, well, you can see it's only gotten worse since then."

"But, what do the doctors say about it?" Sally asked. "Is there a connection between the bite and his…mental condition?"

"The doctors don't think so," Katie replied, turning her head toward the house to reassure herself Bob was all right. "At least, they can't make a connection. Said it's probably just a coincidence." Drawing closer to the table she added, "They said he had a psychotic break of some kind. Maybe something on the fishing trip that triggered it. But they haven't been able to figure out just what happened."

"Have they tried hypnosis?" Paul asked.

"What?" Katie replied.

"You know. Hypnosis," he continued. "A hyper-suggestive state of mind, sometimes very useful for identifying the underlying cause of neuroses. Of course, the patient has to be willing, and of a certain state of mind to be put under. Some people"—glancing back at the house—"may have trouble responding to this kind of therapy. Anyway, it was just a thought."

"What I can't understand is how he can be so lucid at times, but so distant and disconnected at other times," John said. "Like down in the basement this afternoon. Granted, he had me a little spooked at first, with his strange talk about 'curses' and 'time machines.' But I was actually able to carry on a conversation with him. And he seemed to believe what he was saying; he was almost convincing!"

"Well, more than a few persons have been known to change the course of history with their fanciful, but seemingly logical points of view," Paul observed. "Convince a few people, they call you a cult leader. Convince the masses, and you've got a new religion."

Katie ignored Paul's remark and picked up on John's comments. "I know what you mean, John. When Bob is in his…element, shall we say, his 'comfort zone,' he seems almost normal. His shop, his office, he feels most comfortable there. But, put him anywhere else, and well…"

"It's like something gets triggered in his head by certain events," John suggested. "The fireworks display. The exploding grill. Maybe it's all related to something he experienced on that fishing trip."

They mulled this over.

"Maybe you're right, John." Katie said at last. "Or, maybe it's like the docs say, just a coincidence."

The evening continued with coffee and strawberry shortcake that Sally had made for the occasion. Katie let Bobby come down from his room for this, his favorite treat. He apologized to everyone for disrupting the cookout, and said it wouldn't happen again.

Before leaving for the evening, John left behind the legal paperwork for Katie to sign. "Please read through it before signing, Kate. I've signed all that I have to sign. If you have any questions, please, just call me."

*****

That evening, back home in the solace of his study, John poured himself a double shot of brandy. He didn't bother sniffing it this time—just gulped it down in once shot! He was worried about Bob.

How could someone so intelligent, with everything going for him, suddenly, without warning, without any signs, have a nervous breakdown? A "psychotic break." That's what Paul called it. It must've had something to do with that fishing trip. Something must have happened down by the bay that Fourth of July weekend. But what?

John set the brandy glass down, picked up a pencil and notepad and began doodling. Sometimes, just jotting things down on paper helped get his thoughts together, to come up with an idea. Suddenly, a simple thought came to him. Why not go down to the bay myself and investigate, talk to the captain of the fishing boat, find out what happened? He could check Bob's day planner and address book to get the name of the captain, and the boat he sailed on. Maybe next weekend.

John poured himself another glass of brandy

"Hmm. Saturday's not good," he said aloud as he checked his day planner. "That's the day I get fitted for my costume."

He had committed to doing the tour guide gig for the Indian King Tavern Museum, and needed to look the part. He already had the patter down, mainly a recap of what he already knew about the place, but organized in a walk-through presentation for the general public.

But Sunday, the twelfth, was open. He penciled in "Fishing Trip" for that date. Of course, the only thing he was fishing for was information. John looked at the clock: 10:05 p.m. Time to turn in.

The brandy had its desired effect: John had no trouble falling asleep. But with his mind still racing with events of the day, it proved to be a fitful sleep, filled with dreams that were both vivid and vexing, a collage of images from the past mixed out of context with recent events. They say the average dream lasts only two or three seconds. But this wasn't your average dream.

...A great fireworks display showered the football stadium with glowing embers as Dr. Sam Li took to a giant podium set up in the middle of the field on the fifty-yard line. It was more like an altar, or preacher's pulpit, the kind you might find in a large cathedral. Dressed in a long black robe, Sam Li raised his arms over his head and thanked everyone for coming. The giant overhead screen flashed with images of his PowerPoint presentation as

the scoreboard lit up with the words: "GO BACK! SAVE HER!" The crowd erupted in cheers and applause.

   John turned to his left. There was Mary Hogan, his administrative assistant, seated close by. She was busy crocheting and seemed oblivious to what was happening on the field. "How is the baby blanket coming, Mary?" John asked. "Shhh!" Mary gestured, placing a forefinger to her pursed lips. Suddenly, the blanket wasn't a blanket any more. It had changed into a long, richly decorated tapestry, filled with colorful images of horses, stars, and ships, like something John had once seen in a French museum. The tapestry now extended down and across the field, disappearing into the stands on the far side of the stadium. "What does it mean?" John asked. "It tells a story, John," Mary replied without looking up. "Whose story?" John asked. Mary looked up. "Your story, John" was all she said.

   Suddenly, there came a loud announcement, a voice from a P.A. system. "And now, it's time for the half-time show!" Immediately, a herd of little wooden horses took to the field, chasing what appeared to be a young woman dressed in a long, flowing gown, trailing sparks behind her. As the embers from the fireworks and sparks from the woman's gown fell onto the field and into the stands, they began to ignite little fires. John ran around frantically stomping out the flames before they could grow. No sooner had he put out a flame over here, when one erupted over there.

   The stadium had now transformed into a high school football field, the stands into bleachers. John looked to his left. Mary was gone. He was now forced to chase the fires under the bleachers, as the embers found their way between the seats and onto the ground below. The bleachers took on the form of an elaborate scaffolding structure, and as he climbed down through the maze of scaffolding, the space around him grew increasingly dark and confining.

   The fires were gone, now, and John found himself alone in a dark, but familiar, room. He turned to see his good friend, Bob Fenwick, standing by the door. "Hello, John. I'm so glad you could come." Bob smiled. Gesturing toward the door like a carnival sideshow barker he added, "And now, for the main attraction!" Slowly, the door opened with a creak, revealing a blinding white light from the other side. Out of the light appeared the figure of a tall, beautiful woman, floating in a transparent orb of radiance. The sphere hovered and paused, then slowly crossed the threshold, effortlessly transporting the woman to the center of the room. Reaching up she took hold of one of many small, shining globes suspended from the ceiling. As she took the globe, it slipped from her grasp and fell to the concrete floor below, shattering into a zillion shimmering shards of glass in all directions. "Curses!" Bob cried aloud. "Curses! Curses!" his plaintive cries continued...

   John awoke with a start! He continued to lie there, motionless with his eyes closed. He didn't want to lose the memory of the dream as he tried to make some sense of it. He hadn't dreamed that dream since he was a kid— the part with the sparks and embers starting the fires. The "fire starter" nightmare, he used to call it. Only this time, it wasn't so much a nightmare as just a disturbing dream. He eventually rolled over and went back to sleep...and continued to dream.

...*John was now in a cemetery, alone, standing in front of a large, stone mausoleum. It was raining. Inscribed on the marble lintel over the door was the family name: WESTON. He knocked, and the door slowly opened. "Welcome home, John," unseen voice greeted him from within.*

Once inside, John suddenly found himself dressed in colonial garb, standing in the hallway of the Indian Head Tavern. He was alone, but could hear muffled voices emanating from somewhere inside. He tried to find his way, but one room and hallway simply led into another as he searched frantically for the source of the voices. Finally, opening a large, red wooden door he came upon a small, candlelit room, its walls paneled in rich mahogany. Directly to his front was an intricately carved, wooden privacy screen which divided the room in two. Movement and muffled human voices permeated the screen's patterned perforations from the other side. John carefully approached the open end of the screen and peered around its corner. A crowd of people was gathered about a small table located near the center of the room. Nudging them aside he slowly made his way to the table. There, on the table, lay a Ouija board. It was like none other that he had ever seen, elaborately decorated with embroidered graphics. The words "GO BACK! SAVE HER!" were scrawled in red letters across the board—not on the board, actually, but floating a few inches above it. A young man and woman were seated at the table. The young woman looked up and addressed John directly: "John Weston, the chosen one!"

John was now seated at the table. Looking up at the people crowding the room, he recognized many of them. There were his father and mother, and his brother, Matt, as a small boy. The others he didn't recognize, but felt like he knew them, just the same. One whom he thought he knew, but didn't recognize, spoke to John: "When blood lines are at last restored"—as a second voice chimed in—"and the anguished cries of the innocents implore"—and then a third—"the chosen one will at last awake"—and finally, John's father spoke—"to see the path that he must take." When John looked back at the Ouija board, the letters had changed to spell the single word: "CURSES."

John stood up and turned to run from the room, but his feet had turned to lead, weighing him down. Struggling to reach the door, he finally managed to grab hold of the latch, opened the door, and suddenly found himself outside on the banks of a great body of water.

A young man stood on the shore tending a charcoal grill, waving to someone on a boat floating far off on the water. As the boat drew nearer, John saw a young woman standing on its deck, waving to the young man on the shore. John had a strange sense of foreboding. He thought he recognized the woman on the boat. He did not recognize the man on the shore, but felt as though he knew him, all the same. A flock of seagulls hovered closely over the boat. Suddenly, the grill erupted in a great ball of flame! The flock of seagulls was instantly transformed into a great swarm of flies buzzing all about the boat. John cried out, "Noooo!" He tried running to the shore but could not move. "No! No" he repeated over and over again. The woman lifted her hands to her ears, as if she was trying to make out what he was saying. Suddenly, the boat erupted into a great ball of fire, engulfing the woman in flames as anguished cries of pain echoed across the water...

John awoke in a cold sweat, heart pounding in his chest, as he sprang up and flung the covers into the dark naked void. Sitting on the side of the bed he leaned forward and cradled his head in both hands, trying to clear his mind, but to no avail. Looking up to the ceiling he cried out, "No! No! Not again! Not that again!"

He continued to sob.

It had been many years since John had dreamed that dream—the last dream, the part with the woman on the burning boat. It was a nightmare that had plagued John's sleep the several years immediately following that dreadful day in July, 1982. Strange, the only thing different now was the swarm of flies. That was something new.

John sat there, still trembling, as he tried to piece together the events that led up to that day. Slowly, the pieces fell into place, and his thoughts went back to the summer of 1981.

*****

Becky was making good money with her new marketing position at Modeline Fashions, Inc. and John was hoping to finish up his master's degree at Rutgers in December of that year. He had a lead on a good job opportunity at a start-up biotech company outside Princeton, New Jersey: GenAvance Biologics.

It was Monday evening, July 6, when John decided to pop the big question. He and Becky were spending the long Fourth of July weekend at her uncle's horse farm in Sussex County, the northern most county in the state. They had just returned from an afternoon of riding and were relaxing on the front porch swing of her uncle's farmhouse.

"You know what day it is today?" John asked with his arm around Becky.

Becky thought for a moment, pretending not to remember. "Aw, I know!" she said coyly. "It's our anniversary! Two years ago today, our first date."

John smiled and produced a small jeweler's case from his pocket with his free hand. Bringing his other arm around, he opened the case and removed a small silver band with a modest diamond setting. He took Becky's hand in his own.

"And will you, Becky, take this poor graduate engineering student to be your husband, to have and to hold, till death do you part?" he asked as he slowly placed the ring on her finger.

Becky placed her free hand to her mouth to conceal a gasp. While it did not come as a total surprise, John's timing was unexpected. She thought he would have waited until Christmas. But, now was as good a time as any, and probably better than most. After all, it was their anniversary, and the setting was so...traditional. Sitting on a front porch swing with your sweetheart on a warm summer evening, with a chorus of cicadas filling the air with their urgent mating songs.

"Of course, I would," Becky answered, as she flung her arms around John and gave him a long kiss.

She pulled her arm away to inspect the merchandise closer.

"Very nice!" she said, admiring the diamond's glittering facets from different angles as she held it up to the soft light of the front porch lamp.

"You really surprised me," she said, turning to John. "I thought you were going to wait till Christmas for the ring."

"Well, I thought about that, but I just couldn't wait. Besides, how better to celebrate our anniversary?"

Fast forward to Christmas Eve of the same year, 1981. These were exciting times for John and Becky. As they made plans for their future together, they had much to celebrate. John had just received his master's degree in Chemical Engineering from Rutgers University and had been working at GenAvance's Princeton research facility since early November, with a respectable starting salary. In December, John and Becky moved in together—a small, two-bedroom apartment in New Brunswick, New Jersey, not far from Rutgers' main campus. They were branching out, now, trying new things in their young lives. John had grown a beard and mustache, and Becky was developing her culinary skills in the kitchen, as she removed the last batch of Christmas cookies from the oven.

"Ahh, smells good, babe!"

"I hope they taste as good as your Aunt Dee's," Becky replied.

"No way!"

Becky turned and was about to scold him, when he quickly added, "I bet they're even *better* that Aunt Dee's."

John went to grab one—chocolate chip, his favorite—when Becky slapped his hand. "You have to wait till they cool off," she said.

Becky began scooping the cookies from the baking tray and placing them on the cooling rack. "If these turn out, I'm gonna make a batch for our New Year's Eve party at work."

"Yeah, I'm looking forward to that party, babe. I bet Modeline puts on quite a bash. Maybe I'll finally get to meet that Mr. fancy-pants photographer you're always talking about."

"You mean Brad Mathews? And I'm not always talking about him," she corrected him. "He just happens to be an excellent fashion photographer for whom I have great respect."

"You said he travels a lot. Maybe he'll be on the road and won't make the party."

Becky looked concerned, almost hurt. "No way. He'll be there."

Later that evening, as they decorated their Christmas tree, they began discussing their wedding plans for the following summer. John's favorite movie version of Charles Dickens' *A Christmas Carol* was airing on TV in the background.

> "…Before I draw nearer to that stone to which you point," said the TV's Scrooge, "answer me one thing. Are these the shadows of things that Will be, or are they shadows of things that May be, only?"

"You know," John continued, "I like your idea of getting married on your uncle's farm, babe. After all, that's where I gave you your ring. Kind of like returning to the scene of the crime," John chuckled, as he placed the final strand of lights on the tree.

"Return to the scene of the crime? Not really, my dear," Becky tested. "If that really were the criterion, we'd probably be getting married in Harleigh Cemetery." She laughed.

John gave her the evil eye. "What? You don't like Whitman poetry?" Then, backing away from the tree he announced, "Okay, here goes!"

With that he turned off the room lights and plugged in the tree lights, casting the room in a warm glow. In a few seconds the blinkers warmed up, throwing random shadows and changing patterns of light across the ceiling and walls of their small but cozy living room.

> "…Good spirit," the TV Scrooge implored, "your nature intercedes for me, and pities me. Assure me that I may change these shadows that you have shown me, by an altered life!"

"Nice!" Becky said. "Oh, but you forgot the star at the top of the tree!"

"Right! But it's not really finished yet," John replied. "We still have to decorate with glass balls and tinsel. The star's got to be the very last thing to go on the tree."

John turned the room lights back on as they set about finishing the job. Becky took a large glass ball ornament from its box and reached to place it high up on the tree. It was a gift from a favorite aunt, a clear glass ball with swirling colors and engraved frosted lettering that read "Merry Christmas! 1981." Just then, John turned unexpectedly, knocking the ball from her hand and sending it crashing to the hard wood floor below.

"Ohmygod! No! Now see what you made me do!" Becky scolded. "That was a gift from my Aunt Mary."

"Aw geez! I'm really sorry, babe."

John kneeled down to inspect the pieces. "Maybe we can piece it back together," Becky offered plaintively.

John already had four of the larger pieces in the palm of his hand. "No way, hon. We'll have to just try and replace it. Your Aunt Mary need never know."

"But, isn't that bad luck? Sorta like breaking a mirror," she fretted.

"Nonsense! No such thing! We make our own luck, babe," John replied with all the confidence of youth.

"...I will live in the Past, the Present, and the Future," Scrooge continued. "The spirits of all Three shall strive within me. Oh, tell me that I may sponge away the writing on this stone!"

Becky returned to decorating the tree while John finished cleaning up the shards of broken glass with a dustpan and broom.

"And where should we go for our honeymoon?" John asked, getting back to the subject of their wedding.

"Well, I'd really like to do a cruise. Like, maybe the Caribbean," Becky said.

"Yeah, that'd be nice. And we could stop off at all the islands, go parasailing, hang-gliding, snorkeling..."

"And horseback riding along the pink sandy beaches," Becky interrupted, as she tossed a few more strands of tinsel on the tree.

"Took the words right out of my mouth," John hollered back from the kitchen as he dumped the dustpan in the wastebasket. Returning, John paused in the doorway.

"Wow, that really looks nice, babe! I think it's time for the *coup-de-grace!*"

John climbed the stepladder, then turned around to Becky. "Okay, babe, hand me up the star."

Taking the star from Becky, he carefully positioned it on top of the tree and connected its power cord to the nearest plug on the string of lights. "Voila! A new star is born!"

Climbing back down, John returned to the subject of the wedding. "You know, I'd really like to try my hand at boating, or even sailing," he said. "Maybe we could rent a small sloop or something down in the islands. Sail off and find our own private getaway cove."

"Really? I never thought of you as the sailor type."

"No?" John sounded surprised. "Did you forget I descend from a line of merchant mariners from colonial times?"

"So, you're telling me it's in your genes?"

"Could be," John ventured. "Anyway, it shouldn't be that hard. These days I think ships and boats pretty much sail themselves," he added straight-faced.

"You're not serious?"

"Just kidding, hon. Of course I'd take lessons. I think the Coast Guard offers courses. It'd be fun. Like maybe we could try it out beforehand, down at the Jersey shore."

"I take it you mean the *South* Jersey shore," she said.

"Of course! South Jersey has the best beaches and waterways for that sort of thing."

Becky jumped on John and tumbled to the floor together in a playful wrestle. John finally pinned her down and planted a long kiss, then rolled over on his back as she snuggled up close beside him.

"You know, they have a boat show every spring at the Civic Center in Philly. Maybe we could go and check out the merchandise. With our combined salaries we should be able to afford something really nice," he suggested.

"Hmm. Maybe," was all she said.

They continued lying there on the floor, huddled together, awash in the glow of the season.

"...It's Christmas Day!" declared the TV Scrooge. "I haven't missed it. The Spirits have done it all in one night. They can do anything they like. Of course they can. Of course they can..."

It's was now the summer of '82. John and Becky made plans to spend the entire Fourth of July holiday week at the South Jersey shore. They rented a beach house in Ocean City, a popular family summer resort town located about twenty miles south of Atlantic City. The house was situated midway between the ocean and the bay, just three blocks from the Ocean City's boardwalk near sixteenth and Asbury.

Like most New Jersey coastal resort towns, Ocean City lies on one of the many barrier islands running up and down the Jersey coast, a string of islands creating an unbroken network of interconnecting bays and inland waterways, a veritable paradise for fishermen and recreational boaters alike. Ocean City's barrier island is roughly seven miles long and a mile across at its widest point, separated from the mainland by Great Egg Harbor, a wide expanse of choppy bay water broken up by a patchwork of salt marsh islands that offer refuge to a wide variety of water fowl and tidal sea life. In 1982, a narrow four-lane, two-mile causeway and two low bridge spans that hopscotched from island to island, connected the town of Somers Point on the mainland with Ocean City's Ninth Street downtown area, which was located roughly at the midpoint of the main island. Vacationing anglers and crabbers would line the approaches to the smaller islands on either side of the causeway, slowing traffic to a crab's crawl at times. As one crossed the final drawbridge that led to the island, the town of Ocean City came into full view. A tidy harbor packed with marinas, condominiums, and restaurants, running north and south as far as the eye could see, lined the island's bayside community.

Ocean City was a dry town. To buy a drink you'd have to go off the island. From Ocean City's downtown area, the nearest bar or liquor store was across Great Egg Harbor in Somers Point. This fact, together with a three-mile long boardwalk and amusement pier, made Ocean City an especially popular destination shore community for vacationing families far and near. John had fond memories of coming here as a boy with his family. It was their favorite vacation spot. Now he was eager to share it with Becky.

Of course, John was also eager to put his new toy to the test, a twenty-eight-foot Monterey inboard cabin cruiser he and Becky picked up at the boat show in Philly the previous spring, big enough to boast a galley and sleep four, but not so big that you couldn't pull someone on water skis.

"A name. It's gotta have a name," Becky had remarked as they were signing the bill of sale.

"And, traditionally, it should be a *girl's* name," the salesman reminded them.

John nodded knowingly. Before taking possession of the boat, he had the words "Becky Babe" painted on the rear transom in big fancy letters. The name was repeated on both the starboard and port bows.

"Now, that's what I'm talking about!" Becky boasted on seeing it for the first time.

Since buying the boat in the spring, John and Becky had spent almost every weekend on the water and were beginning to feel like old salts. John never did things just halfway. He insisted they both take the Coast Guard course on basic seamanship, which emphasized safety and navigation skills. Just to "get their sea legs," as John put it, they initially put the boat on the Mullica River, a popular recreational inland waterway that flowed through Jersey's Pine Barren wilderness area. Once he felt confident enough, they began inviting friends for weekend outings. He was able to locate a slip at a bayside marina in Ocean City just a few blocks north of the Ninth Street bridge for the summer season.

To kick off the Fourth of July, he and Becky invited two of their best friends to spend the holiday weekend with them at the shore. The three-bedroom beach house was plenty big enough for the four of them. For John, this meant Dan "da man" Kelly, his old college and crew team buddy and designated "best man" for the wedding. Becky invited Sue Wilson, her best friend and college sorority sister, who had agreed to be her bridesmaid. Of course, the weekend together also gave them a chance to talk about their plans for the wedding. The big date was set for next month: Saturday, the twenty-first of August.

The weekend weather forecast for South Jersey called for more heat and humidity, typical mid-summer weather for the area. Weather at the shore, however, was normally tempered by a cool, steady breeze from the ocean, infused with the invigorating scent of salt air. In the evenings, the air even became a bit chilly at times, especially right along the beach and boardwalk.

Late Saturday afternoon, July 3, John and Becky offered to show off their new boat to their friends, and go whale and dolphin watching along the coast. They would take dinner on the boat and would make use of the galley for only the second time since buying the boat. Trolling slowly northward through the bay's "No Wake" zone, they turned east around the northern tip of the island and headed out through the Great Egg Harbor inlet toward the ocean. Staying within the channel, they were able to avoid the rougher waters breaking on the nearby sandbars and pushed on toward the calmer waters of the open ocean. Once through the inlet, John gunned the boat's engines. The clean, salt air spray blew briskly across the bow and bridge as the boat cruised along effortlessly at twenty knots. Traveling north along the coast, about a half mile off shore, they began watching for dolphins and whales. Seagulls, following close behind, soared and crisscrossed overhead, squawking and vying for lead position, keeping a sharp eye out for any scraps of food thrown their way.

"Sorry, no chum today, guys," Dan shouted out at the hovering birds. "This ain't no fishing trip, just an evening pleasure cruise." But that didn't stop them from throwing the birds a piece of stale bread every now and then, just to see them dive and maneuver in flight, competing for the scraps.

Continuing up the coast, they didn't have very far to go to run into dolphins—the dolphins found them. Jumping and surfing in the trailing wake of the boat, four young pups followed close behind off the starboard side, easily keeping pace with the boat. With Becky now at the helm, John took the opportunity to break out his new Nikon 35 mm camera that Becky had given him the previous Christmas. Between the boat and the shore swam a rather large pod of the seafaring mammals, no more than thirty yards off shore, jumping and playing in the shallow surf.

"I can't believe how close they come to the shoreline," Sue remarked. "Do you think the people on the shore can see them?"

"Probably," replied Dan." Good thing, too. I've heard that dolphins keep the sharks away."

Around six o'clock, John shut down the engine and anchored the boat about a half mile offshore. They all had a hand in preparing the evening meal: the guys prepped the veggies and shucked the corn, while the girls fired up the propane stove and oven to broil some steak and bake the potatoes. Before opening the meal's bottle of wine, Dan mimicked breaking it against the bow of the boat. "I christen you *Becky Babe*!" he announced with forced bravado.

Seated at the dinette table inside the cabin, with the heat of the day gone, the men finished off the last of the corn-on-the-cob, as the boat gently bobbed at anchor, slowly turning with the tides to bring the shoreline into John's view over Dan's shoulder.

"Must be Margate," John said with a grin. "What other town has a four-story elephant on the beach that offers a guided tour of its innards?"

Sure enough, there was Lucy the Elephant, tall and proud and basking in the late day sun, a famous landmark in these parts for as long as John could remember.

"Hey, we'll have to go there sometime, John," Becky chided. "That's one place in South Jersey you've never taken me."

"Probably the only place, too," Dan chimed in.

After cleaning up, everyone went up on deck to enjoy the cool evening breeze and watch the sun set over the not-so-distant shore with its unbroken array of white clapboard homes neatly hugging a narrow white band of sand and foaming surf. Extending north and south it slowly faded into the summer haze and cityscape of faraway coastal towns—Atlantic City to the north, Sea Isle to the south—as Lucy the Elephant began to cast long, shifting shadows onto a rust-colored beach, the western sky slowly turning to a blazing crimson. Nature was preparing a glorious exit to a fine day.

"Hey John, another great photo-op!" Dan said. "Looks like the whole sky is on fire!"

John was already on it. While he was busy taking pictures, Dan slipped away to the cabin to use the head. Returning a few minutes later, he remarked, "Hey, John! I'm getting a whiff of some gas or something inside the cabin. You might wanna check it out."

"Sure it wasn't those burritos you had for lunch?" John retorted, leaning up against the gunwale to steady himself for the next picture.

"No, seriously. I'm talking raw fuel, diesel, or whatever it is this thing runs on."

John turned serious. "Then maybe I better have a look."

When John returned from below, he hollered up to Becky who was seated on the bridge talking wedding plans with Sue.

"Hey, babe, can you flip on the bilge exhaust. It's the toggle switch marked 'Bilge Fan.'"

Becky obliged.

"So, what was it?" Dan asked.

"I'm not sure," John replied with a touch of concern. "There could be a small leak in the engine compartment. The exhaust fan should take care of it for now. But, I'll have to take a closer look at it when we get back to port."

The next day was Sunday, the Fourth of July. The foursome spent most of the day at the beach, taking advantage of the gorgeous weather and ocean surf, which was especially active this weekend. A tropical storm lying several hundred miles off Cape Hatteras triggered riptide warnings, which were posted up and down the coast. At least two Jersey drownings were attributed to the rough tides. John and Dan were glad they had brought their boogie boards, though, to take full advantage of the excellent wave action. Following an active day at the beach, they all returned to the house late in the afternoon for an old fashioned Fourth of July cookout with hot dogs and hamburgers.

That evening they braved the crowds and went down to the boardwalk to catch the fireworks display over the ocean. The smell of caramel corn and funnel cakes hung in the air, as the boardwalk vendors hustled to keep up with the bustling holiday crowds—saltwater taffy, cotton candy, and soft-serve ice-cream, all selling at a record pace. The clattering, ringing bells of the arcades and the sounds of the calliope from the amusement piers contributed to the fun-for-all carnival atmosphere. Somewhere along the way, they stopped to do a game of miniature golf before heading further south to Sixth Street and the boardwalk, where the crowds were already gathering for the fireworks display. But they never got closer than Seventh Street. Sue had claustrophobia and didn't want to buck the crowds. Just as well, as they could see the fireworks just fine from where they were.

After the fireworks, Becky suggested they go for a moonlit walk along the beach. The air had turned chilly and they were all forced to break out their Rutgers hoody sweatshirts, which they had brought along and tied around their waists, just in case. The sweet decay of rotting sea life, nature's flotsam washed up on the shore, mingled with the salt air spray to create that oh-so characteristic blend of seaside scents. Going barefoot, they waded into the shallow surf at the water's edge, allowing the retreating foam to caress and tickle their toes and feet, just up to the ankles, as broken shards of clam shell brushed by their feet and small strands of seaweed wrapped uncomfortably around and between their toes. Standing in one place too long, the wet sand would cave in underfoot, washed away by the repeatedly receding wave action, until one's feet became totally buried in the cool, wet stuff.

Walking arm and arm, well ahead of Dan and Sue, Becky turned to John and whispered, "So, how do you think Dan and Sue are hitting it off?"

"Ahh. Now I get it!" John whispered back. "So, that's why you invited them down this weekend. Playing matchmaker, are we?"

"No, not really. Just providing the right opportunity is all. Nature does the rest. Back at school I always thought Dan had an eye for Sue, but was too shy to speak up."

"So, now you just want to give him a second chance, right?" John smirked.

By this time Dan and Sue had caught up with them, and they were forced to change the subject.

Becky was looking up into the clear night sky when a shooting star suddenly darted across the heavens, seeming to fall into the ocean. She jumped. "Did you see that?" she asked excitedly, pointing to the horizon.

"See what?" replied John.

"A shooting star! You didn't see it?"

"Sorry, babe. I was looking down. Totally missed it."

Monday morning, John and Dan were up before the sun to take a long bike ride from one end of the island to the other, and back again—fourteen miles in all. The cool morning ocean breeze was especially invigorating. They stopped once on the boardwalk for a hot cup of freshly brewed coffee. Seated on a wooden bench with their feet propped up on the fence railing overlooking the beach and ocean, they quietly sipped coffee and talked about the future, as they watched the sun coming up over the ocean. A java Zen moment! John scolded himself for not having his camera with him this time.

The rest of the day was spent lounging around the beach house, sharing war stories from college, and listening to Led Zeppelin and Pink Floyd cassette tapes. Dan left for home soon after lunch, but not before exchanging phone numbers with Sue. She left not long afterward. Now, John and Becky had the whole house and the rest of the week to themselves.

"So, have you ever tried skiing?" John asked.

"You mean the water kind?"

"Sure, I mean the water kind!" John looked out the window. "I don't see much snow happening," he added sarcastically.

"Okay, wise guy. So why didn't you just ask me if I wanted to go water skiing?" Becky sniped back playfully. "And to answer your question, no, I have never skied on water, just on snow. How about you?"

"I tried it once at Rutgers. The crew team rented a small boat one weekend and took turns on skis. It's not really that difficult," John said.

"You mean, not for an old sculling pro like yourself."

"Nah. I'll show you how it's done. It's just a question of balance. Got to keep your center of gravity behind your skis."

Becky waivered. "Maybe we should have attempted this when Dan and Sue were here."

"Hey, they can join us next time," John said. "Come on. It'll be fun! And besides, with that bad weather heading our way, the rest of the week might be a washout. Tomorrow might be our only chance."

"But, you do know what day tomorrow is, don't you?" Becky quizzed him.

"Sure, I didn't forget. I called the *Crab Fest* in Somers Point and made dinner reservations for the two of us to celebrate our anniversary. We'll be back from skiing in plenty of time to clean up and head over to the mainland. Our reservations aren't until seven o'clock."

Becky perked up. "Ooo, that sounds real nice! I've been looking forward to some really good seafood."

"So, whadaya say about the skiing?"

"Um. Well, okay," Becky agreed reluctantly. "But, actually, I'm more worried about the other boaters. You have no control over them. What if they run you over in the water?"

"Nah. We just avoid the crowds. It'll be fine!" John assured her.

Early the next day, John and Becky packed a cooler with cold drinks, threw some snacks and a bottle of sunscreen in a gym bag, and headed toward the marina.

"Nice day!" an older marina attendant greeted John and Becky as they approached him on the floating pier. "Will ya be taking the *Becky Babe* out today?"

"Sure thing, Tom!" John replied. "Don't know how long this nice weather's gonna hold out, what with that nasty weather coming up the coast."

"Right," Tom agreed. "So, d'ya want me t'top off the tank fer ya?"

"Sure. Thanks, Tom."

"No problem. Just bring the boat around on around and tie'r up here," Tom said pointing to an open space along the main dock next to the gas pumps.

John and Becky continued to the far end of the floating pier where Becky Babe was docked and loaded on the day's supplies before unleashing the tie lines and climbing on board themselves. The life vests, skis, and tow ropes were already on board. John started the engine and slowly maneuvered the boat out of the slip toward the main dock where Tom was waiting for them.

"Throw me the line," Tom shouted.

Tom and Becky secured the bow and stern with tie lines as John grabbed a camera from his gym bag and climbed onto the dock, motioning for Becky to follow.

"Hey, Tom, when you're finished with the gas, would you mind getting a picture of me and Becky?"

"No, not at all," Tom replied, "happy to oblige"—looking at the Nikon camera John was holding—"If ya'll just show me how to use that thing. Not much used to picture takin'."

"It's easy. I've got it all set. All you gotta do is center us in the window, then push that little button on top."

John and Becky assumed a relaxed pose with their arms around each other's waists, and the boat behind them.

"Okay, here goes," Sam readied himself. "Say 'cheese.'"

Click.

John thanked Tom, then took the camera and began a slow jog back to his car—the '74 Plymouth Gold Duster—parked nearby.

"Be back in a jiff, babe."

"Hey, aren't you going to take the camera along and get pictures of us skiing?" Becky hollered out after him.

"No, not today," John shouted back. "I figure with just the two of us, we better focus on keeping a watch out for each other, and not be preoccupied with taking pictures."

With the weekend crowds gone, they had no trouble finding a relatively secluded patch of open water out on the bay to try out their skis. But, with the offshore tropical storm heading up the coast, the water was a bit choppier than it had been over the last few days. Maybe that was the real reason there weren't many other boaters on the water today.

On the way out they passed a group of teenagers on Jet Skis, the newest form of sport mania to hit the waters.

"Hey, now that looks like fun!" John commented.

"Looks dangerous to me," Becky replied. "They look awfully young to be driving those things out on this open water."

"Well, we'll just have to keep our distance," John said.

Just as he spoke, a black and gold Jet Ski shot out from nowhere about thirty yards off port from their bow and ran directly across their path. The high, shrill whine of the Jet Ski's 400 cc two-stroke engine rose and dipped in pitch as it negotiated the choppy water. John instinctively throttled back the engine and turned to port in the direction the Jet Ski had come. A second Jet Ski, with the name Hornet decaled in red letters on its gas tank, came screaming behind in hot pursuit of the first. John hollered out, "Hey, watch it, damn ya! You're gonna cause an accident!"

The rider of the second Jet Ski—couldn't have been more than fourteen years old—shouted back over his shoulder, "Ahh, up yours, old man!" and continued speeding off in pursuit of the first Jet Skier.

John was stunned. "Old man?" he repeated. "What the hell?"

"We should report them to the Coast Guard, right away, John," Becky said excitedly. "They're a real menace."

"Right! You didn't happen to get their license numbers, did you?" John smirked.

John looked off toward the mainland shore. There must have been a dozen or so Jet Skis skirting about, zigging and zagging in and out among one another. "Geez, like a pesky swarm of flies," he said. "Somebody oughta get the fly swatter and teach those kids some manners."

"Let's just forget it, John, and get as far away as possible," Becky replied nervously.

Once they reached an open area of the bay that seemed right, John trimmed the throttle and let the boat coast to a stop. Putting the engine in idle he looked around to get his bearings, triangulating off known distant landmarks. Best he could tell they were somewhere near the mouth of Great Egg Harbor River. The nearest point of land appeared to be Beesley's Point, on the south side of the river's inlet.

"Looks like a good spot," John said. "So, you want me to go first?"

Becky looked up and removed her sunglasses. "Yes, by all means. You must show me how it's done."

Becky went into the cabin to retrieve the jar of sun block. From inside, she shouted back to John, "Hey, John. I'm getting a whiff of that fuel smell, again. Did you ever check out what was causing it?"

She emerged from the cabin with the sun block. "Did you hear what I just said?"

John was down off the bridge now on the aft deck getting his life jacket and water skis in order. "Yes, I heard you," John finally answered, somewhat annoyed. He wasn't annoyed with Becky, but with himself, for not checking the source of the leak. "Jesus! I forgot all about that leak," he said.

"Well, what should we do?" Becky asked.

John thought a moment. "Not much we can do about it now," he said finally. "Just make sure the bilge fan keeps running to clear any vapors that might build up. Seems to be okay as long as we're moving. So…let's just keep moving."

John had already secured the nylon ski rope to a cleat on the transom and was now proceeding to deploy the portable ladder off the starboard gunnel.

"Here, let me get in the water, then you hand me the skis. Okay?"

Once in the water things started to go more smoothly. Becky took to the helm and eased the boat forward to get the ski line taught. When John signaled that he was ready, some thirty yards behind the boat, Becky gunned the engine. John braced himself. Then, just as the rope became taught, he stood up, a bit wobbly at first, but soon gained control and assumed an upright position. *Piece of cake! Now for the fun part!* Shifting his weight and repositioning the plane of his skis, he started experimenting with turns, first to the right, then to the left, in a lazy S-pattern. But when he tried to negotiate the boat's wake for the first time, he lost his balance and took a spill. *Ker-splash!* Becky saw him fall and immediately throttled down and turned the boat around, dragging the rider-less ski robe behind. As she slowly passed by John, bobbing up and down like a cork in the water, he hollered out, "Hey, that was fun! You really gotta try it!"

John made several more runs until he was feeling fairly confident and in control of his turns. Becky then swung the boat sharply around, as John accelerated in a wide arc away from the boat, sending him into choppier waters than before. He was handling it pretty well until something bit him on his left arm: a large greenhead fly. Releasing his right hand to swat the fly he lost his grip and took a hard dive.

"Son-of-a-bitch fly!" he blurted out just before going down.

As Becky came along side to pick him up, he called out, "Okay, I think it's your turn now. I need to take a breather."

Becky secured the ladder over the gunnel and John climbed on board to trade places with Becky. Donning her life jacket, Becky climbed down into the water and took hold of the ski rope handle for the first time.

"Go easy, hon," she called out, squinting as she faced directly into the sun.

John did go easy at first, and Becky was up and skiing after only three tries. John picked up the pace a bit at a time until she finally found herself skimming comfortably over the water at twenty knots. As she gained confidence, at one point she released a hand to wave back at John, hit some choppy water, and lost her balance. "Ahhh!" she squealed as she took a most ungraceful fall into the bay.

As John circled around and came along side of her, she was still coughing and clearing the water from her eyes. He laughed and gave her a piece of advice. "Ya gotta let go of the rope when you feel yourself falling. Otherwise, it'll just keep dragging you through the water."

"Now you tell me," she complained. "Well, I think I've had enough for one day. Not bad for a beginner, huh?" Bobbing up and down in the water, she turned her head toward the southwest. "Anyway, it looks like we're in for some bad weather. And I can feel the water getting choppier out here."

John looked to the southwest, where dark banks of clouds were beginning to pile up on the horizon. "Yeah, I think you're right. Here let me help you up."

John took Becky's hand and helped her back up the ladder.

"Aren't you going to bring the ladder in?" she asked.

"Nah, not just yet. I'd like to get one more run in."

"Aw, come on, John. I think we've had enough for one day," Becky protested.

"Just one more run, hon," John pleaded.

Boys will be boys. After a quick lunch, and ignoring the admonishments of their elders to wait two hours before going back in the water, the two young Jet Ski riders were back on their powered skis and taking to the water.

"Let's go further out this time," the fourteen-year-old boy challenged his younger companion.

"I don't know," the younger boy replied as he mounted his black and gold Jet Ski. "The water's getting kinda choppy out there. Maybe we should stay closer to shore."

"Aw, don't be a pussy," the older boy teased. "Just stay close behind me. I know what I'm doin'."

Both boys now had their helmets on, and were ready for action.

"Oh, all right," the younger boy gave in. He didn't like being called a pussy, even though he didn't fully know what that meant.

"Okay, let's play follow the leader," the fourteen-year-old commanded. "Everything I do, you gotta do. Get it?"

The older boy, piloting his Jet Ski, the *Hornet*, gunned its engines and was off in a flash. In no time at all he was a good hundred yards off Beesley's Point before the younger boy in the black and gold Jet Ski could even react.

John bobbed up and down in the water after taking a particularly spectacular spill on his skis. It happened so fast, that even he waited too long to let go of the rope handle, making for a powered entry into the water. As he resurfaced he sought to regain his bearings and clear the water from his eyes and ears, and didn't notice right away that the boat had stopped moving. After a few moments, when the boat didn't come alongside him, he finally turned and saw Becky waving to him from the aft deck of the boat, sitting dead in the water about fifty yards away. She was shouting something, but he couldn't make it out. Both his ears were water clogged.

Finally his ears cleared, and he was able to make out some of the words: "…engine won't start…smell fumes…."

"What?!" John shouted back. "Did you try the bilge fan?"

Becky waved her arms and shouted back, "Won't start…a blinking red light on dashboard ."

John figured he'd have to swim back to the boat on his own.

"Okay. Hold on tight, babe. I'll be right there."

The younger boy on the black and gold Jet Ski maintained a tight distance behind his friend on the *Hornet* as he tried desperately to keep control over his Jet Ski through the increasingly choppy waters. He hollered out to his friend, "Slow down, Jeff! It's getting too rough!" But his words were lost in the stiff breeze of the open water.

In 1982, the design of most Jet Skis forced the rider to stand up as he or she rode. The sit-down and tandem seat designs would follow some years later. If the rider were to fall off, a safety mechanism would immediately shut down the engine. Of course, the laws of physics dictated that the ski would continue to travel at its current speed until it finally came to a stop in the water—or collided with another object.

The younger boy was following so closely behind his friend that he had difficulty seeing what lay directly ahead, and the spray from the *Hornet* covering the young boy's helmet visor impaired his vision even further. He did catch a glimpse now and then of what appeared to be a boat lying directly ahead in the water. He shouted out, "Ya gotta turn, Jeff! Gotta turn!"

Suddenly, the *Hornet* made a sharp turn to the left. The younger boy in the trailing Jet Ski now found himself heading directly toward the starboard side of a 27-foot cabin cruiser sitting dead in the water, less than ten yards away. A woman, standing in the aft deck and leaning against the transom, was waving her arms and looking astern, seemingly preoccupied with something else in the water. Having seen the first Jet Ski pass her on her left, she was unaware of the second Jet Ski, which was fast closing on the boat from about fifty degrees off starboard bow, placing it outside her field of vision. Confronted with this situation, the young boy had to make an instant decision. But he froze, and simply shouted, "Look out!" Just then his Jet Ski hit a piece of choppy water and became airborne. The young boy lost his grip on the handles and sailed off into the air, making a very hard but safe landing in the water. Traveling close to forty knots, the Jet Ski continued airborne toward the boat.

As John was swimming back toward the boat, he could see two Jet Skis fast approaching from the right, and recognized them as the same two he and Becky had encountered earlier in the day. As the Jet Skis sped toward the boat, he became concerned and stopped swimming, shouting out to Becky, "Look out, babe! Look behind you!"

Becky put her hands up to her ears trying to make out his words. Suddenly, the first Jet Ski swung quickly to port, narrowly missing the boat. Becky turned with a start as the Jet Ski sped past her.

John couldn't believe what happened next. As the first Jet Ski peeled off, he now saw the second Jet Ski soaring rider-less through the air directly toward the rear of the boat. He shouted out, "Becky! Watch out!"

From that point on everything seemed to play out in slow motion. John watched helplessly as the Jet Ski crashed down through the aft starboard gunnel and bulkhead, ripping into the rear deck where Becky was standing. Becky never knew what hit her. Struck at the knees she was tossed high up into the air, like a rag doll, spinning twice in the air before coming down on the deck out of view behind the wrecked Jet Ski, which came to rest half imbedded into the boat's aft deck just over the engine compartment.

"Nooo!" John shouted out in disbelief. He took a mouthful of bay water and gulped, nearly choking, and began swimming like he never swam in his life. The adrenaline set his heart racing, the blood pounding in his water-clogged ears almost deafening. Even so, for all his efforts, he felt like he was swimming through molasses.

"I've got...to get...to her! Just...get there. She'll be...okay," he kept repeating to himself between strokes and breaths.

Next, the most horrible thing happened. Something he could never have imagined in his worst nightmare. Swimming hard and bearing down on the boat, just yards away now, the muted sounds of splash and heartbeat were broken by a loud *Woomph!* and then a sudden blast of hot air. Startled, he looked up in horror to see the rear of the boat suddenly engulfed in a great ball of flame. John couldn't believe his eyes. How could this be happening? With one great burst of energy he shouted out: "Oh my God! No! Oh my God!?" He shouted till his voice cracked and he could shout no more.

"Becky! My Becky! I'll save you! Please, just stay there! I'll save you!

*****

The hostess at the Crab Fest restaurant glanced up at the clock on the wall. It was 8 p.m. Looking down at her reservation list, she crossed off the entry for *John and Becky – 7:00 p.m. table for two,* then motioned to the bus boy. The bus boy nodded and went over to the table by the window, snuffed out the candle, and began clearing the table.

John was not able to save Becky that day. He was never even able to get onto the boat before it became fully engulfed in flames, and was forced to watch in horror as his one true love was consumed by the floating inferno. The papers simply reported it as "a freak marine accident," and the coroner's report was never able to affix the exact cause of death. Did Becky die as a result of the impact with the Jet Ski, or from the fire? That may have put some closure on the tragedy for John. After all, if it was death by trauma, then getting back to the boat to save her from the fire would not have mattered, right? And the guilt he carried all these years—for failing to tend to the leaky fuel system—may have been assuaged to some degree. As it was, he blamed himself for the entire thing. If only he had taken the time to fix the fuel leak. If only he hadn't insisted on one last ski run in choppy waters with bad weather closing in. If only...if only....

For months following the accident John was plagued every night with nightmares, including the *woman-on-the-burning-boat dream* which had now returned to haunt him after so many years. Initially, he sought distraction in litigation, striking out with a team of lawyers against the makers of the Jet Skis, the boat manufacturer, and even the boys' parents. But that only delayed his inevitable decline and did little to smother the guilt that festered within him. He became depressed, couldn't sleep. Test patterns and infomercials on TV became his best friends. At his wit's end, he finally sought the psychiatric help his mom and dad had insisted upon. The doctor, and certainly his parents, meant well, of course, but to John, the doctor's words remained hollow and trite, never really hitting home; so he switched doctors, not once but two, three times In the end the only thing that seemed to work for John was to take a pick and a shovel to the events of that day and bury them deep in his subconscious. John never set foot on another boat. His Nikon camera remained in its camera case, locked in a desk drawer in his study, untouched, a relic of this tragic history.

John rarely discussed the details of the event with anyone outside his immediate family. His anguish eventually drove him to seek escape from the familiar places and things that tied him to her memory, to get as far away from home as possible. California and GenAvance offered a convenient retreat and it would be years before he returned to New Jersey. In more recent years he avoided the subject altogether, having succeeded, he thought, in burying it deep inside. Even his good friends, Bob and Katie, were unaware of the tragic event and its impact on John's life.

The only thing most people knew about John was that he was once engaged, that things somehow didn't work out, and he now lived alone in a large, restored Victorian house in the middle of historic Haddonfield, devoted to his life's work—most people, that is, except Jennifer Dupree Brady, his good friend and confidante from Thousand Oaks. She knew the anguish he suffered, for she shared a similar pain, having just lost her parents in that fatal airline crash.

Chapter 15

1999
Sunday, 12 September
South Jersey

5:00 a.m. John was up before dawn to do his six-mile run through Pennypack Park. Before leaving the house he set the coffee pot timer to start brewing at 5:45, giving him plenty of time to complete his run and return to the aroma of freshly brewed coffee.

On the table, he had Bob Fenwick's day planner opened to Saturday, July 3. There was only one entry for the day, written in large bold letters: FISHING TRIP! Beneath this entry was the name and cell phone number of the fishing boat captain he was to meet in Fortescue, New Jersey, and the name of his boat.

Captain George Davies
609-783-1882
The Greyhound

Just this past Friday, John had spoken with Captain Davies who gave him detailed directions to Fortescue's state marina, where The *Greyhound* was docked. John made up a story about wanting to see the boat and talk about possibly scheduling a fishing party for himself and some friends. He told the captain he would like to come down Sunday morning to discuss it.

"You came highly recommended by my friend, Bob Fenwick," John had said, waiting for a response. "You took him out on the bay over the Fourth of July weekend. He said you knew just where the fish were bitin'."

"Bob Fenwick, you say?" Captain Davies repeated, pausing. Then, suddenly connecting a face with the name, "Oh, Bob! Yeah, Bob's a regular customer of mine. Only, haven't seen him much this summer. Come to think of it, don't reckon he's been down at all since the fourth. Is he okay?"

"Oh, sure! Bob's doin'…just fine. Just been…very busy, I guess." John was forced to lie.

"Well, tell him ol' Captain Davies was askin' for him."

"Oh, I sure will," John replied, trying to sound sincere.

Now, standing in the kitchen on this sunny Sunday morning in his running shorts and tank top, a towel draped about his neck, John took a small pocket notebook from the kitchen desk drawer and copied the pertinent information from Bob's day planner before setting out for Pennypack Park. He wanted to be on the road by 7:00 a.m., giving himself plenty of time to cover the fifty or so miles to Fortescue by nine o'clock.

After returning from his run, he downed a cup of coffee, jumped in the shower, shaved, and dressed, choosing his favorite khaki cargo pants with the large double-thigh pockets that snapped closed and a navy-blue polo jersey with a single breast pocket for his sunglasses.

Back in the kitchen, John poured himself another cup of coffee and fixed himself a four-egg omelet with fresh diced tomatoes and mushrooms. No cheese, thank you. That's when he noticed the missed call and voice mail message alert on his cell phone.

"Hmm. Must've called while I was in the shower."

It was the captain: "Hi, John. This is Captain George Davies," the recorded message began. The connection wasn't very good, with lots of static and background noise. "I've been trying to reach you since yesterday, but have been out of cell phone range most of the time. Sorry for the late notice. Listen, there's been a change in plans. I had to move my boat up river to Cohansey Mar-…" Just then the signal became weak and began to break up. A few seconds later it returned. "…me a call when you get this message. I'll give you new directions. Hope we can link up. Talk t'ya soon. Bye." *Click*.

John decided to use his landline phone hanging on the kitchen wall to dial the captain's number. He didn't want to take any chances of losing the connection. The phone rang once, twice, three times, and then…

"Hello! George Davies here," said the voice at the other end.

John's face brightened. "Well, good morning, Captain. This is John Weston getting back to you. I got your message about the change in plans, but had some trouble hearing the rest."

"Right! The connections aren't always good down here by the bay. Anyway, what I want to say is, I don't plan to be in Fortescue today. I had to move my boat further up the coast to Cohansey Marina. Do you know where that is?"

John laughed. "Are you kidding? I don't even know how to spell it! You better give me directions."

"Okay," the captain laughed. "Got a pencil?"

John grappled with the kitchen desk drawers, looking for something to write with. He wondered why the captain had to move his boat at the last minute. What was he trying to hide? Something he didn't want John to see at Fortescue? Something that may shed some light on Bob's illness and strange behavior? Oh well, maybe he would just have to make a second trip to Fortescue after he met with the captain at—what was the name of that place again? Cohand-Sea or something? John finally found a ballpoint pen and reached for his notebook.

"Okay, Captain. Shoot!"

"Right! Here we go." The captain let out a big sigh, which came across over the phone as annoying windblown static—he was one of those people who ate the mouthpiece when talking on the phone. "Since you already know how to get to Fortescue from Millville, let me just tell you how to get to the Cohansey Marina from there. That's Cohansey: C-O-H-A…"

"Hey, don't worry about the spelling!" John interrupted impatiently, "Just give the directions to me straight."

"Sure, okay. Whatever you say, boss," the captain replied, sounding a little miffed. "Well, first thing, instead of making the left turn onto Cedarville Road out of Millville, ya wanna continue west on Route 49 for another ten miles or so to Bridgeton. Stay on Route 49 all the way through Bridgeton, following the signs to Salem."

John wrote quickly, trying to keep up, not knowing how long the phone connection was going to last. "Okay, got it. So, go west out of Bridgeton to…where?"

"After crossing a small bridge over the Cohansey River in the center of town, you'll go about…oh, less than a mile and you'll see a sign on the left directing you to Greenwich. That would be Bridgeton-Greenwich Road, or Route 607, I think."

"Okay, left on Greenwich-Bridgeton Road. Got it," John repeated.

"Right!" The captain chuckled. "I mean, *left*. You just want to stay on Greenwich-Bridgeton Road heading south. This will take you into the back country. Roads aren't too well marked in these parts."

"Okay, gotcha," John confirmed.

Just then John's pen began to skip and run out of ink as the captain continued. "…then, after about six miles you'll come to a T-intersection. You'll wanna make a right at the intersection. I'm not sure the name of the road. I think it's …Great Street, or something like that. Anyway, the area is pretty desolate around there, just a few old vacant houses and some low-lying marshes…"

"Wait a minute, George! Slow down! I gotta find another pen. This one isn't writing. Hold it a sec."

Rummaging through a useless collection of used pens in the kitchen desk drawer, John finally located a new flair tip still in its package and ripped it open, momentarily losing his grip on the phone. Okay, fine now.

"Go ahead, George. I'm back again."—picking up where he left off— "So, I make a right at the T-intersection with Great Street…"

"…and take a left at Bacons Neck Road," the captain continued, "just past the ruins of an old brick building. Like I said, there's not much around there anymore."

"Whoa! Wait a minute, George. Can you repeat that? Left on Baconek just past stone ruins…"

"Just stay on Bacons Neck Road, which takes you south toward the bay."

"South on Baconek to the bay," John repeated as he scribbled down the words.

"But, when you come to…"—the signal began to break up—"…you wanna hang a left. This will take you on out past some cornfields. After about a mile, just where the road bends to the right, you make another left on…(more static)…'arbor Road. That'll take you straight to the marina. Can't miss it!" George concluded.

"Wait a minute!" John asked desperately. "Where do I make that first left?"

"…What's that you're sayin', John? You're breaking up…" was all John could make out.

"Listen, George. I think I have enough information to get me to the general area. How 'bout I just call you when I get close. You can give me final directions then."

"…final directions…when?" George sounded confused.

"I said, I'll call you when I get into the area," John shouted into the phone.

"Okay," George replied. "But I'm only going to be there until twelve noon. Then I gotta…(*more static*)…for the rest of the day. Won't be getting back till very late."

"Fine," John concluded. "I'll be there way before noon."

"Okay," George said. "See you when you get here."

"Right. Thanks, George."

John hung up, cursing modern technology under his breath. He took a few moments to clean up his notes before putting the notebook in his left pants thigh pocket and his cell phone in the right pocket. He was anxious to hit the road. But before heading out, he grabbed a couple of cold bottles of Gatorade and V-8 juice from the refrigerator and loaded up a soft-walled cooler for the road.

*****

John glanced down at the dashboard clock of his tan Camry as he cruised west on Route 49 out of Millville toward Bridgeton. Just 8:00 a.m. Excellent! He was making good time, and it was a great day for a drive: warm, sunny, and dry. John had turned off the AC and was driving with both front windows open. He had the radio cranked up, playing a remake of *Dream Weaver*, an old Gary Wright hit tune from the seventies.

Reaching Bridgeton, John continued through the center of town and crossed the small bridge passing over the Cohansey River, just as the captain had instructed, although it was more like a creek or stream at this point.

"Must get wider as it flows toward the bay," John figured. Anyway, so far so good and, yup, there was the road sign up ahead, just where the captain said it would be: "Greenwich" pointing left. John made the left turn onto Bridgeton-Greenwich Road and continued south out of town.

Narrowing down to two lanes, the road meandered through the countryside and crisscrossed with other small country roads along the way, taking the names of the towns they connected, like Barrets Mill and Sheppards Mill roads. Slowly, the terrain changed from rolling farms and cultivated fields to undeveloped woods interspersed with low-lying marsh lands. Crossing over a muddy, slow-moving creek, John sensed a larger river to his left through the tree line just beyond the marshes; less than a mile later the road ended abruptly at a T-intersection.

"Must be Great Street," John figured.

He checked his trip odometer: yup, six miles from Bridgeton. Sitting idle at the intersection for several minutes to get his bearings, John reached over and took a bottle of cherry-flavored Gatorade from the cooler, opened it, took a long, cold drink, and set the half-empty open bottle in the console cup holder.

Strange, he thought. The cross road to his front was unusually wide and straight, like a boulevard or main street of a town. The few houses that remained standing suggested a small town, but were in such states of disrepair, he couldn't imagine anyone living in them. With no other traffic and no soul in sight, not even a single bird in flight, a strange, creepy feeling came over him. The town looked like it may have been populated at one time, but now it seemed more like…"a ghost town," he reluctantly admitted.

No living thing, that is, except for…the flies! It was then that John first noticed them, buzzing all around the car, bouncing off the windshield like ping-pong balls, seemingly excited by the presence of a new out-of-town guest. Several flew in through the open window, possibly attracted by the car's cooler interior, or maybe the scent of John's warm body, which, aside from the flies, seemed to be the only living thing for miles around. One of the flies alighted on the steering wheel, just inches from John's face, and he was able to get a real good close-up look at it. These weren't your ordinary houseflies; they were much larger, with huge green heads. Actually, it wasn't the head so much as the two large, compound eyes protruding from the head which gave them their characteristic appearance. John and the fly continued to study each other, like two adversaries staring the other down, seeing who would blink first. Taken literally, of course, that was a contest John was certain to loose—flies have no eyelids!

John drew closer to the fly. "So, are you the one that bit my good friend, Bob and gave him those hallucinations? Or, maybe it was one of your blood sucking relatives."

The fly twitched, perhaps sensing the ire in John's voice; or, more likely, it was his warm breath. Tiring of the game, the fly bolted out the window. John was able to shoo the two remaining flies away, but it wasn't easy. Unlike a regular housefly, this green-headed variety didn't take to gentle persuasion and John almost had to physically push the flies out the window. Once he had rid himself of the last of them, he rolled up the windows and turned on the AC.

John rechecked his notebook for directions: "Right turn at the T-intersection with Great Street." Looking up, he scanned right, then left. "Hmm, seems to me the water should be to the left," he argued with himself. "Oh, well, the captain says go right, so I'll go right," he finally decided.

John put the car in gear and made a slow right-hand turn onto Great Street. From this new perspective, the view was strikingly serene and peaceful. Proceeding slowly down this especially wide country boulevard John no longer felt alone, somehow. Venerable old sycamore and oak trees, silent sentinels of a bygone era, lined both sides of the street for as far as he could see—about three-quarters of a mile before the road turned and disappeared to the right around a stone wall fence. Set off on either side of the street were the dilapidated remains of old, abandoned farmhouses and the scattered remnants of crumbling, stone foundations overgrown with prickly briars, honeysuckle, and young saplings, all seeking to reclaim the ground as their own.

Coming up on the right was a two-and-a-half-story red brick building, still standing, but inexorably succumbing to the effects of time, weather, and neglect.

"Looks colonial in style," John observed. "Must've been quite a handsome mansion in its time."

Upon closer inspection, John noticed the colored patterns in the brickwork were not the result of weathering, but deliberate patterns worked into the brick façade by the original builder.

Not too far beyond the brick mansion, set back off the right side of the road, were the hollow shell remains of another old stone building. He thought he could make out the word "TAVERN" over the front door.

"Business doesn't look too good," he mused. But the humor was lost on the buzzing flies. The tavern stood opposite a T-intersection with another road which branched off to the left, its street sign post almost completely overgrown with vines, but drawing closer John was finally able to make out the name of the street: "Bacons Neck Road."

"All right!" Checking his notebook one more time: "Left on Baconek Rd past stone ruins." John slowed down to make the left. As he did, he read off the name of the wide boulevard from which he had just turned: "Ye Greate Street."

"Okay. So, it's Bacons Neck, not Baconek. And Ye Greate Street, not Great Street," he said. "Ye gads! Great names! Must go back to colonial times."

John was feeling good, now, humming a little tune as he continued south on Bacons Neck Road toward the Delaware Bay, just as the captain had instructed. Leaving the remnants of the ghost town behind, a small bridge and causeway took him over a narrow tidal creek and adjoining freshwater marsh. Marsh elder, wild rice, and other late-season annuals presented their floral displays among the scattered tussocks of matted switchgrass, as dense stands of tall reeds stood guard at the water's edge. A female swamp sparrow swooped across the road, followed by several more of her species as they disappeared into the safe cover of the marsh's dense vegetation.

John glanced down at his notebook again, but had trouble deciphering the next few lines. He recalled that this was when the cell phone connection with Captain Davies was beginning to break up. He might just have to trust his sense of direction from here on out. He couldn't be too far from the marina, now.

Coming to another T-intersection—Tyndall Island Road—John decided to turn right. Driving on, he continued to read from his notes: "'Make left (?) toward the bay.'"

"So, where do I make that…?" Before he could finish his thought another road appeared to the left. "Bay Side Road," the sign post read. "This must be it," he said hopefully.

Taking the left turn, he headed down a long stretch of road which *seemed* to be heading in the right direction toward the bay. Passing some open fields of corn, he remembered George saying something about cornfields, so he figured he must be heading in the right direction.

John was hopeful, now. He opened the windows halfway so he could hear any signs of marine activity, but the open cornfields soon gave way to tall reeds and marsh grass; growing thick on both sides of the road, they served as a natural sound barrier, muffling all sounds near and far. The muted hum of the car's engine and the peel of tires against the rough asphalt road were all John could hear. The road narrowed, and John became preoccupied dodging the pot holes which were becoming more numerous. Suddenly, a break in the vegetation on the left revealed yet another road; a crude sign was posted displaying a hand-painted left-turn arrow pointing the way: "TO FISHING PIER."

"Fishing Peer equals marina. Sounds right," John figured. He took a chance and followed the sign, but this road was even more primitive than the one he'd left: just a packed dirt surface with loose sand and gravel, becoming increasingly narrow, with basketball-tall common reeds and cattails in ever denser stands crowding both sides of the road. All he could hear now were the sounds of insects buzzing about in great swarms: dragonflies, wasps, and yes, those big greenhead flies! The air became warm and soupy, filled with the ripe, fetid scent of decomposing fish, telling him the bay was not far off.

Just then, something up ahead caught his attention off the side of the road, so he pulled up alongside and stopped to get a closer look. It was a square cage of some sort, framed in wood and covered with insect screening, measuring about two-and-a-half-feet on a side and about one-and-a-half-feet high, set up on four legs about two feet off the ground. On top were two smaller cake box shaped containers located at diagonally opposite corners of the cage, made of a clear Plexiglas-like plastic. Within each container was a small inverted cone fashioned from insect screening, with a hole at the top, like an inverted ice-cream cone with the point bitten off.

Inside the larger cage there were several flies buzzing about. The smaller cake box containers, however, contained many winged insects too numerous to count. Most, or all, of them appeared to be alive. A sign posted over the cage read:

> Please Do Not Disturb
> Agricultural Extension Service and
> Cook College, Rutgers University
> Experimental Station # 105

"Interesting. Apparently some kind of live insect trap."

John wondered if this might have anything to do with Julie Evert's research. He put the car in park and made some notes in his pocket notebook before continuing down the road.

There was daylight up ahead, now, as the road approached a clearing and a large body of water in the distance.

"At last! The marina!" he said triumphantly, expecting to see signs of human activity. But hope quickly turned to disappointment as he reached the clearing, bringing his car to a dead stop. The tall reeds had given way to low scrubby sedge and cordgrass as he found himself stranded on a small, sandy spit of land jutting out into the bay. A rickety wooden fishing pier continued out over the water for another fifty feet or so, but where was the marina? He was isolated and alone, now—except for the flies!

Looking out across the water he was just able to discern a shoreline on the far side. A large oceangoing container ship came within view, plying a steady course up river, left to right, to deliver its valuable cargo in the ports of Philadelphia or Wilmington. The Delaware River widened gradually as it traced its southerly course to the ocean, so it was difficult to tell exactly where the river ended and the bay began. At this point it measured almost five miles across, so it could might rightly be called the Delaware *Bay*.

Turning off the car's engine, John reached into his pants pocket for his cell phone. "All right, time to call in the cavalry." He punched in the captain's number, accenting each spoken syllable with each digit of the phone number. But there was no connection: "No Service," the phone display read.

John tried dialing again.

Still, no service.

"Dammit!" John snapped as he flipped the lid of his cell phone closed and shoved it back into his pocket. He opened the car door and jumped out, hoping to get his bearings from the vantage point of the fishing pier.

The marsh grass grew thick along the edge of the marsh road, washed by the daily ebb and flow of the tides. Though far removed from the ocean, the brackish and freshwater marshes of the Delaware Bay and its tributaries were influenced in a positive way by the rising and falling tides. Like a beating heart, the tides nourished and maintained all life in the marsh, helping to restore nutrients and oxygen to this delicate ecosystem.

Two years prior, in the summer of 1997, things were not so different. A single, tall blade of switchgrass glistens in the sun, bending under the weight of something foreign coating its surface. A gelatinous mass of tiny eggs, about 500 in number, clings to the long, slender blade, biding its time until the unseen hand of nature triggers the next step. Suddenly, one egg hatches. A small larva exits and falls to the moist soil below. Then another, and another; like corn in a popper, the hatching continues and builds, until most of the small creatures are released. The muted cries of the newly born go unheard by the mother, who has long since departed after laying her batch of eggs many days before. She did her job, now her offspring must fend for themselves.

The first of the newborn larvae burrows into the soft, moist soil, rich in detriment and decaying matter. It is soon joined by its blind siblings, each one groping and burrowing for survival, in search of its first meal. Surprisingly, the abundance of detriment does not pique its appetite. Rather, its desire is for the living. It hungers for fresh meat!

Our first newborn sets out in search of what it needs. Foraging through the surface muck and wet vegetation it finally comes upon a small earthworm. It attacks! Viciously tearing into the worm's flesh, it tenaciously clings to its prey as the worm seeks to disengage and wiggle free. At last, with its hunger satisfied, it lets the dying worm go.

The newborn continues to feed and grow over the months that follow: snails, worms, insect larvae, and other small invertebrates all enjoy a place on its menu. It does not discriminate or play favorites. Coming upon much younger and smaller larvae of its own kind, it does not hesitate; its hunger must be placated, even to the point of cannibalism. There is no moral choice to make. The choice is survival, pure and simple.

With winter fast approaching, the larva continues to gorge. Plump and sated, it burrows deep into the mud to avoid the frost, hunkering down until late spring or summer of the following year. It is June, 1998, when our firstborn emerges to enjoy another season of foraging and feasting. Many of its sisters and brothers from the brood are entering their next stage of metamorphic existence; but for our select one, the time isn't quite right for this important transition. Its life of fossorial predation continues through the year, as it prepares to overwinter yet another cold season as a larva.

It is now August of the current year, 1999, and the time has finally come for our larva to enter the next stage of its existence. Coming to the surface, it seeks a warm, safe place in which to begin the process of transforming itself from larva to pupa. In this new, transcendent state of slumber, our chosen one is slowly reborn, emerging at last from its pupal case as a young adult female greenhead fly.

Our young adult greenhead fly, *Tabanus nigrovittatus*, looks out onto a previously unseen world through a pair of large compound eyes. Having among the largest eyes in the insect world, this is what gives the fly its characteristic "green head" appearance. Once her wings are dry, she instinctively takes flight into the deep blue summer sky. She now has a new mission and purpose in life that supplants all that went before: to mate and propagate her species by laying as many eggs over the course of her short adult lifespan as possible. This will mean laying one to two egg batches per week, each numbering up to 1,000 eggs, over the next three to four weeks. This is all the time nature has given her. Finding a male fly with which to mate is her first task. This is not difficult. The male flies are ready and waiting.

The first batch of eggs comes easily. As a new adult female fly, she had emerged from her pupa case with a built-in reserve of protein sufficient to guarantee a successful first batch, supplemented with a normal diet of nectar giving her the energy she needs to subsist. However, for the next and all subsequent batches, she would have to change her diet. In addition to nectar, she would need a good source of protein to guarantee the eggs' proper development. For her next batch of eggs, then, she would choose to feed on the blood of an animal. Her preference: the blood of a warm-blooded animal; a horse, cow, deer…or man.

Our young tabanid greenhead—let's call her "Tabby"—now ventures out beyond the boundary of her marsh home, for the first time in pursuit of a warm meal of blood. An adjoining pasture provides a promising hunting ground. Her keen eyes are attracted by the movement of a large, dark object lumbering across the field. Zeroing in on the object, Tabby picks up the scent of carbon dioxide contained in the exhaled breath of her intended prey. This excites her all the more, driving and directing her toward her target. She is soon joined by others of her kind, all bent on a similar mission.

Suddenly, one among them is snatched out of the air in mid-flight. Tabby looks on as the struggling fly is carried away in the clutches of a slightly larger flying intruder, a black insect with yellow markings on its abdomen. The struggling soon ends as the venom from the insect's sting takes deadly effect. It is the horse guard wasp, patrolling the green pasture in search of greenheads to take back to its nest to feed its hungry brood. But, Tabby shows little interest in this natural predator, for she hails from a chosen bloodline of tabanids which have somehow become immune to the sting of the horse guard wasp. Generations of behavior modification through natural selection have taught her not to fear the horse guard and, likewise, the horse guard has learned not to waste precious energy on so fruitless a pursuit.

Tabby at last alights on the hind quarters of the large beast. She is about to make her mark when…*swoosh*…like a giant broom she and others are knocked aside by the swish of the giant beast's tail. Persistent in her pursuit, she targets another, safer area: the soft, inner pink flesh of the large beast's ears. Unlike other bloodsucking insects like mosquitoes, which are equipped with sharp, slender proboscides for surreptitiously puncturing the victim's skin, our greenhead must take a more direct, obtrusive approach to bloodletting. Her mouthparts, like tiny serrated scimitars, tear and rip into the animal's flesh, producing a flow of blood which she quickly laps up. The ear of the beast flicks nervously; the beast whinnies, then shakes its large shaggy head, but the fly is not so easily dissuaded. Maintaining her grip, she continues gorging herself on the warm, red, oozing liquid; only when fully satisfied does she fly away, quickly distancing herself from her victim and retreating back into the safe damp domains of her marsh home.

The next egg batch follows within a few days of this meal. A bonus brood of 900 eggs! Nice job, Tabby. But there is no celebrating and precious little time for rest. In a day or two she is again in search of a meal of warm blood.

This time she will lie in wait, allowing the meal to come to her. It is a warm, sunny day in mid-September, 1999. She chooses a shady spot by the side of the marsh road leading to the bay. It is mid-afternoon. A large, dark object approaches from a distance down the road. Slowing down, it comes to rest by the side of the road not far from Tabby. Her senses are alerted by the warm abundance of carbon dioxide belching forth from the rear end of the now still object. Suddenly, a second object emerges from the first. This one has all the markings of a favored life form and a source of warm blood. The greenhead takes flight, quickly sizing up her prey. Approaching from behind, she targets a bare patch of warm, sweaty flesh at the nape of the neck, just above the blue polo shirt covering her prey. With surgical precision she alights and makes her strike. Unlike her first prey, this flesh is much softer, with little hair covering to obstruct her efforts. This time she goes deep, gouging out a large pocket of flesh from her victim. The blood oozes profusely, surprising even the fly. Urgently, she laps up the nourishment before her victim can react to the pain of the bite. She makes a quick escape, just as the heavy hand of her victim strikes back. It's a clean getaway.

"Son-of-a-bitch!" John snapped as he slapped the back of his neck with his right hand. "One of those damn greenhead flies got me real good!"

He looked down at the palm of his hand spotted with his own fresh blood.

"Bloody viscous little vampire!"

John found the British expletive entirely fitting. Taking a clean, white rag from the back seat of his car he wiped his hand, and then gently daubed the bite on the back of his neck. To his surprise, the bite was bleeding quite profusely. Taking the rag with him, he walked out onto the pier as far as he felt he could safely go, turned around and scanned the shoreline for signs of a marina. No luck. But looking south he did see what appeared to be the wide mouth of a river emptying into the bay.

"Must be the Cohansey."

John followed the progress of a small sailboat as it slowly made its way up the river and disappeared beyond the first bend.

"The marina must be up river a bit," he figured. He decided to head back up the road and to try to follow the coastline as well as he could toward the river. But with these winding, crisscrossing back country roads, it was easy to get lost, and without a good map, John's sense of direction was poor at best.

Suddenly, John felt a sense of vertigo and had to shift his weight to brace himself from falling. *Must be the pier moving with the tide*, he thought. Regaining his balance, he tested his legs as he walked slowly back from the pier onto solid land, then picked up his pace to a slow jog to help clear his head as he headed back to the car. Getting behind the wheel, he tossed the bloodied rag on the seat next to him, grabbed the bottle of Gatorade and took several long refreshing gulps. He started the engine, turned the car around, and headed out in the direction he had come, anxiously backtracking over the same narrow road that brought him to this isolated place.

When John reached Bay Side Road with the posted "Fishing Pier" sign, he stopped to make some notes and gather his thoughts. That's when he first noticed a small white spot appearing at the center of his field of vision. Imperceptible at first, the spot slowly grew, becoming larger and brighter, eventually obscuring the words he was writing. John blinked and rubbed his eyes, but the spot continued to grow until it became a blinding white light that consumed his entire field of vision. At that point, a loud, unfamiliar voice suddenly reverberated in his head:

"Curses! You must go back and save her!"

The voice was real, not simply imagined: low, growling, almost menacing, at least that's how it seemed. No sooner had the words been spoken, his normal vision returned.

"What the hell was that?"

He checked the car radio. It was definitely turned off.

"Okay, someone's gotta be playing tricks," he said as he threw open the door, got out, and looked around. "Who's there?" he shouted. "Who said that?"

He could feel a headache coming on, the onset of one of those migraines he used to get as a kid when he ate certain foods. He began massaging his forehead and the orbits of his eyes as he circled the car, looking for a loud speaker hidden in the bulrushes, or a van parked nearby with its speakers blaring, but there was nothing that could explain where that booming voice had come from—and that blinding white light, what was that all about? It had only lasted a few seconds, and then was gone. *Maybe an aura that precedes a migraine, or some form of ocular migraine*, he thought. Meanwhile, his heart continued to pound in his chest, his temples throbbing with each beat.

John remained standing there, leaning against the open car door, massaging his temples, when he noticed a boy on a bicycle approaching in the distance, heading south on Bay Side Road. Amazing! The first sign of human life since entering this godforsaken little corner of the world! The boy looked to be twelve or thirteen years old, wore a baseball cap and knapsack decorated with assorted fish hooks and lures, and had several fishing rods attached to the basket of his bike.

John called out to the boy. "Hey, nice day for fishing!"

"Yeah, I'm gonna try out my new rod down on the bay," the boy shouted back in a prepubescent squeaky voice. "How're the fish bitin'?" he asked, assuming John was returning from an early morning fishing trip of his own.

"I don't know. I'm just...sightseeing," John replied.

By now the boy had drawn up alongside of John's car. John looked around nervously as he asked the boy, "Tell me, son. Coming down this road, you didn't happen to...hear any voices, did you? Like maybe from a loud speaker or car radio or something."

The boy looked puzzled. "Nuh-uh," he replied.

John checked the road again in both directions. Not a car in sight. So where was that annoying humming sound coming from?

"Tell me, son, where are you from? Do you live nearby?" John asked.

The hum grew louder, sounding more like a buzzing swarm of flies now.

The boy twisted on his seat, pointing north up Bay Side Road in the direction he had come. "I live about three miles back thataway."

"You mean, Greenwich?" John pursued. He stuck a finger in his right ear and wiggled it, like someone trying to dislodge a piece of wax, or clear water from his ear.

"No, not Greenwich," the boy replied incredulously. "Nobody hardly lives there, anymore! I live in North Greenwich. Some people call it Othello. Up Bacons Neck Road and make a left on Great Street. It's about a mile or so up the road from there."

"Oh, I see," John said. "Past the old stone tavern?"

"Oh, sure, way beyond that," the boy replied. He looked at John and the tan Camry with a measure of suspicion: an obvious out of towner.

"So, Mister…if you're not fishing, what are you doing around these parts?" he challenged.

The buzzing in John's ears reached a crescendo, crowding out all other sounds. "What did you say?" he asked anxiously.

"I said what are you doing around here? You seem…like…lost or something."

"Well, I'm somewhat embarrassed to admit it," John replied hesitantly, not hearing everything the boy had said, "but actually…I think I'm lost. I was looking for the Cohansey Marina. Can you tell me how to find it?"

John was almost shouting now, just so he could hear himself above the din inside his head. The boy didn't quite know what to make of it, but he answered the best he could.

"Well, you go back on Bay Side Road and make a left on Tyndall Island Road…no, make that a right," the boy corrected himself. He began to act out his directions, moving his hands and arms in exaggerated motions, the way people do when trying to adjust to someone who is hard of hearing. "Keep going about a mile," he continued. "You'll pass some cornfields. Just before the road bends to the right you'll see a sign for the marina on your left. Make a left and keep going."

All John could hear was "…go back on Bay Side Road and make a left on Tyndall Island Road…" After that the boy's words were drowned out by the swarm of flies in John's head and all he could see were the boy's lips moving, and his arms flailing about as he gave directions.

John put his head down in the palms of his hands and tried to shake off the buzzing hum of the flies. When he looked up again, the boy was gone, already a hundred yards down the dirt road heading in the direction of the fishing pier.

John got back in his car and grabbed the open bottle of Gatorade. Within seconds of taking a long swig, the buzzing began to subside, but did not disappear altogether.

"I've got to get some help," he mumbled weakly. "The marina may still be my best bet." Or maybe that town. What was its name? Othello? North Greenwich? Maybe they have a doctor.

John put the car in gear and headed north on Bay Side Road and took the first left onto Tyndall Island Road, which was all he could remember of the boy's directions. Opening the car window he stepped on the gas, hoping the breeze would reinvigorate him. It worked for a little awhile. The road curved to the right as it merged with another smaller road coming in from the left. Coming to a fork in the road, John beared right onto Old Mill Road, which seemed to be heading toward a more populated area. The humming and buzzing sounds slowly returned to his head as he began to feel a sense of vertigo, finding it harder and harder to concentrate on what he was doing, and why he was doing it. He blew right through a stop sign at the next cross intersection. Fortunately, there was no one coming the other way. "Gum Tree Corner Road," the sign post read.

"Did I read that right?" he puzzled.

Old Mill Road finally dead-ended at a T-intersection with…Ye Greate Street.

"Ye gads, I'm back on Ye Greate Street!" John exclaimed. "What next?"

Looking around, he appeared to be at the center of a small farming village, but there were no immediate signs of human activity. Sunday morning, everyone was probably in church, or sleeping in. All he knew was he needed to find a doctor. At this point he figured his best bet would be to head back to Bridgeton, where he remembered passing a hospital in the center of that town. But, which way to turn? He decided to go right.

Continuing down Ye Greate Street—north or south, he really didn't know—John left the small village behind and found himself in open country again. A pair of field swallows swooped in from the left, giving John a start as they barely missed his vehicle. Another half mile or so, the road made an abrupt ninety degree turn to the right, continued a short while, and then turned just as abruptly to the left, resuming its original southward direction. The wheels of John's Camry squealed as he negotiated the sharp turns, almost colliding with a low stone fence bordering a cemetery which ran along the left side of the road.

"Not ready for that just yet!" he vowed.

After the second turn, the road widened and became more familiar. This was the same wide boulevard on which he had initially entered town, coming in from the opposite direction! There were the same stately oaks and sycamores lining the street, with their gently swaying overhead boughs creating a shady canopy of forest green for as far as he could see, and up ahead, about three hundred yards on the left, the stone ruins of that old tavern!

"Well, how 'bout that! I've gone in a complete circle, back to where I started!" John exclaimed. "But that's okay. At least I know where I am, now!"

The buzzing in John's head was now driving him to distraction, and he felt like he would pass out if he didn't get some nourishment. The tires skidded as John brought his vehicle to an abrupt stop off the side of the road.

"Need...some...juice," he mumbled as he fumbled with the cooler, finally pulling out a fresh cold bottle of V-8 juice and ripping off the lid. But the open bottle slipped from his grasp, spilling half its contents on the seat next to him, as it all seemed to play out in slow motion. Reacting slowly, John picked up the bottle and drank down what remained; then looked down at the mess he'd just made.

"Damn! Don't know if that stain is gonna come out."

He reached for the bloodied rag he had used to wipe his neck and began sopping up the spilled red juice, doing the best he could with what he had.

"Gotta get back...to Bridgeton," he said, trying to focus on the task at hand. But his mind was becoming clouded and more confused and he could barely remember the name of the town. "Just need to go...to the end of this street and turn...left."

As he said this, he noticed something moving from the corner of his eye. There in the distance, about a hundred yards down the road, was an old wooden farm wagon being drawn by a pair of black stallions, moving at a slow, lumbering pace, but coming straight up the road toward him. He squinted hard, trying to make out the details as the wagon passed in and out of the shadows, and could see that each stallion had a distinctive white marking on its face, sort of diamond shaped. Otherwise, they were completely black.

"Handsome beasts," he mumbled to himself.

As he leaned over his steering wheel to get a better look, the wagon emerged from the shadows as it reached the old stone tavern and began a slow turn to its left. John could now make out an old man and woman in the wagon with the old man at the reins. He was wearing a hat, and the old woman had a white shawl draped about her shoulders.

"That looks to be Bacons Neck street...er, road, they're turning down," he said.

Then it dawned on him. People! There are actually people in this town! He laid on the car's horn trying to get their attention, but the man and woman never even looked up, and the horses never missed a step; they just continued making the wide turn onto Bacons Neck Road.

"What the...?" John leaned his head out the car window. "Hey! Can't you hear me? Where can I find a doctor in this town?" he shouted.

But the man and woman remained unmoved. The horses were already out of sight beyond the overgrowth along Bacons Neck Road. However, John was able to get a good look at the old man, who was seated to the right of the woman, just before they and the wagon disappeared around the corner. The man was wearing a three-cornered hat, and his britches ended just below the knees, where his stockings took over.

"Why…he's dressed in a…*colonial* costume!" John suddenly realized. "What is this? A reenactment weekend of some kind? Gotta get to them before they get away."

John received a new burst of energy as he put the car in gear and hit the gas. He reached the old stone tavern in mere seconds, with tires squealing as he made the sharp right-hand turn onto Bacons Neck Road. He had been here before, less than an hour before, though it seemed like days ago.

Looking straight ahead down Bacons Neck Road, now, John was stunned to see that the wagon was no closer to him than it was before. In fact, it was further away than ever, maybe a half mile or so!

"How can that be?"

Completely perplexed, he put the pedal to the floor, kicking up a cloud of dust in hot pursuit of the lumbering farm wagon. John was quickly closing the distance between them when the wagon temporarily disappeared behind a bend in the road to the right. When it came back into view, it was again no closer than before. As John closed the distance once more, the wagon made another turn, this time to the right, taking a road John hadn't noticed before. When he reached the turn, he stopped the car and looked down the road.

The wagon was nowhere to be seen.

John just shook his head. "Can't be!" he said. "Where did it go? It couldn't have just disappeared into…thin air. It's like…I'm chasing a rainbow."

John looked up at the road sign: "Gum Tree Corner Road." He smiled. "Betcha there's gum at the end of this rainbow," he laughed—but not for long. The buzzing in his head had returned and the migraine was getting worse, bringing with it a strong feeling of nausea. He threw open the car door and ran to the ditch on the side of the road and began to vomit, bringing up a mixture of bile and red juice that burned his throat. That made his stomach feel a little better, but now the dizziness and vertigo set in and his neck was beginning to throb where he had been bitten.

Looking south along Bacons Neck Road he saw that he wasn't far from the marshes where the road passes over a small tidal creek, the same route he had taken less than sixty minutes earlier. It seemed so peaceful and inviting then; now, it was ominous and threatening.

But there was something else this time. A great swarm of flying insects had appeared over the marsh, hovering, growing larger and darker like a gathering storm cloud. The cloud began to move, slowly and inexorably, as a single entity with purpose, up Bacons Neck Road, heading straight toward him. He was feeling sick, now, weak and heavy, his legs no longer capable of holding him up. Dropping to his knees, John tried supporting himself with outstretched arms to keep from falling altogether, palms planted face down against the rough asphalt road surface. The buzzing in his head grew louder, but was now mixed with the real buzzing sounds of the approaching swarm. When he looked up again, there must have been a zillion greenhead flies blocking his view of the road. Strange thoughts began to swim through his head. He knew he was losing it. The small white spot now reappeared at the center of his vision; the buzzing became deafening. Gathering all of his remaining strength, he raised his head and opened his eyes. The great swarm was all around him, now, eclipsing the sun, enveloping him in a cold twilight.

"I'm at the eye—the green eye—of a fly storm!" he muttered incoherently.

But strangely, the flies did not attack him. Instead, they simply hovered about him, keeping their distance. John's mind began to drift in and out, the small white spot grew larger, and he now had the sensation of being entombed—entombed in a swarm of flies! But it was now an almost...pleasant, warming sensation, like they were trying to protect him, somehow. Perhaps more cocoon than tomb. By now, his entire field of vision was consumed by the white light, his body seemingly warmed by that same light, when suddenly, in a flash, his arms gave way and—everything was gone!

John didn't know how long he was out. When consciousness did return, daylight was gone, and he found himself standing under a starry night sky in the middle of the same road, looking back from where he'd come—back up Bacons Neck Road. Or, at least, that's where he assumed himself to be. Spatially, things seemed the same, but the details were different somehow. First, the asphalt road surface was gone, replaced with packed earth and random patches of light soil, maybe sand. He looked around. His car was nowhere to be seen, and back toward Ye Greate Street and the town that once was, there were now the soft, flickering lights of human habitation. And the flies, what happened to the flies? They were gone, too. He patted himself down, doing a quick assessment of his physical state. The pain was gone. The buzzing in his head...gone. He suddenly realized what he felt was...great! Never felt better!

As his eyes acclimated to the dark, he realized that the lighter blotches of ground scattered about him were not patches of sand or earth as he had presumed, but patches of snow made brighter now by a gibbous moon on the wane, unveiled from behind a passing bank of clouds. Looking up at a mostly clear night sky, the stars shown especially bright and numerous. The North Star was an easy find, with the Big and Little Dippers pointing the way. Now, looking over his right shoulder into the southeastern sky, he was astounded at what he saw. It was unmistakable. At approximately thirty degrees above the horizon there it was: the constellation of Orion the Hunter, one of the most beautiful and imposing collections of stars in the heavens. The constellation was easily recognizable by the four bright stars forming a large rectangle, and three lesser magnitude stars within, equally spaced and forming a straight line—the well-known "belt" of Orion. No other constellations had so many bright stars. Now, he wished he had his telescope. There was Betelgeuse, the red giant star, marking the hunter's right shoulder—from Orion's perspective looking down; and Rigel, the brilliant blue-white star of Orion's left knee—or hip, depending on how your imagination connects the dots. The question was: what was Orion doing in the summer sky? John knew his stars, and he knew that Orion was a winter constellation. Looking back down at the ground with its patches of snow, it only took a second for things to click in John's mind. It was no longer a sunny afternoon on a later summer day in September. Somehow, he now found himself standing on a dark country road under a winter night sky!

But, if it really was winter, why didn't he feel the cold? And when pockets of old, dry autumn leaves were stirred up and tossed about him by a cold wind, why did he not feel the effects of that same wind? But John did not waste time pondering such things. He needed to find answers to more pressing questions. Like, where was his car? And how was he going to get home?

He decided to head up the road in the direction of the flickering lights. As he set out, he was struck by the ease of movement; he only had to think about moving and his legs would carry him. Not floating in air exactly—he still had to make the effort and move his legs—it was more like pushing a self-propelled lawn mower equipped with power assist; it only goes as fast and as far as you want it to go, but does so with minimum effort on your part. It didn't take him long to get the hang of movement in the new state he found himself.

"Well, if I'm dead, then this must be heaven. 'Cause there sure ain't no snow in the other place!" he reassured himself.

As he continued up the road, the source of the flicking lights became apparent. He was entering a small farming village, consisting mainly of single-family dwellings variously constructed of brick, stone, and wood. The soft, flickering glow of firelight radiated from the windows of many of the homes, giving evidence of a hearth or burning candles within. As he neared the T-intersection up ahead, the homes became more closely and evenly spaced. Straight ahead of him, now, across the intersecting street, he could see a larger stone building, finely built and better lit than the others. As he drew closer he heard the sounds of human activity from within: voices, and the unmistakable sound of a fiddle, the tinkle of glasses banging together. On reaching the street corner, he looked up at the sign post: "Ye Greate Street" and "Bacons Neck Road." Looking across Ye Greate Street it finally dawned on him: this was the same tavern which just this afternoon had lain in ruins. He couldn't believe what he was seeing. All up and down Ye Greate Street the wide boulevard was now lined with fine homes and shops. The corner store to his right was a large emporium of fine merchandise, now closed for the day. Except for the goings-on in the tavern, the town's population had obviously retired for the night. Why, the entire town of Greenwich—the "nobody hardly lives there anymore" town described by the young boy—had somehow, miraculously been restored. Just since this afternoon!

"How can this be?" he wondered aloud.

But then again—looking up at the sky— it was now winter. He tried putting the pieces together. *Maybe I've been out of it for…three months? But, is that even time enough to restore a town?*

John's mind now became confused as he tried to ponder the bigger questions. He had already stopped thinking about locating his car.

As he began to cross the street, he noticed a commotion far up the street to his left. Coming toward him was a group of men, maybe a dozen—no, make that twenty or more—torches lit, obviously intent on a unified purpose. John remained standing in the middle of the street as the mob of men approached. They were close enough now that he could see their faces and make out their features. Many of the men had painted their faces and fixed their hair to resemble, of all things, American Indians on the warpath. A few had their jackets opened at the front exposing their bare chests, decorated with beads and pendants hanging about their necks. The leader among them—John could only assume him to be the leader, as he remained out in front and was encouraging the others to follow—wore a jacket, knee britches and a three-cornered hat, typical for colonial times.

"On to the Market Square!" one of their party shouted.

"Right! And then to the wharf to get the tea," another replied.

"No," the leader shouted back over his shoulder, "the tea is not there."

"So, where shall we find the tea?" another asked from the rear.

"Not to worry," the leader replied, "the tea is in safe hiding not far from here, biding its time in the tailor's wine cellar."

John remained transfixed as the mob came straight at him, now, appearing not to take even the slightest notice of him. Like a small stone in a fast-moving stream, the men simply flowed about him on both sides. It even seemed that one or two of them walked straight through him, like he was invisible and lacked substance altogether!

As the last of the mob passed by, the tavern door opened and several men emerged, running up to join the group of men as they continued down Ye Greate Street. John was astounded, and felt compelled to follow along, as well.

Not too far along down Ye Greate Street, the mob passed a two-and-a-half-story, red brick colonial mansion on the left. It was a handsome sight. This building, too, John recognized from earlier in the day. Only now it presented itself fully restored to its original greatness. The checkerboard blue and red brick Flemish bond pattern was clearly evident now. Centered in each window facing the street was a lit candle. The front door was decorated with wreaths of holly. The perfect Currier and Ives display for the holidays, John thought.

Upon reaching Maple Street on the left—which John recognized as the Bridgeton-Greenwich Road on which he had initially come into town—the mob suddenly stopped in their tracks. Approaching them from across an open green on the right, a young man was shouting and waving his arms.

"Fire! Fire! There's a fire at the wharf! Come, make haste!"

The leader of the mob shouted back: "You must be mistaken! The tea burning is to happen here, on the Market Square. There should be no tea at the wharf by my reckoning."

The young man had by now drawn up even with the leader.

"Tea or no tea, Master Philip. As sure as I stand before you now, the warehouse down by the river wharf is ablaze."

John looked up. Like red velvet sails in a changing wind, the night sky rippled in waves of orange-crimson, powered by the hidden flames of an unchecked inferno lying somewhere beyond the distant tree line.

Just then another man approached quickly on horseback, coming up Ye Greate Street from the direction of the wharf.

"Come quickly! There is evil afoot! Cries of distress are coming from inside the burning warehouse. I fear someone may be trapped inside."

Philip, the leader of the mob, turned to his compatriots.

"Ben, take three or more men and go to the tailor's house to secure the tea. You other men, come with me!"

As the men departed down Ye Greate Street toward the wharf, John could now hear the cries of a young woman, a mere whimper at first, the sounds seemed to be coming from the direction of the fire. As the flames grew in intensity so did the cries, and soon the whole night sky was ablaze with a pulsating orange glow, alive and breathing with the anguished cries of the innocent. John cupped his hands over his ears trying to mute the sounds, but the cries continued in a rising crescendo, piercing his brain like a hot poker.

Falling to his knees he closed his eyes and shouted out, "Please! No! Make it go away!"

A small white spot appeared at the center of his vision, growing larger and brighter until it consumed his entire field of view, as the world around him became bathed in a soothing white light. The cries quickly faded.

Slowly, John regained his composure. When he opened his eyes again he found himself kneeling beside a tombstone in the middle of a church graveyard. The sun lay low on the horizon, with the bare, twisted branches of giant elms and maples grotesquely silhouetted against a cold, slate gray afternoon sky. Spring, it seemed, was still far off.

John was standing now. There, not too far distant, stood an older man with his head bowed over a newly dug grave, with his back to John. The grave was located near three other, older grave sites, under the low spreading boughs of a large oak tree. All four graves, the tree and the ground immediately surrounding them, were enclosed on three sides by a low, wrought iron fence set about twelve inches off the ground, marking the area as a family burial plot. The iron work was elaborate and well done, obviously the work of a skilled craftsman. There was room yet for several more graves to be dug here.

A second, younger man approached the older man from the left. The two men exchanged nods of recognition, and the younger man joined the older man by the new grave site.

"She was the flower of my life. The very soul of my being," the older man said.

"And mine, as well, sir," the younger man replied, his voice cracking with emotion. "How Providence could ever allow such a thing to happen is beyond my understanding."

The older man placed his left hand on young man's shoulder.

"I have ceased trying to fathom the workings of Providence. My own soul is devoid of purpose. All I feel now is…rage. Rage toward the perpetrator of this evil deed. I tell you now, were it in my power to know and curse the hand responsible for this act, I would do so, though my soul perish in the process."

The two men remained there for a while, standing silently over the grave site. At last the younger man spoke.

"I…understand that Mr. McKenzie perished in the fire as well. I am sorry for that, sir. I know how much you admired him."

The older man did not speak. He simply continued looking down at the grave.

John's presence went unnoticed by the two men. So he drew closer to read the inscription on the tombstone:

Rebecca Whitman
Born: August 16, 1756
Died: Dec 22, 1774

"She is with her mother, now," the older man struggled to say. "May God rest her soul!"

The older man then turned and handed the younger man a small, wooden box he had been holding by his side. John could barely make out a floral pattern adorning the box lid.

"Here, take this," he said, "I know she would have wanted you to have it."

As John continued staring at the grave, the marble face of the tombstone gradually brightened, becoming brilliant as the sun. Raising his hands to shield his eyes, the entire area became engulfed in a bright white cloud. The two men standing there seemed oblivious to this transformation even as they were caught up in its effulgence.

John was forced to close his eyes, and as he did, the vision of an old woman appeared to him. She had a wild, unkempt look about her, with large, buggy eyes protruding from the orbits of her skull. In profile, she favored a mole in appearance—the small furry kind—with a large pointed nose and quickly receding chin and jaw line. Now she was smiling, laughing, as unseen flames cast an eerie orange glow across her worn, aged face. Laughter turned to a cackle as her image morphed into the hideous, prune-wrinkled face of an old hag. The wrinkles slowly melted like heated wax into green dripping ooze and then suddenly…the blood curdling shrieks of agony!

As John's eyes sprang open, the troubling vision was suddenly erased from his mind. Looking about him, now, he found himself in the midst of song and revelry, in what he could only assume was a country tavern. Similar to the Indian King, which he knew very well, with its caged bar and broad planked hardwood floors, this establishment was nonetheless more rustic in its accoutrements and construction. It was past sundown, and the room was sparingly lit with a half dozen or so wall-mounted whale oil lamps.

While the vision was gone, the screams continued for a while, but went unnoticed by the tavern's company of merrymakers. Slowly, the screams faded, melting away into the jovial din of barroom chatter and camaraderie.

"Let us drink a toast to that old hag of a witch. May she burn in hell!" one of their company shouted as he held up a tankard of ale.

Others around him joined in the toast with shouts of, "Hear, hear!"

Another spoke up. "I heard tell she made quite a spectacle of herself. Lit up like the King's own fireworks display, she did!"

This was met with laughter and more cheers.

"She only got what she deserved," another replied.

John stood by the door. Once again, no one seemed to notice his presence. He had long since become accustomed to this new state of anonymity, but remained troubled by the visions, and confused by the direction things were going; he seemed to have no choice but to go with the flow. In frustration he called out, "Can no one hear me?! I need to get back to September twelfth of the current year!"

In an instant the room was awash in a soft white light, and the sound of buzzing flies once more filled John's head. Suddenly overcome by a renewed sense of gravity, John fell back against the wall and slid down, his legs slipping out from under him, his buttocks striking the floor boards with a hard *thump*. Slumping slowly over to one side, he was out cold.

John didn't know how long he remained unconscious. He only knew that when he regained his senses and tried to move, he could feel the burden of his own weight like never before—like a man returning from the moon. Remaining on the floor with his eyes closed, he took a deep breath. Ah! The smell of stale beer mixed with the sweet scent of a wood-burning stove, baked bread, and char-grilled meat on the hearth. All of John's senses had returned, now. With his eyes still shut he could hear and feel the close-up sound of breathing, and from that breath came a voice. It was the gruff voice of an older woman.

"Sir, if you need a quiet place to sleep it off, we can offer you a warm feather bed in an upper chamber...for a small fee. But, mind you, we cannot countenance intemperate slumber on the tavern floor so early in the day. It's like to chase away good-paying customers."

John opened his eyes and looked up. There, staring down at him was the face of a middle-aged woman: large, round, and bright, like a full harvest moon. The moon-face was topped with a puffy marshmallow-white mob cap that covered her entire head and most of her ears as well, looking rather like a deflated chef's hat.

"Wha...What? Where am I?" John struggled to ask.

"Where indeed!" the moon-face spoke. "*That* I can answer. Greenwich of Cumberland County. Now, where did you come *from*? Ha! Now that's a question for the ages!"

There was a measure of firmness and authority in the woman's voice.

John looked around him. He recognized this to be the same tavern as in his vision, but there were only a handful of men sitting and standing about now, no celebrations, no bravado, no talk of old hags and witches, and there was the light of day leaking though the partly closed windows. John slowly brought himself to his feet. No longer the out-of-body traveler, John now found himself in the flesh, feeling the moment. But which moment? In what time?

"So, can you see...and *hear*...me?" he asked her slowly, deliberately—confusedly.

"Pshaw! I see and hear everything that goes on in this establishment. I am the innkeeper's wife. It is my job to know who comes and who goes, and all goings-on around here"

An old sailor sitting in the corner by himself, nursing a pint of hard cider, looked up from a letter he was reading, turned his head and grinned. "Aye, lad, and most of what goes on all about the town and parts beyond, I might add."

The woman straightened up and with her hands on her hips and addressed the sailor directly. "That's enough out of you, Jack McElroy. I don't recall asking for your opinion in the matter."

The sailor laughed and took swig of his brew. "No matter, I'll be headin' north to Haddonfield tomorrow or the day after." He held up the letter he was reading. "The master beckons me to come."

"Well, tell your master that there's a bill waiting to be paid here at the Greenwich Stone Tavern and Inn, if he wants to retain his good credit in these parts," she scolded.

John slowly took a seat at the nearest table and placed his head in his hands. Looking up, he asked weakly, "Please, tell me, ma'am…what day is today?"

"Why…it is Monday, the twelfth day of September," she replied suspiciously.

"Monday, the twelfth," he repeated. Yes, he knew it was the twelfth of September. That much hadn't changed. But…*Monday*? It should be Sunday. Obviously, the only thing that had changed was…the *year*!

After a brief pause he continued. "And, pray tell, what year…" John stopped midway through the question, seeing the confused look on the woman's face, and realizing the response such a question might provoke. She might, after all, think him mad, and that could just make matters worse. If the time and year were as he suspected, he knew madness was a thing not well tolerated. He decided on a different tack.

Leaning across the table and raising his voice just enough to be heard, he addressed the sailor directly. "Pardon my intrusion, Captain, but perhaps you could help me with a small matter."

The captain looked up.

"I take it you are acquainted with the town of Haddonfield?" John continued.

"Aye, if ye be meanin' West Jersey's Haddonfield, I know it quite well. Been there many times meself."

"Excellent! Then you are just the man to help me. You see, I ventured a small wager with a friend of mine as to the age of that fair village. Would you be able to confirm its age for me? The number of years since its founding, I mean."

The captain stroked his sandy bearded chin and thought for a moment. "Aye, let me see. If the town was founded in 1703…no, I think it was 1704…that would make it…seventy years old by my reckoning."

"Ah, I should have known!" John said in pretend amazement. Of course, he knew the captain was off by a few years, but that didn't matter. He now knew the year he was in: 1774.

"Thank you, Captain. That was most helpful."

"Glad to be of assistance."

The sailor studied John a bit further. "Tell me lad, y'appear t'be a bit worn and in need of some…revitalizin'. Can I buy ya a drink, or offer ya something to eat?"

"No, that won't be necessary," John replied. "I appreciate the offer. But, I really must be moving on. I, too, have an urgent need to get to Haddonfield...post haste."

"Aye, and haven't ye a steed, me good fellow?"

John looked up. "A...what?"

"A *steed*, man! A *horse*! Do ye have a horse to take ya there?"

"No, I'm afraid not. I...seem to have...lost it somehow. I think it may have been stolen from me, in fact."

"My! That would be a matter for the constable! Have ye reported the theft?"

"No, but it has been...some time, I am afraid. The trail is probably cold by now."

"That is too bad. Well, it so happens I plan to take the stage boat up river the day after tomorrow. Ye can travel with me and me first mate."

John was anxious to be moving on. He shook his head. "Again, I appreciate the offer, but isn't there anything leaving before then?"

The innkeeper's wife overheard the conversation and chimed in. "Well, there is the stage wagon," she offered.

"Aye, the Cumberland stage! I forgot about that!" the captain replied, slapping his thigh with an open palm of his hand. "It's just that I don't take much t'land travel, is all."

"So, when does the next stage leave?" John asked anxiously.

"Mr. Dare makes a weekly northern run to Cooper's Ferry," the woman said. "And you're in luck. Monday noon is his scheduled departure time." She looked at the clock on the wall. It was ten o'clock. "He should be coming by in about two hours' time. Picks up right outside my door at the stroke of noon, give or take a few minutes. Can't vouch for the truthfulness of my clock, but Mr. Dare is nothing if not punctual," she emphasized. "He should have you at Cooper's Ferry by supper time tomorrow evening."

Cooper's Ferry. That would be Camden, New Jersey, John knew, just a few miles from Haddonfield.

John sighed. "Yes, I suppose that will have to do," he said, rising slowly from his chair. As he did so, he became a bit light-headed and leaned forward against the table to catch himself from falling.

"Ar'ya okay, mate?" the captain inquired.

"Just a little...woozy," John replied, as he sat back down at the table. Then, looking up at the captain, "You know, sir, I just might take you up on your earlier kind offer. I could use a bit of nourishment after all. But, I'm afraid...my purse went the way of my...steed. The same scoundrel made off with both my horse and my purse."

"Aye! A rake and a cur he is, fer sure!" the captain blasted. "At such times as these a body must double up on precaution when traveling alone. D'ya mind if I join ya at yer table? I could use a bit o'grub meself."

"No, not at all." John looked up at the clock on the wall. "It's still two hours before the stage. I would enjoy…having someone to talk to. I do thank you, kind sir, for your generosity."

John was feeling better, more at ease, now. Although, he wasn't really sure how long it would last. He wasn't much sure of anything, anymore. Assuming he got back to Haddonfield, what then? How long would this ramble through time continue? He began to long for the quiet and comfort of his home study and conservatory like never before.

John noticed a slight limp to the captain's gate as he crossed the room. On reaching John's table, the captain set down his pint of ale, pulled up a chair, and sat down next to John. Leaning back in his chair the captain ran his eyes over John, up one side and down the other, giving him a thorough looking over.

"I must say, seein' ya up close, lad, that ye sport a fashion not known in these parts. What manner of dress is that ye be wearin', if ye don't mind me askin'?"

John looked down at his blue polo shirt and khaki cargo pants, realizing for the first time how strange they must seem to an eighteenth-century sea captain. He frantically searched for a suitable reply; one that would satisfy, without revealing the whole truth of the matter.

"Well, I…just happened to come by this ensemble on my recent travels to…France." The captain's eyebrows were raised. "Yes…just this past year," John continued, fumbling for the right words. "It's a new fashion, borrowed from the…foreign military influence on…popular dress…mainly, uh…in the south of France and the French colonies in Africa." He pointed to the trouser pockets. "You must admit to the utility served by the pocket design."

"Aye, very interesting," the captain agreed. Then, slapping his thigh with his right hand, he concluded, "Those French! My, but they do have a knack for quaint fashion, I must admit! Looks like the finest quality cloth! Egyptian cotton, I fancy. Such a fine, tight weave. And ivory buttons on the lapel, to boot!"

John smiled. Of course, he knew them to be white plastic buttons, but that would not translate well and only confuse the matter.

"So, Captain McElroy, may I…"

"Arrgh, ya needn't be so formal here, lad! The name is Jack. Captain Jack, at your service." He held out his hand.

"Okay. Captain Jack it is, then." John reached out and shook his hand.

"And to whom do I the pleasure of addressin', if ye don't mind me askin'?" the captain inquired.

"Certainly not," John replied. "My name is John. John Weston."

The captain seemed surprised, even bewildered, and was slow to respond. "John Weston, ye say?"

"That's right," John confirmed. "Is there…something wrong with that?"

"I suppose not. After all, there is probably more than one 'Jack McElroy' on God's good earth, as well, eh?"

John was confused at first, but finally made the connection. "Oh, so do I understand correctly, Captain, that there is another 'John Weston' known to you in these parts?"

"Aye. He would be the younger brother of me master, Bartholomew Weston, of Haddonfield. They wouldn't happen to be any relation to yerself, now, would they?"

John was stunned. To have stumbled across an acquaintance of his distant great-grandfather and uncle in this faraway place and time. Was it by chance, or the work of an unseen hand? Or was he simply dreaming this whole thing and would suddenly wake up in his leather reclining chair in the comfort of his home study? Too much brandy, perhaps. Not knowing which, and how this would eventually play out, he had to measure his words carefully. If this was not a dream but was actually happening, he didn't want to risk intervening in events of the eighteenth century so as to alter the course of history. On the other hand, acknowledging a relationship with Bart might actually aid his cause and strengthen his chances of getting back to Haddonfield…and the twentieth century.

"Yes, well, as a matter of fact, your Master Bartholomew and I, we are…distant cousins."

"Ye don't say!" replied the captain, reeling back in his chair.

John quickly recalled his family history, which he had memorized like catechism many years ago when he first learned of his colonial connections from his dad and Aunt Dee.

"Yes, although I am not certain of the exact family connections. My guess is that we are…oh, cousins twice or thrice removed, I would say. But, I do know something of the man and his family mercantile business. Tell me, how is his wife, Sarah? And their"—John did quick mental calculation to determine the number and ages of the children, with two not yet having been born—"three children? The oldest, let's see, that would be James. Must be eight years old by now."

"My word! For someone so far removed, ye have an uncanny knowledge of his personal affairs," the captain laughed.

John worried that perhaps he had gone too far. But, the captain's next actions would assuage his fears.

The captain squinted and poked a finger toward John, speaking slowly but assuredly. "Aye, ye may not know it, but seein' ya in the light, ye do bear a certain likeness to Master Bart and his kin."

Turning his head around, the captain shouted across the room to the tavern keeper's wife: "Mary! Please bring me friend, John Weston here, a pint o'cider and whatever ye be featurin' on the menu. And bring me the same, while yer at it."

Mary was about to say something when the captain cut her off.

"And not to worry about the charges, Mary. I'll pick this one up meself."

Continuing in the English tradition, the taverns and inns of eighteenth-century colonial America provided a safe haven for travelers and locals alike from all stations and walks in life, aristocrat and vagabond, itinerant merchant and local farmer—that is, as long as you met the minimum qualifications: you were male, white, and free. More than just a place for food and drink, the tavern was a focal point for social interaction and the exchange of information. These public establishments were places where the common man most often received the news of the day, discussed business, and shared political views and experiences, from local gossip to tall tales of the road.

From the far side of the room a single head, bathed in the shadows, perked up when John's name was spoken aloud for all to hear. As the stranger leaned forward from out of the far corner shadows, his identity was partly revealed: a not so young man with long, dark, scraggly hair and a beard and mustache, wearing a black patch over one eye. His long, lanky fingers fondled his tankard of rum, like a spider playing with its prey. He repeated the name, "John Weston," to himself, and then to his companion, who remained in the shadows. Then, nodding his head, he sank slowly back into the darkness.

John and the captain were served up a fine meal of hasty pudding and roast duck with sugared yams, currant jelly, and wild rice. The cider was especially good. Not the sweet juice John was accustomed to, but what he would call "hard cider," the fermented, home-brewed kind. While most still favored the beer and ale of the old country, hard cider had come to be accepted as a suitable, more affordable and available substitute in the colonies, with apple orchards turning a goodly profit for the farmer.

John thanked the captain again for the fine meal, and said he would repay him some day for his trouble, if he could.

"No need for that," the captain said. "Just put a good word in for me with Master Bart, if ye get to see him in yer travels. Tell me, have ye ever been to Haddonfield?"

John took a swig of cider to chase down a large mouthful of duck.

"I have been there on…two separate occasions," John said recovering from a hard swallow. He was improvising now. "On the first occasion I stayed at the Indian King Tavern on Kings Highway. Very pleasant accommodations. I enjoyed a room overlooking the gardens and kitchens to the rear of the building. On a separate occasion I was forced to take a room at the Estaugh Tavern on Tanner Street just off the King's Highway. Clean, but not as finely appointed as the Indian King."

"Well, ye do seem to know yer way around!" the captain marveled. "Perhaps we can meet there for a brew...when circumstances better suit ya."

Suddenly the outside door swung open as a younger man entered the tavern. Pausing a moment to scan the room, his eyes at last came to fall upon the captain. "Oh, there you are, sir! I was hoping I'd find you here."

The young man approached the captain's table. Taking note of the stranger, he paused and remained standing there, waiting for the captain to make the proper introductions.

"Ah! Where are me manners?" the captain finally said. "John, please allow me to introduce me new first mate, Mr. Paul McKenzie."

John stood up slowly, reached across the table, and offered his hand. "It's a pleasure to meet you, sir," he said. "My name is John. John Weston."

Paul took John's hand and gave a curious glance at the captain.

The captain responded in kind. "Aye, 'tis a seemingly popular name among his kin," the captain said with a wink. "Mr. Weston here is a distant relation of our employee, Master Bart. Just ask him. He can give ya a rundown of his whole family." The captain chuckled.

"My, that is...a curious coincidence," Paul replied quizzically as he continued shaking John's hand.

John thought: *McKenzie? Where have I heard that name before? Yes, of course!* Recalling his recent out-of-body experience in the grave yard, John asked, "Mr. McKenzie? You wouldn't be related to the McKenzie who..." John stopped in mid-sentence. If things were to unfold as revealed in the vision, and the date on the tombstone was correct, then the fiery death of the Mr. McKenzie of his vision would not yet have happened...not for another two months or so. John bit his tongue. "I mean," he continued cautiously, "I did know a McKenzie once, but that was many years ago" – Paul looked at him suspiciously – "in a rather distant part of the colonies. New England, I believe."

"Hmm, I don't believe I have relations in New England," Paul replied slowly, looking askance at his new acquaintance. "The *Old* England, yes, but not the New," he finally concluded, laughing. "Must be an unrelated family line altogether."

The captain interrupted to break the awkward exchange. "So, Paul, are ye going to join us and let me buy ya a pint, or will ye continue to stand there jabber'n away like an old woman?"

"I'm sorry, sir," Paul replied and took a seat at the table. "I have but a few minutes and must return to the piers. But I will join you for a round of *flip*, if that meets with your approval"

"*Flip* it is, then!" the captain beamed. He turned to Mary and relayed the order. John was curious. Not wanting to appear ignorant, he kept one eye on Mary as she prepared this strange sounding concoction, while Paul quickly got to the point of his visit.

"Sir, I've completed my inspection of the *Richelieu*"—turning to John to explain—"that would be our good ship, John,"—then back to the captain—"and I must say, the vessel is worse off than I had first reckoned. I'm afraid we may have to dry-dock for the season to make the necessary repairs."

Mary filled a large pitcher about two-thirds of strong beer, added some molasses for sweetness, then a gill of rum. Setting the pitcher down she went to retrieve something from the fireplace.

"Ooh, that really is too bad," the captain replied. "We will be obliged to make a report to Master Bart on the matter." He held up the letter he had been reading earlier, the letter from Bart. "Master Bart has asked us to join him in Haddonfield as soon as possible. He has a new business venture he needs to discuss…and something about the embargo situation."

John eyed Mary returning from the hearth with a red-hot "loggerhead"—a poker-like rod—and she began stirring the mixture with it. The liquor crackled and foamed as it quenched the hot loggerhead, sending a plume of steamy vapor into the air.

"Do you think I really need to go?" Paul asked.

The captain saw disappointment in Paul's eyes. He knew he fancied a young lady in town—Rebecca was her name—and didn't want to be traipsing off to parts unknown if it wasn't absolutely necessary. His travels at sea left little time in port as it was.

Mary took a beaten egg and a small measure of fresh cream and added it to the brew, mixing it through and through with a wooden spoon to complete the process.

"Yes, I think it's important fer ya t'meet the boss," the captain finally said. "Ye bein' me *new* first mate, and all."

"Fine, captain. As you wish. I shall make the necessary preparations."

Mary approached the table and served up the *flip* in three serving-size glasses.

"Fine it is then!" the captain concluded, slamming down a fist on the table. "So, let us warm ourselves with this fine concoction on this fair September afternoon! Such is the delight of good company, strong drink, and good conversation."

Paul smiled.

John raised his glass to offer a toast, but the captain beat him to it.

"Aye, so it is, as any sailor or well-traveled bloke can attest," the captain said as he raised his flip glass. "So, here's to the tavern…and to the tavern's missus."—casting a devilish grin at Mary who was just passing by gathering up empty glasses— "Where many a happy tongue wagged loose the boastful tale," the captain toasted.

"…and blood oath pried free by fine spirits regaled," Paul added.

"…where many a plot concocted and betrayed ," the captain continued with a wink.

"…and many a friendship lost and made," John capped off the refrain.

The three glasses met over the table with a single clink.

The minutes passed quickly by. John was finishing off a pint of cider and discussing the current political situation with the captain when he heard the stage wagon pull up outside. By the clock on the wall it had arrived fifteen minutes early. Paul McKenzie had long since departed company, having much to do in preparation for the trip north to Haddonfield.

"So, it appears the Cumberland stage is running a bit ahead of schedule today," the captain said.

"Or else the tavern clock is running slow," John replied.

"Aye, that could be," the captain agreed. "Well, ye better grab a seat while there be one t'grab, lest ye be forced to sit upon the roof."

John pushed his chair back and slowly rose to his feet. He was still a bit wobbly on his feet, having sat for so long now he had almost forgotten how to stand.

"Are ye good to go, now?" the captain asked.

"I'll be fine, Jack. Just as soon as I get my land legs back."

The captain chuckled. "Now ye know why I prefer the stage boat to the stage wagon," he said.

John reached out and took a firm hold of the captain's hand. "I want to thank you again, Captain, for your kind hospitality. If you're ever"—he wanted to say, "in the twentieth century, please look me up," but thought again—"were we ever to meet again, you can be sure the meal is on me next time."

"Aye, I'll be sure to take ya up on that offer, me fine lad."

The captain shook his hand and gave him a firm embrace. "Now, be off! If ye don't want t'miss that stage!"

John backed away and turned to go out the door. Stopping in his tracks, he reached across the table and picked up a half-loaf of bread from the bread basket and stuffed it in the hip pocket of this cargo pants.

"Don't want it to go to waste," he grinned.

"Waste not, want not," the captain smiled.

The captain accompanied John outside to the waiting stage, just in case there were any problems with the coachman. John was surprised by what he saw. Not at all the stereotypical stage coach he was used to seeing in TV westerns. It was more like a large wagon, partially open all around, the sides of which rose to about shoulder height with eight posts supporting the roof. The interior was fitted with four forward-facing bench seats, each capable of seating up to three passengers. Rolled up leather curtains were fastened to the roof, and could be rolled down and buttoned to the sides in the event of bad weather. The whole body of the wagon was suspended on springs, with a team of six horses hitched up and ready to go. To enter the wagon one had to approach and mount from the front, like getting into a covered cart. The coachman sat in the front seat, along with the front-seated passengers.

When John arrived there were already two passengers on board, seated in the second seat from the rear, and four more persons—John surmised them to be husband and wife with their two small children—waiting to board. The man was haggling with the coachman over price and baggage. The coachman was a tall lanky man dressed in knee breeches and boots, a white linen shirt and fustian waistcoat.

With things finally settled it was now John's turn.

"And where might you be heading this fine September afternoon, lad?" the coachman asked John.

"I…I am traveling to Haddonfield. I was…told you could take me there," John stammered.

"Well, I can take you as far as Salem this evening. There, we will find lodging for the night at Mr. Dickenson's Inn, and with a fresh team of horses continue the trip north in the morning. But our final stop will be Cooper's Ferry, not Haddonfield. You should have no trouble finding a coach to take you the final leg to Haddonfield. It's no more than four miles inland."

"That would be fine, sir. Camden…err, Cooper's Ferry would be just fine."

"Do you have any baggage?" the coachman asked.

"No, I'm afraid not. Just the body and soul you see standing before you."

"Yes, well…that will be, let's see, three shillings to Salem plus another five shillings to Cooper's Ferry…that will make it eight shillings in all."

"Yes, of course," John replied.

John turned to the captain and mouthed the words, "Can you help me?"

"Ahem! Yes, my good sir," the captain spoke up, addressing the coachman. "You can put these charges to the account of Bartholomew Weston, of Weston Enterprises, Haddonfield, New Jersey. This gentleman, here, is Mr. John Weston, the…"

Just then the two trailing horses gave a great swish of their tails, setting a small swarm of horseflies to flight. The flies buzzed all about the coachman's head as he paused momentarily, like in a daze. Coming to, he waved his hands to shoo the flies away.

"John Weston, did you say?" the coachman continued, confused for the moment. "Why, yes, of course. There will be…no charge, Mr. Weston."

John and the captain exchanged looks of surprise.

The coachman took a slip of paper from his jacket, signed it, and handed it to John. "Here you are, sir. This ticket will take you to Cooper's Ferry. You must pay separately for your night's lodging in Salem."

The captain took out his purse and removed a handful of coins. "Here y'are, John. Take this. It should cover the night's lodging and get ya t'Haddonfield with a few o'shillings to spare."

John thanked the captain and bid a final farewell before climbing into the wagon. Making his way to the rear most bench seat, he nudged his way past the family of four and then the two passengers who were seated directly in front of him. They were an older gentleman and a younger man, possibly father and son, or perhaps just business associates. The older man was well dressed, like a country gentleman, seated with the palms of both hands resting on a walking cane planted firmly on the floor straight up in front of him. John smiled, nodding politely as he passed.

"Good day to you, sir."

The man nodded and smiled in return, but said nothing. The younger man was busy reading a book and seemed to take little if any notice of John as he passed by and took his seat at the rear of the wagon.

John settled back in his sparsely padded, leather upholstered seat and made himself as comfortable as possible, determined to enjoy the ride, with all he had been through this day. The coachman announced that, with the weather being as fine as it was, they should be able to cover the sixteen miles to Salem in less than five hours, including two planned mail stops along the way: one in Stowe Creek Landing and the second at Hancocks Bridge.

The ride began pleasantly enough. The stage wagon traveled north on Ye Greate Street, initially backtracking over the same route John had taken just a few hours earlier—but two centuries hence. There was the same Quaker cemetery just beyond the stone wall fence on the right, with its field of unmarked graves, only this time they were surrounding an old stone building, the original Quaker meeting house, which had somehow miraculously sprung up in what seemed like only two hours' time. A mile further up the road they entered the Head of Greenwich, or North Greenwich, where the townsfolk were setting about their daily chores, some walking, others on horseback, with the occasional carriage or farm wagon carting goods to market or running errands. John was reminded of a visit he had made to Williamsburg, Virginia, as a boy. Only this time the participants were not re-enactors, but real life citizens of a bygone time and place.

Leaving North Greenwich behind, the stage wagon crossed a small creek and continued into the open country. The pace slowed a bit and the wagon's members creaked as the team of horses began its slow climb up Mount Gibbon, the gentle, sandy rise situated just north of town. Approaching the crest of the hill, John turned around in his seat to get a look back down the road. The hill offered a splendid partial view of the town and surrounding countryside, bucolic and serene. John took a deep breath and filled his lungs with the clean, cool pre-autumn air, marked with a fresh scent of pine. Leaning out the carriage window to his left, he closed his eyes for a moment, allowing the noonday sun to bathe his face with a delightful warmth.

John recounted the events of the day, taking inventory of the confusing and often terrifying images and sounds he had experienced in what he was now referring to as his "out-of-body experiences": the winter sky; the mob of men made up as Native American Indians bent on a common mission; the distant screams of agony from the wharf and the blazing night sky; the feelings of anguish and loss at the cemetery; the terrifying specter of the old hag; and the references to a witch burning by the good ol' boys at the tavern. In the end, John was at a loss to make sense of it all.

Then the names at the gravesite flashed across his mind: "Rebecca Whitman"; "Paul McKenzie." Was it the same Paul McKenzie he had just spoken to in the Stone Tavern? Captain Jack's first mate? He didn't know. He couldn't know. How could all this be happening, anyway? How had it all started? With the simple bite of a greenhead fly? *Ridiculous*, he thought. *I must be…imagining all of this. It must all just be…a bad dream. Just wait. I'll be waking up soon in my soft recliner in the safe confines of my home study.*

After about an hour or so of traveling, the wagon pulled into a small settlement of rustic homes and shops clustered along the banks of a wide, slow-moving creek. A flat-bottom ferry with towline was tied up to the wharf, waiting for its next paying customer.

"Stowe Creek Landing," the coachman announced. He pulled a shiny pocket watch from his top vest pocket and flipped open its engraved silver lid. "We'll be stopping here for twenty minutes to exchange the mail and water the horses. If anyone is in need of refreshment, you may step down and avail yourselves of the tavern's facilities. There is a privy located to the rear of the tavern if anyone is so in need."

The young man seated directly to John's front stared wide-eyed at the coachman as he closed the lid and returned the watch to his pocket. The coachman then stepped down and helped the passengers who chose to stretch their legs, which was everyone except John, who desired to interact as little as possible with the people and events of this era, not knowing how it would all play out. But he couldn't help but overhear bits and pieces of conversation from the others.

"That's a handsome timepiece you have there, sir," the young man said to the coachman as he stepped down from the wagon.

"Yes, time is of the essence, my good lad. Not a thing to be squandered. Once spent, it cannot be recalled," the coachman replied eagerly, pleased that someone had taken notice of his fine timepiece. He held it out for closer inspection by the pair of young admiring eyes. "Made in London, you know," he said proudly. "With a fusee cylinder escapement. Very rare and expensive, I might add."

The young man nodded and smiled.

The little girl of the family of four was crying now, saying she had forgotten to bring her dolly along with her.

"We have to go back, Momma. I forgot Lisa," she cried plaintively.

"Oh, darling, we can't go back now," her mother replied. "There isn't another coach for a week, and your grandma and grandpa are expecting us."

The child's muffled cries could still be heard as she clung closely to her mother's dress, and the woman pleaded with her husband. "Oh, Charles, isn't there something we can do?"

The father bent down to comfort his daughter. "I'll tell you what, Sarah. When we get to Philadelphia I'll let you pick out another little doll. They have the best and prettiest to offer in the colonies."

But the little girl continued to whimper. "But I want Lisa. Why can't we go back and get her?" was all she could say.

John looked to the other side of the wagon where the younger man, seated on a tree stump and basking in the afternoon sun, was absorbed in his book: *Mr. Wyngate's Arithmetic.* The older gentleman, having just left the tavern, approached him from behind.

"Can't get enough of the new science and philosophy, eh, my boy?"

"It's all very interesting, sir," the boy perked up. "See here, for example, what a merry riddle that can be reasonably explained by arithmetic means. Would you dare to venture a query?"

The older gentleman reluctantly obliged.

"So then," the young man began, "I bid you to think upon any number at your pleasure."

"Any number at all?" the old gentleman asked.

"Yes, any number at all. But keep its identity to yourself only."

"All right, I have decided upon a number."

"Now, double that number," the young man continued, "and to that doubled number add the number…six."

"It is done," the gentleman said.

"Now, take one-half the sum of this addition, and reject the other half."

The gentleman sighed. "You are trying the limits of my mental faculties, son. But yes, that is done as well. Pray tell, how much longer must I endure these mental calisthenics?"

"We are nearing the end," the young man said with rising enthusiasm. "Now, from this half, subtract the number you first thought upon."

"All right, I have the final number in my head."

The boy closed his eyes as if to conjure up a spirit. "And the number you are now thinking is…the number *three*!" the young man announced triumphantly.

The older gentleman sprang back on his heels wide-eyed. "Why, yes, that is correct!" he said. You are indeed a wizard to have conjured up my own thoughts!" The old gentleman laughed.

"Naw! It's just the power of arithmetic," the young man sought to explain. "There is no wizardry involved."

"Ah, then I am so disappointed. For I would have so liked a wizard to lift the curse of time from these old bones. I would have been in your debt forever."

Both men laughed.

John had to chuckle. *Wizardry and witchcraft*, he thought. Yes, that would be how twentieth-century science and technology would appear even to those living in this age of enlightenment and reform. He thought about his cell phone, which he had all but forgotten about until now, and reached into his right hip pocket. Yup, still there! He carefully pulled the Nokia 8110 from his pocket and turned it on. It was still holding a full charge. Not surprisingly, the phone was showing zero bars and the "Looking for Service Area" message appeared on the screen. Hell, why not? John thought, and hit the "Talk" button. He punched in *8, the quick dial code for Katie's cell phone, and put the phone up to his ear. He was expecting to get the "no service" message tones, but instead heard the quick succession of dialing tones for Katie's number, followed by…silence. The "Looking for Service Area" message on the screen had gone away, but there was no tone or sound coming from the phone, just a steady, faint white static noise that John had never heard coming from his phone before.

John spoke into the phone. "Hello, Katie. Can you hear me?" More white noise. "This is John. I'm calling from somewhere"—he looked around – "from Stowe Creek Landing, somewhere in South Jersey. Can you hear me?"

Just more static.

He hit the "Talk" button again to hang up, but kept the power on just in case, hope against hope, she should call back. Holding the cell phone on his lap, he was attracted to something small to his left. There, resting on the window ledge was a greenhead fly, basking motionless in the afternoon sun. Maybe it was tired and sleeping. John suddenly became sleepy himself.

"So, you might want to tell the sister who bit me just what kind of hell she's been putting me through," he said calmly to the fly. "But, then again, you're not from my time and *century*, are you?"

John shooed the fly away and put the phone back down on his lap, then leaned back in his seat and closed his eyes. He reached up and rubbed his neck. That bite was beginning to bother him, starting to throb and ache just a little. He tried to let his body relax. Soon his mind began to drift in and out of that hyper-suggestive state that immediately precedes sleep. He could hear the little girl crying: "We must go back and get her." Which then became: "*We must go back and save her.*" This was followed by the older gentleman's voice: "…lift the curse from these old bones." The two then became as one, repeating over and over in his head: "*We must go back…lift the curse…save her! Must go back…lift the curse…save her!*"

Before long, John was dreaming:

…Like hordes of angry fireflies bent on a common mission, streams of glowing embers ride the hot currents of air high into the cold, night sky, challenging the moon's dominion over its star-spangled realm, rising ever higher against the broad canopy of stars, mingling at last with the ancient gods-strewn constellations in a final moment's burst of glory…

The young man had retaken his seat in front of John in the wagon. His older traveling companion soon joined him.

…Now, against a backdrop of orange flame and smoke, vague new forms in erratic motion appear and disappear, coalescing at last into more discernible images: human silhouettes in wild, dancing rhythm…

The older gentleman, too, had dozed off as the wagon pulled away from the Tavern. As the wagon jolted forward, the young man heard something drop behind him, striking the wooden deck of the wagon.

…Focusing on the heart of the flames, the vision of a woman's face slowly takes form. It is the face of an older woman, worn and haggard, wrinkled, discernible now as the crackle of flames is replaced by the sinister cackle of an old crone…

Negotiating a rut in the road the wagon tilted forward. The fallen object slid forward across the polish-worn floor boards, coming to rest under the young man's seat. Curious, the young man bent over to retrieve the object. This was the same device he had witnessed earlier in the hands of the stranger seated to his rear. He had observed the stranger speaking into the device, but didn't know what to make of it. He turned around to offer its return, but the stranger was sound asleep. The young man held the device in his hand and studied it for a moment, then flipped open its cover. It seemed to be a small clock or pocket watch of some kind, displaying the correct time in digits rather than a dial, but with so many buttons, and a face that glowed with its own light! A natural phosphorescence of some kind, like fireflies, he thought. He continued to hold it, marveling at its craftsmanship…and wondering at its function.

Chapter 16

1999
Friday, 17 September
Our Lady of Lourdes Hospital

11:00 a.m. Dr. Aldus Caldwell, sitting comfortably with legs crossed in his brown leather upholstered arm chair, spoke slowly, softly to the patient lying before him face-up on the couch in his Lady of Lourdes Hospital office.

"Now, when I count down from five and snap my fingers, John, you will wake up. You will recall everything you have related to me. You will feel refreshed and alert. Are you ready, John?"

John lightly nodded.

"Good," Caldwell said.

The doctor counted down, "Five…four…three…two…one," then snapped his fingers.

John opened his eyes and stared straight up at the ceiling, then turned his head and looked at Dr. Caldwell. "Well, how did I do, doc?"

Caldwell leaned forward and turned off the tape recorder, then stood up and walked over to his desk and put down his notebook. "You did extremely well, John," Caldwell said with a sincere smile. "I think we made very good progress. It certainly was a better start than I was expecting."

John swung his legs around and sat up on the side of the couch. "Never thought I ever would find myself on one of these things," he said, patting the leather upholstering.

"So, do you remember anything we talked about, John?"

John rubbed his face, like a grizzly waking up from a long winter's nap. "Yes, doc, I sure do." John leaned over and cradled his head in his hands. "I remember *everything*. So, what now?"

"Well, I will need some time to study the tapes. But I would think your prognosis looks good. I believe we may have identified an underlying issue that may have contributed to your psychotic episode. John, you apparently harbor intense guilt feelings over the death of your fiancée. It happened years ago. Plenty of time for unresolved feelings of guilt to fester and grow."

John took a deep breath. "Sort of like filling a pot to overflowing?"

"Hmm, something like that," Caldwell replied. "But probably more like a pressure cooker with no relief valve."

"Kinda blew my cork, huh?" John agreed sadly.

John looked up at the doctor. "But what about the other…stuff. You know, the time-travel thing, back to eighteenth-century New Jersey." He glanced over at the cassette recorder. "Did you get all that on tape, too?"

"Yes, well. The mind is a powerful thing, John. It can sometimes trick us into flights of fancy and irrational thoughts that seem quite real at times. I have no doubt that the insect bite played a significant part as well. The psychotropic proteins present in certain venoms and many natural substances can produce a broad range of hallucinatory effects, quite unpredictable and sometimes deadly in nature. The shamans of neolithic cultures were certainly aware of the effects these substances can have on the mind."

"And…the *spirit*?" John quickly added.

"Yes, and *spirit*, if you consider one the mere extension of the other. But this, of course, is beyond the realm of natural science, John.

"Of course," John replied.

Dr. Caldwell sat down on his desk and crossed his arms. "So, tell me, John. How do you feel?"

John cleared his throat. "Well, not too bad, actually. Considering I've been dragged all the way to eighteenth-century America and back." He then thought about his encounter with the sea captain and the trip in the stage wagon. "But then again…it was pleasant at times," he added.

Dr. Caldwell smiled. "Well, I am glad to hear that, John."

John remained pensive. "What troubles me, though, is how I ended up back here, on the streets of Camden, without my car."

"Well, we can only assume you hitched a ride with some Good Samaritan. How else could it be explained?" the doctor concluded. "In your delusional state, your mind simply altered the details of the trip, supplanting the real with the fanciful."

"I suppose so," John agreed reluctantly. But he was thinking about that ticket stub signed by the Cumberland stage coachman. He just brushed it off for the time being.

"So, what now, doc?"

"Well, as you know, Dr. Ritchie has you scheduled for an MRI at one o'clock. Depending on those results, you might be free to go home, John. Check yourself out."

John looked up, surprised.

"Of course, I would recommend that you stay the weekend, John," Caldwell added. "A little more R and R certainly wouldn't hurt. In either case, I would like to follow up with more discussions, more therapy sessions, if that meets with your approval."

John nodded. His mind was clear, now, and he was thinking about his neglected work and the GenAvance study. "Yes, I agree, doc. About the follow-up, I mean. But right now I'm thinking I should be getting back to the office. I've been letting them hold the bag for too long." He thought about giving Jim Connelly a call. "Is it okay if I make a phone call, doc?"

Dr. Caldwell sat back and waved to his desk phone. "Be my guest. You can use my phone. Avoid a room phone charge that way." Caldwell smiled. "Tell you what. I'll just step outside while you make the call."

"Thanks, doc. I appreciate it."

As he exited the room, Dr. Caldwell ran into Dr. Ritchie coming down the hallway.

"So, how is our student of history with the bug bite faring this morning?" Dr. Ritchie asked.

"Much better, Alex, I'm happy to say."

But Dr. Caldwell still looked concerned.

"So, why the glum expression?" Dr. Ritchie pursued.

Dr. Caldwell sighed. "Well, I believe we've identified an underlying condition that may have led to his psychotic break. It has to do with suppressed feelings of guilt over the death of his fiancée seventeen years ago, which he feels responsible for."

"Well, that's good!" Ritchie replied. "Sounds like you're making progress."

"Yes, but I believe there's something else at work, here, Alex. Something that triggered the episode. I'm thinking a psychotropic foreign substance of some kind. But you said the blood tests were all negative for hallucinogens."

"Yes. At least for all known substances. Perhaps this is something new."

They both remained silent for a moment.

"Like, maybe something to do with that insect bite?" Caldwell suggested.

"Perhaps."

"Hmm, well, be sure to let me know, Alex, what the MRI reveals, if anything."

"Certainly. You'll be the first to know."

So far it had been a busy day for John. The three-hour therapy session in the morning with Dr. Caldwell went well. Of course, it didn't seem like three hours, being under hypnosis for most of that time. John actually came out of it feeling quite refreshed—"unburdened" is how Dr. Caldwell put it. John wondered, though, now that the skeletons were all out of the closet, how would he be expected to deal with them? The suppressed guilt feelings were perhaps the easiest to understand and deal with, to John's way of thinking. But what about that time-travel business? And the flashbacks John had been experiencing since waking up yesterday morning? Since the therapy session, the memories of his out-of-body experiences and romp through eighteenth-century colonial New Jersey seemed more real than ever. The hypnosis somehow brought everything out in the open, putting it all together in perfect clarity and focus.

Then there was the MRI ordered by Dr. Ritchie in his search for *real* demons hiding in the nook and cranny lobes of John's brain. The nurse practitioner asked him if he was claustrophobic and in need of Valium for the MRI. "No, I don't do drugs," John replied straight-faced. The NP just smirked and handed him over to the MRI technician. The radiologist would make the final determination, but his preliminary read appeared to give John a clean physical bill of health.

It was now three o'clock. John was sitting in the activity room with a small group of other "walking wounded mentals"—as José, the orderly, referred to the psych patients—waiting for Katie to show up to take them for an afternoon outing. On nice days Katie would arrange to take the patients outside for a healthy walk and a breath of fresh air—very therapeutic. Most of the time it was a leisurely stroll through the winding paths of Harleigh Cemetery, just a stone's throw east of the hospital, but today she had arranged with the Mother Superior of the Dominican Sisters to take the patients on a walk through the quiet gardens of their convent grounds located just next door.

John thought about his therapy session again and the events of the past two months since Bob's original encounter with the greenhead fly on July 4th. Like his own recent encounter, that's what seemed to set things off for Bob: the bite of the greenhead fly. Perhaps *that's* where the demons lurked. He tried connecting the dots, but there were still many pieces missing. On Labor Day, Bob spoke about a "curse that must be lifted," and when he flipped out over the fireworks display and grill fire he talked about "going back to save her."

John then recalled his own experience many years ago with the Ouija board. Again, something about a "curse" the board had said; and "going back to save her." Was that really his great-great-uncle John trying to communicate with him, telling him what he must do? Was the Ouija board's "Rebecca" the same Rebecca whose tombstone he encountered during last weekend's out-of-body experience? Then again, maybe Caldwell was right, that was just his own subconscious trying to deal with the fiery death of his fiancée seventeen years ago. How could any of this be real?

John felt a light tapping on his right shoulder. He turned around. It was Doug Justin, just standing there looking like a scarecrow all made up for Halloween.

"Hi, J-John," Doug stuttered. "Are you g-going for the w-walk today?"

John turned around and faced Doug. "Hi there, Doug! Sure. I'm planning to go. It's been way too long since I did any kind of walking or running. I'm really missing it. You gonna join us? The fresh air will do us both some good."

"Ok-k-ay. Maybe I'll go, since you're g-going."

Over Doug's shoulder, John could see Katie and José entering the activity room. Hospital policy required that a male escort accompany Katie on these outings, and José was always more than willing to oblige.

"Oh, I see the general has arrived," John said smiling. "Time to muster the troops and deploy."

There were about eight patients in all joining Katie and José for the afternoon outing, counting John and Doug. After obtaining the proper passes from security and verifying that everyone was properly attired, she led the motley group into the elevator and down to the lobby of the hospital, with José bringing up the rear. John was wearing his khaki cargo pants and a clean shirt Katie had borrowed from Bob's wardrobe. "Bob wouldn't mind. In fact, he'd insist," Katie had said.

Once in the lobby, Katie took a final inventory and had everyone "pick a partner" before proceeding past security and out the front door of the hospital. Of course, Doug teamed up with John, whom he had come to regard as something of a big brother—even a surrogate father. They filed to the right, heading west up Haddon Avenue alongside the six-foot-high gray stone outer wall that surrounded the convent grounds. At a wide break in the wall marking the main gate entrance, they turned to enter a brick-paved courtyard, used as a parking area for visitors and maintenance staff.

For an instant John thought he was back in colonial America, only this courtyard had an even older feel to it, almost medieval. The buildings were constructed of gray field stone, or at least a gray stone façade. The church and sanctuary were situated to the left of the main gate and courtyard, facing the street, as another line of buildings continued at right angles to the church at the rear of the courtyard. To the right of the last building a second iron gate opened into a grassy yard, filling the space between the inner and outer stone walls of the compound, about forty feet wide. From here a flagstone walkway ran straight back, the only means for outsiders like themselves to reach the gardens located at the rear of the compound.

The patients were gathered in the middle of the courtyard, now, like school kids on a class trip, as Katie approached and knocked on the large red, wooden double door entrance to the building at the rear of the courtyard. A small, square peephole door opened and John saw Katie exchanging words with someone inside. *Like a speakeasy from prohibition,* John thought. He found the comparison amusing. *Was holy water being bootlegged these days?*

The right half of the double door opened just wide enough to allow a small figure to emerge, dressed in a black and white habit, typical of her particular order. John assumed her to be the mother superior. After closing the door behind her, she accompanied Katie to the waiting group of patients.

"I'd like all of you to meet Mother Superior Marguerite D'Esprit," Katie announced. "She was gracious enough to let us come here today to enjoy the beautiful gardens cared for by her order."

The reverend mother was a tiny woman, her face aged and wrinkled but bearing a pleasant smile and penetrating deep blue eyes. Her hands remained clasped together in front of her, wrapped in a string of rosaries.

Katie turned to Mother Marguerite. "Reverend Mother, I want to thank you, both for myself and on behalf of the patients of Our Lady of Lourdes."

"You are quite welcome, my child. Please, enjoy your walk through our gardens." She turned to address the patients. "I will light a votive candle in the sanctuary for each of you, and pray for your speedy recovery. May God bless you all!"

Her voice was sincere and soothing. John felt better already, even without the candles.

Doug whispered in John's ear: "What's a v-votive candle?"

John whispered back: "When you pray for someone or take a vow, you light a candle. It's a symbolic way of wishing someone well, or sealing the vow."

"Oh, I s-see."

Over the course of the next hour or so, John and company soaked up the fresh floral scents and warm vibes of the convent grounds. Squirrels and chipmunks chattered and scampered helter-skelter about the compound, as the sounds and cares of the outside world melted away within the safe confines of these gray stone walls. Time seemed to stand still. The only clue that they were still in the twentieth century were the contrails of a jet airliner streaking high overhead against a dark blue, cloudless sky, the faint rumble of its jet engines trailing far behind.

"So, J-John. When did the doctor say you could go home?" Doug asked.

"Well, if the MRI tests don't reveal anything abnormal, I'm free to go home today."

Doug remained silent.

"How about you, Doug? What's your situation, if ya don't mind me askin?" John chuckled at the thought of his limping friend, Captain Jack, from eighteenth-century Greenwich.

"I d-don't know, exactly," Doug replied, ignoring John's cheap Irish brogue.

John thought a moment. "And where will you be staying, once you leave the hospital?"

Doug didn't say anything right away. "D-don't know for sure. I got friends. That's for s-sure."

John considered his next words carefully before speaking. "Well, listen, Doug. If you ever need a helping hand, just look me up. Remind me to give you my business card when we get back to the hospital. Capiche?"

"Right. Capiche!" Doug replied cheerily.

On returning to the CIU activity room, John was given a piece of good news from the head nurse on duty. The official radiologist's report from John's brain scan gave him a clean bill of health: "No remarkable anomalies found," the report stated. Basically, John was free to go home.

John approached Katie with the good news.

"Whew! That's really great, John. But, are you feeling well enough to go home?"

"Yeah! Actually, I'm feeling much better. I think it was the walk in your little 'Garden of Eden' next door. It really perked me up. Got me thinkin' how much I missed the outdoors."

"Well, okay then. I'll ask José to get your personal things together. And the stuff security had locked away."

"Like my cell phone and billfold?" John asked.

"Right!"

Katie did a double take. "You know, speaking of cell phones," she said, "I received a couple of curious voice messages on my phone earlier this week. They came from your cell phone number. The first one sounded like you, but the second one was definitely someone else. I don't know, maybe they got mixed up in transmission somehow."

"Really? When were they sent?" John asked.

"Well, that's the other curious thing," Katie said. "The voice message said '*Sunday* September twelfth.' But the screen display read '*Monday*, 12 Sept.'"

John thought about that. "Did it tell you the year?" he asked.

"The *year*?" Katie exclaimed. "Of course not! I think it just assumes the current year."

John paused. "Well, like you said, maybe the signals just got crossed up somehow. Or maybe it's a millennial bug or something. You know, how some people are predicting a meltdown at midnight this New Year's Eve. Do you have the phone with you?"

"Yes, but we're not supposed to use them in the hospital."

John looked around. "I think it's okay," he said. "There's no telemetry monitoring equipment operating on this floor. Do you still have the messages?"

Katie took the cell phone from her purse and punched in the commands for message recall. "Sure. Here, you can listen to them."

John took the phone and listened to the first message. There was a lot of background static, but it was definitely John's voice: "Hello, Katie, Can you hear me?...(pause)...This is John. I'm calling from somewhere...from Stowe Creek Landing, somewhere in South Jersey. Can you hear me?"

John's pulse quickened.

He listened to the next message: "Hello! Hello! Is anyone there? Can anyone hear me? " It was the voice of a young man. The accent was British— no, make that *American Colonial English.*

Katie looked at John. "You okay, John? You look like you just saw a ghost!"

John thought: *Not saw...heard.*

"S-sure. I'm fine," he stammered.

John slowly closed the lid of the cell phone and handed it back to Kate.

PART THREE

I wander all night in my vision,
Stepping with light feet, swiftly and noiselessly stepping and stopping,
Bending with open eyes over the shut eyes of sleepers,
Wandering and confused, lost to myself, ill-assorted, contradictory,
Pausing, gazing, bending, and stopping.

Walt Whitman, "The Sleepers," *Leaves of Grass*.

Chapter 17

1774
Saturday, 17 September
Greenwich, Cumberland County

The day started off unseasonably warm. Thomas Whitman, hard at work in his blacksmith shop, had drawn the doors of his shed wide open for better ventilation, but by mid-afternoon the weather was turning cool and blustery and he was thinking about closing them. Looking up from his work, Thomas was startled to see his good friend, Chief Dan Fire Cloud, standing just inside the doorway, quiet and still, arms folded across his chest, his solid frame silhouetted against the intruding daytime glare of the afternoon sun.

Dan was a big man, almost the size of Thomas. As was his custom, Dan wore a blend of traditional Indian and white settlers' garb: buckskin trousers, a vest decorated with beads and trinkets of carved oyster and tortoise shells, a three-cornered hat festooned with turkey feathers, and a splendid pair of black leather boots. The boots were a gift from Thomas.

Thomas didn't know how long Dan Fire Cloud had been standing there silent and unannounced, maybe the entire morning for all he knew.

"Chief! You startled me!"

Chief Dan nodded. "And a good day to you, Thomas, my good friend. May I come in?"

Thomas laid down his hammer and picked up a towel to wipe his hands. "Certainly, Dan. You know you're always welcome here." He walked over and embraced Dan, giving him a firm hug and pat on the back. "And to what do I owe this unexpected visit, my friend?" he asked, drawing himself away.

"I have come to seek advice, Thomas."

"Advice? What advice could I possibly give a wise old man like yourself."

Dan Fire Cloud was a full-blooded Lenni Lenape Indian, one of only a handful of his people remaining in Cumberland County in 1774, a mere remnant of the Unilachtigo nation that once populated the southern regions of New Jersey. Since the arrival of the Europeans over a century before, most of the tribes and villages in the area had scattered to other regions of the colonies, or been relocated to reservations, like the one established in

Burlington County about seventy miles to the north. Brotherton, as it was called, was created in 1758 on a 3,284-acre tract of land as part of ongoing negotiations with the Lenni Lenape to make reparations for lands lost to the new European settlers. Negotiations continued in good faith over the years, and in due course tribes and individuals were compensated for lands and lost hunting and fishing rights. It was a credit to the honorable intentions of both sides that this was achieved without the spilling of blood.

Unfortunately, the old ways and new ways did not always mix well. With the arrival of the Europeans came disease and pestilence. While the white man over the years had developed some measure of immunity against them, they proved devastatingly fatal to the Indians, now exposed to them for the first time, and even the most potent herbs and incantations of their medicine men proved futile against the scourges of smallpox and tuberculosis. It was said—perhaps an overstatement—that "for every white man that settled in this area, six Indians died."[7] However debatable the statistics, the results were a simple matter of history: Native American culture in Cumberland County ceased to exist as it had for countless centuries before the arrival of the Europeans.

Geographical and family divisions overlapped in a rather complex way among the Lenni Lenape.[8] Geographically, the Lenni Lenape in New Jersey were divided into three regions or nations, each ruled by a tribal chief, or sachem, and identified by a unique tribal totem or insignia: the Minsi—"people of the stony country"—lived in the far north (Wolf totem); the Unami—"people who live down river"—occupied the central regions of the colony (Turtle totem); and the Unilachtigo—"people who live near the ocean"—made their homes along the southern shores and inland waterways (Turkey totem).

In addition to one's tribal affiliation, which was based solely geographical area, every Lenni Lenape was identified as belonging to one of three sub-divisions or families which overlapped all three geographical regions. To confuse matters further, the three families were identified with the same names and personal totems as were associated with the tribal nations. There were, then, the Minsi Family (Wolf totem); the Unami Family (Turtle totem); and the Unilachtigo family (Turkey totem). Families in turn were divided into "clans," each with a clan chief who answered to the tribal or nation chief in which he and his clan were located. It is interesting to note that the family clan line was traced through the mother, with all children born

---

[7] Anne Schillingsburg Woodruff and F. Alan Palmer, *The Unalachtigo of New Jersey: The Original People of Cumberland County* (Cumberland County Historical Society, 1973), 16.

[8] Ibid., 2-4, contains a detailed description of geographical and family divisions among the Unalachtigo, forming the basis for this narrative.

into the mother's clan. Therefore, while the clan chief was a male, the position was inherited through the mother and female line.

Dan White Cloud was the great-grandson of one of the last active turtle clan Indian chiefs in the Unilachtigo nation of the Unami family. While he realized that he had no legitimate claim to the title of "Chief"—since he traced his lineage through the father's rather than the mother's line—to the local white settlers, who traditionally traced ownership and titles through the male line, he was known as "Chief Dan."

"Have you heard about the fire at the Stern's farm?" the Chief asked.

Thomas was aware of it. "You mean the barn burning, night before last?"

"Yes. You are correct, my friend. Thursday night. And do you know the cause of this fire?"

Thomas ran his hand through his hair, removing his cap at the same time. He knew what Chief Dan was getting at.

"Say, Dan. Why don't we go inside. I can have Isabel brew a fresh pot of tea for us."

"That would be nice," Dan replied.

Thomas led the way from the shed the short distance through the side yard to the back porch and kitchen door of his cottage home. Thomas hung his cap and leather apron on their assigned wall pegs just inside the back door as he entered the kitchen, with Dan following close behind. The three glass witch balls hanging in front of the kitchen window swayed in the draft created by the two large men as they passed, making a tinkling sound as one lightly knocked against the other two.

Isabel was busy sorting laundry on the kitchen table when the two men entered, but recognized the Chief from of the corner of her eye. "Hello, Chief. I'm surprised to see you so early in the afternoon on market day. Is everything all right?" she asked.

"Yes, Miss Isabel. I am fine, thank you. The market was just…slow today," the Chief replied with some hesitation. "I decided to pack up early. Besides, it looks like rain. Maybe a nor'easter coming through. Thought I'd pay a visit to my good friend, Thomas, before heading home."

Thomas turned to Isabel. "Isabel, would you please prepare a pot of tea for me and the Chief. Make enough for yourself, as well. And please add just a touch of sassafras to mine. My stomach is feeling a bit out of sorts today."

"Yes sir. I'll get right to it," Isabel replied. She cleared the table of laundry and went to fetch a pot of fresh water from the hand pump on the back porch.

Thomas and Chief Dan sat down at the kitchen table across from one another. "So, how are things out by Stowe Creek?" he asked.

"The waters continue to flow to the bay," Dan replied stoically.

Thomas smiled.

Dan Fire Cloud lived alone in a one-room log cabin along Stowe Creek, about a mile upstream from the landing where the main road—the King's Highway—crossed the creek by ferry. Chief Dan had been compensated for the lands forfeited by his ancestors by the terms reached in 1758 between the colonial government of New Jersey and the Lenni Lenape nations. With his holdings, he was able to secure a large parcel of land located along Stowe Creek, near the actual site of his ancestral home. This is where he built his cabin. He leased out a portion of the land for farming and this provided a steady income, which he supplemented by weaving and selling baskets in the marketplace on weekends, which is to say, on Fridays and Saturdays.

Chief Dan did not always live alone. When he'd established his homestead fifteen years ago he was married with four children—a daughter and three sons—with one more on the way. Many of his kin had already relocated to reservations like Brotherton, or to other less settled regions of the colonies. Even his eldest son, newly married, picked up stakes and headed west. Dan was never sure where he ended up, and hadn't heard from him at all since the day he left.

Two years after building the cabin and partly settled into a new way of life, Dan's wife, daughter, and newborn son died from an epidemic of smallpox sweeping the region. Dan himself contracted the disease but was able to fend it off and recover somehow. That just left Dan and his two middle sons: Wild Turkey, the older of the two, and his younger brother, Still Water.

Wild Turkey adapted reasonably well to the new ways of the white man. He learned the shipbuilder's trade and was able to find steady work in the Greenwich ship yards. Though difficult at first, he eventually won the acceptance and respect of his fellow white workers as his fearless sense of balance placed him among a small group of workers valued for their ability to work the ships' highest rigging. Married now with steady work and a modest living wage, Wild Turkey lived with his wife and two young children in a small bungalow just outside of town, within walking distance of the ship yards.

Still Water was a dreamer. Like his older brother he gravitated to the nautical trades, but his spirit of adventure led him to the open seas, not the port-bound life of a shipbuilder. As a young teen, he stowed away aboard a frigate bound for the Caribbean. Once discovered, he was adopted as the ship captain's "cabin boy" for the remainder of the voyage, and from that point on Still Water never looked back. His adopted ship's nickname was Stewey, or Stew for short, a derivative form of "Stowaway."

"So, how are your sons doing, Dan? Your son, Wild Turkey, and his wife, aren't they expecting their third child soon?"

"Yes, you are correct," Dan smiled. "But I sometimes worry that he lacks the means to support a growing family. It's not like the old days, my friend. We have had to learn…new ways."

"I understand," said Thomas. "And your other two sons, do you have any news of them?"

Chief Dan sighed deeply. "I believe that no news is good news," the Chief said.

He reached into his waist pouch, pulled out a small object and set it on the table. Thomas looked closely at the object. It was an amulet of some kind, carved from bone, and bore an inscribed image on its face—the symbol of a flame.

Thomas reached out and touched the amulet, running his fingertips over the ridges of the inscription.

"A shaman's amulet," Thomas said, "for invoking the powers of healing."

The Chief nodded. "Yes. And other powers as well," he added.

Chief Dan Fire Cloud was trained in the art of healing, and other so-called magic arts which claimed to bridge the natural or visible world with the spirit world. Thomas knew this. In fact, it was Dan's shaman skills that first brought Dan and Thomas together. It was about four years ago, not long after Elijah, Rebecca's little brother, died from lockjaw. Rebecca had fallen ill with fever and ague which was not responding to white man's medicine. She had become delirious and dehydrated.

"Isn't there anything else you can do, doc?" Thomas had asked Doc Woods.

Doc Woods just shook his head. "I'm afraid there's nothing else I can do for your child, Thomas. But…"—the doctor hesitated—"Dan Fire Cloud, the old Indian chief living out by Stowe Creek, may have some herbal remedies that could work for her. I've seen it work before in cases like this."

Thomas wasn't convinced, but figured it wouldn't hurt to try. He was desperate. Bundling up the shivering Rebecca and placing her in the wagon, he drove the five miles to Stowe Creek Landing where he was directed upstream to the Chief's cabin. Following a day of incantations and the application of special herbal poultices, Rebecca's fever broke and she soon regained her senses. Thomas repaid the Chief with a new pair of leather boots and they became good friends after that, each helping the other whenever the need arose. Thomas soon developed a deep respect for the Chief and his ancient ways, and shared an unspoken hurt over their personal family losses and the dissolution of tribal bonds that accompanied the diaspora of the Unilachtigo nation.

The amulet now lying on the table was the same amulet the Chief wore the day Rebecca was healed.

"So, the talk in town has it that the recent fires, the Stern's barn fire in particular, are the work of an arsonist," Thomas said. He looked down at the amulet with its flame symbol. "And some even claim to know who the arsonist is." He looked up and across the table at the Chief. "Is that what you are hearing, Chief?"

The Chief nodded. "Yes, my friend. The rumors at the market are pointing the finger…at me, or one of my sons, which is why I left early. No one was buying my baskets."

Thomas sat back and shook his head. "But no one has confronted you directly?" he asked.

"No." The Chief smiled. "They are perhaps…afraid of the consequences."

"Not to mess with the medicine man, eh?" Thomas laughed.

"Perhaps. But it is not me I worry about. It is my son, Wild Turkey. I fear he may lose his job at the boatyards if the rumors continue. That is why I come to you, Thomas."

Thomas looked puzzled. "But what can I do?"

"Perhaps you can talk to the foreman at the boatyards. I know you are acquainted with Master Bart, who has some influence with them."

"Yes, I do know Mr. Weston. But mostly through his younger brother, John."

Thomas noted the drawn and worried look on the Chief's face.

"But, I'll see what I can do, Dan. Try not to fret too much. Perhaps the true nature of these events will be revealed, or it will all simply pass with time."

*****

The tinkle of door bells singled another customer at Mason's Tailor Shoppe. Rebecca looked up from behind the counter, where she had been sorting bolts of cloth for Mrs. Mason, and was surprised to see, by the clock on the wall, it was already past 3:00 in the afternoon. It had been a very busy Saturday and the hours just seemed to fly by. Rebecca greeted the new customer.

"Why, good afternoon, Mrs. Stern! I'm surprised to see you out and about today."

Abigail Stern paused just inside the shop.

"My! The weather certainly is taking a turn!" she said as she removed her scarf and straightened her hair. "The wind is really picking up. Looks like we might be in for a storm."

"Yes, ma'am," Rebecca replied. "I was really sorry to hear about your misfortune. I mean the barn burning and all."

Abigail Stern forced a smile and walked up to the counter. She was holding a satchel in her folded arms. "Yes, thank you, my dear. We've certainly had our hands full picking up the pieces. But, thanks be to God, no one was hurt."

Judith Mason entered the shop from the back room carrying a small bundle of clothes. "I thought I heard a familiar voice out here," Judith said. She laid down her bundle of clothes on the counter, turned and embraced her friend. Backing away and inspecting her at arms' length she added, "I'm so glad to hear no one was hurt. Such a terrible thing! How in the world do you think it happened?"

"We really don't know, Judith. We know it wasn't lightening, and Ralph feels certain it wasn't an overturned lantern. He thinks it started in the hayloft and he keeps no lanterns up there."

Just then the tall, thin frame of Robert Mason appeared from the back room. He was carrying a wire- and wood-framed torso mannequin displaying his latest fashion creation; he intended to position it by the front store window—the only window in the shop with glass windowpanes.

"Rebecca, can you please help me with this mannequin? I'd like to position it by the window and…oh, a good day to you, Mrs. Stern. I didn't see you standing there."

Abigail nodded and smiled. "Hello, Robert. My! That is quite a fetching creation you have there!"

"Why, thank you, ma'am." Mr. Mason stood back with his hands on his hips to admire his creation. The gown's gold lace trim shone brightly, reflecting the direct beams of sunlight coming in through the window.

"Yes, I must say! It looks rather stunning in the direct light of day!"

"It's too bad you don't have more windows to showcase your wares," Abigail noted as she looked around the shop.

She was correct. It's not that the building was constructed without windows, but to avoid the British tax placed upon the number of individual glass window panes found in any home or business establishment, many colonists resorted to bricking up their windows to the bare minimum. For the Masons this meant only one store front window remained to let in the light and allow passersby to view the merchandise. Robert was thinking now that perhaps he had gone too far.

"Alas! The absurd pane tax has forced me to cover most of my windows," he said in exasperation. "When Parliament resorts to taxing the hairs on my head, then I shall be forced to shave my crown and wear a wig!"

Rebecca had to chuckle. Abigail turned and smiled, placing a hand to her mouth to stifle a laugh.

"Eh, what's that I hear to you say?" his soliloquy continued, "Would that the Whigs in Parliament shave the power of the crown instead!"

"Ahem." Rebecca cleared her throat to get Mr. Mason's attention. "Sir, you asked me to help you…with the mannequin?"

Mr. Mason collected his thoughts and turned to Rebecca. "Yes, of course, my dear. I need to position this mannequin to attract the attention of passersby. I would like you to go outside and tell me how to position it for best viewing from the street."

"Yes, sir. I can do that."

Rebecca put down the bolt of cloth and headed out the front door.

On the other side of the room Abigail Stern placed her satchel on the counter top and motioned to Judith to get her attention.

"So, Abby, what can I do for you?"

Abigail reached into her satchel and pulled out a piece of white cloth, laying it out on the table for Abigail's inspection. It was a shawl, a white shawl with the black monogrammed letters:

AG

Abigail gave Judith a moment to study the shawl.

"Judith, would you know who this shawl belongs to?" Abigail said at last. "I figured you'd be the best person in town to ask."

Judith reached for the shawl. "Do you mind?"

Abigail nodded. "Please. Be my guest."

Judith picked up the shawl and examined it more closely. "Hmm, if I'm not mistaken, I do believe this shawl belongs to…Agatha Greene."

She looked at Abigail straight in the eyes. "How did you come by it, Abby?"

"My Ralphie picked it up yesterday afternoon, after the fire. He found it snagged on a branch just a stone's throw from the barn—the barn that burned down."

Judith fondled the cloth, slowly rubbing her fingers over the embroidered lettering. "Come with me," she said.

Abigail followed Judith into the back room, the mending room, crowded with worktables and racks of clothes of every sort in various stages of alteration and repair. They continued into an adjoining room lined with shelves that were stacked with boxes of clothing on one side of the room marked "Clean," the other side marked "Soiled."

"The garments we receive from customers usually need a good washing before mending," Judith explained. "We keep the soiled ones sorted and separate from the clean ones, as you can see."

Judith located one "Soiled" box which was set apart from the others. "These clothes were brought in yesterday by Albert Greene. They belong to his wife, Agatha."

"Why are they set apart from the others?" Abigail asked.

Judith removed and held up a torn dress for Abby's closer inspection. Abby backed away. "Whew! It reeks of smoke!" she said.

That's when she noticed the monogrammed initials on the dress. It matched the monogram on the shawl. Abigail suddenly made the connection. "Oh my God! Do you think it was...Agatha who set the fire?" she exclaimed.

"Sshh! Not so loud, dear," Judith whispered. "We can't go making accusations like that...not without proof."

"But, you know what people are saying? That old Dan Fire Cloud is responsible for the fires. And not just the Stern's fire, but all the previous ones, as well. And what proof do they have for that?"

Judith let out a sigh and nodded. "I know. It's...just not right, is it?"

Chapter 18

1999
Sunday, 26 September
Camden County, New Jersey

John made a right turn off Lakeland Road into the cyclone fenced-in parking lot of Lakeland, Camden County's center for public health and human services. The complex consisted of a cluster of five or so red brick buildings straddling Lakeland Road as it T-intersected with Woodbury-Turnersville Road to the west. Mostly colonial in style, the buildings looked like they could have been lifted from the campus of William and Mary.

John found an empty spot close to the administration building and parked his tan Toyota Camry. There was an early autumn chill in the air, but with the noonday sun beating down and the windows rolled up, the car remained warm and toasty, like a greenhouse or terrarium. John cracked the front windows and was refreshed by a cool cross breeze. *Good thing, no greenhead flies around here*, he thought. He sat there for a few more minutes with the engine running, listening to the final refrains of an old Beach Boys surfing classic on the radio.

Lakeland was situated less than a mile off the Blackhorse Pike in the outskirts of Blackwood, a small crossroads community tucked away in the southwest corner of the county. Surrounded by wooded fields and streams, the area retained much of the serenity and sanative isolation which marked the site as one of the county's original centers for healing and rehabilitation. The area had since become the site for other county functions, as well, with the county fair grounds and 4-H club facilities occupying the open fields on the other side of Woodbury-Turnersville Road

Beyond the administration building, across several hundred feet of rolling fields broken by a hidden ravine and stream, John could make out another imposing six-story structure, also made of red brick. It appeared much older and more austere than the others, as many of its windows had metal grills or bars on the outside, and the wooden trim was in need of a fresh coat of paint. This was Lakeland's Psychiatric Hospital, John's ultimate destination today.

Despite the distance and broken terrain, getting to the hospital was not a problem. Connecting the rear of the administration building to the hospital was an enclosed pedestrian walkway. Starting out at ground level it rose above the falling contour of the land and became a sky bridge, crossing over a hidden gully and stream until it joined with the hospital on the far hillside. It made for a pleasant walk, even in bad weather.

John and Katie had arranged to meet at the snack shop located inside the administration building, toward the rear of the first floor near the entrance to the sky bridge. When John got there, he didn't see Kate, so he took a seat in the lounge area just outside the snack shop. A few minutes later Katie emerged from the shop holding two Styrofoam cups, her face brightening as she recognized John. John grabbed two empty lounge chairs and a small coffee table and motioned to Katie.

"Hello, John. I hope you like instant," she said as she approached. "The coffeepot is being cleaned, I'm afraid."

She held out a steaming cup and John took it.

"Thanks, Kate. Instant ain't so bad. If you cover it up with enough real cream."

John took the seat across from Katie. Studying her for a moment he thought she was looking better than the last time he had seen her at Our Lady of Lourdes Hospital more than a week ago. It was just this past Monday when Bob had been admitted to Lakeland under the care of Dr. Alexander. John was eager to see Bob and talk about certain things, but was also a little anxious about what he might find.

"So, how is Bob responding to treatment here at Lakeland?" John asked.

Katie rested her cup in the palm of her left hand and continued stirring slowly with a plastic swizzle stick. Looking across at John she forced a smile.

"Dr. Alexander is actually quite pleased with the progress Bob has made in such a short time. He thinks the new medication, in combination with the therapy, has produced some very positive results."

"That's great to hear, Kate. And, do you see a difference in him?"

Katie peered down into her cup of swirling coffee. "I think only time will tell," she said noncommittally. "But *you*, John"—suddenly perking up— "you certainly look a thousand percent better than the last time I saw you." She leaned sideways to get a better look at his neck. "Looks like that bite has all but healed."

John reached up and gently massaged his neck. "Oh, yeah. No problemo! I think the doctors and rehab staff at Lourdes nipped everything in the bud! Capiche?"

Katie laughed. "Are you following up with Dr. Caldwell?"

"Oh, you mean the hocus pocus hypnosis doc? I have an appointment with him later this week. The standard two-week follow-up visit." Then, in a more serious tone: "So, tell me, Kate. Have you told Bob about my…recent illness?"

Katie sighed and pursed her lips. "No John. I thought it best not to bother him with any troubling news."

John nodded knowingly. "Good idea. It's probably best to keep it that way. For the time being anyway," he said softly. "If you don't mind, at some point today I'd like to speak with Bob alone. There are some things pertaining to…the business that I'd like to discuss with him."

"Sure, that's no problem, John. Just give me the sign when you want me to go."

"Thanks, Kate."

Changing the subject, John tried to lighten things up a bit. "Oh, by the way, I did my first stint as a tour guide yesterday at the Indian King Tavern. New colonial threads and a wig, the whole nine yards!"

"Nice! How'd it go?"

"Great! It was lots of fun. I only got stumped once. A young kid asked me how much it cost for a night's lodging in those days. I wasn't sure. Said I'd get back to him, if he left his number in the guest sign-in book."

"So, how much did it cost?" Katie pursued.

"Sign the guest book. I'll give you a call."

Katie laughed.

At that moment a thin, middle-aged man in a wrinkled white lab coat, tie and sneakers approached Katie from behind. He was short and mousy looking, with a pair of wire-rim reading glasses set low on the bridge of his nose.

"Mrs. Fenwick?" he said in a squeaky voice.

Katie turned her head. It was Dr. Alexander.

"Yes, hello doctor." She started to get up.

"Please, don't get up." The doctor reached out and took her hand. "Do you mind if I join you…and your friend?"

"Certainly not, please do," Katie replied.

John stood up as Katie made the introductions.

"Please consider John as family," Katie said, as John and the doctor shook hands. "Anything you tell me, you can tell him."

The doctor smiled to seal the deal, then pulled up a wooden captain's chair to join John and Katie around the coffee table. His unbuttoned lab jacket spread apart revealing an especially wide tie so unevenly tied that the smaller end extended well below the wider, front end. Funny how tie styles seemed to cycle over the years between thin and wide; only, in the doctor's case, the spinning fashion wheel had stopped on "extra wide" years ago and remained stuck there.

"Now, before I take you across the bridge to see Bob, let me explain what we know of Bob's condition, and what you can expect to find."

Katie took a Kleenex tissue from her purse, dabbed her eyes, and continued to clutch the tissue firmly in her lap. The doctor sensed her concern.

"First, let me say, I am very pleased with the progress Bob has made in the short time he has been with us, Katie. I think you'll see a significant improvement in Bob's demeanor just since last Monday, the day he was admitted."

Katie forced a nervous smile.

"Having first weaned Bob off of Thorazine before he was admitted, we started him on a combined regimen of Trilafon and Zyprexa. I've had considerable success with this combination drug therapy for the kinds of paranoid schizophrenia Bob appears to exhibit. If it works as planned, it should eliminate the acute episodes and control the severity of symptoms, reducing the swings of mania and depression as well. In time, we may be able to discontinue the Zyprexa to avoid the consequences of long-term use and maintain him with Trilafon alone, or one of the other newer atypical antipsychotic drugs that are becoming available."

"So, what are…the consequences of long-term use?" Katie asked anxiously.

"Well, the usual side effects are weight gain…and an increased risk of diabetes. The drug tends to alter the body's metabolism of glucose, you understand."

"Oh, I see," said Katie, not at all concerned with the details, just the bottom line.

"And of course, we would also be on the lookout for the broader range of side effects, like muscle tremor, tachycardia and, in certain cases, seizures. But at the low doses Bob is taking and responding to, I don't think we need to worry too much about those things."

Katie tensed up at the word "seizures," clutching her Kleenex even harder.

"So, doctor," John inquired, "when you say 'atypical antipsychotic drug,' what do you mean? That his condition is not typical?"

"No, not at all. It's just a term given to differentiate the older, so-called 'typical' drugs, like Trilafon, from the newer class of dopamine inhibitor drugs, what we call the 'atypical' antipsychotic drugs. As I explained to Katie earlier in the week, the dopamine pathways in the brain are involved in a wide range of psychological disorders. Both the typical and atypical drugs act on these dopamine receptor sites. However, the newer 'atypical' drugs, like Zyprexa, tend to be more selective in affecting only certain sites and pathways, producing fewer side effects…"

Boy, this guy's a walking, talking Pharmacopeia!

"…They are also better at treating the so-called 'negative symptoms' of schizophrenia when present, such as a decline in motivation, speech, or emotional response. In Bob's case, his symptoms of social withdrawal have all but disappeared in response to the new drug therapy."

Katie released her firm grip on the Kleenex. "That's really good to hear, doctor," she said. "So, you're saying his behavior is…back to normal?"

Doctor Alexander puckered and smacked his lips. "I said his condition has improved. Greatly improved in fact. But I would hesitate to say 'back to normal.' We still have some ways to go. But I am very hopeful."

John and Katie looked at each other.

"So, when can we see him, doc?" John asked.

Doctor Alexander perked up.

"Well, how about *now*?" He looked down at his wristwatch. "Let's see. Lunch should be over, so we should probably find him in the day room. Bob has privileges. Which means he's not considered to be a threat to himself or others, so he is free to go about almost anywhere in the facility, whenever he feels he is ready. He seems to like the day room best at this time of day."

"Well, let's go, then. Before he gets away from us," John said buoyantly.

After crossing the sky bridge to the hospital, the doctor led the way up an elevator and down a hall or two, until they finally came to a large common lounge area, the day room. Dr. Alexander continued to the far side of the room where Bob Fenwick was engaged in a game of chess with a fellow patient.

"Hello, Bob. I have two visitors that would like to…"

"Shhh! Doctor, you'll spoil my concentration!" Bob interrupted with a wave of the hand, without ever looking up. "The end game! Gotta focus on the end game!"

Bob let out an audible sigh and slumped back into his chair. "Too late," he said shaking his head. Then, looking up from the chess board, he added nonchalantly, "Oh, hello Kate. I didn't see you standing there. And John! When did you guys get here?"

John spoke first. "Just a few moments ago, Bob. Sorry if we disturbed your game."

Katie went to Bob's side and began to lightly massage his shoulders. Bob looked up and gently took Kate's hand.

"Good to see you, babe. Thanks for coming by—and for bringing this other guy with you."

He looked up and gave John a wink. Turning back to Kate he added with a stage whisper, "Tell me, did you remember to bring the cake with the metal file buried inside?"

Kate squeezed his hand and smiled. "No, dear. I didn't think you were looking to escape. Thought you rather liked it here."

"Actually, you're right!" He pushed the chair back and stood up, motioning to his silent chess partner still seated in his leather lounge chair facing Bob.

"Harry, I concede the game!" Then, looking across at John, "You know, Harry, here, he might be crazy, but he's one helluva chess player! I almost had him beat. Finally! But he confounded me toward the end. The best I could hope for was a stalemate."

Harry just nodded and grinned, as he puffed furiously on a cigarette. The ashtray on the table was full to overflowing with butts.

John smiled and took a deep breath, relieved to see Bob behaving like his old self again—perhaps even more than his old self.

Just then the PA system announced: "Dr. Alexander. Please pick up on 211."

The doctor turned his head toward the sound of the PA. "Ah, please excuse me, folks. Duty calls." He turned to Kate "Mrs. Fenwick, would you please stop by and see me when you are able to break away. You know where my office is. Just down the hall, last door on the right."

Katie nodded. "Certainly, doctor."

Addressing John the doctor added, "And it was a pleasure meeting you, John. Please, stay as long as you like."

Or as long as I need to? If the doctor only knew!

Katie found an empty sofa lounge by the nearest window for the three of them to sit; they made themselves comfortable. For the next thirty minutes or so they were able to engage in "normal" conversation, with Katie and John bringing Bob up to speed on events at home and work. John thought he saw Bob's eyes moisten when Katie told him how well Amanda and Bobbie Jr. were adjusting to their new school year. It had been such a rough summer for them, coping with their dad's strange behavior. Next Bob wanted to know how things were going with the project at GenAvance and Dr. Sam Li. John was pleased to hear Bob speak favorably of Sam. He no longer appeared to harbor feelings of paranoia toward him.

"So, when is the next trip to Thousand Oaks?" Bob asked.

"Actually," John was quick to reply, "Jim Connelly and Jacob Carlson flew out last week to meet with Dr. Li's design team and Bruce Hanson, their VP of Global Engineering."

"So, you didn't join them?" Bob pursued.

John squirmed a little in his seat as he was forced to lie to his friend. "No, I was...recovering from the flu, and besides, I didn't think it was necessary this time around. I plan to fly out the middle of next month to deliver the final conceptual design report. Our team is driving up to Rutgers this coming Wednesday to meet with Dr. Julie Evert and survey the future site for the new pilot plant."

Katie looked up at the clock on the wall, then over to John. John nodded, and Katie took her cue to leave him alone with Bob. "Hey, guys, it's getting late. I'd better go see what Dr. Alexander wanted."

Katie got up, leaned over, and gave Bob a kiss on the top of the head. "I'll see you before I leave, hon, when I'm finished with the doctor. Shouldn't take too long."

Bob smiled. "Okay, babe. You know where to find me."

Bob's eyes followed Kate across the room and out the door before he turned around again. As he did so, John noticed a subtle shift in his mood. More subdued, preoccupied.

"You know, John. This is a rather interesting place. You find all kinds of people here."

"I can well imagine," John replied, recalling his own recent experience at Lady of Lourdes.

"I mean, some people have been here for twenty, thirty years or more. Take that sweet little old lady over there." Bob pointed to a white haired woman seated alone on the other side of the room who looked to be in her eighties. "That's Agnes. Claims she was a gun moll for the mob in her early years. Came here 'to escape the mob,' she said. That was over fifty years ago. Been here ever since."

"Do you believe her?" John asked.

Bob shrugged his shoulders. "Have no reason not to." Continuing to stare across the room he added, "But she's one of the lucky ones. The locked wards are on a different floor. Sixth floor, I believe. That's where they keep the real loonies, those that don't respond to treatment. The 'Lifers' as we say around here."

John could see Bob's expression and demeanor continue to change, from friendly and thoughtful, to somber and tense. "So, tell me, John,"—turning slowly and drawing closer to John—"Have you been hearing…the *voices*, too?"

John was totally taken aback. His mind was suddenly flooded with images of Labor Day in Bob's basement, with Bob holding the crowbar in a threatening pose.

"What on earth are you talking about, Bob?"

Bob reached over and touched John on the side of the neck. "That bite is looking better, John. Tell me, did you get to meet *her* in your recent travels?"

What!? How did Bob know about that? Did Katie tell him? No! She said she hadn't.

As John reached up to brush Bob's hand away, Bob took firm hold of John's wrist. "What was her name, John?" Bob asked softly. "Rebecca? Rebecca Whitman? Wasn't that it?"

A chill ran up John's spine. "H-how did you…? How could you know?" John stammered, barely getting the words out.

Bob grinned a broad, Cheshire cat grin. "I told you, John. It's the voices," he said slowly, calmly. "For you see, it is written, 'I am but…a single, lone voice, a messenger, crying in the wilderness.' But you, John, you are…the chosen one."

The sound of buzzing flies began to fill John's head. Suddenly, a bright white flash of light, and then…

…John found himself seated at a table. There, on the table, was a Ouija board, elaborately decorated with embroidered graphics. The words "GO BACK! SAVE HER!" were written in red letters across the center of the board. A young man and woman were seated at the table. The young woman looked up and addressed John directly, "John Weston, the chosen one!" When John looked back at the board, the letters had changed to spell the single word: "CURSES"…

It was the vision of his dream—the one preceding the nightmare of the woman on the burning boat. John's heart was pounding as he emerged from this visionary state. Staring blankly into Bob's glistening eyes, John sensed that Bob, too, had shared the same vision, somehow. Slowly, Bob released his grip, permitting John to regain his composure.

Bob's face now retained an almost radiant glow. Relieved of all tension, like he had finally rid himself of a great burden, he reached up and wiped his eyes. John, though confused, felt a sense of relief as well, like he was no longer hiding a big secret from his friend. But somehow, someway, Bob knew, and John was dumbfounded. Without so much as a few words exchanged between them he had perhaps found out more than he really wanted to know.

But Bob was not finished. "John, you are a stargazer, correct?" he asked, more confirming than asking, like a cross-examining lawyer.

John recalled sharing his hobby interests with Bob, even had him over to the house once or twice to view the night skies through his six-inch Meade reflector scope.

"Why, yes, Bob. You know I like to look at the stars."

"So of course, you realize that the patterns created by the stars in the heavens, the constellations, are simply illusions in perspective, relative to the position of the observer in three-dimensional space."

"Yes, of course," John replied. "When viewed from Alpha Centauri, let's say, about four light years from earth, the patterns would all be different. Same stars, different perspective. Instead of drawing the Big Dipper when connecting the same star dots in the sky, we might be forming who knows what! Maybe The Big Slipper for all we know."

Bob laughed. "Right, John. The Big Slipper! I like that. But Alpha Centauri, that's a relatively close neighbor of ours. Think about Betelgeuse or Rigel, how different things would look from their perspective! More than six-

and seven hundred and light years away! And then throw in the added dimension of time."

"R-right, Bob. Totally different," John agreed—except for the time part; he didn't know where Bob was going with that.

"So, these changing patterns result from the fact that the stars are not all the same distance from the observer, correct?" Bob continued.

"But, of course," John answered, becoming increasingly puzzled by Bob's line of questioning.

"So, tell me, John. How do you think our lives might look when viewed from the vantage point of the stars? Would not the patterns of our lives look different, as well, depending on where we were? And when we were?"

Bob is really losing it!

"The patterns of our lives?" John repeated, bewildered.

Bob didn't say a word at first. He simply reached into his pants pocket and calmly, deliberately, removed a letter-sized sealed envelope. "John, there is one thing I'd like you to do for me," he said finally as he reached out and placed the envelope in John's top shirt pocket. "Take this. When you get the opportunity, sometime this weekend perhaps, go down into my basement shop. But, don't open the note until you get there. It will tell you what to do."

"Okay, sure," was all John could think to say.

After a few moments of silence which seemed like an eternity, Bob offered cheerfully: "Okay! So, how about a game of chess!"

John almost choked, and had to swallow hard and clear his throat. "Ahem. No, I…I don't think so, Bob. I'm not…very good at the game." He reached up and felt the unaccustomed bulge in his breast pocket. "In fact, I think it might be time for me to leave, Bob. You've given me a lot to think about."

Bob nodded. "Certainly," he said pleasantly. "I understand."

As John rose and turned to leave, he looked back at Bob. "I'll keep you posted on developments at GenAvance, Bob. In the meantime, just try to follow the doctor's orders. Okay?"

Bob just sighed and smiled. "Always do, John. Always do."

John left the day room and continued down the hall. Coming to the last room on the right, he stopped to read the nameplate posted to one side of the door: "DR. ALEXANDER." The door was open. Inside, the doctor was seated behind a desk filled with neatly arranged stacks of paper and manila envelopes, busy filling out reports, taking papers from one stack, making some notes, and placing them on a second stack.

Without looking up or breaking stride, the doctor called out in his mousy, high-pitched voice: "Hello, John. Just don't stand there looking confused. You're liable to be taken for a patient." He looked up and smiled pleasantly. "Please, come in!"

John stepped gingerly across the threshold into the office, paused, and looked around. "Where's Katie?" he asked.

"I believe she went to speak to someone about the job opening in the activity center."

"Job opening?"

"Yes, that's what I wanted to talk to her about. We have an opening in our activity center for a recreational therapist. I knew that was her line of work. We're always looking for good, dedicated people, and…"

The doctor stopped mid-sentence and looked up at John. "Say, John. Why don't you take a seat? You can wait for Katie here. Said she'd be back as soon as she's finished downstairs."

John sat down on the wooden captain's chair against the wall to the doctor's right, the one with the foam seat cushion. "Thank you, doctor. If it's not too inconvenient."

"Nonsense! I can use a little sane company every now and then," the doctor smiled. He sat back and gave John a hard, steady look.

"You know, I took the liberty of contacting Dr. Caldwell at Lourdes, and he spoke very highly of Kate."

John perked up at sound of the Caldwell's name.

"Dr. Caldwell? Dr. Aldus Caldwell?"

"Why, yes. Do you know him?"

Somehow, John felt the doctor already knew the answer to that question. "Yes, doctor. I was recently treated at Lourdes for…a nervous breakdown. He was my attending psychiatrist."

"Oh, I see," the doctor said with pretend surprise.

"Yes, he said it was a transient psychotic episode of some kind," John explained. "Possibly triggered by recent events in my life and pent-up emotions of guilt going back to my younger days."

"I see," the doctor repeated. "So, he took the psychoanalytical approach. If you don't mind my asking, did he prescribe medication of any kind?"

"No, I don't mind. He put me on Seroquel, two hundred milligrams a day. I guess it helped. But, actually I've been off of it for about a week, now."

The doctor slowly nodded his head. "And, you haven't had any recurring episodes?"

John thought about the flashback in the day room just minutes ago. "No. Everything's been…just fine."

He lied.

The doctor leaned forward, his elbows resting firmly on the desk, hands folded in a tight fist as he looked straight out into space. "Seroquel," he repeated. "Interesting. One of the newer atypical antipsychotic drugs recently approved by the FDA." The doctor appeared to be taking a genuine interest in John's case. "So, John. If you wouldn't mind, I'd like to ask you about your experiences." He smiled. "Don't worry. This in on the house, so to speak. No charge."

John returned the smile and proceeded to tell the doctor all about that weekend at the bay. The big greenhead flies, his immediate reaction to the bite, and all the "flights of fancy"—as Caldwell put it—into eighteenth-century colonial Cumberland County.

Dr. Alexander was fascinated. "Don't you find it interesting, John, that both yours and Bob's experiences were preceded by an infected bite of the greenhead fly?"

John leaned forward in his chair, arms resting on his knees, like someone was finally ready to listen. "Precisely, doctor! The doctors at Lourdes said there might be a connection, like maybe an allergic reaction of some kind. But no one could nail it down for sure."

The doctor paused and jotted down a few notes as John thought how to phrase the next question

"Doctor, do you believe in the power of…curses?"

The doctor sat back in his chair and folded his arms. "Curses?" he repeated, acting surprised by the question. "As in spells and incantations?"

"Well, I guess. Something like that," John replied.

"Curses. Yes, that is an interesting topic. What would make you ask such a thing?" the doctor probed.

John proceeded to recount his experience years ago with the Ouija board, and Bob's more recent outbursts and delusional pronouncements on the subject. Dr. Alexander knew, of course, about Bob Fenwick's obsession with a "curse" of some kind. He considered it to be an expression of his particular form of paranoia, although a bit unusual for the run-of-the-mill, paranoid schizophrenic, where persecution or conspiracy themes were the norm. But the "curse" was not something new to Dr. Alexander. He had dealt with this delusional theme before.

"And you think there's a connection between Bob's illness, and this séance that happened twenty years ago?" the doctor pursued, rocking back in his chair, hands joined at the fingertips to form a tent.

John smiled sheepishly. "I really don't know, doc. I know it sounds foolish. But you must admit, the connections are…uncanny."

"Hmm, well,"—the doctor scribbled a few more words in his notebook—"I do believe in the powers of positive and negative thinking. I deal with that every day with my patients."

"Yes, but…do you believe that one person's thoughts can directly affect what happens to another person?"

"If you mean the power of suggestion, certainly. A negative thought or idea planted in the subconscious mind of another can certainly affect that person's behavior. If one believes something strongly enough, it can certainly induce psychological or even physical, pathological symptoms."

John shook his head. "Maybe I'm not making myself clear, doc. Let me rephrase it. Do you believe that a person can will something to happen to another, from a distance, through time and space, without any direct communication or contact with the other person?"

The doctor smiled. "Time and space, eh? Well, I'm no Einstein, but I would say what you are suggesting is definitely outside the realm of traditional science and medicine. And while I can't say that such a thing is impossible, it certainly goes beyond the bounds of my personal and professional experience—and training, I might add." The doctor remained silent for a moment, carefully considering his next words. "However, I would say that the *appearance* of such a thing may be possible. There could be some unseen agent at work, some unknown cause and effect mechanism. After all, that's the quest of science. To uncover the cause and effect relationships between seemingly disconnected events in nature. Infectious diseases that were once attributed to the influence of evil spirits are now known to be the result of microscopic agents. Small and unseen, but very real nonetheless. A quite physical, not metaphysical, phenomenon."

John sat back, not totally satisfied with his answer. The doctor let him stew a little while longer before continuing. The tone of his voice changed, like he was about to share a deep secret.

"John, you're an engineer. So you must appreciate data correlations, patterns in design, and such."

"Yes, I suppose," John responded weakly, not sure where this was going.

"Good." The doctor paused. "Let me show you something."

The doctor stood up and went over to a filing cabinet. Opening the bottom drawer, he carefully removed a large file folder filled to capacity and returned it to his desk. He began removing individual files and placing them on the desk, in full view of John, who was literally on the edge of his seat.

"What I have here, John, are case histories that go back to the latter part of the last century, when they started keeping records here at Lakeland. Some of the files even predate that. These are mainly reports from personal family physicians, or articles from medical journals. The earliest are written by contemporaries of Dr. Benjamin Rush—you are familiar with Dr. Benjamin Rush?"

John perked up. "Yes, of course. The famous eighteenth-century Philadelphia physician and one of the signers of the Declaration of Independence."

"Yes, very good," the doctor smiled. "I forgot you are a student of history."

John was intensely interested in what the doctor had to say. Here was a man after his own heart, with a profound, albeit professionally slanted, interest in history—the area's colonial history to boot!

"So, what do these case histories have in common, doctor?" John asked.

"They are all reported cases of what we might today call paranoid schizophrenia, although the term schizophrenia wasn't actually coined until 1908, by Dr. Eugen Bleuler. But more importantly, they all appear to share a common triggering event: an insect bite of some kind. In every case where the culprit is identified, it is our friend the greenhead fly: *Tabanus nigrovittatus*."

"My! That is interesting!"

"Precisely!" the doctor replied. "Normally, schizophrenia first manifests itself in a person's late teens, just as he or she is getting ready to get on with their adult life." The doctor held up a file. "What we have here, however, is quite different. This form of the illness can strike at virtually any age, seemingly triggered by the bite of the greenhead fly."

The doctor picked out a file seemingly at random and began to read from it. "Here's a case from the turn of the century. A thirty-five-year-old woman from Salem, New Jersey."

> ...From most outward appearances the patient appeared normal. She did not exhibit the frenetic movements and rocking motion exhibited by other patients with similar maladies. But the voices and delusions were very real to her. She spoke of a curse that had to be rectified. That it was her mission to find the chosen one who would perform this miracle of absolution...

The doctor picked out another file from the stack. "And here's another from the early eighteen hundreds, a thirty-year-old woman from Shilo, a small town in Cumberland County."

> ...The woman exhibited a strange form of melancholy. She would appease the voices by running naked through the fields, talking to the trees in this manner until physical exhaustion overcame her. Her voices told her of a chosen one who would later come to remove the curse and set things aright.

The doctor took a third file. "Now, here is a very graphic firsthand account of the yellow fever outbreak in Philadelphia in the summer of 1793 from a Mr. Samuel Breck, a merchant from the area."

> ...The burning fever occasioned paroxysms of rage which drove the patient naked from his bed to the street, and in

some instances to the river, where he was drowned. Insanity was often the last stage of its horrors.[9]

The doctor replaced the file and took another. "Now, compare this one from a Cumberland County physician in the following year." He handed the document to John, allowing him enough time to read it to himself.

> ...a strange form of ague affecting the brain has swept the lower regions of the county in recent years. At first thought to be related the yellow fever scourge that ravaged the city of Philadelphia a year ago, this malady, while less severe in its initial manifestations, can be no less pernicious in its long-term effects. The patient does not succumb outright to the fever, but slowly develops a lingering form of melancholy and madness that often requires eventual removal from society and placement into an asylum for the insane. Its sufferers appear possessed and speak of a *curse that must be lifted by a chosen one yet to come*. It is thought by some, that the initial fever is brought on by the bite of the horsefly, of the kind that are common to the tidal streams and marches found in these environs. But such cannot be determined with any degree of certainty, as there are many who, similarly bitten, suffer no ill effects whatsoever.

"The victims were both men and women," the doctor explained as John handed him the file back. "The brain fever or 'ague' the doctor refers to appears to be some form of meningitis, or perhaps tularemia, a serious parasitic disease known to be carried by the horse or deerfly. But in this case the illness takes a turn with the lingering madness aspect of the disease. That is something very different. The fever is short-lived, self-limiting, and goes away, never fatal; but a slow developing madness then takes over."

The doctor held up the four documents. "Notice the text underlining, which is mine," he explained. "They identify the shared delusional themes common to this form of the illness— a 'curse' that must be lifted by a 'chosen one.' I say 'form of illness' because I feel that this represents a truly unique syndrome or collection of symptoms which is not documented anywhere else in medical literature. What's more, it appears to be a limited phenomenon, local to this area. By that I mean mid to south New Jersey, and to a lesser degree southeastern Pennsylvania."

---

[9] This excerpt of Mr. Breck's account is taken from "Yellow Fever Attacks Philadelphia, 1793," *EyeWitness to History*, http://www.eyewitnesstohistory.com/yellowfever.htm (2005).

John was fascinated. Everything the doc said so far fit Bob's condition—and perhaps his own. He gently fondled the envelope in his shirt breast pocket. "Do you think there could be a genetic factor in all of this?" John asked. "Or just environmental? Being local to the area and all."

The doctor sat back in his chair and crossed his legs. "The old 'nature versus nurture' thing," he smiled. "Well, there are patterns of heredity that are often seen in cases of mental illness, like depression and schizophrenia. But unfortunately, I have not been able to demonstrate a genetic link or pattern in these cases."

"But, there is a pattern, nonetheless. Correct?"

The doctor thought for a moment. "Perhaps. But not the classic Mendelian genetic pattern. You know, involving dominant and recessive genes inherited from both parents to offspring."

At that moment Katie Fenwick appeared at the door. "Excuse me. May I come in?" she asked.

The doctor smiled and stood up. "By all means, Katie. How did the interview go?"

Katie walked over and took a seat beside John. "Excellent! I was surprised to find how extensive your recreational therapy programs are. They've even got art, music, and dance therapists down there." She turned to John. "Their activity center is located in the basement, John. You should check it out before you leave...I mean, not that you're in need of..."

Everyone laughed. This was the first time John saw the doctor lighten up.

"Okay, I'll have to do that before we leave," John agreed.

John stood up to leave and offered his hand to the doctor. "Thank you, doctor, for taking the time to discuss my problem."

The doctor took John's hand and held it firmly. "No, I should thank you, John. I enjoyed sharing my thoughts with you. Perhaps we both have gained some greater insight into this...interesting phenomenon."

John and Katie left the doctor's office and continued down the hall in the direction of the day room.

The doctor gathered up the files on his desk and was about to return them to the file cabinet when he had another thought. He sat down behind his desk and began going though the case studies, one by one.

Chapter 19

1999
Wednesday, 29 September
Cook College Campus, Rutgers University

9:00 a.m. The skies were clear and sunny—a good day for a road trip. For some time, now, John had been looking forward to getting back to his old campus and meeting with Dr. Julie Evert to talk about her insect research as it related to the proposed new GenAvance pilot plant and insect cell culture process. On a more personal note, he was eager to see if there was a relationship between what her research team was doing and the recent unpleasant encounters he—and Bob—had experienced with the greenhead fly. Of course, he would not discuss his concerns directly. He didn't want to put her on the defensive. But if there were a connection, he needed to know, especially in light of what he had just learned from Dr. Alexander at Lakeland.

"So, are you sure you know your way around campus?" Jim Connelly teased from the front passenger seat.

Jacob Carlson chimed in from the back seat.

"Yeah, looks like we're taking a round-about way to get there."

"Short-cut," John said curtly. "Believe me, I've been here before."

John steered a course up College Farm Road into the heart of Cook College's bucolic Ag school campus. Taking a left on Dudley, he made his way through the off-campus backstreets of the northwest corner of the campus until he came to Grays Avenue; took a left on Grays; and continued slowly for about two blocks before turning left onto a single-lane, tree-lined driveway, which took them straight back to a cluster of low-profile research buildings and a parking lot on the right.

"Dr. Evert said she would meet us at Shockley Laboratories," John said, reading from his handwritten notes as he drove. "Should be the second middle building on the left."

Pulling into the lot he found an empty visitor's spot. Sure enough, there it was: an unassuming, single-story, red brick building with the name Shockley Research Laboratories blazoned across its top brick face in bold, white block letters. Its full name was the Shockley Research and Mosquito Control Laboratory, noted for its achievements in the practical aspects of mosquito control, particularly the salt marsh mosquito. In more recent years, attention had also turned to other disease-bearing insects, or biological vectors, as Dr. Evert referred to them.

Jacob Carlson took a final sip of coffee from his paper cup before grabbing his briefcase and joining John and Jim who were already outside waiting at the curb. Jacob was the process architect on the project. Not a regular Haddon Life-Tech employee, he would be brought in as needed on a sub-contract basis whenever the job required a process architect. A quiet man in his late fifties, short and stocky, Jacob had served two tours of duty as a Marine in Vietnam, but never talked much about it these days.

John had no sooner punched in Julie Evert's number on his cell phone when he saw her coming down the walk to meet them.

"Good morning, John! So glad you could take the time to come see us."

Dr. Evert reached out and shook John's hand.

"Oh, no trouble at all, Julie. I always welcome the opportunity to visit my alma mater. Of course, I'm not as familiar with Cook campus. I spent most of my undergraduate days on the main campus in town, or out on Livingston campus."

Jim and Jacob exchanged knowing expressions of "See, whatidi tell ya?"

"Yes, of course," Dr. Evert said. "The School of Chemical Engineering. Right?"

"That's right."

John turned to introduce his traveling companions. Julie and Jim Connelly had previously met at the August kick-off meeting in Thousand Oaks. Jacob Carlson was introduced as the team's "Process Architect and HVAC Clean Room expert."

"Yes, Mr. Carlson, you might be interested in seeing the proposed site for the new pilot plant. I've arranged a visit right after lunch. That way you can leave there directly for home. It's located off campus, just a few miles south on Route One."

Jacob nodded. "That would be nice."

Julie led the way up the walk toward the main entrance of Shockley Labs. After ascending a short flight of steps, she produced a plastic ID card and scanned the card reader to the left of the entrance.

"This is a controlled-access building. Don't want people just wandering in off the street."

"No telling what they could catch inside, eh?" John noted wryly.

Once inside Julie had them fill out a visitor badge before proceeding through the lobby down a long corridor to a small conference room at the far end on the right. Along the way they passed a number of laboratories on the left, identified with names plaques over the doors: Microbiology Lab, Vector Biology Lab, Analytical Lab, and so on. Most of the windowed lab doors were either open or unlocked, with teams of lab technicians and researchers in long white coats visible inside, busily huddled about their microscopes, centrifuges, and test tubes, or entering notes in their lab notebooks and laptop computers. There was one lone door on the right, however, with a window that was painted over. An orange BIOHAZARD sign was posted on it, which read: "Controlled Access Only." A card reader to the side of the door guaranteed that only authorized persons could enter.

Once inside the conference room, Julie offered her guests coffee and tea as she took her place at the head of the long conference table. "Please help yourself gentlemen. I brewed a fresh pot just for the occasion," she said, motioning to the credenza, replete with steaming pots and all the fixings.

John wasn't bashful. He was returning with a hot cup of joe when Julie inquired, "So, John, I was sorry to hear of your recent illness. I hope you're feeling better."

The official story was that John had come down with a severe case of the flu and needed to be hospitalized for dehydration.

"Thank you, Julie," John said as he sat down at the conference table. "But I'm feeling much better now."

"Glad to hear that, John."

Shifting focus and assuming a more formal pose, Julie plugged in her laptop computer and switched on the overhead projector. "Gentlemen, I've prepared a PowerPoint presentation summarizing the major findings of our collaborative research here, as it relates to the GenAvance process."

The first slide was entitled: Life Cycle of the Salt Marsh Horsefly, *Tabanus nigrovittatus*. The lettering was superimposed over a super-sized image of a greenhead fly which filled the whole screen. John flinched, squirming at the close-up sight of this green-eyed nemesis, which he knew only too well.

"Are you okay, John?" Julie asked, noting his reaction.

"Sorry, Julie. Just…something I ate. Fried eggs this morning. Not something I'm used to."

"I see. Well, is it okay to continue?" she asked.

John blushed and smiled. "Sure, I'm fine," he said.

Julie resumed her presentation.

"The true greenhead fly, *Tabanus americanus Forester*, can be found throughout the eastern part of the US from the Canadian border to eastern Texas. The salt marsh horsefly, which is often called the greenhead fly, is actually two cryptic species of Tabanus: *T. nigrovittatus and T. contenninus*."

Julie pointed to the slide with a laser pointer. "Now, our friend here, *T. nigrovittatus*, forms the basis of our research with Dr. Sam Li's team at GenAvance." Turning to face John and the others, she continued. "Working with our Agricultural Extension Service, we have produced a genetically altered variety of *T. nigrovittatus* which, in combination with the variant form of baculovirus developed by Dr. Li's team, has given rise to the new

Baculovirus Expression Vector System, or BEVS, described by Dr. Li at the ISPE meeting last month. John, I believe you were there to hear Sam give his talk."

John smiled and nodded. He remembered Sam's little cartoon Trojan horses dancing across the screen at the ISPE conference. Suddenly, he made the connection with his dream: Dr. Sam Li at the podium on the fifty-yard line as a team of wooden horses took to the playing field. And the scoreboard lit up: "GO BACK! SAVE HER!"

"John, are you all right?" Jim turned and asked under his breath.

John shook it off. "Yes…I'm fine," he replied softly.

Dr. Evert proceeded to document the life cycle of the salt marsh greenhead fly, from its beginnings as an anonymous speck of life among a gelatinous mass of eggs clinging to a single blade of marsh grass, to its predacious larval childhood and finally as an adult female fly scavenging for warm blood in preparation for its next egg brood.

"Doctor, if you don't mind," John interrupted. "I happened to be touring the tidal marshlands along the Delaware Bay earlier this month when I came across a cage of some kind. An open square box affair with screened-in sides set about two feet off the ground. There was a "Do not disturb" sign posted identifying it as an agricultural extension service experimental station. Was this at all related to your research?"

Dr. Evert beamed, like someone had just located her long-lost child. "Why, yes! John. You just happened by one of our fly traps. The Ag extension service developed these devices to trap and kill the greenhead in an effort to control their population. We use them to trap and retain the fly for experimental purposes. We screen the local populations of greenhead flies for varieties that better suit our purposes."

"Oh, I see. Very interesting. So, if you don't mind my asking, the variety that proved successful in your experiments, where was it originally found?"

Julie didn't have to think twice. "That's easy," she said. "The fly originated in the lower parts of Cumberland County, along the Cohansey River. That's why we dubbed it *T. nigrovittatus cohansus*."

A chill ran up John's spine. So, that's it! Must be the same fly that bit me—and Bob, no doubt. The same variety that had proven so useful in developing a new baculovirus host/vector system for insect cell culture. Could this be the fly implicated in countless mental breakdowns over the years, as Lakeland's Dr. Alexander had postulated?

"So, we have a celebrity vector right in our own backyard!" John mused.

"Exactly!" Julie replied excitedly. "And who knows! It could just be the next big cure for cancer…or mental illness!"

On her last words, John choked on his coffee and had to get up for a drink of water. "Must've gone down the wrong pipe," he apologized.

Dr. Evert concluded her slide presentation with a discussion of her needs for the new pilot plant. As John understood it, the new facility would include a new cell line development lab, microbiology lab, and entomology lab, or "Insectarium," as Julie referred to it. Evidently, she was fast outgrowing the space allotted her by the university, and GenAvance had agreed to pick up the tab for a new lab as part of the new pilot plant project.

"Well, that about wraps up my little talk, gentlemen. What I'd like to do now is take you through our current Insect Cell Culture Development Lab and Insectarium, to give you a hands-on feel for our needs." She spoke directly to Jacob Carlson. "Mr. Carlson, I believe you will find this of particular interest. I understand the laboratory design is one of your specialty areas."

Jacob Carlson smiled. "Yes, doctor. Lab design has always been my bread-and-butter."

Julie Evert led the way back down the hallway corridor and took them through all the general access laboratories, one by one. Exiting the final lab she turned to them with a grin and said, "Now, I saved the best for last. Please follow me."

She led the team back up the hallway and stopped in front of the mysterious, locked laboratory door, the one with the posted biohazard sign. Swiping her ID card across the magnetic card swipe, she opened the door and entered, inviting the others to follow.

"Is that biohazard sign really necessary?" John asked as he followed her in.

"Well, the cell lab is quarantined, which means, we take all necessary precautions against the accidental release of genetically modified material of any kind or, God forbid, an insect should escape. We're not handling anything pathogenic here, but would rather err on the side of caution when it comes to preventing an accidental release into the environment. So, we abide by NIH guidelines when it comes to biological containment."

"What level of containment are you targeting?" John asked.

John knew the four levels of biocontainment, biosafety levels one through four, with BL-4 being the most severe, reserved for working with the most pernicious of infectious agents, like HIV virus.

"Well, generally, we operate under biosafety level two conditions," Dr. Evert replied. "But for new cell lines which haven't been fully characterized, we strive for BL-3 containment. We originally equipped the lab with BL-4-rated isolators, thinking we would be handling the genetically altered baculovirus in our lab. But that's all being done at GenAvance by Dr. Li's team. We just handle the native and genetically engineered insect cell lines."

"I see," John replied.

Closing the door behind them, they found themselves in a small anteroom—no more than six by eight feet—crowded with wall lockers along the right and left side walls. A small stainless steel bench ran across the floor in front of them, dividing the small room roughly in half. On the other side of the bench, on the far wall, was a second windowed door that opened into the main laboratory.

"Now comes the fun part!" Julie said. "Since this is actually the first step for the GenAvance manufacturing process, we are trying to conform as closely as possible to the current Good Manufacturing Practices, or cGMP's, prescribed by the FDA for medicinal biological products. So the lab space has been upgraded to a validated Class 10,000 clean room."

John, Jim, and Jacob were all quite familiar with the regulations, and the need for special clean rooms and gowning requirements for cGMP operations. The drill varied with the client and the facility, but always involved some form of over-gowning, head cover, latex gloves, and booties to cover the shoes.

"Just do what I do," Julie explained.

The one-piece Tyvek jumpsuit was the first thing to put on, followed by the hair net cover, booties, and latex gloves. The jumpsuit was a chore, but the booties were actually the trickiest part. That's what the "magic bench" was for. It represented a procedural barrier between the "soiled" and "clean" sides of the room. To negotiate this invisible barrier, the bottom sole of the clean bootie, newly removed from its clear plastic bag, could not be allowed to touch the floor on the soiled side of the bench. Likewise, one's street shoes could not be allowed to touch the floor on the clean side of the bench. It goes something like this. First, one sits down on the bench facing the soiled side, places the right bootie on the right foot, and then swings it up and over the bench to contact the clean side floor. Straddling the bench thusly, one places the left bootie on the left foot, and likewise swings it up and over the bench, turning one's whole body in the process. Finally, there are the latex gloves, followed by a hand-wash with an alcohol-based foam lotion.

It takes a trained individual only a few minutes to accomplish the entire gowning procedure. But for the untrained or unaccustomed, these contortions in cramped quarters can come to resemble a party game of Twister!

"You see, we keep the cell lab under negative pressure," Dr. Evert explained. "All exhaust air from the room is HEPA filtered to eliminate any chance of environmental contamination."

John knew that these High Efficiency Particulate Air filters—originally developed by the nuclear power industry to prevent the inadvertent release of fine radioactive dust particles—were a mainstay in the design of a properly functioning containment system for any biologics facility. Pressure control was the second line of defense. If the room leaked, it was best to leak inward rather than outward, for containment reasons.

Once they were all fully gowned, Julie opened the door into the main laboratory. What greeted them was a long room, fairly unexceptional in layout and design. Most of the architectural and mechanical design features required to ensure containment were not apparent to the untrained eye. The only obvious feature was what was lacking: there were no outside windows.

Almost the entire back wall was lined with biosafety cabinets, with two work stations equipped with glove boxes for added containment and protection. Two gowned technicians, their hands inserted into the flexible rubber arm and glove extensions which protruded into the box's interior, were busy manipulating something on the inside. Other portable carts and isolators were scattered about the room in seemingly random, crowded fashion. On the far left side were what appeared to be stacked cages and a series of tall incubators with clear glass doors: refrigerator-sized cabinets used for precise temperature and humidity control. On closer inspection the cages actually resembled glass terrariums.

Julie gave them some time to take in the room before speaking. "This is the heart of our operation, gentlemen. A bit crowded, as you can see. Ergo, the need for more space."

One of the technicians looked up from her perch at one of the glove box work stations. "Good morning, Dr. Evert."

"Hello, Sally. How is the new brood coming?"

"Just fine. Almost ready for the nursery," she smiled. "Should be happening any day now."

Dr. Evert resumed her duties as tour guide. "Sally is working up a new cell line for Dr. Li's research team. We actually develop the insect cell lines right here and ship them frozen to the west coast. Obviously, it would be nicer if we were all working in the same facility. A trip down the hall versus a trek across the country."

"Ergo, the new pilot plant," John ventured.

Julie smiled. "Exactly!"

John took a closer look at one of the other technicians working at a biosafety cabinet. These were basically tables four or six feet in length, featuring a top work surface that was completely enclosed on all sides within a hood. The front sash could be raised or lowered for partial access by the operator. The hood was equipped with a self-contained HEPA filtered air supply and return system designed to provide the correct flow patterns of air to maintain the necessary level of containment, keeping the worker safe from exposure and protecting the specimen from contamination at the same time.

"So, is this where the ovarian cells are dissected from the fly larvae to create the new cell lines?" John inquired.

"Yes, that's correct, John," replied Dr. Evert. "All new cell lines are handled within the glove box isolators, until they're been fully characterized. The established cell lines are handled in the biosafety cabinets, which provide a lesser degree of containment. Once recovered, the cells are washed and grown *in vitro* using those glass culture flasks over there."

Julie pointed to an incubator cabinet against the left wall. Through the glass door John could see dozens of small glass-stoppered flasks with disposable vent filters stacked on the shelves, nestled in wire trays gently rocking in a circular motion.

"Those are the shaker flasks," Julie explained. "Helps keep the cell culture suspended and aerated. Once the culture is fully grown, about ten million cells per cubic centimeter, we harvest the cells, spin them down in a glass ampoule, and freeze them in liquid nitrogen."

She then pointed to a set of double doors located at the far, inside corner of the room. "Here, let me show you the nursery Sally was referring to."

The men followed Julie as she led them through the double doors into a smaller rectangular room lined with double-glass pane terrariums running lengthwise along the two opposing walls, set about two feet off the floor on stainless steel platforms, like something you might find in a pet store or zoo, only much shinier and cleaner. The terrariums were further sectioned off into separate compartments of approximate four-foot lengths. About halfway up at shoulder height, a screened partition separated the upper half from the bottom half. Spaced horizontally at regular intervals along the bottom portion were glove ports, similar in design to those used for the laboratory glove boxes. Alternating between each pair of glove ports were other stainless steel port connections. One of these ports was connected to a portable isolator of the kind seen in the other room. *Transfer isolators*, John thought. Used for making contained transfers from the terrariums to the lab, and vice versa.

John watched as a technician inserted his hands into a pair of gloves inside the isolator, and began transferring something from the isolator to the soil of the terrarium.

"Feeding time," he explained. "Have to keep the hungry little Tabbies happy."

On closer inspection John could see what he was transferring: earthworms.

"They really like night crawlers," the technician said. "We've tried different diets, but night crawlers seem to keep them really happy."

"Of course," John nodded.

"You see," Dr. Evert continued, "with the terrariums we are able to replicate the moist, soil environments of the tidal marshes found along the Delaware Bay.

"Interesting," John nodded. "But how do you simulate the overwintering phase of their larval existence? Wouldn't that require a…cold room terrarium of some kind?"

Julie beamed. "Very good question, John! I can see you were listening to my presentation. Well, that was exactly the problem we faced initially. You may have noticed the large freezer door adjoining this room."

Jacob nodded. He was going to ask about that room.

"Well, that's our cold box, or cold room. It's not really needed anymore, except for storage. But that's where we simulated the cold winter environment when we first started the tabanid breeding program. Not only was it logistically unwieldy, moving larvae and pupa back and forth and keeping track of the adult flies, but, it often took a year or more to turn over a new generation. Not like fruit flies which propagate like rabbits."

"So, how did you come up with this…new arrangement?" John asked.

"Genetically engineered flies!" Julie boasted, holding up an index finger to emphasize the point. "Actually, it was five parts genetic engineering five parts good old fashioned selective breeding. We were able to produce a fly that goes from larva to pupa in a matter of weeks rather than months or even years—as long as the larvae get enough to eat."

"Ergo, the night crawlers," Jim offered.

Julie laughed. "Exactly! And there's one added piece of insurance. They've actually lost their ability to overwinter. So, if they ever get loose in the environment, they'll die in short order, or within a season. A kind of built-in environmental protection and containment system."

"I like it," John said.

At that moment a flickering motion from the other side of the double-paned glass caught John's attention from the corner of his eye. John turned to see an especially large greenhead specimen sitting on a piece of screen in the upper chamber of the nearest terrarium, less than two feet away. John stared at the fly, and the fly seemed to stare back. He drew closer to the glass pane, making the fly loom as large as it did on the conference room projector screen earlier that morning. Large, but not so menacing now, just mesmerizing. He studied its every motion as it preened itself, with little jerky movements of its tiny legs.

"She's getting ready to mate, John," Julie's voice flowed over his left shoulder. "Afterwards, she will be going to the chamber below to lay her egg mass on one of those tall blades of grass you see there."

John backed away, trance broken. "So, how does she get her blood meal?" he asked. "You don't have students volunteering to put their arms through one of those porthole connections at feeding time, do you?"

Julie chuckled. "No, not volunteers, John. Just the failing students who need the extra credit," she deadpanned.

She finally cracked a smile and everyone laughed.

"No, really," John continued, "how do you keep the adults alive?"

"The answer's simple. We don't," she replied.

John raised an eyebrow and looked around at Jim and Jacob who had the same reaction.

"You don't...feed them?" Jim chimed in, with just a touch of concern in his voice.

"No. You see, as new adult flies they have sufficient protein reserves to propagate one time, and one time only. Once they've done their duty, they're...put to pasture, so to speak."

"So, you just let them...die?" Jim pursued.

"No, they continue to feed on nectar, but they can no longer produce any young without a blood meal. We just let them live out their short lives on nectar, another three or four weeks. At this point in our development program, we get all the eggs and larvae we need with a single batch turnover."

"Oh, I see. Very...economical," John said.

"And...humane," Jim added.

John looked at him quizzically and mouthed the words, "Humane?"

Jim shrugged his shoulders as if to say, "Hey, so what!"

Julie was already halfway out the door of the Insectariums and missed this last exchange.

Out in the lab, Jacob was surveying the supply and return vents of the ventilation system. "So, how many room air changes is the lab HVAC system sized for?" he asked Dr. Evert.

"I believe it's about twenty per hour," she replied.

"Hmm, and what room air classification did you say it was?"

Dr. Evert paused a moment. "Well, we are trying for Class 10,000 or Grade C conditions in the lab."

Jake rubbed his chin. "Hmm, you might want to increase that to thirty air changes per hour," he said. He looked around the room. "I don't see any low-return vents for the air. Tell me, did you actually run particle air counts for this room?"

"Yes, I'm sure we did. I can get you all that information. Of course, the Insectarium doesn't really require the same level of cleanliness. It just needs to be contained, or quarantined. But being landlocked the way it is inside this cell development lab, we're forced to impose the same gowning and room air criteria. That will change in the new pilot plant."

"Of course," Jacob nodded as he jotted something down on his notepad.

John looked around the room. "Did this lab have windows at one time?" he asked.

"Yes. Originally there were three outside windows along that wall." Julie explained, pointing to the former window locations. "Actually, the windows are still there. We simply dry-walled over them to blend in with the inside wall. But you can still see the windows from outside the building. It was a lot cheaper than bricking them up. And once we move to the new facility, we can open them up again, no problem."

"Makes sense to me," Jacob said.

John nodded in agreement.

With the tour concluded, the men joined Dr. Evert for lunch in the cafeteria. As he was leaving the laboratory building, John took particular note of where the "missing" windows were located along the backside of the building. On the outside, the windows were partly concealed by shrubbery, but appeared normal in every other way.

After lunch they all drove out to the proposed site, about five miles south on Route 1 toward Princeton, where Jacob was able to take pictures and made more notes in his notepad. John remained in the car with the engine running, waiting for Jacob and Jim to complete their survey of the site.

With a lull in the activity, John's thoughts returned to Sunday and his visit with Bob at Lakeland. He reached over and opened the glove compartment door, removing the sealed envelope containing Bob's note—the one he told John not to open until he was in his basement workshop. But, John couldn't wait. Using his ballpoint pen as a letter opener, he opened the envelope and removed the note.

It appeared to be the left half of a written message and diagram, torn top to bottom right down the middle of the page. John had to chuckle. John could only assume he would find the missing half in Bob's basement workshop.

The half-message was superimposed over a schematic diagram of some kind. In the top left margin was an astronomical symbol for the sun, with lines of light radiating down and outward. Over the sun symbol were the words: "Winter Solstice Male Family Line." Down the remainder of the page were a number of scattered circles—sun symbols—of varying sizes, starting with larger ones at the top of the page and becoming smaller toward the bottom.

At the bottom of the page was the symbol of a "seeing eye" annotated with the cryptic message: "Betelgeuse Portal View; 5 h 43 m 5 s RA; 7° 21' 3" Dec." Radiating upward from the eye were a series of divergent "perspective lines" running to each of the open sun circles. Two of the circles had lines that that ran off the torn page to the right, connecting to something on the page's missing half. Two of these lines were dashed, unlike the other solid "perspective lines."

John studied the note, trying to make some sense of its mysterious markings and symbols. The numbers he recognized as celestial coordinates for locating objects in the night sky. But the rest was just gibberish to him.

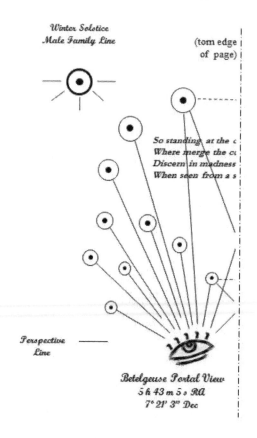

Winter Solstice
Male Family Line

(torn edge
of page)

So standing at the c
Where merge the co
Discern in madness
When seen from a s

Perspective
Line

Betelgeuse Portal View
5 h 43 m 5 s RA
7° 21' 3" Dec

"Looks like something from the Kabbala," he muttered. "Tree of Life? Or an astrological chart of some kind."

The half-message looked familiar, though. Where had he seen it before? Bob's notebook? Labor Day? Yes! One of those crazy verses from the notebook in Bob's basement. John had a sudden sense of urgency, eager to see the other half of the note and what else awaited him in Bob's basement shop. He grabbed his cell phone and punched in *8 for Katie's number. The call went straight to Katie's voice mail. He left a message after the beep, asking if it would be okay to drop by this weekend, say around eleven o'clock Saturday morning, to check out something Bob wanted him to see in his basement shop. "…Just leave me a voice message to confirm. Thanks, Katie. Talk to you soon."

John returned the note to its envelope and put it back in the glove compartment for safekeeping.

Chapter 20

1774
Thursday Evening, 29 September
Greenwich, Cumberland County

Young Roger Walker sat at a table in a far dark corner of the Stone Tavern, slouched over a pint of cider with both arms wrapped around his mug, hugging the drink like an old friend. He wore simple homespun wool trousers with suspenders and a shirt, which hung loose from his thin, boney frame. A wide-rimmed farmer's hat concealed a thick, dirty shock of blond hair.

The drinking companion seated to Roger's left was an older gentleman, sedate and a bit portly, wearing a colorful, gambler-style vest, one button missing and two more getting ready to pop. A red bulbous nose and patchy rose-colored cheeks evidenced a man well-accustomed to drinking. A noisy breather—sounding rather like a draft horse hauling a heavy load—the man busied himself carving apples and popping the smaller peeled pieces of the fruit into his mouth as he nursed a tankard of rum. No words were exchanged as he and Roger sat there, as though they were waiting for someone, or something to happen.

Suddenly the front door to the tavern burst open. A gust of northeast wind mixed with rain swept into the room snuffing out two candles on the table nearest the door, as a tall man with a coachman's cape and three-cornered hat stepped inside. Slamming the door closed behind him, he stood there for a few moments shaking off the rain, then removed his hat and cape and headed instinctively toward the far back corner of the room where Roger and his friend were seated and waiting. With the long strides of a savanna giraffe he covered the twenty feet or so quickly in just a few steps, and after hanging up his hat and cape on a nearby wall rack, he took a seat at the table.

The newcomer was a dark-complected man with long, dark straggly hair trailing behind a tightly wrapped bandana. He sported a mustache and goatee that called out for a good grooming, but was otherwise arguably attractive in a roguish sort of way. He wore a handsome, full-length blue coat with brass buttons and gold cord trim, the kind that might have been worn by a naval officer. But the thing that distinguished him most was the black patch he wore over his right eye.

"Evenin', Cap'n," Roger greeted the newcomer. "A bit of nasty weather we're having, eh?"

The man whom Roger addressed as "Cap'n" wasn't a captain at all. While he did put to sea on numerous occasions, whenever it served his purposes, he never commanded a ship of his own; he was just another signed-on member of the crew. Roger didn't know much about the man's past, or how he lost his eye, only that his grandfather was one of the last of the privateers licensed by the British crown to conduct "lawful" raids on French or Spanish merchant ships. It was also rumored that one or several of his uncles had engaged in the more "unlawful" form of robbery on the high seas: piracy.

The Delaware Bay and its tributaries offered ideal hideaways for the hit and run tactics of pirates operating along the east coast well into the eighteenth century—the "golden age" of piracy. This included the enterprises of certain shadowy individuals operating in and around Greenwich on the Cohansey. But by 1774, piracy had largely disappeared from the North American colonies, and those inclined toward illegal pursuits were forced to resort to other, arguably less hazardous livelihoods, such as bootlegging and smuggling, prompted largely by the high taxes and import duties imposed by Parliament on a broad range of items. The more profitable of these involved the bootlegging of rum manufactured from molasses smuggled in from the British colonies of the Caribbean. The high duties on molasses imposed by the Molasses Act (1733) were largely responsible for kick-starting this illicit cottage industry.

The Cap'n did have a name: it was "Jacob," a man born a half century too late for the pirate's blood flowing in his veins.

"So, tell me, my young squire," Cap'n Jacob inquired as he reached across the table and grabbed the lad's mug of cider right out of his hands, "are you ready to hold up your end of the bargain?"

After taking a healthy swig, Jacob set the mug down in front of him, caressing it gingerly with his long, spidery fingers. He smiled, and a large, bright gold tooth sparkled where an upper front incisor used to be.

Roger gulped. "S-sure," he stammered. "That's right, isn't it, George?" he replied, turning to his portly drinking companion.

George took a needed raspy breath before responding. "That is correct, my good man. The rum will be ready for shipment at the appointed time, at the appointed place. You have my word."

Jacob leaned forward and took a hard look into the puffy red eyes of his rum supplier and partner in crime. "That is good to know, George. I wouldn't want anyone drinking up all the profits before the deal is consummated."

Jacob eyed the last remaining whole apple lying on the table in front of George. Reaching down to his side he pulled a dagger from the inside of his leather boot and in one swift motion he swung it overhead and brought it down with a thud, slicing the fruit in twain, missing George's outreached fingers by inches. Roger jumped in his seat. George just grunted, leaving his hand where it was as the dagger remained imbedded in the table top, vibrating like a tuning fork. Jacob took one-half of the apple and raised it to his mouth.

"Fifty-fifty. That was the deal. Right, George?"

Jacob pushed the remaining piece over to George's side of the table. George just played with it as he replied. "That is correct. Fifty-fifty. Roger and I provide the rum, and you arrange for the shipping and molasses delivery."

"Which reminds me, Cap'n," Roger spoke up. "Did you have a chance to speak with John when he was in town the week before last?"

"John? You mean John Weston?"

Roger nodded. "Yes. You said he might be persuaded to aid our cause, what with his inside knowledge of shipping schedules and the habits and whereabouts of customs officials."

Jacob pulled the dagger from the table top and sat back in his chair, wiping the blade with his shirt before returning it to his boot.

"You know, appearances and namesakes can be deceiving, my young squire," Jacob said with a crooked grin. "I later spoke with our good friend Paul McKenzie, who informed me that the Mr. Weston I saw a fortnight ago Monday wasn't the same young John Weston of Weston Enterprises. It turns out that our John Weston is visiting the southern colonies arranging for a shipment of special goods to be shipped to our fair port-o-call."

Roger thought about his last encounter with the young Miss Rebecca Whitman. Oh, well. No need to apologize. Just an honest case of mistaken identity.

"So, who was this…imposter gentleman, then?" Roger asked.

"A distant relation, cousin. Who knows," Cap'n Jacob replied. "Anyway, it no longer matters."

George looked puzzled. "How so?"

Jacob leaned back in his chair and cocked his head. "Well, with my good friend, Paul McKenzie, now in the employment of Weston Enterprises, we have all the inside connections we need. And I think we're better off not involving John. While he may vie with the best of scoundrels for his disdain of the crown, he values too much the authority of good conscience to suit our purposes."

George nodded and breathed a raspy sigh of relief. "Yes, my sentiments all along. I think we have the better champion in Paul."

*****

With a large pot of stew bubbling on the hearth since early morn, the Whitman kitchen had grown warm and uncomfortable; but Izzy, who was busy organizing and folding three large baskets of laundry on the kitchen table, didn't seem to mind the heat. In addition to the Whitman's laundry she had taken on doing the laundry of some of the townsfolk, as a kind of side job. Mr. Whitman allowed her to keep half the money she took in, saying it would help prepare her for the day she was manumitted, on Rebecca's twenty-first birthday or upon her marriage, whichever came first. The laundry, then, gave her a real sense of purpose and self-worth. She was doing this as much for herself as anyone else, so she tended not to mind the heat. But then again, weathering the heat was something a girl from the islands was very much accustomed to.

But not so the young and fair Rebecca Whitman.

"Whew! It is stifling in here!" Rebecca exclaimed as she entered the kitchen from the back porch. She had just returned from her chores at the tailor shop with a new package of clothes for mending.

"There's a beautiful breeze blowing outside, Izzy. Why don't you open the other window and get a little ventilation in here?"

Izzy looked up. She had opened the one large window on the far wall to the right of the hearth, but the smaller, high garden window on the other side of the room was firmly closed and locked. It hadn't been opened in quite a while, probably not since last season. This was the window with the three glass witch balls hanging in front, just as you enter the kitchen from the back porch. The globes' frosted surface patterns caught and reflected the sun's beams, casting dancing patterns of light throughout the room, not unlike a modern-day disco ball. Izzy knew, of course, that these glass orbs served a more serious purpose. Positioned as they were near the back door, they served to ward off evil influences both coming and going, one ball for each person in the household.

"No way that window is gonna open," Izzy said. "Don't even try, Miss Rebecca."

But Rebecca was already at the window, reaching up on her tippy toes trying to unlatch the lock.

"Be careful!" Izzy warned. "Don't wanna hurt yourself!"

Rebecca grunted as she gave the window latch a good pull. It started to budge, but then she lost her grip. As she backed away, her head knocked against one of the glass globes and set it gently swaying. Izzy caught her to keep her from falling, and reached up to still the glass ball.

"Please take care, Miss Rebecca. You don't wanna go breakin' somethin'!"

But Rebecca remained determined. Looking around the kitchen she spied a three-legged stool by the hearth. "Ah, that's just what I need!"

Rebecca picked up the stool and positioned it beneath the stubborn window.

"I don't trus' that stool ma'am," Izzy warned. "It got an unsteady wobble to it."

"So, are you suggesting my weight exceeds its proper limits?" Rebecca chided.

"No, ma'am. Jus' don't wanna see you fall, is all."

Ignoring Izzy's warnings, Rebecca stepped up on the stool and reached for the window latch. "Perfect!" she said.

The window finally opened for her, letting in a refreshing puff of cool autumn air. The witch balls swayed gently in the breeze not far from Rebecca's head as she remained standing there, silhouetted against the brightness of the open window, enjoying the fresh scent of the autumn air.

"You see, that wasn't so bad, now, was it?" she said as she slowly turned around on the stool. As she did so, shafts of sunlight illuminated her face, bathing her in a special glow. For a while, it appeared to Izzy that she was just floating there, a foot or so off the kitchen floor, enveloped in a transparent orb of radiance.

Then it happened.

Izzy watched as one of the legs of the stool—the wobbly one—collapsed under the weight of one even so light and fair as her young mistress. The startled Rebecca, instinctively reaching out to grab something to break her fall, took hold of the nearest of the three hanging glass globes with her left hand.

To Rebecca it all happened much too quickly; but to Izzy, it seemed to play out in slow motion. The glass ball's leather tether tore loose from the ceiling as Rebecca tumbled from the stool, her shifting weight propelling the broken stool out from under her in one direction as she went in another. Letting go of the glass ball to free up both hands to brace herself for the fall, the glass ball went flying off in a third direction toward Izzy, who reached out and tried to catch it, but came up short. The ball struck the hard flag stone floor a few feet in front of her and shattered, sending a million shimmering shards of glass in all directions.

Rebecca picked herself up off the floor and patted herself down. "Well, no broken bones. Just a little ruffled," she said as she adjusted her dress and apron.

But Izzy just remained there, silent, frozen with fear, both hands cupped over her mouth, like she'd just seen a ghost.

"Izzy, I'm fine. Really!"

There was no reaction from Izzy.

"Izzy? What's the matter?"

Bringing her hands down to her side Izzy finally spoke, shaking her head slowly as she did. "You…broke it! It…jus' shattered…like an egg!"

Rebecca kneeled down and began picking up the pieces and placing them in her apron. "Yes, I know. That's a real shame. But no one's hurt. And we can always get another."

But Izzy remained unconsoled. "No! You don't understand," Izzy said fearfully. "It's…bad luck! And someone gonna pay!"

"Nonsense!" Rebecca exclaimed. "It's just an ornament. Nothing will come of it."

Izzy remained visibly shaken as Rebecca finished cleaning up the pieces. Just her old island superstitions, Rebecca thought. She'll get over it.

There was no further mention of the incident. It even took several days for Mr. Whitman to notice the glass orb was missing. He promised to have Mr. Turner, the town's glass smith, produce a new ornament.

And Izzy did her best to hide her concern.

Chapter 21

1999
Saturday, 2 October
Moorestown, New Jersey

11:00 a.m. John Weston pulled into the driveway of Bob and Katie Fenwick's Moorestown home and parked alongside their Dodge Caravan. Bob's Ford Taurus was also sitting in the driveway, in front of an open garage door, one of three. John was surprised to see a FOR SALE sign posted on the front windshield, facing the street. It's a sad day when Bob is forced to sell his baby buggy, John thought.

John picked up the envelope lying next to him on the passenger's seat, removed the note, and studied it for a few moments before returning it to the envelope and placing it in his top shirt pocket. He was just getting out of the car when he saw Katie step out onto the front porch.

"Good morning, John. Right on time, I see," she shouted.

She had been expecting him. Eleven o'clock he told her. John was out of his car by now and remained standing by his open driver-side door.

"Good morning Katie. Never like to keep people waiting—especially not friends." Pointing to Bob's Taurus he added, "Are you really looking to sell the Bob's baby buggy?"

"Yes, afraid so. I tried to talk Bob out of it, but he insisted."

"Really!" John was surprised.

On reaching the porch John gave Katie a little hug.

"Thanks for letting me into Bob's inner sanctum, Katie. I know you've got a ton of things to do. I promise not to take too long."

Katie shook her head. "Take as long as you like, John. If I need to go somewhere I'll just let you know. You can let yourself out."

John looked around. "Where are the kids?"

"Oh, around," Katie said, squinting as she peered down the street. "I sent Bobbie out to Wawa's for a half gallon of milk. He should be getting back any minute."

John followed Katie into the house and headed straight for the basement door.

"I promise not to return until I find the buried treasure!" John quipped.

"Or the dead bodies!" Katie retorted.

John did a double take.

"Just kidding," Katie snickered. "Anyway, you'll find his shop just as he left it. He insisted that it remain undisturbed. You're the only person he's allowed in."

"Are the shop lights working?" John asked, remembering his last dark encounter on Labor Day.

Katie looked puzzled. "Sure! They work fine."

"Okay. Just checking," he said. "I'll holler if I get into trouble."

John headed down the stairs and continued through the family and utility rooms to Bob's shop. He tried the door. It was unlocked, just as Bob promised. However, it was not without a small measure of trepidation that John entered the room, remembering his last encounter with the crowbar-toting Bob and the remnants of his bad dream. John flipped the wall switch. The fluorescent ceiling lights flickered a few times, but eventually came on with a hum. There was plenty of light this time.

The room didn't seem so threatening, now—strange and weird, yes, but not threatening. The room was pretty much the same as John remembered it: the suspended, open wooden lattice structures and glass orbs scattered and hanging throughout the room, like stalactites in a limestone cave. John ducked as he stepped into the room, avoiding the first and largest of the glass globes. Spelunking his way across the floor toward the smaller workbench at the far end of the room, there was something about the orbs he hadn't noticed before: the largest globes, about the size of cantaloupes, were located near the entrance; the closer he got to the workbench, the smaller they became until they were no larger than Christmas tree ornaments. Also scattered among the orbs and suspended at varying heights was a forest of letters and numbers carved from blocks of wood, with no apparent meaning or connection to one another. They did, however, follow the same size order as the orbs: the larger alphanumeric symbols located near the door, the smaller ones closer to the workbench.

Another feature that had escaped his earlier observation—or perhaps Bob had added it since the Labor Day cookout—was a floor-to-ceiling room divider located about three feet from the workbench, between the bench and the first cluster of hanging orbs. The partition was constructed of two hinged panels, each about two feet wide by six feet high, set up like an open book. This resulted in the outward face of each panel being oriented toward the two far corners of the room. Approaching the panels from the front, John noticed a round peephole, about one-inch in diameter, drilled through the face of each panel about five feet off the floor. Their purpose was not immediately apparent.

Preoccupied with the panels, John failed to notice the large, wrinkled fold in the throw rug lying across his path, causing him to catch his foot and trip. Trying to catch his fall he instinctively reached out and grabbed whatever was available. Unfortunately, this turned out to be a piece of lattice work with several wooden letter blocks attached. Like dominoes they came down, one falling into another, as John attempted to redirect his fall. He succeeded, but not before a number of the letters and block symbols had fallen, bouncing off the concrete floor like a toppled set of child's blocks.

"Oh, shit! Bob's gonna be pissed for sure. Maybe I can fix it."

But he never was very good at puzzles. He gave up after a few tries and continued his original pursuit. Reaching the workbench, John took Bob's note from its envelope and laid it out flat on the bench top, next to Bob's notebook and a second envelope with the words "OPEN ME FIRST," written on the outside. John obliged. What he found was the missing right half of the Bob's note. Laying it flat up against the left half of the original note, the two edges matched up perfectly.

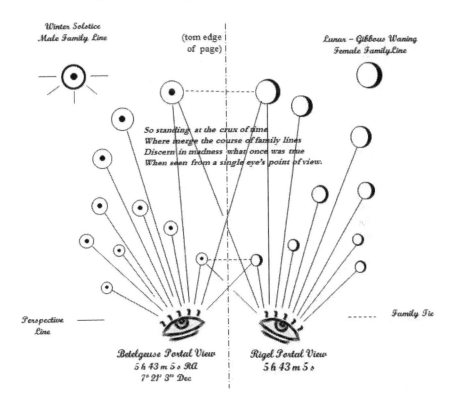

The symmetry in the arrangement of symbols was now apparent, although their meaning remained a mystery. The full message was now revealed as a complete quatrain of verse. John read it aloud: "'So standing at

the crux of time…Where merge the course of family lines…Discern in
madness what once was true…When seen from a single eye's point of view.'"

He looked up and across the room.

"So, where is this 'crux of time'?"

The Betelgeuse and Rigel star references below the two eye symbols he
knew well. They were two of the brightest stars in the nighttime winter sky,
located in the constellation of Orion the Hunter. John also recognized the
numbers below them as astronomical coordinates of Right Ascension (hours,
minutes, and seconds) and Declination (degrees, minutes, and seconds), used
to chart the location of celestial objects in the sky. John made a mental note
to check these numbers against his sky charts when he got home.

Standing at the workbench, John turned around to examine the hidden
sides of the room divider panels, and he had to smile at what he saw. There,
spread across both panels, was an ornately drawn picture of the constellation
of Orion, complete with hunter, upheld club in his right hand and lion in his
left. All the stars were carefully represented and labeled, even the ones you
couldn't see with the naked eye. The only thing different was the way the stars
were oriented. Instead of the normal upright position, the whole grouping of
stars was rotated ninety degrees to the left, placing the hunter on his side. On
closer inspection, it became apparent why this was so. The star Betelgeuse,
which marked the hunter's right shoulder, was located directly over the hole
in the left side panel; and the star Rigel, marking Orion's left knee, was
located over the hole in the right panel. For this to work, Orion had to
assume the supine position.

Directly under his feet were two bold black lines painted on the
cement slab floor. The lines started where each of the two star peepholes
were located on the panels and ran toward the workbench, crossing under his
feet. In the acute angle formed by the intersection of the two lines was an
infinity sign: ∞

"So, is this the cross, or crux, of time?" he wondered aloud.

John turned to the workbench and read the words one more time,
repeating the last line of the verse: "When seen from a single eye's point of
view."

John turned to face the panels again. Of course! The eyes! He bent
down and placed his right eye over the left peep hole, the one marked
"Betelgeuse."

Suddenly, the spheres and symbols occupying the open space in the
left half of the room came together in a most fantastic way, forming patterns
and spelling out words that could only be discerned from this uniquely
positioned one-eyed perspective. From this "single eye's point of view," the
normal three-dimensional world afforded by stereo, two-eyed vision was
reduced and flattened into a two-dimensional plane. The letter "J," carved in
wood and hanging from a nearby ceiling joist, close enough to reach out and

touch, now lined up exactly with the letter "O," which was actually located on the far side of the room. Their real size difference was now negated by perspective, so that all letters and numbers appeared the same size. The letters "H" and "N," likewise, lined up perfectly to spell out his full first name: "JOHN." And so it was with the remaining letters and numbers that filled the space of the room, spelling names and dates with uncanny precision.

Even more amazing were the patterns created by the hanging orbs, which, like the letters and numbers, now appeared to be the same size: the larger, far away globes were the same as the closer, smaller globes, and the wooden beams and members comprising the open scaffolding structure suddenly became the connecting lines between disparate and, now, seemingly adjacent spheres. It was now clear to John what he was looking at, for he had seen it all before. This entire collection of spheres, wooden beams and scaffolding, letters and numbers, hanging in apparent disarray throughout the room, now formed a pattern, a precisely drawn picture as only an engineer of Bob's caliber could fashion. Like the message said, it was something that "once was true." It was…his family tree! Just as Aunt Dee had described and drawn it up years ago on a dinner napkin, and in the Weston family bible!

John drew back from the panel, smiling as he recalled Bob's words from last week's visit to Lakeland: "So, tell me, John. How do you think our lives might look when viewed from the vantage point of the stars? Would not the patterns of our lives look different, as well?"

John smiled. "So, I am viewing the pattern of my life as seen from"— looking at the words beneath the peephole—"the star Betelgeuse, of the constellation Orion."

John ran his hands through his hair and shook his head as he looked out across the room. The collection of spheres, lines, and symbols resumed their former haphazard and meaningless arrangement in three-dimensional space.

"I've got to hand it you, Bob. This is quite an elaborate setup you have here. You really outdid yourself. But, why?"

He then turned to the other peephole, the one labeled "Rigel," lying on Orion's left hip.

"Okay, so let's see what Rigel has to offer."

He leaned over and placed his right eye over the second peephole. Now, the globes and latticework adorning the right side of the room fell neatly into place, a family tree of a different kind. It only took him a few moments to realize that this family tree traced a parallel line, not through the male line, but through the direct female bloodline on his mother's side: from mother to daughter, daughter to granddaughter, and so on. This was evidenced by the change in last name with each generation, as each daughter took on the family name of the father.

It was then that John noticed two special orb pairs which cross-linked the parallel male and female lines of descent at two points in time. The first pair occurred in the distant past—colonial times—and was labeled: Samuel Weston Jr., lying on the Betelgeuse or male line side; and Amanda Jay on the Rigel or female side. The second pair of orbs occurred in more recent times. They were labeled: Richard Weston, John's father, and Mandy Richards, John's biological mother.

John pulled away from Rigel and switched back to the left Betelgeuse peephole. There they were! The same linked family connections between the same orb pairs! He continued studying the two family lines in this manner as it became apparent what he was seeing. They were his two family lines: one traced directly through his father's male bloodline, the other through his mother's direct female bloodline, or, as Bob's schematic identified them, the solar winter solstice male line versus the lunar female line. The two lines first diverged with the union of Sam Weston Jr. to his second wife, Amanda Jay, and re-converged two centuries later with the union of John's father with his first wife, Mandy. The connecting orbs told the story. Sam Weston Jr. and Amanda Jay Weston were John's many-times removed great-great-parents, traceable through both his father's side and his mother's side! Similarly, John Jay Weston—of revolutionary war fame—was his many-times removed great-great uncle, traceable through either bloodline! The important difference was that the maternal bloodline was traced through a direct female line of descent, while the paternal bloodline followed the more traditional male lineage.

This was all beginning to give John a headache as he tried putting the pieces together. It didn't help that some of the names and dates were missing from the maternal family line, thanks to his bumbling fall halfway across the room.

"Dammit!" he scolded himself. "I hope Bob has that information recorded somewhere in his notebook."

But how did Bob know the details of his family line in the first place? And how in the world would he have been able to trace his mother's line, when John didn't even have this information!? Then he remembered Bob's words: "But I really think it was the voices that brought you here, to this place in history."

"The voices?" John repeated aloud.

"Yes, John. Not just from your past alone, but from your family's past."

So, was it the voices that instructed Bob how to build this thing? This "time machine" as he called it? Yes, indeed, a time machine of sorts, tracing the patterns of family lines woven through time, stories told and retold. Whose story? "Your story," echoed a voice from his Labor Day dream. They were Mary Hogan's words—the Mary Hogan of his dream, the weaver of baby Afghans and tapestries! Even the weaver of dreams!

And now here he was, standing at the crux of time, where family lines re-converged. But was this present moment in time truly the crux? Or was the crux of time yet to be? Or had it come and gone, in a distant colonial past, destined perhaps to come around again, like a recurring alignment of stars and plants, a conjunction that foretells disaster, a king's pending birth, or an opportunity to set things right—even, to lift a curse! Yes, that must be it! The curse that Bob spoke of, the curse of the Ouija board, the curse of his dreams!

As these thoughts and images swirled in John's head, a growing spot of white light appeared once again in the center of his vision. Then, in a flash…

…*The flickering light of a small fire sent shadows dancing over the man's face. This was the same man whom John remembered seeing standing over the grave of the young Rebecca Whitman in the churchyard cemetery. Seated next to him is an older man with long hair—a Native American Indian—sitting cross-legged on the ground, wearing leather boots and assorted beads and trinkets. Staring straight ahead, the older man speaks from a trance-like state:* "I see an old woman. She wears a shawl marked with the letters A and G. She is laughing as she dances before the rising flames. I know this woman. It is a sad happening."

The first man takes a cup from the older man. Standing with outstretched arms, he begins tossing sprinkles of powder from the cup into the flames, which brings new sparks and bursts of orange light with each flick of the wrist. As he performs this rite, he speaks these words:

"A curse be on the bloodline of one whose sinister deeds this night did spill the innocent blood of so fair and pure a child as she. That henceforth empowered the greenhead fly…by noxious bite will so devour…the minds of the guilty and their descendants…for acts committed and un-repented. When summer solstice days return…the fly awakens, the noon sun burns…the unsuspected being bitten…with withering madness will be thus smitten."

Another smaller figure seated by the fire—a young black woman—looks up into the starry night sky with upraised arms and adds these final words:

"And ne'er the curse shall it be lift…till the time of the winter solstice rift…And The One whom time henceforth reclaims…returns to barter with his good name…"

John had fallen to his knees. Exhausted by his most recent vision, he found himself leaning against the workbench to keep from toppling over completely. It took him a few minutes to regain his strength.

"Those last words. Where have I seen them before?"

Then it dawned on him.

He turned around and reached for Bob's notebook. Thumbing through the pages, he finally came to the one he was looking for. Yes, there it was, word for word, in beautiful calligraphy style!

And just below this quatrain was another, more freshly penned in a different color ink:

The patterns of our lives through time
Trace out the course of family lines;
Converging on a distant past,
Then and now the same at last!

This verse appeared to carry the same intent as the crux of time quatrain. Reading these verses together, John began to understand their connected meaning. Suddenly popping into his head came the words spoken by the young woman in his dream as she looked up from the Quija board table: "John Weston, the chosen one." These were the same words Bob used during his Lakeland visit: "I am but a single, lone voice, a messenger, crying in the wilderness; but you John, you are the chosen one."

Incredible as it seemed, the coming together of male and female bloodlines was somehow presenting a unique opportunity, a challenge, to go back in time, to lift the curse! And now, from his latest vision it appeared to have something to do with the greenhead fly. Why was he not surprised by that?

John opened Bob's notebook to a blank page and scribbled the words of the curse contained in his most recent vision—quickly, before the words faded from his memory, or became locked away in his subconscious, requiring the magic key of Caldwell's hypnotic spell to unlock.

Then, turning to a fresh blank page, he sketched the connecting elements of the two family bloodlines, taking his time to fill in the details of his maternal line of descent through the female bloodline—the lunar line as seen from the point of view of the star Rigel. He did the best he could with the missing information—at least he hadn't destroyed any of the glass orbs— but he needed to know if it was all true, or just a fabrication of Bob's demented, albeit creative, mind.

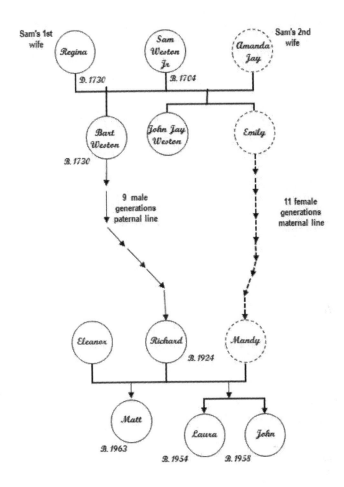

John counted the number of generations on his father's side separating him from Samuel Weston Jr., his six-times paternal great-grandfather. There were nine. On his mother's side, there were eleven generations separating him from Amanda Jay, his eight-times maternal great-grandmother, Sam's second wife and the mother of John Jay Weston.

Strange at first, but it made sense after thinking about it, when you consider the average female married and bore children at a much younger age than the average male. That would account for the difference in the number of generations.

John re-focused on the time elements of Bob's sketch: the winter solstice and waning gibbous moon references, along with the location coordinates for Rigel and Betelgeuse. He knew these positions changed over time. Hopefully, they would all direct him to a common point in time: the crux of time.

So, why not just ask Bob? Then he realized, Bob probably wouldn't even know. After all, he was just the messenger, the recorder of words, numbers, and symbols as they were revealed to him—by the voices! It was John—the chosen one—for whom these words were intended, who had the job of making sense of it all.

Finished with his notes and sketches, John closed the notebook and pushed it aside. He had seen about as much as he was going to see, absorb about as much as he was going to absorb, and now he just needed time to ruminate, think things over. He made a mental note of certain things he needed to follow up on. How much did his stepmom know about his natural mom and her family? Maybe he should try and contact her, somewhere in New England.

As he turned to leave the shop, John picked up Bob's notebook and tucked it under his arm. He was sure Bob wouldn't mind.

*****

It was late afternoon when John finally pulled into the driveway of his Haddonfield home. After this most recent experience in Bob's basement, he could use a little Tylenol—and maybe a good shot of brandy!

John grabbed the mail from the front porch and was opening the door when he saw a folded piece of paper wedged in the door jamb drop to the porch floor. A flyer of some kind. He picked it up. There was a handwritten note on the back:

> Hi. I'm sorry I missed you. I'll try again later.
> Hope you are feeling well.

John turned the note over, but there was no signature. He folded the note, stuffed it in his pants pocket, and entered the house.

Chapter 22

1999
Sunday, 3 October
Haddonfield, NJ

Sunday morning, John decided to sleep in, having been up late the night before trying to decipher the astronomical coordinates for Betelgeuse and Rigel from Bob Fenwick's notes. They didn't quite match any published coordinates he was able to find in his astronomy guidebooks, so he finally decided he would have to consult one of his stargazer club friends who just happened to know an astronomer on staff at the Franklin Institute across the river in Philly. If anyone could figure it out, he could.

It was nine o'clock when the chirping bird sounds of John's alarm clock radio awoke him for the first time. He hit the snooze alarm and rolled over for a nine-minute reprieve. He had just dozed off again when...*blaaaaat!*...he was jarred awake by a long and annoying buzz. Not the chirping alarm clock this time. This was the front door.

"Jehovah's Witnesses! Please, no!"

Either that or some high school kids selling magazines for a free trip to Disney World. John pulled the pillow over his head but couldn't crowd out the sound. The caller was persistent.

"I gotta change that doorbell," John vowed groggily. A nice set of chimes would do just fine. Set it to ring only once with each push of the button. He had the plans all drawn out in his head when...*blaaaaat!*...went the buzzer again.

"Okay, okay! I'm coming!"

John tossed the covers aside, threw on yesterday's dirty pair of jeans over his pajamas and bounded down the two flights of stairs to the front hall lobby. He went to the front door and peaked through the tiny fish-eye lens peephole: a distorted, bigger than life Humpty-Dumpty head greeted him on the other side, its green Mohawk haircut only adding to the grotesqueness of the form. Though a bit shaggier than he had remembered it, the Mohawk unmistakably belonged to the young man from Our Lady of Lourdes's psych unit...Doug Justin!

John didn't open the door right away. He had to get his thoughts together. Once again he looked through the peephole. The head was turned sideways now, bobbing up and down, lips moving a little, like he was listening to some bebop tune on a Walk-Man, only he wasn't wearing a Walk-Man.

Just what I need on a Sunday morning...!

John took a deep breath, reached for the door knob, and opened the door.

"Well, if it isn't Doug Justin!" John exclaimed in pretend amazement.

Startled, Doug stepped back, turned, and smiled. "G-good morning, J-J-John. D-did you get my n-n-note?"

"Note?"

John then remembered the unsigned note he found the day before lodged in the door jam. He reached into his pants pocket and pulled out a crumpled piece of paper. "You mean this one?" John said as he unfolded the note and held it out. "It's not signed, Doug. How was I to know?"

"Oh. S-s-sorry. I f-forgot to s-sign it."

Doug looked pretty much as John remembered him, only a bit scrawnier and more unkempt. His brown hair roots were beginning to push out the green and the youthful stubble on his chin cried out for a shave. He just remained standing there, hands in the pockets of his baggy jeans, rocking back and forth on the balls of his feet, seeming to wait for John to make the next move.

"So, Doug, how long have you been out of Lourdes?"

Doug pursed his lips and tilted his head, looking up to the sky for the answer. "Hmm. Guess it'll be a week tomorrow," he said. "They said I was okay, as long as I continued with my meds." He pulled three bottles of pills from his pants pocket and held them up. "Gotta take 'em every day."

John checked the labels: Haldol, Cogentin, Topamax. The first was an antipsychotic drug, the second treated the tremor side effects of the first drug, and the third was for bipolar disorder. Looking back at Doug he asked the next obvious question: "So, tell me, Doug, do you have someone looking after you? A place to stay?"

Doug squirmed and looked down. "W-well. I was st-staying with my s-sister. But she up and left t-town with her b-boyfriend."

He reached in his other pants pocket and pulled out a wrinkled business card. John recognized it as one of his own. "You s-said if I ever n-needed help I sh-should look you up."

Yeah, like call me at work! Not come knocking on my front door at eight o'clock on a Sunday morning!!

Okay, so John did remember giving him the card and making that promise. Never thought he'd have to make good on it, though. Anyway, Doug looked like he could use a bite to eat. John cleared his throat. "Ahem. Well, Doug, I was just about to put on some coffee and make myself some eggs and bacon. Care to join me?"

Doug perked up. "S-sure! That'd be g-great!"

Doug followed John into the house, down the hallway, and through the kitchen onto the back porch veranda where he plopped himself down on a wicker lounge chair while John set about preparing breakfast.

"Real nice p-place you have hear, J-John," Doug said staring out across the backyard and garden.

"Thanks. I like it."

"My f-folks used to have a p-place like this when I was little. B-but that was a long t-time ago," Doug said with a touch of sadness in his voice.

John took advantage of this opening to ask about his family.

"So, Doug, tell me about your mom and dad. You never really said much about them in the hospital."

Over the next two hours John learned a lot about Doug and his troubled past, how his mom fought off the debilitating roller-coaster swings of manic-depression, or bipolar disorder, until one day she simply lost her grip on the handlebars. She came down with a hard splash as she ended life with a high dive off the Ben Franklin Bridge. Doug's father retreated into the bottle and was killed three years later in an automobile accident, DOA, DUI. Doug was ten years old at the time. His older sister, Teresa, continued to raise him, moving to Washington Township, where they shared a two-bedroom apartment. She had to juggle two waitress jobs to make ends meet, so often wasn't around to keep tabs on Doug. At the age of seventeen, he started doing hard street drugs and dropped out of high school. He would sometimes hitchhike the ten miles or so to Camden to turn a drug deal, often ending up wandering the Admiral Wilson Boulevard at two in the morning. Somehow, his sister almost always knew where to find him. What she didn't know was what drove him to do drugs. That came to light one day in May, 1996, when Doug had to be talked down from a high water tower in Washington Township, insisting that he could fly and was ready to prove it to the world. When asked how he knew he could fly, he responded matter-of-factly, "The voices. They tell me so."

So began the first of Doug Justin's many stays at Our Lady of Lourdes psych unit. Diagnosed as a functional schizophrenic with bipolar disorder, Doug responded well to medication and was released once he was stabilized on an effective drug regimen. But Doug became a "revolving door" case, going in and out of the hospital as he repeatedly fell off the treatment wagon, owing largely to his unstable home environment. His sister had taken up with an aspiring rock musician, part-time drug dealer, and was now pregnant. In the past she was always there for him. Now, she was gone, off to parts unknown, and Doug had nowhere else to turn.

John poured himself another cup of coffee. Was that his fifth or sixth? He'd lost count. Doug refused the coffee, saying it interfered with the Haldol.

Trying to put the pieces of his timeline together, John figured Doug had to be at least twenty, maybe twenty-one.

"So, Doug, how old did you say you were?"

Doug thought hard about this. "Guess I'm…about twenty." Then he thought again. "No, twenty-one. Just had a birthday. Yeah, definitely twenty-one."

John figured it out, now. Doug's sister had waited till he turned twenty-one before hitting the road with her druggie rock star boyfriend—terribly considerate of her.

By now, Doug wasn't stuttering nearly so badly; he seemed more relaxed and in tune with his surroundings. He looked around and stared out the window at the backyard. "Ya know. It's really n-nice here, John. Peaceful. Kinda like that garden p-place near the hospital. W-what was it?"

"You mean the convent grounds next to Lourdes? Hmm, never heard my yard compared to a church monastery before."

"Well, I think you're r-real lucky to have a place like this."

"Yes, thank you, Doug. I surely am."

John then asked a question that had been gnawing at him since this whole conversation began. "So, Doug. You grew up in Shilo, down in Cumberland County, right?"

Doug nodded.

"Growing up," John continued, "were you ever bothered by those big nasty greenhead flies?"

After asking the question, John realized how crazy and out-of-the-blue it must have sounded. But Doug didn't even flinch.

"Oh yeah! All the time, whenever I'd go down to the bay in the summer. Real pesky critters!"

John was relieved. "And your sister. Was she ever bothered?"

Doug thought for a moment. "Don't really know. She hardly ever went down to the bay. She liked the ocean best. The boardwalk in Ocean City, that's where she liked to go in the summertime. But me, I preferred fishin' in the bay. Used to go there on my bike with friends all the time."

John felt redeemed. Maybe there was a connection after all.

"So, Doug. You're gonna need a place to stay. At least until you get on your feet and maybe get a job." *Or until I can find an aunt or uncle willing to take you off my hands!* "I can put you up for a while."

Doug took a deep breath. "B-boy! That'd be g-great, John!"

John looked around. "So, did you bring any clothes? A suitcase or something?"

"Oh, yeah, I forgot! My s-stuff is still out on the porch."

Doug sprang from his chair and bounded down the hall toward the front door. That was the fastest John had ever seen him move.

"Just put everything in the foyer, Doug. Until I figure out where to put you."

John considered the third-floor spare room, but then remembered Doug's "flying problem." It was a forty-foot shot straight down to the driveway. No sense risking that. And the first floor guest room was out of the question. That's where his stepmom stayed whenever she visited, usually on weekends.

"Tell you what, Doug. You can have the small spare room on the second floor. It needs a little straightening, but should do just fine. I'll show you the way."

By now it was past two in the afternoon. John had missed his morning run. Still not too late, he thought. Maybe I can get Doug to join me.

Chapter 23

1774
Monday, 3 October
Greenwich, Cumberland County, NJ

Major repairs to the *Richelieu* were at last complete, but the ship would remain in the Greenwich shipyard another day or two for final repairs and inspections before being moved to the wharf for cargo loading. Over the past two weeks, teams of skilled carpenters, sailmakers, ropemakers, blacksmiths, and riggers scoured the ship stem to stern, working long days to make her seaworthy again, all under the able watch and direction of ship's first mate, Paul McKenzie. Repairs to the bulkhead required the ship to be careened in shallow water, first one side and then the other, as rotten planks were replaced with fresh timber, and all seams tarred and sealed anew. The ship was then uprighted to make the final repairs to the deck and rigging; the shorter mizzen mast was replaced and damaged spars repaired; worn sails were dressed down with beeswax, while the worst of the tattered sails and rigging were replaced.

Paul McKenzie and his captain stood some distance away, taking in a full view of the ship as they assessed the progress of the repairs.

Captain Jack complemented his first mate, slapping him on the back.

"She's looking mighty fine, lad! Ye actually did more than I was ever expectin' t'be done in such a short time. I thought we'd have t'dry dock'er fer sure."

"Yes, sir. Just a few final touches to be made. Once the decks are payed we can move her to the wharf and begin loading the cargo and provisions for the voyage."

The consignment of furs from New Jersey was already in the warehouse biding its time. Freshly milled lumber from Pennsylvania had arrived just yesterday on a barge from Philadelphia and was being off-loaded at this very moment for the planned transfer to the *Richelieu*. One of the two shipments of cotton and tobacco from the southern colonies was presently moored in the bay at the mouth of the Cohansey waiting for more favorable conditions to move upriver, and the second would arrive in a day or two.

"I think I'll have a closer look at 'er, if ya don't mind," the captain smiled.

Paul nodded approvingly. "Be my guest," he said. "But it looks like someone else beat you to it."

The captain squinted to see a tall well-dressed figure of a man already on board slowly pacing the deck with hands clasped behind him. It was Master Bart. There was a second figure as well, a bit frumpy in his attire and makeup.

"Ah, the master has decided to honor us with a visit, I see," the captain noted. "And who, pray tell, is the other gentleman with him?"

"Yes, well, Master Bart wanted to be here when the shipments arrived, and to be double sure everything goes smoothly with the customs officials." Paul motioned to the ship. "The other gentleman is Mr. Mathew Philips, the local customs official."

"Yes, of course," the captain replied slowly. "Mustn't forget the King's duty"—thinking about his recent sojourn at the Stone Tavern—"and certain accounts needin' t'be settled."

Paul smiled and waved the captain off.

As Jack moved away and up the gangplank, a tall, one-eyed figure approached Paul from behind, emerging from the shadows of an alley way between two workman's shacks.

"Yes, we surely mustn't forget the King's well-deserved duty," the shadowy figure spoke

Paul turned with a start. "Jesus! You startled me, Jacob! Must you be all the time so— conniving?"

Cap'n Jacob took this as a compliment and smiled. "Ah, yes. Every day, in every way, my good friend, if ever we are to survive in this world."

Jacob eyed a young man hauling two buckets of steaming pitch that hung at opposite ends of a poll balanced between his shoulders and across his back. He was walking up the gangplank to join a team of laborers on their knees, busily paying the seams of the deck with oakum and hot tar.

Jacob nodded in the ship's direction. Paul turned to follow his directed glance. "You see there?" Jacob challenged. "I'd sooner pay the devil than give the King and Parliament their unjust due!"

Paul smiled. This play on words was not wasted on Mr. McKenzie. He well knew, even as any young apprentice seaman knows, that the "devil seam" was the most difficult deck seam to pay, or seal, due to its curved form and intersecting position with the straight deck planking. It was one of the more unpleasant and tedious tasks of ship's maintenance.

Suddenly aware of an unwitting glance from the customs official and his own vulnerable position in the open, Paul turned nervously to place himself between Jacob and the ship. "Yes, well, I really don't think it is so wise for us to be seen together in a public place like this, Jacob. Please, state your business and be on with it, and let me be about mine."

Jacob drew close and put an arm around Paul's shoulder, then speaking just above a whisper: "As we now speak, my friend, the good ship *Intrepid* is moored offshore in the bay awaiting our swift attention."

Paul appeared puzzled. "Yes, of course, the *Intrepid* carries cotton and tobacco from the southern colonies, as arranged by our associate, Mr. Stewart of Annapolis. But, what has that to do with…our enterprise?"

Jacob shrugged. "What Mr. Stewart doesn't know cannot hurt him," he said sheepishly.

Jacob proceeded to inform Paul of the other cargo aboard the *Intrepid*, the cargo that didn't appear on the ship's manifest. It was their cargo, the smuggled molasses from Barbados. He explained how the contraband was able to find its way from British ports in the Caribbean, through a series of drop-offs and ship transfers at safe havens along the North American coast, until its final transfer to the *Intreprid*, outbound from Annapolis, near the mouth of the Chesapeake Bay. The entire coastline was littered with hundreds of isolated coves and safe harbors well-suited to the smuggler's purpose, and Jacob knew them all. Of course, he also knew most of the ship captains involved, if not personally, then at least professionally, and with Paul's help he further knew which customs officials to approach for a bribe when necessary.

"You are quite the magician, my friend," Paul said at last.

"Thank you," Jacob replied with a gracious nod. "And now, the final leg of the journey comes tonight, with the full moon."

"Where will the transfer be made?"

Jacob studied Paul for a moment before responding. "Tindall's Island. I trust George and Roger will be ready with the long boats."

Paul sighed. "I can only hope so. My job is keeping track of customs officials, not the rowdier elements of your scoundrel team."

Jacob laughed. "Ah yes, of course. That would fall to my charge! I must see to it at once."

With that Jacob casually saluted his friend and turned to leave.

"So, what of the return trip?" Paul pursued as an afterthought.

Jacob paused. "Ah yes. The return leg. A good captain and merchantman must never return with an empty hold. Not good business."

Jacob explained the plan. Once the ship had off-loaded its contraband at Tindall Island, it would proceed upriver and dock at the Greenwich wharf, where it would off-load its legal cargo. Jacob would sign up as a member of the ship's crew for the return southbound trip. Departing late in the day, they would drop anchor at the mouth of the river for the night. His "business associates" on Tindall Island would then transfer the bootleg rum by longboat to the waiting ship, completing the exchange of rum for molasses.

"You won't be seeing me again around these parts till early December," Jacob added. "I'll be returning then for another rum run. I trust you will be here, my friend, to clear the way with the customs officials."

Paul shook his head. "I'm afraid not. My own travel plans will be taking me to England on the *Richelieu*. If all goes to plan, I will be returning in mid-December on the *Greyhound*, accompanying Captain Allen with a shipment of tea..." Paul bit his lip and stopped abruptly.

Jacob raised an eyebrow. "A shipment of...tea?" he smiled deviously. "In these troubled times you are bringing tea to the colonies?"

Paul stared nervously past Jacob, avoiding eye contact and a direct response.

"And I thought I was the daring one!" Jacob laughed.

"Yes, well. Just try to keep this between the two of us," Paul implored.

"Mum's the word."

But Paul knew he'd let the cat out of the bag. He could only hope that where Jacob was going, there could be no repercussions.

"So, if our business is concluded I shall be on my way," Jacob said as he noticed Bartholomew Weston accompanying the customs official down the gangplank. "And none too soon, I might add."

With that, Jacob gave Paul a smart salute, turned, and slithered back into the shadows.

*****

Night time on the Cohansey. A young seaman leaned out over the ship's railing, peering intently across the black, open water to the dark shoreline of Tindall Island some three hundred yards away—as though a few feet closer would actually make a difference.

"Dark as a mummy's tomb," he whispered to himself, though he really didn't know how dark that was; just an expression he picked up from the crew on a recent voyage to the Mediterranean.

The young man reached around to tend the signaling lantern on the deck at his rear, adjusting its wick to conserve its whale oil fuel reserve.

"Great night for a rum run!" he muttered to himself.

Looking up at the dull, overcast sky that concealed the harvest moon, he adjusted his feathered headband and returned to his post at the rail. Even better than before, he thought, thinking back four nights ago to the successful ship-to-shore transfer of contraband molasses. That went well, despite the moonlit sky. During the three days hence, he took the opportunity to visit his brother and father in the port town of Greenwich as the ship's legal cargo was being off-loaded. It was almost four years since he had last seen them. The reunion went well, much better than he had expected.

Suddenly, he spied the dim light of a distant lantern showing through the nighttime mist that clung low to the still surface of Cohansey Cove. He waited. The light reappeared.

The young seaman lifted and rested his signal lantern on the ship's rail. After raising the lantern's wick to intensify the flame and adjusting its inside mirror, he began flipping the shutter on the lantern's window, open and closed, in regular intervals, in response to the shoreline signal. The distant shoreline signal stopped, as expected. The seaman put down the lantern and prepared to receive the longboats from the shore with block and tackle. It didn't take long. The slurping sounds of water lapping at the ship's waterline signaled the arrival of the longboats.

"Stewey! Is that you?" came a hushed voice from below.

The young seaman with the feathered headband leaned over the railing and called back in a low whisper. "Yes! Do you have...the cargo?"

Stewey was joined by two other men at the rail. One of them, a tall man wearing a long blue coat with brass buttons and gold trim, a patch over one eye, put his hand on Stewey's shoulder.

"Well done, my good lad! Well done, indeed!"

Chapter 24

1999
Wednesday, 6 October
Haddonfield, New Jersey

John had just returned from lunch and was settled behind the desk of his Haddonfield office when Mary patched a call through. It was Dr. Alexander from Lakeland. John thanked Mary and punched in the outside line.

"Hello, doctor. To what do I owe the pleasure of this call? Is everything okay with Bob?"

The doctor got right to the point. "Yes, John. Bob is doing very well. But that's not what I called about."

John sensed urgency in the doctor's voice.

"Go on, doctor."

The doctor took a breath. "Do you remember our little discussion last weekend, those historical case studies documenting a particular form of schizophrenic disorder?"

"Yes, of course. A syndrome, you called it. You said they were all related to the bite of the greenhead fly."

"Precisely!" the doctor said excitedly. "Actually, it was your questions concerning a genetic link that got me thinking and challenging some of my original assumptions."

Dr. Alexander proceeded to tell John of his recent discoveries following a systematic epidemiological and statistical analysis of the case histories going back more than two centuries. It took some time to complete, the doctor explained; there were hundreds of cases, missing links here and there, but in the end the results all pointed to same conclusions.

"So, you're saying there is a hereditary link, after all?"

"Yes, of sorts," the doctor replied. "The illness passes through the maternal line, yes, but it does not follow the classic Mendelian patterns of heredity. As every schoolboy knows, the nucleus of every cell contains the genetic material, or DNA, that serves as a blueprint for our hereditary makeup and metabolism. Both parents contribute equal amounts of this nuclear DNA at conception which, when combined, determines the final genetic makeup of the individual offspring. However, in our case, the nuclear DNA is not involved!"

The doctor paused, expecting a response.

"I'm still listening," John replied. "Go on."

The doctor continued to explain that not all DNA is found in the nucleus. A small portion of genetic material is actually located in the mitochondria, those specialized organelles located in the cell's cytoplasm that function as tiny power stations producing the energy needed for the cell's metabolism. What is unique about mitochondrial DNA (mDNA) is that all of it—one hundred percent—comes from the mother, starting with the mDNA found in unfertilized egg! But just as with nuclear DNA, certain variations and mutations in mDNA can lead to serious illness.

"So you're saying that our mental cases result from a mutation of some kind in the mitochondrial DNA, passed down from mother to child."

"Yes, but not entirely."

The doctor explained that it was only the tendency or potential for mental disease that was passed through the direct maternal line. In our particular case, for the illness to manifest itself in the individual, it needed a triggering mechanism, and that trigger came from something in the environment.

"The bite of the greenhead fly?" John posited.

"Precisely!"

The doctor then offered his hypothesis on the epidemiology of the syndrome, tracing its origins to the back-bay regions of eighteenth-century Cumberland and Salem Counties. The evidence pointed to a single progenitor and mutational event occurring sometime between 1770 and 1780. But he couldn't narrow it down any better than that.

"My word, doc, you're quite the forensic sleuth!" John exclaimed. "Any idea what the triggering mechanism is? I mean, how does the bite of the greenhead fly actually trigger such a response?"

"Well, I can only guess at a mechanism. It may be epigenetic in nature, something from the environment that triggers the expression of the gene or genes responsible for observed trait or illness. Like royal jelly fed to selected bee larvae that turns on those genes responsible for turning the bee into a new, fertile queen. In our case, it's the bite of the greenhead fly! What's interesting is that only certain flies from that area appear capable of eliciting this response in susceptible individuals carrying this mutated genome. As implausible as it may seem, it's as though the required mutations and the emergence of a complementary vector system developed at the same time, but independently of each other."

John thought about Julie Evert's genetically altered fly research.

"Perhaps," he suggested, "the mutations and the emergence of a new variety of greenhead fly, or vector, shared a common cause or triggering event, somewhere in the dark shadows of eighteenth-century Cumberland County."

The doctor paused a moment. "Hmm, that's an interesting thought, John. Do you have any idea how that could have happened?"

John was taken slightly off guard. *Why is he asking me? Does he think I was there?*

Suddenly, in a flash of white light...

...*The man now stood with outstretched arms, tossing sprinkles of powder into the flames, which brought new sparks and bursts of orange light with each flick of the wrist. As he performed this rite, he spoke these words: "A curse be on the bloodline of one whose sinister deeds this night did spill the innocent blood of so fair and pure a child as she; that henceforth empowered the greenhead fly, by noxious bite will so devour, the minds of the guilty and their descendants, for acts committed and un-repented. When summer solstice days return, the fly awakens, the noon sun burns; the unsuspected being bitten, with withering madness will be thus smitten..."*

The vision lasted only a second or two in real time. It was the same vision he experienced in Bob's basement on Saturday, just three days earlier. But this time it was much more vivid—and more meaningful. He could feel the warmth, hear the crackle of the flames, and study the details of the amulet worn by the old man seated at the fire. It was the symbol of a flame, carved into bone.

"You still there, John?" spoke the voice on the other end of the phone.

"Yeah...sure, doc. Just trying to put the pieces together," John responded haltingly.

The doctor asked John if he wouldn't mind coming down to Lakeland for a second visit. Said he'd like to follow up on their earlier discussions and possibly probe further into the incidents John had described. If John wouldn't mind, he'd even like to put him under hypnosis again, to further explore his "delusions of time travel," as the doctor put it. John knew the doctor was fishing for something, and it wasn't bay flounder! Anyway, John said he had already scheduled an appointment with Dr. Caldwell at Lourdes for a follow-up hypnotherapy session. He, too, was eager to get to the meaning of these visions, though probably for different reasons. John promised Dr. Alexander that he would share the results of his session with Caldwell on his next visit to Lakeland to see Bob.

*****

That evening John did something he knew was long overdue. It had been almost two months since he'd visited his mom at Lakeview Estates, just a few miles from his old childhood home in Stratford. She knew about John's hospital stay, but he never told her the real reason. As far as she was concerned, it was just a bad case of the flu.

He would have gone straight from work, but had to stop at the house first to check on Doug, his newly adopted boarder and former fellow inmate from Lourdes' psych unit. Doug had just returned from his first solo run through the neighborhood and was on the back porch veranda reading an article from one of John's fitness magazines when John arrived home. He was surprised how readily Doug took to running when he first suggested joining him for a run Sunday afternoon. Doug literally jumped at the idea.

Without looking up from the magazine article, Doug spoke as John entered the kitchen. "So, J-John, you said something about a 'runner's high' the other day. You said that's all the drugs you ever need."

"Yeah, that's pretty much it," John replied as he poured himself a glass of skim milk from the fridge. "Of course, that's not to say drugs aren't ever necessary. But the body does some pretty amazing things with the 'drugs' nature has given it."

"Yeah, well this article talks about that. As m-much as I can tell, this ananda-something-or-other is some pretty serious sh-shit!"

John smiled as he wiped away a milk mustache with a dish towel. "Well, the final verdict isn't in on *anandamide*. But whatever the active chemical turns out to be, it really works!"

John knew that what exactly causes this natural high has been subject to debate and controversy over the years. For much of the eighties it was felt that endorphins were responsible, but the nineties produced a more likely candidate: anandamide, a naturally occurring substance produced by the body. Discovered in '92, it behaves similarly to THC, the active ingredient in marijuana, binding to the same brain receptor site as THC and producing similar feelings of relaxation and pain relief often described by runners and pot smokers alike.

"So, you're going to visit your m-mom?" Doug inquired, suddenly changing the subject.

"Right, Doug. I'm way overdue for a visit. And...there are some things I need to talk to her about," he added.

Doug just looked down. "Yeah, well, at least you s-still got a mom to visit," he replied woefully.

John promised Doug he wouldn't be gone long, but if he needed anything, he could be reached on his cell phone.

*****

Eleanor Weston had developed quite a reputation as a cardsharp at Lakeview Estates retirement community, a place she'd called home for the past six years: hearts, gin rummy, pinochle, take your pick. Even sheeps-head, a not too common card game she learned growing up in the midwest. But, bridge?

Well, that required a partner. And she had lost her bridge partner five years ago the day her husband, Richard, died suddenly and unexpectedly.

That was almost a year to the day after selling their Stratford home and moving to Lakeview Estates. "Couldn't handle the yard work anymore," Richard had said. His wife agreed, though she couldn't give up doing what she loved most, and continued tending a small flower garden in the backyard of their new townhouse.

While officially retired, Richard was called in from time to time to substitute teach at Sterling High. Though almost five times the average age of his students, he still connected, and the kids loved him—right up to the day he collapsed in the teachers' lounge. He was pronounced dead on arrival at Voorhees West Jersey Hospital. Official cause of death: Ruptured asymptomatic aortic aneurysm…the silent killer. He was sixty-seven.

For John, this was the second most traumatic event in his life. While he always had the deepest respect for his dad, it was only in later years, after John's return from California, that he and his dad had really become close, and now, suddenly, he was gone. Like burning boats and smoke on the water, that old familiar, helpless feeling of loss and guilt returned to haunt him. Why guilt? His dad had been complaining of low back pain the week before. John convinced him he didn't need to see a doctor, just had to exercise more and "work it out."

It was raining the day of his dad's funeral, with family, friends, and an endless line of students, teachers, and well-wishers attending and paying their respects. Cold and numb, John remained at the gravesite hours after everyone had gone, standing there alone in the drizzling rain, snot running from his nose, mixed with tears and rain.

Harleigh Cemetery, that's where his dad was buried.

*****

John gave his mom a gentle hug as she greeted him at the door. "So, how're you feeling, mom?"

"Oh, I'm hanging in there, Son."

She hugged him harder and kissed him on both cheeks. "It's so good to see you, John."

She stepped back and held him at arm's length. "But you, John. How are you doing? You look tired. Are you fully recovered from the flu? You don't look like you're getting enough to eat."

John smiled. "Yes, Mom. And I'm doing just fine, really."

"Well, promise me you won't forget your flu shot next year, John. Promise?"

"I promise, Mom. 'Flu shot, next year,'" he wrote down in an imaginary palm-held notebook.

"So, how about a nice fresh pot of herbal tea," his mom asked as she backed away and shuffled into the kitchen.

"Sure, Mom. Do you have any honey to go with that?"

"Of course, John. I remember how you like it."

As Mrs. Weston left the room, John walked over to the entertainment center with its generous collection of knickknacks and family photos displayed in glass-door shelved cabinets on either side of the TV. There was the book-framed 8" x 10" of his dad and stepmom on their wedding day, opposite their twenty-fifth wedding anniversary photo. That was just ten years ago, July '89, one year after John's return from the west coast and the start-up of his new consulting business. On the next shelf down was a picture of John with his dad, posing with their bikes soon after their return from France in 1990. John smiled. Those were happy days. He and his dad started out taking long hikes together, sometimes overnighters along the Appalachian Trail. His dad, an avid biker, got John interested in cycling not long after returning from California, and in 1990 they even flew to France together to see the Tour de France. John's sister, Laura, and editor brother-in-law put them up in their villa just outside Paris. It was the first time he had seen his sister since leaving for California in the early eighties.

"You know, Mom, that trip to France with Dad was probably...one of the best times of my life," he noted wistfully.

Mrs. Weston smiled as she returned with the tea and some cookies on a tray. "Yes, I know," she said, setting the tray down on the coffee table and taking a seat on the sofa. "That was a really special trip for your dad, too. He was always talking about it."

On the other side of the TV was another framed picture located toward the rear of the cabinet and almost hidden from view. John had to move a ceramic elephant aside to get a better view. He recognized the pretty, young woman in the picture, smiling and holding a baby, with a little girl of five standing by her side. The woman was Mandy "Richards" Weston, his natural mother; the little girl was his older sister, Laura; the baby, of course, was John.

"Better drink your tea, John, before it gets cold."

John walked over and joined his stepmom on the sofa and took a sip of tea. "Mom, you know all that family tree stuff that Aunt Dee was into. Do you know if she ever"—pausing for the right words—"investigated my mom's side of the family. You know, my natural mom."

Mrs. Weston smiled and thought about the question for a moment, her cup of tea shaking just a bit on as she cradled it in her lap. "Well, dear, I don't believe Dee ever looked into it, at least, not to my knowledge. What makes you ask?"

John tightened his lips and took a deep breath. "Oh, I don't know. You know how people get to thinking about family origins as they get older. Like trying to tie up loose ends in their life before it's too late."

"Well, dear, I think you have quite a few years left before you need to worry about 'tying up loose ends,' as you put it."

"Yeah, I know. But, I just think it would be nice to know something of my mom's side. If I ever did decide to get married and have kids, I'm sure that's something they would want to know about. You know, there's the whole question of medical history, inherited traits…genetic illnesses."

That got a raised eyebrow from Mrs. Weston. "Oh, yes. Well, I can understand that."

Setting down her tea, she stood up and walked into the next room. A minute later she returned with two manila envelopes, one labeled "John," the other "Laura."

"I've been meaning to give these to you, John. I found them going through some storage boxes this summer, and you and Laura should really have them. Don't know when I'll get to see your sister again, so maybe you should take them both."

John took the envelope marked "John" and spilled its contents onto the coffee table. They were birthday cards in their original envelopes addressed to himself, from his fifth to tenth birthday. The earlier ones were signed, "Love, Mommy," the later ones, simply "Mandy."

"As you can see, none of the cards have a return address. Just the postmark, 'Stockbridge, Mass.'"

John opened and studied each of the cards. Funny, he didn't recall ever seeing them before. Maybe he just forgot. For this tenth birthday there was even a personal check for ten dollars signed, "Mandy Richards." It was drawn on the Bank of Springfield, Massachusetts, but was never cashed.

After some time, John finally spoke. "Stockbridge, Massachusetts. Isn't that somewhere up in the Berkshires?"

Mrs. Weston sighed, "Could be. I don't really know. Never was very good at geography."

John nodded.

"Hmm, I remember Dad saying how she took up with some hippie guru in one of those new age mountain communes. Do you think he was just making that up?"

Eleanor just shook her head. "Well, I really don't know, John."

"But, do you think she's still alive, living up in the Berkshires?"

"I don't know that either, son" Eleanor replied, growing a little impatient. John sensed this.

"I'm sorry, mom. I didn't mean to be so…pressing. I guess maybe there're some things we'll never know."

John gathered up the cards and put them back in the manila envelope. "Thanks for sharing these with me, Mom. At least it tells me something."

Eleanor just closed her eyes and smiled.

John decided to change the subject. "So, Mom. What have you heard from Matt?"

She perked up. "Oh, Matt calls me every week to chat and bring me up to date on things. I do so look forward to his calls."—*So why don't you call me more often, John, like your brother?*—"You know, little Sammy is a senior in high school this year! I can't believe how time flies!"

"Yes, well, Matt and Sammy were supposed to have paid us a visit this summer visiting colleges and campuses back east," John said. "I was really looking forward to that. But Matt called at the last minute to say they had a change of plans."

"Oh, yes. That was too bad," Mrs. Weston pouted.

"It seems that Sammy was invited to join his girlfriend on her family vacation. Beverly, I think Matt said her name was. And you know what they say: 'Girls rule.' Or at that age, I think it's 'hormones rule.'"

"Oh well. He's got a whole year to look at colleges. I think he made the right choice," Mrs. Weston conceded.

*****

Thursday afternoon, October 7. John received a phone call at work from his stargazer friend, Sean, who claimed to have the lowdown on those celestial coordinates John had laid on him Sunday night, the ones he'd copied from Bob's basement notebook on Saturday.

"Okay, Sean, so what exactly did your friend at the Franklin Institute say about those coordinates?"

A high-pitched, nerdy voice came from the other end. "Well, he confirmed them as the stars Rigel and Betelgeuse, sure enough. Just like you said. But..."

He drew out the last word like a whiny school girl, and then paused. "Okay. Bu-u-ut what?" John asked impatiently, imitating the irritating inflection in Sean's voice.

"Well, it's the time, John. Those coordinates are not from our time."

"Whadaya mean, 'not from our time'?"

"What he told me was they were the precise coordinates of Rigel and Betelgeuse in the year of our Lord seventeen-seventy-four."

John repeated the words "seventeen-seventy-four" to himself.

"Could he be more specific than that, Sean?"

"Well, he couldn't pinpoint the exact day. But he was able to narrow it down to sometime late in that year, close to the winter solstice."

"December twenty-second." John offered.

"Right. Give or take a week or so."

John closed his eyes as his office became awash in a white light, and then...

...The older man did not speak. He simply continued looking down at the grave. John's presence went unnoticed by the two men. So he drew closer to read the inscription on the tomb stone:

Rebecca Whitman
Born: August 16, 1756
Died: Dec 22, 1774

"She is with her mother, now," the older man struggled to say. "May God rest her soul"...

John slowly opened his eyes; the light was gone. The visions were coming much easier now: no more sweating, no throbbing headaches.

"Thank you, Sean, for following up on this. I owe you one."

"No problem, John. Glad to help."

After hanging up, John looked around at the scattered notes on his desk and credenza and realized he was beginning to accumulate more information than he could keep track of in his head, or on so many loose pieces of paper. So, like any good engineer, he set up a loose-leaf binder, labeling it: "Greenwich – The Final Project, Book Two," a takeoff on Bob's original basement shop notebook which John kept safely locked away in his top desk drawer.

He took a clean sheet of paper and made the following entry, marking the connection between his vision and Bob's prophetic timeline utterances: "The 'crux of time'—December 22nd, 1774—the winter solstice."

He leaned back and sighed. "So, that's *when* I gotta be."

Reaching into his middle desk drawer John pulled out the Triple-A map of South Jersey, the one José gave him at the hospital, opened it and stared at the little fishing boat Doug had drawn at the mouth of the Cohansey River. "And that's *where* I gotta be!" He made some wiggly doodles on his desk pad calendar. "But...how?"

The sudden rustle of a venetian blind to his rear caught his attention, followed by a desperate buzzing sound. John turned around. A housefly was trapped between the blinds and the window pane, a lone survivor of the hot summer season.

"A distant relative—a 'cousin thrice removed,' perhaps—longing to escape and renew old family ties. Hmm, I wonder," he muttered softly, then jotted something down in his notebook.

Chapter 25

1999
Saturday, 9 October
South Jersey

A cool autumn breeze started up through the trees as John negotiated the final bend in the trail of his early morning three-mile run through Pennypack Park. Barely breaking a sweat, John called out over his shoulder to the tall, lanky figure struggling to keep up about twenty yards behind.

"C'mon, Doug. Just another hundred yards. You can do it."

As the path faded into a clearing marking the trail's end, John stopped and turned and held up the digital stopwatch dangling from a cord around his neck.

"C'mon! You can beat your previous time by a full thirty seconds! Counting down, ten, nine, eight, seven…"

On the count of "six," a huffing, puffing Doug Justin jogged past John and came to a stop, bent over with hands braced on his knees.

"I d-did it!" he gasped. After a couple of deep, quick breaths he looked up smiling at John. "I did it! I b-beat my old record!"

John smiled back and patted him on the back. "All right! Great job! Now, don't forget the warm down routine. You don't wanna cramp up those calf muscles."

On the drive back to the house, Doug talked nonstop about how good running made him feel.

"Never thought it c-could be like this! Like, m-maybe I can run a m-marathon someday, huh, John?"

"Sure, Doug. But marathons, well, they're pretty special. Gotta build up to them, gradually. Takes a special diet, too."

Doug took a moment to consider. "Okay. I can do that. Whatever it takes, right?"

John smiled. "Sure, Doug. Whatever it takes."

Doug sat back and relaxed, peering out the window as they entered downtown Haddonfield. "So, John. Are we still going to Greenwich today?"

Earlier in the week, John had asked Doug to join him for a road trip to Cumberland County, the area around Greenwich on the Cohansey River. He said he needed to do some research for a project he was working on and could use the help of someone familiar with the area.

"Sure thing, Doug. I'd like to hit the road as soon as possible, once we get cleaned up. We can grab breakfast on the road."

Back at the house John let Doug shower first. For as large a house as this was, it had only one shower, located on the second floor just off the master bedroom. There were numerous half-baths—toilets and sinks—like the one he put in for his mom on the first floor. John had scolded himself repeatedly for never adding a second full bath, but just never got around to it.

Once John heard the water running he figured Doug was okay, so he just settled into his study, waiting his turn, using the time to review the route he planned to take to Greenwich. He'd done his homework this time and was well prepared, maps and all, planning to follow the old King's Highway—or the portions that still existed—from Haddonfield down to Salem, and from there to take the lesser-traveled backcountry roads to Greenwich, backtracking the approximate route he had taken during his "delusional" eighteenth-century time travels a month earlier. He thought by doing so he might rekindle a memory—or perhaps trigger a vision—by association, and might even encounter another one of those greenhead Tabby monsters down near the bay, wondering what another bite from a pair of those serrated mandibles might do—maybe take him back again. Go back! Save her! Wasn't that what Bob and his visions were asking him to do?

John was too absorbed in his preparations to notice a blue '96 Ford Bronco pulling up in front of the house. A middle-aged woman, pretty, with jet black hair tied up loosely in the back, got out and jaunted up the walk toward John's front door. She was carrying a white cardboard box tied up with string, the kind you might get from a bakery.

Blaaat! Blaaat!

John jumped at the sound of the buzzer.

"Yes, definitely gotta change that doorbell!"

When John opened the front door, a smiling Sally Fielding in tight cut-off jeans and bulging halter top greeted him, bold tan cleavage and all.

"Sally Fielding!"—*you are indeed a sight for sore eyes!*—"To what do I owe this surprise visit?"

Sally's pulse quickened as her green, sparkling eyes scanned the tall, handsomely athletic and sweaty figure standing before her. John followed her gaze with some measure of embarrassment.

"Sorry, Sal. I'm not really dressed yet."

"No need to be sorry, John. You look…fine."

John quickly got things back on track. "So, what have you got in the box?"

"Ah! I come bearing delectable gifts from the baker's oven!"

John's eyebrows were raised. "And who is the baker?" he asked as Sally followed him through the vestibule into the foyer.

"Why, me of course! I remembered how much you loved my strawberry shortcake at Katie's on Labor Day. So, I took the liberty of baking one for you."

John reached over and opened the lid. "My! That looks good enough to eat!" he said.

Sally laughed. "Why of course! What else would you do with it?"

John closed the lid and took the box from Sally. "So, what's the occasion, Sal?"

She cocked her head coquettishly. "Oh, nothing special. It's just that we haven't seen you since you left the hospital. And with no one to take care of you, I thought you could use a little...support."

John looked past Sal toward the front door. "So, did you come alone, or is Paul waiting out in the Bronco?"

Sally glanced quickly over her shoulder and shook her head. "No, Paul was busy with some yard work, so I came alone...all by myself."

She batted her long, glossy eyelashes and waited for a reaction. John took a deep breath, exhaling slowly. "Well...I better get this thing in the fridge. It does need refrigeration, right?"

Sally smiled. "Yes. It does keep...longer that way."

The few moments of awkward silence that followed were suddenly broken by a loud, stammering voice from the main staircase. "I th-think we're out of sh-shampoo, John. I just used the last of it."

John and Sally both turned and looked up. There was Doug standing on the lower landing, stripped to the waist with a wrapped bath towel covering the rest of him, holding up an empty bottle of shampoo.

"Oh, I'm s-s-sorry. Didn't know you had c-c-company, John."

Sally's expression suddenly changed from sensually charming to shocked and bewildered and, yes, just a touch of betrayed. She was having trouble figuring out what a good-looking, half-naked young man was doing coming out of John's shower and down the stairs so early on a Saturday morning! "Not dressed yet," was probably an understatement.

"Well...I can see I may have...chosen the wrong time to...drop by," she said, groping for the right words.

John didn't pick up right away on her reaction. "No, this is fine, Sally. As good a time as any."

Sally thought otherwise. "I...better be going, John. Just...give us a call if you need...anything else," she stammered as she turned to leave.

John finally got it. He turned to explain, but it was too late. Sally was already out the door and halfway down the path to her car.

By now Doug was standing in the foyer looking out the front porch window. "So, who was that pretty lady, John? She seemed to be in an awful h-hurry."

John let out a sigh. "That was Sally Fielding, the wife of my good friend, Doctor Paul Fielding, Chief Medical Examiner for Camden County."

John, still holding the box of strawberry shortcake, smiled and turned to Doug. "She was just…a little confused. You see, I haven't told anyone about you." *After all, I thought you'd be gone in a day or two!*

John looked out the window and followed Sally's Ford Bronco as it peeled off down the street. Well, Johnny boy. Like Ricky told Lucy, "You got some 'splainin' to do!" He then turned to Doug. "It's okay, Doug. I just owe her, and others, an explanation, is all."

*****

The first part of their road trip proved uneventful: no flashbacks, no visions, just a pleasant ride through a beautiful South Jersey countryside—farms, fields, and woods under a fair-weather autumn sky. They reached Salem in just under sixty minutes and stopped at a diner just inside the city limits for a quick breakfast. Typical of an older blue-collar working town, modern-day Salem was quaint and charming in spots, worn and torn in others. Waiting for their meal, John took out his cell phone and dialed the number for George Davies, the fishing boat captain he had tried contacting a month earlier. Maybe there was something about that boating trip in July that would shed more light on Bob's condition. But the call didn't go through. In the display window was the message: "Call Failed. Non-Working Number."

"Damn!"

John returned the phone to his pocket.

After breakfast, John studied the map one more time before setting out. Back in the car, he reached around to check the rear seat for a package he'd placed there before leaving the house: a large shoe box with a double wrap of twine to secure its lid. He gave the package a little OCD tap. Good! Still there! Then he turned to Doug.

"Here, Doug, you take the map. I'll drive, you navigate. Capiche?"

"S-sure. But h-how do I know the way?" Doug asked as he unfolded the map and laid it out on his lap.

"Not to worry. I've highlighted the route in yellow. Just like Triple-A. Can't get lost."

"Okay. I'll d-do my best."

From Salem they headed south on a two-lane country road toward the town of Hancock Bridge, sight of the 1778 massacre of about two dozen rebel militiamen in their sleep by a force of British regulars and colonial sympathizers. Less than 300 yards past the bridge over Alloway Creek lay the Hancock House, site of the massacre. The well-preserved building was an excellent example of early colonial architecture and brickwork. John parked the car to admire the red and blue vitrified brick patterns in Flemish bond.

"Potassium nitrate!" was all he said as he continued staring at the house.

"W-What did you say?"

John smiled and turned to his young traveling companion. "That's how they made the blue color in the brick. Potassium nitrate. The clay was treated with the chemical and held a certain distance from the open flames in the kiln to develop the blue tint. The quality and size of the brick was actually established by law."

John pointed to the zigzag patterns of red and blue brick decorating the outside end walls of the building from top to bottom. "See that pattern? Looks like a giant staircase going up to the sky."

"Cool! Like a 'Stairway to Heaven.'" Doug began humming a few bars from his favorite Led Zeppelin tune.

John smiled, noticing the Led Zeppelin name, complete with dirigible, Doug recently had tattooed on his left arm. "Nice artwork!"

"Oh, yeah, th-thanks. Had it done Fr-Friday while you were at work." Doug looked out the car window at the Hancock House. "So, what happened here, John? I mean, back in the olden days."

John explained how about three dozen or so Cumberland County militiamen protecting the bridge against a British advance were holed up in the Hancock House the night of 20 March, 1778. Just before sunrise on the morning of the twenty-first, a British element proceeding upriver surprised and silently overcame the sentries at the bridge. No shots were fired, which would have alerted the townsfolk and main contingent of rebels. With fixed bayonets, the redcoats silently surrounded and entered Hancock House, where they viciously attacked and bayoneted the rebels as they slept. Even William Hancock, the establishment's Quaker owner, wasn't spared. He died of his wounds several days later.

"So, do you think the place is haunted?" Doug finally asked.

John paused a moment. No auras or white flashes of light. No flashback visions. "Well, I really don't know, Doug. Not by my reckoning, at least."

Leaving the Hancock House behind, they picked up Canton Road (County Route 623) heading south and east out of town, generally paralleling the Delaware Bay's coastline toward Cumberland County and points south. As they approached and crossed Stowe Creek, the dividing line between Salem and Cumberland Counties, that's when déjà vu and the strange sensations started setting in for John: fleeting cognitive moments of knowing what was around the next bend—but not so much knowing as feeling.

And then there was the other thing.

Putting the car on cruise control, the dashboard cruise control indicator light came on as it should. Suddenly, the word began to flash "CRUISE"..."CRUISE"..."CRUISE"...which then became..."CURSE"..."CURSE"..."CURSE"...and then..."GOBACK"..."GOBACK"..."SAVHER"..."SAVHER."

John shook his head, rubbed his eyes and looked again: he was back in "CRUISE" control. "Okaaay!" he said nervously.

He turned off the cruise control and turned to Doug. "Look, Doug. I want you to tell me if you see me doing anything...weird. You might even have to drive." He looked over at Doug. "You can do that, can't you?"

Doug squirmed a little in his seat. "S-Sure, John. I can d-drive. If I really h-had to."

He looked down at the map. "But I c-can't drive a-and navigate, too," he said.

John smiled. "Don't worry. If it really comes down to you driving, navigating will be the least of our worries."

Coming to Gum Tree Corner, John slowed down and brought the Camry to a stop as the road forked in three directions. "Okay, Doug, which way do we go?"

Doug traced the highlighted path on the map with his finger, and then pointed toward the middle road veering off to the left. "Th-that one! Take that one over there. Ch-Chestnut Road."

Following Doug's direction, John took off down the road. Within minutes they passed Davis Mill Pond and were descending the gentle slopes of Mount Gibbon toward the outskirts of North Greenwich.

Nice view, John thought. *I've seen this before; been here before.*

John recalled his trip by stage wagon from eighteenth-century Greenwich. The hill offered a splendid view of the town and surrounding country side, bucolic and serene. John took a deep breath and filled his lungs with the clean, cool pre-autumnal air, marked with the fresh scent of pine.

Reaching the bottom glen, they slowed down as a sign just ahead welcomed them to the village of North Greenwich, a collection of quaint cottages and farmhouses arranged in haphazard fashion along both sides of the road. Just past Mill Road on the right, they crossed a small, tree-lined stream—"Pine Mount Creek" the sign said—where and the buildings became more closely spaced and regular, typical of a small village center. An old cemetery nestled in a wooded glade on the right caught John's attention. John pulled over just past where another road T-intersected the main road from the left. John quickly surveyed the grounds.

Looks ancient. I know this place!

"Yeah, I know this place!" Doug blurted out, echoing John's private thoughts.

"W-what was that?" John asked, flustered momentarily by Doug's seeming prescience.

Doug pointed up the road to the left. "Sh-Shilo, the town I grew up in. It's just up that road to the left, about f-four miles."

John turned his head and checked out the posted street sign: Ye Greate Street and Sheppards Mill Road.

"So, we're on Ye Greate Street!" John suddenly realized. *Ye gads! I've definitely been here before!*

"Right!" Doug confirmed. "And that's Sheppards Mill Road. I used to c-come this way all the time as a kid on my bike, on the way to the b-bay to fish."

John smiled. "So, now you know why I asked you to come along."

John took the map from Doug's lap and folded it up. "This map won't do us much good from this point on. Not enough detail. I'll be relying on your dead reckoning, Doug, to get us to the marina. Of course," he added with a smile, "I also happen to enjoy your company."

Doug took a deep breath, suddenly taken with his own importance "Right! Don't worry, John. I'll g-get us there."

"I'm sure you will."

John looked past Doug at the cemetery. Doug followed his gaze. "So, d'ya wanna g-get out?" Doug asked.

John paused a moment, then nodded. "Sure. Let's have ourselves a closer look."

The air was turning cooler now as the sky had become mostly overcast. A brisk, stiff wind greeted John as he stepped from the car, stirring up a whirligig of autumn leaves newly fallen from the line of trees bordering the cemetery grounds—old, enormous trees, mostly buttonwoods and oaks, which still offered a good deal of shade despite an early seasonal loss of foliage. A six-foot high perimeter fence, black wrought iron, paralleled the line of trees, set back a comfortable distance off the road. There were no buildings on the grounds, but a small clearing near its center provided evidence of an earlier stone foundation. *A church used to be here*, John sensed. Looking further down the road, on the other side of street, he noticed a modern, red brick Presbyterian church with a newer cemetery to its rear. He turned his attention back to the clearing. *My guess is this was the site of the original, "mother" church.*

Doug followed John through an open gate onto the cemetery grounds. The tombstones—those that remained after years of weathered neglect—varied in size, from eight-foot tall marble obelisks to modest stone tablet markers. As they walked slowly down the regularly spaced rows toward a far distant corner of the cemetery, John felt that he was looking for something, but didn't quite know what, not until he actually found it, or it found him: a lone, tall, ancient oak tree, its low-hanging boughs hovering over a small collection of crumbling, green algae-encrusted stone markers symmetrically arranged at its base. Four stone posts marked the corners of this small plot, with the tree positioned just off center. Only two of the posts actually remained; John surmised the other two must have once existed, as their stone bases were now worn level with the ground. Orange rust-stained depressions bore into the sides of the posts, the sole remnants of a low iron rail fence that once bordered the plot and had long since vanished to the elements. It appeared to be an old family burial plot.

As they drew closer, John began to feel light-headed and had to kneel down; then, in a flash of white light, he re-experienced his original churchyard vision of the two men at the grave site of a young Rebecca Whitman, near and dear to the two of them, only this time it was much more vivid in every detail.

...There, not too far distant, stood an older man with his head bowed over a newly dug grave, with his back to John. The grave was located near three other, older gravesites, under the low spreading boughs of a large oak tree. All four graves, the tree and the ground immediately surrounding them, were enclosed on three sides by a low, wrought iron fence set about twelve inches off the ground, marking the area as a family burial plot

...A second, younger man approached the older man from the left. The two men exchanged nods of recognition, and the younger man joined the older man by the new grave site. "She was the flower of my life. The very soul of my being," the older man said. The older man placed his left hand on the shoulder of the young man. "I tell you now, were it in my power to know and curse the hand responsible for this act, I would do so, though my soul perish in the process"

...The older man turned and handed the younger man a small, wooden box he had been holding by his side. "Here, take this," he said, "I know she would have wanted you to have it." As the young man took the wooden box, John was now able to see its every detail, from the gentle curvature of its brass-hinged lid to the vivid, colorful floral engravings.

Emerging slowly from his vision, John's mind's eye held firmly onto the image of the box with the floral carvings. "I've seen that box!" he mumbled; then thought again: "I *have* that box!"

"John, are you okay?" Doug asked, gently shaking him by the shoulder.

John continued to stare at the grave markers as he regained his senses and rose to his feet. "I know who is buried here," he said softly.

John walked closer and began inspecting the five stone markers for a name. But the inscriptions were terribly worn and impossible to make out with the naked eye. Like a blind man reading Braille, he had to feel them to read them. One after another he traced out the names: "Elizabeth," "Elijah," and "Reb...c...W...tman..." John had to fill in the missing letters, so worn they couldn't even be felt, but he knew the name: Rebecca Whitman.

John gasped in disbelief. "So, it is true!"

"W-What's true, John?" the bewildered Doug asked.

"Rebecca Whitman. She really does…or did exist!" Looking back at the car, he added: "And now I know where the box came from!"

Doug scratched his head. "So, w-who is Rebecca W-Whitman?"

John looked up. "Why, she's the girl of my dreams! The Quija board girl! John Weston's one and true love!"

Doug backed up a few steps. "J-John. Are you…o-k-kay?" making good his promise to say something if he saw John acting weird.

John stood up smiling, wiping his hands on his jeans. "Couldn't be better, Dougie boy! At least I know I'm not going crazy. Not just yet, anyway."

Doug looked relieved. "So, you g-gonna take any pictures of this place? Just to p-prove what you saw, I mean."

John gave a faraway look. "Nah! Didn't bring my camera."—turning to Doug—"That's why I brought you. To be a witness to anything that might happen." John laughed. "So, what d'ya say we head on down to the marina before we provoke whatever other spirits reside here."

"Sure, let's go!"

The fearless duo returned to the car. Before getting back in, John checked the back seat to make sure the shoebox was still there. Good! Don't want no Houdini disappearing box tricks!

"The marina shouldn't be that far from here," John said as he climbed behind the wheel. "You just gotta show me the…" John stopped mid-sentence, alarmed by the look on Doug's face.

"We g-got a visitor," Doug said softly as he stared past John out the driver-side window.

John turned and was startled to see a bearded old man in ragged clothes standing not arm's length away by the open car door window.

"Whoa! You startled me, old timer"—*Where the hell did you come from?!*—"What can I do for you?"

There was intensity in the old man's gaze that belied his years. He remained standing there, slightly hunched over with a dirty, worn duffel bag slung over his shoulder.

"Ye wouldn't happen t'be headed me way, would ye now?"

John was taken aback. The voice and Irish brogue were familiar somehow, but the face…?

"Well, that depends on where you're heading," John calmly replied.

The old man put the duffel bag down on the ground. "Bridge-town. That's where I be headin'."

John smiled. "You mean Bridgeton," he corrected.

"Aye! Have it your way, lad."

"Well, sir, we plan to be in Bridgeton eventually. But right now we're on our way to Greenwich, just down the road a piece."

The old man's eye twitched, then squinted as he rubbed his fingers through a long, scraggly beard. "Ahh!" he moaned. It was a long, ghastly moan. "That cursed place!"—pronouncing it *kur-sid*, with the emphasis on the first syllable—"Hardly any soul, living or dead, goes to Greenwich these days!"

A chill ran up John's spine as he realized who this old gentleman might be. Can't be! He tried convincing himself. It didn't look like him, but then again, two hundred years might tend to age a person a bit!

"Well, I'm afraid that's where we're heading, nonetheless, my good man" John replied.

Surveying the old man's worn condition, John reached down and pulled out his wallet. "Here, old man. Take this." John handed him a crisp, new twenty dollar bill from his wallet, the one with an "X" mark drawn over the serial number, like a cashier might do to mark it for counterfeit tracing. "Get yourself a bite to eat. And maybe there'll be a…bus or something coming by soon to take you to…Bridge-town."

The old man smiled and took the bill, stuffing it into his jacket pocket. "Much obliged, my good lad. God be with you."

"And…a good day to you, old man."

With that, John slowly pulled away and continued down Ye Greate Street. Not a few seconds later he checked his rearview mirror, but the old man was nowhere to be found.

"Where did he go?"

Doug turned around to look. "Don't know. But he sure disappeared quick. Like, right into thin air, huh, John?"

"Right!"

Okay, doc, just check us both back in to the loony bin, why doncha!

Continuing down Ye Greate Street they headed south out of town, and were soon back in open country. Doug pointed ahead. "Be careful, the road takes a quick turn to the right about a half mile down the road, then turns left again,"

Yes. I remember that. Almost ran off the road last time!

After making the final left turn into the old part of town, John slowed down to get his bearings. He remembered the last time he was here: the long, wide boulevard down the center of town; the remains of the old Stone Tavern across the street; the phantom farm wagon pulled by two black stallions with the old man in eighteenth-century knee britches and three-cornered hat. But that part of his memory was hazy and blurred—not vivid like the time-travel portion of it.

Approaching the corner of Bacons Neck Road on the right, John pulled off to the side of the road.

"Okay, Doug. So where do we go from…"

Without warning John was overcome by a vivid flashback to the Stone Tavern of 1774. It lasted but a second and he was back in the present. Then, like freeze frames from a frenetically edited movie trailer, the flashbacks continued, one after another in quick succession—then and now—old and new: the Stone Tavern alive with the sound of the fiddle—the crumbled Stone Tavern dead and silent—the Gibbon House with Flemish bond and candles in the windows—the Gibbon House in overgrown ruins—Ye Greate Street filled with the colonial mob bent on a single mission—Ye Greate Street deserted and abandoned on a bright, hopeful autumn day…a flame-filled night sky with the dying cries of a young woman!

John buried his face in his hands, trying in vain to dispel the visions. Finally, as quickly as they started, the visions ceased.

Slowly, John removed his hands and looked up.

"You okay, J-John?" Doug asked nervously.

"We…gotta keep movin', Doug. Quick! Show me the way to the Cohansey Marina."

"S-sure, John, okay. Well, you take a right here onto Bacons Neck Road, then go down about a mile through the marsh where the road dead-ends. Not sure of the name of the other road. But I'll know it when I see it. That's where you'll make a left."

"Great! Let's go!"

Driving down Bacons Neck Road brought back more memories of the phantom wagon and…that swarm of flies.

That's where the wagon turned and disappeared into thin air, John recalled as they approached the intersection with Gum Tree Corner Road. John stopped the car just before reaching the intersection.

"This is where they found my car, Doug, the day before I was admitted to Lourdes."

Of this there was no doubt. It was well documented in the police report; but the rest? Well, maybe it was all just a drug-induced dream, as the doctors had said.

Looking down Bacons Neck Road toward Pine Creek marsh, John's pulse quickened as he half expected to see a large swarm of flies emerge from its muddy banks. He leaned out of the open car door window and looked around. "The flies? Where are all the flies?"

Doug shrugged his shoulders. "Dunno, but I think they go back to the swamps for the winter."

Yes, of course, John knew this. Not the flies themselves, they die; but their offspring, the larvae, they survive the winter burrowed safely in the marsh mud. He learned this from his friend, Julie Evert. But he was half hoping there might be a few hangers-on from the summer season. After all, he had to go back! To save her! How else could this happen if not by the bite of the greenhead fly!

But that wouldn't be happening. Not today, anyway.

John put the Camry into gear and proceeded slowly across the bridge and causeway leading through the marsh. The air was cool and damp; all was calm and still.

Not far beyond the marsh, the road dead-ended with a stop sign at a T-intersection, just like Doug said it would. John looked up at the road sign: Tindall Island Road.

"Okay, so you wanna make a left," Doug said. "And then another left a half mile or so down the road. That'll take you straight to the marina."

John looked past Doug down the road to the right. "So, if I made a right turn here instead, where would that take me?" John already knew the answer.

Doug followed John's gaze to the right. "Oh, yeah. Well, that way will take you to the old fishing pier down by the bay. That's where we used to go fishin'."

And where I got bit! John thought.

John followed Tindall Island Road south for about a half mile and took the first left where a road sign directed them to "Cohansey Marina." The road passed through a field of tall corn ripe for the harvest, and John could hear the sound of seagulls and marine activity up ahead. Suddenly breaking into the open, there it was: Cohansey Marina and the wide open water of the Cohansey River.

"So, this is where all the living people are hiding," John said.

"Yup! A popular boating spot ever since I can remember," Doug confirmed.

The marina was bustling with activity, weekend sailors and anglers trying to get in just one more outing, one more fishing trip for the season, before the weather turned bad. Others already had their boats dry-docked for the season or were busy winterizing and making needed repairs. As John trolled the parking lot toward the main building, he couldn't help but notice all the license plates from every adjoining state: Delaware, Pennsylvania, even New York.

"Popular is right," John said.

Doug nodded.

John parked the car near the main building down by the dock, under the sign: "Cohansey Marina – Tackle Shop and Restaurant."

Before going inside, he quickly surveyed the boats tied up along the dock for a familiar name.

"Whadaya lookin' for?" Doug asked.

John peered out across the forest of masts in the harbor, shielding his eyes from the glare of the sun with his hand. "The *Greyhound*," he replied. "It's a large fishing yacht. Tell me if you see it anywhere."

Doug joined him in his futile search.

"Why d-don't we just go in and ask someone?" Doug finally said.

John turned and smiled. "Good idea."

Inside, John approached a young man in a Led Zeppelin T-shirt sitting behind the counter leisurely assembling the contents of a tackle box.

"Excuse me, but I was wondering if someone might be able to help me."

The young man looked up.

"I was looking for a Captain Davies," John continued. "George Davies. Captain of the *Greyhound*, a fishing yacht."

The young man cocked his head, trying to recollect. Finally, he shook his head. "That name don't ring a bell. You sure he docks here at the marina?"

"Pretty sure. The last time I spoke with him he said to meet him here. Though I think he normally operates out of Fortesque."

The young man hollered out to an older, grizzly looking man working in the back room. "Hey, Tom! There's a man here looking for a Captain George Davies. You know him?"

As they waited, Doug complimented the young man on his choice of fashion. "N-Nice T-shirt, man! Led Zeppelin really r-rocks!"

The young man gave a half smile.

A moment later the older man stepped through the door. "Who's wantin' t'know?" he growled.

John smiled, raising a finger to signal "over here!" "I just wanted to talk to him about booking a fishing trip. He came highly recommended by a good friend of mine. Actually, I spoke with him just…"

"Don't know no Captain Davies," the old man rebuffed firmly.

John backed off, rethinking his approach.

"Well, actually, my friend owes him money. I was hoping I might be able to settle the account."

"Hmm," the older man grunted suspiciously. "Wait here just a sec. Let me get someone might be able t'help ya."

The older man disappeared into the back room and re-emerged a few minutes later with another gentleman, thirty-something, beer gut, and balding, but who carried himself like someone in charge. He held out his hand to John.

"Frank Kilroy at your service."

John shook his hand. "John Weston. Pleased to meet you."

"So, Tom tells me you're looking for George Davies. Something about owing him some money."

John explained the situation, about his failed attempt to link up with George a month earlier. Of course, the part about owing him money he just made up, baiting the hook, so to speak.

"Well, old George does drop by from time to time…but not on a regular basis," Mr. Kilroy was quick to add. "Like you said, he normally operates out of Fortesque, about thirty miles south of here."

"Is there any way I can get in touch with him?" John asked. "The cell phone number I had doesn't seem to work anymore. Must've been disconnected."

"Hmm. Well, I don't feel right about giving you his personal number. But…"—he did a quick double take—"…you say it's…a business matter?"

"Er, right! Kind of…a matter of business." John just went along with the curious spin Frank was putting on his simple inquiry.

Frank reached under the counter, pulled a notepad from a desk drawer, and began jotting down some numbers.

"Here, this number should work. Been a while since I used it, though. The second number is the marina at Fortesque, if you have trouble getting hold of George directly."

John took the slip of paper. "Thanks, I'll give it a try. But I'll have to wait till I get further inland. My cell phone doesn't connect way out here."

Frank smirked. "Yeah, ain't technology wonderful!"

John thanked him for his trouble and was turning to leave when Frank added, "Say, listen, if you leave me your name and number I can have old George give you a call next time I see him."

John considered this. "Actually, George should already have my number. But here it is anyway," and wrote his contact information on the notepad.

As John and Doug returned to the car and were preparing to leave, Doug asked, "So, who is this Captain Davies, anyways?"

John recounted the story of his partner Bob's Fourth of July fishing trip, and his own misadventures and foiled attempts to contact Captain Davies to get the facts. Then he told him about the flies. Not the whole story, of course, and certainly not the part about going back to eighteenth-century Cumberland County, but just enough to explain his delirious state, abandoned car, and eventual admission to Our Lady of Lourdes.

"Coming down here today, well, I just had to finish what I started four weeks ago."

Doug just nodded. "S-Sure, I get it. Okay. So, w-what now?"

John started up the engine. "Bridgeton! And the Cumberland County Historical Society!"

Doug smiled. "All right! Let's do it! I know the way!"

Actually, John also knew the way. He only needed to backtrack his way into town, turn right at the Stone Tavern ruins, and then follow the reverse route that first brought him into town that unforgettable Sunday four weeks ago. John was granted something of a reprieve this time: the trip back through town went smoothly—no flashbacks or visions—and they covered the six miles to Bridgeton in less than fifteen minutes.

John had phoned the Historical Society in advance, so they knew he was coming. He told them he was a freelance writer researching an article about colonial life in Cumberland and Salem Counties, Greenwich, and the areas along the Cohansey River in particular. They were more than willing to oblige him.

John pulled into an empty parking space marked "For Museum Patrons Only" and cut the engine.

"Okay, let's go learn some history!"

Doug jumped out as John reached into the back seat and grabbed the shoe box package. Together they headed for the main entrance of the Cumberland County Historical Society and Museum, the shoe box held securely under John's left arm. The office and museum remained closed to the public through the week but—lucky for John—was open on weekends if you called in advance to make arrangements.

John was greeted in the lobby by a silver haired sprite of a lady, Miss Emily Grady, document custodian and curator of the Society's museum. Austere and demure, Emily was a no-nonsense woman who took her job very seriously. In her brightly flowered, full-length dress she brought to John's mind a Sunday school teacher he had as a child. She did soften a bit after John explained that he was volunteering as a docent at the Indian King Tavern in Haddonfield. Yes, of course she knew of it! What student of New Jersey history didn't know about Haddonfield's Indian King Tavern?

She went on to explain that Cumberland Country had its fair share of historic taverns, as well. Unfortunately, the oldest of them—the Stone Tavern in old Greenwich—had fallen into disrepair over the years. She said there was a proposal in the works to raise money for its restoration, along with some other of the more prominent structures that once stood proudly in that historic town.

"You mean, like the Gibbon House," John offered.

Mrs. Grady almost gasped with surprise. "Why yes! It appears you've done some homework before coming here, Mr. Weston!"

John just smiled. *If you only knew!*

John and Doug were given a personal tour of the museum, which occupied most of the second and third floors of the Society's three-story building. Pausing in front of a large glass-faced display case—actually an old eighteenth-century china closet—Mrs. Grady pointed out one of the items on prominent display.

"Now, here is a very interesting article. Actually, a favorite of mine."

Taking a key chain from her apron pocket, she unlocked the glass door and carefully removed a clear, hollow glass globe—about the size of a grapefruit—from its display stand. The glassblower had created a masterpiece of swirling surface patterns of frosted glass.

"This was a gift from a Mrs. Harriett Rodgers. It's called a 'Witch Ball,'" she explained as she held the globe it up to the light shining through a nearby window. "In colonial times they would hang this in a window to catch the sunlight, and"—casting a mischievous smile—"keep away evil spirits!" She laughed. "Of course, I can't vouch for the latter, but it did provide some embellishment to perhaps an otherwise austere décor. Many of them had colorful, swirling patterns as well. This one is clear glass with frosted swirls."

John studied the globe. "It looks like an oversized Christmas tree ornament." Then he thought about the glass spheres of various sizes hanging from the ceiling of Bob's basement shop. "Did they come in different sizes?" he asked.

"Oh, I suspect they probably did," she replied. "Why do you ask?"

John just laughed it off. "No special reason. Just the engineer in me, I guess, looking for precision in all things man-made."

Then another thought came to mind: his Labor Day dream, the one with the woman floating in a transparent orb of light reaching up for a shining globe suspended from the ceiling. Slipping from her grasp the glass globe fell crashing to the floor, shattering into a zillion pieces. "Curses!" the Bob in his dream had shouted out.

"So, tell me, Mrs. Grady. What happens if you break one of these things? Seven years bad luck?"

Mrs. Grady held the globe close to her bosom, like a mother protecting her threatened child. "Why would you ask such a thing?" she asked suspiciously.

John chuckled. "Don't worry, ma'am. I have no intentions of putting it to the test!"

"Well, you know, there are many legends surrounding the Witch Ball," she replied as she gingerly returned the glass sphere to the display case. "One has it that misfortune will befall a person within a year's time, if he or she causes a ball to break. 'As perish the Ball, so perish the Bearer,' I believe is how it goes."

A distant memory was resurrected in John's mind: Christmas Eve, 1981. John and Becky are decorating their first Christmas tree together. Becky reaches up to place a glass ornament on the tree. It is a clear glass ball with swirling colors and engraved frosted lettering that reads "Merry Christmas! 1981." Losing her grip, the ball drops to the hardwood floor below and shatters into a thousand pieces! Eight months later...

For a moment John forgot where he was.

"Whoa! You okay d-dude?" Doug asked.

John regained his composure and shook it off. "Sorry. Just felt a little...woozy there for a second."

"Well, it is rather warm in here today," Mrs. Grady offered. "Let me turn down the heat a notch or two."

While she tended to the thermostat in the next room, John turned to a map on the wall: Salem and Cumberland Counties, The Jerseys, circa 1770. The town of Greenwich was prominently displayed as one of four major towns in the area, the others being Fairfield, Salem and Bridgeton, identified as "Bridge Town." The larger, elaborate calligraphy style and area cross-hatching employed by the cartographer indicated their greater significance. The smaller towns and villages located at crossroads and river crossings had their names, too, but were identified with a more modest font.

"So, it appears that the town of Greenwich once enjoyed some level of prominence within the Jersey colony," John remarked loud enough so Mrs. Grady could hear in the next room.

"Oh, yes, indeed it did!" she responded enthusiastically as she re-entered the map room. "At that time, the port of Greenwich was one of only three official ports of entry for the Provence of West New Jersey. The others being Salem"—pointing to the map—"and the city of Burlington, which is off the map, of course, about fifteen miles north of Philadelphia on the Delaware.

"So...what happened?" John inquired bluntly. "The town we drove through this morning was no more than a..." John paused.

"Go on, you can say it," Mrs. Grady frowned. "A ghost town, right?"

John smiled. Yes, that's what he wanted to say. Not just figuratively speaking, either. He didn't think she'd believe him, anyway.

"It was right around the time of the war—the American Revolution—when the town entered a period of steady decline."

"You mean, because of the war? That would be understandable," John suggested.

"Well, no, it was...more than that." Mrs. Grady said hesitantly. "Actually, it had more to do with...disease. A kind of pestilence swept through the region"—she gestured with a sweeping motion of her arms over the map—"which pretty well decimated the local population. By all accounts, it appeared to be some form of meningitis or sleeping sickness. Some people likened it to the great yellow fever outbreak in Philadelphia in 1792. But this was different. The yellow fever outbreak was self-limiting, lasting only a season."

"So, you're saying this, whatever-it-was, continued to plague the area?"

"Oh, yes. Well into the next century. The folks who weren't affected directly by the illness simply decided to move out of the area, until there was hardly anyone left. Even the waters along the Cohansey became overgrown, making navigation difficult. And without the shipping industry, the town lost its economic base—its raison-d'être."

John could have chosen his next words more carefully, perhaps.

"It sounds almost as if the area was under a spell, or…curse!"

Emily froze in her tracks, the color almost draining from her face.

"I'm sorry, ma'am. Did I say something…wrong?" John asked.

With a blink of her eyes, her color slowly returned as she glanced over toward the display case housing the Witch Ball.

"What exactly do you know about…the curse, Mr. Weston?" Her words came very slowly.

John felt like he may have touched a nerve.

"Not very much, really. It's just one of the many things on my 'to-do-or-find-out' list."

Emily closed her eyes and sighed. "Well, there are many versions to the story. Which one do you want to hear?"

"How about the one that involves a young Rebecca Whitman?"

Emily pulled back. "My! But you have done your homework, Mr. Weston! I am impressed. These stories are not well-known and certainly not published, to my knowledge. It would"—choosing her words carefully—"give the county a bad name."

Mrs. Grady proceeded to recount the version that made the most sense to her, although she prefaced it by saying she considered them all to be "old wives' tales."

"Just people trying desperately to make some sense of events and situations they have no control over," she opined.

"Yes, I'm sure. But, please, indulge me."

She paused. "Okay. But you may want to sit down for this. It may take a while."

She led them into an adjoining room with a table of chairs. "Please, make yourselves comfortable," she said, taking a seat at the head of the table.

John and Doug took flanking seats as John lay the shoe box package on his lap out of sight.

"Can I get either of you a glass of water, or something from the vending machine?" Mrs. Grady offered.

John smiled and shook his head. "No, thank you, ma'am. We're fine. Please continue."

Emily took a deep breath and began. "It all goes back to the night of the warehouse fire down by the Greenwich wharf, December twenty-second, seventeen-seventy-four. Certain of the townsfolk had learned a week or so earlier that a shipment of tea, recently arrived from England, was being secretly stored somewhere in town. The merchant who had arranged the shipment was fearful of a repeat of events in Boston Harbor less than a year before. His fears were not unfounded. As recently as October of this same year—just two months prior—a merchant ship, the *Peggy Stewart*, was burned in Annapolis Harbor for carrying a consignment of tea from England to the

colonies. Another was turned away in Philadelphia, not being allowed to dock
and unload its shipment of tea."

"My! Even the peaceful Quakers were caught up in the patriotic fervor
of the day?" John smiled.

"Apparently so. But at least they did not resort to violence!" She
sighed. "Well, returning to my story. On the night of the twenty-second, a
torch-bearing crowd of angry men, disguised as Native American Indians,
marched down Ye Greate Street intent on confiscating and destroying the
tea."—*Yes! I remember! I was there!*—"When they saw flames rising from the
wharf they became confused, thinking perhaps that someone had beaten
them to the punch, so to speak. In any event, they never did complete their
self-appointed mission. It turns out the tea was not in the warehouse, which
was now engulfed in flames. Some of the men reported hearing the cries of a
woman coming from inside. So, the attention of every able-bodied man
turned to the wharf fire, trying to save whomever was inside…"

As she spoke, John recalled the event forever burned into his memory:

*…As the men departed down Ye Greate Street toward the wharf, John could now
hear the cries of a young woman. A mere whimper at first, the sounds seemed to be coming
from the wharf. As the flames grew in intensity so did the sound of the cries. Soon, the
whole night sky was ablaze with the pulsating orange glow of a not too distant inferno, alive
and breathing with the innocent cries of anguish and pain…*

"…With the light of dawn," Emily continued, "the grizzly facts
became known. In the dying embers of the warehouse fire lay the charred
remains of two bodies: our young Rebecca Whitman, and a Mr.—" She
paused, trying to remember.

"…A Mr. Paul McKenzie," John finished the sentence for her.

Mrs. Grady was dumbfounded.

"Why, yes! But h-how did you know that?"

John shrugged his shoulders. "Just a lucky guess…I guess."

"So, you have heard this story before," Emily concluded.

John looked down at the package in his lap.

"Well, not so much heard," he said, then looking up, "It's all been just
a scattering of information that I've collected over the years. This is the first
time anyone has managed to put it all together for me."

"I see. Well, perhaps you even have some missing information that the
Historical Society would be interested in acquiring?"

"Perhaps."

John lifted the package from his lap and placed it on the table. Emily
peered wide-eyed as John untied the twine, opened the shoe box lid, and
removed a wooden jewelry box decorated with colorful, engraved floral
patterns, setting it down in front of her. He allowed Emily to study it for a
moment before speaking.

"This is an eighteenth-century jewelry box which has been in our family since…well, since the death of our dear Miss Rebecca Whitman."

Emily's face brightened. "Oh, my! That is a splendid piece of colonial craftsmanship! And you say that it once belonged to Miss Whitman? The same Miss Whitman said to have perished in the fire?"

John smiled. "Precisely. You see here?" He turned the box over. "These engraved initials, 'R.W.' And there's more inside."

John opened the lid and removed several of the letters.

"These are letters written by my many-times-removed great-uncle, John Jay Weston, whose name I happen to share…except for our middle names. He used his mother's maiden name, 'Jay.' You see can see…"—pointing to the signature—"he would sign his letters 'Jay-Bird' or 'J.J.' The letters are all addressed to Miss Rebecca Whitman, whom he addressed as 'Missy.'"

After studying the letters, Mrs. Grady seemed a little puzzled.

"Yes, but…there are no direct references to a Rebecca Whitman. Have you been able to authenticate this by other means?"

John squirmed a little in his seat. Okay, so which will she believe? That a Ouija board told me so almost twenty years ago? Or that I time-traveled back to eighteenth-century Greenwich and verified it myself? No, I don't think so!

"Let's just say…I have several independent corroborating sources, but I wouldn't want to disclose them this time. Suffice to say, they're the same that revealed her name to me, and the name of Mr. McKenzie."

"Yes, I see," she said half convincingly.

John redirected the line of questioning. "But, you still haven't answered my first question."

Mrs. Grady paused, confused at first, before responding. "Oh, yes! The curse! Well, allow me to continue."

As she did, John returned the letters to the box and closed its lid.

"You see, two mysteries surrounded the fire. First, what were two young people, a man and a woman, doing so late on a winter's evening, alone in a deserted warehouse? Well, you can imagine the rumors that flew! And there was little that the father of the young Rebecca—Thomas Whitman, a blacksmith by trade—could do to quell the suspicions of the local populace, if you know what I mean."

John acknowledged with a slight nod. Thomas Whitman! So, that was the older man at the cemetery standing over Rebecca's grave.

"Secondly," Mrs. Grady continued, "How did the fire start in the first place? Of course, it was first assumed the mob had set fire to the warehouse, thinking the tea was stored there. But that possibility was quickly put to rest during the ensuing legal inquiry over the weeks that followed. Then, thoughts turned to a string of fires that had recently plagued the area, all of unresolved origins. Suspicions initially fell on an old Indian man who lived by himself outside of town, or one of his sons. Others suspected Agatha Greene, an old crazy woman some of the townsfolk referred to as the 'Town Witch.'"

John's eyes widened. "Town Witch! You mean they still believed in such things? I thought that went out with the Salem Witch Trials a century before."

Emily frowned, tilting her head in the direction of the Witch Ball in the display case. "Old ways die hard, you know."

John chuckled. "Yes, but that's almost funny, actually. So, is that how the town got its name: Greene Witch?"

Mrs. Grady continued like she didn't hear his last remark. Or maybe she had heard it just one too many times to suit her tastes.

"Well, in the end, when the dust finally settled on the whole affair, no one could point a firm finger of blame to anyone or anything. The fire remained a mystery. Even to this day."

"So, what has that got to do with the cur…"

"Hold your horses, young man! I'm getting to that."

Her last rejoinder put a smile on Doug's face.

"You see," Emily continued, "from this point on there is no real documentation as to what happened next, except for one disturbing event which I am about to describe."

She shifted in her seat to get more comfortable.

"As you must know, John, being a man of science, 'nature abhors a vacuum.' As do desperate people looking for answers in troubled times. What they often do, in the absence of any firmer evidence, is to concoct their own. That opportunity came six months later to the day, on the twenty-second of June, seventeen-seventy-five.

"It was mid-afternoon when Agatha Greene showed up alone on the Market Square with a team and wagon, and a small keg of kerosene. Setting the team loose, she was reported to have doused herself with the liquid. Then, standing alone and tall in the back of the wagon she pulled a match from her apron and…"—John grimaced. He could see it coming—"set herself afire!"

"Whoa! Totally awesome!" Doug exclaimed, breaking his long silence.

"Awesome, indeed!" Emily frowned disapprovingly.

"So, there must have been others who witnessed this, right?" John quickly interjected, recalling an event from one of his time-travel visions….

…"I heard tell she made quite a spectacle of herself. Lit up like the King's own fireworks display, she did!" This was met with laughter and more cheers. "She only got what she deserved," another replied…

"Yes, of course," Emily replied. "There were many witnesses, and just as many varying accounts of what exactly happened, or more importantly, what the old woman said, her final words."

Emily got up and went to the next room where she retrieved a photocopy of a contemporary *Pennsylvania Gazette* article reporting the event not long after it happened. The article was entitled: "'Witch Burning' Stuns Citizens of Greenwich, Cumberland County." The article gave conflicting accounts of Agatha Greene's last words by various eyewitnesses. To some, she spoke about it being "her destiny" to share in the fate of young Rebecca Whitman. Others said, no, she was referring to "Destiny, her first born child" whom she lost in a fire so many years before. Still others quoted her as saying: "Cursed and abandoned, I leave this lonely place!" While still others thought she said: "...I leave this place cursed and abandoned!"

Emily handed the paper to John.

"So much for eyewitness accounts," John said. "It could be taken either way. I mean, either she was cursing the town, or she herself was cursed. So, what do you believe, Emily? Was Agatha Greene really a 'Witch'? Responsible for this...Curse?"

Emily sighed. "It doesn't much matter what I believe. What matters is that what others decided to believe two hundred years ago. Not so much at the time, mind you, but later, in retrospect, when deteriorating conditions forced people to seek an explanation for something they did not understand."

John nodded. "A scapegoat, then, for events beyond their control."

"Hmm, yes. History does it all the time, am I right?"

John spent their remaining time going over documents, maps, and other memorabilia from that time and place. He was especially fascinated by the Indian artifacts—bone needles and fish hooks, grooved granulated quartz axe heads, and other stone tools, gorgets and bannerstones, brown flint arrowheads and fish spearheads, drill points, clay pots and decorated smoking pipes, copper beads, and yes, even carved bone amulets. But none carried the carved flame image like the one from his vision!

As John and Doug prepared to leave, John thanked Mrs. Grady for her time and generous hospitality. He asked if she could make him a photocopy of the newspaper article to take home with him. She more than willingly obliged.

Back in the car he reached into his pants pocket for his keys and was surprised to find a clean, crisp, new twenty dollar bill. Holding it up to the light he saw it bore a hand-drawn "X" over the serial number.

No way! I could've sworn I gave this to that old man by the cemetery!

Chapter 26

1999
October
South Jersey

The evening of his Cumberland County day trip found John in the comfort of his Haddonfield home study sipping brandy and updating his Final Project loose-leaf binder with new information gathered that day. The *Gazette* article from 1775 became the newest page.

Trying to pull the pieces together, John leafed through the notebook until he came to an entry from a week ago, the "Campfire Curse" he called it. They were notes from the vision he experienced exactly one week ago in Bob's basement—the one with three persons seated around a campfire in the midst of casting a spell or curse of some kind:

> …The first man took a cup from the older man. Standing up with outstretched arms he began tossing sprinkles of powder from the cup into the flames, which brought new sparks and bursts of orange light with each flick of the wrist. As he performed this rite, he spoke: "A curse be on the bloodline of one whose sinister deeds this night did spill the innocent blood of so fair and pure a child as she."

John closed his eyes as he recalled the vision. He recognized this man as the same man of his time-travel vision at the churchyard cemetery in Greenwich—his "cemetery vision" as he called it—who, standing over the freshly dug grave of Rebecca Whitman, had declared, "I tell you now, were it in my power to know and curse the hand responsible for this act, I would do so, though my soul perish in the process."

John took a sip of brandy.

"So, that was Rebecca's father, Thomas Whitman, the town blacksmith, who conspired with others to cast this curse!" He turned to the *Gazette* article. "It wasn't the old 'town witch' after all!"

Then he thought about the old man at the campfire, the one wearing the bone amulet with the flame symbol carved into it. Could he be the Indian Emily referred to? If so, then it certainly wasn't he who started the fire.

"Must've been the old woman...what was her name?" He checked his notes again. "Yes, Agatha Greene, 'The Greene Witch'!"

He turned a page and rubbed his chin. So, who was the third person at the campfire—the young black woman?

Looking down again he reread her final words recorded in his notebook:

> ...And ne'er the curse shall it be lift...till the time of the winter solstice rift...And The One whom time henceforth reclaims...returns to barter with his good name.

A chill ran up John's spine as his mission became reinforced in his mind. He was indeed the chosen one, as Bob—and yes, even the Ouija board—had declared! "The One whom time henceforth reclaims!" So, he must return in time to lift the curse! And somehow, for whatever reason, he must do it by the twenty-second of December—the winter solstice. But how? That was the problem. The flies! Those green-headed monsters that brought all this on in the first place were no longer available to complete the job.

John closed his notebook, sat back in his genuine Naugahyde recliner, and took a final sip of brandy. Looking at the flowered jewelry box sitting on his desk, he wondered: so, if those letters were all from John to Rebecca, then what ever happened to the return letters Rebecca must have written? Too bad they never turned up in Grandpa's attic; and if they were signed in her name, that would have clinched the authenticity of John's letters.

Putting down his empty brandy snifter, John opened a desk drawer and removed a second box, a simple metal lockbox with the word "Artifacts" handwritten on the lid. Unlocking and opening the box, John took a crisp twenty dollar bill from his wallet and placed it inside the box to join the other items located there: a one-way ticket by stage wagon from Greenwich to Cooper's Ferry, and a handful of assorted coins which John had retrieved from a hidden pocket of his cargo pants, the ones he wore back to eighteenth-century Greenwich.

"There, I think this is where you belong," he said as he laid the twenty dollar note in the box. Maybe not an artifact in the strictest definition of the word, but he figured it was a relic nonetheless. After all, it did touch history—thinking about the old man at the cemetery in Greenwich—and mysteriously return from somewhere...from some time."

Closing the lid of the box, John's thoughts turned to tomorrow. It would be Sunday, and he planned to do nothing. Rain was in the forecast, so doing nothing seemed like a good idea. Maybe he'd just relax and watch the Eagles game on TV. Monday would come soon enough, and it promised to be a busy week.

*****

Monday morning. John assembled his project team leaders—Jim Connelly, Jacob Carlson, and Maggie Stoebels, his automation and controls engineer—in the conference room to review the final conceptual design package for the GenAvance pilot plant which they planned to present to Dr. Li and his project team in Thousand Oaks next week. Ann, the newest member of the team, was a bright, attractive woman in her late twenties: a short, mildly stout, and spunky brunette with a pixie cut, possessing a sensual, seductive charm that bordered on voluptuous. An electrical engineer by training, having received her BS from Drexel University in '92, she worked six years for an instrument and controls company right out of school before joining Haddon Life-Tech less than a year ago.

Mary Hogan arranged to have lunch brought in as they planned to work through the lunch hour.

"So, what'll it be, guys? Chinese takeout or pizza?"

"Hey, how about hoagies?" Jim hollered out. "Haven't had a good Philly cheesesteak or hoagie in quite a while."

"Hogan's Hoagies! Sounds good to me!" Maggie agreed.

"Or...Hogan's Heroes!" Mary retorted, "depending on what part of the country you're from."

"Okay!" Jim chuckled. "Whatever you call them, just be sure they got extra onions and hot peppers."

The plan for next week was for the team to fly to LA first thing Monday morning and spend the remainder of the day fine-tuning their presentation for Tuesday's meeting with the client. Breakout sessions were scheduled for most of Wednesday, followed by a tour of the insect cell seed development lab late in the afternoon. "That's were our microbiologists work their recombinant DNA magic!" Dr. Li boasted. John had requested to see just how the baculovirus DNA was modified in the lab, incorporating the required genetic information that codes for the target protein in the infected insect cell. To John, all the engineering technology that he could ever bring to bear on the process was dwarfed by this elegant piece of high-tech twenty-first-century sorcery.

The team would catch an early flight home Thursday morning, except for John. He would stay an extra day, returning home Friday morning. He had already arranged to spend the extra day with his good friend, Jennifer Dupree Brady. Jennifer's eight-year-old daughter, Renee, had the day off, as well. Teacher's conference or something like that. Anyway, Renee planned spending Wednesday night at a friend's sleepover, and wouldn't be getting back home till later in the day on Thursday. Which meant John and Jennifer would have most of the day—and prior evening—to themselves. John promised they would all go out to dinner Thursday night, his last night— John's treat.

Later that afternoon, John gave Katie a call to see how Bob was doing, and to let her know he would be traveling next week, would she mind driving by the house once or twice just to check on things. And oh, yes, he told her about Doug, his new boarder.

"You must remember Doug from Lady of Lourdes. He was the young man with the green Mohawk."

Yes, of course, Katie remembered Doug.

John recounted the story of how he found him on his front porch doorstep a week ago Sunday and had been caring for him ever since. How Doug's sister left him fending for himself and he didn't appear to have any other close relations nearby.

"That's interesting, John. So, how is he doing?"

"Well, he seems to be doing much better, now…as long as he takes his meds. I've even managed to get him interested in running. He's taken to it like a veteran. Says he wants to run a marathon some day."

Katie chuckled. "Well, then I'd say you may have done more for Doug than the doctors were able to do."

John smiled. "Thanks, Katie. But I really think it's the medications that are keeping him on track. That's what worries me about next week. Without me around, I'm afraid he may forget to take them, or just decide to skip them altogether."

"I'm sure he'll be okay, John. From what you tell me it sounds like you've been a good influence and role model for him."

"Maybe. But I'm afraid this running thing has got him believing he can do without his meds. That all he needs are the body's own natural store of drugs. Endorphins, anandamide. He's really become quite the disciple of au natural health treatment. And I'm afraid I haven't helped."

Silence.

"Say, listen, John," she said at last, "if you'd like, I could drop by the house and check up on Doug while you're gone."

"Oh, no, Kate. I don't think that'll be necessary," John said halfheartedly. "You've got your hands full as it is. You don't need another…"

"Mental patient?" Katie completed the sentence for him.

John bit his lip. "Anyway, I don't think it's necessary. I'll only be gone a few days. But…if you wouldn't mind just dropping by, maybe once. That would be nice."

Katie agreed, and suggested coming by the house one night this week just to get reacquainted with Doug and his med schedule. John thought that might be a good idea.

"Oh, and one more thing," John added. "If you wouldn't mind, I'd appreciate it if you could talk to Sally and explain the situation to her. I think Doug's presence threw her for a loop Saturday morning when she dropped by to give me one of her famous strawberry shortcakes. No doubt she got the wrong...impression."

Katie gave a hearty laugh. "Well, I guess that explains it!" she said.

"Explains what?"

"When I ran into her on Sunday, all she had to say was, 'maybe I should've given him a banana cream pie instead!'"

John grimaced. "Well, tell Sal I definitely prefer ripe strawberries over bananas any day."

"Oh my God!" she laughed. "I won't say that. I'll just tell her how much you enjoyed the cake. Don't worry; I'll straighten things out with Sal."

"Thanks, Kate. And tell Bob I'll be down to see him as soon as I get back from the west coast."

"Sure, John. He always looks forward to your visits."

After hanging up, John went to see Mary at the front desk to check on the mail. He told her he was expecting a package from Dr. Li, something about tickets to a Lakers game.

Mary put down the Afghan she was working and double-checked his mailbox.

John noticed the Afghan. "Hey, that's coming along pretty nicely, Mary. Think you'll have it done by...when is it, the end of December?"

"Yes, December twenty-second, the baby shower."

Mary picked up the unfinished Afghan. "See this? I'm gonna hafta rip it out and start over from this point. I made a mistake with the pattern, but it's okay, I can still use the yarn. Just have to unravel and reweave it with the correct pattern."

John picked up and studied the Afghan. Yes, he could see what she meant. Then he thought about his dream—Mary in the bleachers with the Bayeux tapestry, weaving history through time and space—and then about his own space-time dilemma.

"Wouldn't it be nice if life were that easy," he intoned wistfully. "If we could just go back in time and...reweave life, to fix our past mistakes."

Mary looked up and cocked her head. "Hey, that's pretty deep coming from a chemical engineer!"

John just smiled and gently laid the Afghan back down on the table.

Chapter 27

1999
October
GenAvance, Thousand Oaks, California

Dr. Sam Li was in rare form, ebullient over the recent news that capital funding was finally approved for the new biologics pilot plant to be built near Rutgers University's New Brunswick campus, as planned. The design team from Haddon Life-Tech, led by his good friend John Weston, had arrived on Monday, October 18th, to make their final conceptual design presentation to Sam's project team on Tuesday. The final report had been forwarded to Sam's team the week before, so he knew what to expect. In effect, then, this week's scheduled meetings amounted to a "kick-off" of the next phase of the project. Even more exciting, he had been able to convince his management to pursue a design-build approach, which basically awarded all subsequent phases of the project to Haddon Life-Tech, from preliminary engineering design through detailed design and construction.

"And so, I want to thank all of you for a job well done," he said addressing the standing room-only assemblage filling the Pod-A conference room. Raising his arms in grand theatrical style, he looked like the Pope giving his blessings on the adoring crowds in St. Peter's Square.

A sultry smile from the lovely Jennifer Brady, who was seated to Dr. Li's side and directly across the table from John Weston, did not go unnoticed by Sam. It elicited a blush from John that threatened to reveal his inner thoughts.

"And now," Sam continued, "it gives me great pleasure to turn the meeting over to Mr. John Weston of Haddon Life-Tech. He and his team will make a formal presentation of the scope of design for the new pilot plant." He was about to sit down when he added with a wink and a nod to Dr. Julie Evert seated at his right side, "...and I promise it will be a real sweetheart of a presentation."

John rolled his eyes and others in the audience gently moaned, recalling the Sweetheart of Sigma Phi Delta story from their kick-off meeting back in August.

After introducing his team and giving an overview of the project, John turned the PowerPoint presentation over to Jim Connelly, who proceeded to describe the process basis of design for the project with the help of schematics—or Process Flow Diagrams—of the insect cell culture process. Maggie Strobels chimed in on cue to elaborate on automation control philosophy and cGMP electronic batch recording capabilities. Wrapping up the process, Jim segued to the next and most anticipated portion of the presentation.

"The architectural design of a cGMP biologics facility is dictated by the needs of the process," he said as he handed the laser pointer to Jacob Carlson. "Mr. Carlson will now take us through the architectural and HVAC aspects of the facility design."

Like a relay runner taking the baton, Jacob approached the podium with laser pointer in hand to present the final series of slides detailing the layout and space programming requirements for the new facility. This was the coup de grace, what everyone was waiting for: a detailed view of how the facility would actually look! Starting with a perspective artist's rendering of the proposed pilot plant, the design assumed a new reality. Then, as Jacob activated his 3-D walk-through model, the renderings suddenly came to life! Down hallways, up stairways, in and out of clean rooms and laboratories, they roamed freely, taking a virtual tour of a facility that did not yet exist. For John, the illusion of effortlessly floating through time and space was an all-too-familiar one, and he had to turn away more than once to quell the uneasy sensation it revived in him. He was finally saved when Bruce Hanson, VP of Global Engineering, perked up and unloaded with a barrage of technical questions. But Jacob and the rest of the design team were well prepared and satisfactorily addressed each question and concern in turn. Approving nods from around the room evidenced an attentive and accepting audience.

Following a quick working lunch, Dr. Sam Li rose in his seat to kick off the afternoon session as folks were still finishing off their Cobb salads and avocado wraps.

"Before we continue with reviewing the conceptual cost estimate and financials for the new facility, John would like to share something he and his team at Haddon Life-Tech have come up with. It's an invention he says may increase our chances of success by improving the production yields of our new insect cell culture process." Dr. Li turned to John and smiled. "I know something of this…invention of yours, but look forward to learning more of its details. John, if you please." With a partial bow at the waist, Sam retook his seat at the table.

John acknowledged his host with a return nod and then took his place at the presenter's table.

"Thank you, Sam. As Dr. Li indicated, I'd like to share an idea that may prove useful in turning a batch cell culture process into a continuous process by the application of a continuous cell harvesting device. I regret that the brainchild for this device, my partner and good friend Bob Fenwick, is not able to be with us today, but I will do my best to explain the workings of the device and cell recovery system which he has devised. Bob was in the process of building a prototype for testing, but this work was interrupted by his…recent illness…from which, I am happy to say, he is well on the road to recovery."

This good news was greeted with polite nods and smiles from around the room. John pressed a key on his laptop and the images of the McDonald's golden arches and Colonel Sanders flashed up on the screen. He scanned the roomful of confused expressions for a moment before continuing.

"So, what does cell culture harvesting have to do with making french fries, or frying chicken for that matter?"

There were no takers.

He went to the next slide, entitled: "Hydro-Cyclone Continuous Clarification of Frying Oil." It was a schematic representation of a commercial frying machine with raw sliced potatoes entering one end on conveyor belts and coming out the other end as french fries. A system of tanks, pipes and pumps recirculated the hot frying oil through a cylindrical device with a cone-shaped bottom, labeled: Hydro-Cyclone Clarifier.

"Having worked in the food industry for many years," John continued, "Bob realized that many of the processing problems faced by the food processer are shared by our industry. Hydro-cyclones are sometimes used to remove cracklings and other suspended solids from the hot oil used to fry foods. The clarified oil is returned to the fryer, exiting the top of the cyclone, while the solid cracklings exit the bottom cone as a sludge which is pumped away and discarded."

Next slide: "Hydro-Cyclone Continuous Cell Culture Recovery System." Four slender vertical cylinders with long cone-shaped bottoms appeared on the screen. Tying the cylinders together was a network of interconnecting pipes, pumps, and other boxes of various sizes and shapes with labels like "Filter," "Recovery Vessel," and "Bioreactor."

"What we have done is to adapt the principal of the hydro-cyclone to achieve continuous separation of cells from liquid media for continuous perfusion cell culture processes. The cell culture enters here"—pointing to the side entrance of the hydro-cyclone—"and the concentrated cell mass exits the bottom to be returned to the bioreactor. The clarified culture media exits the top. The greater portion of clarified culture media is sent back to the bioreactor, while a small fraction is diverted into a recovery tank. A clarifying filter may be inserted here to remove fine particles and cell debris that gets through the cyclone."

John turned to face his audience. "What's nice is the process lends itself especially well to the recovery of extracellular protein products—or proteins that are excreted into the media"— looking at Dr. Li—"Which, I understand it, is the main focus of your continuous BEV insect cell culture process. Am I correct?"

Dr. Li beamed. "Yes, indeed! This is definitely something we would be interested in exploring!"

John turned to Ted Salmonson, the Fermentation Group Leader, seated directly across from him. "Ted, I know this is something your group has been looking into for some time. Spin-filters, alternating tangential flow filtration technology, and the like. Perhaps you can share the results of your investigations with Life-Tech. What has worked, and what hasn't worked."

Ted responded, but not directly to the question. "So, tell me, Mr. Weston. Do you have a working prototype of this device? Something we could test in the lab or pilot plant here in Thousand Oaks?"

John had anticipated this question. "Yes, indeed. We are in the process of assembling a prototype and plan to run tests in our shop"—*uh, basement*—"with yeast culture."—*Beer, anyone?*—"The major components for the system are ready and need only be assembled onto a skid for final testing."

"And you will share the results of those tests with our development team?" Ted asked.

"Yes, of course."

There were nods of approval from around the table.

Ted paused before finally asking: "And who would own the intellectual property rights for this device."

John was prepared for this question, as well. "We would consider this a joint venture under the terms of the current confidentiality agreement. The IP rights would be shared between GenAvance and Life-Tech. I'm sure the details can be worked out by our counsel working with your legal department."

Ted chuckled. "And which millennium did you say you wanted this completed by?"

Light laughter rippled through the room. John put the last slide on the screen—a repeat of the Golden Arches and Colonel Sanders—and waited a few moments before asking, "Are there any more questions?"

After a moment of silence, Ted deadpanned, "So, tell me, Dr. Li. Are we planning to give away Happy Meals with our finished product?"

*****

The tour of the insect cell culture seed development lab on Wednesday afternoon was led by the effervescent Samantha Joyce. Although Sammy now headed up the Downstream Processing Team, she actually started out in the seed lab and probably knew more than most about the modified BEVS, developed under her watch.

Before heading to the seed lab, John was briefed by Sammy on the underlying technology and protocols used for creating a recombinant baculovirus seed stock for insect cell culture and target protein manufacturing.

"Let me explain the basics," Sammy began, "so you better understand what you're looking at when we get in there."

"Sure. Fire away!"

John opened his notebook to an empty page and readied his ballpoint pen.

"Okay," Sammy continued, "First, how much do you know about homologous recombination?"

Sammy explained that homologous recombination is a type of genetic restructuring in which genetic material—single genes or groups of genes—is exchanged between two similar or identical molecules of DNA. A nearly universal biological mechanism, it finds many uses in nature, from the repair of a cell's DNA to the creation of new genetic varieties during reproduction. But in the hands of the modern molecular biologist, it has become a powerful tool for the genetic manipulation of a cell's genome in which the cell—"in our case, the insect cell"— is "tricked" into replacing a section of DNA with a gene of interest, or GOI, which codes for the desired target protein.

"Unfortunately," Sammy lamented, "current standard methods for generating recombinant viral DNA within host insect cells are terribly inefficient, resulting in less than one percent recombinant virus particles. Recovering the particles presents an even greater challenge, like finding a needle in a haystack, and can take up to forty days to complete, including the subsequent purification and amplification steps."

"Sounds tedious and time consuming," John offered.

"Precisely!" Sammy delighted. "Which is why"—Sammy sat back and paused, like she was starting a new chapter—"alternative methods have been sought and developed by various researchers in the field to streamline the process."

"I see. So what method does GenAvance use for generating the recombinant virus seed stock?"

Sammy gave a little "funny you should ask" smile and a drawn out "Well…" as she continued, "with the discovery of our variant baculovirus strain and greenhead fly host vector system, we can generate a recombinant virus seed stock"—snapping her fingers—"in less than one week! And, achieve 90 percent recombinant progeny in the process!"

"Sounds impressive! So, how is it done?"

Sammy sketched the process on the white board as she explained the details.

"You may remember from Dr. Li's ISPE presentation, how we've developed a variant form of the baculovirus, what we call 'vBV,' that is capable of infecting the larva cells of the greenhead fly while achieving a balanced symbiotic relationship with the host cell."

"Yes, Dr. Evert briefed me on her work with her greenhead fly: *Tabanus nigrovittatus cohansus.*"

"Wow! I'm impressed," Sammy replied. "But what they didn't tell you is that we've succeeded in developing a stable insect cell line which incorporates the vBV virus as inclusion bodies within the cell. We call it our Tnc cell line, short for *Tabanus nigrovittatus cohansus.* All we need to do is infect this parent cell line with a suitable transfer vector containing our gene of interest and voila! Ninety percent recombinant progeny virus! Purification and amplification of the recombinant virus becomes a simple two-step process, requiring only eight to ten days to complete!"

It was impossible for Sammy to hide her excitement when given the chance to expound on her favorite subject. Like a formula-one dragster out of the gate, it took a parachute to slow her down.

Glancing up at the clock on the wall, John thought it was time to deploy the chute.

"Don't mean to be a party pooper, Sam, but it's already past three o'clock. Doesn't Dr. Li want us back for a wrap-up session at four?"

Sammy drew back, checked the time, and smiled. "Oh, right! Better keep things moving!"

The tour of the seed development lab that followed amounted to something of a personal tour for John, as he had missed the previous opportunity during the last design review meeting a month earlier.

"Mind if I tag along?"

Dr. Julie Evert seemed to come from nowhere as Sammy led John down the hall toward the clean room suite containing the seed development lab.

"No, not at all!" Sammy replied. "The more the merrier!"

The seed development lab was located in a Grade A/B clean room space which carried a BLS-3 biosafety containment level rating. Getting into the core space of the lab was a bit like peeling back the layers of an onion, as one passed through a series of rooms and air locks of increasing cleanliness and containment, each having its own gowning and over-gowning requirements.

"A little bit more involved than our insect labs back at Rutgers," Dr. Evert remarked.

"Yes, more like Dante's nine circles of hell," John quipped.

By the time they reached the seed lab's innermost circle, John was covered head to toe in disposable clean room garb, consisting of hair nets, masks, latex gloves, Tyvek body suits, and booties covering a body stripped down to one's skivvies.

"How can you ever get anything done in these get ups," he fidgeted.

"Oh, you get used to it pretty quickly," Sammy giggled.

But John was having trouble getting used to it: the body suit, gloves, face masks, all very confining. And what was that humming noise? He looked up at the ceiling. Could be the fluorescent lights. Or maybe the HVAC, or...*an embracing swarm of greenhead flies, wrapping body and soul in a gray, buzzing cloud. A cocoon of sorts, at once frightening and somehow soothing...*

"John, are you okay?" Dr. Evert asked.

John shook it off. "Y-yes. I'm fine. Just a little...claustrophobic, is all."

Once inside John surveyed the room. The working core of the seed lab was a well-lit, medium-sized Grade B clean room, approximately fifteen by thirty feet. Arranged in a row along the wall on the right side were two six-foot long biosafety cabinet workstations and two smaller glove box isolators. The other side of the room contained two peninsular lab benches, a chemical fume hood work bench, and two floor-mounted cabinet CO_2 incubators. A sterilizing autoclave, an upright double-glass-door refrigerator, and a liquid nitrogen (LN2) chest freezer took up the remaining wall space in the room. The freezer contained the working cell banks for the insect cell lines being developed.

Two lab technicians were busy at work in front of two biosafety cabinets and didn't seem to notice the three visitors entering the room. A third technician, having just deposited a tray of tissue culture plates in one of the incubator cabinets, turned to greet the newcomers. He was tall, thin and dark complected, which was not readily discernible, as the Tyvek body suit left only a trace of bare skin remaining around the eyes and cheek bones. Despite the unisex attire, he was still able to recognize Sammy as she entered the room. Maybe it was her bouncy gate.

"Ah, good afternoon, Sam!" the dark-skinned man greeted her. "So, it is show-and-tell time again, heh? Eh, eh, eh!"

The man spoke in a high-pitched tone, attacking each syllable with the choppy rhythm of an African who had learned the King's English later in life. But it was his patented eh, eh, eh laugh—a slow, syncopated monotone—that was markedly unique and humorous.

Sammy chuckled. "Yes, Manny! Do you have anything of interest to show my guests? I promised them the grand tour of our seed development lab."

"Ah, yes! You are in luck today, Sammy! We are running a special on *re-com-bin-ant bac-u-lo-vi-rus-es.* You know, when two spiral strands of DNA unravel and then recombine with a new snippet of foreign DNA inserted."

"Yes...just like Mary's Afghan tapestry," John said with a faraway look in his eyes.

Three blank faces stared back at him.

"Er, it's just...an inside joke," he chuckled nervously.

"Yes, well, let us continue," Manny replied. "Please, allow me."

Manny led the trio to the nearest biosafety cabinet workstation where a technician was manipulating a glass pipette over a six-well tissue culture plate.

(There was that humming sound again! Only louder, and more buzz than hum, actually.)

"You see, Sidney here is a real wizard, eh, eh, eh! He is performing the first step of our transfection protocol," Manny explained. "Please observe. He is inoculating each well with inoculum from our Tnc seed bank in several milliliters of a special serum-free medium which has been optimized for our particular cell line. The plates will then be incubated at twenty-eight degrees centigrade about an hour to allow the cells to attach."

The room was suddenly bathed in a soft, white light. John blinked hard, and then...

...*the old Indian with the turkey feather hat and carved bone amulet pendant gently picked up four small, squirming larvae from a pewter dish and placed them, one by one, into a small clay mortar on the kitchen table. Opening a small leather pouch he reached in and removed a pinch of a powdery substance and sprinkled it over the larvae. He turned to Thomas, the blacksmith, standing next to him and nodded. Thomas took a small glass vial filled with an amber liquid—a mixture of nectar and sap from several varieties of evergreen—and poured it into the clay pot. The old man picked up a stone pestle and began grinding the contents of the mortar until he achieved a smooth, pearly-white consistency. Walking from the kitchen table to the open hearth, he placed the mortar with its gooey contents on the warm mantle shelf just above the hearth...*

John was nudged out of his reverie by Julie Evert.

"C'mon John. Gotta keep up with our escort."

Manny was already there, hovering over Brenda, the second lab technician, busy at work at another biosafety cabinet.

"Now, Brenda here is performing the next step in the transfection process. It's a little marriage ceremony of sorts between the transfer vector, which contains our gene of interest, and our healthy little Tnc cells. Pose for the camera, Brenda!"

(John's vision was becoming somewhat blurred. He didn't want to rub his eyes, so he did a hard double-blink. There! That's better!)

"The transfer vector," Manny continued, "is contained in that little glass vial Brenda is holding"—John leaned over to get a better view of the straw-colored suspension—"It consists of plasmid DNA from E. coli in which our little snippet of DNA, the gene of interest, has been inserted. She will use a special cationic lipid reagent to effect the liposome-mediated transfection process."

"Liposome-mediated...?" John asked.

"Yes. Let me explain," Sammy interjected. "Liposomes are microscopic particles of fatty material that combine with the DNA to help it get through the lipid cell wall of the target cell. Without it, the transfection of essentially foreign DNA couldn't happen."

"Yes," Manny added, "it's rather like trying to crash a party without an invitation. The liposomes form a lipid/DNA complex which serves as a kind of forged invitation to get the DNA past the bouncer at the cell wall door, you understand."

"And then…it's 'party time'?" John said, forcing a smile, although he wasn't feeling very well or much in the partying mood.

"Precisely!" Manny exclaimed. "Party time! I like that, John! Okay, Brenda, let's get the party going, eh, eh, eh!"

Brenda took two sterile test tubes and prepared two solutions, labeled "A" and "B." Carefully combining the contents of A into B, she mixed gently and allowed the mixture to incubate at room temperature for about fifteen minutes. As Brenda performed these tasks, Manny explained the procedure, but his words were crowded out by the buzzing in John's head. John closed his eyes…

…The old Indian turned to a young black woman—the same black woman from his initial campfire vision—and took the soiled articles of clothing she was holding. They were monogrammed with the initials, AG. He examined them, nodded his head approvingly, and proceeded to remove the stain patches with a pair of shearers.

"These blood stains are from her monthly flow?" he asked.

The young girl nodded.

After shredding the blood-stained patches of cloth, he put them into a small copper pot, picked up a small glass apothecary jar, and poured its contents over the shredded fabric. He turned to the blacksmith and asked, "Do you have what I asked of you, Thomas?"

Thomas nodded and removed a small leather pouch from his pocket and handed it to the old Indian.

"Yes, Chief. Dried tea leaves obtained from the last shipment of tea to arrive in port aboard the brig Greyhound back in December."

The Chief emptied the tea leaves into a second mortar and pulverized them to a fine powder. Chanting words from his native tongue, he removed a pinch of powdered tea leaves and threw it hard into the pot. He repeated this action several times, accentuating each toss with the accented words of his chant. When finished, he gently mixed the brew and placed the pot on the mantle over the hearth, next to the clay mortar with its pearly-white concoction of larval remains…

"…and so, while the lipid/DNA complex is forming," Manny explained as he removed a previously prepared cell culture tray from the incubator, "Brenda will wash the incubated cells from the first cell culture step with a few milliliters of serum-free medium."

He handed the cell culture tray to Brenda who proceeded to perform her sleight of hand laboratory magic on the prepared cell culture.

"Now comes the marriage ceremony!" Manny said with a laugh.

Right on cue, Brenda began to overlay the washed cells with the diluted lipid/DNA mixture. When finished, she covered the tray and carefully removed it to the incubator.

"Now, we will allow the cell culture to incubate at twenty-seven degrees centigrade for five hours," Manny continued. "At that time we will remove the tray, overlay with fresh medium, and return to the incubator for another seventy-two hours. Kind of like basting the holiday turkey, eh, eh, eh! And voila! You have your transfected insect cells! The virus particles containing the recombinant gene of interest will then be harvested from the liquid medium…"

Manny's words faded as a new, but not totally unfamiliar, vision took hold:

…As Thomas looked on, the Chief poured the gooey contents of the clay mortar into the copper pot with its shredded remnants of blood-stained cloth. Mixing the two with his fingers he created a kind of poultice as he continued to chant in his native tongue. When finished, he handed the vessel to Thomas and instructed him on what to do. He spoke softly, in a low whisper, and John could not make out the exact meaning of the words. After carefully setting the copper pot down on the kitchen table, Thomas reached out and took a second cup from the Chief. Standing up with outstretched arms he began tossing sprinkles of powder from the cup into the flames in the hearth, which brought new sparks and bursts of orange light with each flick of the wrist. As he performed this rite, he repeated the words spoken earlier around the campfire: "A curse be on the bloodline of one whose sinister deeds this night did spill the innocent blood of one so fair and pure a child as she…

That henceforth empowered the greenhead fly…

By noxious bite will so devour…

The minds of the guilty and their descendants…

For acts committed and un-repented…

When summer solstice days return…

The fly awakens, the noon sun burns…

The unsuspected being bitten…

With withering madness will be thus smitten."

The young black woman, staring into the roaring, open hearth with upraised arms, added these final words:

"And ne'er the curse shall it be lift…

Till the time of the winter solstice rift…

And The One whom time henceforth reclaims…

Returns to barter with his good name."

A familiar but frantic voice broke through the veil of John's visionary state.

"John! Are you all right, John?"

John slowly opened his eyes and was surprised to find himself lying prostrate on the laboratory floor. "Wh-What happened?" he asked weakly.

Dr. Evert was kneeling beside him and taking his pulse. "You passed out, John," she said, giving him back his wrist.

John looked up at the concerned ensemble staring down at him. "Did I…have a seizure of some kind?" he asked.

"I don't think so," Julie answered nervously. "There were no convulsions, and your tongue looks to be intact. No bite marks or signs of bleeding."

"But you should have yourself checked, Mr. Weston," Manny offered. "We have a clinic on campus. Do you want me to call for a paramedic?"

"No, that will be quite all right," John said softly as he slowly came to his feet. "Although the clinic would probably be a good idea." He paused before asking, "Tell me, did I say anything while I was…passed out?"

They all looked at each other. "No, not to my knowledge," Julie replied for all of them, a little perplexed by the question.

"That's good…I mean, I'm feeling much better now. I really think it was all this gowning I'm not used to…and not enough fluids."

"Well, that could do it," Manny commented hopefully. "Dehydration. Electrolyte imbalance. Maybe all you need is a little Gatorade!"

"Yes…Gatorade," John said a little nervously, thinking about his ordeal a month earlier.

"Well, okay then." Sammy interjected. "I rather think that concludes our little tour for today."

"Yes, I certainly appreciated it, Sam. And I apologize for the…interruption."

Sammy gave a little nervous laugh. "No problem, Mr. Weston. No problem at all."

Chapter 28

1774
Annapolis, Maryland

Wednesday, October 19. Seated by the front window of the Harbor Coffee House, the young Mr. John Jay Weston took another sip of coffee as he silently gazed across the open waters of the Chesapeake Bay, which were especially calm this afternoon, in marked contrast to the commotion and human drama unfolding on the shore. More than the usual maritime activity, a large crowd of townsfolk, men, women, and even children, had been gathering since mid-morning along the docks, trying to get a better look at the goings-on in the harbor.

Coffeehouses were enjoying a surge of popularity of late, vying with taverns as a public venue for social interaction, as coffee was fast replacing tea as the politically correct beverage of choice in the colonies. The Harbor Coffee House offered a particularly fine selection of domestic and imported coffees, with the prized mocha beans coming all the way from the terraces of Yemen on the Arabian Peninsula. The proprietor knew his coffee. The beans were freshly roasted and ground, not pressed, to capture all of the essences that contribute to the superior flavor of this much sought after berry.

John hugged the hot mug of coffee close to his chest, allowing the tantalizing scent of the freshly brewed mocha beans to waft upward to his nostrils, which flared with each breath. The afternoon sunlight filtered through the laced window curtains, highlighting the strong angular features of the young man's face. A pair of piercing blue eyes sparkled from the depths of their shadowy sockets. Capping his well-groomed crown was a thick crop of chestnut-brown hair, with one feisty lock that refused training falling carelessly to one side. An off-white cotton shirt and gold-laced waistcoat covered a torso of modest but handsome proportions, set off with a simple white linen cravat worn loose about the neck, importing a free spirit of youth and rebellion.

Peering out the window, John was just able to make out a tall rumpled figure of a man with dark, wavy hair, jostling his way through the crowd toward the pier. He knew this man. It was his good friend and business associate, Anthony Stewart, a fine gentleman in his forty-seventh year, upon whom John and his older brother, Bartholomew, had relied for making all of their shipping arrangements from the southern colonies. Normally fastidious in dress and demeanor, the events of the past few days had taken their toll on the poor man[10].

And who were the other two gentlemen with him? Ah, yes! They would be Joseph Williams and his brother, James, two local merchants who figured strongly in this affair. After all, it was the third brother, Thomas Williams, safely planted on the distant shores of merry old England, who was ultimately responsible for setting in motion the confused and tumultuous events of the past six days. From what John now knew of the trio's intent, he was glad to be viewing this from the safe confines of the coffeehouse.

It all began last Friday, the 14th of October, with the arrival from England of the brig *Peggy Stewart*, a merchant ship owned jointly by Mr. Stewart and his father-in-law, James Dick. The ship took the name of Anthony's daughter, the pretty Miss Peggy Stewart.

John Weston and Mr. Stewart were in this same coffeehouse that day discussing future business arrangements when the ship came into port on the morning of the fourteenth. The ship's captain, James Jackson, immediately sought out Mr. Stewart with a piece of troubling news. It happened that the ship's hold contained seventeen chest of tea—about 2,320 pounds in all—consigned to Joseph and James Williams by their brother, Thomas, who represented the family firm's business interests in England. Thomas had tried to conceal the identity of the cargo, listing it as chests of "linen"; but the captain refused to go along with the ruse, fearful of reprisals with customs officials—and colonials—should it be found out that he was hiding tea and be brought up on charges of smuggling. Furthermore, he was fully aware of the sentiment in America on such matters, with tea embargoes being enforced in many of the colonies in response to the Tea Act of 1773. So it was that he rightfully declared the true nature of the cargo on his customs forms before making the Atlantic crossing, and so listed it on the ship's manifest upon his arrival in the port city of Annapolis.

Upon hearing this, Anthony Stewart immediately sought out the Williams brothers and demanded that they pay the duty on the tea. But they wanted no part of their brother's hapless scheme and refused to pay the tax.

Anthony now had a problem. He knew that unless the duty was paid, the customs official would not allow any off-loading of the ship's cargo. He feared a repeat of the events of four-plus years ago when the brig *Good Intent*, with much tea on board, was forced to turn around and go back to England

---

[10] Anthony Stewart, a Scottish immigrant from Aberdeen, born in 1738, owned and operated a successful family merchant business along with his father-in-law, James Dick. While every attempt has been made in this narrative to remain faithful to historical accounts surrounding the burning of the brig *Peggy Stewart*, character interactions and dialogue are a matter of the author's own interpretation and are not intended to be taken as fact.

still fully loaded. That was in February, 1770, when a similar embargo was in effect resulting from the Townsend Acts of '67.

Mr. Stewart returned to the coffeehouse to discuss the matter further with his captain.

"Well, it appears that your stay in port may be short-lived," Anthony warned. "The Williams brothers refuse to pay the tax due on the tea, and so, I fear that none of the cargo may be off-loaded."

"So, are you saying the ship and its cargo must return to England?" John chimed in.

Anthony sat back in his chair and let out a long sigh. "Yes, I'm afraid so."

Captain Jackson shook his head. "Well, sir...er, the ship...she is leaking quite badly. It was all I and the crew could do to keep her afloat for this single crossing. Without the proper repairs...well, with the autumn gales approaching, I'm afraid she may not survive the return trip."

"Hmm, yes, but I don't know what else to do. Perhaps, once out to sea, you could...lighten the load, if you catch my meaning."

"Yes, well, er...sir, there's just one other small problem," the captain added with some hesitation.

"And just what would that be?"

"Well, you see, the ship's cargo includes a rather large number of indentured servants. Fifty-three, to be precise. As you know, they are bound by the same conditions of release and may not disembark until duties are paid on all cargo."

Mr. Stewart raised an eyebrow. "Are you suggesting that those poor souls may have to return to England along with the rea?"

"Maybe so. Maybe not," the captain replied. "But one thing is for certain. As long as this tea situation remains unresolved, those poor blokes must remain confined to the ship."

Mr. Stewart let out a sigh. "My, but we are well-placed on the horns of a dilemma, are we not, my good Captain?"

The captain nodded.

"Well, then," Mr. Stewart continued. "There is but one recourse remaining for a good Christian man to follow, tea embargo or no tea embargo."

With that, Mr. Stewart excused himself and went forthwith to the customs office where he proceeded to pay the duty due for the seventeen chests of tea, allowing for the human cargo to disembark. Of course, the tea would remain on board pending a final decision by local officials on the matter.

Meanwhile, the Williams brothers quickly arranged for a meeting with the Anne-Arundel County Committee to inform them of the current situation and to seek advice on the disposition of ship's tea and cargo. Only four committee members were available at the time, so the meeting was reconvened for 5 p.m. that same afternoon and opened up to the general public. Certain members of the Provincial Court, which happened to be meeting in Annapolis at the time, also joined the citizens of Annapolis to address this new crisis. Statements were read from the Williams brothers intending to absolve them of any wrongdoing, citing the ill timing of the tea's departure from England, which predated the enactment of the resolution establishing the current tea embargo. When it was learned that Mr. Anthony Stewart had actually taken it upon himself to pay the duty on the tea—with no mention of the humanitarian motives for this action—the ire of the committee and local citizenry was piqued, turning the focus of blame to Mr. Stewart. Eventually, a consensus was reached giving permission to unload all of the brig's cargo except the tea, and a committee of twelve persons was appointed to supervise the unloading. A final determination on the disposition of that "detestable weed tea" would have to wait for a full meeting of the committee, which was scheduled for the morning of Wednesday, the nineteenth.

News of the affair spread quickly. One of the more radical committee members, a Mathias Hammond, immediately set about distributing handbills advertising the Wednesday meeting and attacking Mr. Stewart and his business associates directly, rousing much public furor over his payment of the Tea Tax, which many saw as a deliberate and willful violation of the colony's recently enacted embargo resolution. Of course, the fact that Mr. Stewart was not a signatory to the resolution, and there being no mention made of the mitigating circumstances surrounding the plight of the human cargo aboard the *Peggy Stewart*, did not enter into Mr. Hammond's discourse on the matter. The issue was pure and simple: an example must be made of Mr. Stewart and his complicit abidance to the King's duty on imported tea! Anthony Stewart increasingly found himself stuck between the proverbial rock and hard place, or in this instance, the tea and the sea.

Hoping that calmer heads would prevail, Mr. Stewart and the Williams brothers continued to negotiate with others on the committee, notably Charles Carroll, committee chairman. On Monday, Mr. Carroll proposed that if the consignees and Mr. Stewart were to destroy the tea and publish a public apology in the *Maryland Gazette* denouncing their froward actions, then all would be set aright. Stewart and the Williams brothers readily agreed. Unfortunately, the proposal was rejected by the assembly at large. Public sentiment had continued to deteriorate, calling for stricter penalties, particularly with regard to the actions of Mr. Stewart and his "cheerful compliance with the act of Parliament taxing the tea." As the feverish pitch of discontent rose higher, there were even those very much "disposed to present him with a suit of tar and feathers."[11]

Diverging views quickly developed over what to do with the tea and the ship that brought it to these shores. To many, the offer to destroy the tea was reparation enough. Others pressed for the destruction of the vessel itself along with the tea. Some even questioned whether the tea needed to be destroyed at all! However, in the end, a small emerging minority of men, some of "respectable influence in their respective neighborhoods," vowed to take it upon themselves to destroy the brig *Peggy Stewart*, with or without the express approval of the committee. At this point, following the advice and admonition of Charles Carroll, Mr. Stewart offered to "destroy the vessel with his own hands."[12]

John J. Weston put the mug of hot mocha to his lips and took a cautious sip.

So how did John, the young firebrand patriot of Boston Tea Party fame, fit into all of this? He had attended this morning's public proceedings at which time Mr. Stewart formally presented his offer to burn the ship together with the seventeen chests of contraband tea. In the end the offer was well received, and seemed to satisfy the will of the people, although rumblings of discontent could be heard from certain disgruntled individuals who had rather looked forward to a good tar and feathering.

Needless to say, John's feelings were mixed. One part of him—the part that had participated as a nameless war-painted face in Boston's harbor ten months prior—readily identified with the more defiant sentiments of the mob and would have gladly offered to light the first match. Another part—the dedicated businessman desiring to find an equitable balance between duty and profit—cringed at the thought of seeing so fine a ship and so much equity go up in smoke. And still a third part—the human part that harbors a God-given sense of fair play and discernment, and which had served him so well in bonding with this man of good conscience—recoiled at the seeming injustice of it all. After all, the tea did not belong to Mr. Stewart, nor was he responsible for its loading in the first place; his only concern for paying the duty was, in his own words, "to save the vessel from seizure and of having the opportunity of releasing the passengers from a long and disagreeable confinement." At the time, the impropriety of securing the duty and the furor that it would cause did not occur to him.

Now, looking past the crowd toward the piers, John could just make out the figures of Mr. Stewart and his two accomplices boarding the vessel, *Peggy Stewart*. Within minutes the sails became unfurled with colors flying from the mast tops. Cheers and jeers went up from the crown as the ship's masts

---

[11] "Annapolis's 'Tea Party'," *New York Times*, November 19, 1892.
[12] Ibid.

drifted slowly to the left, past the docks toward a primitive section of shoreline. The crowd followed en masse. The motion of the top masts stopped abruptly as the ship was deliberately run aground on the shore.

A few minutes of silence followed. John could only surmise that Mr. Stewart was now reading his public apology as a prelude to the next and final act. And now, in his mind's eye, he saw Mr. Stewart striking the match. Was that smoke? Yes, definitely! There, just rising up through the ship's rigging. More cheers from the crowd as the smoke thickened and took on a flickering orange glow with hungry flames lapping at the ship's sails. Then suddenly, whoosh! The ship's masts went up like a stand of dry timber pine! Soon the entire ship was ablaze, engulfed by a great inferno. A spectacular sight! Red sails in the sunset, indeed! With a crackling boom, one mast fell, and then another, accompanied by the exuberant cheers of the great throng of people gathered along the water's edge, patriots all! High into the pewter gray sky the embers rose, carried by soft evening breezes across the fair city until, cooled and dying, they fell like sprinkles from a baker's spoon on the far flung and unsuspecting citizenry.

And so, the fire continued far into the evening, consuming the ship in due course until, by dawn's light, nothing remained but a charred, burned-out hull, bobbing precariously in shifting tides, right down to the water line.

Chapter 29

1999
Wed, 20 October
Simi Valley, California

The televised wide screen image cast an eerie, fuchsia glow to the room, bouncing and flickering from wall to wall in the small confines of an otherwise darkened space. The TV commentator spoke into his hand-held mic as flames leaped high into the night sky on the distant hills behind him. Fanned by the Santa Anna winds the brush fires had already destroyed twenty homes in the Lake Sherwood area and threatened many more. However, with the TV muted, the only sound was the hum of the AC and the rhythmic groans of lovemaking from beneath the rumpled sheets of the nearby queen-sized water bed.

Joined in conjugal bliss, the two naked bodies rocked and sloshed about on the waterbed like a lost dingy in a storm. On climax John's sweaty body fell limp, collapsing in spent delight on his willing partner as their two hearts beat as one, throbbing hard against the other through the protective confines of their padded rib cages, rising and falling in near unison with each breath.

Jennifer's eyes remained closed. She smiled, reliving the sensation over and over, a slowly fading echo of passion and desire. Would that it lasted longer! But, then again, this was the first time in a long while…for the both of them.

John rolled over onto his side and Jennifer turned to cuddle and spoon him from behind. The TV cut to a commercial. For several minutes they simply lay there in a quiet embrace. Jennifer spoke first.

"Renee is really looking forward to tomorrow, John," she said softly. "You made a real hit with her when you suggested going horseback riding."

An old memory flashed through John's mind. Long ribbons of white corral fence winding though the undulating fields of Sussex County, New Jersey. He was trying his best to catch up to the young lady on the palomino galloping far ahead of him, her long blonde hair trailing carefree in the wind.

"Yes. Well, you said she was fond of horses. And it promises to be a nice day tomorrow."

Jennifer smiled. "When isn't it a nice day in Simi Valley?" she asked.

John turned over on his left side to face Jennifer. Drawing himself close, with one arm folded beneath him, he reached down with his free hand to feel the warmth of her inner thighs, smooth as silk. She relaxed, allowing him to caress her thighs with slow, gentle strokes. The strokes became longer as his hand found its way to the warmer, moist upper regions.

Like a purring kitten she sighed and drew closer, totally embracing him with arms and legs.

"Do you think the gun is still loaded?" she whispered in his ear.

He smiled. "Not to worry, my dear. It's cocked and ready to fire!"

Their next round of lovemaking took them well past the late evening news hour. It was much better than before. With relaxed expectations and all inhibitions removed, he was able to make it last, now, to the point of satiated exhaustion. He didn't even recall drifting off. And then...

A soft, timid voice broke through the fog of sleep.

"John! Is that you, John?"

It may have been the voice of a child...or perhaps a young woman. John opened his eyes.

"It is me, John. Rebecca."

Without thinking, John replied, "Rebecca, my one and only love!"

An image now appeared before him. It was the form of a young, beautiful woman, hovering over him as he lay there.

"Yes, my love! Your sweet and abiding Rebecca. Biding my time, until your return."

John was standing now beside the bed. He turned his head and looked into the dresser mirror. Surprisingly, the image, while familiar, was not his own; a younger version of himself, perhaps, wearing a light banyan, a nightgown of sorts, seemingly from another era.

Where have I see that face before?

John turned toward the bed. Where was Jennifer?

When he turned back there was the lovely figure of young Rebecca standing before him, wearing a dainty, lacy nightgown, loosely tied across her bosom. Reaching out she took both of John's hands in her own and gently pulled him toward her.

"Come to me, John. Please, you mustn't forget."

John swallowed hard. Her touch was both gentle and electrifying. The words *Go back ! Save her!* echoed in his head.

Slowly, she released her grip, the pads of her fingers caressing his palms as she withdrew.

"Come to me, now, John!" she said repeatedly, as her form slowly evaporated into the darkness.

John turned and looked in the mirror. It was his own image, now, staring back at him; and there on the bed was Jennifer, just as before.

*****

John was up at the first light of dawn. He hadn't slept very well following his nighttime visionary experience. It all seemed so real! The scattered remnants of dreams and half-dreams that filled his head on awakening quickly faded with each passing minute of daylight, but closing his eyes, he was able to force their recall: he and Jennifer, passionately embraced, making love again and again—and then, her sudden transformation into…Rebecca! The girl of his dreams! He had become someone else, somehow; or rather someone else had occupied his body, an unwitting vessel and accomplice to ecstasy! She would call out his name, again and again: "Johnny! Johnny! Johnny Jay!"

John tried to shake it off as he put on a fresh pot of coffee.

"Good morning," came a groggy voice from the doorway.

John turned and smiled. "Yes, it looks to be a rather good morning in the making. A perfect day for a ride in the country."

Though disheveled and without her morning makeup, Jennifer's natural beauty and sex appeal needed no artificial embellishment to entice. Pausing at the threshold and leaning against the door frame with arms folded, like she had something important to say, she opted for something less contentious.

"Coffee smells good," she said. "Always smells better than it tastes. Ever notice that?"

John took a sip. "Taste and smell are bound up together," he opined. "I don't think the brain can tell the difference."

Jennifer approached John seated at kitchen table and gave him a little peck on the cheek before sitting down.

"I trust you slept well, cheri," she said in a questioning tone.

John was forced to lie. "But of course. Lovemaking is the perfect sleep aid. Releases all of those pent-up endorphins." Then, still thinking about the dreams, he asked, "So…how many times was it, exactly?"

Jennifer sat back in her chair and cocked her head. "So, you are keeping a scorecard, now, *mon amour*?"

"*Pas du tout!*" he replied quickly, realizing his mistake as soon as the words were uttered. "I didn't mean it that way." No, just trying to figure out what's real and what's not!

He leaned forward and took her hand. "Just trying to savor the memory of it all," he said softly with lingering emphasis on "savor" and "all."

"Oh, I see," she smiled.

Not convinced, and with a slightly troubled look remaining on her face, she finally asked, "So, tell me, John. Who is…Rebecca?"

Wha...? Ohmygod! Talking in my sleep! What else did I say?

"Rebecca?" John repeated the question to buy time.

"Mm. Qui, mon cheri. You must have said her name...many times, in your sleep."

In my sleep, yes! Thankfully not while we were making love!

John took a moment. He didn't want to lie, and he knew that sooner or later he'd have to level with her about his visionary episodes, even the time-travel thing. But this wasn't the time.

"Just someone from my...past life," he said at last.

Though not totally satisfied with his answer, Jennifer was willing to let it drop for the moment.

"I see," she said with a sigh. Then, glancing up at the clock on the wall, "Well, if we're going to pick up Renee by ten, we'd better get a move on. I'll shower. You make breakfast."

"Sure," he simply said, glad to be off the hook for the moment.

In the course of the day John did tell Jennifer about Doug, his new house guest, and how it all came about. He explained his concern for Doug, having to leave him alone even for just a few days while he made this trip. Fortunately, Katie had promised to drop by after work each day to check on his condition and make sure he was taking his meds. In her last voice message Wednesday night she assured him that everything was all right.

Their day of horseback riding went exceptionally well. For John, this was the most fun he'd had since making that Tour de France trip with his dad nine years ago. John was also a big hit with Jennifer's daughter, Renee. They struck up a rapport right out of the gate. Of course, it helped that John knew horses, though it had been almost twenty years since he'd been in the saddle; but it all came back to him—like riding a bike—you never forget.

What John did forget, however, was his cell phone—he'd left it on the dresser in Jennifer's bedroom, plugged into the charger. It was past five o'clock when they returned to Jennifer's condominium and were freshening up before heading out to a new sushi restaurant Jennifer wanted to try, when John first noticed the light flashing on his phone: ten unanswered phone calls and five voice messages.

"Oh, shit! Pardon my French."

John picked up the phone. His heart raced as he listened to the first message. It was a man's voice, unfamiliar, unemotional, direct and to the point:

"...This message is for a Mr. John Weston. Sir, this is Detective Blane of the Haddonfield Police Department. Please contact our department at your soonest availability. It concerns a matter of utmost urgency involving your property and a person of interest. You may reach us at..."

"Definitely not good!" John mumbled. The time of the message was ten o'clock this morning, which would make it one o'clock in the afternoon east coast time.

"Damn! Couldn't have missed that call by more than ten minutes!"

The next message was from Kate:

"…hello, John. This is Katie. Pleeease call me as soon as possible! It's very urgent (she sounded upset) It's about Doug. There's been…an accident. Please! Just call me as soon as you get this message…"

Her other two messages basically said the same thing, but in more urgent tones, providing some additional information:

"…Doug has taken a fall…he's been taken to Cooper Hospital and is in critical condition…the doctors don't know if he's going to make it…"

"Oh my God!" John said aloud.

"Que-ce que c'est?" Jennifer asked from the other room.

"Bad news on the home front, I'm afraid" John replied. "I'll fill you in once I get the full download."

The final message was from Lady of Lourdes Hospital, asking whether John had any "next of kin information" on Doug Justin. John's pulse quickened.

"So, are you going to go to dinner wearing your riding boots, or are you going to change into something else?" Jennifer asked tongue in cheek as she re-entered the room.

John put up his hand to signal, "Shh! Sorry, hon. Just give me a minute. Gotta make an important call."

John hit *8 to quick dial Katie's number. Katie picked up on the first ring.

"My God, John, where have you been? I've been trying to reach you all day!"

Before John could explain, Katie opened up with a nonstop description of events as she knew them. She had phoned the house during her lunch break, something she did every day at this time to check on Doug's condition. Today there was no answer. She tried again an hour later, but still no answer. Becoming concerned she decided to leave work early to make her nightly stop by the house. What she found this time took her breath away. Parked out front and in the driveway were two police cruisers, with yellow crime tape running through the yard and around the porch.

"The police said a neighbor called to alert them to a man perched on your third-floor roof, screaming that someone was after him. When they arrived they found him sprawled out in the driveway, unconscious and bleeding from the head."

John shook his head, not believing what he was hearing.

"What the…? Good God! How bad was he hurt?"

"Well, he was still alive when the paramedics arrived, but barely. They took him to Lourdes, where he was stabilized and transported to Cooper Hospital's trauma unit."

"Well, that explains the call from the hospital," John surmised. He then changed his tone, becoming almost accusatory. "But, what the hell happened? He was taking his meds, wasn't he?"

"Yes, John. Absolutely!" she responded defensively. "As far as I could tell. When I dropped by last night he seemed just fine. I counted the pills. Unless he was throwing them down the toilet."

There was a pause.

"Well," John sighed. "I really should take the next plane home. Not much that I can do at this point, but I do feel responsible somehow."

"You shouldn't feel that way, John! It's not your fault. It's nobody's fault. Just…an unfortunate turn of events. Would it have been any different if you'd been here?"

"Perhaps. I might have seen it coming."

After hanging up, John turned to Jennifer, who by this time had tuned into what was happening. Disappointed, she agreed that the best thing would be for John to go home as soon as possible. There was always room on the red-eye flight, which would get him into Philly around seven o'clock the next morning—Friday, the twenty-second.

Chapter 30

1774
Sat, 22 October
Annapolis, Maryland

John Jay Weston was enjoying a late evening meal at the Harbor Coffee House—a plate of steamed clams harvested fresh that day from the bay—when a young man, not five years his senior, entered the establishment alone. Shaking off the dust of the road, he took a seat at an empty table to John's left. John studied the man as he opened a satchel and produced a handwritten journal which he began to peruse by lamplight. John gave him a few minutes to himself before approaching.

"Please pardon the interruption, sir, but you do bear a strong semblance of familiarity. Have we had the pleasure of meeting before?"

The man leaned back in his chair, looked up, and smiled weakly. He had a reverent bearing, like that of a school teacher or minister.

"Why, no. I don't believe"—pausing to take a closer look at John as he stepped into the light of the table lamp—"well, yes, you do strike a familiar chord as well. Perhaps...have you ever been to Cohansie? Cumberland County, West New Jersey?"

John let out a hearty laugh as he finally made the connection. "Yes, of course! You are a Fithian, are you not?"

The man smiled. "Indeed! Philip Vickers Fithian at your service."[13]

The man stood up and held out his hand, which John took and shook in earnest.

"My name is John. John Jay Weston, of Weston Enterprises. Perhaps it is the family resemblance or name that strikes the familiar cord. You may

---

[13] Philip Vickers Fithian (1747-1776), patriot and native son of Greenwich, Cumberland County, West New Jersey—or "Cohansie," as he commonly referred to this region—is best known for his journals and letters which provide detailed accounts of colonial life and customs in New Jersey and Northern Neck region of Virginia, where he served as tutor to the Carter family on their "Nominee Hall" plantation. Hunter Dickinson Farish, ed., *Journal and Letters of Philip Vickers Fithian: A Plantation Tutor of the Old Dominion, 1773-1774* (Charlottesville: The University Press of Virginia, 1957).

know my brother, or half brother, Bartholomew Weston. A more engaging gentleman than myself, I assure you, with long-standing business and social ties to your fair city."

Philip took John's hand firmly with both hands.

"Yes. My father has had numerous dealings with him in the past. A good man of good repute!" He squeezed John's hand one last time. "It is always good to meet a familiar name and face so far from one's home, is it not!"

John invited Philip to join him at his table to share a bowl of freshly steamed clams, which Philip graciously accepted.

"So, where are your travels taking you, Philip?" John asked.

"To Greenwich, God willing. I tried making the crossing to Kent Island earlier this evening, but the winds did not favor us. We were forced to return."

"Ah, yes, we are ever at the mercy of the tides and winds. So, you will be staying the night, then?" John asked.

"Yes, I'm afraid so."

Philip explained that he was returning to his home on the Cohansey after having spent the last twelve months in the very agreeable service of "Councillor" Robert Carter III of Nominee Hall, Westmoreland County, Virginia. A third-generation American, Robert Carter III was the current patriarchal head of the Carter clan, a very wealthy and influential plantation family in the Tidewater region of Virginia. Nominee Hall, the manor house of his estate, was situated on a hilltop overlooking the Potomac River. His estate comprised seventy thousand acres in the Northern Neck region between the Rappahannock and Potomac Rivers.[14]

"Yes, I believe I have heard the Carter name spoken by my business associate, Anthony Stewart," John acknowledged. "A very enterprising planter. The products and produce of his labor regularly pass through this port."

"Yes, very enterprising," Philip assured him. "And quite prolific as well, with nine surviving children to boast of!"

---

[14] The notion that John may have encountered Philip in his return travels through Annapolis is a matter of conjecture, but certainly plausible, as Philip's journal entries for Saturday, October 22nd, and Sunday, the 23rd, record his overnight stay in this port town on the Chesapeake. For Saturday, he records: "Left Annapolis at 6 no wind returned at 8 to the Coffee-House." His Sunday entry reads: "Tuesday evening last the people of this Town…obliged one Anthony Stewart a Merchant here to set fire to a Brig of his lately from London in which was 17 Chests of Tea…" Hunter Dickinson Farish, ed., *Journal and Letters of Philip Vickers Fithian* (Charlottesville: The University Press of Virginia, 1957), 209.

"Impressive!" John replied. He took a clam from the bowl. "There must be some truth, then, to the adage that Chesapeake clams increase the vigor in men!"

"And make barren women fruitful. Yes, I have heard this said," Philip responded with a grin.

John chuckled. "So, tell me, Philip. In what capacity were you employed by Mr. Carter, if you don't mind my prying?"

"Not at all. But, it's *Colonel* Carter," Philip corrected him. "Like I said, very influential. By virtue of serving as a member of the Governor's Council, he earns the title of "Colonel" in the militia."

John bowed his head. "I stand corrected, sir."

Philip proceeded to tell his own life story. How he had graduated from Nassau Hall—later to become Princeton University—in September of 1772. Returning to Greenwich he decided to pursue a ministerial career and so took up the study of theology under two friendly pastors. A year later, in the autumn of 1773, he heard through a friend that Councillor Carter of Nominee Hall desired a tutor for seven of his nine children and a nephew. Philip Fithian eagerly responded to the offer of "sixty pounds a year, a servant, a library, and a room to study in."

As men are want to do in such circumstances, their conversation soon turned to politics and the current state of affairs with the crown. John shared his experiences with the Sons of Liberty, even admitting to his participation in that Boston tea dumping affair last December. For his part, Philip Fithian was not shy about expressing his own fervent views on liberty, to the point of waxing prophetic on the bright future and destiny of the American people.

"I do believe that the westward movement of commerce and improvement is so compelling that before too long we shall have towns and cities overlooking the Pacific Ocean," he asserted. "But, not before this distended bladder of British rule, filled to bursting with the venom of discontent, splits outright with rage!"[15]

John was most impressed by the fervor and zeal of his pronouncements.

"Have you seen this week's issue of the *Maryland Gazette*?" he asked.

---

[15] Such prophetic pronouncements and sentiments of rage against the Crown are later recorded in Philip's journal entries for June 1, 1775. Referring to the "hell-inspired" British blockade of Boston in that month, he writes: "...All along the Bladder has been filling with Venom. Now it is distended with Poison—full, ready to crack, to split with Rage!" He further exclaims, "O America! With Reverence I look forward and view thee in Distinguished Majesty...The March of Commerce & Improvement to the westward is so rapid, that soon...we shall have Towns overlooking the Banks of the Pacific Ocean." Quotations are taken from Joseph S. Sickler, *Tea Burning Town: Being the Ancient Story of Greenwich on the Cohansey in West Jersey* (Bridgeton: The Greenwich Press, 1950), 54-59.

Philip shook his head. "No, I'm afraid my travel has taken all my attention of late."

John related the events of this past week, concerning the burning of the tea-laden brig, the *Peggy Stewart*. Philip was intrigued, and expressed disappointment for having missed it by so few days.

John was so absorbed in conversation that he failed to notice a shadowy figure approaching him from the far side of the room.

"Well, if it isn't the young and dashing Mr. Weston, in the flesh. It is you, sir? Is it not?" he bellowed sarcastically so all could hear.

John knew the voice in an instant.

"Yes, Jacob. It is I, in all corporeal form and fitness. What is your pleasure?"

Cap'n Jacob was holding a tankard of rum and was already teetering from the effects of it and who knows how many before. He glanced at the other gentleman seated at the table.

"Where are your manners, my good lad? Aren't you going to introduce me to your friend, or just leave me here standin' to dry out in the wind?"

Reluctantly, John motioned for Jacob to have a seat. After a quick introduction, John asked, "So, what brings you to these parts, Jacob. I would have placed you in Port Royal, or some other pirates' haven."

"Shh! Don't say the 'P' word! You might offend our distinguished guest," he said, nodding to Philip.

"I assure you, I'm not easily offended," Philip responded without flinching.

"Well, that is good to know. Because it so happens that I bring some news that some may find to be offensive."

"Pray tell, offend us with your news, Jacob!" John insisted.

"Well, I know your sentiments regarding the crown and the current embargo situation." He looked at Philip. "And I suspect that Mr. Fithian, here, may share in your...seditious views."

"Sedition is hardly the word I would use to describe a lover of liberty, my good man." Philip rebounded.

"Hear, hear! Well stated, Mr. Fithian!" Jacob replied, raising his glass in the manner of a toast.

John let out an audible sigh. "Please, curtail the obfuscations, Jacob, and get on with it! What is the news that you bring?"

John was quickly becoming impatient. Jacob took a quick swig of rum and produced a folded copy of the most recent issue of the *Maryland Gazette* from his inside coat pocket and laid it upon the table

"It so happens that a notably sized shipment of tea, that 'detestable weed,' if I may borrow an appellative from the local *Gazette*,"— pointing and underscoring the reference with a lank forefinger—"is due to arrive on board the brig *Greyhound*, bound out of Liverpool for the fair shores of New Jersey, destined for none other port of call than your own fair town of Greenwich on the Cohansey."

John and Philip both looked down at the paper. John picked it up and gave it a careful perusal. "I see no reporting here on such a matter as you say."

Philip then addressed Jacob directly. "Where did you come by this scandalous piece of news, my good fellow?"

"Ah, from a protected but reliable source, I assure you," Jacob replied with a conquering grin. "I was further told that they have arranged storage of the tea in a safe house, as it were, to avoid public scrutiny and a repeat of the Boston affair."

"I see," John said, not knowing whether to trust the man. "And when is this…untold event due to unfold? Do your sources divulge this?" John pursued.

"Yes! In point of fact, they did! It shall be in the early days of December, assuming the ship and crew are blessed with fair weather and a timely passage. You know how the gales can blow in the Atlantic this time of year."

There was a moment of silence as John and Philip considered this.

"And the safe house, as you put it, have you any information on where this might be?" Philip asked.

Philip shook his head. "No, I'm afraid not. My source was careful not to divulge that little detail."

Philip turned to John. "I shall be in Greenwich within the week. I can look into the matter then, to verify its authenticity."

Jacob stifled a laugh and shook his head.

"Don't trouble yourself, Mr. Fithian. I assure you that lips are sealed tight on this matter. It was only by the slip of the tongue that I chanced upon it myself."

"A slip? Or perhaps a slice?" John challenged, glancing down at the exposed handle of a dirk tucked inside Jacob's boot.

Jacob gave a pouting sigh of feigned offense. "Come, come, John! You chafe me with your insinuations. Do you think I have no power of persuasion beyond the dagger in my boot?"

John glanced at Philip, then back to Jacob. His thoughts went back to the turmoil of the past few days and their life-transforming effects on his good friend and business associate, Anthony Stewart.

"Tell me, Jacob, why do you favor us with such disturbing news?"

"What you mean to say is, how can it benefit me?"

"Precisely!"

Jacob leaned back and grinned broadly. "Well, let us just consider it…collateral for a future favor. After all, I am always in the market for reliable information from someone as well connected with customs officials as you, John."

Jacob smiled a bright, gold-toothed smile. John and Philip remained unmoved.

"Yes, well I can see that you fine gentlemen have other...business to discuss. I will bid you my leave."

As he was turning to go, Jacob paused in his tracks

"Ah, yes, John. There is but one additional, small item that may interest you."

John gave a deep sigh and reluctantly lent an ear.

"It seems," Jacob continued, "you have a relation in these Jersey colonies who bears a Christian name that is almost one and the same as your own: a John Samuel Weston. He was seen rummaging about the taverns of Greenwich laying claim to be a distant cousin of your older brother, Master Bartholomew."

Jacob had John's full attention now.

"And, I might add,"—sitting back and studying the boyish figure before him—"but with a few more years to his credit, he did bear a strong resemblance to you, sir. Enough to be your full flesh and blood."

John shook his head. "That's not possible! I have no knowledge of such a relation as you say. He must be...a pretender, an imposter!"

"Have it your way. But then, I must wonder why he would assume the Weston name and be so bold about it," Jacob replied, the double ss in "assume" sounding like the hiss of a serpent. "And he did convey an intimate knowledge of Master Bart's family situation. Even knew the missus' and children's names."

John was speechless for the moment. Then just shook his head. "You must be mistaken, Jacob."

The pirate puckered a frown and placed both hands down on the table.

"Very well, then. I've said what I came to say. I must away." And with a partial tip of his hat, "Gentlemen, I bid you my leave."

Early the next morning John and Philip met for breakfast. For John there was one more item to discuss with Philip before seeing him off— something of a personal nature. Reaching into his inside vest pocket, John produced a sealed envelope and laid it upon the table.

"If it is not too inconvenient, Philip, would you be so kind as to deliver this letter to my sweet Miss Rebecca upon your return to Greenwich. You may know her, or know her father, the town smithy, Thomas Whitman. His home and shop are situated on the road to Shilo in the North Head section of town."

"Why, it's not inconvenient at all, John. I should only be too happy to comply with your request." Philip took the letter and placed it in his satchel.

"In fact, I pass by that very place on making my way home, which is just on the outskirts of town."

John smiled. "Excellent! I am much indebted!"

Philip nodded and continued. "I should like to contact you, John, regarding this...business of the tea shipment, once I return to Greenwich and am able to confirm or refute Jacob's claims. Where shall I be able to contact you by posted letter?"

John took a quill pen and letter paper from a nearby credenza and wrote something down, then handed it to Philip.

"Please, take this. It is the address of my good friend and business associate, Anthony Stewart, where I am presently boarding. I will be in and about over the next several months, but will be checking my mail on a regular basis," he assured Philip.

Later that evening, in the privacy and darkness of his own room, John thought about the second piece of news that Jacob bore—that business about the other John Weston.

There was just something disquieting about it.

PART FOUR

Weave in, weave in, my hardy life,
Weave yet a soldier strong and full for great campaigns to come,
Weave in red blood, weave sinews in like ropes, the senses,
sight weave in,
Weave lasting sure, weave day and night the wet, the warp, incessant
weave, tire not,...
...We know not why or what, yet weave, forever weave.

Walt Whitman, "Weave In, My Hardy Life"

Chapter 31

1999
Fri, 22 October
South Jersey

The red-eye flight from LA to Philly was smooth and mercifully uneventful. The plane was only one-quarter full, so John had three seats to himself on the starboard side of the big 747. Folding up the middle armrests, he lay in a crosswise, scrunched up fetal position, striving desperately for some needed shut-eye. Flying high above the clouds, the plane gave chase to a larger than life full moon, shining gold and bright in a star-studded, ebony sky. It was around eleven o'clock when Orion first appeared, skirting low along the southern horizon before fading away into the pre-dawn light. Another two months from now the Hunter would dominate the winter skies, but for the moment he took a low profile. As John tracked the constellation's progress through the early morning hours he thought about his own rendezvous with upcoming winter solstice events as foretold in verse by his good friend Bob and his basement "time machine." Actually though, Orion served more as a diversion, an attempt to take John's mind off the more disturbing thoughts and images racing through his head.

"I shouldn't have left him alone! It's all my fault!" he repeatedly scolded himself.

Dozing off, he would awake with a jolt from that hypnagogic state of half-sleep where thoughts and images meld into an amalgam of the surreal. For a moment it seemed the plane had become frozen in time and space, no sense of motion, just the drone of the engines and the occasional jounce through choppy air.

The sun was just coming up when the plane's huge tires screeched against the tarmac of Philly's International Airport waking John with a start. He had managed to fall asleep after all. Rubbing his eyes, he filled the palm of one hand with water from his water bottle and splashed the cool stuff across his face, letting it drip dry as the plane found a parking spot at the gate. Ah, sweet terra firma!—and the sobering light of a new day.

After picking up his car from long-term parking, John drove straight to Cooper Hospital in Camden, about a twenty-minute ride. Numb from lack of sleep, he put himself on autopilot, barely remembering the drive. Fortunately, traffic was light and his car seemed to know the way.

This was John's first visit to Cooper, so it took him a little while to get his bearings from the parking garage. It was after nine o'clock before he finally made it to the front desk where he was directed to the trauma intensive care unit.

A "Turn Off All Cell Phones Before Entering" sign greeted him as he stepped off the elevator. John willingly obliged and approached a nurse manning the central ICU monitoring station, with its banks of beeping, fluorescent screens and rows of green, amber, and occasional red blinking lights.

"Excuse me, ma'am," John offered timidly, "My name is John Weston. I'm here to see one of your patients, a Mr. Doug Justin."

The nurse, a middle-aged veteran well-accustomed to the multitasking demands of emergency medicine, answered John without looking up from a green screen display of jagged wavy lines.

"Are you a relative, or next of kin?" she asked, testing his need to know.

"Well, no, not exactly. Doug has been in my care for the past several weeks. I haven't had much luck locating his family"—the nurse looked up— "but until someone does, then I suppose I must assume responsibility for him."

The nurse sat back and breathed a deep sigh. "Well, Mr. Weston. Your friend took a really bad fall yesterday and is very lucky to still be alive. That's all I am free to say at this point. You will have to discuss the particulars with Dr. Wilson"—pointing—"He's the tall gentleman over there."

John turned to see the doctor in a white coat standing by the door to a patient's room about halfway down the hall.

"Yes, thank you, ma'am."

John approached the doctor and introduced himself.

"Ah, yes," Dr. Wilson responded, "You are the home owner the police, er, should I say, the hospital has been trying to contact."

"Yes, I'm afraid so. I've been away on business," John confessed apologetically.

John peered into the room. It was Doug alright, though barely recognizable. He had lost his Mohawk to the orderly's razor and was connected ten ways from Sunday with life support and monitoring equipment.

"Please tell me, doctor, is he going to...survive?"

"Well, It's really too early to say," the doctor conceded. "We've placed him in a drug-induced coma to help with the brain swelling. He's responded well, but these things are difficult to predict with any certainty. Tell me,"—

shifting his tone from doctor to investigator—"what exactly is your relationship to the patient?"

John gave the doctor a quick rundown of recent events, how he came to be Doug's de facto guardian, how he'd been trying to contact Doug's sister or any next of kin without much success, how Doug seemed to be getting it together.

"So, what exactly happened, Doctor?" John asked at last. "The voice message I received said he was perched on my rooftop trying to…fly?"

Must've gone off his meds. Or worse, gotten hold of some street drugs!

"Well, according to the police account a neighbor tried talking him down. When asked how he got up on the roof in the first place, he was reported to say, 'why, I flew up, of course!'"

John thought about Doug's obsession with flying and the episode on the water tower as a teen. *Damn! This wouldn't have happened if I was here!*

"So, you think he was…*tripping* on drugs, or something?" John probed.

The doctor shrugged. "Yes, well of course, that is, er…the *unofficial* police position on what happened. Perhaps, Mr. Weston, you could shed some light on the subject."

John did a quick recap of Doug's medical history, going down the list of medications Doug was taking…or supposed to be taking. Did they test his blood for drugs? Yes, of course, the doctor assured him. The results confirmed that Doug had not neglected his daily regimen. That was a relief! Katie had apparently done her job well. He felt bad for thinking maybe she hadn't. *No, it was me. I'm the one who neglected him!*

John felt helpless, and finally resigned himself to just waiting it out in the unit's visitor lounge area. He gave Katie a call from the public phone to let her know his whereabouts. He thanked her for all her help over the past week and assured her that this wasn't her fault. He believed it this time.

The minutes slowly passed by.

Just before noon, Dr. Wilson approached John in the lounge with a worried look. "I think I may have found the 'smoking gun,'" he said, holding up a clear plastic specimen bag.

John stood up for a closer look. Inside was a small rumbled wrapper or bag of some sort with markings he couldn't quite make out. "What's it say? Saliva something or other?"

"Close. Try *Salvia Divinorum!*" the Doctor corrected.

"Salvia…Divinorum?" John repeated.

"That's right. *Diviner's Sage. Seer's Sage. Ska Maria Pastora.* Or just plain *Salvia.* Take your pick. It's got a number of popular street names. Your friend had it tucked away in a hidden inside pants pocket. We ran some tests and confirmed it's identify."

"So, what is it exactly? Some kind of marijuana?"

"Not quite. It is a plant, and normally smoked, but that's where the similarity ends. Its effects are totally different, normally of short duration, maybe ten minutes or less, but much more extreme in terms of its dissociative hallucinogenic effects. The Mazatec shamans of Mexico have long used the plant in religious ceremonies to facilitate altered states of consciousness during spiritual ceremonies. Unlike alcohol or cannabis, it's definitely *not* a party drug. They say you should really have a friend with you when you're doing it…a 'trip sitter,' as it were."

"So, you think Doug was…*tripping* on this stuff when he climbed the roof?"

The doctor shrugged. "Can't say for sure. Our normal battery of blood screening tests don't include *Salvinorin A*, the active psychotropic ingredient in Salvia. And by now it's well out of his system. But, I would say the chances are very good this may have precipitated a psychotic episode in Doug's case, considering his underlying psychopathology and susceptibility."

John was stunned. "But…why…how in the world could he have gotten hold of it? It's not legal, is it?"

The doctor grinned. "That's the sad part. Or best part, depending on your tastes in recreational drugs. It's *totally* legal! Because it's non-habit forming and has not been shown to produce any long-term toxicological effects, the drug eludes all current federal and state statutes for controlled substances. You can even buy it on the internet, for God's sake!"

The doctor excused himself and left John alone with his thoughts. John was convinced more than ever now that he was to blame. Stewing in self-recrimination and overpowered by fatigue, he drifted into a tortured half-sleep, and was about to sink deeper into a welcomed sleep when— *Blaaat!…Blaaat!…Blaaat!*— he was abruptly aroused by a code blue alert. It took him a few seconds to come to his senses. Rising slowly to his feet, he left the lounge and headed back down the hall to the unit.

What greeted him was ordered pandemonium, all seeming to head in the direction of Doug's room: nurses and green-robed technicians rushing past him with push carts, defibrillators, and other emergency response equipment, like he wasn't even there, being sucked into Doug's room like a giant vortex. He tried to swallow, but couldn't get the saliva past the dry lump in his throat.

It all seemed like a bad dream. But, then, John had been there before: events playing out in slow motion; senses numb; the feeling of moving, speaking, reacting in robotic fashion, but only when prompted to do so. Of course, it didn't help that he'd hardly had any sleep in the past forty-eight hours. The notion of a "trip sitter" lodged in the back of his mind. *Could use one of those right about now*, he thought. *That's what I should have done for Doug. Been his "trip sitter."* Too late for that.

John carefully approached Doug's room.

"One...two...three...clear!" someone shouted.

Doug's body jolted as the defib paddles were applied to his naked chest.

Again. "One...two...three...clear!" *Zap!*

No response.

Doug's heart monitor continued to draw a straight green line.

"The IV epinephrine isn't working," the doctor barked. "We're going direct intramyocardial! Nurse, give me a ten c-c syringe, stat!"

Dr. Wilson took the syringe handed to him and plunged the needle directly into Doug's chest clear up to the hilt. Then standing back he took the paddles again.

"Clear!" *Zap!*

Still, no response.

John turned away, staring blankly into space as the sounds and commotion of the paddles, the monitors, the urgent commands all faded into one foggy blur. Then all at once...the commotion ceased.

Doctor Wilson slowly emerged from Doug's room. Appearing tired and defeated he just stood there in the hallway, silently peeling off his latex gloves. Looking up he caught John's eye and slowly shook his head side to side.

"I'm sorry, Mr. Weston. We did all we could do."

John inched forward past the doctor to see into the room. The nurses had already drawn a sheet over Doug's face.

"How c-could this have happened?" John asked, his voice trembling with a mixture of anger and grief.

The doctor gave him a few moments before asking, "Can I assume, Mr. Weston, that you will be taking responsibility for the young man's...remains?"

Sure, who else is there?

"Yes, I will make all the necessary arrangements," John replied calmly.

John thanked the doctor for all he had done, then spent the next few hours making good on his promise, getting tangled up in all the red tape associated with the business of dying. *Did Doug have a next of kin?* Yes, an older sister, but I have no way of getting in touch with her. *Was there a last will and testament?* No, not to my knowledge. *Would you prefer cremation or burial?* Hmm, never discussed this with Doug while he was alive. I suppose I'll have to get back to you on this. *And of course, you realize, Mr. Weston, there will be a postmortem. Unfortunately, it is required in cases such as this.* Yes, I realize that. Actually, I welcome it. Maybe we'll find out something we don't already know.

On the matter of the postmortem, John had the presence of mind to contact his good friend at the County Medical Examiner's Office, Dr. Paul Fielding. He asked Paul if he wouldn't mind doing the autopsy himself.

"Sure, John. I can do that, no problem."

It was close to three o'clock before John was able to leave Cooper Hospital and head back to Haddonfield. There would still be time to touch base with Mary at the office and check his voice- and e-mail messages.

Driving down Haddon Avenue he could see the not too distant white marble statue of Mother Mary standing high atop Our Lady of Lourdes Hospital in bold contrast to a leaden sky. Slowing down as he passed the hospital, his car took a sudden left turn through the gates of Harleigh Cemetery. He was not sure what made him do it, but no matter—he was on the cemetery grounds now.

The car took him past Walt Whitman's family tomb and on down the narrow, winding roadway into the heart of the cemetery; over gently rolling hills; past manicured lawns, ponds, and landscaped waterways; and across a narrow bridge toward the large mausoleum situated near the rear of the cemetery. He knew where the car was taking him. Not far from the tree-lined banks of the Cooper River the car came to a halt. John cut the engine, got out slowly, and walked unsteadily toward a modest, white stone marker, flanked by several undisturbed future grave sites. The tombstone read:

Richard T. Weston
Born 4 Sept, 1922
Died 23 Nov, 1991
"Beloved Father, Husband and Teacher!"

John knelt down, leaned forward, and grasped the cold stone monument with both hands. A light drizzle began to fall.

"Why?!" he sobbed. "Why is it, Dad? Everything I touch, or dare to care about in this world, just...*dies*?"

Suddenly, the floodgates of his mind opened wide as memories of Becky, his one true love, came gushing forth in a spate of tortured images, feelings, and regrets. Mixed in with this were thoughts and memories of his dad, mainly from the final few years of his life, the really best years of their lives together. And Doug? Well, John had really just started getting to know him. But a certain kinship had begun to develop, and Doug seemed like the son he wished he had. Now he felt responsible for his untimely death.

The drizzle became a light rain that mingled with the tears and snot running down over his upper lip like the wax drippings of a burning candle. Wiping his face on his sleeve, he looked up and surveyed the family plot left to right.

"So, Dad, would it be all right if I asked you to share this space with a non-family member?"—doing a quick mental calculation—"I think there is room enough here for all of us."

As he knelt there, half expecting an audible reply, a panicky, paranoid thought flashed through his mind. *Jennifer! I forgot to call Jennifer!* Groping for his cell phone he pulled it from his turned inside out pants pocket and did a quick message check. Ah, there was one unread message from Jennifer! Apparently she called this morning when he was in the trauma unit, incommunicado: "...Hello, John. Is everything all right? You said you were going to call when you got in. Please call me as soon as you get this message. I'm getting a little worried."

John breathed a sigh of relief as he punched in her quick dial call-back number, but all he got was her voice mail.

"Dammit! Should've called from the airport. Should've, could've. Damn red eye!"

Frustrated, he stood up and looked around. Frustration turned to agitation, and he felt an overwhelming need to talk to someone—someone living!

Looking back over his shoulder toward the hospital, the towering the stone figure of Our Lady of Lourdes seemed to be beckoning: *The body is often curable, the soul is ever so.*

John tried desperately to recall. *What was her name? I should remember it. It was a French name. Sister...Mother...*"Yes! Mother Superior Marguerite D'Esprit!" he said aloud.

Scrambling back to his waiting Camry, he revved the engine and did a tight one-eighty, peeling off back up the winding trail toward the exit of the cemetery grounds.

A light rain was still falling as he pulled into the brick-paved courtyard of the Dominican Sisters Convent grounds adjacent to the hospital. It was just as he remembered it: that protected, cloistered, back-in-time, medieval feel. Parking as close as possible to the rear building, he got out and approached its large, red, wood double door, the one with the small speakeasy peephole door. He went to knock, but held back for a moment, wondering if he was doing the right thing.

How is she going to help? What does she know about this...time-travel thing? Maybe...I can talk just talk around it. See if she picks up on it.

John rapped lightly on the door, then listened and waited.

No response.

Just then he noticed a small sign posted below a button to the right of the door: "Please Ring for Service."

He pressed the button.

Still nothing.

He looked at his watch: 5:10 p.m.

"Hmm, maybe they're taking their evening meal."

He pressed the button again, and knocked a second time.

Still no reply.

"Oh, well, three strikes, I'm out."

Just as he was turning to leave, he heard the slow creak of the speakeasy door opening.

"Yes, young man. What can I do for you?"

John knew the voice. Unmistakable! It was the Reverend Mother Marguerite D'Esprit! He introduced himself, recalling their previous first encounter five weeks ago. He said he needed advice, a confidante to talk to, it was urgent; would she be so kind to give him a few minutes of her time?

There was a moment of silence, and then…"Yes, my child. Please, just give me a moment."

John waited. A slight breeze, amplified by the narrow confines of the courtyard, stirred up some newly fallen leaves, adding them to a growing pile of debris trapped against an inside corner of the outer stone wall.

Creeeeak! The large red door opened slowly. John paused a moment, then stepped gingerly inside, closing the door behind him. He found himself in a small, candlelit room, its walls paneled in rich mahogany. It had a warm, woody feel to it and he had an immediate, strong sense of *déjà vu*. Directly to his front was an intricately carved wooden privacy screen which, except for a small passageway to the right, blocked further entry to the room. Yes, he knew this place. It was the room of his dreams!

There's a table and Ouija board on the other side, he thought, but then quickly dismissed the notion as patently absurd.

"Please, come no further," spoke a gentle, unseen voice from behind the screen. "You may have a seat, if you like."

As John's eyes became acclimated to the dim light, he noticed a chair to his right. He sat down.

"So, you have something urgent to discuss?" the gentle voice asked in soft tones just above a whisper.

John shifted his weight in the chair. "Yes, ma'am, er…sister…I mean, Your Reverence. You once said, if ever we were in need, that help was just a prayer away."

Pause.

"Yes, my child. God answers all prayer. In His own manner, and in His own time."

John thought. *In his own time?*

"Reverend Mother, would it not be a good thing if 'God's own time' included past time as well as present and future time?"

Pause.

"Past time is for learning, child. The present is for doing. And the future…the future is a time for hope fulfilled, God's will revealed."

John struggled with this. "And when is the time for healing, for setting things aright?"

"God is ever willing and ready to forgive. But you must be willing to forgive yourself for the healing process to begin. That, my son, is truly the hard part."

John deliberated carefully before responding. "Mother, wouldn't it be nice if it were possible to…go back in time, to fix past mistakes, to make things right?"

"Hmm, perhaps. But wouldn't that make things much too easy?" she replied. "Life would be no more than a hit and miss, trial and error affair. Cheapen the act of forgiveness, the quest for perfection."

"But, do you think such things may be possible…if God willed it so?"

Pause.

"I cannot say what is possible for man, but only that for God all things are possible. However, I cannot offer you false hope, my son." She breathed a sigh and continued along a different line. "While I do believe that God is all knowing, what he chooses to reveal, to whom, and how is totally His prerogative, at His own discretion, whether in dreams, visions, or engraved on cold, hard, stone tablets."

Dreams, visions, hard stone tablets. Yes, John knew all about those things!

"Hard stone tablets," he repeated. "You mean, like tombstones?"

"Why, yes, I suppose."

Another pause.

"Please, tell me, my son, exactly what is bothering you?"

John finally opened up, telling Mother Marguerite about his dreams, his visions of time travel, his regrets and feelings of guilt over the loss of Becky, his dad, and now most recently, Doug. She listened patiently, sympathetically. Indulging his seeming preoccupation with time travel, she confessed her own fascination with modern scientific thought on relativity and quantum theory, time travel, and the ultimate nature of things, right down to the *God particle* sought by men of science.

"I believe that science and religion will ultimately converge on the same universal truths," she offered, "while approaching it, perhaps, from seemingly opposing starting points of view."

"So, what *is* that universal, converging truth?" John asked.

Mother Marguerite responded without hesitation. "Love. Compassion, my son. A shared consciousness and oneness with the Creator."

John smiled. "Sounds nice. Kind of like…a unified field theory of the spirit!"

Mother Marguerite gave a little laugh. "Yes, I suppose you could say that."

John thought about the time machine in Bob's basement, the seeming randomness of objects floating in space taking on perfect geometric harmony when viewed from the *crux of time*…the unique God perspective, perhaps, where time lines converge and all things are revealed.

"…'Then and now the same at last'!" he said under his breath.

"The *Alpha* and the *Omega*," she added.

"Wha- What?"

"God's view on time, my son. As stated in scripture, God is timeless— no beginning and no end."

On leaving the convent, John felt relieved and unburdened. He came away not with definitive answers, but with a newfound hope and purpose, and perhaps that was enough, replacing the feelings of guilt he had carried with him like so much weighted baggage all these many years. While not expressly stated, his exchange with Mother Marguerite confirmed what he already knew: that somehow he had to get back to eighteenth-century Greenwich to avert certain tragedy that would befall young Rebecca Whitman. Only problem was, he hadn't a clue how he was going to do it— not without the help of those obnoxious, green-headed flying monsters, whose populations now lay dormant for the winter season in the tidal marshes of the Delaware Bay.

Jumping into his Camry, John continued on to Haddonfield. First stop: the Haddonfield Police Station, with more annoying questions and forms to sign. But this gave him the opportunity to read the full police report, including the accounts of eyewitnesses. One eyewitness account from a Mrs. Fleming, a chance passerby, was especially disturbing:

> Police Officer: "Did the victim say anything else before falling from the roof?"
> Mrs. Fleming: "Oh, yes. He said something about being 'cursed,' and 'having to go back and save her,' or something like that…"

John's heart nearly skipped a beat. "What the—!?"

Taking a moment to collect himself, he tried to rationalize the statement to the interrogating police officer. "Yes, well, he did have an older sister. Maybe he thought she needed help, or something. Or maybe just his delusional state of mind."

The police officer nodded absently.

Interrogation over, John headed over to his office on Tanner Street to check on things. Mary would probably be gone for the day, but he did want to check his e-mail and phone messages.

The words in the police report came back over and over again to haunt him: "Cursed! Gotta get back to save her!" What the hell? How did Doug know about that?

He then asked himself the million dollar question: Okay, buddy boy, you need the flies to go back; the flies are gone for the winter; so, where are you going to get live adult greenhead flies this time of year, out of season?

As expected, everyone was gone when he reached the office. A legion of sticky notes in assorted rainbow colors covered his desk calendar pad, Mary's favorite form of communication ever since the 3M Company unleashed them on the office world. At least half had to do with recent events surrounding Doug's accident and the missed calls from Katie. John took the important notes and pasted them in his day planner as reminders, just below the "BEVS" anagram he doodled during his last meeting at GenAvance:

B aculovirus
E xpression
V ector
S ystem

He then dialed up his voice mail for the latest unheard messages. The last message was from his brother:

"Hi, John. Your brother Matt here. Listen, John, I'm sorry to say I'm gonna hafta postpone our planned trip back east. Turns out Sam, your godchild and favorite nephew, has decided to vacation with his girlfriend, Beverly, and her family before heading back to school in the fall…"

"That's weird," John said scratching his head. "That's an old message I thought I deleted. How'd it end up with my new messages?"

He let the message run out: "…Sorry, but you know how it is. He's just got Bev on the brain! Anyway, give me a call when you get in. And give Mom a hug and a kiss for me. Later."

"Bev on the brain!" John repeated aloud. He glanced down at his notes again: BEVS. Suddenly, the lights came on in his head.

"Yes! Of course! BEV'S on the brain! That's it!"

John fumbled with his cell phone and dialed in Dr. Paul Fielding's number.

Rring…Rring…Rring…Click.

"Hello. Doctor Fielding. County Medical Examiner's Office."

John exhaled. "Paul! It's me. John."

"Oh, John. Hey, I'm glad you called. Listen, about the autopsy—"

But John didn't let him finish. "Paul, I need your professional help, and may need you to pull a few strings for me. Are you okay with that?"

"Well, er, sure, John. As long as it's legal. I'm guessing this has something to do with Doug?"

"Yes, unfortunately."

John proceeded to explain his theory of Doug's demise, about the greenhead flies, the recombinant baculovirus research, that strange form of schizophrenia endemic to the region where Doug grew up, and Dr. Alexander's genetic theory of mitochondrial DNA transmission through the female line.

"Whoa, that's quite a theory, John. You got anything to back it up?"

"No, but you do, Paul. Doug's brain. I need a sample of Doug's brain tissue to send to Doctor Li at GenAvance. They can confirm the presence of baculovirus particles."

There was a moment's pause. "I see. Well, if what you say is true, John, then the CDC may have to be informed. This could be a significant finding impacting public health."

John was afraid he'd say that.

"Paul, can't that wait until we determine for ourselves if the virus is present or not? Don't want to create an unnecessary scare."

Another pause.

"Okay, John. I'll give you the brain specimen. If you'll sign for it."
"Done!"

Chapter 32

1999
Sat, 30 October

It had been a busy week for John, making final burial arrangements for Doug and following up with Jennifer at GenAvance for special tests to be run on Doug's brain tissue specimens. She hesitated at first, but John was able to convince her of the importance of running these tests. After all, if BV virus particles were found, it could change the course of their research and even threaten to shut them down once the CDC caught wind of it. Not that they were responsible for Doug's contracting the virus, but they could not dismiss the possibility that their proprietary strain of virus was related somehow to the one responsible for a particular form of mental illness endemic to this region since the late eighteenth century—the so-called "curse" of Greenwich. After all, they both appeared to share a common vector of transmission: the greenhead fly. And not just any greenhead fly, but their prized *Tabanus nigrovittatus Cohansis*, the same greenhead Tabby strain that sent John packing back to eighteenth-century Cumberland County.

There was just one more thing. Recalling his recent telephone conversation with Dr. Alexander from Lakeland, John contacted Dr. Paul Fielding to request tissue samples be taken from Doug's remains for DNA testing.

"So, let me get this straight," Paul replied. "You want me to test his *mitochondrial*, not nuclear, DNA?"

"That's right, Paul. It's like I said, Dr. Alexander believes there's a genetic link through the female bloodline, passed on through the mother's mitochondrial DNA. Can you do it?"

"Sure, that's no problem, John. Should I send the results to Dr. Alexander?"

"Yes, if you wouldn't mind. I'll alert the doctor that it's coming."

But John didn't stop there. When he phoned the doctor at Lakeland, he further arranged to have Bob's blood, and his own blood tested for m-DNA matching as well. Dr. Alexander was only too willing to oblige.

John finally succeeded in contacting Doug's older sister, Teresa, on Monday evening. She had just returned from a concert tour of the Pacific Rim with her heavy metal rocker boyfriend. John met her for the first time at the gravesite early Wednesday morning when Doug was laid to rest in the Weston family plot at Harleigh Cemetery. She appeared visibly shaken by the latest turn of events—or maybe it was just the jet lag. In any event, she had no problem with John's taking charge of things, and expressed her sincere appreciation for the gravesite.

"I don't know what I would have done," she confessed. "Probably just...cremation. I'm so glad Doug had a friend to turn to."

Family would've been better, John thought.

"Yes, I only wish I could have done something to avert this sad outcome. Doug was a fine young man."

And so would read the words on his modest tombstone:

> Here lays a fine young man
> Too soon lost
> Too late found.

On Friday John alerted Mary that he would be taking Monday off. He was planning to get away for the weekend and thought he may decide to stay over.

"Don't forget Sunday is Halloween," she reminded him.

"Oh, right. Well, I may just have to get dressed up and go trick-or-treating, or something," he said with a grin.

He then noticed Mary's Afghan folded neatly and lying on the credenza nearby. "So, how did your rework go?" he asked, nodding toward the credenza.

"Oh, you mean the Afghan."

Mary reached for the Afghan and held it up for inspection. "Ta-da! See, wha'did I tell you! All fixed and rewoven. All it needs now is the border."

John picked up and studied the Afghan carefully, gently feeling the rewoven pattern with his fingertips. "You're right. A seamless fix. Great job. Can't tell where the old ends and new begins."

Mary smiled as he handed her back the Afghan. "So, where are you going for the weekend?" she asked.

"Oh, I don't know. Someplace where I can start doing some...reweaving of my own," he replied with a touch of mystery in his voice.

Back at his desk, John made a list of things he was going to need for the task: a portable, rechargeable drill and ¾" drill bits; saber saw; keyhole handsaw; bolt cutters; glass cutters; duct tape; an arm-length, right-handed rubber glove (clear up to the elbow); window screening; wood framing materials; ¼" plywood; three pull-handle vacuum suction cups; a sheet of neoprene rubber; a small CO_2 fire extinguisher (the kind you might keep in your kitchen or auto); a set of night vision goggles; and, oh yes, two out-of-state license plates from Bob's plate collection, which covered the back wall of his garage.

After a quick call to Katie, John made final arrangements to stop by the house Saturday morning to borrow the tools on his list from Bob's basement shop and garage. The license plates and pull-handle suction cups would come from Bob's garage—Bob used the cups for body work, pulling out dents and lifting auto glass. John would pick the building materials up from the nearest Home Depot. He already had the night vision goggles covered. Friday evening he stopped by his amateur astronomer friend's home in Runnemede for a nice pair of flip-up binocular goggles that he used for stargazing.

"I'm taking my six-inch Meade to the country this weekend to do some serious stargazing," John explained. He promised Sean that he'd have them back by Wednesday at the latest.

Saturday afternoon found John in his home basement, busy assembling a small cage measuring roughly 18" on each side. The front, back, and bottom were constructed of solid ¼" plywood; the top and two sides were open frames covered with window screening. On the front end, he fashioned a hinged door that swung open to the inside; on the back end, were two round openings, side by side, each one just large enough to fit a man's fist. The right opening was sealed with a thick sheet of neoprene rubber forming a kind of drumhead covering. Through the upper port he inserted the long rubber glove, securing and sealing its open sleeve end against the round opening, which effectively turned the cage into a glove box. He stood back and studied his work.

"Needs just one more thing."

John cut two, 2¼" diameter circular openings near the top two corners of the front panel, each hole just large enough to snuggly fit the two pull-handle suction cups that were secured with epoxy and positioned with their handles inside the cage, their cups laying flush with the outside surface of the panel. A makeshift handle placed on the top completed the glove box's construction.

Setting the cage aside, he proceeded to load a large gym bag with the tools he would need: keyhole saw, bolt cutters, duct tape, glass cutter, night vision goggles, latex gloves, a screw driver, and the license plates from Bob's garage. From his bedroom closest he added a ski mask, then took the bag and placed it in the trunk of his rented Celebrity, which he had picked up just that morning from a local car rental agency. A small, wooden, three-step painter's ladder he had picked up from a local thrift store earlier in the week—didn't want any telltale store tag or serial number giving him away—lay folded next to the gym bag.

After washing up and changing into a pair of black jeans and a dark sweatshirt, John adjourned to his study to make his final plans. He took a map of the Rutgers University New Brunswick campus from his middle desk drawer and laid it out flat across his desk. With a snifter of brandy in one hand and an orange fluorescent marker in the other, he studied the map carefully and began highlighting a path through the campus, ending with a circle drawn around a small square, labeled *Shockley Research Labs.*

"Should get there before dark to reconnoiter the area," he strategized. "If nothing has changed, the rear of the building is not well lit, and my window of opportunity"— giving a little self-congratulatory chuckle—"is partly concealed by the bushes."

John smiled as he raised his glass of brandy. "Mischief night! Well, here's to my little plan of mischief!" and he quaffed the remaining brandy.

John had left little to chance. The previous Saturday, just one day after Doug's demise, the wheels were already turning in his head. That evening he visited the campus to get the lay of the land and check on night security in and around the targeted research building. On Tuesday, he arranged to meet with Julie Evert at Shockley Labs, ostensibly to review plans for the new pilot plant, but in fact to evaluate internal building security measures and develop plans of his own. From inside, he noted the location of the outside windows, covered in drywall. Two of the window locations were obstructed with biosafety cabinets, but the middle one was located above an open lab bench. *Perfect! I can step in right down onto the lab bench from the outside.*

It was almost four o'clock when he finally set out Saturday afternoon. Traveling north on the Jersey Turnpike, traffic was relatively light, so he made good time, reaching exit nine in just under an hour, with plenty of daylight to spare. He knew that what he was about to do was, well, wrong and against the law, but if everything went right, no one would get hurt, he rationalized, and maybe no one would need ever know—not for a while at least.

Not far past the Hilton Conference Center he picked up US Route 1 South, drove two miles, and took a right onto College Farm Road into the heart of Cook College campus. Following the highlighted path on his map, he wound his way to the far side of campus to a quiet off-campus side street and parked the car. Checking to be sure no one was watching, he took the two out-of-state license plates from Bob's garage and quickly changed out the plates on his rental vehicle.

Climbing back into the car and continuing on, he made a left onto Grays Avenue, then another left into the driveway of the research complex. There it was just ahead at last: Shockley Research Laboratories, the second of four buildings just off the parking to the right.

But instead of turning into the parking lot this time, he continued straight back down the narrow drive past the end building—the Vivarium— and looped around behind, bringing him to the rear of the laboratory. Here the area was fairly confined, isolated and off the main track, serving mainly as a receiving and utility service area for Shockley and two other nearby research buildings. Being Saturday evening, things were pretty quiet, the only noise coming from some kids playing in a public playground to the rear of the complex on the other side of the tall cyclone security fence. But where John planned to make his entry, he was well out of sight of any prying neighborhood eyes.

John studied the backside of Shockley. Yup, there were the three windows, just as he remembered them: double-hung, single-pane secured with padlocked grills on the outside, covered and sealed with drywall on the inside. The middle window, partially concealed by shrubbery, offered the best cover. It was also the one with the open lab bench on the inside. Perfect! Yes, that is where he would make his ninja entry under the cover of darkness. The only challenge would be the outside windowsill height, as the basement's low-laying casement windows elevated the first floor by four feet or so above ground level. That's what the stepladder was for.

For the next few hours John lay low, grabbing a quick bite from a nearby fast food spot. Parking the car on an obscure, residential side street, he took a long walk back through campus as he rehearsed in his mind what he was about to do. He thought about the consequences of failure. If he were caught that would be the end, not just of this adventure, but his career—and his life! *I'd be committed for sure,* he thought.

"So, please tell the jury, Mr. Weston, just how you planned to return to eighteenth-century Cumberland County from the single bite of the greenhead fly."

"Oh no, you got it wrong, judge. Not just one bite. It might take several. Don't know for sure how genetic engineering has altered the psychotropic time traveling effects of the native fly species, Tabanus nigrovittatus. It may take more than one bite."

"I see. So, please tell us, John, why you feel compelled to return to a prior point and place in time."

"Don't you see, doc? I must go back! To save her, to lift the curse, to set things, right. Yes, even to redeem myself!"

Pregnant pause.

The judge pounded his gavel.

"John Weston, the court has no recourse but to award you the maximum sentence for failure to complete your mission: a life time of self-recrimination, anguish, and guilt! Next case!"

It was almost ten o'clock when John returned to Shockley Labs. Two cars remained in the parking, and area lighting was minimal; but there was one, well-lit window on the near end of the building which John found troubling.

"Someone working late on the weekend," he figured, "unless they just forgot to turn off the lights. Damn!"

Discretion being the better part of valor, he decided to head back out to Grays Avenue from a safer vantage point and wait it out. He could still see the lighted window from this distance.

At about five minutes to eleven, the bright light went out, leaving only the soft backlighting of a hallway nightlight.

"Good, now get out of there and go home! Get a life, it's Saturday night, for God's sake!"

A few moments later he heard the rev of a car engine, and within minutes a blue sedan exited the driveway, just a few yards from where he was parked. The driver didn't seem to notice his presence.

John let the sedan pass from view; then took a deep breath. "Okay. Here goes."

He started the engine and pulled slowly forward. Turning into the driveway, he continued slowly toward the research complex, past the parking lot, down the narrowing driveway, and around the Vivarium to the rear of the research building. Good, no one there! Pulling up as close as possible to the research building on his right, he came to a stop by his "window of opportunity," put the car in park, then cut the engine and killed the lights. Reaching down to his left, he pulled the trunk release latch—*Clink*—and watched the trunk lid rise open in his rear view mirror.

"Okay. Showtime!"

From this point on John entered a kind of Zen state where everything played out mechanically, as he remained intently focused on the job at hand. No extraneous thoughts, no more doubts, he knew what he had to do, having rehearsed it many times in his head; and now his mind, body, and soul seemed to meld with his surroundings, taking charge over the obstacles confronting him, like Moses parting the Red Sea.

First, the latex gloves, the stepladder, gym bag, and night vision goggles. The bolt cutters made quick work of the padlock on the window grill, now fully opened on its hinges. The double-hung window presented no problem. It was actually unlatched, so he needn't bother with removing the glass pane. He was able to simply raise the lower window sash.

"Okay, so I won't need the glass cutter and third suction cup after all," he said under his breath, almost disappointed that that it would be so easy.

With the window raised, he came face-to-face with his final obstacle: the layer of drywall that covered the window opening from the inside. Using his cordless drill, he made four ¾" holes located just inside the four corners of the open window. With the keyhole saw, he made three straight cuts through the drywall from one hole to another, across the top, down the left side, and across the bottom. He applied several overlapping strips of duct tape over the entire length of the left vertical cut, then three horizontal strips equally spaced top to bottom in the manner of door hinges. He then made a final vertical cut on the remaining right side to complete the door.

Inserting a finger into one of the corner holes on the right side, John gently pulled on the makeshift trap door until it opened, with little crackling sounds, revealing the dark interior void of the insect lab. The duct tape hinge worked fine. A cool rush of night air swished by him, trying to equalize the slight negative pressure within the room.

John leaned his head into the room to get his bearings. "Dark as a mummy's tomb," he mumbled to himself. "And just as quiet."

But the night vision goggles proved their worth, and he had calculated right: the lab bench lay just before him, mere inches below the opening, and all he had to do was climb in. Stepping back down off the ladder to retrieve his glove box cage, John quickly scanned the area to see if he had been noticed. All was quiet.

"Good! Now comes the tricky part!"

Heading back up the ladder he carefully passed the cage through the opening and laid it on the lab bench, then climbed down inside, being careful not to knock anything off the bench. Looking around the room, everything was pretty much as he remembered—only darker, just the dim glow of instruments and blinking status lights from the incubators and other ancillary lab equipment. Stepping down off the lab bench, he took the glove box cage and headed toward the double door in the back corner of the room—the one marked "Insectarium." That's odd, the door was closed. During all of his daytime visits the door had remained open. Now it was closed. A paralyzing thought gripped his mind. Quickly, he tried turning the door knob.

"Dammit! Locked!"

He wrestled with the knob a few more times, but it was no use. His heart sank. That's when the buzzing sound began, blending with the soft background hum of the AC.

"Oh, shit! What now?" he grimaced. "Got to get hold of myself. Think! Think! Where would I put a set of keys if this were my lab?"

He checked the lab bench drawers. No luck. The buzzing got louder, but as he moved toward the other end of the room, the noise gradually subsided. Walking back past the upright freezer cabinet the buzzing grew louder again.

"Maybe just a bad compressor."

Wishful thinking; he knew that buzzing sound.

"Damn greenhead flies!"

As he approached the freezer cabinet the sound grew louder, and he swore he could hear voices this time, buried deep down in the buzzing sound. The closer he came to the freezer, the more intense were the voices, until he could actually make out the words: "*Save Her! Go Back!*" they said. "*Save Her! Go Back!*"

The sounds and voices filled his head now, becoming almost unbearable. Breaking out in a cold sweat he reached for the freezer door handle, and with one spasmodic jerk popped the door open. There, hanging from a hook on the left inside cabinet wall was a key ring with six keys. It took John a moment to make the connection. Then, as if to keep the keys from suddenly disappearing, like in a dream, he reached out and snatched them off the hook.

Almost instantly the buzzing and voices stopped, fading like a distant echo until they were no more. John removed the night vision goggles and wiped his sweaty forehead, puzzling over what had just happened.

"So, what's this? The voices are my friends? Or, my *Masters*?"

He put the goggles back on and moved over to the locked door of the Insectarium. Holding his breath he tried each key. The sixth and last key was the charm. "Yes!" He breathed a deep sigh of relief.

Retrieving the glove box cage from the lab bench he headed into the insect room with its floor-to-ceiling, wall-lined, glass-faced terrariums harboring the lab's precious stock of greenhead flies. Suddenly, he had a sick, sinking feeling in the pit of his stomach as the reality of what he was about to do actually hit him:

"So, you're planning to hijack these flies so you can do what?"

"No, I need just a few, really. They'll never be missed. You heard what Dr. Evert said: they just let the adult flies live out their lives once they've delivered their first brood. It's the 'humane' thing to do, right, Jim? So, I'm just providing added purpose to their spent lives. Don't know how much longer they've got to live anyway. So, I better take plenty…"

Inserting his right hand into the glove of his glove box and placing the front face of the cage up against the safety glass of one of the terrariums, John aligned the cage door with the stainless steel port on the terrarium and activated the two corner vacuum suction cups from inside. Great! They held firm with no problem. He then opened the cage door from inside and unlatched the port which opened into the terrarium, directly connecting the two interiors. Now, how to coax the adult flies into his cage?

John took the small CO_2 fire extinguisher from his gym bag of tricks and released a small cloud of CO_2 into his cage. Nothing happened at first. Then, after a few minutes, some of the more curious members of the greenhead fly community began hanging around the opening. He gave it another spritz and smiled as one of the more curious flies venture inside his cage.

"Gotcha!"

Soon the first fly was followed by another, and then another, until John began to lose count.

"Amazing! It really works!"

He had been listening well and taking notes when Julie Evert described how the greenhead fly was attracted to the breath of warm-blooded animals, like livestock. "It's the carbon dioxide in their exhaled breath," she had explained.

When he figured he had enough flies, he reached in with his gloved hand, closed and re-latched the doors, and broke the vacuum on the two suction cups, one at a time, releasing the cage from its docked position. He looked up at the clock on the wall: a few minutes past midnight. Not bad.

"Now, to get out of here without being noticed."

After taking quick inventory of the tools in his gym bag, he zipped it up and headed for the lab bench window and gently lowered the cage to the ground with a tied length of rope, followed by the gym bag. Taking one last look back into the room, he suddenly remembered. "Oh, shit! Forgot to return the keys."

But he had already removed his night vision goggles. He thought he knew the way in the dark, but wound up slamming into a lab cart sitting in the middle of the room. The sound of broken glassware reverberated through the lab.

"Dammit!"

Well, so much for leaving the scene of the crime undisturbed.

Groping for the freezer cabinet door, John returned the keys to where he found them, and then carefully retraced his steps to the lab bench window. His heart was racing now. That Zen feeling was wearing off and the reality of what he had done was sinking in.

Climbing back out the window, he groped for the step ladder with his feet, found it, then turned and resealed the drywall opening with duct tape and closed the window, leaving it the way he'd found it. That's when he heard the distant sound of an approaching vehicle. Couldn't tell exactly where it was coming from, or how far away it was. With heart racing he doubled his efforts to return everything to the car trunk, then climbed in behind the wheel and listened. The vehicle was definitely closing in from the direction of the Vivarium and would be turning the corner of the building any second now. Too late to start the engine without drawing attention, so he decided to "play dead." Pushing his driver's seat back as far as it could go, he crouched down low in the floor well and assumed a fetal position, his head butting up against the console, becoming virtually invisible in the shadows to any casual passerby.

The vehicle—sounded more like a truck—approached him from behind, slowed down and idled for a moment. After what seemed like an eternity it slowly pulled away toward a loading dock on the far end of the building where it came to rest. He heard the truck door open and slam, and then another, followed by muffled human voices and activity, sounding like trash cans being handled. After a few more minutes, John heard two more door slams, and then the sound of the truck pulling away, apparently exiting the far end of the building area through a service exit.

John exhaled. It seemed like he had been holding his breath the whole time. The sound of the truck faded slowly into the distance and was soon gone.

John waited. Five minutes passed.

Slowly, he lifted his aching body from its cramped position and peaked out the window. The coast seemed clear.

Sitting up behind the wheel he put the key in the ignition and started the engine. Slowly backing up and turning around, he headed back around the Vivarium the way he had come. The driveway leading from the complex stretched long and forbidding before him, but he resisted the urge to gun the engine. On finally reaching the exit, he stopped, looked both ways and made the right turn onto Grays Avenue.

Home free at last! With at least a dozen living, adult greenhead flies to his credit.

Chapter 33

1999
Sun, 31 October
Halloween

Braaaat! John's radio alarm clock woke him with a jolt, rescuing him from a bad dream.

"Jesus!"

It was one of those "fire starter" dreams again, the one with the pretty lady in the floating orb. John sat up and looked at the clock: 9:00 a.m.

It was six hours ago when John had finally arrived back home from his midnight raid of Dr. Evert's laboratory. Even that seemed like a dream, now. The entire ride home was spent checking his rearview mirrors for the blinking red lights of a state police cruiser. In his rush to get away he had forgotten to change back the license plates on his Celebrity rental, which he finally did at the first rest stop on the Jersey Turnpike. But that was after the toll booth. He just hoped the surveillance cameras didn't catch him.

After checking the condition of his booty—the flies were all doing well, thank you, feeding on fresh sugar water—John jumped in the shower and got himself ready. It was going to be another long day.

First things first, he returned the car rental—didn't want that "hot" vehicle hanging around any longer than it had to—and stashed the bogus license plates in his basement for the time being. He wasn't so sure about ever returning them to Bob's garage—no need to risk implicating his friend any more than he already had.

Pulling a hanger from his closet clothes rack and removing the sheer plastic dry cleaner's wrap, he held the garment at arm's length for close inspection.

"Nice! As good as the day it came from the tailor."

It was John's colonial costume, the one he used as tour guide—or *docent*—at the Indian King Tavern. Complete with knee britches, cotton shirt, and waistcoat, all authentically hand stitched with carved bone and ivory buttons, with a little gold trim thrown in, but not too ostentatious. A three-corner hat completed the ensemble. He didn't want to arouse suspicion, so if he was going back to colonial Greenwich, he would do it this time as a colonial, and being it was Halloween, there was no chance he would arouse any twentieth-century suspicions.

From his special metal lockbox—the one labeled "Artifacts"—John removed the handful of coins he had kept there, those remaining from his previous trip to eighteenth-century Greenwich, and placed them in a leather purse tucked away in his right pants pocket.

Now, there was just one more thing to do. Going to his study John sat down at his rolltop desk, removed a blank sheet of parchment paper from the top right-hand drawer, and laid it down before him. From the bottom drawer he removed a glass bottle of black ink and an authentic goose quill. With a penknife he carefully sharpened the tip of the quill and cut a small slit at its point, turning it into a functioning eighteenth-century pen. Pausing a moment, he opened the carved wood jewelry box sitting on his desk and removed one of the letters addressed to "My Dearest" and signed "J.J.," dated 22 October (no year given) and read it to himself:

22 October

My Dearest Missy,

Alas! Like a ship in unchartered waters we are jostled about by the vagaries of fortune, both good and bad. Our course, though well intentioned, is as uncertain as flotsam upon the whimsical seas of the gods. I dare say, events have taken a dour turn in this southern colony. Our business associate and good friend, Mr. Stewart, whose kindness and long-suffering I owe my very sustenance these past months, has just of late fallen upon severe misfortune. I must remain here to assist him by whatever means avails me, to soften the blow and tend to his recovery. His missus also ails, suffering from a form of consumption which prevails in these maritime climes. Events, I fear, have overtaken us. Please convey to my brother, when opportunity presents itself, my sincere wishes for a speedy and successful conclusion to our enterprise.

Pray he abstains from any dealings in that detestable weed, dare I utter the word "tea," which has so ruined the fortunes of honorable men as to be avoided like the plague, which contagion I am told is soon to visit upon your fair village! Please be warned that a consignment of the King's tea bound for these colonies is soon to foul our shores, even the very port of Greenwich itself!

I will next write when opportunity presents itself
as to when we might be united again, which it pains me to
say may not be until well into the New Year.
With my undying love and devotion

J.J.

The letter was one of many from the prized family collection of love
letters which had been preserved down through the generations of Westons
from colonial times to the present. The other family heirloom was the journal,
or ledger, that his five-times great-grandfather, Bartholomew Weston, had
kept of the family business. John had spent the past week going through
every letter and every journal entry, looking for some cross-reference that
would provide contextual evidence identifying where, when (the year), and
under what circumstances the letters were written.

The first thing he noticed was that the letters were signed either "Jay-
Bird" or "J.J.," depending on the content of the letter. Letters of a more
personal, affectionate nature were always signed "Jay-Bird"; those simply
reporting events or business dealings were signed "J.J." They were all
addressed to *My Dearest Missy*, who John now knew to be the lovely Miss
Rebecca Whitman.

But it was Thursday evening when the real breakthrough came with the
letter of 22 October and several journal entries dated 1774. He was amazed
that his dad and Aunt Dee had failed to make the connection.

The journal entries made reference to a "Mr. Stewart" or "Anthony
Stewart," a business associate and fellow sea trading merchant living and
operating a mercantile business in Annapolis, Maryland. These entries
spanned a period of time from 3 July to 8 November, 1774, and the reference
to a Mr. Stewart in J.J.'s letter of 22 October matched this same time frame.
Checking his notes from his conversation with Miss Grady, the Cumberland
County historian, John further connected the burning of the *Peggy Stewart* in
October of that same year, which tied everything together.

So, young John Weston must have been in Annapolis working with
Mr. Stewart when the ship burning took place. What's more, the letter of 22
October appears to have been the final communication between John and
Rebecca before the tragic events of 22 December claimed her life. While
other letters bore November and December dates, their context obviously
placed them in prior years.

Laying the letter to the left of the blank parchment paper, John picked
up the quill pen, dipped it in the ink, and began to carefully pen a letter of his
own, pausing frequently to study the handwriting on the left.

It was almost twelve noon when John finished his one-page letter. He
studied it one more time, comparing it to the writing on the left. Nodding his

approval, he carefully folded the letter and placed it in an improvised envelope of brown paper, wrapped and sealed with string and notary hot sealing wax.

"There, I suppose that might pass for a genuine eighteenth-century epistle to the untrained eye."

Now, all there was left to do was pack up and hit the road. The weather was promising, partly cloudy with just a mild chill in the air, but no rain in the forecast. John packed a change of clothes in a canvas knapsack and placed the letter in one of its button-down pouches. He put the knapsack and the cage with the greenhead flies on the back seat of his tan Camry, a retractable utility knife in the glove compartment with the maps, and a small cooler of Gatorade on the front passenger seat before finally heading out.

John took the quick route to Greenwich this time, heading down Route 55 past Glassboro, where he picked up Route 553 over to Bridgeton. This was a particularly scenic and little-trafficked route, with mile after mile of rich farmland and quaint crossroad villages like Olivet and Centerton. It was easy to see why New Jersey had been coined the "Garden State." An anachronism, cruising along at 60 mph in his stylish eighteenth-century Ben Franklin suit, John just had to smile. He popped a CD of his favorite new indie rock band, The Gantry, into the console player and scanned forward to *Green Eyes*, a tune which had taken on special meaning in recent months:

> …You were the same girl, I knew back in high school when
> And you had those Green Eyes, killing all the young boys' pride
> And I can hear your old laugh, with those hips that matched the lips
> And I didn't know you, but I heard that you just died
> And floated away…[16]

Passing through Bridgeton, John noticed that things began to look familiar. Continuing down Bridgeton-Greenwich Road for another six miles brought him once again into that abandoned part of town that had greeted him on his first encounter with Greenwich in September. As he came into town, it appeared that nothing had changed, except those majestic trees bordering Ye Greate Street, which had lost half their leaves to the shorter days of autumn—and, oh yes, those greenhead flies were nowhere to be found!

---

[16] Kevin Goldhahn, "Green Eyes," *Years and Years*, compact disc recorded by The Gantry, copyright 2012 by Kevin Goldhahn. Reprinted with permission.

Turning right onto Ye Greate Street, John had no chance of getting lost this time, as he pretty much knew his way around town by now and knew exactly where he had to go. Continuing slowly down the wide boulevard past the crumbling remains of the once-thriving colonial village, John sensed a vitality that had eluded him on his first visit to this ghost town. Maybe it was the rush of adrenaline and the hope of what lay before him, or perhaps just the fear of failure. After all, he really didn't know for certain if the flies in his cage had retained the ability to transport him back in time. Maybe that was a one-time deal. Maybe these laboratory specimens had been genetically engineered to the point of losing their transcendent power of time travel. Well, he had to try at least. It was his only hope of restoring the past, of setting things right.

Passing that handsome two-and-a-half-story red brick mansion, he remembered how it looked over two hundred years ago: candles in the windows, smoke rising from the chimney, a white picket fenced-in yard—a genuine Courier & Ives picture postcard image.

Coming up on his right now were the dilapidated hollow shell remains of the Stone Tavern, overgrown with dried bramble and sumac. John pulled over and came to a stop in front of the tavern, then turned off the engine, put the keys in his pocket, and took a deep breath.

"Okay, I'm ready for this," he said, trying to convince himself, like someone about to undergo open heart surgery.

Grabbing the utility knife and duct tape from the glove compartment, John got out and looked around, studying the area for possible passersby. There was no one this time, no prepubescent boy on a bicycle going down to the bay to do some fishing. John was alone.

He removed the cage from the back seat and placed it on the ground with the glove ports facing him. With the utility knife he made a careful incision, top to bottom, in the rubber diaphragm covering the opening beside the glove port; then, he made another cut, left to right, turning the diaphragm into a penetrable port with four folding, self-closing flaps.

"Okay, here goes."

After taking a healthy swig of thirst-quenching Gatorade he proceeded to roll up his left sleeve and slowly penetrated the diaphragm port with his hand until his bare forearm was fully inside into the cage.

It didn't take too long for the flies to react, as they were thirsty too—for warm blood!

The first fly to alight went for his wrist. John watched and felt the pinch of its mouth parts, the oozing of blood. It was all he could do not to flinch and retract his arm, but he held fast. A second joined the first, choosing a more tender spot on the back of his hand. A third and fourth fly soon followed. John wondered how many it would take, how many was enough—or too much, perhaps! Could he OD on the venom from these pernicious pests? After taking the bite from a fifth fly, John figured that had to be enough.

"Okay. You've had your fun. Bet you've never feasted like that back in Doctor Evert's lab!"

John gently shook the flies away and pulled his hand from the cage, allowing the rubber flaps to close behind. He tore off a strip of duct tape and pasted it across the hand port, sealing off the flaps just to be sure no flies escaped.

As he knelt there he began to feel a little woozy—just like the first time. He took another swig of Gatorade and that seemed to help.

Before returning the cage to the car, John was careful to replenish the feeder with some fresh sugar water.

"There. That should hold them till I get back, whenever that is."

That's when a small white dot appeared at the center of his vision. The spot began to grow.

"Okay. Haven't got much time."

He grabbed the knapsack and slung it on his back, then finished off the Gatorade in just a few gulps.

The spot grew larger and brighter as that old familiar buzzing sound began to fill his head. He knew what was coming; it had all happened before, only this time things were moving much faster. John stumbled forward, feeling for the car door as the white spot became a blinding light, obscuring his entire field of vision. Shoving the car doors closed, the buzzing in his head grew louder, followed by the sound of bells—and the voices, loud growling voices.

"Good boy, John! Good boy!" they repeated over and over again.

Groping for his car keys, he pushed the lock button twice, but couldn't hear the confirming click or car horn. The sounds in his head were crowding out everything from the real world, a cacophony of buzzing flies, clanging bells…and the voices! He instinctively cupped his hands over his ears, but it was of no use; the sounds were coming from within. Growing faint, he fell to his knees, his vision now totally consumed by white light.

"Just a little bit longer," he struggled. "Gotta hold out just a little longer!"

Then, in a flash his arms gave way—and all consciousness was gone.

When John regained his senses, he found himself standing outside the old Stone Tavern under the same starry, winter night sky that had greeted him on his first trip into eighteenth-century Greenwich. There was Orion, shining high and bright in the southern sky. The voices and buzzing in his head were gone. The blinding white light, all pain and discomfort—gone! He looked around for his car. That was gone, too. No surprise.

This time he knew where he was, and *when* he was—and where it was he had to go. As he set out down Ye Greate Street in the direction of the river and wharf he had to smile. He almost forgot how easy it was to move around in this anonymous, altered state. It was earlier in the evening this time and he was glad of that. He was hoping to see events at the wharf as they happened, before that mob of colonials in Native American dress appeared on the scene.

There was that same handsome, two-and-a-half-story, red-bricked mansion on the left, just as he remembered it. The red and blue checkerboard brick Flemish bond patterns seemed more vibrant and detailed than ever before. The candles in the windows flickered bolder and brighter than before.

"Must be the higher dose. Five flies are better than one!"

John continued down Ye Greate Street past closed shops and shuttered homes until he came to the intersection with Maple Street on the left, with the Market Square and open green on the right. Looking down Maple Street he saw a sign for *Mason's Taylor Shoppe and Haberdashery.* He recalled his first out-of-body experience and the mob on Ye Greate Street the night of the warehouse fire, someone shouting out something about a "tea burning," and the "safe hiding" of tea in the tailor's wine cellar.

Continuing past the Market Square he passed the rectory and St. Stephen's Episcopal Church on the left, and not far beyond that, on a rise overlooking the Cohansey River, a massive red brick building looking to be of new construction. A posted sign identified it as the *Orthodox Friends Meeting House.*

The road ended at the ferry and wharf. Nearby stood an elegant, clapboard-framed house, presumably the home of the proprietor and operator of the ferry service. All was quiet, as all business had ceased for the day.

Except…over to the right of the wharf there appeared to be some minor activity in the vicinity of several windowless warehouse structures. Drawing closer John could make out an Appaloosa tied to a post, and the figure of a man standing nearby in the shadows.

Suddenly, John's attention was drawn to the clatter of a horse-drawn carriage coming down the road toward him. He instinctively turned to hide, but quickly recalling his anonymous state, he thought it best to remain in place. The carriage, a fashionable canopied buggy with isinglass windows, drawn by a single horse and driven by a young lady, the carriage's only passenger, pulled up close and came to a stop by one of the warehouse structures.

The young lady exchanged some words with the man, and then dismounted. Drawing nearer, John recognized the man as the same Mr. Paul McKenzie, first mate, whose acquaintance he made at the Stone Tavern during his first journey to eighteenth-century Greenwich.

It was only then that John noticed a third figure lurking in the shadows on the back side of the warehouse, appearing to be that of an older woman, of medium build. John moved to the right to get a better look, and was sure he saw the back end of a farmer's wagon parked there, partly hidden in the tall grass.

Firing up a lantern, Mr. McKenzie unlocked and removed a cross bar from a small side-door entrance to the warehouse, and then accompanied the young woman inside. The only other door to the warehouse—a large double barn door, wide enough to pass a large wagon—was closed and padlocked from the outside. The light of the lantern flickered and shown from inside through the narrow crevices in the outer walls.

Almost immediately the older woman appeared from out of the shadows carrying two small wooden kegs. Proceeding quickly to the side-door entrance, she put down the kegs, then closed and re-barred the door from the outside. Opening one of the kegs, she began pouring its contents along the perimeter of wood-framed structure. That's when John noticed the piles of thatching spread out along the base of the walls: straw, twigs, kindling—anything that could easily burn, obviously prepared in advance. With the first keg depleted, the woman opened the second and continued in the same manner, until the entire perimeter of thatch material was saturated with the liquid.

Disappearing momentarily into the shadows by the wagon, the woman reappeared with a lit torch. By the light of the torch John could now see her face and his heart skipped a beat. It was the face of the old hag, bug-eyed and worn, the same face that had tortured him in visions and dreams. The name Agatha Greene popped into his head, the old woman whom the local Cumberland County historian, Emily Grady, had referred to as the "Town Witch."

So, it was the old "town witch" after all, he realized. And now, as she labored at her evil task, the woman laughed and sang, haltingly humming a little tune, with occasional words interspersed. This was something new. In all his visioning, this was something he hadn't seen or heard before:

"…Come little baby…don't you cry
…Mamma gonna see you…by and by
…And if you die…before I wake
…Destiny…and fire…will seal your fate…"

John now realized the young woman in the warehouse was Miss Rebecca Whitman, the blacksmith's daughter. He tried to get closer, to somehow warn the two inside, but something prevented him from advancing any further. All he could do now was watch as the old woman pranced along, humming and singing, igniting the thatching as she went. Quickly the flames grew and spread up the side walls, lapping at the overhanging roof shingles. John could now hear pounding on the barred door from the inside, and cries for help. He had seen this all before, but from a distance. Now it was up close and personal. He tried closing his eyes, but the flickering orange glow shown through his eyelids. When he next opened his eyes, the entire warehouse was ablaze, and the farm wagon, pulled by two handsome black stallions with white diamond markings on their foreheads, was coming straight at him at a full clip, just yards away, the vapor from the beasts' nostrils gushing forth with the power of a runaway steam locomotive, their eyes glowing red with the reflected light of the growing inferno. In an instant they were upon him, the beasts, the wagon, and old woman passing through him like so much smoke, as a cold-to-the-bone chill racked his soul. Closing his eyes he cried out, "Enough! Take me from this place!"

Immediately, the pulsating orange glow turned to a bright, diffuse white light.

When he next opened his eyes he was standing by a hearth in what appeared to be a modestly appointed colonial kitchen. Nearby two frosted glass globes hung by an open window, through which he could see the naked branches of a maple tree against a gray, winter sky.

At the kitchen table, roughly hewn from half-log timbers, sat a man of middle years, solid frame, with long, unkempt, chestnut-brown hair, his entire countenance and attire evidencing personal neglect. John looked closely at the man. This was the same man he had seen at the churchyard grave site of young Rebecca. He was also the man of his campfire vision—*the curse ritual*—conducted by the young black woman and old Indian chief. He knew him now. This was Thomas Whitman, town blacksmith and father of young Rebecca Whitman.

John watched as Thomas gulped the remaining contents of a pewter mug and threw the empty mug across the table. Wiping his mouth with his sleeve and pausing momentarily, he reached out and picked up a flintlock pistol that lay on the table in front of him, his hands shaking, face covered with beads of sweat. The pistol was half cocked, indicating it was loaded and primed. One shot was all it had. But one shot was all he would need.

Thomas took the pistol in his right hand and positioned the muzzle over his right temple. Taking a deep breath, he pulled the hammer to its full-cocked position, hands trembling.

"Thomas! Please! Do not do this!" a strong but gentle man's voice reverberated from behind.

John turned. There was an old man, a native America Indian, standing in the kitchen doorway. John hadn't heard him entering the room, but now recognized him as the Indian from his visions.

"There is a better way, my friend," the old man said.

"I didn't want you to have to see this, Chief," Thomas stammered weakly as he continued to hold the pistol against his head.

"Then, please, put the pistol down, Thomas. Let us talk together on this."

The Chief's voice was soothing and had an immediate calming effect on Thomas. John was reminded of Mother Superior Marguerite and her soothing, understanding way.

After a moment, Thomas slowly lowered the pistol, unlatched the hammer, and set the loaded pistol on the table in front of him.

"What is there to talk about, Chief? She is gone. My whole world is gone! And it's all my fault! I cannot bear the loss, or the guilt, any longer."

The Chief moved slowly to the table and took a seat next to Thomas. He chose his words carefully. "Thomas, it was not your fault. You had no hand in what happened."

"But, I sent her there, Chief! I sent her to the warehouse that night, and to her death."

"Not true," the Chief was quick to respond. "You sent her to the warehouse with good intent and purpose. Good intent, my friend."

It was as if Thomas hadn't heard. "She is gone. My whole world is gone!" he repeated, sobbing inconsolably. "I cannot bear the loss, or the guilt, any longer."

Chief Dan decided to take a different tack. "Thomas, you have every right to be angry, but not with yourself. It was a senseless tragedy, cold-blooded and deliberate, nothing less. But, you must try to harness your guilt…and your anger. Like a wild stallion, it can be trained."

Thomas regained his composure and turned to his friend. "Trained? You mean, like *vengeance*."

The Chief shrugged his shoulders. "Call it what you like."

Thomas shook his head and leaned forward. "If I only knew who was responsible, I could channel my anger. Call it justice or vengeance; I would serve it up hard and cold."

The Chief took a long, deep breath and began fondling the amulet that hung about his neck. Carved from bone, it bore the symbol of a flame. "Perhaps, my friend, there is something we can do…together," he said.

John's focus remained on the Chief's amulet with its mesmerizing flame symbol. As the Chief rubbed its polished surface with his thumb, the flame began to glow, emitting a white light that grew in intensity, until the entire room was filled with its brilliance, so bright that John had to shield his eyes with his hands.

When the light finally faded, John found himself in a green, open field. Scattered about were various vacant vendor stalls and tents with people cleaning up from an apparent farmers' market morning. Judging from their attire, it seemed to be a warm summer afternoon. Of course, in his transcendent state, John could not feel the warmth, or appreciate the scent of livestock and dying embers from the smokers and barbeque pits. Studying his surroundings a little more closely, he came to realize he was standing in the middle of Greenwich's Market Square.

Suddenly, there came a commotion from behind. John turned to see a wagon pulled by two black stallions recklessly careening across the green at breakneck speed, barely missing several men caught unawares as they were taking down their tents. He could hear the men hollering out after the old woman at the wagon's reins. John looked closely. Yes, it was Agatha Greene, the same woman he had just witnessed setting fire to the warehouse at the wharf, taking the life of young Rebecca Whitman and Paul McKenzie. But that was winter; this was now summer. At least six months had passed since that awful December night. He now recalled the tale of the so-called "Witch Burning," reported by the *Gazette* in the summer of 1775, as told to him by Emily Grady, the county historian.

John carefully approached the wagon as it came to an abrupt halt at the center of the green. Agatha Greene tossed down the reins and braked the wheels, then climbed down and released the team of horses, waving her arms to shoo them away, allowing the team to quickly distance themselves from what they appeared to sense was about to happen. Agatha climbed back up on the wagon and moved to the rear deck, all the while shaking and muttering to herself, gesticulating wildly, caught up in the throes of an argument with unseen persons or things.

John was closer now than anyone else dared to come. He could hear her words, the harsh gravel ramblings of a woman gone mad.

"...Don't go tellin' me what I gotta do!...Don't need no one tellin' me...I know what I got to do...."

And then, from out of nowhere, a low, growling voice, or was it "voices": *"You are cursed! Agatha Greene. Cursed for your sins! You must stand the test of fire! Burn now in life or forever burn in hell!"*

A chill ran up John's spine as he realized he was hearing the same voices that now tormented Agatha Greene! He was being drawn in to her madness! Her ranting continued:

"...Damned! Cursed and abandoned I leave this lonely place! My sweet Destiny, your momma is comin' child...your momma's soon to be comin' to ya!...Wait up for me, child!...I share your fate!...the fate of young Rebecca...she did not deserve...did not deserve...it was the captain, damn him!...his fault...now I must pay...I must pay for his transgressions...yes, he deserted me...now I must pay...but I will not desert you child...no, oh no...my sweet Destiny!"

Now, picking up a small wooden keg from the deck of the wagon, Agatha began to dowse herself with its smelly liquid contents, as several of the townsfolk who had ventured near pulled back in horror. Murmuring among themselves, one lone voice cried out, "Oh my God! She's going to set herself afire!"

Her clothes now totally soaked in the flammable liquid, Agatha stood straight and tall and, looking skyward, announced to the world: "Cursed and abandoned, I leave this lonely place!"

And with a single stroke of flint against hard steel, Agatha Greene went up like a torch, totally engulfed in flames! As the flames rose higher, she remained standing there, arms outstretched and looking skyward, for what seemed to be an eternity, screaming out to the heavens above. It was a bloodcurdling scream, resurrected from John's worse nightmares.

John had seen and heard enough. He closed his eyes and thought hard and fast.

"I must get back to the present!" he said, turning his head from the flaming spectacle before him. "Now!" he commanded.

Immediately, like a blinding supernova from the end of times, the sun grew in size and intensity until his whole world was consumed by its brilliant white light. John closed his eyes as his head began to spin. The screams of agony were replaced by the sounds of buzzing flies, millions of flies, rising to a feverish pitch, becoming as screaming jet engines, until suddenly—nothing!

The vacuum of silence and sudden stillness almost knocked him over, or was it just the return of gravity that weighed him down? Regardless, John welcomed it, and slowly opened his eyes as a warm calm returned to his soul.

Looking around, John was not surprised to find himself once again in the midst of familiar surroundings. *Same place, different time,* he thought. Standing by the road outside the old Stone Tavern, he surveyed his surroundings. Things were just as he'd left them over two hundred years ago: Ye Greate Street and the town of Greenwich, in all its resurrected charm and glory.

A man on horseback trotted leisurely by, tipping his three-cornered hat to John as he passed. John smiled and returned the greeting with a tip of his own three-corned hat. Taking a deep breath of clean eighteenth-century air, John turned and entered the tavern. He was relaxed now, coming to feel almost at home in these once upon a distant time surroundings.

It was mid-afternoon and the establishment had only a few customers, but there was one familiar face that he could not fail to recognize: Mary, the innkeeper's wife. He'd never learned her last name.

"A good day to you…Mary," John announced boldly as he claimed a seat at a table by the window.

Mary looked up from her sweeping chores, studied him for a moment, smiled and returned the greeting in cheerful fashion. "Ahah! Well, if isn't Mr. Weston, the other John Weston! What would be your pleasure, sir?"

"A pint of ale would do just fine, ma'am, thank you," he replied as he removed his knapsack and placed it on the floor by his side.

The missus nodded. "A pint of ale it is, then," she replied. Setting down her broom she made her way to the beer kegs locked safely behind the bar cage.

"So, Mr. Weston, if you are seeking to board the stage, then I am afraid you're a trifle too late. It departed these premises not more than two hours ago. Haddonfield, wasn't that where you were heading?"

"Yes, ma'am, Haddonfield. I must say, you do indeed have a memory for fine detail." They exchanged knowing smiles. "But for today," he continued, "my business *brings* me to Greenwich, not *takes* me away. In fact, I will need lodging for the night, if you have a room available."

"Yes, that can be arranged," she replied.

John then produced an envelope from his knapsack.

"I have a message here for the lovely Miss Rebecca Whitman, the blacksmith's daughter. Do you know where I may find her?"

"Well, I cannot say for sure," she replied as she delivered the pint of ale to John's table, "but you might find her over by Mr. Mason's tailor shop, just off the Market Square on Maple Street, not four furlongs from here. She assists Mrs. Mason about the shop, learning the seamstress trade. You might say she has a fine eye for the needle."

Mary smiled and winked, proud of her little play on words.

John laughed. "Aha! Well played, Mary, well played!" he commended. "And I thank you for the information"—lifting his mug of ale—"and for the fine ale."

"You are quite welcome, Mr. Weston."

From a table in a far back corner of the room, a young man, tall and thin, with long, mousy brown hair, rose to his feet and approached John's table, leaving his two drinking companions behind.

"A good day to you, kind sir. Roger Walker at your service. Begging your pardon, I could not help but overhear your request. If I may be so bold, I am well acquainted with the young lady about whom you inquire. Indeed, we are longtime friends. If you give me the message, I can vouch for its safe delivery."

John studied the young man standing before him. Two rows of crooked, damaged, or missing teeth barely showed through a wide, thin smile. He had an overall deportment bordering on slovenly, which forced John to reject out of hand the notion that this individual could have any relationship at all with Rebecca, other than sharing the same town. Nonetheless, he played along.

"Good friends, you say?"

Roger smiled harder, revealing more evidence of dental neglect.

John thought for a moment "So, tell me, Roger. Are you a betting man?"

Roger cocked his head and squinted, sizing up this strange question. "Well, sir, that depends on the wager," he said finally. "I only bet on sure things."

"Yes, of course. I am sure you do. Now, my good man, I will wager this letter against whatever is in your purse, that I can read the contents of your mind."

Roger smiled and straightened up like a winning cock at a Saturday night cockfight. "Well, that hardly seems like a fair wager, a letter for my purse. But no matter, you would surely lose the wager."

"Well then, you have nothing to lose and everything to gain," John replied. "Am I wrong?"

Roger took a seat at John's table as his two drinking companions joined him from behind. This was shaping up to be the makings of some fine, unexpected entertainment, and they didn't want to miss it.

"If you would match the contents of my purse, then I might consider such a wager," Roger offered.

John feigned careful consideration. "I tell you what I'll do, my young challenging lad…" Reaching into his purse John produced two crowns, six shillings, and a sixpence and laid it on the table on top of the letter. He pretended this to represent only a portion of his purse, but in fact this was all he had. "…If you can match this, I would consider it a sealed wager."

Roger looked back over his shoulder at his two companions, who smiled and nodded approvingly. "Okay. I agree to the wager, Mr.…"

"John Samuel Weston. The senior John Weston.

"Ah, yes, I have heard of you, sir, from a good friend of mine. You are…the other John Weston. I am pleased at last to make your acquaintance."

"Yes, well, lest pleasure and daylight wane, shall we get on with the wager," his more portly drinking companion interjected from behind.

"Ah, Mr. Weston, you must make allowance for my friend, George. He is a man of little manners, and little patience."

John smiled. George just grunted.

"I take no offense," John replied. "That is, if George wouldn't mind serving as witness to the outcome of this wager. Please, have a seat my good friend."

George nodded and took a seat at the table.

John took a piece of parchment paper from his knapsack and asked to borrow a quill and ink from Mary.

"I trust you are versed in the skills of basic arithmetic?" he asked Roger.

Roger nodded. "Yes. I *can* add and subtract," he said condescendingly.

"Well, then," John began, "I bid you to think upon any number at your pleasure."

"Any number?" Roger asked.

"Yes, any number at all. But keep its identity to yourself only…and to George, of course. You may record it on the parchment, but keep it from my sight."

"All right, I have decided upon a number."

"Now, double that number," John continued, "and to that doubled number add the number…*six*."

Roger labored a bit and conferred with George. "It is done," he said at last.

"Now, take one-half the sum of this addition, and reject the other half."

"Whoa! Slow down, sir! I thought you were going to read my mind, and instead you try my patience!"

"Not to worry. We are nearing the end," John reassured him.

Roger began to struggle a little with the math, but George helped him out, double checking the figures.

"Okay. What comes next?" Roger asked looking up from the paper.

"Now, from this half, subtract the number you first thought upon, and record the final number."

"You mean my starting number?"

"Yes. The first number you recorded," John replied nervously.

Finally, Roger looked up for the last time. "All right, I have the final number."

"George, do you concur with the results?" John asked, worried that a single miscalculation would totally ruin the outcome.

"Yes. Everything appears to be in order," replied George.

"Fine! Now, think hard upon the final number, that I may pluck it from your mind."

John placed one hand on Roger's grimy forehead and his free hand over his own eyes to enhance the illusion.

"Ah yes! The number you are now thinking, the final number recorded on the parchment is…the number three!" John announced triumphantly.

George and Roger looked down at the number "3," then back to John.

"How is that possible?" Roger exclaimed. He muttered something about it being by "pure happenstance" that John was able to "guess" the correct number. He then insisted on being given the opportunity to reclaim his bet, double or nothing. John pretended to protest at first, but then "reluctantly" gave in. To vary the outcome, John had Roger add the number *fourteen* to the original doubled number. When John correctly "conjured" the final number, *seven*, Roger was beside himself. Forced to honor the wager, he reluctantly counted out the total sum from his purse and pushed it across the table to John, objecting the whole while, insisting that John must be "in league with the devil himself" to be able to do such things.

John collected his winnings and bid adieu to Roger and his two companions, who were more than eager to part company with the likes of this "miscreant."

John had quadrupled his purse, and now had sufficient funds to cover expenses for the near term. He certainly couldn't depend on the generosity of Jack McElroy, the sea captain who had come to his rescue the last time he was in town. When John asked Mary the whereabouts of Captain Jack, she said he had taken to sea four weeks ago, bound for England, and she didn't expect to see him back in these parts much before year's end.

John recalled Jack's association with his five-times great-grandfather, Bartholomew Weston—"Master Bart" as the good captain referred to him. And the ship, what was its name? Ah yes, the *Richelieu*! That's the name first mate, Paul McKenzie, used.

"So, I assume he is about Master Bart's business," John replied. "And did Mr. Paul McKenzie set sail with him on the *Richelieu*?"

"Of course! He wouldn't set to sea without his first mate, now, would he," she replied, like he should have known this.

John figured the timing was right. Assuming best case sailing conditions, Paul could be back in time to perish in the warehouse fire the night of December twenty-second. And then there was that mob on Ye Greate Street the night of the fire and all that talk of "burning tea," and hiding tea in the cellar of the tailor's shop, "biding its time." Working at the tailor's shop as she did, could Rebecca have gotten caught up in these happenings, leading to her great misadventure and demise?

John thanked Mary for her pleasant company and the fine ale. Then, after paying in advance for one night's lodging, he picked up his knapsack and headed down Ye Greate Street toward Market Square and the tailor shop. It was mid-afternoon, and with any luck he would run into young Rebecca.

When he reached the Market Square, where Maple Ave intersects with Ye Greate Street, John paused awhile to take in the serenity of the place. He knew his history. Even a place like this, seemingly off the beaten path of the main course of history, would not remain untouched by tumultuous events soon to unfold.

"The Revolution will come," he said softly. "Even to this charming, industrious hamlet."

Looking down Ye Greate Street toward the wharf, John thought about the events in his earlier vision, the warehouse fire the night of December twenty-second, the *winter solstice*, just as described in Bob's crazy quatrains. Maybe there was something he could do to stave off the events of that terrible night. He thought about setting fire to the warehouse himself, tonight; then there would be no warehouse for Rebecca and Paul to meet in on the night of the twenty-second! Right? Wrong! They could easily have the warehouse rebuilt between now and then. Even if they couldn't, would this really change the course of history? Or would these events, as inexorable as the movement of the planets and stars, simply play out in a different setting? If not that particular warehouse, then perhaps another, or any other building, would do. The fates would have their way. "I'd have to burn down the whole town, to avert the tragedy of that night!" he finally concluded, and he really hadn't come prepared for arson. Not knowing how much time he had before the effects of the fly venom wore off, carefully conceived schemes requiring time and resources were not luxuries he could count on now.

John mulled these things over as he headed down Maple Street toward the tailor shop. In the end he fell back on his original plan, concluding that his best chance at averting tragedy would be to change the opportunity, or motivation, and not the place, for their meeting. He would have to give Rebecca a reason to change her plans that night. This is what he hoped to do with the letter he had written and brought with him, tucked safely away in his knapsack. But before giving her the letter, he had to be sure of young John Weston's whereabouts—that he in fact was in Annapolis and would remain there, and whether there had been any recent communications between the two of them. For, you see, the letter in his knapsack was addressed to "My Dearest Missy," and signed, "With my undying love and devotion, J.J."

The tinkling of bells announced John's arrival as he opened the door to Mason's Tailor Shoppe and stepped inside. He was greeted by the warm scent of burning candles and fabric, reminding him of something between a new age head shop and modern-day carpet store.

"Yes, sir. Can I help you?" came the voice of an older woman from behind the counter. She had her back to John, and was tending to some bolts of cloth on the far shelves.

John paused to survey the room, then smiled and tipped his hat. "Yes, ma'am. And a good day to you. I came by to retrieve an article dropped off by my business associate, about a week ago. He brought it in for mending and cleaning."

Mrs. Mason turned to face John. "Yes, of course. Please tell me, what was the gentleman's name?"

"A Mr. Robert Fenwick."

John figured it wouldn't hurt to implicate his good friend and business partner from another century. How would it ever catch up with him?

"And you are...?"

John approached the counter and nodded politely. "John Weston, ma'am. The name is John Samuel Weston."

Judith Mason did a double take. "John...Weston?" She did a quick study of the figure standing before her. "I see. Are you any relation to the Westons of Haddonfield? Bartholomew and his younger brother, also named John."

"Yes, I am. By my reckoning we are distant cousins, perhaps thrice removed."

Judith smiled and eyed him thoroughly up and down. "Yes, I can see the family semblance. You cut as fine a figure as either one of them."

John smiled and removed his hat. "Thank you, ma'am. You are most kind."

"Not at all," she smiled. "Please wait here while I recover your coat. Mr. Mason keeps all mended items for cleaning in the back room."

Mrs. Mason turned and left the room. John could hear her conferring with someone, most likely her husband, in the back room. Then she hollered out, "can you please describe the item for me, Mr. Weston?"

John though a moment, then stretched his neck and hollered back. "Yes, of course. It was a heavy, full woolen greatcoat, tan in color, with a high collar and deep cuffs. About knee length, I would say."

Some further murmuring and rustling in the back room. A minute later Mrs. Mason emerged accompanied by her husband.

"I am having trouble locating your article," said Mr. Mason, scratching his head. "You say you brought it in a week ago?"

"Well, not me personally. My business associate dropped it off. I'm just retrieving it for him, since I was in town."

"And what was this gentleman's name?"

Mrs. Mason spoke up, slightly annoyed. "I told you, Robert, his name was Fenwick. Robert Fenwick."

"Yes. Approximately the same age as myself," John clarified, "but less tall by a few inches, with a slightly wider girth about the middle."

Mr. Mason thought for a moment, stroking his chin. "I'm afraid I don't recall such a gentleman. And the article you describe doesn't sound familiar. Are you sure it was this shop, and not some other. Perhaps Lippincotts' haberdashery in the northern part of town?"

"Ah! That must be it!" John conceded with feigned sudden realization.

Mr. and Mrs. Mason smiled, relieved that they were not to be blamed or held accountable by a disgruntled customer.

With all parties relaxed, John began to engage Mr. Mason in polite conversation, bringing him news of recent happenings in the southern colonies, which he had recently visited. He reported verbatim the events surrounding the burning of the brigantine *Peggy Stewart*, as reported by the *Maryland Gazzette* in October of 1774. John had thoroughly researched the affair after the event was initially described to him by Emily Grady, the Cumberland County historian, and alluded to in young John's letter to Rebecca.

"Of course, I was not present at the time of the burning," John clarified in all honesty, "but I did read the reports of eyewitnesses."

Further testing the waters, he added, "I understand young John Weston was there, in association with the family business partner, Mr. Stewart."

Mr. Mason appeared a little distressed over these last remarks.

"Yes," he replied, "John is handling the business arrangements for his older brother, Bartholomew, in the southern colonies. Annapolis, I believe. That would indeed place him at the scene of the events that you describe."

Bullseye! I was right! John is in Annapolis!

"And when does…Master Bart expect his brother, John, to return?"

Mr. and Mrs. Mason exchanged worried glances.

"Well, according to Rebecca—that's John's sweetheart, you know—we don't expect his return before the end of the year," Mrs. Mason replied with some reluctance. "I wouldn't offer this information so freely, except knowing you are family and all."

"Ah, yes! Young Rebecca Whitman! John speaks of her all the time. As a matter of fact, I have with me a letter from John which I promised to deliver to her in person. I much look forward to finally meeting the young lady. I was told I might find her here, in your premises. Even that she works for you."

"Yes, you were told correctly," Mr. Mason assured him. "But I'm afraid you just missed her today. She came in early but only stayed until just past midday."

"She often takes her work home where she can tend to the mending at her leisure," Mrs. Mason explained.

"I see," John said. "Please tell me, do you expect her in the shop tomorrow?"

"Oh, yes. I would expect her by mid-morning," Mrs. Mason replied. If you'd like, you can leave the letter with us. We will certainly see to it that she gets it."

Hmm, might be wise, John thought. *If the time-dilatant effects of the fly venom wear off tonight I'd be plum out of luck!*

"That's most kind of you," John said, "If it wouldn't be too much trouble."

"No trouble at all," Mrs. Mason assured him.

John produced the letter from his knapsack and gave it to the Masons. Then, bidding adieu to the tailor and his wife, he set off and headed back into the main part of town.

Coming to the intersection with Ye Greate Street, he thought about his first encounter with Greenwich on Sunday, the twelfth of September, just seven weeks ago. This was the exact spot he'd driven to in town, where he'd been greeted by silence and the buzz of greenhead flies. So much had happened since then—and changed over the past two hundred twenty-five years.

John figured he'd take the opportunity to explore the wharf and warehouse area down the road to the left, to do a little reconnoitering just in case it all came down to taking more drastic measures. Anyway, it was a good day for a walk: sunny, not too cool.

It was about a half-mile walk to the wharf where Ye Greate Street terminated at the river's edge. Everything was laid out just like in his earlier vision, but seeing things in the light of day made a big difference. There was the ill-fated warehouse, the largest of three wooden structures which provided enclosed protection for incoming and outgoing cargo. The remaining structures were open sheds, more like lean-tos in construction, providing temporary cover for traded goods. There was also a small, enclosed shack with a sign: "Customs Official."

Down by the wharf John was greeted by the two men operating the ferry service between Greenwich and Fairfield. The older gentleman introduced himself as John Sheppard, and the younger man as his son. John wondered where they were the night of the fire. Didn't they see what was going on? They could have saved Rebecca. Studying the young Sheppard more closely, and hearing his voice, he then recalled him as the man who rode into town announcing the fire at the wharf.

John asked about "security" at the wharf. "Don't they have guards or police patrolling the area at night?"

The two men laughed.

"Where do you think you are, Boston?" the older Sheppard rebutted.

John smiled sheepishly. Then, after thanking them for their time, he headed back into town and the Stone Tavern, where he planned to spend the night. The sun was beginning to set, so he figured it was getting close to six o'clock by now.

"Good evening, Mr. Weston," Mary greeted John as he entered the Stone Tavern.

"And a good evening it is, indeed!" John replied as he planted himself at a table by the front window. He wanted to see all the comings and goings—no telling who might show up with useful information. "That's a heavenly scent coming from the kitchen, Mary. Pray tell, what's on the menu tonight?"

"Venison stew with jams and wild rice," Mary hollered back. "Can I fix you a plate?"

"By all means! And a pint of ale if you don't mind."

John relaxed and enjoyed the meal as the tavern began to fill up with what John assumed to be the usual Monday evening crowd: merchants, farmers, craftsmen, and other men folk eager to share a brew and catch up on the news of the day. By seven o'clock the place was nearing full capacity with standing room only, and John was forced to share his table with three other men.

"Is this a typical crowd for a Monday night?" John asked the men. The youngest among them responded.

"No, sir. Not so typical. I seldom frequent the place so early in the week, but with the rumors about town, I had to find out for myself."

The "rumor" the man spoke of was the burning of the *Peggy Stewart* in Annapolis just a fortnight ago. Apparently, the news first surfaced last week when a prominent and trustworthy local, by the name of Philip Vickers Fithian, returned from that southern port city with a firsthand accounting of the event, which was later corroborated by other news sources. But the local scuttlebutt went beyond this. It was now being rumored that someone was planning to actually bring tea, that "detestable weed," into the port of Greenwich in the not too distant future. No one was quite sure how the rumor started, but some suspected it may also have come from Philip.

"I think it's pure fabrication, plain and simple," ventured the eldest of the three gentlemen. "That's always the way of it. A piece of news from afar gets embellished to bring it home, stirring up the locals. Makes for good conversation, and"—holding up a pint of ale—"good business."

"I don't know, Elmer. I think there may be some truth in it," countered the third gentleman. "My cousin in Philadelphia wrote me that a ship laden with tea was recently denied port entry into that city. Actually turned back to sea!"

Talk then turned to the "embargo" situation in certain of the colonies, like the one in Maryland that prompted the *Peggy Stewart* affair. Maybe the same should be done here, some suggested.

John had finished his evening meal and was enjoying his second tankard of ale when he spied a familiar face across the room. Excusing himself from present company, he got up and approached the gentleman from behind.

"Good evening, Mr. Mason. Excuse me, but I never caught your first name."

"Ah, if it isn't the *other* Mr. Weston!" he replied turning around. "Robert. You may call me Robert," he said as he reached out and shook the hand being offered.

"I wasn't expecting to see you so soon, or in a place such as this," John said with a smile.

"That so?" Robert responded with raised eyebrows. "Yes, well, I do enjoy the bawdy company of travelers"—giving John a wink—"and other vagabonds of the road from time to time."

Time to time, indeed!

"So, are you suitably sated of food and drink, my good man?" Robert continued.

John laughed. "Oh, my, yes! I am particularly fond of the ale."

"Yes, I agree. English ale is so much preferred over the local cider." Then, looking about the room and taking a more somber tone he added, "But, I fear all things English are fast becoming, shall we say...unfashionable?"

John nodded and followed his glance. "Yes, it appears the local populace is taking to heart the news from Annapolis"—turning to Robert—"about the tea situation, I mean."

With a worried frown, Robert drew closer to John, his next words coming in a near whisper. "John, may I confide something in you?"

John gave a single affirmative nod. Looking about the room, Robert wrapped his free arm about John's shoulder to draw him aside from the main crowd.

"Just this past week, Rebecca shared with me a letter she received from the younger John Weston who, as you know, is in Annapolis tending to the affairs of the family business for his brother Bart."

John feigned a look of expectancy. Of course, he knew of this letter, having read it two hundred plus years into the future, but couldn't let on.

"Somehow," Robert continued, "John found out about the consignment of tea his brother had arranged for shipment to these colonies, to arrive here in Greenwich some time before the end of the year. Of course, John doesn't know it was ordered by his brother, but unleashed rumors abound nonetheless."

John shook his head. "I see," was all he could say.

"Yes, well, beyond that, I have offered my services to harbor the tea in the safe confines of my own wine cellar, which, of course, puts me and my household at risk should circumstances become, shall we say...unsavory."

John nervously cradled his tankard of ale with both hands, recalling his initial out-of-body experience in Greenwich and the words of the leader of the mob on Ye Great Street: *"Not to worry, the tea is in safe hiding not far from here, biding its time in the tailor's wine cellar."*

"Yes, I can understand your concern," John replied at last.

Robert took a sip of ale. "Yes, well, my concern is also for young Rebecca. This puts her in a rather difficult situation. You see, unbeknownst to Rebecca, it was Mr. McKenzie, the ship's first mate—and Rebecca's former suitor—who approached me about providing a convenient safe haven for the tea. Rebecca knew nothing of it."

John thought a moment. "Until last week?" he offered.

"Precisely!"

Robert proceeded to explain what he knew of the family situation as it was explained to him by Mr. McKenzie: about young John's involvement with the Sons of Liberty and his participation in the Boston Harbor tea dumping incident last December; how brother Bart sent him to Annapolis to keep him from knowing anything about his plans to bring in tea to the colonies.

"How John ever found out about the tea is beyond me. When Rebecca challenged me with news, I was forced to confide in her. And now I wish I had taken a different approach."

John nodded. "I see. So now she must decide between the truth, or protecting the Weston family business interest, hiding what she knows from her one true love."

Robert sighed. "Precisely!"

*****

John lay on his back, motionless, eyes closed, as self-awareness slowly replaced the remnants of a good night's sleep. It was his best night's sleep since this whole Greenwich thing began almost two months ago. But, where—or when—would he find himself when he dared open his eyes? Encouraged by the not too distant sounds of human voices and activity mingled with the chirping of early morning songbirds, he figured he remained in eighteenth-century Greenwich. But then again, if the letter had the effect he was hoping for, he could be back in his own century with the curse lifted, lying in that same tavern room in a modern-day Greenwich transformed, resurrected, and preserved. He opened his eyes and scanned the room. Nothing had changed from the night before. Getting up he looked out the window: packed dirt road and colonial dress. Yes, it was still 1774.

Actually, that was probably a good thing. Having retired rather late after an evening of good conversation and moderate drinking, he had neglected to attach his knapsack to his body. He wasn't quite sure what would have happened if the effects of the drugs had worn off. Would the knapsack have returned with him? Probably not.

John quickly readied himself for the day. Judging by the sun's position, he figured it couldn't be much past 7:00 a.m. and he should be able to reach the tailor's shop before Rebecca. Splashing cold water across his face from a porcelain wash basin, the final words of the campfire curse suddenly came to mind: *...And ne'er the curse shall it be lift...till the time of the winter solstice rift...And 'The One' whom time henceforth reclaims...returns to barter with his good name...*

The words ran over and over in his head. It was all making sense now. "Winter solstice rift." Sure, everything was pointing to the twenty-second of December as the day of reckoning. And he was definitely "the One"—as his good friend, partner, and latter-day prophet, Bob, had foretold—to go back in time to set things right. So far no one else had come forth in either century with his credentials and good name. But it was the last part, about "bartering his good name," that bothered him. What did that mean?

*****

When Rebecca Whitman arrived at Mason's Tailor Shoppe and Haberdashery the next day—Tuesday morning, the day after Halloween—John was already there, engaged in friendly conversation with Mr. Mason over the current political situation in the colonies. Up until now, the mood in Greenwich had been rather mixed, with little support for the notion of breaking away from mother England. Most people considered any talk of independence as too radical, and that differences between the colonies and the crown could yet be resolved to everyone's mutual satisfaction. However, recent events in Annapolis and Philadelphia, vis-à-vis the tea burning and embargo situation, began to polarize public opinion on these matters. Certain townsfolk—Mr. Philip Fithian among them—began to express strong concern over the status quo, feeling that a break with England was fast becoming inevitable. Mr. Mason, while endorsing the notion of self-rule for the colonies, did not share the more extreme views calling for complete independence.

"Good morning!" Rebecca announced cheerfully as she entered the shop. "Sorry I'm running a bit late, but I happened to run into an old childhood friend of mine whom I haven't seen in quite a few years. You remember Cynthia Greene, the youngest daughter of Mr. and Mrs. Albert Greene? We had a most pleasant reacquainting!"

Mrs. Mason smiled. "Yes, dear. I do recall you mentioning her as an old childhood friend."

"My, how time has flown," Rebecca continued as she lay her bundle of mended garments on the counter top. "She is so grown up now! Not at all as I remembered her."

"Ah yes! It is indeed a good morning, Miss Rebecca," Mr. Mason chimed in. "All the more so when greeted with news from a favorite suitor."

Mr. Mason removed John's letter from the countertop drawer and held it out to the young Rebecca. "I have a letter for you from your Johnny Jay, which Mr. Weston"—giving a nod in his direction—"was kind enough to deliver in person."

All John could do was smile, rendered momentarily speechless by the young lady's sudden and real appearance. Having at last come into the presence of one who had so captured his imagination and thoughts these past many weeks, he found her even more beautiful and captivating than he had envisioned, even more so than he remembered from his dream experience less than a fortnight ago in Thousand Oaks, California. Had he actually made love to her ghost as the surrogate John Jay? He brushed aside the notion as, looking now into her sparkling, emerald green eyes brought to mind his own true love—his sweet Becky. Seeing Rebecca now in the flesh, he wanted to reach out and touch her, and by so doing might somehow connect with his once true love. It was all he could do to hold back and control the urge.

"Why, thank you, Mr. Weston?" Rebecca replied with a question, appearing somewhat confused as she took the letter in hand.

"Yes, ma'am. I am John *Samuel* Weston, at your service," he said, emphasizing his differentiating middle name. John went on to explain his relationship with the Westons of Haddonfield; that he was a cousin "thrice removed" from Bartholomew Weston, and yes, it was an interesting coincidence that he shared the same first name with the young John *Jay* Weston.

"So, you were in Annapolis and actually met with my Johnnie Jay?" she asked, holding up the letter.

John explained that he received the letter through an intermediary; that he did not actually see or speak with John.

"I see," she said. "It's just that it comes so quickly on the heels of another letter delivered by Mr. Fithian just last week. I hope everything is all right."

Sitting down on a nearby stool, she opened the letter and began to read silently to herself.

26 October

My Dearest Missy,

I can scarce contain my joy with the latest turn of good fortune, which comes so quickly on the heels of my most recent epistle. Mrs. Stewart is fairing much better, so much so that Mr. Stewart has given me leave to return to New Jersey once all business affairs in these southern colonies are in order. The good news is I will be home before the end of the year and plan to celebrate Christmas with my brother in Haddonfield. Please do not reveal my plans to brother Bart, if perchance your paths should cross, as I wish to bring him the news myself.

Missy, it is my most urgent desire that you spend Christmas with me and my brother in Haddonfield. If at all convenient, you should plan to be in Haddonfield before the twenty-second of December, as this would best suit my timed arrival. You need not respond to me with your answer, as I would likely not have opportunity to receive it, not knowing where my travels will take me in the interim, as I have business dealings to complete in sundry places.

My heart races with the thought of seeing you again, my fairest Missy!

With my undying love and devotion,

J.J.

"I trust it is good news?" John asked, knowing full well the content of the letter.

Rebecca looked puzzled, taking a moment to respond. "Odd," she said, shaking her head; then, looking up at John, "Yes, I suppose it is good news, if taken at face value. But, well, it just doesn't sound like John. I mean, it takes such a turn from his most recent letters."

"What do you mean child?" asked Mrs. Mason.

"He wants me to meet him in Haddonfield to spend Christmas with him and his brother. But, he wants to keep it a secret. Says I need not respond with an answer. He would just hope to see me on the twenty-second, or sooner, in Haddonfield."

"Well, I should think that is good news," Mr. Mason offered, adding with a sly grin, "Perhaps he wishes to take that opportunity to—how shall I say—tie the knot with a proposal of marriage."

Rebecca blushed and shook her head. "Yes, that would be nice, I suppose. But, I just have a feeling that something is…amiss. A meaning hidden between the lines, as it were."

She is an astute and intuitive young lady, John thought. *I hope I didn't press this thing too far.*

"Perhaps your apprehension is misplaced, Rebecca," John suggested. "After all, for most men, when it comes to matters of matrimony, all well-meaning attempts to communicate are too often confused and confounding."

"Well stated, my good man!" Robert Mason applauded.

"And if you ask me," Mrs. Mason chimed in, "Christmas in Haddonfield sounds like a good idea to me, whatever the reason. Perhaps you will have opportunity to see Philadelphia as well. That has been your dream, child, has it not?"

"Yes, that would be nice," she conceded with a sigh.

Rebecca folded the letter and placed it in her apron pocket as she set about her daily shop chores, starting with the mending. As John watched her, he thought about how to make his next move, but finally just plunged in.

"So, tell me, Robert, what can you tell be about Agatha Green?" he asked in a stage whisper. "Rumor has it that she is some kind of…town witch!"

Total silence as all heads turned to John.

"I'm sorry," John said, returning their frozen stares. "Did I say…something wrong or offensive?"

Mr. Mason measured the expression on his wife's face before responding. "No, John. Not really. Just curious why you would ask such a thing."

John decided to go out on a limb. "Because, Mr. Mason, I have reason to believe she has an unnatural preoccupation with fire. Shall we call it pyromania?"

Robert was taken slightly aback as he and Mrs. Mason exchanged knowing glances.

"Are you referring to the recent rash of property fires in these parts?" he asked at last.

My, there was pay dirt to be found here, after all!

"Why, yes. You might say I am conducting an investigation into such matters. I cannot say who has charged me with this. But, any information you can provide—apart from hearsay I might add—would be most helpful."

Robert and Judith Mason proceeded to tell John everything they knew about Agatha Greene, from the loss of her first child, Destiny, to a fire in Boston; the infamous wolf peach affair which many say made her the way she is today; to the recent barn fire at the Sterns and the smoky shawl remnant found nearby with Agatha's monogrammed initials.

"So, you think she had something to do with setting that fire?" John asked.

Judith took a deep breath. "I cannot say for sure; but it does seem to point that way."

John took a pencil and journal from his knapsack and made a few notes in the manner of an inspector, further conferring a certain measure of legitimacy to his "investigation."

"So, please tell me, in your opinion, does Agatha Greene represent a threat to anyone? Would she intentionally cause anyone any harm?"

Robert shook his head. "Other than herself, I would say not," he affirmed. "But then again..."

"Yes?"

"One can never know, with a troubled mind, what imagined wrongs may need righting, if you understand my meaning."

On his way back to the Stone Tavern, John thought about Rebecca's reaction to the letter and how it might not play out as he'd hoped. What if she wrote John or contacted Bart about their holiday plans and discovered it was all bogus? Hopefully, it would create just enough confusion to alter events for the better—or maybe just make matters worse!

Back at the tavern John decided to take an even bolder course of action. Finding an empty table in an isolated corner of the room, he took quill pen to paper and drafted a second letter—this time in his own handwriting, so it went a lot quicker this time. Placing the folded letter in a sealed, addressed envelope, he asked Mary to post the letter to the person named. She would know where to send it.

Satisfied, John spent the remainder of the afternoon walking the streets of Greenwich, getting a better lay of the land and noted points of interest: the wharf and boatyard, the Market Square, and the Friends Meeting House. He even had time to walk the mile or so north up Ye Greate Street to North Greenwich, or the "Head of Greenwich," as the locals called it. This was the same path he had traced by stage wagon on his first venture into eighteenth-century Greenwich; but this time he knew where he was going.

Coming to the Presbyterian church yard and cemetery on the left, located where the road to Shilo tees off to the right toward the northeast, he had no trouble finding the Whitman family plot. It was located under the same—though much younger and smaller—oak tree he encountered on his modern-day trip to Greenwich just a couple of weeks ago. Of course, there were not five, but only three, stone markers this time, contained within a newly fashioned and well-maintained, low wrought iron fence. John took a piece of paper and pencil from his knapsack and wrote down the easily discernible inscriptions:

Thomas Whitman, Jr., 1753-1754, Our Little Angel
Elizabeth Whitman, 1736-1764, Beloved Wife of John
Elijah Whitman, 1764-1770, Child of God

There was one more stop he wanted to make before heading back downtown to the old Stone Tavern: the blacksmith shop of Thomas Whitman. The directions were not hard to come by, as everyone knew where to find the town smithy—like asking for the nearest auto mechanic in John's day and age. He didn't have far to go, less than a furlong down the road to Shilo, or about two modern-day city blocks.

John found the carriage doors to the shop half open, with the sound of hammer against hard steel reverberating from within. *PING-ping-ping! PING-ping-ping!* One loud ring followed by two softer rings, as the hammer struck and bounced against steel and anvil in well-practiced rhythm, the cadence of the smithy's song. *PING-ping-ping! PING-ping-ping!* The red-hot, semi-molten piece of steel was pounded into submission by the might and skill of the smithy's arm and forge. *Ssssssss!* With a hiss the piece took final hardened form as Thomas plunged it into a bath of cold water. With a pair of tongs he held it up for John's inspection.

"A new half-door hinge for Ralph Stern's new barn. Lost it in a fire about a month ago." He motioned to another piece lying on a nearby workbench. "That's the mating half-hinge over there. This is the last of four hinges in all."

"Nice work," John replied with a smile.

Thomas put down the tongs, picked up a rag, and wiped his hands. "And what can I do for you, sir?" he asked, squinting hard and looking askance at his new visitor. "I don't believe I know your name, but your face is familiar, if I may be so bold to say."

"Please forgive me. I am John Samuel Weston, a distant cousin of Bartholomew Weston of Weston Enterprises."

"Well, I'll be the King's own chambermaid!" Thomas replied straight-faced "You do indeed favor the likes of Master Bart. And there is bit of the younger Weston in you as well. Even share his name, I see." Holding out his hand he finally broke a smile. "I am Thomas Whitman, blacksmith by trade."

"I'm honored to make your acquaintance, Thomas. You and your work are very well spoken of in these parts."

Yes, this was indeed Thomas Whitman, the father of young Rebecca, in the flesh! Funny thing, dreams and visions; they can trick you into thinking you know something or someone, but reality is so much more searing on the soul.

"Thank you, John...I may call you John?"

"Why yes, of course."

Thomas leaned back against his workbench, almost sitting. "So, how may I help you, John?"

"You spoke of a fire, the one that destroyed the Stern's barn. It so happens I am investigating that incident, and others that have occurred in recent months. So as to avoid a repeat occurrence we would certainly like to apprehend the person or persons responsible."

John stiffened and took a non-conciliatory tone. "And you believe I may have some connection with that person or persons."

"No, not necessarily. I just need to know what you know, if anything, about the event."

"I see. So, does this have something to do with rumors surrounding my good friend, Dan Fire Cloud, implicating him in these events?"

Ah, yes. The Indian Chief in my visions! Makes sense.

"No, not at all. Rest assured, Thomas, I am quite confident that Chief Fire Cloud is not involved in any way with these fires. Actually, I suspect another."

Thomas eased up.

"So, Thomas, what can you tell me about...Agatha Greene?" John asked.

"Agatha Greene?" Thomas repeated with a puzzled look.

Thomas proceeded to tell John what he knew, which wasn't very much. He started by inviting John in for a cup of hot tea, prepared by the slave girl, Isabel. John recognized her, too, as the young black woman of his visions around the campfire. He figured he'd just hit the mother lode! He knew he wouldn't be around to continue the investigation, but by planting the idea in their minds, perhaps they would investigate her on their own, or maybe get the local constable to pick up the lead. It was a long shot, but he let them know what the Masons thought, and the monogrammed shawl that appeared to place Agatha Greene at the scene of the crime. If successful, she would be apprehended and incarcerated—or committed—before she could do any further harm, before the tragic events of the coming the winter solstice—the twenty-second of December. It was perhaps a coldhearted approach to take, but he was desperate to avert disaster by whatever means necessary.

John left the blacksmith shop with renewed hope. As he headed back down Ye Greate Street toward the old Stone Tavern, he figured that between getting Rebecca out of town for the holidays and having Agatha Greene apprehended and possibly put away, the warehouse fire could be averted. Or at least Rebecca wouldn't be there to suffer a tragic and torturous end.

Passing the Friends cemetery where the road took a double bend, John began to feel a little light-headed, like maybe the effects of the drug were wearing off, or maybe it was just a touch of dehydration. There was no Gatorade this time to quell the effects. He picked up his pace as he rounded the second bend, bringing him within view of the Stone Tavern about a half mile down the road on the left. The sun was beginning to set to his right, casting long shadows across Ye Greate Street. There was a slight ringing in his ears, now—no buzzing, just ringing. He urged himself onward as an extreme fatigue began to overtake him. *Like I've been drugged, he thought*, laughing at the irony of it. *What if someone sees me as I make the transformation? They'd think me a wizard, or maybe that they'd seen a ghost!*

As John approached the tavern his leaden legs could barely support his own weight any longer, let alone the knapsack which now seemed to weigh a ton. He figured he'd get off the main street and go around the side where no one would see him. But just as he did, two gentlemen emerged staggering from the side door, each carrying a tankard of rum and leaning on one another for support. John instantly recognized the one as Roger Walker, the young man he had encountered on his initial arrival, the one whose purse he'd plundered on a sure bet.

Even in his inebriated state, Roger recognized John. "Well, if it isn't mishter Weston, the master reader of minds and wizard of numbers!"

John forced a smile, but was in no condition to banter. He simply nodded and tried to excuse himself, mumbling something about being late for an appointment.

Roger drew close and wrapped his free arm with the tankard of rum around John's neck, coming within a hog's breath of John's face, and offered a sloppy toast, sloshing and spilling rum on John's vest.

"To John Weshton—the other John Weshton, mind you—wizard extr'ordinaire!"

At this point the ringing in John's ears had become as loud as cathedral bells; he felt like a man trapped in a bell tower as the bells drowned out all sounds from the natural world. He could still see Roger's lips moving, but there were no words. Then suddenly…there was nothing.

When Roger later recounted these events, he would tell how Mr. Weston suddenly "turned to smoke," causing Roger to lose his hold and fall straight to the ground, "like a condemned man falling through the gallows doors!" he would elaborate. While his drinking companion corroborated his story, the reliability of both men was severely questioned, owing to their intoxicated states and Roger's own reputation for tall tales. Nonetheless, the story did quickly gain momentum as something of an urban legend. After all, what ever did happen to Mr. Weston? No one had seen "neither hide nor hair of him" since that day. Maybe he was a wizard or ghost after all, as Roger supposed.

*****

When John came to he found himself face down in a pile of underbrush and sumac with the weight of his knapsack pressing him against the ground. Good, he hadn't left it behind! His head was pounding, though, and it took a few minutes for the pain to gradually subside.

Slowly raising himself to his knees he took inventory of his surroundings. To his utter disappointment, the deteriorated remains of the Stone Tavern lay to his right. Nothing had changed! He was back in twentieth-century Greenwich and everything was just as he had left it. Apparently, his efforts were all in vain: Rebecca did not spend Christmas in Haddonfield, and Agatha Greene remained on the loose.

"Dammit! My letter never got delivered! I should've burned down that frigging warehouse!"

Rising to his feet John took a few moments to regain his land legs as he looked around. Good! His car was still there, parked in front of the Stone Tavern just where he'd left it yesterday morning. Groping for his car keys, he unlocked and opened the doors, then checked out the fly cage on the back seat. Several dead flies littered the bottom of the cage, but as he shook the cage he was glad to see most of the flies were still alive.

"Good. Maybe I can still go back to finish the job," he said anxiously.

Without thinking twice he plunged his right forearm through the flap door into the cage. But the flies showed no interest.

"Must be gorged after yesterday's free meal."

Disappointed, John removed his arm and studied the cage. "Wonder how long I can keep you buggers alive?"

No reply. He took the bottle of sugar water and replenished the feeding tray before placing his knapsack on the rear floor and climbing in behind the wheel. The engine started up on the first try. Good old reliable Camry!

Chapter 34

1999
Thursday, 4 November

6:00 a.m. John studied the swollen face staring back at him from his bathroom mirror. This was his first case of poison ivy since he was a teenager running cross-country at Sterling High School. And this time it was a doozy! The rash and itching started Tuesday morning. He figured there must've been some ivy in those bushes he landed in when he touched back down in twentieth-century Greenwich Monday evening. The swelling kicked in that same Tuesday afternoon, and he didn't waste any time heading over to the Lady of Lourdes Emergency Room. The docs put him on the usual steroid treatment, starting out with a heavy dose the first day and gradually weaning off over the next five to seven days. This was only day three, but he thought he was starting to see some improvement. At least it wasn't getting any worse.

After a quick shower and a shave—skipping his usual morning run—he forced down a bowl of lumpy oatmeal, washing it down with a cup of coffee and a bottle of Ensure. Swallowing had been difficult, but was getting easier now.

Before leaving the house for the office he checked on the condition of his little Tabby friends. Their head count (make that "greenhead" count) had diminished overnight, down from six to five. "Damnable short life span!" he complained. He knew the adult fly didn't live very long, but he was hoping enough would survive to take him back to eighteenth-century Greenwich at least one more time, and now with this poison ivy and steroid situation, he dared not challenge the combined effects of the fly's venom, no telling how his system would react.

On the way to the office he thought about that 1775 *Gazette* article, the one reporting on Agatha Greene's fiery demise in the Greenwich Market Square in the summer of 1775. Tuesday night he gave it a reread as he leafed through his Final Project loose-leaf binder. Funny he hadn't noticed it before—the article that followed, about a "mysterious interloper" claiming to share the same family name of Weston Enterprises, a man who some say "appears and vanishes as a spectral vision into the night." He had to smile. It looked like he had influenced history after all, although not in the way he had hoped.

And he now realized how it all worked, this greenhead fly venom-induced time-travel thing. He could travel "in the spirit" to any time in the past he chose—or was chosen for him—but he could only directly interact on matching days. Whatever day it was in the present time—1999—he could interact with people and events on the same day in 1774, but on no other. Somehow, the two time lines were on a parallel course, like two trains running alongside each another on separate tracks. He could jump from train to train, but had no influence over the course or speed of the two trains. He figured at some point in the near future, perhaps the new millennium, their paths would once again diverge, removing all hope at reconciliation. This was indeed the meaning of "crux of time" from Bob's time machine. To directly influence events of 22 December, 1774, he would have to travel back on that day precisely in the current year, 1999, and as Bob prophesied, "time is running out." The problem now was how could he go back without the flies? Surely his captive specimens would be long dead by then.

At the office Mary gave John the "news" about the break-in at Shockley Labs over the weekend. She had just received a phone call from a very upset Dr. Evert who had been on vacation until yesterday, which is when she'd first learned of the incident. John did his best to act surprised.

"My! Who could've done such a thing? Was anything…taken?"

"No, apparently not. Just some broken labware. According to Dr. Evert the police feel it was the work of local vandals, with it being "mischief night" and all."

"I see. And how did the culprits get in? I thought the place was pretty well secured."

"She said they broke in through an outside window. But that's the strange part."

"Oh?" John responded with genuine interest.

"Yes, she said whoever it was must have known about the false drywall. They apparently did a very neat job of cutting through. Unlike the police, she doesn't feel it was neighborhood mischief makers at all, but someone who knew exactly what they were looking for."

John swallowed hard to clear the lump in his throat. "I see. But you said nothing was missing?"

Mary looked back at her computer screen. "Well, I only know what Julie told me. Apparently the police and campus security are still investigating the matter."

That afternoon John received two very important phone calls. The first was from Lakeland's Dr. Alexander. John was in the conference room when Mary transferred the call.

"Hello, Doctor. It's good to hear from you."

"I've got some very interesting news for you, John. The results of the genetic testing are in."

There was a pause.

"Yes? And what's the verdict," John asked nervously.

"John, it appears that you and the late Doug Justin share a common maternal family line. Your mitochondrial DNA shows a near match."

John took a deep breath. "So, that would make us, what, distant cousins?"

"Yes, indeed. It's hard to say for certain how many generations separate you, but you do both share a common link—a grandmother several times removed in the maternal line—in the not too distant past."

"Like, maybe, our *colonial* past?"

Dr. Alexander chuckled. "Yes, most assuredly within that time frame."

"And what about my friend, Bob?" John pressed.

The doctor was slow to respond. "Well, those results aren't as conclusive. But there is a close match of sorts."

"What kind of 'sorts'?"

The doctor explained that while there wasn't a clear match, it was close enough to suggest a common ancestor, perhaps pre-dating the colonial era.

"But the important thing is," he continued, "all three of you share a common aberration in your mitochondrial DNA at a locus often associated with certain forms of mental illness. This supports my theory—or I should say, our theory, John—of a common triggering mechanism inserted into the maternal line some two hundred years ago."

"Ah yes! And by that you would mean 'the curse of Greenwich'!"

Images of the campfire flashed through John's mind: Thomas Whitman, the blacksmith; the old Indian Chief; the young slave girl; followed by the ritual in Thomas's kitchen paralleling the modern "ritual" of transgenic manipulations performed by GenAvance's modern wizards of genetic engineering. The parallels were uncanny.

"Be sure to footnote me, doc, in your upcoming AMA article!"

A light chuckle was heard on the other end of the phone.

"Yes, John. I surely will."

The second phone call came less than an hour later. John took the call in his office. It was Jennifer Dupree Brady, calling from the west coast. There was a measure of urgency and concern in her voice.

"John, the results of tissue culture tests are in on the brain tissue sample you sent us."

There was a pause.

"And—?"

"Unfortunately, your suspicions were right, John. Doug's brain tissue was loaded with viable BV virus particles."

John took a deep breath. "Are you sure, Jen?"

"Yes, quite sure. We ran the test three times on three separate samples. They all gave the same results. And what's more, the virus particles bear a striking similarity to our proprietary variant strain of baculovirus."

For Jennifer and GenAvance this was not good news. But John immediately saw an opportunity as he began to connect the dots. If the BV virus particles from Doug's brain could be made to infect insect cells in the lab, then the cells might express the same psychotropic protein that produces the effect of time travel in John's brain. What was it Dr. Alexander said? *We both share a common aberration in our mitochondrial DNA at a locus associated with certain forms of mental illness.* Maybe they could even grow up a batch in the pilot lab to produce enough time travel juice to last a lifetime!

"Jen, I really think we need to take this to the next level."

"What do you mean? Report it to the CDC?"

"No. Not just yet. I think we need to first characterize and better understand exactly what it is we have here. Maybe it's nothing. No reason to raise a red flag, at least not until we understand it more fully."

John proposed trying to inoculate their genetically engineered Tnc insect cell line with the virus particles from Doug's brain, to see what would grow, what proteins might be expressed.

"It might shed light on the so-called 'Greenwich curse' that Dr. Alexander alluded to. Maybe lead to some form of treatment." *And maybe get me back to eighteenth-century Greenwich while we're at it!*

"I don't know, John. I'll have to speak with Sam Li about this. He doesn't even know the results of the testing. It may take some convincing."

"Yes, I'm sure. But if it helps, have Sam give me a call. I could even set up a conference call between the medical examiner, Dr. Alexander, and myself and—"

"Whoa, John! Let's just keep it in the family at this point. Trust me. I can handle Dr. Li."

"Sure, Jen. Okay. Just keep me posted on any developments."

Late that same evening, John got a phone call at home from Dr. Sam Li himself. John had never heard him so flustered, almost at a loss for words. Recounting his conversation with Jennifer earlier in the day, Sam said he had to hear it "straight from the horse's mouth"—John being the "horse" in question.

John told him what he knew of Doug's history and condition, how they met in the hospital, the friendship that followed. But more importantly, he recounted Dr. Alexander's research into a peculiar form of schizophrenia endemic to the region that appeared to be genetically linked to mitochondrial DNA passed down through a common maternal line of descent. Apparently, Doug suffered from this same illness and was shown to share the same mitochondrial genome characteristic of this disease. What was new, of course, was the apparent involvement of the baculovirus as a possible vector for this genetic aberration. Of course, John avoided any mention of his own personal experiences, and the fact that he, too, shared this same genetic aberration.

In the end, John was able to convince a very reluctant Dr. Li of the need to run further studies to better characterize the proteins expressed by the vector genes, that is, the protein or proteins responsible for the mind-altering effects of the disease. In the end, Dr. Li agreed.

"Yes, John, there may be an opportunity here. But we will need to scale up the cell culture process in order to produce sufficient quantities of protein for analysis. That's assuming, of course, we can get the BV particles to infect our line of insect cells."

John understood the challenges involved. Like trying to resurrect an ancient Mesopotamian beer brewing process, he thought. And doing it right the first time—without a recipe!

"I will have Sammy write up a test protocol and arrange for a test batch in the pilot lab," Dr. Li continued.

"Will you go for a continuous or batch-fed process?" John asked.

"Batch for the seed train, continuous for the production reactor. We'll use the five-hundred liter bioreactor with the alternating tangential flow-recovery process Sammy and Ted Salmonson have been developing. I'll send you a copy of the protocol, if you'd like."

"Thank you, Sam. I'd appreciate that."

"Yes, well. I am hoping in the end that this may all be much to do about nothing. There may be no connection at all between the BV particles in Doug's brain and Dr. Alexander's schizophrenia theory."

"Yes. I hope you're right, Sam."

In reality, though, John was banking on just the opposite.

On Friday morning, John's cell phone sent him a reminder for Monday's appointment with Dr. Caldwell. This would be his second follow-up visit since being discharged from Lady of Lourdes Hospital over two months ago. "Hypnotherapy," that's what the good doctor called it. The last session hadn't gone particularly well, it being on the eve of John's trip to the west coast; he'd been especially anxious and not very susceptible to the power of suggestion. Both he and the doctor were hoping for better results this time, although for different reasons.

Chapter 35

1999
Mon, 8 November
Our Lady of Lourdes Hospital

10:00 a.m. Dr. Aldus Caldwell sat comfortably with legs crossed in his brown leather upholstered arm chair and spoke softly to the patient lying before him faceup on the couch.

"So, tell me John, how are we feeling since our last visit? Any more—unusual episodes, or out-of-body experiences?"

John looked straight up at the ceiling, avoiding eye contact with his interrogator. He thought it curious how Dr. Caldwell would always refer to him in the first person plural: the royal "we."

"No, doctor, *we* are actually feeling much better. Less anxious and sleeping more soundly—since going off the meds."

The doctor smiled and nodded. "That's good, John. I'm glad to hear that. You do appear relaxed. Are you comfortable?"

John just grunted and nodded "yes."

"Good. Let's proceed then."

While the last session didn't go well, this time would be different. It would provide both John and the doctor the breakthroughs they were looking for, although for totally different reasons. While holding out the possibility of a genetic link—a theory advanced by Dr. Alexander, his colleague at Lakeland—Dr. Caldwell was seeking a behavioral or Freudian basis for John's psychosis. He considered the creative fantasies of John's time-travel experiences as an expression of suppressed fears and guilt feelings lurking deep in his subconscious mind.

John, on the other hand, took these "flights of fancy"—as the doctor referred to them—at face value, and was hoping to unravel the secrets of his family's past to help him connect the dots on his quest to lift the "curse of Greenwich"—to "go back and save her!" Ever since the first successful hypnotherapy session at Lourdes unlocked the memory of his first time-travel experience, John had been eager to continue the investigation, to pick up where he left off so many years ago on that long, bumpy road from Greenwich to Camden. He was hoping this session would provide the answers.

"Your body is weightless now, John," Dr. Caldwell continued. "Mind and body set adrift with the tides of time. It is the twelfth of September, 1774, and you are traveling by stage wagon from Greenwich to Salem..."

...The wagon lurched forward, waking John from a fitful sleep. He looked around to get his bearings, forgetting where he was for the moment. The young lad seated in front of him turned around and held out his hand.

"Here, sir. I believe you dropped this."

John reached out and took the cell phone from the young lad.

"Thank you, son. It must've slipped from my pocket while I was napping."

The young man's eyes remained fixed on the cell phone. "That is quite a magical timepiece you have, there, sir. May I be so bold as to ask where you came by it?"

The boy's older traveling companion turned to John. "You must pardon my son's inquisitiveness," he apologized with a smile. "He is truly a child of the current enlightenment."

"No, I don't mind at all," John replied. "An inquiring and questioning mind, it is a good thing. Especially in these times."

Striking up a conversation with the lad and his father, John learned they were heading north to Princeton to enroll the boy in Nassau Hall, the institute of advanced learning located there.

"Yes, I am very familiar with the school," John acknowledged, although he better knew the place, of course, as Princeton University.

"Some very fine men"—hesitating as he was about to say "and women"—"have hailed from those fine halls of learning."

"So, you never said where you came by that timepiece," the young lad pursued.

"Ah, yes. Well, it so happens it was a gift," John replied. "I'm not completely sure of its origins, but I believe it is old world-made, German or Swiss perhaps."

The boy nodded, seemingly satisfied with John's answer.

It was almost 5 five o'clock when the wagon rolled into the town of Salem. Linking up to King's Highway north, the wagon hauled its load of weary passengers up Main Street into the heart of town: weary not just from a general lack of comfort, but from the added burdens exacted by the primitive conditions of the road. More than once the able-bodied male passengers were obliged to assist the coachman in freeing a wheel from a muddy rut, or guide the wagon on and off a ferry, even to assist the ferryman by taking to the poles.

Coming to a final stop in front of Dickenson's Inn, John was very much looking forward to a good meal, a bath, and a good night's sleep, if that was in the cards—or the stars. Having no luggage of his own, he offered to help the other passengers with theirs. That's when he noticed a rather large, well-appointed coach parked in an alleyway to one side of the inn, its team of horses still hooked up, waiting for the stable hand to tend to them.

"That's a very handsome coach," he commented to his coachman.

"Quite! English made. Some well-to-dos, no doubt. My guess is it arrived from Philadelphia."

John joined the other passengers inside at the reception desk where he was asked to sign the register and pay for the night's lodging: nine pence, just like the captain said. "Is a bath included with the price of the room?" he asked the clerk, a tall, thin middle-aged gentleman with impeccable bearing and attire.

The clerk simply smiled and pointed to a sign posted on the wall:

Amenities available for a surcharge:
- Bath: 4 d
- Hot Water Bath: 10 d

John gulped. "So, a hot bath costs more than the price of a room?"

The clerk just shook his head. "Please understand, sir, I don't set the prices here. You would have to take that up with the innkeeper, Mr. Dickenson."

John paid for the room and signed the register on the next available line, noticing a familiar name several lines above his own. Looking up at the clerk, he asked: "You have an 'Amanda Jay' registered here?"

"If it's written in the book, then it must be so," the clerk replied stiffly.

"When did she arrive, if you don't mind my asking?"

"Don't mind. Not twenty minutes before you and your company arrived. Came in on that handsome coach parked just outside."

Amanda Jay. Could it be the same Amanda Jay? John turned and gave the establishment a quick study. The dining room lay just off the hallway and lobby area; the stairs directly ahead down the hall.

"What time is the evening meal served?" he asked, turning back to the clerk.

"Six o'clock is when they start serving."

John thanked him, then took the key and headed up the stairs.

"It's the second room at the top of the stairs," the clerk called out after him. "The rope springs may be in need of some tightening," he added as John topped the stairs.

After freshening up with a pitcher and bowl of cold water and a towel—he decided to forego the pleasures of a hot bath, not knowing how long his cash reserves would hold out—John took the opportunity to rest up until dinner. The bed was the typical rope spring and straw mattress design. John flopped down to test the ropes. Yes, they definitely needed tightening.

He thought about that old saying: *Sleep tight, and don't let the bed bugs bite!* He had to smile.

"Just hope that second part doesn't come back around to bite me!"

That evening at dinner, John finally got to meet the real life Amanda Jay Weston, the mother of John Jay Weston and second wife and widow of the late Samuel Weston Jr., John's six-times great-grandfather on his father's side. The Ouija board turned out to be correct, but the oracle never told him how stunningly attractive she was! Even in her mid-forties—she was approximately the same age as Bartholomew Weston, Sam's only son by his first wife, Regina—her fair complexion and handsome figure retained the vitality of youth, while her bearing exuded a confidence and a boldness John found refreshingly attractive in women, but which he had assumed, perhaps wrongly, was largely relegated to women of his century. Yes, of course, there were your Dolly Madisons, Sarah Bartons, and the occasional Queen Elizabeth, but in a largely man's world they were the exceptions, right?

Amanda wasn't dining alone. A young lady, appearing to be about sixteen years old, sat across from her at the table.

"So, Mr. Weston, you say you are related to my late husband, Sam? I find that altogether intriguing. I thought I knew the entire Weston family pedigree."—looking across the table—"So, you see, Emily, there are always new things to learn in this life. Even for your aging mother!" she laughed.

So, Johnnie Jay had a younger sister! The Ouija board never mentioned that!

John would later learn this from Bob's basement time machine. But now, in his current state, this was just a distant future memory.

Amanda went on to explain that since Sam's death—Emily was only two at the time—she would use her maiden family name, "Jay," in all her business dealings. The Jay family name was prominent in Boston business and banking circles, so it made sense to do so.

"So, what brings you to these far reaches of our fair Jersey colony?" John asked.

Amanda laughed. "I was visiting Philadelphia on family business. You see, we have family represented at the Congress which is presently convening in that city."

John made the connection. "You don't mean John Jay, the New York barrister?"

"Why, yes. Do you know him?"

The whole world knows of him, my dear! Founding Father! President of the Second Continental Congress! First chief justice of the United Sates! Later governor of New York!

"Well, I have heard tell of him, but our paths have never crossed," John simply said. "But, you still haven't said what brings you to Salem. After all, two attractive women traveling alone."

"But we are not alone. We have each other," Amanda smiled, waving to her young daughter. "But I do appreciate your concern, John— may I call you 'John'?"

"Yes, please do."

Amanda sat back and took a quick, deep breath. "Well, you see, John, being this close I decided to take advantage of the situation to visit a dear cousin of mine whom I haven't seen in over twenty years. She is a first cousin on my mother's side. We were very close growing up, but in forty-nine she left Boston with her new husband and migrated to Cumberland County"— pausing—"for health reasons."

"Cumberland County?"

"Yes. Greenwich, a port town on the Cohansey River. I am told it is just a half day's ride from here."

"Yes, of course. I know it well. I left there just this morning. What is your cousin's name, if you don't mind my asking? Perhaps I know her, or her husband."

Amanda paused. "Her name is Agatha Greene, the wife of Albert Greene."

John strained to recall the name, but finally just shook his head. "No, I'm afraid I'm not familiar with that name."

Although deep in the recesses of his mind the name did strike a familiar chord. A kind of *future* déjà vu from events not yet realized in his current hypnotic state.

Amanda went on to explain how she had recently received a letter from a very distraught Albert Greene who expressed extreme concern over his wife's rapidly declining health. "An extreme form of melancholy that borders on madness at times," is how he put it. He was nearing his wit's end. Amanda responded by letter that perhaps there were doctors in Philadelphia that could help her. One in particular came highly recommended: a Dr. Benjamin Rush, well respected, with a sound reputation in the healing arts.

Agatha Greene? How do I know that name? John struggled.

With dinner finished and most of the inn's company adjourned for the evening, Amanda finally had to excuse herself. It was getting late and she and Emily were hoping for an early start in the morning. She expressed her gratitude for John's company and hoped they would someday meet again.

John remained in the dining room for another hour or so, finishing off a bottle of English porter before turning in. The effects of the porter had the desired effect: he was sleeping within minutes—and dreaming…

…*Now, against a backdrop of orange flame, new forms appeared. Vague shadows at first, the images became sharper and discernible. Human silhouettes in wild, dancing rhythm…*

Tossing and turning, John tried to shake off the disturbing images, but to no avail.

...Focusing on the heart of the flames, the vision of a woman's face slowly took form. It was the face of an older woman, worn and haggard. Her wrinkled face was discernible now, as the crackle of flames was replaced by the sinister cackle of an old crone. A frightening specter!

An unseen but familiar voice broke through the hypnotic veil and turmoil of his dream. "So, John. What can you tell me about this vision?"

"Wha—?"

John finally made the connection. "Yes, doctor. I know this! The old woman, she is the 'Witch of Greenwich,' Agatha Greene. I know this now!"

"I see. And, this Agatha Greene person, she is related to the lovely Amanda Jay Weston?"

"Yes! Apparently they were cousins. First cousins."

"And you, John, are also related to the lovely Amanda Jay?"

"Yes, I know this from Bob's 'time machine.' We are related on my mother's side. Through my maternal bloodline."

"This would be your biological mother, who deserted you as a child?"

John hesitated before responding.

"Yes."

"So, that would mean you are also related, though many generations apart, to Agatha Greene, the 'Witch of Greenwich,' as you refer to her?"

John's subconscious mind considered this. Suddenly, breaking through to his conscious mind, there shown a bright new light of awareness. It all made sense now! This was the connection he and Dr. Alexander were looking for: the genetic connection through the female line on his mother's side! And what was the triggering event for the "curse"? The campfire and kitchen ritual that altered Agatha Greene's mitochondrial DNA for all future female generations! A genetic alteration that somehow makes the carrier susceptible to the mind-altering effects of the bite of the greenhead fly. And not just any greenhead fly, but one whose own genetic makeup was itself modified by an altered strain of baculovirus. Three separate genetic events occurring at the right time in history to produce a single lasting effect. A trifecta of recombinant DNA magic!

"Yes, doctor," John replied from his transcendental hypnotic state. "We are all related."

*****

Dr. Caldwell removed his eyeglasses and looked up from his notebook.

"So, John, I believe we have made a real breakthrough today. Do you want to know what I think?"

Sitting across from Dr. Caldwell, cross-legged and relaxed, John took another sip of coffee. He was already convinced of the significance of today's session, although he was sure Caldwell's interpretation of events would differ from his own.

"Yes, of course, doctor. I'm all ears," he calmly replied with a smile.

Dr. Caldwell returned the smile and proceeded to give his professional opinion of John's condition, punctuating major points with a nod and simple hand gestures. According to Caldwell, the elaborate history of persons and events contained in John's visions represented a playing out of deep feelings of guilt and betrayal. Young Rebecca's tragic warehouse fire death mirrored Becky's equally tragic boat accident death, also by fire. Amanda Jay and Agatha Greene represented opposing aspects of his birth mother's personality: Amanda was the free and bold feminine spirit of adventure which John respected; Agatha was the dark side which forced John's abandonment as a child, something John saw as "sinister" and "bewitching." To help deal with the latter, Caldwell recommended that John make every effort to find and meet with his real mother, to assess her real personality and come to terms with her motives for leaving. In the end, he need not agree with her motives, but it would provide the necessary closure to this traumatic past event in his life.

"Capiche?"

John smiled and took a final sip of coffee. "Capiche," he replied.

One thing he and Caldwell did agree on: the need to meet and speak with his real mom, but for different reasons. For John, it would offer an opportunity to confirm the maternal bloodline represented by Bob's time machine; nothing more, nothing less.

Chapter 36

1999
November
South Jersey

The flies were dead! That's what John discovered when he returned home Monday evening from his recent visit with Dr. Caldwell. There were three still alive when he'd left for work in the morning, and now they too were gone. Too bad, just as he was coming off his steroid treatment and was considering the possibility of another road trip—or time trip—to Greenwich.

John made a second unwelcome discovery that evening. Going through his Final Project collection of artifacts and letters from John Jay to Rebecca, John was surprised to come across one he hadn't seen before—at least, not before his most recent trip to eighteenth-century Greenwich. He had already picked up on the updated 1775 *Gazette* article, but never thought to check the trove of love letters tucked safely away in the carved wood jewelry box. This one was dated 8 December. Again, no year was given, but from the context John knew it had to be 1774 and represented the newest final letter from John Jay to Rebecca:

8 December

My Dearest Missy,

Forever longing for the perfumed scent of your kind and loving words, I was delighted to receive your latest epistle, as it had been far too long between correspondences. I must say, howsoever, I remain perplexed by its content and implications. Unless I have taken leave of my senses, I have no recollection of the invitation you make mention of, and while I would sorely welcome our reunion during the coming Christmas season, I must say your acceptance of this "invitation" came as a shock to me—it seemed almost as if it were intended for someone other than myself! Please assure me that this is not the case.

You mention another "John Weston" as the deliverer of this letter, an older gentleman with claims to family connections. This too is as much a revelation to me as it was to you, I am certain, although I also have heard rumors to this same effect. News travels quickly among seafaring men in these climes! My firm and freely offered admonition would be to avoid contact with this person, as I fear he may be an imposter whose true intentions I would fail to trust. Could this person be connected in any way to rumored plots to bring tea, that detestable weed, into your fair town? Or the rash of fires ravaging the countryside as you reported on?

While my plans have not yet changed for the remainder of this year, the pain of our separation becomes all the more intense as I fear the implications of these recent developments as regards to your safety and the welfare of your fair town. Please remain on your guard, and keep me informed of any developments in this regard.

Forever and devotedly yours,

Jay-Bird

"'An imposter whose true intentions I would seriously question,'" John reread aloud. "So, besides being a wizard and 'mysterious interloper'"—tossing the revised *Gazette* article aside—"I have become something of a sinister fellow in the eyes of my long-lost relatives. Not exactly the impact on history I was hoping for."

John refolded the letter and placed it back in the jewelry box. He got to thinking about the letter from Rebecca that surely must have prompted this unfortunate response. And all those other letters from Rebecca over the years, where were they now? Surely John Jay must have kept them safely tucked away as he did with the letters Rebecca received from him. Maybe they just became misplaced and lost somehow or inadvertently destroyed over the years. Whatever the reason, they never made it into the collection of family heirlooms handed down through the generations which John now found in his possession.

But you know what they say about bad news coming in threes. Well, bad news number three came Tuesday afternoon when John received a surprise phone call from a Sgt. Stan Kowalski of the New Jersey State Police. The sergeant explained that he was investigating a recent break-in on the Rutgers campus and was just following up on a few leads. John was identified as a "person of interest" who may have information helpful to the investigation. Would John mind him dropping by to ask a few questions?

"Er, no, of course not," John replied hesitantly. "What makes you think I could offer anything to the investigation?"

"It's just routine, sir. Your name came up as someone renting a vehicle fitting the description of the vehicle identified at the crime scene. Of course, there are hundreds of rental cars fitting this description, so there's probably no connection. But we need to follow up on all possible leads, you understand. It's just routine, sir."

The blood was thumping in his ears now. "Yes, of course, sergeant. Just routine, I understand."

After hanging up John thought about those bogus out-of-state license plates. They were still in his basement, sure to be discovered if there was ever a search.

"Mary, I'm going to step out for a while," he said as he passed by the front desk. "Should be back before closing."

Mary looked up. "Sure, John. Is everything alright?"

"Er, sure. Just remembered...I think I left the iron plugged in this morning."

John grimaced and bit his tongue.

That was stupid! Couldn't I come up with anything better than that?

But Mary just chuckled. "Boy, I thought only I did things like that. I don't hear any fire sirens, so you're probably okay."

John returned a half-hearted smile, grabbed his jacket, and left the office. He hoped he would have a better explanation than that if that state trooper ever found that license plate in his basement:

"Well, you see, sir. I found it on my front lawn. Someone just...tossed it out their car window as they were passing by."

"I see. And what was this someone driving, if you don't mind my asking?"

"Er, well, I think it was a Celebrity. Late model. Blue."

No, that just wouldn't do. John had to rid himself of this incriminating evidence before the state trooper showed up at his door asking questions. He put the plate in a plastic bag, drove all the way to Philly, and placed it in a dumpster in one of those narrow alleyways somewhere in Old City. He made sure no one was watching. Paranoia runs deep.

The remainder of the week went pretty well for John, who kept busy in order to take his mind off the state trooper. By week's end all the swelling in his face was down and the rash had all but disappeared. On Thursday he phoned Dr. Evert to get an update on the project, but all she could talk about was the break-in.

"Why would anyone want to go to all that trouble? And for what? Nothing was missing so they must not have found what they were looking for."

Apparently Dr. Evert's team doesn't inventory their adult fly population.

John also phoned Sammy at GenAvance on a daily basis to check on the progress of the cell culture batch. She said they wouldn't really know anything until next week when they would start harvesting from the production bioreactor. She promised him he'd be one of the first to know.

On Tuesday afternoon of the following week—the sixteenth of November—John got the news he'd been anxiously awaiting. He was in his office when the call came through from Sammy.

"So, John, I've got some good news and some bad news."

John took a deep breath. "Okay Sam. Shoot."

"Well, the good news is, the insect cells grew well during the batch seeding process, and as far as we could tell the BV inoculation took hold, but—"

"Okay, so what's the bad news?"

"Well, the continuous cell culture process went terribly wrong, somehow. As far as we could tell, the tangential flow membranes on the ATF harvest recovery unit became fouled early on. Without the continuous harvest draw off we weren't able to keep the culture nourished with fresh media feed."

"I see," John replied dolefully. "Has that ever happened before?"

"Well, yes, very early on in our development process. But we thought we had ironed out all the bugs, no pun intended. Apparently, the BV particles you supplied from Doug's brain tissue, while resembling our variant vBV strain, are different enough to sufficiently alter the cell's chemistry, taking us back to square one."

"Hmm. That's not good. So, could you tell at all whether any proteins were expressed after the cells were infected with the BV particles?"

A disappointing sigh from a usually exuberant Sammy. "No, I'm afraid not, John. The cell culture, well, just died without the proper nutrients. Crazy!"

Crazy? No, I'll tell you about "crazy"!

John thought about his friend, Bob, and an idea popped into his head. "Listen, Sammy, this may be a long shot, but do you remember Bob's 'happy meal' invention with the liquid cyclone separators?"

Sammy laughed. "Oh yes, I remember: His rather unique continuous cell culture recovery and harvesting system."

"Right! I'm thinking it just might provide the proper hydraulic dynamics not afforded by the ATF unit," John suggested.

"Hmm, I guess it wouldn't hurt to try. So, do you have a working prototype we could use?"

Ah, therein lies the rub!

"Er, sure," John stammered, "I'll have to check with Bob. He was working on a prototype that wasn't too far from completion. I think we could have something finished and shipped out to you by end of the month, or the first week in December at the latest."

A little wishful thinking, perhaps, but he did think it was at least possible. And it might be his last hope for getting back—way back—to Greenwich for a winter solstice rendezvous with destiny.

The next day John paid Bob a visit at Lakeland. He hadn't seen him in several weeks, but according to Katie he was showing much improvement and would probably be coming home for the holidays for a trial outpatient visit.

John took along a set of assembly drawings and details for the cyclone recovery system that he'd retrieved from Bob's drawing file cabinet. He called ahead just to be sure Bob was okay with that and was feeling up to having visitors. They met in the same day room where John had received that first revelation from Bob—"a voice in the wilderness"— almost eight weeks ago.

"So, how's our time traveler?" Bob asked without looking up from his chess board.

"Okay, Bob. Just…okay," John replied. He took the empty seat at the table across from Bob and studied the board. "So, who's winning, Bob?"

"Shh, the end game. Gotta concentrate on the end game." He looked across at John and smiled. "You know how difficult that can be, John—right?"

John took the tube of drawings he'd brought with him and placed it on the table next to the chess board.

"Bob, I need your help with these drawings. Got a minute?"

Bob leaned back and gave a quick glance around the room with a wave of his arms. "I have all the time in the world, John. However, I do understand your dilemma with time."

John was unfazed. By now he'd grown accustomed to Bob's oblique prophetic references.

"Bob, we need to complete the fabrication of your prototype. Any chance of you getting a weekend pass from this place?"

"For good behavior? No way," Bob smiled. "Did you bring a note from the governor?"

John explained the most recent developments with GenAvance and the importance of getting this insect cell culture process to work. Bob unrolled the drawings and laid them out on the table. Borrowing a mechanical pencil from John, he began marking up the drawing as he explained its construction and operation. Apparently, fabrication of the actual physical prototype was much further along than John had realized, but remained mothballed in Bob's garage since the Fourth of July, when Bob's attention turned to other things.

Their conversation and activity did not go unnoticed. Before long several robed patients were standing by the table looking over Bob's shoulder.

"Did you do that, Bob?" an older patient finally asked incredulously.
"Sure did," Bob replied without looking up.
"No way!" a second, younger patient challenged.
Bob paused, looked up and addressed the challenger.
"Listen, sonny. I may be crazy. But I'm not stupid."

PART FIVE

Catch the sound of windfull night,
A frosty anthem to Winter's might;
And stars froz'n still against the sky
Shine brightly cold to catch the eye.

Anonymous

Chapter 37

1774
Early December
Delaware Bay

Sunrise found the brig *Greyhound* moored at anchor off Cape Henlopen under fair skies and a gentle seaward breeze. Paul McKenzie joined Captain Allen at the rail, eyes peeled toward the coast as they awaited word from the harbor master in Lewes, Delaware, on conditions in the bay.

"We made the crossing in good time, sir," Paul said as he tossed a piece of hard tack in the air toward several gulls hovering overhead. The gulls squawked, weaved, and dove, competing for the tiny morsel arcing past them, the victorious gull taking flight with his booty, trailed by others in close pursuit.

"Yes, the weather has been our ally," the captain replied. "If it maintains, we should make port by the twelfth."—turning to Paul—"That would be Greenwich, not Philadelphia. Am I right?"

Paul nodded. "Yes. Those are our instructions. Young Jonathan was well up to the task. Last night's lamp signal confirmed it. We are to put in at Greenwich."

Jonathan Bigelow, Master Bart Weston's young apprentice, was good at his word. He had arrived in Lewes, Delaware a fortnight ago, keeping watch for the *Greyhound* every day since to confirm and communicate by signal lamp the intended final port-o-call destination: one lamp for Philadelphia, two lamps for Greenwich. The first lamp signal from the *Greyhound* came at six bells during yesterday's dog watch—or 7:00 p.m.—two hours after the *Greyhound* first dropped anchor in the mouth of the bay, and confirmed Paul's presence on board. From the shore, Jonathan breathed a sigh of relief as this spared him the trouble of having to personally deliver the message to the captain aboard the *Greyhound*. Jonathan responded with two lamps, confirming Greenwich as the final destination. The lighted reply from the *Greyhound* signaled: "message received and understood."

This would be Captain Allen's first trip up the Cohansey. He was glad to have Paul along to help him navigate its serpentine course to the port of Greenwich.

"I appreciate your captain's giving up his first officer to accompany me on this voyage, Paul."

"Yes, well, they were Master Bart's parting instructions. Fortunately, the *Richelieu* handled well for our outbound crossing. Captain McElroy was of the opinion that the ship is reparable, and I shared in that assessment. So, he made the decision to remain behind in England to oversee repairs in dry dock and, of course, to settle our accounts for goods delivered."

Captain Allen watched as the ship's dinghy approached on the port side, returning with important information from the harbor master on tide and channel conditions in the bay.

"So, I imagine you are eager to return to home port, Paul. Do you have family in Greenwich?"

"Only the remote prospect of family, sir. There is a young lass whose affection I have been seeking to win for some time. Unfortunately," Paul confessed hesitantly, "I find myself competing with another."

The captain smiled. "A triangle of love. What is it the bards tell us: 'better to have loved and lost than never to have loved at all.'"

Paul gave an audible grunt. "Please, spare me, kind sir. Stale platitudes are no substitute for requited love...and prospects of marriage."

The captain smiled. "You are right, Paul. Please forgive me."

"No offense taken, sir. It's just that, well, the more I live and see of the world, the more I come to value home and family. My biggest fear, as I approach my thirtieth year, is that I should pass through this life without progeny to carry on the family name and pedigree."

"So, what are your intentions?"

"To sway her attention from her other suitor and make a proposal of marriage as soon as the opportunity presents itself. He is presently away, occupied with business ventures in the southern colonies, so I should have no trouble making ripe this opportunity."

Progeny and pedigree, things shared by all life forms—even greenhead flies and the tiniest of living things: viruses.

Below deck, securely tucked away in the ship's cargo hold, wooden crates packed with West Indies tea successfully weathered the long sea voyage to the colonies. Stenciled with the Dutch West India Company name, the crates were listed in the ship's manifest as being consigned to a Mr. Bartholomew Weston of Weston Enterprises, Haddonfield, West Jersey Province.

Unbeknownst to all, however, were stowaways of a silent but pernicious kind, eluding even the most vigilant and conscientious customs official of the day. In fact, one would need a microscope with a power not to be invented for centuries to discern the presence of these minute trans-global drifters: viruses. Or more precisely, baculoviruses, minute life forms capable of infecting their unwary insect host with devastating effect.

Hitching a ride on the dried leaves of West Indies tea, these virus particles would lay low and dormant until given the opportunity to infect the unwitting larvae of the fall armyworm moth. That's how it was in the old world. But the new world of the American colonies would provide the opportunity to breed and propagate within a new host organism, the larvae of the greenhead fly: *Tabanus nigrovittatus*. And not just any Tabby, but a special variety with its own unique pedigree—to be dubbed *T. nigrovittatus cohansus* by a future generation of naturalists—whose genetic makeup complemented that of the foreign viral DNA, which itself was a near perfect match for the new host species of fly, a serendipitous pairing made possible by the trans-Atlantic trading routes of a new global economy.

This special pairing would prove beneficial in several ways. First and foremost, the migrant virus would come to enjoy a symbiotic relationship with its new host larvae allowing it to survive into adulthood and propagate new generations of BV-bearing greenhead flies. Special proteins coded by the viral DNA would further confer a new survival feature: immunity to the sting of the horse guard wasp, a natural enemy of the native greenhead fly. That these proteins would later prove to have unique psychotropic effects on human hosts was inconsequential to the fly, but would significantly alter the course of local human history.

However, rendering the baculovirus capable of infecting a human host would have to await yet another very special enabling event at the hands of a Native American shaman, a new world blacksmith, and a young black slave girl from the islands.

Chapter 38

1999
November - December
GenAvance, Thousand Oaks, California

John worked frantically for the remainder of November assembling the final working prototype—serial number 001—of Bob's continuous cell culture harvest and recovery unit, which John dubbed: the Hydro-Cyclone Continuous Recovery System, or HCCR for short. Teaming up with Carl, a local metal fabricator whom Bob knew and recommended from his food processing days, and drawing on Maggie Stoebel's expertise for process controls, John's team worked through the Thanksgiving weekend to complete its fabrication and assembly. Bob already had the major components in his garage—hydro-cyclones, pumps, and instrumentation—and the design drawings were complete enough to give Carl, the fabricator, sufficient information for its construction. John would call on Bob for any further clarification, if needed. He was even able to arrange a pass for his friend for the long holiday weekend, which both Dr. Alexander and Katie agreed would be good therapy for Bob.

On Monday, the twenty-ninth, John had the unit crated up and shipped to GenAvance. He phoned Jennifer to give her a head's up to expect delivery toward the end of the week, with himself, Maggie Stoebels, and Jim Connelly planning to fly out on Thursday to oversee the installation and start-up of the HCCR once it arrived. He then called Sammy Joyce to make arrangements for a new cell culture batch. Hopefully, with the HCCR in place, the continuous cell culture and harvest would go much better this time.

"Sorry, Sam. No time for factory acceptance testing at our end. We'll just have to hope it works the first time. We can make adjustments on site."

"Sure, John. I'll start making preparations for a new cell culture batch right away. We should be able to start growing up a new batch early next week."

John knew that they would be cutting it close if he was to have any chance of making a rendezvous with eighteenth-century Greenwich on the twenty-second of December. Assuming the BV particles from Doug's brain were capable of expressing the desired proteins within the *in vitro* cell culture, there would be no time to characterize or purify them. If the culture was successful, he would have to settle for the crude cell-free supernatant from the initial harvest and recovery steps, and could only hope that the active psychotropic protein material would be present.

Of course, this was John's personal agenda, which no one shared except his good friend, business partner, and time-bending oracle, Bob Fenwick. But not to worry, after all Bob was *crazy*, and any leak of the tongue would simply be taken as a delusional rant, not to be taken seriously. As far as Dr. Li, Sammy, and Jennifer were concerned, the objective of this study was to prove, or hopefully disprove, a potential threat to human health which threatened to alter the entire course of their research.

One thing did bother John, though: pangs of guilt for not leveling with Jennifer on the real nature of his intentions. They had shared their inner thoughts and feelings on just about everything else in their lives, especially those events that pained them the most, leaning on one another to ease the suffering of personal loss. Now, he found himself shutting her out, unable to reveal his true motivation for pursuing this line of investigation, essentially lying to her and to others as well. But he felt he had no choice, figuring if they knew what he was really up to, he'd be forced to check himself into Lakeland and share a room with Bob—that is, assuming the courts deemed him mentally incompetent to stand trial for breaking and entering!

The next two weeks went pretty much as planned. John, Jim, and Maggie flew out on Thursday, the second of December, and spent the weekend assembling and testing the HCCR apparatus in the pilot plant with Ted Salmonson assisting and supervising them at every turn. After all, as head of Fermentation Development, he was the hands-on guy when it came to large-scale cell culture and fermentation and needed to know more than anyone else how this thing was going to work.

Anticipating their arrival, Sammy had already begun growing up a new batch of insect cells in her cell culture lab, the first step in initiating a production batch. The whole idea was to start out small, growing up cells in small shaker flasks which would then be used to inoculate larger and larger vessel volumes in a step-wise fashion until, after about sixteen days, the desired production batch size and cell mass would be reached, 300 liters in this case. At this point the batch would be ready for the final and most important production phase: inoculation with BV virus and subsequent protein expression and harvesting. Normally, the virus would be a genetically altered variant form of the baculovirus (vBV) developed by the GenAvance research team. However, for this special test run they would be using BV particles isolated from Doug Justin's brain tissue—dubbed "jBV" by the research team.

Up to this point in the cell culture process, everything was conducted in a batch mode intended to simply increase total cell mass. Once inoculated and fully infected with baculovirus, the 300-liter production bioreactor would transition to *continuous perfusion mode*, with fresh liquid media being added, as spent media and cell culture was continuously drawn off, maintaining a constant level and viable cell mass concentration in the bioreactor. This was the most critical step in the process, where Bob Fenwick's invention—the HCCR system—would come into play.

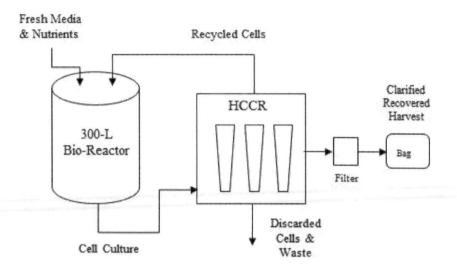

The hydro-cyclone device was designed to separate live cells from the liquid culture media, a small fraction of the cells being discarded with the greater portion being returned or re-cycled to the bioreactor. The liquid phase, containing the desired target protein expressed by the viral DNA, would be collected, clarified, and concentrated as finished harvest product.

Hopefully, after a week of continuous cell culture and harvesting—assuming the HCCR unit was up to the task—John would have enough product to take home, while production and further testing would continue at GenAvance. John had set a target date of the eighteenth, based ostensibly on the demands of the medical examiner back home in anticipation of a CDC inquiry, but in fact driven by John's own secret agenda and time line. Of course, no one at GenAvance had any idea that John planned to use the clarified harvest material on himself!

In was now Thursday morning, December 9. In less than one week's time John's team had been successful at installing the HCCR unit and getting it operational. On Wednesday, they made several test runs with water to work out the remaining kinks in the control system. Hopefully, the unit would perform as intended when it came time to harvest live cell culture. They were all keeping their fingers crossed.

"So, today's the day of reckoning," Sammy said with a nervous laugh, seated at the conference table in her usual legs-curled-up-and-under yoga-like position. They had been meeting each day for the past week at the same time—8:00 a.m.—in the small pilot plant conference room to review progress and discuss the day's planned activities.

"I have no doubt the inoculation will go well," Ted Salmonson said confidently. "I'm shooting for one o'clock. The live jBV test virus is ready to go."

"So, assuming it works, how long after inoculation before protein expression begins?" John asked.

"Well, the first thing that has to happen is for the batch to become thoroughly infected with the virus. This should take about two days."

"And what do you see as obstacles to successful protein expression?"

Ted leaned back in his chair, hands folded behind his head. "Well, first of all, the cells could simply lyse and die. But based on the results of the last test batch, we don't expect this to happen. This particular wild type BV virus appears to behave much like the variant BV line of virus particles developed in our lab. Assuming the cells do live, however, we don't really know how long they will survive in culture, or there may be some kind of environmental factor required to initiate protein expression that we've failed to replicate *in vitro*. Finally, the level of protein expression may not be high enough even to detect. Hell, we really don't even know what proteins we're are looking for!"—looking directly at John—"And all this assumes your recovery system even works."

There was a moment of silence before John spoke. "So…you're saying our chances are pretty good, then?"

That got a little chuckle out of everyone—even Ted—although it wasn't the effect John had intended. He was deadly serious. For John this *had* to work; failure was not an option!

Jennifer noticed the shift in John's demeanor since his arrival a week earlier. Understandably preoccupied and concerned at first, as they all were, he had become increasingly obsessed with the success of this run. For the rest of the team, if it didn't work, well okay, they could try again. But for John it had become something of a life or death struggle, and timing was of the essence. Everyone sensed it, but of course, no one really understood why.

Friday night found John pacing the balcony of Jennifer's condo. All night long he was up, thinking and rethinking the testing protocol over and over in his mind.

"John, it's three o'clock in the morning. You must try to get some sleep," Jennifer pleaded with him.

John didn't say a word

"I don't understand," she continued. "Why is this test run so important to you?"

John continued staring up into the heavens. The stars of the constellation Orion dominated the night sky.

"Do you see those two bright stars up there?" he asked softly.

Jennifer stood next to John and took his hand. "Yes. I see many bright stars in the sky."

John pointed with his other hand. "That one there, the star with the reddish hue, that's Betelgeuse, a red giant. See, it forms the right shoulder of Orion, the Hunter. The other lower and much brighter star is Rigel. It marks the hunter's left knee."

"Hmm, if you say so, *cheri*. They all look the same to me. I guess it all depends on how you connect the dots."

"Yes, I suppose so," John conceded. "But there are those who say our lives are controlled by the stars, or at least influenced."

"And what do you say?"

John gave a long sigh. "I don't know. I suppose it's possible. But I rather think, like you say, it is we who connect the dots. And if the patterns so formed turn out wrong, then we have only ourselves to blame."

"Yes. It would be nice if we could go back and…reconnect the dots in our lives, no?"

John smiled and drew closer to Jennifer. "Yes, m'love. It would indeed."

Fortunately, connecting the dots this weekend went as well as anyone could have hoped. The jBV-inoculated cell culture passed the first major hurdle: the insect cells did not lyse, but remained intact and viable as the virus infection spread throughout the cell culture population. By Saturday afternoon, the batch was ready to transition to perfusion cell culture mode as the HCCR apparatus was brought on line. There were a few anxious moments in which the transfer pumps failed to start, but the problem was quickly resolved as Maggie went through her start-up checklist and discovered the source of the problem: a control wire inside the panel which had come loose during last night's final system checkout. Sighs of relief were heard all around.

The first hour or so was spent balancing the pressures and flows in and out of the cell recovery unit and adjusting the control loop parameters for live cell culture. The loops had been pre-tuned running on water, but live cell culture altered the fluid dynamics enough that adjustments had to be made— kind of like trimming the controls of an airplane with and without a passenger load. Once the system was stabilized, Ted and Sammy took over, sampling and testing the major process streams and calling out instructions to John and his team.

Cell recovery and harvesting was the critical step where the first trial batch failed a month ago, and it required all hands on deck to ensure success.

Whereas the first trial batch resulted in a rapid loss of cell viability over the first twelve hours of continuous harvesting operations, the current cell culture remained healthy through the first night and well into Sunday. A small decline was observed that afternoon, but with a small adjustment in nutrient composition and cell removal rate, the decline was reversed and a viable cell mass maintained. Ted and Sammy were forced to acknowledge the success of the HCCR unit. Apparently it had made all the difference.

By Tuesday afternoon it was becoming clear that the trial batch was a success. How long the culture would remain viable was anyone's guess, but they had already recovered almost a thousand liters of clarified harvest into pre-sterilized 100-liter plastic bags, more than enough for their purposes. There was just one more processing step to perform: concentration of the clarified harvest to produce a more stable, concentrated protein mixture that would be easier to characterize in the lab. Concentration would be performed using a tangential flow ultra-filtration (UF) module—a standard downstream unit operation of biotech processing.

Ted and Sammy wanted to wait until Thursday for the first UF run, but John was becoming increasingly anxious to take something back to Jersey with him. The winter solstice deadline was fast approaching—only a week away—and he was eager to do his own little "test run" over the weekend. And what if something went wrong with the UF run? That would at least give them another day to make a fix.

So, they reluctantly agreed to take the first 600 liters of clarified harvest out of cold storage for a UF run on Wednesday. The run went well, resulting in about 20 liters of concentrated clarified harvest. The final bulk product—tagged "jBV Harvest"—had an almost straw-like appearance, slightly viscous. The 20 liters was sterile filtered into forty smaller, more manageable 500-cc plastic bottles. John had them further subdivide one of the bottles into one hundred 5-cc aliquot vials—"as requested by the medical examiner." The bottles and vials were placed in frozen storage. Those that John was to take with him were further placed into shipping containers packed with blue ice packs.

Thursday evening the team celebrated with Japanese takeout and sake in the Pod-A conference room, the location of his first meeting with the GenAvance team back in August. Jennifer was there, and Dr. Sam Li joined them as well. Dr. Li congratulated John and his team on the success of their star performing invention, the HCCR unit.

Pleased with the success of the run, there was nonetheless a certain pall which hung over the gathering, an unspoken uncertainty over the future of this particular line of research, Sam's pride and joy. While the jury was still out over the implications of the jBV particle, there would certainly be repercussions and possibly delays in funding until all the loose ends were tied down. John would be returning home on Friday with his frozen booty, while

Jim and Maggie would remain behind to assist the GenAvance team with operation and training on the HCCR unit.

John spent his last evening in Thousand Oaks with Jennifer and Renee. He thought it strange, though pleasing, how Renee had come to regard him as more than just her mother's friend, but almost as a father figure. John, too, had come to look upon her as the child he never had.

Chapter 39

1999/1774
18 December
Haddonfield, N.J.

Back home in his study, John studied the frozen, straw-colored contents of the small glass vial on the desk in front of him as he contemplated his next move. It had all came down to this genetically engineered concoction, this time-bending psychotropic potion spawned in the crucible of natural selection, ancient rituals, and modern science; his last chance to fix history, to "go back and save her," the girl of dreams and visions, visions which had plagued him since the first bite of that greenhead fly three months ago, the week after Labor Day.

But would it work?

When John arrived home Friday night there was an official looking letter in the mailbox. It was a summons from the New Jersey State Police. He was being cited as a "person of special interest" in the ongoing investigation of the break-in at Shockley Laboratories, Rutgers University, on Saturday, 30 October. He was to appear at the courthouse in Trenton on Wednesday, the twenty-second of December, promptly at 9:00 a.m.

"Wednesday, the twenty-second?" he read aloud. "'Please be prompt.'"

That was now just four days away. The summons was dated December 2, more than two weeks ago, the day he and his team left for the west coast. The summons gave him two weeks to respond, or to request a stay for any special circumstances. That date, too, had come and gone. Now he would be "in contempt" if he did not appear in court as summoned.

But, of course, John had no intention of going to Trenton on Wednesday, the twenty-second. He had a prior commitment, an appointment with history in eighteenth-century Greenwich, Cumberland County. Assuming things worked out this weekend and the elixir had the desired effect, he would be well on his way to Greenwich come 9:00 a.m. Wednesday morning, in plenty of time to catch up with later events of the twenty-second —the "crux of time," the marking of the winter solstice, his rendezvous with destiny, and the opportunity to reweave the very fabric of history, to reconnect the dots of tragic, star-borne events, past and present. No, he could not postpone this happening; the opportunity may never come again. And if he failed in this endeavor? Well, he would just have to face the music on his return. But he had no intention of failing—or at least failing to try. Now, as he considered his next move to test this vile concoction in the safety of his home, John had two decisions to make: exactly *where* to do it, and exactly *how* to do it.

The where part was easy, once he thought it through. If he remained in his home and the drug worked as he hoped, he had no real assurance of where he would end up. Yes, hopefully eighteenth-century Haddonfield, but John's house didn't exist back then, and its location was well outside the limits of downtown colonial Haddonfield. For all he knew he could end up in a barn or pigsty, or some farmer's daughter's boudoir, or much, much worse—an outhouse or privy! No, he would have to go somewhere safe, a place that was today just as it was then. In John's mind there was only one such place: the Indian King Tavern. No problem. As docent he could come and go as he pleased at the Tavern, and was expected to show up in traditional colonial garb anyway.

Okay, now the second question: how to administer the drug. This was the part that made him nervous. His aversion to drugs of any kind made him shiver at the very thought of it. Should he drink it down, like Doctor Jekyll? No, he had no assurance that it could be absorbed through his GI tract, or simply destroyed by stomach acid and digestive enzymes. Mainline it with a hypodermic like some street addict? Heaven forbid! The very thought was anathema to him; and besides, way too risky. Should he go with an intramuscular injection, like insulin? Hmm, perhaps; but even that may be too risky. Then he considered the obvious, asking himself the simple question: how does the fly do it? Yes, that was it! He would administer it subcutaneously, pricking his skin with a needle dipped in the stuff. Yeah, just like a smallpox vaccination, or—suddenly recalling the Led Zeppelin tattoo on Doug's left arm—a tattoo! Sure, all he needed was a tattoo needle, or something like it. Yes, given his general aversion to drug use of any kind, this was definitely the way to do it. "Vaccination" sounded far more innocuous than "injection"; and "tattoo" sounded better yet!

John checked the local Yellow Page listings and found a place in Berlin, New Jersey—about six miles away—that carried a full line of tattooing supplies. He gave them a call. Great! They were open till noon. He headed over and got the complete lowdown on needles and the art of tattooing from a guy who obviously knew his stuff. He wound up buying about a dozen disposable tube/needle combos, going with 7 magnum needle/tubes with 5/8" combo grips. He figured that would give him the area coverage he needed. He even picked up an illustrated book on tattooing techniques.

Returning home after a hearty diner lunch—didn't know when his next meal would be—he made final preparations for his test run journey. After dressing himself for the occasion in his freshly pressed colonial garb, he took a thawed vial of jBV harvest from the fridge and placed it in an empty Sucrets tin, then put the tin and six disposable tattooing tubes into his eighteenth-century cartridge box attached to his belt. He took the remaining eighteenth-century coins from his box of artifacts and placed them in the leather coin purse hung around his neck and tucked it inside his vest. After checking himself out one last time in the mirror, he headed out.

2:00 p.m. Things were slow at the Indian King Tavern. The next scheduled tour wasn't for another half hour, and the docent on duty was in a back room filling out some paperwork. John headed straight upstairs to one of the guest rooms and closed the door behind him, checking carefully to be sure he was alone, that there was no one else on the second floor.

Placing the Sucrets tin and the tattoo tube/needle combos from his cartridge box on the dresser, he removed one of the glass vials from the tin and began filling the tubes with equal portions of the straw-colored liquid until the vial was empty, ending up with three partially filled tubes. Returning the empty glass vial and the three unused tube/needle combos to the cartridge case, he studied the three filled tubes and took a deep breath.

"Well, here goes."

Sitting on the edge of the bed he rolled up his left sleeve and picked up one of the liquid-filled tube/needles. Gingerly, but deliberately, he began applying the needles. He went a little deeper than the illustrations in the tattoo book showed, just deep enough to draw some blood. After all, that is what the greenhead fly would have done. Only thing was, he wasn't really sure how much to apply. He figured he'd start low, see what the effects were, then increase the dose if necessary, keeping the two remaining tubes as spares. If he was able to go back in time, and the effects began to wear off too soon, they would serve as a backup supply in order to—what was the word?—keep on tripping!

John sat there, waiting for something to happen.

But nothing did.

He decided to widen the application area, effectively giving himself an area tattoo of straw-colored "ink." He paused, waiting, but nothing—hold on! What was that, a faint humming sound? Had the AC kicked in? No, this was a non-directional hum that sounded as if it was coming from inside his head. The room began to brighten, and the humming grew more intense as John holstered the partially spent tube/needle in his cartridge pouch. Yes, something was indeed happening! The transition seemed smooth and painless this time, not as before with real live flies. There were no voices, no headaches—at least not yet. Soon the hum turned into the more familiar buzzing sound and further intensified, crowding out all ambient noise from the street below. The room became awash in a brilliant white light; then a very faint voice, barely audible at first, but definitely discernible: *"Go back, John! Save her!"* It was not at all threatening, but almost reassuring. John was

forced to close his eyes as light and sound intensified in a flood of
otherworldly images. The single voice became several voices, then a choir of
voices raging against a sea of blinding white light. Suddenly there came a new
and different voice—a much calmer and gentle voice—from somewhere
above him.

"*Open your eyes, John! Open your eyes…NOW!*"

John responded reflexively to the command and there came an instant
silence, a sudden rushing vacuum devoid of sensation, drawing him into a
new state of consciousness, like an egg sucked into a bottle—that old eighth
grade science trick—a feeling both rejuvenating and fleeting, transitioning
him to that transcendent, out-of-body, visionary state which by now had
become quite familiar to him. Yes, he had successfully transitioned back in
time. And yes, he felt quite well and alive, and very much at peace with
himself.

John looked around. He found himself in yet another bedroom, about
the same size as the guest room he'd just left, but much more finely
appointed with signs of being lived in. Several shirts and pairs of pants lay
across the canopy bed waiting to be folded; two leather saddle saddlebags lay
open over the backs of a reading chair, one empty, the other half packed with
undergarments and various personal articles. Next to the bed was a small
trunk, empty with raised lid waiting to be packed. An open armoire revealed a
modest collection of jackets, waistcoats, and footwear.

But it was the wooden box on the dresser that really caught John's
attention. Could it be? Yes! It was the same ornately carved wooden box with
floral patterns he now had in his modern-day possession, handed down from
generation to generation, containing the love letters written by John to
Rebecca. Next to the box was a leather satchel filled to stuffing with what
John could only assume to be more papers and letters.

Then there came the sound of footsteps on the stairs, followed by a
voice as the footsteps paused in the hallway just outside the room. It was a
young man's voice, responding to another more distant voice from below.

"Thank you, Bart. I look forward to joining you and Jonathan for
dinner at the Tavern. This being my last night home for some time, perhaps, I
could surely use a good meal and a few stiff pints of English ale as a
sendoff!!"

"Yes, indeed!" bellowed a baritone voice from below. "This certainly
calls for the proper patriot send off."

The bedroom door opened and the young man entered the room. John
recognized him instantly: John Jay Weston, his many-times great-great uncle
of revolutionary war fame.

John instinctively rose from the bed with the intent to hide himself—
he was after all the intruder. Forgetting for the moment his incorporeal state,
this minor effort took him almost instantly to the far side of the room. He

had to smile. He was invisible, of course! And this time and place was but a shadow of the past.

The younger John was carrying a musket, ammo pouch, and powder horn, which he set down in the corner of the room by the armoire. Taking a seat at the desk, he opened the middle drawer, removed a document, and studied it.

The older John drew close, peering over young man's shoulder. The document was a letter of commission conferring upon John Jay Weston the rank of Captain in the 8th Massachusetts Regiment. It was dated 9 July, 1775, and signed by Colonel Paul Dudley Sargent, Commanding Officer.

John drew closer still, close enough for physical contact had he been in a corporeal state. As it was, it was more an overlapping of two consciousnesses, a kind of mind meld similar to what John experienced that night in Thousand Oaks when he traded souls with young John Jay and made love to the lovely Rebecca. This time his senses were taken on a toboggan ride of sight, sound, and fury as young John Jay's life suddenly flashed before him. More than a mere visual reprise, the experience evoked the same feelings of hope, joy, passion, and pain that accompanied them in real life.

It began with John Jay as a boy growing up in Haddonfield; his trips to Greenwich with his older half brother, Bartholomew; his first meeting with little Missy Rebecca at the Greenwich Fair in 1763; continuing through his teen years in Boston, where his mother, Amanda, relocated following the death of John's father, Samuel Weston Jr., in 1765; his later involvement with the Sons of Liberty and the Boston Tea Party. Finally, there were the war years, a collage of images presenting John's valiant service to the cause of liberty played out in rapid succession: his regiment's crossing of the Delaware with Washington on Christmas Day, 1775; his distinguished service at the battles of Trenton, Princeton, and Saratoga; the encampment at Valley Forge through the harsh winter of 1777 to 1778 where he was attached to Brigadier General Anthony Wayne—whose fiery and daring exploits would win him the moniker "Mad" Anthony Wayne.

The mood quickly changed as a subsequent series of increasingly disturbing images flashed through John's mind's eye: young John shivering from the cold, then from the "fever"—typhoid most likely; intermittent bouts of "old soldier's disease" and other forms of dysentery, that recurring and dismal companion to eighteenth-century army camp life. Beyond the imagery, John could feel the pain, physical and emotional, of young John's suffering. Weakened by illness, John Jay eventually succumbed to consumption in the spring of '79, an open letter from the young Rebecca slipping from his hand as he took his last breath.

Drawing back and away, the connection between the two Johns was immediately broken—a welcome reprieve from the young man's pain and grief of having lost the love of his life just seven months before. The older John knew this feeling all too well; it resonated within him like shattered glass.

John Jay rose from the desk and went to the dresser, opened the leather satchel, and removed the papers from inside, which were tied together with string like bundled mail. Untying one of the bundles, he began going through the papers one by one. They were letters, all addressed to John, sharing the same handwriting and signed by a "Missy" or simply "RW."

John realized what he was seeing. These were the missing, long-lost love letters from young Rebecca to John Jay! Combined with John's letters they would tell the complete story of their love. Oh, how John wished he could reach out and grab these letters and take them back home with him to twentieth-century New Jersey! Like newfound treasure in a child's dream, if one could but hold on and believe strongly enough, perhaps it would remain in one's tight grasp upon waking!

John Jay sat down on the side of the bed and reread each letter, one by one, rekindling the memory of young Rebecca with a smile, a nod of the head, even a little chuckle from time to time. Several times he had to rub his eyes to wipe away a tear, to clear his vision to read further. Finally, he let out an audible sigh, re-bundled the letters, and carefully returned them to the satchel. Pausing a moment, he took the satchel and placed it in the empty saddlebag.

So, he would be taking the letters with him into battle. There would be the letters from home, from Bart, perhaps, and from his mother, Amanda; but the Rebecca letters would be his main solace, his means of connecting with the familiar, his one true love and the world he left behind, as he faced the uncertainty of the coming conflicts.

Yes, of course! Which is why the letters remained lost to this day—or at least never made it into the Weston family archives. Perhaps they still exist; perhaps someone picked them up with good intentions to return them with his personal effects; perhaps they'd found a good home and now resided in someone's collection of war memorabilia or in a museum somewhere— perhaps.

John's attention was drawn to movement outside the bedroom window and he went to look. When he got there he realized it wasn't movement at all, but changing shadows cast by an ever-brightening afternoon sky. The intensity increased and began to spill over the windowsill into room, like a creeping fog. He suspected that he was in for another change of venue. The room became bathed in a familiar, soft, white light, his consciousness fading as he closed his eyes and thought the words: *Okay, take me there!*

On regaining consciousness, John found himself back in the same guestroom at the Indian King Tavern where his out-of-body travels began. He now felt the full weight of his own body against the bed, and with it came a deep disappointment. Had he returned so quickly to his own century without experiencing an in-the-flesh encounter with eighteenth-century Haddonfield?

Must've been the dose, he thought. "Need to increase the dose."

But on further inspection he realized the room was different: different furnishings, curtains on the windows, an overcoat hanging a coatrack that wasn't there before, clear evidence of occupancy.

"So, I'm still in colonial Haddonfield after all!" he said, relieved. "And apparently I've barged into someone else's room uninvited."

Getting up too quickly he became a bit light-headed, soon recovered, then went to the door and listened: no one there, just the muffled sounds of voices and human activity from the floor below. He carefully opened the door, walked out into the hallway and down the stairs to the ground floor below. Tipping his hat to a passing guest, he stopped and looked around the main hall lobby area to get his bearings. A well-dressed young man standing at his post behind the concierge desk, not ten feet away, looked up and addressed the newcomer.

"Can I help you, sir?" the young man inquired with a smile.

John returned the smile.

"Thank you. You wouldn't happen to know where I could find…a Mr. Weston? A Bartholomew Weston?"

"Why yes. As a matter of fact I do. Master Bart, as he is often called"—punctuating his remark with a wink—"typically takes his Sunday evening meal in the dining room, just there to your left." The young man looked up at the grandfather clock in the hallway. "He should be by within the hour. If you don't mind waiting in the tavern, I could alert you upon his arrival."

John considered this. "Yes. That would be fine."

"And who should I say is calling?"

John paused. "Tell him…John Samuel Weston, a distant relative."

"Yes, indeed, Mr. Weston," the young man replied with a raised eyebrow, jotting down a note to remind himself, "I shall be sure to inform him of your presence."

Just then, the sound of a guitar, a violin, and a woman's singing voice could be heard spilling from an adjoining room. John walked past the young man at the counter and entered the tavern bar room on the left, the source of the music.

As it was not yet evening, there were but a few patrons scattered about the dimly lit room. The smell of stale beer and burning wood from the fireplace hung in the air. John took a seat at an empty table near the performing duo: a young woman on guitar and vocals, and an older male accompanying her on violin. John nodded and exchanged smiles with the two performers, as a waiter approached him and took his order:

"A pint of English ale, if you please."

The waiter nodded and backed away.

John decided to just settle back and enjoy the music and the beer while awaiting word of Master Bart's arrival. One tune in particular caught his fancy. It was a haunting melody, set in a minor key, played on guitar with an open string tuning, imitating the plaintive drone of the bagpipe, an entirely suitable emulation for the matching lyrics. The pleasing lilt of the young woman's voice lent a special, mesmerizing quality to the rendition:

> Catch the sound of windfull night,
> A frosty anthem to Winter's might;
> And stars froz'n still against the sky
> Shine brightly cold to catch the eye.
>
> What purpose have these winds of rage,
> That solstice lengthened nights engage
> To pound and shred man's mortal fibre,
> To strip the earth of life's own fire,
> Till all is covered cold and clean
> By midnight's wrap...gray moonlit sheen.
>
> A prelude to some holocaust?
> A purging clean of all things past?
> Or just a change the seasons bring
> When time encircles back again
> And Spring at last the heavens tame,
> Earth's remnants warmed...and life reclaimed.

The words struck home with John. The last verse in particular. *A purging clean of all things past?* Yes, that's what it was all about. Setting things right! *Earth's remnants warmed...and life reclaimed.* That's why he was here, why he had come back. Only thing was, he couldn't wait for spring. He had to do it now, *when solstice lengthened nights engage!*

Absorbed in music and thought, John didn't notice the young concierge standing by.

"...I beg your pardon, sir."

John looked up, a bit flustered. "Wha...? I'm sorry, what was that?"

"Master Bart has invited you to join him for dinner"—motioning to the adjoining room—"there, in the main dining room."

"Yes, of course. Thank you, son. Please inform Mr. Weston that I shall be there presently."

John spent the next few minutes gathering his thoughts. What story would he present to his five-times great-grandfather, Bartholomew Weston?

How were they related? How did he know so much about Bart and his family situation? He decided it would be best to shift the conversation as soon as possible to other topics, like the tea shipment and threats of retaliation from the local populace sympathetic to the growing patriot cause. That would hopefully pique Bart's interest more than family matters.

On entering the dining room, John did a quick survey for the most Bart-like figure. A gentleman seated alone on the far side of the room—late forties, well groomed, handsome, sipping a glass of brandy—seemed the most likely candidate. Almost at the same time, the gentleman looked up and, seeming to recognize John, smiled and motioned John to come join him at the table. John smiled and nodded in return and proceeded to the table.

"So, you must be John Samuel Weston," Bart said, rising to meet his guest with an extended hand. "At last, I now have a face to match with the name I've heard spoken on several occasions of late. Someone claiming to be a distant relative of mine, I believe."

John shook his hand, but sensed a slight testiness in Bart's voice. "Yes, sir, the same, at your service. And you must be Bartholomew Weston," John replied with a handshake. "And as to the matter of relations, I cannot say precisely how, but our surnames would surely suggest a past family connection."

"Hmm, yes, perhaps. Please, have a seat."

John took a seat at the table across from Bart

"I must say, I was surprised when my ship's captain first told me of your encounter in Greenwich," Bart continued. "I thought I knew the Weston family line and was surprised to learn of a distant unknown cousin."

"Well, it is not uncommon for family lines to diverge," John offered, "especially given the circumstances of colonial expansion and exploration in the new world. It is easy to lose touch."

"Perhaps," Bart simply said, lingering on the word. "As I think upon it further, it does occur to me that my grandfather, Samuel Weston, who came to settle these colonies eighty or so years ago, spoke of a cousin who accompanied him on the crossing. I believe he said his name was...let me think now...Andrew. Yes! Andrew was his name."

John was quick to make the connection. Andrew Weston was mentioned in his Aunt Dee's family bible, but it wasn't clear whether he was Sam's brother or some other relation.

"Yes. Well, there you have it then," John replied, going a bit out on a limb. "Andrew was my grandfather. So, that would make us, let's see, third cousins, would it not?"

John's assertive tone, and the simple logic of it, was enough to convince Bart.

"Yes, I suppose it would," he agreed.

Bart appeared more relaxed, now, but there was something else bothering him. "Now that we have met, John, I find it hard to believe the rumors that circulate concerning your appearance in Greenwich."

John was puzzled, and more than a little concerned. "What…kind of rumors?"

"Forgive me for saying, but I only repeat what I have heard."

"Which is…?"

"That you may in fact be responsible for the rash of fires that have plagued the region of late. That you come and go at will—like a wizard in the night, disappearing in a puff of smoke!" he added with a chuckle.

"Me? A wizard? My, those are…wild assertions! The fact of the matter is, it is I who has been investigating these same events, and I believe I have picked up the scent of the fox, the true culprit! I can only surmise that these rumors are the nefarious work of the real perpetrators of this mischief, to misdirect and obfuscate the course of my investigation."

John sat back in his chair, rather pleased with his cross-examined defense.

"Well stated, John. As I said, I place no credence in these rumors. I consider myself a good judge of character, and while I must admit to sensing something…mysterious in you, I detect no malice or flaw of any measure that would support these allegations."

John expressed his appreciation as Bart poured him a glass of brandy from his favorite reserve stock and ordered dinner for the two of them. John felt it was the proper time to broach the subject of the tea shipment, a sensitive topic. He told Bart he learned of it during his recent visit to Greenwich and feared that the growing fervor of popular dissent in that town may cause some to take drastic, even violent action.

"Yes, I am aware that 'the cat is out of the bag,' as it were," Bart fretted. "The brig *Greyhound* arrived in port with our consignment of tea on the twelfth, Monday of last week. We had hoped to avert public disclosure, but somehow word of its anticipated arrival leaked out. I was told that a certain Reverend Philip Vickers Fithian may have been responsible, but that is just hearsay."

"Yes, I have heard the same name spoken, and other names as well."

"Really? And what names might they be? Please, speak freely, John."

"Well, I believe your brother, John, has also caught wind of it, although, to my knowledge, he does not know of the company's involvement, only that the *Greyhound* would be bringing it into port at Greenwich."

Bart seemed visibly shaken by this piece of news. "Oh my, I was hoping not to involve John in any of this. How in God's name did he find out?"

John shrugged. "I don't know. I only know that John communicated his knowledge of it by letter to a Miss Rebecca Whitman, the blacksmith's daughter, the young lady whom John has been courting of late."

"Yes, I know Miss Whitman. A very fine and lovely young lady. This 'courtship,' as you put it, goes back quite a few years, to childhood, in fact."

John smiled. He knew this, of course, from the family letters, but couldn't let on. From his visions, he also knew of other pending events which none, other than himself, could possibly know or foretell.

"There is just one more thing, Bart."

Bart cocked his head to one side. "Which is?"

"My sources in Cumberland County informed me of a plan to take the tea by force and destroy it—in fact, to *burn* it!"

"Really? A repeat of the *Peggy Stewart* affair?"

John nodded. "Yes, it would appear so."

"But I am told the tea has been off-loaded and is in safekeeping, in a secret place?"

Recalling his conversation with Mr. Mason, the tailor, in the old Stone Tavern, John added, "Yes, indeed it has. But, do you know where?"

Bart thought for a moment. "No, Paul did not divulge those details to me."

John leaned forward, speaking just above a whisper. "In the wine cellar of the Masons' tailor shop, the same shop where young Rebecca is employed."—pulling back and taking a normal tone—"But I fear that this particular cat may have also slipped from the bag. The tea's whereabouts is known, I'm afraid."

Bart raised an eyebrow. "So, our plan has been completely compromised, then. When do your sources say that this...hijacking is to occur?"

John was quick to answer. "Next Thursday evening, the twenty-second of December, the marking of the winter solstice." He let Bart absorb this detail before adding, "Bart, I fear not only for the tea, but for the safety of Miss Rebecca. She spends a good deal of time at the shop, and is good friends with the Masons."

"So, do you think she may be responsible for leaking this information?"

John shook his head. "I really don't know. But given the circumstances, she may have been forced to choose between conflicting loyalties."

Bart sat back, massaging his brandy snifter with both hands. "John, are you planning to return to Greenwich before the twenty-second?"

John didn't have to think twice. "Yes, God willing."

"Good. I wonder if I could impose upon your good graces to request a favor?"

"Certainly, if it is within my power."

Bart explained that he would like John to contact his associate Paul McKenzie, first mate, who had signed for the release of the tea with the customs officials, and had arranged for its safekeeping in town. John recognized the name, and indicated that he and Paul met on a previous occasion in Greenwich, and that he would know him on sight.

"That's good. What I'd like for you to do is give him a letter, which I will pen this evening and give to you in the morning—I trust you are staying the night?"

"Why…yes, of course. Though I haven't yet made arrangements for lodging."

"That is not a problem. I will arrange it for you," Bart assured him.

"So, is that it? Just deliver a letter?"

Bart hesitated before responding. "If it's not too much to ask, John, I would like you to work with Paul to arrange transfer of the tea to another safe location for the tea. Paul knows the area well and"—pausing as though he was going to say something else, but decided against it—"should be able to come up with an alternate safe haven. Of course, it must be done at night to avoid detection."

Bart took a sip of brandy. "I would go myself," he added, "but I have pressing business to tend to here in Haddonfield and Philadelphia."

"Yes, of course. I will do what I can," John said.

"Good! It is settled then!"

The waiter approached the table with a tray of fine food: pheasant under glass, wild rice, and candied yams.

"Splendid! Thank you, Thomas."—turning to John—"I hope you are hungry, John. The chef refuses to take anything back!"

They both laughed.

But John had one more thing on his mind.

"Speaking of 'letters,'" he said. "I had written your brother John more than a month ago to explain my situation and concern for Rebecca's safety. Of course, I made no specific mention of your involvement with the tea shipment, or anything relating to its whereabouts."

John paused to gauge Bart's reaction.

"Yes, go on," Bart said.

"Well, not knowing where to send the letter, I had the innkeeper's wife from the Stone Tavern post it for me. But there has been no reply or indication that he ever received it."—*as my future state confirmed*—"I was simply wondering if you might know of its whereabouts. Perhaps it was routed to your care."

Bart played with his snifter of brandy and leaned back, speaking to the rafters above him. "Hmm. Jonathan, my trusted apprentice, handles all of my correspondence. I would have to check with him. Perhaps it was overlooked, or misplaced." He took a sip of brandy and looked back at John. "But, I assure you, if it does turn up here, I will make certain it gets delivered to young John."

"Thank you, Bart. I'm much indebted."

Chapter 40

1774
19 December
Greenwich, Cumberland County, NJ

Monday afternoon, December 19. The town of Greenwich was abuzz with news of the tea. No longer a mere rumor, the brig *Greyhound* had made port one week ago to the day with its "contraband of that detestable weed," and by the afternoon of Tuesday, the thirteenth, word was out. As news spread through the countryside and to neighboring towns, local patriotic fervor was fanned as citizens and town council leaders considered what should be done. Nowhere was the discussion more focused and intense than at the local taverns, and no tavern was better situated than the Stone Tavern in Greenwich to get the latest information and voice one's opinion. While a few stalwart loyalists remained, public opinion had definitely shifted in favor of the patriot cause.

"I hear the county elders in Bridge-town have called for an indignation meeting to be held at the courthouse there come this Friday, the twenty-third, to decide the fate of the tea," one man said.

"Bridge-town! Why Bridge-town?" said another. "We can handle our own affairs!"

"Aye, but this goes beyond local concerns," said a third. "It's a question of principle. What happens here needs to be heard and announced to the world!"

"The twenty-third? That's four days from now!" said another. "It's been one week already. I don't think we can wait that long."

This was met with concurring grunts and murmurings of "remember the *Peggy Stewart*" and "should never have let them land the tea in the first place."

Seated at a distant table, a very nervous Paul McKenzie and Captain Allen listened for signs of new developments as they finished their evening meal.

"The *Peggy Stewart* affair? Well, at least *my* ship may be spared," the captain sighed with weary resignation. "I'm just glad we managed to off-load the tea that first night before anyone knew we were in port. But, the next day, they showed up in droves, almost like…they were expecting us."

Paul didn't say a word. He was thinking about that conversation he'd had with Cap'n Jacob two months ago, just before he set sail for England— that ill-fated slip of the tongue.

"Well, my job is done," the captain said with a satisfied smile. "Goods delivered, safe and sound. But, I'm afraid yours is just beginning, my friend." He took a swig of ale. "How do you think they knew where the tea was to be hidden?"

Paul took a deep breath. His thoughts turned to Rebecca. "I don't know. I thought the Masons' shop would be a safe house. I suppose I was wrong."

Paul hadn't spoken to Rebecca since arriving back in Greenwich the week before. Mrs. Mason had said she was ailing and hadn't shown up at the shop in several days.

Captain Allen sensed his preoccupation. "So, if you don't mind my prying, how are things between lass and swain?"

Paul forced a smile and shook his head. "Not so good, I'm afraid. I am told she is not well, and what with all the commotion over tea, I haven't been able to break away to see her."

But there was one other thing on Paul's mind, which he had no intention of sharing with the captain. It turned out that Cap'n Jacob was back in town arranging for another shipment of contraband rum. Paul ran into him on Saturday at Wood's Emporium as he was shopping for the week's provisions. He thought it uncanny how Jacob always seemed to know where to find him—and always at the most inopportune times.

"Well, this *is* a surprise!" Paul groaned. "I'm almost afraid to ask what brings you back to Greenwich."

Jacob took an apple from a bin, flipped the clerk a penny, and proceeded to slice and eat the fruit as he spoke. "Why, I came back for the apples, Paul! They are hard to come by in Barbados."

"Yes, I am sure. Please, state your business, Jacob."

"I have a proposition to make, Paul. And there is a pretty profit in it for you if you care to partake."

John looked around. "Let's take this conversation elsewhere, Jacob. This is not the place to discuss such matters."

Walking back toward the wharf, Jacob revealed his plan to smuggle out rum and other contraband concealed in crates of beaver pelts. They would pay the necessary duty on the skins; however, this was but a very small fraction of what they would receive for the rum. "Just the cost of doing business," as Jacob put it. He wanted Paul to arrange for warehouse storage of the crates at the wharf and make the necessary arrangements with the customs officials, like any normal shipment.

"Why don't you just use your normal pickup and transfer point off Tindall Island?" Paul asked.

"Hmm, yes, well, that's become somewhat risky of late," Jacob said rubbing his chin. "The new commander of the local British guards is beginning to catch on. Almost intercepted our last outbound shipment."

"So, you think you have a better chance smuggling the rum right under their noses?"

"Aye! I do!" Jacob guffawed. "Beyond the monetary reward, just think of the personal satisfaction it would bring!"

"So, when is this all to take place, Jacob? As you must know, I am caught up in the middle this tea debacle, which I suspect you may have played a part in, somehow."

"Why, Paul! You cut me to the quick with your insinuations! I am just a hard-working businessman like anyone else, trying to eke out a living in these tumultuous and uncertain times."

"Cut the blarney, Jake. Just tell me when."

The two paused at the crest of Ye Greate Street where it overlooked the Cohansey River, wharf, and warehouse complex below.

"This Thursday evening, the twenty-second," Jake said, pointing to the largest of the warehouse structures. "That one there, the one with the padlocked door. I believe it to be the most secure. Be there at six. I will have the goods there by seven o'clock, eight at the latest."

Paul reluctantly agreed, as long as he could disavow direct complicity if the hidden contraband were discovered.

"Not a problem!" Jacob assured him. "You may throw me to the sharks if ever I point a finger at you!"

Captain Allen was alone when he left the Stone Tavern that afternoon, leaving Paul behind nursing his tankard of ale while strategizing on how to win the heart of young Rebecca. The captain struck a handsome and imposing figure as he strode down Ye Greate Street in his ship captain's uniform. Passing the Gibbon House, he greeted two crew members coming in the opposite direction and making their way toward the tavern.

"Good day, gentlemen," he offered with a nod.

"G'day to you, Captain Allen," returned one of the sailors, doffing his hat.

Captain Allen!? The name rang out, striking a familiar chord with the old woman seated in a passing horse-drawn farm wagon being pulled by a fine team of black stallions with distinctive white diamond markings on their faces. Captain Allen! Like a sprung trap, the name unleashed a torrent of memories in the old woman's mind, memories of romance, of a young British leftenant, her first true love and father of her firstborn and ill-fated child, Destiny. Yes, Leftenant Jacob Allen would surely be "Captain Allen" by now, she reasoned. This is him! At long last, he has come back for me!

Agitated and distressed, assuming a totally different persona, the old woman abruptly turned to the man seated beside her and shouted out with girlish glee: "Father! You must stop the wagon at once! Young Jacob Allen has returned! Jacob has come back to me!"

And with that she leaped from the wagon to the ground with all the vigor of newfound youth. Albert Greene pulled up smartly on the reins, bringing the whinnying team and creaking wagon to an abrupt halt.

Agatha Greene raced forward and flung her arms about the astonished Captain Allen.

"Jacob! At last! You have returned home to me!"

Captain Allen was at a loss for words. Prying himself loose from her hold, he held the woman at arm's length, shaking his head.

"Madame, I am afraid you have mistaken me for another. Please, take hold of yourself."

The exasperated Agatha remained undeterred.

"But, Jacob! Little Destiny waits for us at home. She speaks of you often and has been longing for your return."

By this time, Albert Greene had arrived. He tried to console his distraught and confused wife. "Now, now, my dear. You must let the captain be. He surely has important matters to tend to aboard ship." Addressing the captain with a hard wink, "I am sure he will come home once these matters are settled. Won't you, Captain?"

Captain Allen played along. "Why, yes...of course. I shall...be along presently, my dear."

"There, you see, my dear child," Albert consoled, "Let us go and leave the captain to tend to his business."

*****

Thursday, December 22. It was late afternoon when Cynthia Greene and her older sister, Alberta, returned from town with the week's provisions. Their father, Albert Greene, was busy in the barn when the wagon pulled up outside their home, a humble, if not slightly ramshackle farm cottage located about half the distance to Stowe Creek Landing. He dropped what he was doing to tend to the team and help the girls unload the wagon.

"Did you remember the lamp oil?" he asked.

"Sure, Pa," Cynthia replied. "Two small kegs was all they had, so we bought them both."

"Fine. Just leave them in the wagon for now, I'll tend to them later. Let's get the rest into the house."

He sensed a certain excitement in the girls' giggling demeanor as they brought the supplies into the kitchen, like they were holding onto a delicious piece of gossip dying to be shared. Living with a house full of women his whole life, he knew the signs.

"You two look like cats that just ate the canary. What conniving have you been up to?"

At eighteen years old, Cynthia was the youngest of four sisters. Taking more after her pa than her ma, she was also the most comely and outgoing, so whenever the opportunity arose to take the wagon into town she was quick to volunteer. Lately, she had re-established acquaintances with an old childhood friend, Rebecca Whitman, whom she hadn't seen since Pa stopped taking them to church on a regular basis, some six years ago.

Cynthia knew it all had to do with her ma. Although she didn't quite understand it, she knew her ma wasn't like the other women, and had a mean streak in her, too, as Cynthia received more than her fair share of beatings as a young girl growing up. In later years she and her sisters just did their best to avoid any confrontation, for Pa's sake. The oldest sister, Samantha, just turned twenty-four, had recently married and was now living in Salem City. Did she love the man? Perhaps, but Cynthia felt it was mainly to escape her mother and family situation.

Roberta, the second oldest, was working in the kitchen when her two younger sisters arrived with the supplies—and latest gossip—from town.

"I have the most delicious tidbit to share, Bert! Do you care to hear it?"

Roberta shook her head and continued with her chores, feigning indifference to Cynthia's breaking news.

"C'mon, sis! I know you want to hear!" Cynthia insisted.

Cracking a smile, Roberta broke down. "Okay. What is it Cynth?"

"Well, you know that handsome first officer from Captain Allen's ship…the one with the dreamy eyes? And you remember Rebecca Whitman, the blacksmith's daughter?" Not giving Roberta a chance to reply, or even take in what she was saying, Cynthia continued. "Well, he is planning to make a proposal of marriage to Miss Rebecca! She told me so herself!"

"Captain Allen and Rebecca Whitman? Can't be! I thought Rebecca had an eye for that young John Weston feller."

"No, no! Not Captain Allen!" Cynthia corrected her. "His young first officer. Only I can't remember his name."

"Well, then, maybe she'll make you the maid of honor!" Roberta chided.

They all laughed, and the conversation soon shifted to other things.

Agatha was in the other room, just within earshot, rocking to and fro in her rocker, when the words "Captain Allen," "Rebecca Whitman," and "proposal of marriage" broke through her veil of consciousness. It had taken Albert the better part of a day and a half to calm his wife down, to get her to focus on other things besides seafaring captains and ghosts from the past.

Now, it all came back to her in a raging flood of emotion. In her delusional state she began piecing things together into a new and distorted reality, guided by the voices in her head which suddenly came alive, telling her what she must do: *"So, the great Captain Allen thinks he can do as he pleases! Desert his family, cavort and carry on with that young whore, Rebecca Whitman! You must not allow this to happen! You must stop it in its tracks!"*

Then another, deeper, more sinister voice commanded her: *"He must stand the test of fire! 'Refiner's fire!' as scripture says. You must purify his soul with refiner's fire!"*

"Yes," the first voice responded, *"Purify with fire! Better to burn once in life than burn forever in hell!"*

Albert hadn't witnessed the likes of what happened next since that terrible wolf peach incident many years ago revealed to the world the demons that lurked inside Agatha Greene's troubled mind. The girls were equally astonished and aghast at their mother's actions.

Without warning Agatha burst into the kitchen in a fit of rage, glowering, waving arms and screaming: "That cheating scoundrel! I will have his twiddle-diddles in my purse by day's end, mark my word!" With that she grabbed the largest carving knife from the wall and ran out the back door toward the wagon before anyone could to stop her. By the time Albert could chase her down, she was already at the reins, and with a crack of the whip the team was off down the road with a lumbering Albert in fading pursuit.

"Agatha! Stop! What are you doing?" he shouted after her.

"Gotta do what I gotta do, Pa! Teach that varmint a lesson he won't ever forget!"

She was soon long gone, leaving Albert in the dust, panting and clutching his chest. Cynthia caught up with him a moment later.

"Pa, are you alright?" She asked.

"I'm...okay. Just let me...catch my breath a minute."

Chapter 41

1999/1774
22 December
South Jersey

John glanced in his rearview mirror. Good, no flashing lights; no sign of pursuit. Loosening his jacket to get comfortable, he reached over for his bottle of Gatorade and took a healthy swig. A quick OCD glance at the back seat confirmed everything was in order: knapsack, change of clothes, tri-corner hat, overcoat, and his cartridge pouch with his tattoo paraphernalia and vials of time-travel potion. He had left the house in a hurry and didn't have time to stash them in the trunk. Just glad he hadn't forgotten anything. He even brought along a box of matches and small can of lighter fluid, just in case he needed to cause some diversionary mischief. *Fight fire with fire*, as he put it.

This was the day he had been planning for, the day of reckoning, the "crux of time" where life lines converged, his last chance to change history, to set things right—to "go back and save her"! And this morning everything almost came to a screeching halt when a patrol car pulled up in front of his house at ten in the morning.

"Cant' be!" he uttered incredulously.

He ignored the knock on the door, knowing full well what the police officer wanted, or at least he thought he knew. He had ignored the summons to appear in state court in Trenton and now they were coming for him, but he didn't think they would be so prompt! After all, he was due in court at nine, and now it was eleven. Maybe it wasn't the summons after all; maybe it was something else, but he couldn't take any chances. He remained quiet, standing away from the windows, figuring he'd just outwait the officer. Fortunately, he had parked his car in the garage with the garage door closed. Had he locked the door? He couldn't remember.

He heard the officer going around to the rear of the house, followed by a knock on the back door.

"Damn persistent!"

Just then the phone rang and John nearly jumped ten feet in the air. He couldn't answer it, of course; that would be a dead giveaway. Anyway, it was probably the court or Sheriff's office. He let the call go to his answering machine.

"Hello, John." It was Katie's voice. John breathed a sigh of relief. "Just wondering how things are going. Haven't talked to you in quite a while. I tried your cell phone but you must have it turned off, so I left a message. Are you back from California? Give us a call when you get in. Hope everything is okay."

John took out his cell phone. Sure enough, it was turned off. He checked the time: 11:45 a.m. Glancing out the front door at three days' worth of neglected morning newspapers lying on the porch, he got an idea.

"Can't call her. Too risky. I'll have to text her."

He hadn't used the new texting feature since texting across networks on cell phones became possible this year. Fortunately, his Nokia mobile phone was so equipped. Dialing Katie's cell phone number he punched in the text:

GOT YOUR MESSAGE. GOT BACK FRIDAY BUT ON VACA THIS WEEK. TRAVELING. CAN YOU DO ME A FAVOR? I LEFT THE HOUSE AND FORGOT TO STOP THE MAIL AND PAPER. CAN YOU PLEASE STOP BY TODAY AND PICK IT UP FOR ME. SHOULD BE BACK END OF WEEK. TELL BOB HIS MACHINE WORKED! THANKS.

He hit the send button. When he looked up again, the police officer was gone, but only for a moment. Peering through the veranda window blinds John spied the young officer nosing around the garage, trying the door—it was locked—then, looking through the garage window he took out his notepad and made some notes.

"Damn! Should've parked around the block!" John scolded himself.

The officer walked back to his parked cruiser, got in, and just remained there. Ten minutes passed.

"Dammit! Don't you have somewhere else to go? A donut shop or something?" a frustrated John mumbled.

John jumped again as his cell phone buzzed, signaling a new text message. It was from Kate.

SURE JOHN. NO PROBLEM. WENT OUT FOR LUNCH IN NEARBY WESTMONT. CAN DROP BY THE HOUSE ON MY WAY BACK. HAVE A NICE VACA.

John breathed a sigh of relief. The officer meanwhile remained undeterred, having apparently decided to play a waiting game as he enjoyed his own paper bag lunch break right there in the parked cruiser.

It was around 12:30 when Katie's minivan pulled into the driveway. Immediately, the parked cruiser's door opened and the police officer exited and walked toward Katie's van, his right hand palming the holstered revolver by his side. Katie, a smile on her face, turned to face the officer as he approached.

John couldn't hear the conversation, but could only surmise what transpired from what happened next. After a few minutes, the officer smiled, tipped his hat, and backed away toward his cruiser. Katie paused before proceeding up the brick path to the front porch where she gathered up John's mail and morning newspapers and returned to her minivan. After a quick call on his police radio, the officer started his engine and slowly drove off, disappearing from view around the next corner, apparently convinced that John was gone, "on vacation," and would not be returning home anytime soon. John waited another five minutes or so before gathering up his things and heading out.

It was two o'clock when John reached Greenwich, which by now he could find in the dark with his eyes closed. He made just one stop on the way, a gas station in Bridgeton, to change into his colonial garb before heading on. The station attendant barely gave him a second look.

Entering town, John pulled up to the now familiar, crumbling remains of the old Stone Tavern, cut the engine, and took a deep breath. The air was cold, crisp, clear, and still, the only sound being the soft pinging of engine parts cooling down under the hood. The next step, too, had almost become rote as John prepared to self-administer the time-travel potion, returning the unused vial portion of the straw-colored liquid to his cartridge pouch. John didn't have long to wait, having administered just the right dosage this time. He was getting the hang of it, and that did bother him a bit.

The humming sound began ever so faintly, blending in with the ping of the cooling engine, such that John did not at first differentiate the two. Once it became apparent what was happening, he got out of the car, gathered up his things and waited. He came prepared for the winter weather this time, having brought along a wool overcoat fashioned with brass buttons and a high upturned collar.

By now John knew what to expect and this transition offered no real surprises. The fair weather cumulus clouds began to slowly melt away against a deepening blue and vibrant sky, as the afternoon sun grew larger and brighter, like a supernova, flooding the world with an intense, all-consuming brilliance. The humming became a buzzing, and then the voices, firm but gentle, commanded John to "Go back! Save her!" John closed his eyes as sight and sound intensified, forcing him to his knees, the buzzing becoming like the roar of a jet plane accompanied by a choir of a thousand voices. Cupping his hands over his ears John knew the time had come, and hollered out, "Please, take me there—NOW!"

When John came to, he found himself in a familiar eighteenth-century setting. He had been here once before when Thomas Whitman was rescued by his good friend, Chief Dan Fire Cloud, from taking his own life. It was the kitchen of Thomas Whitman, the blacksmith. This time he had landed in the midst of a heated argument between Thomas and his daughter, Rebecca.

"Please don't tell me how to run my life, Papa! I know what I am doing and must abide by the dictates of my heart and soul."

"You are still but a child!" came his booming reply. "I cannot stand idly by and let you ruin your life, running off with this...this merchant of mischief who has no better regard for your welfare and safety than to perpetrate these irresponsible acts of defiance against authority. I have no doubt that he is behind all of this talk of a tea burning."

"Oh, Papa, that just isn't true. John loves me and would do nothing to bring me harm."

"Aha! You cannot deny that he was involved in the Boston tea dumping affair. And you would call his presence in Annapolis at the time of the *Peggy Stewart* burning a mere coincidence? And now, he threatens to bring violence and treachery to our fair town! I tell you, you deserve so much better than this!"

"That's not fair, Papa!" Rebecca cried out. "You have no proof of his involvement in any of this. You're just upset because I have no intention of accepting Paul McKenzie's proposal of marriage."

"Indeed! A proper proposal from an upstanding man of impeccable character and excellent credentials. What more could a young woman ask for?"

"Happiness, Papa, just happiness!" she sobbed.

Thomas took a deep breath. Taking a few moments to calm down and gather his thoughts, he drew closer to his daughter, reaching out and wiping the tears from her eyes.

"My dear Rebecca, I want nothing more than for you to be happy. Please, just consider his proposal. Think it through. Not just with your heart, but with an open mind as well. Please, promise me you will do that."

Rebecca looked down and nodded. "Yes, Papa. I will do that. I promise."

"Fine. That is all I ask."

Thomas backed away and was about to turn when he added, "By the way, there is a shipment of hand tools from England waiting for me down at the wharf. When you are finished with your chores at the shop today, please be a good girl and retrieve them. Could you do that for me?"

Rebecca hesitated. "Yes, I suppose so. But I am expecting to work late today, making up for lost time while I was sick. It may be after dark. Is that okay?"

Thomas nodded. Just yesterday he had spoken to Paul, who he knew would be at the warehouse tending to some "important" business. But he needn't tell Rebecca this.

"Yes, that's okay," Thomas continued. "I know there is usually someone there well into the evening. You shouldn't have any problem." *And if you should happen to make a chance encounter with Paul, well, that would be okay, too,* Thomas thought.

As Thomas headed out the back door to his blacksmith shop, the room seemed to gradually brighten, the glass witch balls hanging by the window casting an eerie glow and making strange humming noises, like vibrating tuning forks. John knew what was coming. Closing his eyes he waited for the next transition, not really knowing where he would end up next.

When he next opened his eyes, he found himself kneeling in front of the intact Stone Tavern, obviously not the twentieth century, presumably the eighteenth. Standing up took something of an effort, and the cold, he could feel the cold air against his face and hands. He remained there for a moment, getting his bearings, not realizing he was standing out in the street directly in the path of an on-coming horse-drawn wagon traveling at breakneck speed. A young gentleman passerby grabbed and yanked him out of the way just in time to avoid being run over, and the two of them fell in a heap off the side of the road as the wagon passed by, its team of black stallions snorting and puffing great clouds of vapor from their nostrils, seemingly oblivious of the near miss, as was the old woman at the reins. John instantly recognized her as the old woman of his visions, the wizened hag with the cackling laugh destined for self-immolation. He recognized, too, the black stallions, black as pitch, with their distinctive diamond markings on their faces, the last thing he saw before being rescued and pulled to the ground.

John and his rescuer stood up, brushed themselves off, and recovered their composure. It was the gentleman who spoke first. "Mr. Weston, you must take more care in crossing the street."

John recognized the voice, and the face. They belonged to none other than Paul McKenzie, ship's first mate, the very person John was hoping to meet up with.

"It just seemed to come out of nowhere," John said, a bit flustered.

"As did *you*, sir," Paul chuckled. "In truth I didn't see you there but a minute ago."

John did not pursue it. "Good fortune surely follows me, Paul. I am much indebted to your quick response. Otherwise, I don't know how I would have ended up."

He thought about what would happen if he met his end here in eighteenth century America. Would his remains be simply transported back to present times, or remain forever trapped in the past?

"A bag of broken bones, I would presume," Paul responded with a laugh. "You look like you may be in need of a pint, sir, to quell the nerves as it were. Let me treat."

John was beginning to get his footing again in eighteenth-century Greenwich and accepted Paul's invitation. Accompanying him into the Stone Tavern, they found a table at a far corner of the room, far from prying ears, as Mary brought them each a pint of ale.

John brought up the subject of the tea shipment, saying he had some urgent instructions from Master Bart, with whom he had met just this past weekend in Haddonfield. He took a small bundle of folded, sealed documents from his knapsack and handed them to Paul.

"I was asked to deliver this personally to you, Paul. Bart said it was important."

Paul opened the documents and took a few moments to study them before responding. "Yes. I must tend to this immediately," he said finally.

"And one other thing," John added. "Bart would like you to arrange for the transfer of the tea from its current hiding place in the Masons' wine cellar to another secure location."

"Yes, John, I have already taken steps to move the tea, knowing that its current location has gone public, as it were."

"That's good," John nodded.

But John had more pressing concerns. Leaning forward across the table, he spoke softly. "I must warn you, Paul. There is much more mischief afoot this day than you may realize. I fear not for the tea, but for your own safety, and for the safety of young Rebecca. Please, you must avoid the warehouse this evening at all costs."

Paul was taken aback. What did John know about the rum shipment? Was that cat out of the bag, as well? He carefully scrutinized John's expression for any telltale signs.

"How do you know of happenings this evening at the warehouse?" he finally asked.

"I cannot say *how* I know, but only *what* I know, that young Rebecca will be dropping by warehouse this evening to retrieve some articles for her father, and that there is one who has designs on your destruction."

"Wha-? So who is…this *one* with nefarious intent?" Paul asked hesitantly, fearing what the answer might be. Had the British Guard caught wind of their smuggling enterprise? Or worse, would he face a double cross from competing smuggling pirates?

John considered telling him the truth, that there is a certain Agatha Greene, a delusional old woman with a penchant for starting fires, whom he suspected was responsible for the late rash of fires, and who intended to torch the warehouse tonight with Paul and Rebecca locked inside.

But he thought better of it.

"I cannot say with certainty, Paul. Only that the threat exists. I would only ask that you allow me accompany you this evening. I promise to be discreet and not interfere with any part of your business, personal or otherwise."

"Yes, I suppose that would be fine." He paused a moment. "John, can I ask you one favor?"

"Certainly, if it's within my power."

"Please contact Rebecca and tell her to stay away from the warehouse tonight. Tell her I will retrieve her father's articles myself. I would seek to tell her, but"—looking down at the letter—"I have some very important business to tend to, and must away as soon as possible."

John smiled. "Yes, I was planning to do that anyway."

"Thank you, John. Then you can meet me later this evening at the warehouse, as you propose."

Paul began to rue the day he ever decided to team up with the scheming Cap'n Jacob and his gang of smugglers.

John remained behind in the tavern while Paul hurried out to tend to this very important new order of business. John could not imagine what it might be, but Paul appeared to have things well in hand. John ordered another pint of ale from Mary and sat back, confident that things were now under control. He knew exactly where to find Rebecca: working late at the tailor shop as she had told her father.

He then thought about Agatha Greene. Where was she at this moment? Would he find an opportunity to thwart her plans before heading down to the wharf? No matter. He knew exactly what to expect and would intervene at the warehouse at the appropriate time. After all, she was just an old woman with delusions of betrayal; no match for an adult male who knew her intentions.

John finished off his pint with one final quaff, tossed a few pennies on the table, donned his coat and his knapsack, and said good-bye to Mary. A cold breeze met him as he exited the tavern and made his way down Ye Greate Street toward the Market Square. But he hadn't walked ten paces when a voice shouted out from behind: "THAT'S HIM! That's the scoundrel who stole my purse through wizardry! And mark my word, he is the one responsible for the fires, as well!"

John looked around to see to whom the man was referring. Then it dawned on him: the accusations were directed at *him*!

Not recognizing the voice at first, John turned around to confront his accuser. It was Roger Walker, that young ne'er do well whom he'd encountered on two previous occasions. Roger was accompanied by his partner in crime, George—old fat George, nose glowing red with drinker's rosacea. But it was the third individual that concerned John the most. By his dress and demeanor he took him to be the local constable.

"Are you quite certain?" the constable questioned.

"Yes, of course I'm certain! That's the imposter who claims to be John Weston! As sure as the nose on my face! I recognized him the moment I saw him walk into the tavern with Mr. McKenzie."

"And you claim that this man, this imposter by your words, drugged you and your friend into submission, taking that opportunity to abscond with your purse. Is that your story?"

"Yes, with God as my witness, that is what happened!" Roger exclaimed.

The constable turned to Roger's companion. "And you, sir, do you corroborate your friends story?"

George grunted and shook his head "yes."

The constable turned and addressed John directly. "I'm sorry, sir, but I'm afraid I'm going to have to take you in for questioning."

"Secure him well!" Roger shouted, taking pains to position himself well beyond John's reach, "You don't want him to go disappearing in a cloud of smoke!"

Ignoring Roger's last remark, the constable reaffirmed his earlier request. "Please, Mr. Weston, if you don't mind, would you please accompany me."

"But, constable, I have some very urgent business to attend to. It's a matter of life and death."

"Yes, I'm sure it is," the constable condescended. "But whatever it is, sir, I'm afraid it will have to wait. I promise this shouldn't take very long. More a matter of course, I'm afraid."

John was quick to recognize the irony of it all, to have escaped the law of his native century only to be picked up on some trumped up eighteenth-century charges! John protested, denying the charges, but reluctantly agreed to accompany the constable to the guardhouse. Roger and George tagged along behind, eager to be compensated for their losses.

On reaching the guardhouse, John was asked to show some form of identification. When he wasn't able to produce any, the constable became more suspicious and asked John to empty his pockets and knapsack on the table.

"What are these?" the constable asked, holding up a small carton of twentieth century matches and the small tin can of lighter fluid.

"Er, those are…matches," John replied nervously.

"And the other? It appears to be an incendiary fluid of some kind," the constable offered, reading the label on the can.

"Ah, yes. A form of…naphtha," John explained.

"Can you demonstrate their use?"

John hesitated. "Yes, I suppose so. Do you have a ceramic plate or ashtray?"

The constable produced a small ashtray from the desk and handed it to John, then backed away from the table as John took the can of lighter fluid and directed a small stream into the ashtray. He then took a match and stroked it against the rough band on the outside of the box, igniting the match instantly. Before they could react John tossed the lighted match onto the ashtray. *Woosh!* The ashtray was aflame in the blink of an eye.

"Quite impressive!" the constable conceded.

Roger was quick to pounce on this. "Don't you see? That's how he started all the fires! Without so much as flint and steel! That proves what I've been saying all along. This man is an evil wizard! Why else would he carry such devices on his person?"

The constable remained thoughtful, carefully studying John's person and demeanor. He eyed the partially exposed cartridge pouch hanging about John's neck.

"If you please, Mr. Weston, would you kindly show me the contents of that pouch."

The beads of sweat forming on John's brow did not go unnoticed by the constable.

"You have no right detaining and searching me in this manner!" John protested.

The constable laughed. "Whatever do you mean, my good man? I am the law around here. It is well within my right to question whomever I please if I believe there is cause to do so. And you, sir, are giving me ample cause."

John reluctantly removed the pouch and laid it upon the table.

"Please, empty the pouch, Mr. Weston."

From the window, John could see that the sun had already set. Time was running out.

"Mr. Weston, the pouch, if you please."

"Yes, of course," John stammered.

John opened the pouch and removed the Sucrets tin and four tattoo tube/needles. The constable looked at the tin, then at John, as if to say, "fine, now please open the tin."

John snapped open the tin, exposing two small partially filled vials of travel potion.

"Potions!" Roger exclaimed. "See! What did I tell you! That's what he used to put a spell on me and George!"

Roger was good at improvising tall tales.

The constable studied the paraphernalia on the table. "This is all very interesting, Mr. Weston. Could it be a mere coincidence, or do we have evidence that corroborates Mr. Walker's story, here? You tell me," he challenged.

"I can explain everything."

"That may be. But I'm afraid that will have to wait until morning when we visit the magistrate."

John couldn't believe what was happening. "What do you mean, the magistrate?"

"I mean, Mr. Weston that I'm going to have to detain you until morning. I cannot release you, as you have no identification, and there is ample evidence here that supports Roger's claim. We'll let the magistrate decide."

"But I told you, I have very urgent business to attend to! The warehouse is about to go up in flames and it must be stopped before…"

John bit his tongue, not believing what he'd just said. But by this time he was exasperated and losing patience.

"Before what, Mr. Weston?" the constable pursued.

At this point John lost control. After all his careful planning and hard work, had it come down to this? Thwarted by a country bumpkin and his drunken companion! No, this could NOT be happening. He must do something, quick.

John's basic survival instincts took over. Grabbing his knapsack and what paraphernalia he could from the table he lunged for the door, and would have made it, too, if it hadn't been for someone deciding to enter the room at that very moment, giving the constable sufficient time to react. Tackling John from behind, the two men went tumbling to the floor. Roger just stood by hooting and hollering, cheering on the constable with unbridled enthusiasm. It was payback time for Roger!

John was bound and taken to a holding cell in the gaol next door, while his personal items were bagged and stored in the guardhouse. The cell was sparsely appointed with a straw mattress, a pitcher of water, and a piss bucket. A single, small, barred window high on the wall was his only communication with the outside world.

Totally disheartened, John slumped down on the straw mattress to consider his fate, and the fate of those he had let down. It had all come to naught. Sometime tomorrow he would return to his century—"in a puff of smoke," as Roger put it—having accomplished nothing. He hoped it would be in the middle of his arraignment before the magistrate when it happened. That would surely give everyone something to ponder! No doubt it would make the *Gazette*: "Greenwich Man Vanishes into Thin Air!" Maybe enough to bring back the witch trials of the last century!

As John lay there, he became aware of a dim, orange, flickering light reflecting off the walls of his cell. At first it appeared to be coming from a candle or lantern in the adjoining room. As the light grew more intense, he realized it was coming from outside, through the window. He got up and walked to the far side of the cell to get a better angled view of the barred open window and night sky. What he saw struck him with horror.

"Oh my God!" he exclaimed. "The warehouse is burning! It's really happening this time!"

John watched helplessly as the distant night sky became ablaze with a sickening, pulsating orange glow. The memory of his earlier visions and nightmares came back in haunting reality. He was too far away to actually hear anything, but the memory and sound of anguish and pain reverberated in his head nonetheless.

Pressing his hands against the sides of his shaking head, he cried out, "No! Please no! This can't be happening! It's all my fault! I could've done more! I should have burned down that damn warehouse myself when I had the chance!"

Overcome with grief and regret, John collapsed on the floor in a heap, exhausted, as his body retreated into a deep sleep, and with that sleep a disturbing dream, a familiar dream, the one he'd dreamed that first night back in September:

...Like hoards of angry fireflies burnt on a common mission, streams of glowing embers ride the hot currents of air high into the cold night sky, challenging the moon's dominion over its star-spangled realm, rising ever higher against the broad canopy of stars, mingling at last with the ancient gods-strewn constellations in a final moment's burst of glory. Their fiery tracks, traced back to earth, reveal the source of their being: flames rising from a great fire, spawning and spewing forth fresh embers in crackling pangs of birth, the newly born gushing upward in great swarms, playing catch up to their brothers and sisters gone before, dispersed on cushions of a calmer air high above. Orion the Hunter looks down from his celestial perch with passive, star-eyed wonder...

...Now, against a backdrop of orange flame and smoke, vague new forms in erratic motion appear and disappear, coalescing at last into more discernible images: human silhouettes in wild, dancing rhythm; men, some naked to their waists, joined in common celebration around a raging bonfire; human voices, chants, and shouts of victory; and then an odor, pleasant, sweet, and familiar, but difficult to place...

When John awoke the next morning, he found himself in the same eighteenth-century holding cell, wishing it were all just a bad dream; but the reality of yesterday's events hit like a blunt two-by-four, complete with a hangover style headache. He thought about the dream. That sweet scent, he was able to place it now.

Tea! Yes, definitely "tea"!

As John contemplated this, his senses were jarred by the sound of clanking keys in the cell door lock. The cell door opened with a creak and a scruffy old man with a scraggy three-day beard greeted him

"Mr. Weston," the jailer said, "please, come with me."

John stood up—a little too quickly for his throbbing head—and followed the jailer into the next room, out the front door, and into the neighboring guardhouse. Seated at the table in the center of the room was the constable, with the bag of John's personal effects laid out before him.

"Mr. Weston, you are free to go," the constable declared curtly. "Mr. Walker has decided to drop all charges, and it appears that your nephew here"—giving a nod to John's left—"has solved the mystery of the recent fires."

A bewildered John turned to see a young man seated in the corner of the room. He had to do a double take.

"John Jay Weston!" he exclaimed. "Wha...How can it be?"

"Yes, John Jay in the flesh and at your service," young John beamed. "And you must be John Samuel Weston, a lost uncle with some mysterious family connection, I'm led to believe. At long last we meet face-to-face!"

"But...How? Why...?"

John was at a loss for words, a rare event in either century.

"Not to worry," John Jay laughed. He stood up and approached John with a firm embrace.

"You look like you could use a good meal, John. Grab your things and I'll have Mary prepare us a fine breakfast at the Stone Tavern."

"But, what about last night? The fire? I saw it through the jail cell window."

"Ah, yes, and a fine blaze it was, indeed!" John Jay took a deep, exaggerated breath. "Ah, the sweet scent of liberty! You should have been there, Uncle!"

"Wha...?

"The tea burning, my good man! The sweet aroma of burning tea leaves in the crisp winter night air. You missed quite a show."

"So...the warehouse didn't...burn down?" John asked hesitantly.

"No, not at all. And we have you to thank for that, Uncle."

John Jay let his "uncle" ponder this for a moment before continuing. "You see, John, I finally received the letter you sent me two months ago, warning me of the pending danger this very night. In truth, I don't know how you could know such things, and with such detail, but it prompted my concern and curiosity, especially as it concerned the safety of my lovely Rebecca."

"So, Rebecca is...alive?"

"Very much alive and well, thank you."

"So, when and how did you finally receive the letter?" John asked.

"I returned to Haddonfield two days ago, cutting short my business in the southern colonies to address my growing concerns with rumors of an imposter posing as me and inserting himself into my personal affairs. Brother Bart said you had been by inquiring about a letter that you posted to me. Apparently it had become misfiled, but Jonathan was finally able to recover it."

"How very fortunate!"

"Very fortunate indeed! Had I not pursued your lead, events could have turned quite tragic, as you suggested in your epistle. As it happened, I was able to intervene just as Agatha Greene was preparing to ignite the naphtha-soaked tinder she had so methodically piled up against the warehouse. It was only then I heard the muffled voices of Rebecca and Mr. McKenzie from inside—Agatha had barred the door with a sturdy timber!"

John could scarcely believe the good turn of events. Even his headache was gone.

"Yes, she is quite the lunatic, I'm afraid," young John continued. "Kept going on about a 'destiny' and having to 'teach him a lesson'—yes, I believe they were her very words. From what I could piece together, she claimed to be the victim of unrequited love, abandoned in her youth by a British seaman by the name 'Allen,' a leftenant in the King's Navy. Apparently, in her madness, she mistook Paul McKenzie for this jilting bloke and was intent on doing the two of them in, both the leftenant and his 'jaded whore'!—a.k.a. the fair and lovely Rebecca Whitman. Quite a story, I must say!"

"Quite a story, indeed," John echoed.

"But there's more! In all her raving rants, she actually admitted to being responsible for the recent rash of fires about the county! So, John"—giving a nod and a wink to the constable—"that puts you clean off the hook for those charges."

"Yes, I'm afraid Agatha Greene will have a lot to account for in the coming weeks," the constable rejoined.

John picked up his things from the table, thanked the constable for his kind hospitality, and the two Johns headed out the door toward the Stone Tavern.

"But what about Roger? Why did he drop his charges?"

"Oh, you mean our fellow compatriot and smuggler in arms?" young John laughed. "Well, in the process of defusing Agatha's wicked plan, I happened to uncover Roger's rum contraband scheme as well. Paul was good enough to share what he knew. He owed me that much, at least. While Roger certainly wasn't the ringleader, his involvement would not have gone unpunished if the British guards had been alerted. When I learned of your incarceration—as you know, Mary knows all the goings-on in this town—I simply did a little horse trading. I promised Roger I would not divulge his dirty little secret, if he promised to drop all charges against you."

"My, you've been quite the enterprising fellow!" John chuckled.

"It's in the blood, John, in the blood."

The two Johns headed over to the Stone Tavern where Mary greeted them with the promise of a hearty breakfast of smoked ham, beans, eggs, and freshly brewed mocha coffee. She led them to a small room toward the rear of establishment where they could dine and discuss matters in private.

"So, tell me about the tea," the elder John inquired, once they were comfortably settled in.

The young John Jay proceeded to recount the events of the previous night, leaving no stone of detail unturned. After his initial encounter with near tragedy at the warehouse, he drove a shaken Rebecca back to town in her carriage, leaving Paul at the wharf to tend to his other, more clandestine, affairs. As for Agatha Green, she simply vanished into the night with her wagon and loyal team of black stallions, headed for parts unknown, ranting all the while in fits of rage against the demons and voices in her head.

As John and Rebeca approached the Market Square from the south, they saw in the distance, coming down Ye Greate Street from the opposite direction, a great throng of men, many naked from the waist up, costumed in the manner of Native Americans, chanting and whooping in the cold night air with shouts of "burn the tea!" and "Patriots all!" Drawing near, John had recognized many of the men, local citizens all, their apparent leader none other than the Reverend Philip Vickers Fithian, whom John knew instantly, war paint notwithstanding, from his most recent encounter in Annapolis, Maryland. [17]

"John! Is that you?" Philip shouted.

"Yes, indeed. It is I," John replied aloud.

John was told that they sought the illicit shipment of tea—"that most detestable weed!"—which they intended to gather up from Mason's Tailor Shoppe and take to the Market Square where they would set it ablaze "in a glorious act of defiance in the name of liberty!"

Of course, John knew of their plans, having learned from Paul of the threat against the tea, and he could well read the determination and fervor of this throng of men written on their faces and carried in their stride: they would not be deterred in their enterprise! He knew what they felt, for he had felt the same way one year ago in Boston's harbor, on that night of what had since become known as the "Boston Tea Party."

"Come join us, John!" a voice in the crowd shouted out.

John turned and looked at Rebecca, still shaking from a combination of the cold night air and her recent near encounter with death. She shook her head "please, no!"

John turned back to the crowd. "I'm sorry, Philip. I will pass on this opportunity. But, I do wish you and your band a most successful endeavor."

John had also learned from Paul that the tea was no longer to be found at the Tailor Shoppe. With memories of the *Peggy Stewart* affair fresh in his

---

[17] While direct documentary evidence may be lacking, Philip Vickers Fithian is generally credited with having participated in the Greenwich tea burning the night of December 22, 1774. Several attempts were made to prosecute those believed to be responsible, but in the end no one was ever brought to trial. Joseph S. Sickler, *Tea Burning Town* (Bridgeton, New Jersey: The Greenwich Press, 1950), 40-42.

mind, and fearful that some harm might come to the Masons and their establishment once the tea was not found there, John thought the better part of valor would be to divulge the tea's true, new location. A relieved nod from Rebecca told him he had done the right thing.

"On to Dan Bowen's cellar!" a cry went up from the mob. "There we shall find the tea!"

John drove Rebecca back to the Masons, where she safely remained for the rest of the evening, while John returned to the Market Square just in time to see shadowy figures of men dumping crates of tea in a great pile onto the center of the green. There was no hiding their fervor, as chants and shouts of victory filled the air; torches were lit, casting long erratic shadows of men in dancing rhythm, mimicking the movements of Native Americans on the warpath. One by one, the arcing trails of flaming torches flung through the air ignited the pile of wood and weed and the town green was soon illuminated with the blaze of a great bonfire, sending sparks high into the nighttime sky to mingle with the stars against a cloudless sky, filling the air with the sweet scent of burning tea.

"A sacrificial pyre to liberty!" remarked young John.

The sights and sounds of the bonfire aroused local residents from their homes, who, initially fearful that the nameless arsonist had struck yet again under the cover of night, were quickly caught up in the celebration, joining in with chants of victory and the shared camaraderie of mounting patriotic fervor. And so it went on well into the night, long after the flames had died down, creating a common bond, igniting the quest for liberty in the hearts of the local citizenry, a feeling that would grow to unprecedented proportions in a land that was about to experience the birth pangs of a new nation.

The elder John S. Weston sat back, sipping his morning cup of java as he listened intently to his many-times great-great-uncle recount his tale. When finished, he posed the obvious question. "So, tell me, John. Was the night's celebration worth the cost to Weston Enterprises? That was a tidy profit to see all go up in smoke!"

Young John smiled. Leaning back in his chair he produced a document from his coat pocket and held it up. The elder John recognized it as the same document he had delivered to Paul just one day earlier.

"I hold in my hand the bill of sale," young John explained, "re-assigning our consignment of tea to, shall I say, a competing merchant based in the fair city of brotherly love. It is dated and signed by all parties and attested to by the local customs inspector here in Greenwich."

John laughed. "So, that was the urgent business Paul had to rush off to when I gave him the papers! A visit to the customs office!"

"Precisely!" young John replied. "Of course, we didn't achieve the profit we had hoped—our buyer was, after all, a good negotiator," he added with a wink. "But, neither did we absorb the loss."

"I would say, then, that your timing was—impeccable."

"Indeed. Profit or loss, it all depends on the timing!" young John asserted.

After breakfast John Jay escorted his "Uncle" John to the tailor shop to see and speak with Rebecca, as the elder John had requested. He needed the reassurance, to see with his own eyes, to hear with his own ears, proof that she had indeed survived that fateful night, escaped the judgment of time, which in John's mind was nothing less than a miracle, a miracle of circumvented destiny, avoiding the precipice of personal disaster that set a ruinous course for the entire region and its progeny. The question was: would the curse be lifted now and for evermore? Or would fate simply conspire to reconstruct a temporarily disrupted timeline into the same pattern of tragic future events, like a stream whose flow is locally altered by a large boulder tossed in its path, but whose downstream flow remains indistinguishable from before? Would the thread of time be simply mended, or actually rewoven, like Mary's Afghan and the tapestry of his dreams and visions?

Of course, John would not know the answer to this vexing question until he returned to his native century.

*****

...A young man stood on the shore tending a charcoal grill, waving to someone on a boat floating far off on the water. As the boat drew nearer, John saw two young women standing on its deck, waving to the young man on the shore. He recognized the two women on the boat. He did not recognize the man on the shore, but felt as though he knew him all the same, as a thick swarm of flies hovering overhead blocked his view. Suddenly, a flock of seagulls came sweeping down over the water and consumed the flies! Flying back out to sea, the gulls paused over the boat and spoke out with a common voice, "Rejoice! And live forevermore!"

When John awoke from his dream, he found himself lying flat on his back in the middle of Ye Greate Street, his knapsack by his side. With his eyes still closed he recalled his last hours in eighteenth-century Greenwich, his delightful visit with John and Rebecca at Mason's Tailor Shoppe, and the sparkle in her eyes, like emeralds in the sunlight, as she embraced young John with hope for a future filled with promise, shared with the young man of her dreams.

As John's senses slowly returned, the sounds of nature, revelry, and voices filled the space around him. With his eyes still closed he wondered if perhaps he was still in eighteenth-century Greenwich. Had the drug produced a permanent time shift effect? Frightened at the prospect, he remained reluctant to open his eyes to learn the truth.

"Are you okay, sir?"

It was the voice of a young man. Strange to say, the voice was familiar to him. Where had he heard that voice before?

John opened his eyes and looked up at the young man staring down at him. "Doug! Doug Justin! Is...is that really you?"

The young man, dressed in colonial garb and accompanied by several other men in similar attire, reacted with surprise.

"How do you know my name, sir?"

John propped himself up on his elbows to get a better look. Yes, it was definitely Doug—only without the green Mohawk!

"Doug, don't you remember me? I'm John Weston, from Lady of Lourdes Hospital?"

Doug just shook his head. "I'm sorry, sir, but I've never even been to Lourdes Hospital, wherever that is. Here, let me help you up. Sounds like you may have hit your head or something."

Doug's friends just smiled, muttering something about "losing it," while Doug reached down and helped John to his feet. John thanked him as he dusted himself off and gathered up his knapsack. Looking around to get his bearings, he was amazed at what he saw. No longer the deserted "nobody hardly lives there anymore" ghost town etched into his memory, Greenwich seemed alive and well, restored you might say, to a semblance of its former self. Not exactly as he remembered the eighteenth-century version, but close enough to say it had never really gone away. There was the Gibbon House, with a placard advertising it as the home of the Cumberland County Historical Society, obviously relocated from the Bridgeton location John had once visited. And there, just down the street, was the old Stone Tavern, not much changed since the eighteenth century, as all up and down Ye Greate Street people were strolling and reveling, some in colonial dress, some modern.

John turned to Doug. "So, what is this? Some kind of reenactment?"

Surveying John up and down in his colonial outfit, Doug replied with a surprised chuckle. "Well, surely you must know! It's December twenty-third, the two-hundred-twenty-fifth year anniversary of the Greenwich Tea Burning! Right down there on the village green," he said pointing south toward the Market Square.

John thanked him, wishing him and his friends well as he bid them a fond adieu before heading up Ye Greate Street toward the Stone Tavern. He breathed a sigh of relief at the sight of his Camry parked outside the tavern, just where he had left it. On the windshield was a parking ticket for violating the temporary no parking ordinance posted along Ye Greate Street for the reenactment celebration. John smiled as he placed the ticket in his inside coat pocket.

"Yup, looks like I'm back in a restored twentieth century, alright."

Chapter 42

2000
Early December
Haddonfield, NJ

Safely seated at his desk in the study of his Haddonfield home, John
nervously wiped the dust from the fissure-marred imitation leather cover
of the picture album lying unopened before him. It had only been a month
since he was discharged from Lakeland Hospital and he was just now getting
up the nerve to revisit past memories—memories documented in bolder than
life Kodachrome color; memories that were, as far as he could recall, not
entirely his own, but somehow refashioned into a new, or rewoven time line;
memories that had to be relearned, and what better place to start this process
than his own picture album.

Slowly, he opened the album to roughly its center, page twenty or so.
There he was posing with Becky in front of their new pride and joy, the
twenty-eight-foot Monterey cabin cruiser, the *Becky Babe*. The picture was
dated July 5, 1982. Yes, John remembered that very well. It was the day that
marked the traumatic turning point in his life, the day Becky perished in that
tragic boating accident, right?

The pictures and scrapbook memorabilia on all subsequent pages—
and there were enough now to fill the album—were strange to him, however,
for he had no living recollection of putting them there, or even of the events
they recorded, but had to accept on faith that they were true.

The first series of pictures documented the remaining days of their
Fourth of July weeklong vacation. There was a picture of the two of them
smiling, seated close together at a table at the Crab Shack restaurant in
Somer's Point, New Jersey, enjoying a fine seafood feast in celebration of the
anniversary of their first date. Becky looked vibrant and stunning. *I wish I could
remember that*, John thought.

The next few pages included pictures leading up to their planned
August wedding, complete with an actual wedding invitation and a wedding
list, and then—one blank page, followed by some letter entries. One, dated
August 5, 1982, addressed to John from Becky, read:

Dear John,

It pains me to write this, John, but after a long period of agonizing soul searching, I have come to realize that I cannot in all honesty proceed with this wedding. To be honest with you, John, I must first be honest with myself, and face the truth that I have fallen in love with another.

What we had was special, John, but I cannot live a lie, which is what I would be doing if we continued our current course. You are young, John, and I am certain, over time, you will get over this, find another, fall in love, and continue with your life, which is so full of hope and promise.

Please don't despise me for this, John, for you would despise me all the more if I continued to live a lie, ultimately making life miserable for the both of us. Better to fix it now, than have to mend things later on, entailing a complete reweaving of life's tapestry.

Sincerely loving you,

Becky

John wiped his eyes and was forced to look away. Ironic, her mention of life's rewoven tapestry; was that just a coincidence, or was it in fact what prompted his delusions and break with reality—as the doctors insisted—in the first place? Or did events actually play out as he experienced them, as he knew them to be? He really couldn't say for sure, but he suspected the latter.

Several pages later there was a newspaper article announcing the marriage of Becky Bowman to Brad Mathews, fashion photographer par excellence at Modeline Fashions. Yes, John remembered meeting him at the company Christmas party when Becky interned at Modeline. She'd spoken highly of him and the two worked closely together—John just never realized how closely.

Further on were pictures of John posing with fellow workers, palm trees in the background. He recognized the place—GenAvance, Thousand Oaks, California—and the people: Dr. Sam Li, Jennifer Dupree, and others.

And then more pictures of John and Jennifer, a wedding announcement, followed by—could they really be wedding pictures? John broke out in a cold sweat as he realized what he was seeing. There were John and Jennifer in their new apartment, then—what's this? A series of baby pictures of little Renee and John, one captioned: "New proud father with little Renee."

"My God! Can this really be true?"

John closed the album and sat back, trying to take it all in, trying to make sense of it all.

"Well, I asked for things to be set right. Didn't realize what I was bargaining for!"

Over the past ten months John had learned other things, too. He was ultimately connected to the break-in at Shockley Laboratories at Rutgers University. All criminal charges were dismissed, however, once he was diagnosed with Schizoaffective disorder and deemed unfit to stand trial. He was committed to Lakeland Hospital for treatment, but it wasn't the same hospital that he remembered. No, apparently the old hospital had been torn down in "life's reweave," and a brand new facility erected in its place. But the biggest surprise came when he received a visit from both his mom and dad! He thought he was hallucinating at first, but sure enough, it was his dad, in the flesh. Apparently, in life's reweave John had insisted that his father see a cardiologist when he first experienced those shoulder and neck pains. Good thing, too. They were able to stave off a pending heart attack with a few well-placed stents, and he was able to resume a normal life under the care of the cardiologist ever since.

And what of his good friend and business partner, Bob Fenwick? Well, it turns out his condition was not schizophrenia after all, but a somatically based illness: *Tularemia*, is what the doctors called it, an often serious parasitic infection resulting from the bite of a greenhead fly! Bob responded well to treatment and was better in no time at all. Good thing, too. He had to fill in for John, who was suffering from bouts of delusional paranoia that culminated in his eventual commitment to Lakeland.

And Doug Justin, what about Doug?

"A fanciful creation of John's delusional psychotic state," the doctors declared.

That would probably explain Sally Fielding's reaction on that Saturday morning in October of last year when she surprised John with her homemade strawberry shortcake. As John turned to converse with an "imaginary" Doug Justin—who, in John's mind was standing on his stairway landing wearing nothing but a bath towel—she obviously became confused, a little frightened perhaps, and simply bolted out the front door.

John smiled. "And here I thought she just didn't approve of the company I kept."

There were other revelations, too. Like Captain George Davies being picked up on charges of smuggling whiskey, rum, and the occasional marijuana (he drew the line at the heavier illicit drugs) into the country along southern Jersey's intercoastal waterways using his chartered fishing business as the perfect cover. Of course, his sixty-foot cabin cruiser, The *Greyhound*, was impounded as evidence and subsequently auctioned off by the Feds. A carryover from the rum running days of prohibition, George would pick up contraband from a larger oceangoing ship sitting just beyond the three-mile (4.8 km) limit of US jurisdiction and bring it in under the cover of night to any one of hundreds of coves and inlets along the Jersey and Delaware Bay shores. Thinking about it, John just had to smile. "The more things change, the more things remain the same," he chuckled.

It had only been in the past few weeks that John had resumed his normal routine at Haddon Life-Tech. His office was pretty much the way he had left it—not as he remembered it, mind you, but the way life's reweave left it. On first entering, he thought he had gone into Bob's office by mistake, but this was no mistake. The walls remained covered with the Escher-like prints of impossible three-dimensional mechanical renderings, glass ball mobiles hung from the ceiling, notes and loose papers were scattered about with those strange, all-too-familiar doodles, along with quatrains written in elaborate calligraphy style. Though he had trouble reconciling this "new reality" with events as he remembered them, the doctors said it would help in his recovery if everything remained just as it was.

John did not resist the healing process, but allowed the new reality to sink in. It didn't replace the old reality, mind you, but took its place right alongside it, for deep down inside, John knew that what he'd experienced— the reweaving of history to set things right—was in fact true. After all, did he not have proof, the physical and circumstantial evidence of his trips back in time? There were the coins, authentic from that time period, and the stage wagon ticket, "good for one-way passage" from Greenwich to Cooper's Ferry, all secure in his metal lockbox, the one marked "Artifacts." And how did he recognize Doug Justin on waking up in twentieth century Greenwich if they had never met during in his earlier stays at Lourdes? The doctors just shrugged their shoulders on that question.

And then there were the entries in his many-times great-great-uncle Bart's business journal making reference to a mysterious "cousin John Weston" who's exact lineage no one could seem to trace; and the 1775 *Pennsylvania Gazette* article about a "mysterious interloper" claiming to share the same family name of Weston Enterprises, a man who some say "appears and vanishes as a spectral vision into the night." Of course, the good news was, in this new time-revised version, there was no longer any mention— none at all—of the infamous "witch burning" on Greenwich's Market Square, and most importantly, no mention of the "curse of Greenwich," or a curse of any kind, for that matter! The way John figured, it was the burning of the tea that destroyed whatever threat it carried with it from foreign shores, whatever infestation or vector of infection it brought with it that would have been responsible for setting the curse in motion in the first place—the "triggering mechanism," as Dr. Alexandria put it. From his campfire visions, John knew the tea leaves were a key component of the potion concocted by Thomas Whitman and his friends. Exactly how, John couldn't say, but he knew it required all three: the leaves of that detestable weed from the *Greyhound*, the larvae of the greenhead fly, and the blood of Agatha Greene. Eliminate any one, and the curse was null and void.

So, was it all worth it?

Yes, John thought so. Even though he would be forced to suffer the repercussions of these time-altering effects on his own life and reputation, for while saving young Rebecca and fixing things for all of Cumberland and Salem Counties and, yes, even saving Becky, Doug Justin, his own father, and who knows how many countless others over the course of the past two centuries, he had, in effect, totally screwed up his own life in the process! He now understood better than ever before those last four lines of the now nonextant curse uttered by the young black slave girl back in 1775:

> *And ne'er the curse shall it be lift*
> *Till the time of the winter solstice rift*
> *And The One whom time henceforth reclaims*
> *Returns to barter with his good name.*

But the thing that bothered John the most, the one thing he had trouble reconciling since his return to a rewoven twentieth century, were the missing love letters from John Jay Weston to the young and lovely Rebecca Whitman—and the missing carved wooden box that contained them! What he found in their place when he first went looking for them after his release from the hospital, was a simple cardboard box held together with twine that contained the long-lost letters from Rebecca to John! Yes, apparently those letters survived, having remained in the safekeeping of his older half brother Bart while John went off to fight the war, but not before John Jay and Rebecca married early in the summer of '75. With Rebecca safe and sound in Greenwich, John no longer felt the need to take her letters along with him into battle, looking forward only to receiving new epistles as she would pen them in the ensuing months, and eventually years, of the war. Unfortunately, unlike the letters, John Jay would not survive the war—this much of history remained unchanged. One could only assume that Rebecca retained all of the letters from John Jay, that she eventually remarried, and then either destroyed the letters to better get on with her new life, or hid them away for future disposition by her heirs. In any event, these letters never made it to the Weston family archives, as they had in the previous, uncorrected version of John's life. It would be John's quest in subsequent years to search for those letters and the wooden box that housed them.

In a related quest, John was eventually able to track down his natural mother, Mandy, living in New England, not far from where his dad once thought her to be residing. His dad, living in retirement with his stepmom, was now able to help him in his search, but John had to make the road trip alone. His biggest revelation came when he learned from Mandy that Becky, his once true love, was actually a blood relation through his mom's side. It turns out that Becky's great-grandmother on her mother's side, and Mandy's grandmother, were second cousins, making John and Becky third cousins! Although stranger and closer pairings were well-known throughout history— did not John Adams, a Founding Father and second president of the fledging United States of America, marry his third cousin, Abigail Smith!—John figured things probably worked out for the best. The important thing was, she survived!

John thought about those wooden block letters in Bob's basement time machine, the one's he had stumbled into and knocked to the floor that Saturday back in early October of last year. Associated with the a more recent time period on his mom's time line—the lunar female bloodline as viewed from the perspective of Rigel's portal— John could only assume that in their intact configuration, they actually identified this elusive link!

*****

Friday, 22 December, the year 2000. Fortunately, the doomsday millennial meltdown never quite happened the way many predicted. For John, however, it had amounted to a kind of personal meltdown, but he was coping as well as he could, managing to put the pieces of his life back together.

Yesterday had been the office Christmas party and many had already left for the long holiday weekend. He was looking forward to doing the same. Stopping by Mary's desk in the middle of the afternoon, he noticed her engaged in a familiar activity.

"So, knitting another Afghan, I see."

Mary looked up and smiled. "Not knitting, John, crocheting!" she corrected him.

"Oh, yes, of course. So, expecting another addition to the family?"

"Yes. Nancy and Paul are expecting again! Can you imagine?"

John smiled. "That's great, Mary. Please wish them my best. Family is so important. Got to keep the family line going, you know."

Mary put down the Afghan for a moment, giving John a sincere, inquiring look. "So, how are you doing, John?"

John paused and took a seat on the edge of Mary's desk. "I'm doing fine, Mary. Just fine, thank you for asking." He looked down at the Afghan. "Trying out any new…patterns or stitches," he asked hesitantly.

Mary cocked her head and smiled. "No, just the usual, like last time. I think I finally got it right."

"Hmm, yes. I know what you mean," he replied wistfully.

"So, tell me John, where are you going for the weekend, if you don't mind my asking?"

John sighed. "No, don't mind at all," he said, then paused. "I think I'll be taking a ride down by the Delaware Bay. Greenwich is having their annual Tea Burning celebration and reenactment. Should be fun."

"Greenwich?" Mary inquired.

"Yes, it's such a charming town," John said, looking off into space. "It's almost like...going back in time."

The End

Acknowledgments

Greenwich offered me the perfect opportunity to combine a love of history and writing with my lifelong career experience as a process engineer working in the biotech consulting field. My desire to bridge the gap between my two brain hemispheres climaxed in the summer of 2007 when I launched this writing project at the urging of my wife, Janet, following our own "off-the-beaten-path" day trip to the quaint town of *Greenwich*, on the Cohansey River near the shores of the Delaware Bay.

First and foremost, I wish to thank my wife, whose passion for reading inspired me to take on this challenge. A seemingly daunting task at first, it quickly turned into a labor of love.

And thank you to family members and friends for their candid and constructive feedback on the manuscript at various stages of completion: Richard Kral and Young Heinbockel, two very talented engineers, coworkers and confidantes (thank you, Richard, for your careful reading of the final draft; and Young, for pointing out, among other things, that Sam Adams beer comes in a bottle, and not a can!); Walter Bowne, freelance writer-editor and high school English teacher extraordinaire, for his early comments on structure and narrative; Rich Flamini, longtime friend, fellow musician, and drummer par excellence; my twin sister, Susan Bowne, and our good friend, Nancy Foster, whose opinions I value as avid readers of fiction; and most significantly, my wife for her continued encouragement and meticulous proofing of the final draft.

Finally, I wish to thank my editor, Nikki Busch, without whose professional assistance the book would simply not have made it to the finish line. Going beyond the editing process, Nikki shared her experiences and advice on the world of publishing, which, as a first-time author, I found to be invaluable information. You can visit Nikki at: http://www.nikkibuschediting.com.

About the Author

Stephen Goldhahn is a consulting process engineer, a part time musician, singer song writer and history buff. He received his master's degree in chemical engineering from the University of Maryland, and has spent the major portion of his professional career working in the food and biopharmaceutical manufacturing industries.

While honing his professional technical writing skills, Steve has tapped into his artistic side over the years as a singer song writer and musician. In the eighties he helped to establish an original rock band and, together with his brother, Ron, formed an independent record label to record and promote their music, and has since then collaborated on other projects. His appetite for creative writing evolved from his song writing experience, which until lately had largely remained a private passion, focusing on short stories, travel journals, and personal memoirs. *Greenwich* is his first novel.

Steve and his wife, Janet, have called south New Jersey their home for the past thirty-some years, and are the proud parents of two grown sons, Kevin and Michael.

Selected Bibliography

Andrews, Frank D. *The Tea Burners of Cumberland County Who Burned a Cargo of Tea at Greenwich, New Jersey, December 22, 1774.* Cumberland County Historical Society, 1974. 200th anniversary commemorative edition reprinted from original publication. Vineland Historical and Antiquarian Society, 1908.

Belote, Julianne. *The Complete American Housewife 1776.* Concord, California: Nitty Gritty Productions, 1974.

Chu, Wai Lang. "Schizophrenia Gene Function Offers Hope for Drug R&D." *William Reed Business Media SAS* (April 24, 2006). Accessed January 10, 2015. http://www.outsourcing-pharma.com/Preclinical-Research/Schizophrenia-gene-function-offers-hope-for-drug-R-D.

Cumberland County Historical Society. *Fithian: The Beloved Cohansie of Philip Vickers Fithian.* With an introduction and explanatory comments by F. Alan Palmer. Cumberland County Historical Society, n.d.

Dorwart, Jeffrey M., and Elizabeth A. Lyons. *Elizabeth Haddon Estaugh 1680-1762.* Haddonfield, New Jersey: Haddonfield Historical Society, 2013.

Dunlap's Pennsylvania Packet. "At a General Meeting of the Inhabitants of the County of Cumberland, in New Jersey, held at Bridge-town, on Thursday, the 22nd day of December, 1774." January 9, 1775. Limited Edition reprint of excerpted article. Cumberland County Historical Society, December, 1974.

EyeWitness to History. "Yellow Fever Attacks Philadelphia, 1793," www.eyewitnesstohistory.com/yellowfever.htm (2005).

Farish, Hunter Dickinson, ed. *Journal and Letters of Philip Vickers Fithian: A Plantation Tutor of the Old Dominion, 1773-1774.* Charlottesville: The University Press of Virginia, 1957.

Haines, Felicity J., Robert D. Possee, and Linda A. King. "Baculovirus Expression Vectors." *Encyclopedia of Virology.* 3rd ed. London: Elsevier (2006): 451-54.

Hansen, Elton J. and Stuart R Race. "The Greenhead and You." Rutgers University Department of Entomology (2008). Accessed September 8, 2015. http://esc.rutgers.edu/fact_sheet/the-greenhead-and-you/

Harper, Douglas. "Slavery in the North." On-line publication, 2003. http://slavenorth.com/slavenorth.htm.

Historical Society of Haddonfield. *History of the Town of Haddonfield.* http://haddonfieldhistory.org/about/history-of-the-town-of-haddonfield/.

Hunt, Ian. "From Gene to Protein: A Review of New and Enabling Technologies for Multi-parallel Protein Expression." *Protein Expression and Purification* 40 (2008) 1-22.

Invitrogen Instruction Manual. "Guide to Baculovirus Expression Vector Systems (BEVS) and Insect Cell Culture Techniques." *Invitrogen Life Technologies*, 2002.

The Maryland Gazette. "Annapolis, October 20." October 20, 1774. Excerpt of article reporting the burning of the Peggy Stewart. Sultana Education Foundation. Accessed October 4, 2014. http://sultanaeducation.org/teacher-programs/roots-of-nation-curriculum-aids/the-revolutionary-era/primary-documents-and-images/.

Megget, Katrina. "AstraZeneca's Schizophrenia Drug Gets the Nod in the Netherlands." *William Reed Business Media SAS* (August 8, 2007). Accessed January 10, 2015. http://www.in-pharmatechnologist.com/Ingredients/AstraZeneca-s-schizophrenia-drug-gets-the-nod-in-the-Netherlands.

New York Times. "Annapolis's 'Tea Party'." November 19, 1892.

Outsourcing Pharma. "New Dopamine Mechanism Equals New Drugs?" *William Reed Business Media SAS* (August 2, 2005). Accessed January 15, 2015. http://www.outsourcing-pharma.com/Preclinical-Research/New-dopamine-mechanism-equals-new-drugs.

Przekop, Peter, and Timothy Lee. "Persistent Psychosis Associated with *Salvia Divinorum* Use." Letter to the editor. *American Journal of Psychiatry* 166, no.7 (2009): 832.

Peterson, Robert A. *Patriots, Pirates, and Pineys: Sixty Who Shaped New Jersey.* Medford, New Jersey: Plexus Publishing, 1998.

Sickler, Joseph S. *Tea Burning Town: Being the Story of Ancient Greenwich on the Cohansey in West Jersey.* Bridgeton, New Jersey: The Greenwich Press, 1950.

Strobbe, Mike. "Brain-eating Amoeba Kills Man, Two Kids." *Courier-Post*, August 18, 2011.

University of Cambridge. "Introduction to the Baculovirus Expression System." *Department of Biochemistry, University of Cambridge* (2007). Accessed January 10, 2015. http://www.bioc.cam.ac.uk/baculovirus/expression

Werner, Kirk D., ed. *The American Revolution.* San Diego: Greenhaven Press, Inc., 2000.

Whitman, Walt. *Leaves of Grass.* 150th Anniversary Edition. Forward by Billy Collins. Introduction by Gay Wilson Allen. Afterward by Peter Davison. New York: Signet Classics, 2005.

Wikipedia, s.v. "Haddonfield, New Jersey." Last modified January 25, 2008. http://en.wikipedia.org/wiki/Haddonfield,_New_Jersey.

Wikipedia, s.v. "Peggy Stewart (Ship)." Last modified December 7, 2007. http://en.wikipedia.org/wiki/Peggy_Stewart_(ship).

Wikipedia, s.v. "Salvia Divinorum." Last modified August 15, 2011. http://en.wikipedia.org/wiki/Salvia_divinorum.

Wikipedia, s.v. "Schizophrenia." Last modified September 27, 2007. http://en.wikipedia.org/wiki/Schizophrenia.

Wilkinson, Matt. "New Schizophrenia Target Found in the Glutamate System." *William Reed Business Media SAS* (September 26, 2007). Accessed January 10, 2015. http://www.outsourcing-pharma.com/Preclinical-Research/New-schizophrenia-target-found-in-the-glutamate-system.

Wood, Gordon S. *The American Revolution: A History.* New York: Modern Library, 2003.

Woodruff, Anne Schillingsburg, and F. Alan Palmer. *The Unalachtigo of New Jersey: The Original People of Cumberland County.* Cumberland County Historical Society, 1973.